Theft of Decks

Book Three

Lars Machmüller

CONTENTS

DEDICATION

Yo, I love dedication pages! They're a break from expectations, from any expected tropes or paths.

Listen, where anything else in a book, from the start onward, has pre-determined paths showing

Up, telling you where the story is going, which mood, and content you can expect, here is different.

Here's a safe spot, a wildcard, where you're allowed to do exactly what you want. I can do a poem.

A limerick. Rant on about the insanity that is English grammar. Today, instead, I will tell you all a

Story. A story showing why I have the best wife! Now, at this point, we'd known each other for

About a few months and dated sporadically. We were slowly getting to know one another. Then,

A lazy afternoon at my then job, the tempo was turned up. She called me, asking, "Want to go on a

Little adventure with me? We're climbing Kilimanjaro." I asked for time to consider. She said "My

Guy, I have an offer for tickets that expires in about two hours. Consider away!" Right then! At

That moment, I knew that I had something special on my hands. I was right. Over the years, our

Lives have been many things. Adventurous. Filled with love, travels, a desire to *learn*! Yet, even

in fifteen years and counting, they have never been dull.

A thousand things have happened. Our lives have changed drastically, again and again. I have been

Blue with you, happy, exhilarated, downcast and furious. Yet, Tina, you will always remain my

World. My rock! Thank you for everything!

Lars

<u>The path we traveled thus far</u>

I hesitate to say this... but I have hope. In the brief span of my life thus far, that sensation has occurred on despairingly few occasions. Yet now, I cannot help but feel it, a warm sensation burgeoning deep in my chest.

We started from nothing. With nothing. Street kids, running wild in the streets of Isarn, with expected lifespans shorter than our list of self-preservation skills. Grew up further on the Waves, slightly wiser than before, yet with a life expectancy that barely moved. We were bound for an early, impoverished death. Things went off-track from there.

One of Chase's harebrained schemes actually *worked*, and we might have found a smidgeon of lucky growth, only to be derailed by the presence of an inquisitor of the Church of the Circle. This saw us, in short order, beaten, captured, and turned into living fodder among the indebted in the forces of the Light. Our life expectancy... well, let's be fair. It was probably still the same as on the Waves. Yet, we were expected to live out our short lives as meat shields, fending off the worst of hostile Guardians, dying instead of their valuable trained soldiers. I'm glad we managed to ruin their plans.

It was none of our doing, though. Nothing we planned for, at least. We were plotting a clever escape, rushed due to an infection to Kith's arm, when the Lightborn army was beset by unknown forces. These were Guardians of Darkness, creatures that had been thought defeated for hundreds of years.

The next few days were a horrid mess. Anybody who wants to take a stab at making sense of it can rummage through my annotated comments in Arnault's journal. (A weak word to describe the concentrated madness in those pages, but it shall have to do.) Suffice to say that we survived and emerged from the ordeal with three things we had never had before. Hope. The original Deck of Darkness, thought lost for the ages. And one wayward Lightborn noble healer.

For a while, things got a little confusing. In no particular order, we fought with our healer, walked the Steps and got stronger, lost the healer and found her again, gave Dark cards to the powerless lower class of Isarn, and realized that history as we knew it was a sham. Those were some *strange* days. The good part was that the healer actually turned out to be a wonderful person, and her inclusion among our number remains an absolute boon to us.

We also, eventually, managed to snag a Deck of Light for ourselves, even though we were forced to kill a few Lightborn in the process... among these, another inquisitor. That really got us on the shit list of the Church and Lightborn in general. Still, it didn't matter much to us. Now that we had Light cards, we'd be able to hide safely somewhere in the lands of Light.

Or so we thought. Turns out that inquisitors gain one specific card, granting the ability to sniff out Dark wielders. This "lovely" revelation left us floundering, unable to make a home for ourselves within the lands of Light. With that in mind, we made our way toward the one shining beacon of learning in the entirety of Ordei. Earth's Ward. The single, huge, overwhelming wonder of a city, home of Elementals and the Elemental towers themselves. Bulwark against the Lightborn and all else.

Turns out there's a reason the Elementals aren't outbred or pushed out of their own city by outsiders. You're not allowed to stay, only visit. Meaning, in order to stay, we had to come up with something. So, we joined the recruitment process to become part of the Protectors and protect the Elemental towers.

It still sounds ridiculous to me that we made it past the vetting process.

What was even more ridiculous was the fact that the following months were amazing. Surprisingly, being Protectors could very well have *worked* for us. Training was harder than hard, but so *giving*. Our growth was untethered, our potential endless, and our teachers were inspirations. Also, I had full access to the vaunted Library of Earth's Ward! I miss it all so much. That Professor Brookwatch! Yet, it was not meant to be.

Unbeknownst to us, a conspiracy was brewing in the towers. Most of the resident Lightborn Protectors, and even a few of the Elementals, were working to gain access to the Elemental decks and steal them for the Church of the Circle, thereby forcing the towers to finally surrender and become a puppet state under the Lightborn.

We uncovered the conspiracy, partly by accident, and secured the Elemental decks. I still remain confused at how we managed to survive that ordeal. Among the highlights were being ambushed from the sky by grimbolds and fighting our way up through the entirety of the towers. Oh, and Chase *tossing himself off the top of said towers!* By rights, we should have died that night. But we didn't. Which brings us to today.

High Elementalist Tatiana Skysworn, leader of the Elementals, is clever. She is powerful. She is also fully aware of the position of her people, and their relative lack of power. She saw something in us. What, I am not sure. But she set us on a course for the lands of the Furyborn, with a crafted wooden contraption as a message for a leader of theirs, Half-Swart.

Now, I am not simple. I am aware this scheme is a gamble on her part. One which is likely to end with us dead—by Furyborn, Lightborn, or raving Guardians. Yet, if it works, it might—just might—end up procuring us a permanent home of our own. A home where *we* call the shots. No nobility keeping down the powerless. No churches or secret police lurking behind the screen. Simply a place for all.

With that thought often lurking at the back of my mind, I am hopeful. Hopeful that this insanity may come to pass, and we can win the support of the Furyborn and gain the decks needed for a safe haven. Hopeful that we won't be forced to spend our lives looking over our backs. That we can earn the strength we need to stand tall against whomever may come against us.

Oh, but I'm never telling any of the others. They would think I finally cracked. Better play down my excitement until we make it. And I am *definitely* not telling them that I rather enjoy being the one who pens down our stories and plans. It allows me to settle everything in my head. I don't want them to take it for granted, though.

And Kith, if you read through my notes again, and read this? I *will* stab you.

Chapter 1

"Forty years. Forty years of negotiation, of broken communication and oft-interrupted trades. All our toil and frustrations have resulted in this tome. Dear reader, you hold in your hands the assembled wisdom of the Elemental towers regarding the lands of the Furyborn. Please approach it with reverence." I struggled against the task, at first. I didn't want to be the one responsible. However, now I know it's for the best. If I get to be the first to peruse gems like these, there are perks to the job. Besides, who else is supposed to be in charge of gathering knowledge on our destination? Liam? Please! (Page 1.)

Chase ran through the glow of the early evening, pursuit hot on his heels. The lazy Lightborn town of Vitras, plagued by an uncommon heat wave, barely stirred at the sound of his soft leather shoes pattering over the well-lain cobblestones. Most shopkeepers were already in the process of closing shop for the day, with only the occasional street taverns making brisk business in the oppressive heat.

Chase's gait was fluid, natural, and smooth. His frame had always been thin; however, over the past half year, he'd evolved from looking like somebody on the verge of starvation into his current state: sinewy muscle moving effortlessly beneath his swarthy skin.

He veered to avoid a chaotic arrangement on the street. This one looked more like an impromptu party in progress, with a bunch of people having dragged furniture out into the center of the street and draped bolts of cloth from one side of the street to the other to cover the sweating clientele below. A shadow of a thought, and Chase activated Steps of Brilliance, glowing platforms erupting mid-air as stepping stones, leading *over* a trio of middle-aged, laughing merchants playing jedak on a rug. The platforms, Chase knew, would be visible only to himself, and he sprinted above and past the trio before the first merchant even spotted him, ducking and cursing as he dropped his drink to the derisive laughter of the others.

It wasn't the first time Chase had been hunted. Pits, it wasn't even the fiftieth. Growing up as a dirt-poor Darkborn in a city of Lightborn, with pilfering and begging as his only recourses, had seen to a wide range of experience in that department. However, he'd hoped that the last few months had taken him past the point where he'd need to flee for his life. Except, whoever was following him was testament to the opposite.

The start of their journey had been promising. They'd managed to travel several weeks from the city of Earth's Ward without any issues. If nothing else, their time in the towers had left them with sharp senses and a healthy smattering of suspicion—they knew people were out to get them and acted accordingly. Yet, for the past two and a half weeks, they'd managed to move nearly straight west, with no incidents. It had nearly been enough for them to let their guard down and think they'd made it away from any pursuers.

Thankfully, they had stayed alert.

It started like a regular complaint from Kith, their low-set Furyborn scout, of his head hurting like a right bastard, something straining at the edge of his vision when he was watching through his summoned shadows. That seemed unconcerning on the surface—the low-set summoner's hangovers were matters of legend, and, left to his own devices, bloodshot eyes with wild-colored sclera half-hidden under the earth-toned ruffian's unruly hair would be the standard look—only, they'd deliberately eschewed alcohol for the sake of moving through Lightborn lands fast and without leaving too much of an impression. The innocuous complaint led to a brief onslaught of questions from Cilia.

Cilia could look intense. The uncommon mixture of Darkborn and Liberty blood in her veins, coupled with an extreme lack of tolerance for nonsense, made for an almost scary level of focus when the slight, dark-skinned scholar turned her full attention on you.

Knowing that she wouldn't stop until she got what she wanted, Kith immediately responded and got straight to the point. Yes, he had been drinking. Only water, though. Yes, he had his shadow summons active. That was the deal. He was the scout. In the wilderness, the shadows would be ranging far out, searching for any distant movement. Moving through populated territory, he'd keep them near, glancing from the shadows, placed front and back, to keep an eye out for any pursuers. No, he hadn't seen anything, or he would have said something. Yet, the headache had been slowly building over the past twenty minutes. It was like there was something right there, on the edge of his vision.

Since leaving the Waves, they had all trained like madmen and -women. During their time in the Elemental towers, obviously, they'd been constantly put through their paces. Afterward, however, they'd kept up the self-imposed pressure. They knew that they would likely face new challenges soon and needed to improve. Nobody, it seemed, trained harder than Kith. Especially when it came to his shadow summons. He'd spent a large part of his waking hours keeping the summons active, using them both as reconnaissance—as extra eyes alerting him to surprises in the middle of fights—and as nighttime roamers. Hence, they knew that, at this point, nothing about simultaneously using both summons, no matter how actively, was likely to strain Kith's Mental Power.

That was enough for them. There was something out there.

Chase asked a question. One word. "Split?"

"Split!"

A second later, they took off in separate directions. The rest of their group ran for the western edge of Vitras, while Chase, faking a slight limp to attract any pursuers, made for the center of the city.

It was one of a handful of planned and rehearsed contingencies they'd cobbled together over the course of their travels. Before even entering the place, they'd found and agreed on a spot where they'd reconvene if they were divided—and in case they managed to get some heat on them and needed to split up and meet again later once they'd lost it. There were other plans: for ambushing, different responses to a fight, to distractions... even to a last-pitch defense.

This one was sheer avoidance. Chase would present himself as the inviting target to any pursuit, lead them on a merry chase before losing them and circling back to where they planned to meet.

Only, whoever or whatever was following, they were catching up to Chase.

They were good. There was no discussing that. He only spotted them out of the corner of his eye because he already suspected somebody to be following. What was worse was that they were definitely using some sort of card. Their presence was blurred, vague, like Instructor Swansong, the head of the Cloaks in Earth's Ward had been, only this looked like a shimmering heat haze instead of a cloud of fog. And they were *fast*. Faster than Chase, which, at this point, was a rather scary prospect, given that he'd eclipsed thirty Agility, where your average person had *ten*.

Chase made his way through the center of the city, using his cards sparingly, combining Steps of Brilliance and Race of Life to give himself the highest possible speed and avoidability, while still not making it overtly obvious to the world what and who he was. Bad enough that people might be able to spot a one-handed Darkborn racing through the streets. If he showed off

Elemental or Dark cards on top of that, he'd be too easily recognizable.

In the adrenaline-heat of the moment, he did consider using his Sticky Fingers card. He was racing at a speed where he wasn't easily spotted, and the attributes he'd be able to steal might help him get away. Only... no. Again, somebody racing through the streets would be forgotten in a minute. Somebody stealing one of your attributes, perhaps permanently, most definitely would not.

Chase used everything he'd learned in a hard-lived life. He bumped into pedestrians, making them crowd the streets angrily to make it harder for his follower to power their way through. He spilled produce and crates, shimmied his way through the smallest of openings, and took shortcuts across stalls, people, and once even a rooftop.

The pursuer remained on his heels. They were even gaining on him.

Chase was panting heavily as he made it to the meeting place. It was the butcher's yard. In Vitras, they'd had the questionable wisdom of deciding that they wanted the slaughter of all animals to be handled openly, inside the city. That way, everybody would be able to ensure for themselves that the butchery was well done, the animals were in fine shape, and nobody was cheated. Of course, it also made for a spectacle: dark colors permanently staining the cobblestones, and clouds of flies buzzing to and fro. In the center of the plaza, the others waited, waving away insects, ready for anything.

He didn't waste time on the blood and filth. Yet, his brain did swell with a sudden burst of pride as he realized he wasn't entirely winded. A mere two months ago, he'd have been face down on the cobblestones, vomiting from the effort, half a mile ago. Now, he only had to take two deep breaths before he was able to shout out, "We've got company!"

All at once, his body was filled with several sensations. He felt a burst of energy as Sera activated her Spark of Divinity, focusing on Toughness. The sensation swelled as her Blessing of the Night stepped into effect, substantially increasing his Agility boost. He raced the last hundred feet at a dead sprint, with the others opening ranks to let him into their midst to present a common front against whatever was chasing him.

Liam stepped up. His chain-linked armor was dust-covered and the leather underneath was sweat-stained after the weeks of travel. However, the tall, handsome Lightborn looked anything but worn. The blue eyes were alert behind the rim of his shield, the threatening truncheon unwavering and steady.

Kith moved up to flank him, with Sera and Cilia providing the secondary rank.

Cilia's hands were at her waist, hands ready to pick any of a dozen different crafted items attached to the belts crisscrossing her body.

Sera, meanwhile, had her swordbreakers out, eyes roaming the area Chase had just vacated.

"Show yourself," Liam demanded loudly. "Who are you?"

Sera pointed. "There! In the shadows. I saw something!"

Chase turned around, heart pounding in his chest. His hand wavered between his sling and short sword, before choosing the sling, easing an iron pellet into it.

At the far end of the plaza, a window slammed shut, as somebody took a look at the group assembled and decided it was likely more trouble than it was worth. Halfway between the building and them, a shape slowly coalesced into being.

The transformation was disturbing. One moment, nothing was there except perhaps a shimmer, a barely observable disturbance in the air. The next, the air *folded*, and a person stepped out. *I guess that confirms the use of a card.* The tall, regal figure wore a form-fitting dress in yellow, white, and gold; a gold-wrapped braid almost reached her waist. She did *not* look like somebody who'd just sprinted several miles.

"You spotted me. But then, they always say that evil, because of its duplicitous nature, is more aware than good."

"Light scour me." Kith groaned. "Another inquisitor."

"Yes. Another inquisitor." The tall Lightborn did not look as if she were afraid. "I must admit, I doubted your existence. The clergy always seemed to inflate the threat of the Deck of Darkness, with no real proof. Yet, now I see you, I see how you all *glow*. That tainted, vile light. No wonder the mentally weak are drawn to your offers, like moth to the flame."

Chase cursed to himself. He'd hoped that tidbit they'd learned was exaggerated. A high priest of the Church of the Circle had claimed that inquisitors got a card that let them suss out Dark cards. Apparently, that was anything but hyperbole. "If you think we're so vile, why even talk to us?" he called out.

The woman inclined her head respectfully. "I owe it to you. If I am to bring your doom, I will do it in the light."

"Wait, what?" Kith coughed. "You're going to kill us, but you wanted to say *hi* first?"

She shook her head, looking every bit like an image from one of the church murals, the very image of goodness and benevolent judgment. "No. I will not fight you. Yet, you cannot hold me. My gifts will not allow it. Thus, I wanted to give you this chance to present your perspective and repent, before I bring the forces of Light down upon you."

Sera tilted her head, frowning in concentration. "So, whatever happens, whatever we say, you intend to bring Lightborn soldiers down upon us? Yet, you still claim to have the moral high ground?"

"I do." The inquisitor, entirely serious, held up a hand. "Also, do stop edging closer, or you will lose your chance to repent your sins."

Chase's mind whirled. She really wasn't worried about them catching her. Wearing those clothes, it did make sense. There was no way she had actually outraced him. It had to be a card. Or, two cards, more likely. One to hide her, the other to move as fast as she had. Possibly other cards, as well. Her dress was dark enough that he couldn't see whether she sported any cards on her legs. Meaning, they didn't know which threat level they were dealing with, only she had the guts to take on five Tier twos and threes by herself.

What else? Well, she clearly wasn't going to fight them. That meant all her cards were focused on hiding and moving. Meaning... one of her cards was most likely something along the line of his Heart card, only stronger. Something that would hide her. Something using her Mental Power.

Smoothly, Chase directed his mental attention to his cards. With a thought, he swapped his Tier three card from his training card, Spoils of the Undeserving, to Free of Perdition. Without any gestures or drawing attention to himself, he activated the card. Instantly, he felt his Mental Power blossom and burgeon. The attribute more than doubled as he copied the attribute from the Lightborn. He felt his mind clear and checked. Forty-five Mental Power. No wonder she didn't fear any of them. "Swarm!" Chase gasped. "Cut her off!"

The inquisitor faded from existence the moment that his power came into being.

Only, she hadn't accounted for his strengthened Mental Power. Chase grinned as, clearly, Sera had arrived to the same conclusion he had and changed her buff to Mental Power. His Mental Power increased to just past fifty, and suddenly the Lightborn was no longer entirely invisible, but was a vaguely defined blur speeding toward the thoroughfare leading to the western side of the city.

Chase shouted as he ran, pointing. "There! Bring 'em down on her!"

His voice was nearly drowned out by the buzzing.

It was Kith's new combination of cards. Twice the Fun doubled the number of two of his other summoning cards. Meanwhile, Apian God not only allowed him to summon a huge number of insects, it also let him draw in and control any *existing* insects. And the reeking, offal-filled butcher's plaza was a birthing place out of the lowest horror stories for any sort of buzzing, humming pests.

At a gesture, they all converged down upon the area where Chase pointed... stinging, biting and tearing in a frenzy by Kith's orders. Within seconds, a high-pitched wail rang out from the area.

Chase sprinted toward her, anything but speed thrown aside, as the blurry area wavered, strengthened, and reformed. For a split second, the inquisitor's image solidified, dress sporting red blotches along with the bright, happy colors. Then she disappeared in a flash. Chase's mind worked overtime. That was a new card. *Not the fast-moving one, or the illusion one. Teleportation? Where would she—* His head jerked around to try to catch her form.

Sera beat him to it. "There she is! Behind the table!"

Chase turned, spinning the sling, and spotted the inquisitor, overturning a large table and stumbling into cover inside one of the wooden stalls that had been abandoned following the day's business. Dark spots amidst the red blotches showed that whatever card she'd used had transported the insects on her body *along* with her. He sprinted into motion to get closer to the stall and attack her.

Cilia beat him to the punch. A tiny object sailed through the air and struck the ground behind the table.

An inhuman scream erupted, even as a large flame ignited from within the stall. The Lightborn stood up, beating at the flames on her arm, on her neck.

Tamping down any empathy, Chase let the iron pellet fly, empowering it with a burst of air from his Squall Sling.

The impact of the half-inch pellet didn't look impressive. It didn't have a lot of mass, and wasn't enchanted. It did, however, hit with insane speed, tearing right through her shoulder. The inquisitor ignored the wound, stumbling slightly, as she kept beating on the flames. She kept screaming... a horrid, ragged sound. Meanwhile, blood slowly spread from where Chase hit her. Another burst of flames erupted, lighting the entire *stall* on fire. Seconds later, the inquisitor lay still, even as the city woke up in panic around them.

They froze for a moment, undecided, as they turned to take in the situation: The flames roaring for the heavens. The city erupting into shouts and activity. The bright body of the inquisitor blackening in the background, along with any fancy items she might have worn on her.

Kith sighed. "I'm guessing we won't be sleeping in a real bed tonight?"

Chapter 2

"You search for a measure of wisdom? Take common knowledge and dig a few steps deeper. For instance, the Furyborn. Ask anybody about them—Elemental, Lightborn... even a rare Liberator, if you can find one. Their comments will be full of mockery, about how they are brutish, uncivilized, even animalistic. They will criticize their manners, their lack of culture, their clothing. Yet, rarely will you find anybody who is willing to mock their prowess in battle." I do approve of that approach. Listen to what is not being said. (Page 2.)

"I'm just saying, they could've given us a *real* guide instead of just a handful of maps," Kith complained. He gestured at the throng of dead trees surrounding the barely existing animal path they were following, illuminated by the rising morning sun. The town of Vitras was already well behind them.

Sera's face, studiously composed behind her blonde curls, contorted in a momentary frown. "No. They could not. We have discussed this a plethora of times, Kith. Yes, the High Elementalist surely had the funds and the connections to do so. She could also have given us fully enchanted gear, two squadrons of Protectors, a cart load of gold, and forced Ænima on us until we were Tier five. She did not. Why?"

Liam snorted. "Even I remember this one. Possible reliability. If it's possible that we relied on her, the Lightborn will have an excuse to complain, and that in turn will justify their trying to steal the decks, so it *needs* to look like we were kicked out of the school because we failed to meet the requirements."

Sera nearly tripped over a branch, stood still, and stared at the big guy who kept trotting on ahead of her, oblivious. She spluttered. "No. That..." She stopped herself and huffed. Then she turned to Chase, who came plodding after the two. "Possible reliability. I am *furious* with how he almost made that make sense." Picking up the pace, she spoke louder. "It is *plausible deniability*, Liam. That is the entire point. If we are caught, the towers cannot afford for us to be associated with them. Besides, you would not claim that they have done nothing for us, would you, Kith? They have helped us with rations, information, and obscured our leave-taking. They even gave us something that will help us with our introduction to the Furyborn and promised future aid. What else do you want?"

"A decent bed and steak for breakfast," Kith responded immediately.

Chase snorted and put his arm around Sera's shoulder. "That one's on you. You should've seen it coming. Besides, Kith's just bitching to stay awake. It's not like these are real complaints. But I do want to hear what the rest of you think. What's the overall plan now? The idea was that the Skysworn lass created a bunch of false trails for anybody trying to follow us. Now, we got unlucky. There's no denying that, and we were *most definitely* spotted. In a week or so, the entire region will be swarming with inquisitors and Lightborn soldiers."

Cilia spoke from behind the pair. "I have taken that into account. There's a reason we're going cross country right now. At least, we now have *good* maps, and some good information too. Round up, please."

The others halted, then huddled into a semi-circle behind her as she unfurled a long piece of vellum. She pointed on the map, indicating Earth's Ward. "This is where we started. We've gone straight west for nearly two weeks now. Another two and a half weeks would see us straight to the main Furyborn territory... but we're not going there anymore."

"Why's that?" Kith asked.

"Because of the state of the Furyborn territory. This tome they gave us with information on the Furyborn is excellent. It also does make our situation somewhat more challenging." The diminutive crafter frowned. "Look at the map. You'll notice how the Lightborn are at the center of everything, right? They've managed to dominate the center of the map, with a few exceptions. The notable ones, of course, are Earth's Ward where we just came from, and the Liberty Fields that take up a huge portion of the central to northernmost lands. Apart from that, however? It's all Lightborn."

"Yeah, sure." Liam shrugged, gnawing at a piece of hardtack with delight. "Furyborn are pushed back everywhere and the Liberators are in hiding. Even kids know that."

"Sure," Cilia said, with a deceptively sweet voice. "Do they also know where the Fury cities are, then?" She rolled her eyes, continuing before he had a chance to respond. "Of course they don't. Because the Furyborn have been in a constant state of war for decades, and they're nomadic! That means, if a settlement is about to get overwhelmed by Lightborn? They just pack up their things and *move*."

"Wait. How's that work? Where..." Liam squinted down at the map.

"Exactly. There is one well-known Furyborn settlement, Heart Halls, that they have managed to hold against any armies and besiegers for years and years. They even let traders approach, because the Lightborn nobles are hypocrites and want what the Furyborn can create, which, of course, would be our way in. However, the Lightborn always have forces near Heart Halls. What's worse, they have ways to mobilize in speed, when they choose. Given our recent meeting with that inquisitor? Them mobilizing and cutting us off if we tried to approach that way isn't as much a possibility, as it is a certainty."

Chase frowned, looking at the map. All it showed was a vast swathe of lands in a north–south stretch in front of a huge ocean, all clearly marked as *Furyborn Wilds*. Farther south, the area blurred into an intermingled zone, aptly named *Unaspected/Furyborn Wilds*. "That means we're going south to avoid any soldiers ready to catch us... and then we'll go west into Fury lands where there's less of a chance that there'll be armies or inquisitors waiting to catch us?"

"Exactly. With all that entails. It means we'll be closer to unaspected areas, at a bigger risk of being caught out by both unaspected Guardians and wild Furyborn Guardians, *and* there's a bigger risk that any Furyborn are more likely to attack us than listen to any explanations we have." Cilia grimaced. "On top of that, the item we were supposed to present to the Furyborn leader as an introduction will be less likely to have an impact on somebody fighting out in the wilds."

Kith snorted. "Don't sugarcoat it on our behalf, Cil. Tell us the *bad* news!"

"*That is the bad news, you cretin,*" she snapped. "But if you absolutely want more? We will need to travel south for at least a week before we move past areas regularly controlled by Lightborn soldiers. In that time, there is ample risk that we will run into somebody looking for us or Guardians, and I see no other way of approaching this. Running straight west will see us going straight for the greatest concentrations of Lightborn around."

"You get *cranky* when you don't get your beauty sleep, Cil. You know that?" Kith laughed unapologetically. "I'm with you, though. I mean, at this point, what's the alternative? Move back to Lightborn lands and try to hide from inquisitors? We haven't done too well on that point, historically speaking. We're just lucky the last one actually sought us out instead of staying at a distance and following us until she could lead their armies in our direction."

"Lucky," Liam said. "Sure."

Chase cleared his throat. "I agree with you both. We've stirred up the beehive, but there's no going back. Hiding or trying to sneak our way past their armies is not going to happen.

Meaning, we move onward and take on any comers. Then we make a case at any Furyborn settlement we find. Worst thing they can do is turn us away, right?"

"Actually—" Sera started.

"Okay, I was trying not to dwell on the whole *kill on sight* approach, which is also a possibility." He glared at the healer. "Ignoring that... we might be seeing more action in the weeks to come than we'd like. Who's up for a quick status to pass the time and make sure we spend our down time properly?"

With the exception of Sera, they groaned and complained, but eventually agreed.

"I'll start us off," Chase said, "by repeating a few of the advantages that we tend to forget we have. When we absorbed the Deck of Darkness, it gave us an additional two to our class attributes per Tier. Absorbing the Deck of Light improved our general fortitude while reducing the duration of detrimental effects. And the Elemental Deck gave us all an additional plus one to all attributes. Most everybody else just has *one* of these... and nobody else has the Deck of Darkness boost but us. So, whoever we face, we're always a step ahead. Remember that."

Personal Info:
Name: Chase
Title: Dark/Elemental/Light rogue
Step: 19 (Tier 3)
Strength: 18 (+1 Tier bonus) = 19
Agility: 21 (+11 Tier bonus) = 32
Toughness: 17 (+1 Tier bonus) = 18
Mental Power: 17 (+1 Tier bonus) = 18
Potential: 28 (+1 Tier bonus) = 29

"Obviously, my Spoils of the Undeserving card stays on, as often as I can spare the slot. Even if we've only used limited time for training while on the road, and it *has* slowed down some, it's gotten me two more points since we left the towers. At this point, I think that my training should focus on Mental Power, Strength, and Toughness, in that order, while any points from new Steps will go to Potential. My Agility, at this point, is adequate for pretty much anything. That's why my ability to make proper snap decisions and the Strength to really make a difference should come first." He smiled hopefully. "I know I'm going to jinx this, but I kind of hope that we meet some Guardians along the way. I feel like I am *this* close to Tier four!"

Liam tsked. "You *do* know that means we are going to be attacked by something completely out of our league, right?" He shook his head. "Can't say I disagree with your thoughts, though."

Personal info:
Name: Liam
Title: Dark/Elemental/Light fighter
Step: 15 (Tier 3)
Strength: 15 (+11 Tier bonus) = 26
Agility: 14 (+1 Tier bonus) = 15
Toughness: 26 (+1 Tier bonus) = 27
Mental Power: 13 (+1 Tier bonus) = 14
Potential: 10 (+1 Tier bonus) = 11

The big guy shot a quick grin at Chase. "Obviously, I'm going to need to learn how to steal that training card from you, because it's *insane*. You're even catching up to me in Strength. I remember back when I used to have to help you lift your spoon because you were too weak to feed yourself."

"That never happened," Chase protested.

"Aah. Those were the days. Your weak mewling. The cute way you drooled..." He snorted. "Okay. I haven't been slacking either, and Kith's been pushing me around enough that I've gained a point to Toughness since we left. I am going to continue this exact route. Strength and Toughness for me, with enough Mental Power and Agility to not hold me back. That, with my cards as they are, should be able to handle most things, as long as they come straight at me." He blinked and rubbed his nose. "Unless they're trying to run away instead. That inquisitor had me looking like a fat merchant caught with a finger up my nostril. Anyways. Any complaints? Comments?"

The others shook their heads and murmured noes.

Cilia spoke up. "One comment. You might want to look out for that. Focus a bit on Agility or, for the next Tier, plan to get some fast-movement skills. Being tough and strong are all well and good, but not if you're in the wrong place. Now, as for me? I have been practicing as well."

Personal info:
Name: Cilia
Title: Dark/Elemental/Light crafter
Step: 14 (Tier 2)
Strength: 12 (+1 Tier bonus) = 13
Agility: 18 (+1 Tier bonus) = 19
Toughness: 14 (+1 Tier bonus) = 15
Mental Power: 25 (+9 Tier bonus) = 34
Potential: 11 (+1 Tier bonus) = 12

"I got a single point to Agility since we left—and that's the way I'll be going. You remember that exhibition fight with the top-rank Protectors taking on all those Guardians? Well, it hit something home for me, that I've been thinking about ever since."

"Okay? Clue us in." Chase smiled.

"First thing is my own role. The fights out on patrol with the Protectors proved to me how important it is that we have somebody who stays back, keeps alert, directs and reacts where it's needed. That should be me. I have the Mental Power and attention span for it, and soon, I'll have all the items I need to step in and assist if we're in trouble. Sera could do the same, but keeping us all alive is enough of a job."

"That's bloody brilliant," Kith agreed. "Can't believe we haven't thought of that before."

Cilia nodded, a pleased smile lurking at the corner of her mouth. "Second point is in continuation of that. We're a team. We don't all need to be on the front line."

Liam said, "'Course we don't. We never asked you to, and, like Kith said, we *like* your idea."

"Mmm-hm. Fact is, though, we've still been working off the assumption that we all need to do damage, so we can walk the Steps. Only, that's stupid. You remember that Protector, the all-defensive guy who only had a shield?"

Chase slapped his forehead. "You're entirely right. I... Fury rend me. I can't believe I never thought of that before. With your new fire droplets, we can *all* do damage, even if we don't move into close combat."

Cilia looked at him until he shut up. "*Thank* you. You are still getting only half of my point. What I mean is, we have been mostly reactive, letting fortune and circumstances dictate who walked the Steps. We haven't even discussed who earned the Ænima from our fight with the inquisitor." Her voice rose at the end, turning the exclamation into a question.

Sera raised a cautious hand.

"Wonderful! That was entirely by chance, but I'm happy it went to you." Cilia nodded. "My point is, as our powers grow, we will increasingly be able to dictate the battles and control outcomes. That also means deciding for ourselves where the Ænima should go, define what we need as a group and act accordingly."

She pointed at Chase. "You are capable of draining enemies of their attributes." Her finger continued, resting on Liam. "Your Tainted Earth can slow down and hobble them; your clay armor can capture their weapons and you're strong enough to knock out most enemies as you please." Kith was the next on display. "And your summons can blind, sting, and overpower most enemies... while Sera ensures that we all stay alive, and I help where it's needed. Can't you see it? We have everything we need to *choose* who earns the Ænima. For instance, sorry,

Chase, I'd say that it's more important for our healer to reach Tier three than for you to hit Tier four."

Chase shrugged sheepishly. "Don't be sorry. I completely agree. I'm here for the part where she makes sure we stay in one piece... and I completely agree with your points. We've spent a lot of fights on the back foot, reacting instead of acting. That should change. Now, obviously the chaos of battle isn't going to allow us to dictate *every* damn movement of a fight, but we should be able to be more conscious about our choices—starting with the fact that we need both our healer *and* our crafter at Tier three. Anybody disagree with that?"

Cilia blinked. "That wasn't—"

"Good. That's settled then." Chase interrupted her with a wide grin. "Kith, you're up next, aren't you?"

"Damn right I am. Fire burn me, but I've been waiting to show off!"

> Personal info:
> Name: Kith
> Title: Dark/Elemental/Light summoner
> Step: 16 (Tier 3)
> Strength: 17 (+1 Tier bonus) = 18
> Agility: 18 (+1 Tier bonus) = 19
> Toughness: 14 (+1 Tier bonus) = 15
> Mental Power: 18 (+1 Tier bonus) = 19
> Potential: 11 (+11 Tier bonus) = 22

The Furyborn preened and flexed his muscles, warm colors swimming in his eyes. "Although I have no ridiculous training cards like Chase, I've still managed to increase my Strength *and* my Mental Power. And that, if you're interested, is my goal as well. I need to keep increasing my Mental Power, while still keeping up with Chase in the Strength department. On top of that, my Potential has increased to where I'm pretty much ensured to only draw Uncommon cards or better."

"Mental Power and Strength," Sera mused. "I believe I agree, but I should like to hear your reasoning."

"Sure. Mental Power, like I've had drummed into me, is all about control. I'm not a single fighter. I'm a one-man army. That means I need to be able to handle my summons optimally, make the most of them. I already have a decent Agility, and what I need the most is the Strength to make sure that, when my summons create an opening for me, I can personally do enough damage to capitalize from it."

The healer tapped her upper lip. "Agreed."

"Good enough for me." Kith grinned. "Now, tell us how you've done, Sera. There's no way you've gained as much as Chase and me!"

She rolled her eyes. "You are right on that count. I have only gained a single point to my Toughness *through our training*." She stressed the final three words, then beamed at them all. "However, even if I appreciate your intentions to make me stronger... I already hit Tier three. The fire droplet I threw was the one that finally ended the inquisitor. That earned me a full two Steps."

> Personal Info:
> Name: Serafine
> Title: Dark/Elemental/Light healer
> Step: 16 (Tier 3)
> Strength: 14 (+1 Tier bonus) = 15
> Agility: 17 (+1 Tier bonus) = 18
> Toughness: 16 (+1 Tier bonus) = 17
> Mental Power: 32 (+11 Tier bonus) = 43
> Potential: 12 (+1 Tier bonus) = 13

"Forty-three Mental Power." Kith groaned. "Forty-three. Darkness hide me. That's insanity!"

Sera ducked her head. "My focus is a bit obsessive; I know. But I believe that is the right choice for me. I will best be able to keep you all alive and well, with the Mental Power to make the right choices in a stressful situation and make my cards as effective as possible. On top of that, my training has, so far, done quite well for me in maintaining a decent level of physicality."

Chase coughed. "There is one thing."

"Yeah?"

He looked ill at ease. "Nobody here's going to question your dedication. I do believe, though, that you're forgetting something."

Her brows furrowed. "Being?"

"Being yourself." He took her hand in his. "You tend to focus on the well-being of the group at the exclusion of yourself. Well, you can't save us if you're dead in a ditch somewhere."

Liam gaped. "And you say *I'm* trash with the ladies!"

"Well, I mean it," Chase finished, awkwardly. "We need something that helps us make sure that you survive. Have you chosen your Tier three cards yet?"

She shook her head, still frowning. "No. I wanted to wait until we had discussed our approach."

"Consider that our approach, then." Cilia spoke up emphatically. "When he's right, he's right. We want to keep you around. If you keep focusing on Mental Power, at least choose some cards that will help keep you safe. We don't want a stray arrow to rob us of our favorite noble."

Kith barked a laugh. "As if we liked more than one."

Sera's lips drew to a thin line. Then she nodded. "All right. I will try. Does anybody else have any opinions?"

The Furyborn rolled his eyes. "You have the Mental Power and schooling of everybody except Cilia combined. I *think* you'll make the right choices, princess!"

At that, the healer looked down, and froze in concentration. Over the next seconds, then minutes, her face danced through several different ranges of emotion, from disgust over disappointment to glee and curiosity. Finally, she erupted into an all-body shudder that lasted for several seconds. "I am never going to get used to that sensation." She looked up to face the assembled group and smiled. "Before we dig into it, I did get my Tier three card upgrade. I went with my Blessing of the Night. Both for the boosts on everybody, and because I am certain that the future will bring further clashes with Lightborn."

[**Blessing of the Night**
Epic, Dark healer
Tier One
Passive, long duration
Once tapped, any attribute increases on you and group members in range are further boosted. Any active Light card effects of nearby hostiles are reduced to a third, sometimes outright quelled.
Long cooldown
"You dare come into this, my domain, and challenge my superiority?" The king of Fury is brought low.]

"The duration is unchanged. We shall see if the attribute boost is increased—but the effect on any enemies with Light cards is undeniable."
The others nodded. Having the effect of being able to negate enemy Lightborn effects almost entirely? That was impressive indeed!
"As for my chosen cards, I will not draw it out. I followed your recommendations."

[**The Flame Within**
Uncommon, Elemental healer
Tier three
Active, medium duration
This card will light a boosting fire within the healer. The benevolent flames of the fire will increase all attributes of the healer,

growing in strength and effect for a full ten minutes before burning out.
Medium cooldown
"At the apex, there is a sensation of becoming... what I was supposed to be. Approaching the divine. As if I could reach out and touch it. Yet, you cannot touch this." Mareus Corex Hammer.]

She smiled. "This, I can combine with everything else regardless of what happens, with no downsides, to boost my own attributes. On top of that, I got another card I can switch to, if push comes to shove."

[**Warhammer of the Ancients**
Uncommon, Light healer
Tier three
Passive, long duration
Activating this card summons the Warhammer of the Ancients. A massive, magically enhanced—though not unbreakable—warhammer that will circle the healer for the duration of the card, fending off attacks and striking against any enemies who come too close.
Long cooldown
"What do you mean, the whooppening? That is not a word. Now draw your weapon, you imbecile." Lord Actrus of Standale, seconds before the whooppening.]

Cilia looked up, musing. "Am I getting this right? Passive? That means it'll work independently of your own mind?"

"Exactly. I can activate the card and forget all about it. Of course, with my Mental Power, I should be able to multitask and handle the warhammer on top of everything else, but there *is* something to be said for the fire-and-forget approach."

The smaller crafter nodded, tight-lipped. "Not the least that it can defend you from somebody approaching from the back. Those are *solid* picks, Sera! What is the third one?"

Sera gave a warm smile. "The others were to make you happy. The final one? That one is *all* for me!"

[**Heart of Hearts**
Rare, Dark healer
Tier three
Passive, permanent
When equipped, this card takes that which your companions hold in their hearts and makes it stronger. Effects are drastically increased, as are durations, while cooldowns may be reduced. Beware, however, that the card may also increase existing drawbacks to the use of Heart cards.

"You've always had the power, my dears; you just had to learn it for yourself. Also, I've nudged the power along a bit." Famous high priest of the Circle to his congregation.]

"No *goddamn* way!" Liam burst out, then held a hand over his mouth and blushed. "What does that mean, though? I need to try."

The next few minutes had them all frantically running around, trying out their Heart cards, seeing what, if anything, the boost changed. Their card descriptions didn't change much, but the effects most definitely did.

Liam marveled. "My range is increased. The heat doesn't need to come from my body. Also, I can light things on fire now, if they're dry? That, or I can create and hold a larger change in temperature all told. It won't let me go so far as to fling fireballs or anything, but I can really raise the temperature by a lot."

[**Heart and Hearth**
Heart card (amplified)
Long duration
From the heart comes that which we love. It provides life, love, and heat. For a while, you are able to control the heat around you, at short range. You may banish the cold for your loved ones, make your friends comfortable, and make annoyances overheat and leave.
Long cooldown
"Come close, love. Do you feel this? This, from my heart to yours."]

"That *is* impressive." Chase nodded. "Say, if somebody was in a small guard room, you could heat up the room enough that they'd want to leave."

Sera frowned. "Your mind went straight to theft. How surprising." She perked up. "Mine has increased the range as well! Now, when I learn about the personal info of others, I can use it from twenty feet away. Also, I get more details now. I believe the effect of my Mental Power has increased the effect, on top of everything."

[**Look Deeper**
Heart card (amplified)
Instant, short duration
With a mental activation, the card wielder can pit their Mental Power against anybody, disclosing information about them up to a maximum distance of twenty feet. The higher the difference in

Mental Power, the more information is disclosed about a person's Step, class, current active effects and cards, even their attributes.
Medium cooldown

"Sire, I regret to inform you that this cad has used his Mental Nudge card to influence your decisions." A merchant loses his head.]

Cilia clapped her hands like a noble girl who just got her first pony. Then she blushed, deeply for it to be that visible against her dark skin. "I am *so* sorry, Sera. That's an amazing improvement. But..." She waved her hands, searching for words.

"Out with it, or you'll burst, Cil," Chase shot.

Her eyes gleamed with joy, and she looked at Chase.

Then... nothing happened. Only, the others looked as though they were falling over themselves laughing. Except, Chase couldn't hear anything at *all*. No voices, no annoying birds chirping overhead. "Oh, very gods-cursed funny."

The others looked as though they laughed even harder.

Sound returned in a rush. It took longer for order to be restored.

[**Death of Distractions**
Heart card (amplified)
Active, permanent
The Hand of Liberty keeps everything in check. Even distractions. Those pesky, tiny outside influences and sensual bombardments that constantly derail our thoughts, leading us to reduced productivity, minimal output, and any number of mental irrelevancies. This card can be activated at will, without cooldown. It will activate a small area of perfect control within fifty feet of the card holder, preventing anything auditory or olfactory from entering.
"Yeaaargh." The death of the scribe. He never heard the goblin sneaking up on him.]

Finally, Cilia, wiping tears from her eyes, concluded, "The range is limited. Still, I can see how it could be useful. Keeping a mark from crying out."

"Drowning out Liam's snoring," Kith offered.

"Please. I've done that for years for myself," she responded. "Chase? How about your card?"

Chase gestured at Sera with his hand. "It's... insane."

[**Nothing to See Here**
Heart card (amplified)
Active, medium duration

The attention span of the average person is a fickle thing. What will keep you interested one moment will seem dull and unimportant the next. Sometimes, to get from one to the other, all it takes is a nudge. For a limited time, become less interesting to anybody around you. Those with much higher Mental Power than yours may be less affected or unaffected.
Medium cooldown
"Now, to all those watching, I would love to extol upon you the forty-eight virtues of clean living. The first..."]

"It's gotten better all around. Not only does it last longer, the effect has also improved. From your reactions when I was testing it out, only Cilia and Sera—that is, people with Mental Power above friggin' thirty—have a chance to keep an eye on me, unless I'm dancing around naked right in front of them. I don't think I need to explain how Light-scourged insane that is!"

"Can you use it in combat?" Liam asked.

Chase cracked his neck, considering the question. "Yes and no. I mean, if somebody already has their eyes trained on me, it won't do any good. I won't just disappear from view. But if I'm trying to slip past a group who aren't looking straight at me, it'll definitely mean less attention. It demands some testing."

"Sure does," Liam said.

A companionable silence fell over the group. Only one person looked uncomfortable. Finally, Liam said what they were all thinking. "Kith? You have anything you want to share with the group?"

Kith, looking down on the dirty soil between his feet, shook his head. "Can't. Sorry."

That was different. In all the years before, he'd always treated his Heart card like a joke, as if it were something useless or embarrassing.

Chase cleared his throat. "Mate. I don't know what's going on, but it's clearly bothering you. At some point, you'll have to tell us."

Kith sullenly kept on glaring at the ground.

Eventually, Liam changed the subject and they moved on.

Chapter 3

"One other detail to keep in mind on the topic of wisdom. Even though the Furyborn are the subject of much mockery, there is one thing to be said for them. What they are doing, works. They have managed to not only hold back, but, on many occasions, fend off and cause horrible damage to the Lightborn forces. No other force on Ordei can lay claim to the same." It's not wrong if it works? Well. It's not the worst argument. It might also be attributed to the relative ineptness of Lightborn leadership, but... sure. (P. 3.)

"**T**his is perfect!" Chase's voice broke the silence. They were camped out on a hillock overlooking a nearby village below by the name of... Lily's Brook, or something else eminently forgettable. Kith had been scouting through his shadow summons, taking in everything about the place and its inhabitants.

The others nodded. Kith rubbed his hands together.

"Perfect?" Sera asked. "Why is that?"

"We talked about this," Chase said, clearly ill at ease. "We're getting closer to our target. A couple more weeks will likely see us there, and we're ready to veer off from the lands of Light and into less civilized straits. Yet, our rations are low. The climate around here is too dry, and we've had little luck hunting. We *need* to replenish our rations."

"But we agreed that we cannot show our faces... oh. Oh no. We are not robbing those poor villagers!"

Cilia put a hand on Sera's arm. "Yes. Yes, we are. We've been over this. The High Elementalist was good in granting us provisions for the trip. Only, she didn't plan for this massive detour."

In retrospect, Chase was rather annoyed with himself about that. He'd granted Dark cards to a full ninety Elementals before leaving, hidden behind a dark curtain, and given the new deck to the High Elementalist for safekeeping and, eventually, spreading the cards among the Protectors in the towers. Ninety persons. Of *course*, the secret had escaped. However, amidst all the last-minute plotting in Earth's Ward, they hadn't spent a lot of time going into alternative plans, focusing on speed.

At least they'd gotten a bit out of it, too. Adding further decks to their repertoire as well as spreading the Dark cards among the populace both provided additional bonuses to the first ten wielders of the original deck that Chase carried. Meaning, Chase's group and Gunnha and her people back in Isarn, however they were doing.

[By bestowing cards to a hundred Wielders, you have created a subservient Deck of Darkness. The subservient Deck will work in the exact same manner as yours, with two exceptions:
—It cannot birth additional Decks.
—The Titles granted to the Wielders from this or any future subservient Decks will not be augmented.
When five hundred Wielders have been granted cards from any Deck of Darkness, an additional subservient Deck will be birthed from the original.]

[You have continued working to restore the balance. As a reward, the first ten card wielders of Darkness are granted an additional bonus to their Title. You have received +2 to Agility from the rogue class.]

Chase's mind boggled. He hadn't really taken in the importance of that final point earlier on. Absorbing additional aspected decks granted them further strengths and advantages to their Title. That was amazing. Yet, there was a definite limit there, with only the Furyborn Deck and the Liberty Deck still missing.

Independent of whether they'd be able to hunt down a full set of decks or not, they'd earn additional class attributes automatically, simply for spreading the cards to the rest of the world, and birthing further decks. As the cards spread, this would keep on working even if they did nothing, to improve their class attributes, granting them subtle advantages over regular card holders. It would, however, also spread the news and let the world know that the Dark cards were back for good, with the subsequent hunts for heretics that would ensue. As such, attempted secrecy was still the name of the game, for now at least.

For the next plateau? Four hundred additional wielders to hit five hundred total? Good luck keeping that hidden. Even so, the idea of growing his Agility to inhuman proportions simply by existing? Very tempting.

Cilia continued, somehow in key with Chase's trail of thought. "We can't afford for anybody to know we've come this way. Some food and water going missing? Could be anybody. Us going in to buy stuff? That will bring the inquisitors down on us."

Sera looked from one to the other. "Can we at least leave some money?"

Not unkindly, Cilia answered, "Will that bring more attention down on us?"

Sera cursed and turned away. "Okay. But I want to be part of the planning."

"Wait. What?" Kith blinked owlishly.

"If we need to do this, I want to be sure we do it right and have it happen to the right people."

Before the sun set, they were able to pinpoint their target, as well as their approach. Sera also managed to ascertain for herself, through Kith's overheard conversations, that Mayor Emperlinger was eminently deserving of a visit by karma. The mayor's estate—a large, solitary, walled-off building at the center of the village, partly constructed from stone, whereas all other buildings were wooden—had seen a couple of people in the past hours arrive, carrying sacks and crates. The goods were unceremoniously lowered directly into an outside access to a root cellar.

The two guards on the estate were less than professional. They spent as much time chatting and sharing a wineskin near the gate as they did actually patrolling the grounds.

Chase slipped over the low walls at the far end from the gate. At his side walked Raudt, the current official name for one of Kith's shadow summons. The other was named Svart, and Kith hadn't elaborated on the meaning. Chase was simply happy it wasn't as silly as some of the earlier attempts. With the shadow floating silently at his side, he moved straight for the root cellar, but deviated slightly at the last moment and activated his card. The three platforms coming into being were bright and visible from afar – to him. With three effortless leaps, he rose into the air and slipped smoothly into the open second-story window.

"The mayor won't be back for a while. He's *visiting* one of the maids. You're free to move." Kith's whisper came from the shadow, disconcerting when there wasn't even a face the voice could originate from.

Still, Chase simply nodded and moved. Ignoring the valuables sprinkled liberally over the room cost him, especially as he saw a small, open money chest filled to the brim with coins. But today was not about money. It was about provisions, and— heh—"possible reliability." Somebody raiding the pantry? Could be anybody. Somebody pillaging the mayor's private goods? That would be something else, and less easily forgiven.

He didn't wait, didn't listen at the door or spend his time scouting for any surprises. Raudt had already preceded him to the door, floating straight through and into the hall, double-checking any neighboring rooms for activity. All was quiet; the few staff members mostly having retired at midnight.

He entered the hallway, rolling his eyes at the puffed-up self-importance of the ostentatious series of portraits arrayed on the walls, then slid down the hall, down two flights of stairs and into the root cellar.

It could be locked from within, like Kith had already cleared. Only, nobody ever bothered. In a household as small as this, and a smallish village, locking the pantry would be a waste of time. Now, Chase went straight for the goods they'd already planned to take.

"Be quiet for the next minute. They're doing their rounds." The voice came calmly from next to him.

Chase obeyed, eyeing his surroundings and readying himself for how he'd best arrange his ill-gotten goods, before dumping them into the large backpacks he was carrying. He took a moment to marvel at the insanity of it. There was no real stress, so little risk. With one shadow roaming the house in search of anybody still awake, and the other keeping watch outside, they'd have to be supremely unlucky to get caught. And even if they did... well, the mayor *himself* was only a Duo and out of shape to boot, and Chase couldn't imagine him having access to any real surprises.

A minute later, he got the signal from Kith and bustled into activity again, packing the two backpacks full to bursting. He walked out, and slowly eased the door closed. With the door unlocked, the suspicion should fall on the entire village.

As he vaulted the low walls, he allowed himself a tight smile. A year ago, he wouldn't have been able to *lift* the filled backpacks, let alone jog effortlessly as he did right now. Yet, now, he barely felt the straps on his shoulders as he loped around with what might be close to a hundred pounds of foodstuffs.

Also... this had just been Kith and him. They'd discussed what might be necessary and wasn't and had been surprised at how many contingency plans they had available to them *and just didn't need*. Liam wasn't needed to slow down pursuit or knock heads together. Sera would not be needed to heal wounds or shield their back (though her buffs did lend Chase a nice spring to his steps), and Cilia wasn't needed to fling shadows, silence, or blinding lights. They were all still out there in the darkness, just in case... but they weren't needed. What did that say about their capabilities, should they need to plan a truly elaborate heist? Chase wasn't sure, but he felt good about it.

A minute later, his family welcomed his arrival, Liam took the heavier of the backpacks, and they escaped out into the darkness. Chase's teeth were white in the darkness, as he couldn't stop smiling.

"Fury rend me, there's a lot of them." Liam's tone was part reverent, part disbelieving.

The day was hot and threatening to grow hotter still. They'd only moved a few hours away from the unremarkable village before camping for a handful of hours. They'd originally planned to sleep in, but the sun rose high and hard, ruining any chance of a comfortable slumber. Hence, grumbling and under protest, they eventually agreed to further distance themselves from the crime scene.

Noon saw a hot day turning downright oppressive, and when their route turned westward in the direction of Furyborn lands, they spotted a lone forested hilltop that promised some relief from the heat. They debated spending the afternoon in the shade and walking into the evening instead. The tall, majestic trees with the wide leaves looked like the perfect place to celebrate a successful theft with a well-deserved rest. Only, when they made it to the top of the small hill, the view over the stretches of land before them ruined any notion of rest.

The lands by themselves weren't anything special to their untrained eyes. Dirt-colored stretches as far as the eye could see, covered with splotches of hard-bitten vegetation here and there. Broken earth, a few uneven hills, and a solitary river cut the terrain in two at least a handful of miles west of them. In short, nothing to catch the eye.

Well, some of it might have been interesting enough to catch the eye. Only, the horde of beasts milling across the ground, breaking the soil with their heavy hooves, took all the attention.

"I'm counting eighty-some. Less than ninety." Sera's eyes were glued on the tableau before them. "I do not recognize their kind, however. Might they be regular herd animals?"

"No." The words from Kith were hard and no-nonsense. "Svart is halfway down there. They're clearly carnivorous. A few of them are still blood-spattered from an earlier encounter, and one's chewing on a small creature. Also, I'm seeing weird sparks from their hooves. They're Guardians."

"Describe them to me," Cilia demanded.

"Well." Kith hesitated. "They're maybe waist high. Heavyset animals, like a mix between pack animals and scavengers, and with what looks like heavy, bristling fur. Long teeth, long snouts, and shiny hooves that almost look like steel. They're—"

"Can you see their eyes?" Cilia interrupted.

"I can if I tell Svart to get closer." He frowned and fell silent for a moment. "Yes. Their eyes are weird—"

"Said the kid with eyes as inconstant as a Lightborn preacher," Chase shot out.

Kith sneered. "They change from one color to the next when they blink. The entire eye, except for the pupils. It's unnerving."

Cilia harrumphed. "I know what they are. Now, the hours spent in the library pay off. They're spark manes." She turned to the others, saw that she had their full attention, and continued. "Unaspected Guardians. Yes, Kith, they're carnivorous, and herd animals. They are also, even for Guardians, suicidal and bloodthirsty. Any living beasts they may fall upon, they will tear to bits, with no thought on self-preservation whatsoever."

"Do they have any powers?" Sera asked.

Cilia nodded. "As expected, the hooves. Their eyes flash between different colors and any kicks by their hooves will have added powers. The book didn't mention it as being too outlandish, but still. I recall one of them was a stunning attack. All close-combat capabilities, though, that need to hit for the power to step into effect."

Chase grimaced. "Anything on their hunting and tracking capabilities?"

Cilia looked on the herd in the distance. "No. From what I recall, they were only remarkable in their ferocity and refusal to flee."

The rogue exhaled in relief and sat down with his back against a tree. "Well, that's that then. They're veering past us. We'll just sit tight and we can continue in a couple of hours. No issues."

A chorus of agreeing murmurs and relieved chuckles were drowned out by a single, emphatic, "No." Sera had her arms crossed over her chest and a hard look in her eyes.

Silence fell over their group.

Kith cleared his throat. "Sorry, princess, we'll need a *bit* more than that to go on."

"I said no." Sera's face, normally half-hidden behind her curls, was steel-set, and her eyes sparkled with challenge. "You, as well as I, can see the direction that the pack is traveling." She pointed to the southeast, close to the direction they'd just come from. "They are moving for the village. The same village which we just robbed."

Eventually, Chase said what they all thought. "We know. Nobody likes it. But let's be honest here. They." He pointed behind him, back at the village, the outside wall barely visible at this distance. "They're the enemy. Not by choice or anything. Yet, if we try anything *heroic...*" He sneered the word. "Try to join their forces and defend them? How do you think they'll act? When they figure out their precious inquisitors are after our necks? When their lovely mayor is done fiddling the staff and realizes we robbed him?"

Sera shook her head. "You believe I say it out of a guilty conscience? Some misguided sense of loyalty to other nobility? No. This is a matter of simple humanity. My father..." She grimaced, searching for the words. "He is not a nice man. Yet even he admits that those who make their homes on the outskirts like these frontier villages live unenviable lives. They take a chance, hoping beyond hope that the Lightborn empire will grow to engulf and protect them, making their questionable refuge into a permanent, blossoming one. More often, they end their lives like this, snuffed out in a Guardian attack, or forced to retreat, impoverished after Furyborn raids. Do I think we owe the Lightborn anything? Water erase me, no. Do I think we should help this village? Yes."

Cilia spoke up, softly. "You'll have to explain that to us. It makes little sense to me."

"First off, although I do not believe we owe the Lightborn anything, I believe we owe it to the people down there, as humans. We have the chance to do something, divert the beasts if not destroy them outright. We can save them from a horrible destiny, hence we should. Even if you disagree with me there, we owe it to *ourselves*. Where we are going, we are going to need strength more than ever. This pack of Guardians might be the perfect way for us all to grow, to reap Ænima, to ensure that we are not just tossed aside by the Furyborn when we encounter them."

Kith snorted. "Princess. I think you're—"

"Onto something," Chase interrupted.

Blinking furiously, Kith turned on Chase. "Not in a *million* years was that going to be what I was trying to say."

Chase didn't face his confused gaze. Instead, he looked, troubled, down upon the large herd of killers slowly crossing the lands ahead of them. "Maybe it should've been." He grinned, heart starting to pump faster. "Kith. How fast would you say those beasts are?"

"Fast? Hard to tell from here. Besides, if they're half as bloodthirsty as Cil says, their speed wouldn't be the issue—getting overrun by *eighty of the Light-scourged things* would!"

"Humor me, please?" Chase asked.

Kith huffed, clearly annoyed. "Not too bad. I mean, right now they're just loping ahead, but they'll obviously be able to sprint a lot faster. Still, you'd definitely be able to outrun them over a short distance. So would I, for that matter."

Chase nodded. "How about Liam? He's only four Agility lower than you."

He grimaced. "I... really can't be sure."

Chase didn't back down. "What if we added Sera's group buff on top? Added by her Blessing of the Night? That's a full plus nine Agility on top."

"Plus ten. My Mental Power has increased," Sera interjected.

"Are you really suggesting..." Kith's gaze traveled between the herd and Chase.

"*Yes*, I am," Chase said. "Sera's entirely right. This is the perfect matchup for us. Not because we ought to take them down or owe anybody anything... but because we're in a position where we'll be able to grind down their numbers in a way where they won't be able to catch up to us and overwhelm us with numbers! Pits, half of the strategies we've thought up revolve around this very thing—huddling down behind Liam, while we slowly grind down the enemies' numbers! It's just that we never get the chance to fight on our terms. Not until today, at least." He held up a finger. "Whatever else happens, we're likely to be able to kill a few dozen of their numbers and still run away safely. But riddle me this. How much Ænima do you think we'll be able to leech from that damn herd, if we actually manage to defeat them?"

The Furyborn looked undecided. Yet his eyes betrayed him. As his eyes shot back to the spark manes, a tiny glimmer of avarice lit up. He turned silent, considering, before speaking up again. "Hypothetically... I mean, just speaking out loud... what would you suggest?"

Chase smiled and started to elaborate, announcing the ideas the moment they popped into his brain. He didn't try to think too hard on his decision. Because a piece of his brain—a tiny, infuriating piece—told him that it ultimately didn't matter. That they'd eventually have taken on the herd anyway, because it was the right thing to do. Chase did *not* want to deal with the idea that he might be turning into a moron.

Chapter 4

"They have constructed nothing. That is one of the main detractions of those who would belittle the Furyborn. That they do not build. There are no towers, no works of art to commemorate their passing on Ordei. Even if we disregard how ridiculous that kind of criticism is on a nomadic people, we should lavish scorn upon it for being patently untrue. Because the Furyborn do build. But their monuments, their contributions to Ordei, are created in flesh, in pack animals, in Guardians and living, thriving tribes. And considered like that? The Furyborn have managed a construction to rival even the Lightborn." Interesting argument. It's easy to see how you could discount the Furyborn on that basis. Who doesn't build? But can that even be right? I am unsure. (Page 4.)

"**G**o dark!" Liam's roar drowned out the whinnying of the manes, their snarls and the frenzied cries. He stood alone. Planted right in front of the entirety of the incoming herd, shield and truncheon raised, he did not give an inch. Instead, he simply raised his mace and roared defiance.

Once they agreed on their plan, and Cilia vetoed a few of the less well-considered aspects, they raced down the hill and circled around, in order to approach the herd from the northeast. That way, whatever happened, as long as the beasts went for them, they wouldn't be led in the direction of the village, but farther into Lightborn territory, with a full week to the nearest settlement. Not that they planned for anything but the ultimate destruction of the beasts.

The others responded. With a series of flashes and movement, their cards engaged, just in time, in order to ensure that they had as much time to run on as possible before the cards went on cooldown.

Sera engaged her Spark of Divinity and Blessing of the Night, along with The Flame Within, ensuring that her attributes would be as high as possible for the first, crucial clash.

Kith was a dozen steps behind Liam and to the left. He activated Apian God. The air burst into a buzzing, high-pitched mess, and the sky grew dark where insects started to descend on the mass of animals. There weren't as many as last time, but soon, any local insects lazing about on the warm day would start amassing as well.

Chase snapped his first Sticky Fingers, stealing a point of Mental Power from a beast, while he kept Winds of Change selected, ready to switch any cards at a moment's notice.

Cilia, Sera, and Chase enacted the crux of the plan at the same time, simultaneously tossing stakes of darkness right in front of the charging beasts. Three overlapping circles of darkness burst into existence, hiding all the beasts of the advance group of the enemy for a brief, crucial moment. Baying and howling erupted along with a few pain-filled howls from beasts that stumbled and fell. Then, the second part of the plan came into being, as the foremost beasts made their way, confused and blinded, through the patches of darkness.

The bloodthirsty and enraged beasts, eyes straining to see anything in ultimate darkness, were met by another three items flopping down onto the ground. Small, stitched pouches. They didn't slow. Didn't even react. Right up until the pouches erupted into a blinding, brilliant light.

Chase closed his eyes and focused on activating another card. His Tier two Elemental card Among the Raindrops came alive, and in seconds, puddles started to emerge ahead of him. He didn't open his eyes, didn't bother to aim, just summoned puddle after puddle of acidic, slippery patches of liquid among the enemies. Once the flashes disappeared from behind his eyelids, he opened his eyes and grinned.

Kith finished his kicker, summoning his Tainted Earth. The large circle of bubbling, shapeless mess also arrived ahead of Liam, turning the unbroken soil into a roiling mess of living earth, its sole intent to grasp onto any enemy stupid enough to come close.

There was no lack of enemies. The initial darkness and the following blinding light caused the front-runners of the charging beasts to fall and crash, many getting hurt in the process. Now, they were followed by their unhurt brethren who did *not* care to stop, simply because a dozen of their own were fallen and hurt.

The acidic, slippery surface, the Tainted Earth, and the fallen beasts all resulted in one massive collision. Chase took potshots here and there with his sling, Kith directed his insects to sting and bite indiscriminately, and Cilia flung a few fire droplets at downed beasts, fire adding to the absolute chaos. Sera waited, expectant.

Liam stood tall, shield raised.

A single beast made its way, near unscathed, from within the sea of fur and fury. Its hooves clattered against the ground as it raced on through. Spotting Liam, its eyes changed color, and it made a noise deep within its throat as it charged.

Liam made his move first. He took one step forward, two. Then, with a thought, he activated Waterfall of Light. He sprinted ahead, arm moving in a blur. Suddenly, the front legs of the beast were swept out from under it, and it struck the ground jaw-first as the trample effect activated.

The brawny Lightborn didn't waste his time. The truncheon rose and fell twice in short succession, crunching down on the front legs of the beast. Then Liam looked up at the other manes leaping past the downed beasts (and in many cases trampling them or rocking them aside), and promptly ran away.

The second part of their plan unfolded. This was not a battle. It was a grind, a slowly unfolding punishment. It felt all wrong, too. Their group didn't actually *engage* with the manes. They pulled back continuously, veering slightly to ensure they'd be going in a huge circle. Meanwhile, they allowed for three parts to have an actual impact on the herd.

Chase did his part there, casting Sticky Fingers every chance he could, slowly building his own attributes while he reduced those of the beasts and continually summoning acidic puddles that ruined the footing of their pursuit and ate at the skin of any beast unlucky enough to fall into one of them. Kith's Tainted Earth also did what it could to slow down the charging beasts, draining their Toughness here and there.

Meanwhile, Liam stayed in front, in between the front-runners and the rest of their group. He stunned the beasts with Waterfall of Light and sapped them of their Agility with Draining Ward. As if that wasn't enough, he'd gained a new overwhelming weapon in Unleash the Elements. Now, when his weapon connected, it carried the power of the elements with it. Manes burned, were buffeted by aerial blasts, had their legs pulled from under them by localized rogue waves, or even found themselves momentarily caught in fistfuls of clay hardening unnaturally fast. They were minor effects, but surprisingly efficient, even if their randomness almost caught Liam once or twice.

For a handful of minutes, that was all they did: draining the enemies, fending them off, falling back and spending as little energy as possible, while costing the enemy and punishing the front-runners. At every moment, insects buzzed around their pursuers, stinging, biting, and distracting.

Chase's energy reserves bubbled and threatened to spill over. Every attribute point he stole from the beasts was doubled by Sera's buffs and more. His Sticky Fingers card wouldn't be enough to have a serious impact on the herd in itself. Neither would any of the other cards by themselves. Yet, in combination, they weren't to be underestimated. The same went for Liam, whose Agility was ever increasing following every clash with the rare beasts escaping the combined slowing effects of the Tainted Earth and Among the Raindrops.

A handful of the beasts were already lagging behind the herd. Whether they'd been hurt by the crashes, were weaker than the others, or had been drained of vital abilities, they found themselves unable to keep up with the rest of the herd. Unfortunately, they weren't the only ones to find themselves too slow.

"My Tainted Earth is falling behind!" Kith cried out. "We need to circle around!"

Grunting with the effort of flinging a mane bodily back into two others, Liam shouted, "No. Push back. *Now!*"

Again, they repeated the trick with the shadow stakes, followed by the blinding pouches. This time, however, that wasn't all. Preceded by Liam and fire droplets thrown by both Sera and Cilia, Kith and Chase flanked the Lightborn warrior in a charge meant to punish the beasts.

For a while, everything disappeared in the baying of the manes, the stabbing of downed, confused beasts, and the ever-present thunder of the rest of the herd charging in heedlessly from behind the globes of shadow. Chase stabbed one howling mane in the neck, swung a warding strike with the short sword to fend off another animal. The beast lunged blindly, near impaling itself on the sword, and still pushed to get closer to him. The hooves themselves burned fire, releasing heat and smoke that obscured his vision and threatened to burn off his eyebrows. When the beast finally shut its eyes, slobber hanging in cords off its snapping mouth, the flames died as well.

Liam stood at his side. Following his first card-infused rush that made the leading mane tumble end over end, he planted his legs and didn't move. Where Chase was in constant motion—dodging, sliding, leaping about to evade any attackers—the Lightborn fighter was a wall. A solid wall, taking on any comers, weathering their blows and punishing them for the temerity of attacking. On his left arm, his Draining Ward card flashed with every strike. The Dark card increased Liam's defense while sapping any attackers of their Agility. Following his swings, the elements made the colors fly, as he punished any beast to get within the reach of his truncheon.

On Liam's right side, Kith reigned supreme. There was little finesse to the Furyborn's attack, but oh so much aggression. The squat summoner's hand axes struck out in quick, punishing strikes, hitting anything close enough to bleed.

"Split!" Cilia's voice rang out from behind.

They acted at once, breaking from their entanglements and rushing away immediately. Behind them, another blinding pouch unleashed blinding light to help them get away.

This time, Kith left a surprise behind. As he ran, his sweat-streaked face showed a furious concentration, and when it faded, animal howls of pain arose behind them.

Coils of Shadow was clearly a card meant for night ambushes, not for open conflict. However, in the absolute chaos of the melee, the surprise it provided worked just fine. The card summoned a near-dozen venomous vipers in the midst of the ambushed beasts. Vipers which immediately got to biting any exposed skin, attaching themselves to any downed beasts and pumping them full of venom.

Spark manes were straightforward beasts, not easily distracted. As Guardians, even unaspected, this aspect of their behavior was even stronger, bloodthirst drowning out most animalistic caution. Even so, certain instincts could not be quelled. And for a roaming herd focused on catching up to their prey to suddenly find itself beset by what looked like an entire swarm of venomous vipers? The herd went berserk—striking, biting, and kicking at anything that moved.

It took nearly a minute for the herd to regain a semblance of coherence. At that time, Cilia's blinding effect had long since faded, the summoned vipers were stomped or bitten to death—sometimes fully torn apart—and a huge number of the spark manes reeled from venom or suffered wounds from the panicked fury of their brethren.

Also, the Tainted Earth had caught back up with their numbers.

"Change targets for the insect swarm, Kith!" Cilia shouted. "Go for the healthy ones, one at a time. Take their sight!"

The insect swarm, at this point, had been reduced in size. The warm, open plain didn't hold as many insects as they'd hoped for, and the spilled blood hadn't yet settled to call in the local buzzing population. Also, the fiery hoof attacks of the manes were especially lethal to the insects. Even so, the remaining flying insects swarmed with undiminished fervor at the leading beasts, going for their heads and eyes with suicidal zeal. They didn't kill. However, enough bites or stings left manes with swollen eyes and ruined vision, ambling about, trying to hunt by scent.

Their brethren didn't care. The following manes never stopped to help, sometimes barreling straight into their own family in their desire to finally devour their targets. However, little by little, the strategy started to work. Chase kept stealing attributes from any leading beasts, the Tainted Earth kept draining the Toughness of anything it lay its misshapen limbs on, and the insects singled out those who were yet unharmed.

Chase, Sera, and Cilia started to do the same, attacking any beasts that looked unharmed. Fire droplets lashed out from the healer and crafter, while Chase was surrounded by the constant hum from his sling. This they did in fits and starts, stopping only for a moment to attack, before continuing to drop back against the onslaught of the herd. Liam never wavered in his defense.

By now, the herd was flagging. A few beasts were unhurt, but had been drained of Agility to where they simply couldn't keep up. Others had lost Toughness from the Tainted Earth and were panting, tongues lolling as they tried and failed to keep up. A good number endured smaller wounds, but suffered the indignity of being properly caught by the Tainted Earth. Finally, the mewling, howling beasts were strung along in a long, bleeding line of wounded after the chasing herd—those who were blinded, had suffered broken legs, or were simply too hurt to follow. One and all, they were stumbling along, slipping in the constantly emerging acidic puddles of Among the Raindrops.

Cilia caught the moment where the balance shifted. A large mane—the pack leader, from the looks of it—caught fire from one of her fire droplets, and as a handful of other manes shied away from the howling torch of an animal, the remaining pursuit finally devolved into an unorganized, chaotic line. She shouted, "We stand our ground now. Sera, switch to shields and heals."

Sera called out in the affirmative. Their group Agility buff faded away, and her shoulder flashed as she switched to the Cry for Blood card.

Then they went fully on the defensive. Liam's form changed as he swapped to his Become the Clay card, his shoulders and arms layered with defensive magical clay. He planted himself, feet wide, ready for anything. Chase and Kith took up their positions on either side. Behind them again, Cilia and Sera were prepared to aid.

They held the line. The first few minutes, the manes arriving were still in decent shape and proved a danger to them. However, the debuffs had taken their toll, and Chase, at this point, had every single attribute nearly doubled. He danced among the beasts, causing damage and death, while Liam, defense topped out by Draining Ward, was the rock they crushed themselves against, and Kith took on any beast that tried to move around Liam. On top of his Become the Clay card, Liam activated Ravenous Shadows, his Tier three Dark card, which actively took the hostile magic from the manes and converted it into a Strength buff for him. The voracious beasts never stopped being shocked by the sparks or fires from their jaws being actively sucked away from them as they neared.

If, at any point, they were in danger of being over-whelmed or overrun, Cilia called out short, terse commands for them to follow or flung fire droplets at the threatening beasts. Otherwise, Sera kept them protected. Shields burst into being on the few occasions where one of the beasts managed to enter a threatening position, their wounds healed almost immediately, and somehow, she even found the surplus attention to use the third ability of her Cry for Blood card, granting the three an impressive boost to Toughness.

Eventually, Cilia cried out, "Enough."

A beast sunk down at Liam's feet with its head smashed in. Chase leapt back, leaving a mane—with both front hamstrings cut—still trying to follow him with its drooling maw open and snapping. Kith stood there, panting, blood and worse dripping from his axes as his eyes flicked about, ready for any challengers. Not a single beast was still able to attack.

For a moment, the scene froze. It was a slaughter, a streak of battered and bloodied beasts more than a mile long following their trail.

"Cilia?" Sera shouted, to drown out the pain-filled braying of the surviving Guardians. "You're up."

The tiny crafter looked at the Lightborn. Her gaze shot out over the plain, taking in the thirty-plus manes that were wounded, but still alive. She croaked in protest, "We need our fighter to—"

"Our fighter is doing good," Liam interrupted, wiping blood off his face. "We've *just* talked about this." He leapt forward, shield unceremoniously backhanding a mane trying and failing to escape from the grasp of the Tainted Earth. "We work as a team. And the team needs their crafter to grow." He held out his truncheon haft-first toward Cilia. Unmentionable fluids dripped from the head.

She blanched but didn't back down. With a grim nod, she instead asked for and accepted Chase's short sword. Then, she went to work.

It was a grim job and bloody as anything. Weakened and wounded, the manes still refused to give up, and they tossed about—struggling, attacking even in their death throes. Within a minute, Cilia's hands were blood-soaked. After ten, her entire body was spattered with the blood of the dead and dying manes. Yet, she persevered.

One after the other, they did the rounds. They made sure to keep it as safe for her as possible. Chase constantly used Sticky Fingers, the Tainted Earth stayed focused, draining and restraining, and Liam made sure to knock down the few remaining beasts that weren't already near-dead.

Finally, the diminutive caster rose from the corpse of the final spark mane with a full-body shudder. "I never thought I'd say this. I've seen dysentery on the Waves. I've suffered Kith when he was convinced that water equated weakness and he should drink and touch only alcohol."

"That was *one week!*" Kith protested.

Something slid from her neck and into her shirt. She gritted her teeth, another full-body shudder going through her. "I have *never* met a person who needed a bath more than I do right now!"

Chapter 5

"Constructions or no, few people walk away from a meeting with the Furyborn culture unchanged. Unrefined, they may be. Uncouth, even bestial in some ways. Yet, there is an undeniable nobility to them, a sense of honor and dedication that even we Elementals could learn from. The Furyborn are a force to be reckoned with." Now we get to the good stuff. I can't wait to see what actually *makes* the Furyborn what they are. (Page 5.)

It was two hours of warm, uncomfortable trekking, worsened by the residues from their fight, before they made it to the low river trickling across the plains. For a while, Liam had Chase in a princess carry while he suffered the backlash from Sticky Fingers running out. Obviously, the others abused that to bring up comments about his lack of staying power. Chase, for himself, couldn't wait until his Toughness rose to the point where he'd be able to shake off the backlash of even the worst of these escapades.

When they finally reached the river, they took turns scrubbing any remnants of the battle from their skin in the placid water, while the others watched the surroundings, both for any beasts and for a reaction from the Lightborn village. Eventually, they crossed the river and started their westward-bound journey for the Furyborn lands. Kith, who, after the cooldown for summoning was over, had resummoned his shadows, let them roam as far as his control would let him. He said that he couldn't spot any Lightborn near the place of the battle.

"Of course," he continued, "that doesn't prove they aren't there, watching. Just proves that they aren't entirely idiots. Anybody scouting on a huge group of slaughtered Guardians should be clever enough to not want to draw attention to whoever or whatever did the slaughtering."

That left them all wandering in silence for a while. Knowing that they had no way of learning whether anybody had spotted their presence or not was a sobering thought.

Finally, Chase exclaimed, "Well, that's enough worrying. We've done what we could, and hopefully, even if we were spotted, they won't be quick to fetch somebody to follow. Now, what we *can* do... is press our lovely crafter on whether or not she actually made it to the third Tier."

Cilia frowned. "I have never been lovely in my life, and don't you start. You know I don't react well to flattery."

Liam nodded sagely. "She punched me once, when I complimented her eyes."

"I would do it again." Cilia nodded merrily. "That being said? You best believe I hit Tier three. I actually made it to the seventeenth Step. Three full Steps!"

"Nice!" Chase offered. "What did you put the points into?"

Personal info:
Name: Cilia
Title: Dark/Elemental/Light crafter
Step: 17 (Tier 3)
Strength: 12 (+1 Tier bonus) = 13
Agility: 19 (+1 Tier bonus) = 20
Toughness: 14 (+1 Tier bonus) = 15
Mental Power: 27 (+11 Tier bonus) = 38
Potential: 11 (+1 Tier bonus) = 12

"Two in Mental Power, one in Agility, on top of the additional two to Mental Power I got from the Tier bonus. I'm swiftly catching up with Sera," Cilia proclaimed.

Sera tossed her head, sodden curls bouncing. "That is not happening, and you know it."

Cilia smirked. "So you claim. A full lifetime of training, and you're just five ahead?" She snorted. "Now, as for my new Tier upgrade. I went with one specific upgrade, for a reason. Let me tell you."

[Ritual of Fire
Rare, Elemental crafter
Tier two
Passive, activated
Crafting by itself can be draining, both on willpower and stamina. Now, however, you can decide whether you want to sacrifice your energy for improved results. Once activated, this card will continually siphon small traces of stamina from the crafter to remain working. While in effect, for the purposes of crafting, the crafter's Mental Power is increased by seventy-five percent.
"Donande-tak, donande'tek, eru menthala-ze... damn. Candle blew out. Lousy secondhand candle makers. Kill 'em all when I rule the world."]

"The increase to Mental Power rose by another twenty-five percent with this upgrade. The reason why I chose this one?

It's all across the board. I could've improved my Manipulate Light, or the A Hint of Permanence card that improves the chances that any single thing I craft becomes permanent. However, this will ensure that *any single thing* I craft while I have Ritual of Fire active will have a better result, because my Mental Power is increased."

Sera looked like she was about to burst with impatience.

Cilia rolled her eyes. "*Yes*, Sera, we know. Your boosts will also improve the increase even further, and you can raise my Toughness, allowing me to keep the ritual going for longer."

Chase frowned. "Wait. I'd forgotten that part. So... let me make sure I get this right. You're currently at thirty-six in Mental Power?"

"Thirty-eight. Tier increase."

"And the ritual adds seventy-five percent on top of that? That's... sixty-something?"

"Sixty-six and a half, yes."

"Only..." Chase frowned. "Sera's boost increases our buffs even more... more than double now. Wait. I hit a hard limit at some point! When we attacked the estate of Sera's family, I couldn't increase my attributes beyond double the actual number."

Cilia gave him a tight smile. "Sorry. That limit's apparently only for combat. Last time I crafted with Sera's help, I reached seventy-two total, which was more than double my past attributes. With the increase, it will be even higher."

Chase whistled. "I can't even make out those numbers. So, what's it do? I mean, having a higher Mental Power, when you craft?"

Cilia frowned. "It's hard to put into words. Obviously, it helps with the mental aspects... visualization, compartmentalization, figuring out exactly what I need to do and add and when, holding a good image of my task. However, there is also an intuitive part of it. It helps me *feel* how to apply my Mental Power, where and how to introduce the magic." She wrinkled her nose, and her eyes lit up. "It also lets me push the limits. Say I craft everything flawlessly... there's a limit to how big an effect I can put into my creations. With higher Mental Power, I can craft effects that work for longer, have a bigger oomph. Over the next couple of days, I will be restocking what we just used, and you will be able to see the difference for yourself."

"That's all well and good," Kith said. "And I enjoy a good math discussion as much as a nice throat punch. Didn't you say you just tiered up? What the Pits are you waiting for? We aren't getting any younger! New cards, now!"

Cilia raised a single eyebrow, just to show him who was in charge. Then she closed her eyes and focused. Expressionless, the others waited and continued to walk, Sera with a hand on Cilia's shoulder. A while later, she sagged and gasped. "Okay. That was the biggest one yet. Three cards at a time is... a lot. Do they get more intense with higher Tiers? I think they do."

[**A Testament to Light**
Uncommon, Light crafter
Tier three
Passive, activated
There are cards which help with given aspects of the crafting process. Some help shut out distractions. Others help with the stamina cost. This card, instead, holds a tiny collection of recollections, from Light masters of old. These assembled tidbits of brilliance aid with any single creation that involves the use of Light magic. The boost is lower overall, yet the card will aid with every part of the process, and may even aid with intuitive leaps in the creation processes.
"They say that having voices in your head is madness. Only, when those voices keep being right and result in better creations? People shut up."]

"This one is simple. If I'm crafting blinding pouches or anything Light-related, it'll make it easier, *and* it will make it easier for me to improve crafts and learn new crafts by myself. I can switch it on if I'm trying to experiment."

[**A Dearth of Materials**
Uncommon, Dark crafter
Tier three
Passive, activated
Darkness is often associated with a lack, something missing. Why should it surprise people so that it also is a fantastic tool for filling out those missing links? This card allows the crafter to use their magic to replace some regular materials. Depending on the materials at hand, the result may even become better for it.
"Ah. We are out of thread for the needle. Magic will suture that well and tight." A proper battle doctor improvises.]

Cilia's dismissive handwave made no secret of the fact that she didn't think much of the card. "For most crafters, this would be a waste. They are able to order the materials they need. However, I don't see us in a situation in the near future where we'll be free to stay a long time in any given place, where I can actually get proper deliveries made. This should help me make do."

Liam nodded slowly. "Well, sounds like it may even make things better sometimes. Also... damn. Summoning material out of nowhere? Can you make like... gold? We can sell it!"

Cilia frowned at him. "Obviously, I haven't tried out the card yet. Even so, I can tell you with a one hundred percent certainty: That's not how it works!" She opened and closed her mouth a few times. "I think. Stop messing with my head, Liam. Now, as for my final card. It's my favorite of the lot."

[Chosen Focus: Fire
Common, Elemental crafter
Passive, activated
At third Tier, everybody gets this choice, for all their decks. It can also be chosen at later Tiers, and you can only have a single focus. When activated, this will increase your control and output of Fire at any stage of the crafting process. It will allow your creations to hold more of the element, will grant you a better understanding of the bindings, and will drain you less during the crafting process.
"Hearken my words, knave! There is a purity to Fire, a clarity you do not see in other elements. It burns, but it also cleanses!"
"Sire, art thou aware thou hath entered Wendie's domain?"]

Kith stared open-mouthed at Cilia for a while, until she caved. "What?"

"Well... this sure looks like one of those things you'd scold me over. So, you've got Darkness, Fire, and Light to pick between for a focus? You just said having something that affected all aspects was better. And still you chose Fire... which you yourself have said is notoriously bad, combined with leatherworking?"

Cilia huffed. "Your memory really is inconvenient—"

"Hah! I knew it! I was right!"

"Inconveniently wrong. What I said, back in the towers, was that the combination of Fire and leatherworking is notoriously *difficult*. Not that it's bad. Generally, when you try to combine a fiery Element with a material that's flammable, the result can be... prone to combustion. But the point is that it's so difficult that few crafters manage it at all!"

Kith squinted. "Meaning... when you nail it, you can charge higher prices for your work?"

"That, sure. But have you noticed the wording? *Increase your control and output of Fire at any stage of the crafting process.* What *else* is a part of the crafting process?" She looked at Kith for a long while, until she flung her hands up in disgust. "My ritual card, dammit. This will ensure that my Ritual of Fire *which improves my Mental Power* will work even better and be less draining. In short, the two cards in combination are going to improve my focus and results even higher."

"Oooh. Okay. No scolding, then," Kith admitted.

"No scolding." Chase laughed. "Though, when you manage to make a fiery leather armor that won't burn the wearer? I want first in line! That'll look so intimidating!"

With a wry smile, Cilia said, "I'm pretty sure that's not how it works. Besides, it would make stealth really hard, I feel."

Kith grinned. "So, am I the only other one besides Cil who earned a Step from that fight?"

Turned out he wasn't. All of them got a Step and increased their respective attributes. No surprises, for once. Kith went with Mental Power, as did Sera, Liam with Strength, and Chase opted to continue increasing his Potential, aiming for better cards.

They continued their march for a few minutes before Sera said, "Wait a minute. You earned a Step too, Chase? But weren't you at nineteen?"

Chase's grin threatened to bisect his head. "I wondered when one of you was going to remember!"

She punched him, not gently, as the others added abuse. "You stupid... butt! Tier four? Really? Well? Have you selected your cards yet?"

He shook his head. "Nah. You know I like to make a spectacle of myself."

Rolling her eyes, Sera admonished, "Get on with it, then! Tier four..."

"I know, right? Back on the Waves, I dreamed about getting a single card and here I am, at Tier four. It sounds unreal, even to me." Chase focused, then whistled softly. "First, my Agility boost just earned another permanent plus two increase from the Tier boost. Also, the battle proved that Sticky Fingers is absolutely viable long-term. *Two* of the ability increases I stole became permanent. That's just the start, though. Pushing everything else aside, this last battle showed me just how insane Among the Raindrops is. A card that allows me to damage any enemy, without even having to focus, while I'm running away? That, combined with the fact that, at this point, I'm faster than almost everybody out there? That's a winner. Meaning, that's the one I picked for my Tier four upgrade."

"Not the training card? I was sure you'd pick that one."

Chase shrugged. "I really considered it. Only... that's extremely long-term. And long-term won't do me any good if I don't survive to get there." He waggled his eyebrows. "Besides, I already made the choice. And it was totally the right one!"

[Among the Raindrops
Epic, Elemental rogue
Tier Two
Active, medium duration
Upon activation, this card will start summoning puddles for the duration of the effect in a thirty-foot radius around the wielder. The puddles of water have a triple effect, all working only against enemies. First, they have an oily, slippery effect and will make it hard to keep your equilibrium. Second, they have an acidic effect, causing ongoing damage against any exposed skin or equipment. Third, the puddles have a viscous quality, clinging to anything and anybody unlucky enough to enter.
Long cooldown
"Your fancy power is to make me stand in a puddle of water? Hah. Wait. Why are you laughing?"]

Liam gawked. "Let me get this straight. First, that water makes people fall over. Then it starts eating away at their skin. And now it sticks to them as well?" He shuddered. "I'm so glad you're on our side. You're on our side, right?"

Chase grinned. "As far as you know. Now, silence, lowly peon. I've cards to pick!" He rolled his shoulders and turned his gaze inward.

Sera walked up to him and laid a hand on his shoulder as they walked, guiding him away from the worst of obstacles.

A minute went by. Two, then three before Chase suddenly halted, falling to his knees, panting as he slowly folded up.

"Are you okay?" Sera asked.

He held up his hand, head resting against the ground. When he finally spoke, the words were rough, as if he'd just spent an evening in one of the coarse smoke tents of the Waves. "That was *intense.* I can tell you it doesn't get any smoother, Cil!" Shaking himself like a wet dog, he slowly got to his feet. "My first card... well, I'd been thinking about this for a while. I needed an escape card. Something that could help me get away if I was caught out, like with those kidnappers. On top of that, Kith's shown me how efficient shadow can be at getting away from pursuit. My new Dark card is the combination of that."

[Circle of Darkness
Uncommon, Dark rogue
Tier four
Active, short duration
Darkness is the friend of any rogue. That is a well-known fact. This card allows a rogue to bring the Darkness with them, even in broad daylight. Upon activation, a thirty-foot circle of absolute darkness surrounds the wielder, staying with them, even if they move. Meanwhile, the darkness will be fully see-through for the

rogue. Even enemies with higher Mental Power than the wielder will have trouble gazing through this short-lived circle of shadows, allowing them to get in a cheap shot, get the goods, or get away.
Short cooldown
"An eclipse? No, my stupid, stupid friend. This is theft."]

Kith nodded approvingly.

Liam's brows creased. "That seems a bit underwhelming for Tier four. Doesn't it?"

Sera shook her head, smiling. "Not at all. The versatility of the card is amazing. If Chase were not to use this for escape, but for combat, how many times would he be able to stab you, if you were blind? On top of that, it moves with him, allowing him to *stay* hidden."

"Huh. But against other Tier fours..."

"He will still have that Winds of Change card."

Kith's mouth turned into an O. "So, he'd be able to turn the day to night, do whatever he wanted, and switch over to another card without any penalties."

"And switch back when the cooldown is over. Yup." Chase grinned, eyes ablaze. "As for those other cards? My Elemental choice was rather weird. But I like it."

[A Friendly Wave
Rare, Elemental rogue
Tier four
Active, short duration
Rogues, more than any other class, are aware of their surroundings. They learn how to use the terrain to their advantage, always on the outlook for cover, for hiding places and terrain that will aid them and work against their enemies. This card allows the wielder to take a more direct hand in adjusting the surroundings to their advantage. For a short duration after activation, the wielder is able to command any water in their surroundings, making the water splash onto pursuers, soak clothes, ruin footing, and even drown an unlucky pursuer.
Medium cooldown
"Getting your hands dirty is part of being a criminal, they say. But... look at me. My hands have never been cleaner!" A crime scene is swept clean by a rogue wave.]

Liam and Sera looked doubtful, while Kith squinted, considering.

Cilia, meanwhile, clapped. "Finally! You've started thinking like you should!"

Chase grinned proudly. "You got it, didn't you? I've been paying attention."

Liam scratched his short hair. "I haven't, sounds like. What am I missing?"

"The word *water*," Chase said. "It's what Cil's been talking about. How you can really make your cards shine, when you start looking for synergies. Check this out." With a flash, his Among the Raindrops card activated, and small puddles of water appeared around them as they walked.

"You're not telling me that—" Liam started.

Chase interrupted him without words. The new card flashed on his right leg. Then, with a loud rushing noise, like a large wave surging over an edge, the puddles all soared as one, joining together in one enormous pool, that grew taller and wider, as his other card kept summoning puddles. The pool of liquid grew taller and wider, almost reaching shoulder height, in defiance of any logic.

With a grunt, Chase relaxed, and the pool collapsed into a large, wide puddle. "I'll need better Mental Power to truly make the water do my bidding... but I really think Cilia has the right approach. Find the cards that are not only powerful by themselves, but work well with your other cards or those of the rest of us. That's where the real power lies."

Liam shuddered, eyes still fixed on the puddle of water. "Yeah. That 'water' right there is acidic, will make you trip, *and* will stick to you and you can make it move and wash over a full group? That's scary. I... almost don't dare ask what the last card was."

Chase's smile was more fragile this time, less self-satisfied. "I... had better just tell you."

[Clothed in Living Light
Rare, Light rogue
Tier four
Active, long duration
The one constant for rogues, ironically, is a need for versatility. They need to adjust to their surroundings, often on the fly and under unhealthy or threatening conditions. This card allows the wielder that versatility. Upon activation, the card bestows the wielder with a quantity of living material that he can move, fix, and adjust with a mental nudge. A weapon? A shield? A set of skis? Any of these can be created and adjusted with this card. Any damage to the material reduces the pool of material available to the wielder. The material can be every bit as sharp as the wielder's Mental Power allows.
Long cooldown
"It's my time to shine." The Thief of Valkeer makes his move.]

Kith gulped. "No way. Will that..." Wordlessly, he pointed at Chase's left arm.

Chase smiled softly. "I... let's see." He switched to the Light card. With a soft flash, the card activated. A bright cloud billowed around the rogue, slowly solidifying into a cape. A glittering, brightly shining cape, enfolding Chase as snugly as if it had been tailored to him. He closed his eyes, and the material flowed like something living, parting and shifting. The material split, and half ran down his shoulder, across his arm and pooled around the stump. Eyes wide open in wonder, he raised his arm and flexed his new hand. His brilliant, bright new hand.

Sera grabbed the hand and held it, marveling. "It feels cool, but otherwise just like a normal surface. Can you feel my touch?"

He didn't dare speak. Merely nodded. The bright, sparkling fingers of his new hand moved ever so slightly. Hoarsely, he said, "They—" He had to clear his throat and try again. "They feel... removed from me. Not entirely part of me. Also, my control doesn't feel natural. I will have to practice. A lot. But with this, I can become, I don't know. Whole." The last word was close to a whisper.

"Yeah, well. I still say you're just compensating," Kith said.

"Kith!" Cilia cried, disbelief and affront struggling for supremacy.

"What? You all thought it. I just said it. Sparkly? It can grow? Clearly bigger than it used to be? Dude is compensating something bad."

Chase didn't respond. He merely held up his new appendage. The middle finger extended and grew to double size, to the laughter of all.

Chapter 6

"As much as I hate to admit it, there's one place where the Furyborn entirely live up to their bad reputation. Organization. Whether it's due to lack of planning, bad leadership, or simply their major focus on individualism, I cannot say. Yet, their organizational structures are horrible, compared to something as structured as our towers, let alone the massive tapestry of organization among the Lightborn. You ask to speak with somebody in charge, and they spit at you." I guess I see what he means. The Lightborn did seem rather hit-or-miss, when it came to leadership, with what we saw. But thinking about how fast they got the inquisitors to look for us and what that entailed? That is rather impressive. (Page 26.)
The main Church of the Circle, Inner Sanctuary.

"I have to thank you for the cooperation, Archbishop de Arcour. This could easily have become a major debacle. Allowing us to handle this bloodlessly will, in the end, be a boon both to your church and to the lands of Light as a whole." The voice was warm, sincere, and entirely at odds with the smirk only half-repressed on the handsome features of the tall male. Lord Beforant looked every bit what he was—one of the most powerful nobles in the lands of Light.

Archbishop de Arcour inclined his head in the barest of nods. Between the two, blood spread on the floor, surrounding Lord Beforant's boots in a growing pool. His two bodyguards had put up an impressive struggle against the superior numbers of the attackers. Meanwhile, the archbishop himself had seen the folly of it and succumbed to the inevitable instead of struggling.

He did not deign to comment on the irony in calling this bloodless. They both knew that personal protectors, by their nature, were too dangerous to keep around for transitional phases like this one. Whether he would be in a position to get some new ones at a later date was still to be decided. There was a good deal of unknowns to the current situation. For the moment, the sole certainty was that he, despite all his preparations, had been outplayed. "I see no reason to waste energy unnecessarily. I respect your professionalism. How will you present this to the public? Unknown attackers? Perhaps Darkspawn?"

The noble sneered, though it faded almost instantly. His features *were* handsome—frustratingly so. The naturally curly locks, the strong jaw, and the open, honest face looked like something that belonged on statues across the nation. Which, of course, it already was. "Oh, we shan't bother the public with something as simple as this. A tiny military exercise, I believe we will call it."

The archbishop did not hint at his thoughts. Yet it shook him. At first, he'd expected that this was a simple murder. Yet, there had been no disturbances, no deaths except for his personal protectors. This meant that the fortress of Light had been purposefully opened to the noble and his military retinue, granting them all access. This was an internal coup. It could potentially be really bad, depending on how deep it went. "There is something to be said for keeping unnecessary turmoil from the public. No need to challenge their small minds with nuances they are incapable of grasping."

Lord Beforant tittered. It was a weird look on the statuesque face, this model of self-control and flawless masculinity. "Small minds. Yes. That does sound about right. I hope you do not mind that I point something out, Esteemed Father. You are being... how should I put this? Surprisingly levelheaded about this."

That took him aback. A tiny frown appeared on the archbishop's brow. "What is there to be surprised about? I have been outmaneuvered. Your presence here portends a threat to my physical well-being. In normal circumstances, I would have two options—either to stall you with conversation as my stalwart defenders tried to come to my rescue, or to hold you off myself, until such time as my brothers were able to bring their numbers to bear." His eyes roamed over the attackers, assessing, considering. "Three Quattros, a dozen Trios, and you, a very impressive Tier five. Normally, I would be more than capable of handling you by myself—or at least, holding you back, until every inquisitor, every soldier of the Light in the entire capitol flooded the sanctuary to bring me your heads."

Bowing his head in acknowledgment of the accomplishment, he continued. "Alas, you have me outplayed. There are no alarms, no cries of outrage or sounds of fighting. Meaning, you were helped from the inside and I have no martial aid coming."

Lord Beforant raised a perfectly manicured eyebrow, a hint of a smile at his lips. "Most people would see that as an even better reason to struggle. Fighting against inevitability, as it were."

The archbishop's chuckle sounded cold and mirthless, even to himself. "Which inevitability? You have me at a disadvantage. You may kill me at your leisure. Yet, you are not a rube, a newcomer to believe that holding the reins of power is the only thing that matters. You and I are presenting blades, facing the most important fight of all. The fight of succession. You know for yourself the struggle you will face, should you choose to murder me in cold blood. Hiding something like this is not an option, and I have safeguards. Oh, so many safeguards."

"Ah." The noble bowed deep, granting the point. "At that, you do have a point. Murder as a path to take-over is so often portrayed as crude. People choose to take offense, to view it as an illegitimate choice, as something, dare I say, evil?" With a flippant tone of voice, as if he were debating the price of a cheap bauble, he waggled his index finger. "People are so short-sighted. If I order my guards to have you run through here in the most holy, I must surely be evil, somebody to be struggled against at all costs, with all that entails. Trade embargoes. Slander and gossip. Protests and posturing during the day, blades in the night." The powerful man rolled his eyes. "Such pettiness over something that has already been decided and cannot be taken back."

"I agree," the archbishop granted. "Yet, it is undeniable to my advantage that—"

"Alas," Lord Beforant continued.

The archbishop's eyes boggled. Ignoring him like he was a common serf? Yet, everybody painted the noble like somebody well-versed in the games of the court. What did he hold back?

"Alas, I know all too well who you are, dear archbishop. You are a political animal, and a ruthless one at that. Your path to the vaunted Deck of Light has corpses of the powerless and wielders aplenty left strewn in your path. If I were to leave you alive, I would have a month, at most. By then, you would have traded in favors, used blackmail, pulled any strings you hold, to have the noble houses and whichever parts of the clergy you have under your thumb go against me. No. A vital part of diplomacy is knowing at which point the sword is the cleanest kind of diplomacy."

The archbishop of all the realms of Light did draw back at that. He truly dared? Was he such an ignoramus that he would simply attack and curse the results? He hissed, barely holding back the venom. "That is truly what you think, *Thomas?* I thought you were a real player, not a pretender. You believe that killing me will lead to blades in the night? *It will be civil war!* Four of the largest noble houses are *mine.* Within a week, you will have armies besieging Stradeburg. Within a month, you will be dead, your legacy in flames. Any survivors of House Beforant will be cursing you for ages to come. Whichever member of the clergy you have pressured into doing your bidding, it will not be enough to keep the Church of the Circle from pronouncing you anathema."

That was not an idle threat. It had taken him close to a decade to ensure that this was the case. The noble was not wrong when he spoke about ruthlessness. Yet, it had been necessary, and it had led him to where he was. He was *not* going to let a simpleton take everything from him because he did not comprehend the nuances of the game.

The nobleman did not react the way he anticipated. He did not deny the point, or lose his patience. With a low chuckle, he moved past the archbishop and pulled the string to the bell, calling for a servant. Then he stepped back, holding up a hand for patience, brushing back an errant lock of hair from his forehead, plastering on that blasted smile again.

A man walked in. As opposed to Lord Beforant, he did not stride. He walked painfully slowly, one leg half-dragged behind him, near unable to carry his weight, even as a Lightborn soldier supported his arm. The man was maybe middle-aged, dressed in the clean, white robes of the church, adorned with the golden wings of a high priest. His looks were unfamiliar, ravaged by scars, some still reddened as if they had been badly inflamed. The hair had been shorn off, only a spattering of uneven stubble showing the golden colors of a Lightborn.

"You!" The archbishop's voice was equal parts vitriol and condemnation. He sputtered, unable to summon all the words he wanted. "High Priest Desahl. I thought—"

"You thought I'd died." The usual sly voice was changed. Hoarse, ruined. "As well you should. You were the one who tried to have me killed. Nearly succeeded too." He spat, then made the sign of the Circle. *"Esteemed Father."*

The archbishop sneered. "So that is what this is? Petty revenge? You will be the one to argue to the Church that nothing evil has happened, while this upstart takes over the rule of the realms. Do you not know what this rube plots? If you take over as archbishop, it will be in name only. His disdain for the influence of the church is well-known. You will be the sole cause for having dismantled the Church of the Circle and allowing darkness to take over the lands. *Is this your desire, High Priest Desahl?"*

The high priest sneered and coughed. "Ah. Who would've thought that Old Bloodless had that sort of heat in him? Or is it still just a game to you? Pushing, prodding to find weaknesses?" He pointed at the foremost noble of the lands of Light. "Even if I were to forget that Lord Beforant saved my life, I would still follow him." His voice rang out stronger, with zeal and ardor. "Archbishop de Arcour. You have strayed. The Church of the Circle is meant to protect the Lightborn from evil. To be the shield between the Pits and man, the guiding force to those in charge.

Instead, you have grasped the reins of power for yourself and tried to make the Church the leading power."

The nobleman looked on, nodding in satisfaction. A look at the open hatred on the face of the archbishop made him chuckle. "Oh, don't worry. We won't kill you outright. You will surrender the Deck of Light, with all that entails. Then, you will be questioned, quite thoroughly, ensuring that we know anything of value. As long as you do not hold back information, you will not be unduly harmed, beyond perhaps a token effort to ensure you see the gravity of the situation. Finally, you will be escorted into exile. It will be a lonely life, but one not entirely bereft of luxury. You will, of course, hope that you will be able to eventually manipulate your way out of there... let us call it an incentive for your future."

The most powerful man of the realms looked around. Everywhere, he saw his power evaporating, threads he had sown now proving to be little but cobwebs, falling apart in his hands. Yet, he had not reached the heights of power he had for a lack of patience. "If I go along with this... what will happen with the church? And the wielders of Dark?"

Thomas Beforant nodded amiably, as if they were debating an everyday occurrence. "Little will happen to the church. It is well. However, there will be no further attempts at the church trying to steer the politics of the lands of Light. The nobles will reign, in accordance with our collective desires."

"You mean they are going to do what you say."

He shrugged, not debating the point. "The nobles are not always that easily led, but... sure. As for the church, it will rest in the capable hands of Archbishop Desahl. We have had some productive, amiable conversations on the future. Archbishop Desahl, if you would?"

The burned high priest hadn't looked away from him. He'd barely blinked, taking in everything with a gleefulness that bordered on obsessive. "Whatever you think, Lord Beforant has no interest in dismantling our church. But he can also see where things have gone astray. There will be a few changes. The preachers all around the realms will be withdrawn and repurposed. We will no longer be trying to stir up religious fervor without reason. On that note, we will also call back a lot of the inquisitors. Many are little but ridiculous zealots, stalking the realms, inciting hunts on any who are slightly different. No, they will return to their real purpose, as shields. Fighters, to be put into action, when we have a real target."

"We *do* have a real target," the archbishop hissed.

"We do at that. The confirmation that the wielders of Dark cards are out there has been proved true. Yet, we still have inciters in every village, inquisitors touring the north, churning up spurious notes of heresy, while we have a real enemy. *That is not of the Light.*"

Lord Beforant nodded. "It took us a while to come to an agreement on this topic. Yet, eventually, we reached it, and it is, if I may say so myself, rather elegant. We have come full circle, as it were."

Desahl laughed. A low, mirthless sound.

He caught the reference immediately. But... that would turn *everything* on its head. Ruin years upon years of indoctrination. "You will burn everything."

"No. We will not." High Priest Desahl smirked, a terrifying look on the ruined, inflamed face. "I should know what burning is like. We have spent years upon years to tell people that wielders of Dark are demons in the night, boogiemen everybody should look out for, so they don't look too closely at the depredations of the Church of Light itself. Now, as soon as we find the Deck of Darkness, we will be able to bring it back to the fold. Cleanse it."

"It will be a gradual thing, of course," Lord Beforant said, openly and eagerly. "First, we will tell the world that we have finally triumphed. Then, we will have to show them that we have conquered the evil lurking in the decks. Then, we will be able to show the world how select people receive the training and protection needed from the Church to wield these powers safely, for the protection of all. The Church of the Circle will finally again command the powers of the entire circle: life, death, rebirth. Then, we will *finally* be able to bring the Furyborn to heel and bring down the towers. Bring the entire world into the Light."

The archbishop reeled. It was all too much. It would work, too. He could plot out the steps needed to complete the plan in his mind. "Obviously, these *select people* will mostly be faithful priests and high priests, and those who do not oppose you on your pathway to power over the other nobles."

"Put like that, it sounds rather devious." Lord Beforant tittered again. "Also, effective. Do you see anything wrong with our plan? Your brother in faith here has divulged the truth of the schism in the church back in the day."

Grasping for control, he answered, sneering, "Destroying the priests of Dark was always a ruse. Something to appease the masses while we cleaned house. My predecessors had the right of that move, even if they failed in obtaining the original deck for themselves. But there are two, rather obvious flaws in your plan."

"Do tell." Beforant smiled.

"First. You do not *have* the deck. Everything you're plotting is based on that, yet you don't even know where it is."

"True." The nobleman didn't look all too disturbed at that fact. In fact, he was disturbingly stoic. "We have plans, of course. However, what we *really* have is dedication. The good Desahl and I are not afraid to truly play with our metaphorical muscles, once we need to do what needs doing."

"Second." The archbishop continued, determined to wipe that self-satisfied smile off the man's face. "You do not have the political acumen or power for this. Desahl? He's clever enough. Only, he doesn't wield the control that I do. He doesn't have the stranglehold I have over the nobles... the knowledge of their missteps, the depths of their depravity. In short, if you attempt to do this, *you will need me!* Anything else will lead to your ruin."

High Priest Desahl spoke up. His rasping voice had a weird tone to it. Was it... empathy? "This, at least, was one thing Lord Beforant and I wholeheartedly agreed on. Any attempt to include you would only backfire or lead to our betrayal. Removing you from the position? It gives us a chance to start over. Our reasonings may not always be entirely of the Light. But if I do nothing else with my life, the afterlife will surely see the removal of your taint as an action of the Light."

Chapter 7

"Yet another reason why the world as a whole has little but disdain for Furyborn? Their poverty. They have been pushed to the outskirts, to the least enviable living grounds. Living in dirt, in barren surroundings? That must be a sign of losing. Yet, if you talk to a Furyborn, their perspective differs. This is their crucible, their grinding stone. The life that will help them grow strong and tough." Somebody would choose life in the wilderness and poverty *on purpose*? Yeah, that sounds like somebody lying to themselves. (Page 12.)

For a full week, their travels resumed nearly uninterrupted. They didn't hurry—their successful theft had left them with enough provisions that they had ample food and drink. On top of this, they decided that they'd made it away without getting caught, and needed to focus on training and preparation more than they needed to create distance between themselves and theoretical pursuit.

Chase focused on his new abilities almost exclusively. He did spend time learning how to manipulate water as well as possible. Yet, most of his time, unsurprisingly, was spent trying to adjust to his newfound limb. How to make it into a spear. A shield. An axe for chopping firewood. Slowly, he learned the limits and advantages of the glittering, attention-demanding material. It turned out that the "living light" was able to withstand attacks from most everything slashing or stabbing—yet, any slashing damage especially consumed large amounts of the material, making it less useful for defensive use in protracted fights. Against crushing damage, from Cilia's quarterstaff or Liam's truncheon, it was nigh useless. You needed to create a thick layer to ward off blunt attacks, and the material was crushed and rendered inert and useless from a few attacks, even inside a glove. Where it excelled was in the versatility, as a defense against daggers and arrows... and in the strength. Using his new "hand," if he managed to clamp down on anything, only Liam had the Strength to wrestle it free from his grasp.

During their downtime, Liam and Kith were almost constantly embroiled in training sessions. Kith focused on improving his Mental Power, pushing his control over his minions, attempting to become better at forming cohesive attacks and strategies and pulling them off flawlessly.

Liam, meanwhile, took everything he'd learned from the Elemental towers about footwork and weaponry and tried to polish it to a blinding sheen. Although he did participate in their common talks about strategy, building or improving their combined cards, he was near-obsessed with learning how to hold his own, to ensure that he'd be able to go toe-to-toe with anybody and win through sheer physical prowess and skill.

Sera pulled back slightly from the combat training. In part, it was due to her perceiving more of a need for somebody to act as the trainer, to pinpoint flaws and weaknesses. However, she also took it upon herself to act as the prime author of strategies and possible card combinations. Some of them were simple strategic choices, such as Kith summoning his Apian God to harass and sting anybody caught in the caustic, slippery mess of Chase's Among the Raindrops. Others were combinations that needed a lot of practice before they'd want to try them out in actual combat, such as Sera inviting an attack, funneling the damage back on an attacker with Unexpected Spillage, followed by Liam trampling the attacker with Waterfall of Light and finishing them.

Cilia stayed out of training entirely. Unsurprisingly, nobody complained about this at all. Because she dedicated her every waking hour to learning and crafting. She read as they walked, ensconced in the bubble of her Heart card. Whenever they were on breaks, or safely encamped for the night, she focused on crafting. The High Elementalist had provided her with a backpack full of basic crafting materials and equipment. There were leathers, thread, and string. There were needles, scissors and knives, mallets, awls, and other, more esoteric equipment. In short, there was enough to keep her busy for quite a good while. On top of that, she'd insisted Liam carry one of the manes along so she could skin it and experiment with the material. Whatever else she needed, she used her newfound Dearth of Materials card to summon into being.

Every evening, she was there, wrapped in her bubble of silence, with Sera nearby, boost active to increase Cilia's Mental Power and the efficiency of her crafting. On top of that, Cilia activated her ritual card, surrounding herself with a circle of lightly glowing runes as she worked, casting an eldritch light over whichever creation she was working on. And her theories were being proven correct.

On the first evening, she triumphantly exclaimed that her Ritual of Fire card combined wonderfully with her new chosen focus on fire. The resistance she had initially experienced every time she tried to use fire workings on leather were minimized, while the capacity to work as much of the element into the leather as possible was greatly enhanced. On top of that, the drain on her stamina was increasingly reduced. She went from exhausting herself creating a single fire droplet a night to completing three and four, which, in her words, "carried more oomph" than her earlier creations.

Once she had a full dozen fire droplets for herself and the others had at least one, she changed tacks. She switched her cards often, testing combinations, figuring out which effects worked best for which of her known creations. Then, she experimented with the combinations that aided with the different aspects. She almost always had her Heart card active, cutting off sound from the outside, but the others grew accustomed to seeing flashes of elements from within, and, more often than one would expect, snippets of material getting angrily tossed out of the circle of silence.

The landscape changed slightly as they traveled, moving from browns and greens to yellow-orange earthy tones. The rivers grew smaller, and trees were less verdant, trending more toward spikes and dry, skeletal tapestries. The soil became clammy, dominated by plateaus of blue-gray clay, and their travels appeared increasingly lifeless.

At night, the wilderness came alive, though. According to Kith, the lack of shrubbery and natural hiding places on the surfaces simply meant that the wildlife was predominantly active at night and tended toward diggers and cave dwellers. A disturbing number of snakes and rodents only emerged after dark, and their sleep was often interrupted by the cries and howls of life being taken and spilled on the dark plains.

Only once did they meet any Guardians. A trio of large, shambling humanoid beasts roamed the place north of their approach. They debated attacking for the Ænima, but when Kith came closer, he was able to put their height at around fifteen feet, and saw a weak haze hanging around each of them. Considering neither Cilia nor Sera could place their race, they decided the risk of the unknown wasn't worth it.

Their maps had no exact line where they'd cross into Furyborn territory. Partly because of the constant conflicts with the Lightborn, and partly because the Furyborn rarely stayed in one place for a long time. However, they were aware that, within a day or two, they would be approaching what was likely to be contested territory.

At the end of the first week of marching since they turned west again, Cilia approached the others.

They'd arranged themselves for the evening inside a low depression that kept them hidden from plain view. Liam was cooking a brace of hares Kith managed to catch with his viper summons. Kith insisted their venom was short-lived and didn't linger in the flesh, and the smells coming from the small bonfire was hard at work dispelling any doubts the rest might have.

It was a, by now, common arrangement. Liam enjoyed cooking; Kith was half-present and half-distracted, scouting the wilderness even as he teased Liam. Chase prowled the outskirts of their camp, incorporating his new hand into his movements, using it to leap over obstacles, push off tree trunks and others. Years of practice had to be reversed to incorporate having a hand again.

Sera was deep in her own thoughts, having borrowed one of Cilia's books as she had her buff active to help Cilia.

"Get your asses over here. I've got something to talk to you about," Cilia said.

The others stopped what they were doing. Even Liam only took one long look at his meat before leaving it cooking and focusing entirely on Cilia.

The crafter had a different look to her. Usually, her every action carried a decisive undertone, an arrogance of sorts. It could appear offensive to outsiders, but their small group knew by now that her know-it-all attitude was backed up by years of taking in and absorbing all knowledge she could put her hands on. Tonight, however, she looked… unsure. Decided, but shaky.

She cleared her throat. "I've come to a conclusion. I… wanted to talk it over with you all, however."

That was unlike her, as well. Chase frowned and then simply blundered ahead. "Why? You never ask for advice."

She sneered and snapped, "That's because I know what's right, you idiot!" She grimaced. "That came out wrong. What I mean is, usually, if I search, I can find the knowledge I need to back up my opinions. That way, I don't have to wonder at the right answer to any given question. This? My crafting? It's different. Even the crafting teachers back in the towers didn't claim to have all the answers. Instead, they had hard-won experiences, educated guesses, notes from decades of crafters, and a ton of disclaimers."

She searched for the words, eventually coming up with, "There are a lot of known combinations of cards. Yet, there are precious few clear-cut solutions. Two Tier three crafters, both wielding only water cards, may have wildly different results attempting the same creation." Cilia hesitated, then added, "Even if they hold the exact same cards, which, of course, is a rarity. In the classes, they talked about three main focus points for crafters."

The tiny crafter looked up, lost in the effort of remembering the exact lessons. She ticked off on her fingers. "First, we have our attributes. Mental Power. Focus is key, for any craft. If you cannot focus properly, your creations will suffer. Toughness. The process can be draining. Agility and Strength are necessary depending on your chosen craft."

"Second, we have our cards. The exact combination of cards you have will determine what you are able to craft well and where your focus should lie. I know, this is not exactly deep."

Liam held up a hand, then chuckled at himself when he realized he'd done that. "Shouldn't that be reversed? That you pick the cards that, like, have the kind of effects affecting what you want to build?"

Chase patted Liam's shoulder. "Mate. There're quite a few cards out there. Also, it's not like Cilia knew which craft she wanted to pursue when she started out."

Cilia simply pointed at Chase. "Exactly. Knowing up front precisely which path you intend to take, and then getting the exact cards that you need to follow that path? That is a rarity. And the ones who manage that, and keep walking the Steps? They are the legends we tell stories about. Almost everybody else is reduced to picking the best of many sub-optimal or obscure choices, and figuring out afterward how to make the best of things."

She held up the third finger. "The third, and arguably most important part, is our crafting experience. The better you are at your chosen craft, the better a product you are able to craft, and the more powerful magic your creations will be able to hold." She met their eyes in turn. "You can hear what I'm aiming at, of course. I am lacking."

At that, the others spoke up as one, denying her claim.

Cilia shook her head vehemently, scoffing. "Stop that. You think I am aiming for pity? I *am* behind most other leatherworkers of my age when it comes to skill and knowledge. The High Elementalist was kind enough to gift me a tome on leatherworking, but that doesn't change facts. For the most important part of imbuing your aspect into crafting, craftsmanship, I fall behind the curve. For the two others, I am *ahead* of the curve. My Mental Power is very much above average for somebody our age, and the range of cards I have access to grants me some tangible advantages over most everybody. This is what my experimenting over the past week has covered. Choosing the best course of action for my crafting."

Kith blinked. "Wait. But... I thought you also created a lot of things? The fire droplets?"

She rolled her eyes. "Sure. But that was just the start. Figuring out what I *can* do best and pinpointing the way forward? That has been my main focus." She took a deep breath, then nodded to herself. "There is one clear-cut truth among the many pieces of advice among crafters. If you seek to create something permanent, you need a good grasp of your craft, good materials and cards to aid you. I have the cards. I might swing the materials, especially with my new Dearth of Materials card. But my lack of craft lays that to rest. I will not be able to craft something like actual, proper armor until I have learned a lot more. Not only will the armor itself be subpar, but the magic imbued into it will not last."

"Makes sense," Liam mused. "You do have that card that helps making things permanent, but you'd want better materials, better tools, and more experience before working on something like that."

Kith snorted. "You'd also want a better workplace than a rotten tree trunk and a clay pit in the middle of nowhere."

Cilia seemed a little taken aback by the quick acceptance. "Yes. Well. Instead, I decided that I would do better experimenting for now. Once I have a simple set of creations for each of you, including at least a fire droplet, shadow stake, and light pouch, I would want to try seeing what I can create. Push my limits when it comes to the magic. That way, once I actually find a place to truly learn my craft, I know what my other limitations are. Obviously, I have the cards to create some good Fire creations, but I should also be able to create some good combinations, or pure Light items. If you have any ideas, I will try to see what I can do. Otherwise, I would try to simply... experiment."

"Sounds good." Chase nodded.

"Right on. I'll try to think up something wicked." Kith grinned.

Liam just held up two thumbs, while Sera patted her shoulder.

Cilia looked slightly confused. "Why are you so understanding about this?"

"What? You're the expert here. Are we supposed to fight you?" Chase asked.

"No, but... Liam needs better armor."

"Sure." The big man shrugged. "I'm sure if you could, you'd make it. I'd also like that armor to not fall off mid-fight. So, experiment away."

The crafter sprouted a tenuous smile, opened her mouth to say something.

A loud voice rang out from behind them. "Now, that *is* touching. A really heartfelt moment for all of us. Too bad we're going to have to interrupt."

Chapter 8

"A few large groups insist that the Furyborn are apolitical. That they only care about conflict, survival, and self-defense. That is entirely wrong, and at least the Church of the Circle seems to spread that lie willfully. The truth is that the Furyborn are wildly individualistic. Many of them care little about politics, and a good deal would see the rest of the world burn if it meant they could live their lives in peace. Yet, that doesn't mean people should think they are all the same." This is essential, I think. Entering their territory, expecting to find a unified people can only result in errors being made. I'll have to keep my mind open. They... can't all be like Kith. I hope. (Page 16.)

The voice was loud, rough, with a dark undertone to it that rang of cruelty and a dark humor. "We'll want you all facedown on the ground. No moves toward any of those fancy weapons I can see around the place, or things are going to spiral out of control rather fast."

Chase looked around and cursed inwardly. They'd been caught out nicely. In the one moment where Kith was distracted, they'd let down their guards. None of them were close to their weapons, except for knives, and Cilia who was wearing her tool belts filled with tricks. "We're not going to do anything unless we're forced into it. Mind if you show who you are?"

A man appeared at the edge of the depression, around thirty feet from the group, beside a large boulder. At first, they didn't even spot him appearing. He wore an ensemble that was both smeared with clay and with branches strapped on everywhere. Even his short, coarse hair was smeared with a thick layer of clay to make him blend into the background. It would have made him look comical, if it weren't for the absolute lack of a smile on his lips.

The man was a Furyborn, and looked almost archetypical for his kind. His eyes swam with dark colors and repressed violence. The heavy crossbow in his hands made no secret of his readiness to bestow violence upon them. Below the thick layer of clay on his bare arms, a couple of cards were barely visible. "Now, there are two ways this can go. You can surrender unconditionally. We'll relieve you of your valuables, and of course end those pithy Lightborn you've got in the group. Then we'll let the rest of you go on with your lives, to regret freely challenging our borders. The other way is where you try your luck, and we kill you all."

Chase spoke up. "You might want to reconsider. Attacking would be a mistake. We've been given a message from the High Elementalist for your leader, and we don't have any ill intentions."

The man chuckled, a sound with little humor in it. "You outsiders rarely have any ill intentions. Especially when you've been caught out. I don't care about your lies. You transgressed. Now you pay. *Face down.* And for any of you who should think that I'm alone... think again. You are outnumbered."

Chase's mind whirled. Now, he did spot movement around the edge of the depression. Not only that, a large, winged beast flew overhead. A summoned creature, perhaps? They'd have to stop this, make sure they got out alive and unharmed... and, if possible, not kill anybody. He held up his arms and started to get on his knees. Just as he bent forward, he shouted, "Go dark! Full defensive!"

Even before he finished the sentence, he barreled forward. A circle of darkness erupted into being as an impenetrable layer of night all around him, while he grasped his dagger. This wasn't his own darkness, but one of Cilia's spikes. If this was going to work, he'd have to use his Tier four card for something else.

He couldn't see anything, only hear, as shouts and cries burst out all around the low depression. Five. Eight. Too many voices to count. Shouts, sounds of cards being activated, arrows being loosed and panicked screams. He didn't care. Chase sprinted straight for where the leader had been, while he activated his Race of Life, feeling the Agility boost double and more, as Sera's boost came into being. He arrived at the edge of the darkness at a full sprint. His vision panned, failing to fix on his target. Then he saw him. The man had flung himself to the ground and was aiming at the darkness, slightly to the right of Chase. However, the man did not look as shocked as Chase would've liked.

That tip of the crossbow bolt occupied quite a bit of Chase's attention. Especially the part where it didn't waver in the least. Instead, it corrected and aimed straight at him, even as a card flashed on the attacker's arm.

In a split-second decision, Chase activated Steps of Brilliance. Three platforms came to life, allowing him to run up into the air.

The world erupted into light behind him. He was ready for it, but his vision still became a blur of colored circles.

A "thwack" sounded, but Chase didn't feel an impact. He soared through the air, straight at the Furyborn.

The man was slowly getting to his feet, clearly blinded, reaching for some weapon at his side.

Chase hit him first. He activated Free of Perdition, feeling Strength soar into his limbs as he sapped it from the attacker. Then, his new hand of Light crystallized into being and locked like a sparkling slave band around the neck of the attacker.

Even blinded and outmaneuvered, the man didn't panic. He grabbed for his weapon and simultaneously tried to fling himself back and away. Except, Chase's card had hardened now. The man's Strength was reduced to rival Chase's own, and he was unable to break the stranglehold of the card as it closed around his windpipe, threatening to pull tighter.

With the shining light tied to the man's neck, Chase pushed him off-balance and to the ground, putting his regular dagger to the man's throat. "Call them off!" he growled.

The eyes of the Furyborn locked on to Chase's. They were filled with tears from being blinded. His sclera whirled in dark colors, showing fury, hatred, and embarrassment. "Your people are already dead."

"Think again, idiot," Chase spat. "It takes something stronger than a random pack of bandits to take my family out... even if you did catch us at an unfortunate time. Now *call them off.*" The edge of his dagger bit into the side of the Furyborn's throat, while the edges of the living light pressed in on the sides of his throat.

The man's eyes tightened in rage and defiance.

Chase cut deeper, drawing blood.

The furious fighter bared his crooked, yellow teeth at Chase. With a furious growl, he subsided. "Hold!" he shouted. "Hold, Fire scour you! The blood wills it!"

In short succession, the flashes of light and sounds of battle died down around the depression, revealing a near-dozen people in attack positions around the edges. Half of them trained their weapons on Chase, while the rest kept their focus on their original targets. Seconds later, the shadowy area based at the center of the bowl died, revealing Chase's friends.

At first, he could barely see them. A massive, moving bulk undulated in the middle of the depression. Surrounding the bulk, a huge, buzzing shape was the Apian God, the summoned horde of insects, moving in a frenzied circle, daring anybody to enter. One Furyborn fighter was inside the cloud, fending off insects with both hands. Another stood right on the edge of it, panting with his two-handed axe moving back and forth, covered with some roaming, earth-colored energy that devoured clumps of insects wherever he waved it.

At the center of the bowl, the huge figure slowly unfurled slightly. It was Kith's Crescendo of Might summon. It had been riddled with arrows and in a few places, chunks had been blasted out of its body. However, their number were nearly unharmed, having hidden beneath it. Liam stood tall, Become the Clay covering him in a layer of protective might as he rose, shield and truncheon held up defiantly. Two arrows were stuck in the clay. Sera glowed with power as her Warmth of the Circle healed a touch of damage from Kith. Cilia held a fire droplet in each hand, ready to pitch in.

The Furyborn under Chase gawked and made a half-strangled sound.

Chase realized he was probably pushing a bit too hard and eased his grip. He shouted, "This is all a misunderstanding. We traveled here to *find* the Furyborn and reach Heart Halls. We have brought a message for Half-Swart the Mountain from High Elementalist Tatiana Skysworn. If you attack us, it's going to cost you all!"

"Don't listen to him! This is a trick." The man under Chase squirmed and surreptitiously tried to reach a bolt on the ground.

Chase tightened his stranglehold again.

A steel-set, young voice rang out from the far side of the depression. "Screw you, Slate. You said to attack because this was a bunch of raiders trying for our lands. That clearly isn't the case."

"Shut it, Naley! You forget who's in charge here!"

Chase had to begrudgingly admire the stubbornness of the fighter in his grasp. He was sealing his own doom, yet even so, he kept arguing to attack, kept squirming and trying to reach some of the weapons around him. He sighed, then raised his dagger and struck. Once, then twice. Then he stood up slowly and shouted, "I had to knock out the bastard. Sorry. He's not dead. Can we perhaps sit down and talk about this like normal people?"

The mood was tense. Some of the bows were fully trained on him, trembling as if their owners wanted nothing more than to punish him. Then, eventually, an older, tired voice rang out. "I'm calling it. No bloodshed today. Stand down, everybody."

With a lot of grumbling, the Furyborn lowered their weapons. One of them slowly walked down the edge of the depression.

Chase slowly let the fighter, Slate, drop to the ground, and moved down to rejoin his people and the other Furyborn.

The other man was the owner of the tired voice. He looked exhausted too, like Kith, strained from directly controlling too many summons at once. The gray of his long, frazzled hair whipped about in the wind. His face, along with his well-worn coarse clothes, made him appear more a feature of the landscape—a craggy, wind-worn rock—than a person. His grip on the curved, twisted, five-foot staff at his side looked like he was using it to keep him upright. He halted at the edge of where the insects still circled, waiting for Chase to join them. With a couple of fast and confusing hand movements, he gestured at the other fighters still in the bowl, and they pulled back, taking their weapons with them.

With a loud sound, like that of an indrawn breath, multiplied by a dozen throats, the Crescendo of Might summon disappeared, having reached the limits of its growth.

Chase spoke up over the buzzing. "The insects too, Kith."

"You sure, man? They're not pulling back." Kith nodded at the edge of the depression, where most of their attackers still hung back. Many still held their weapons ready.

"I'm sure. I just knocked out their leader, and they're still not attacking us. We need to show some goodwill too."

"Leader is stretching things a bit. Slate was picked to lead us on this outing. Once we get back, I doubt he's earning that privilege for a good long while." The man looked as if he'd bitten into a lemon and found that it had also spoiled. "That being said, there's a difference between not attacking somebody who's clearly not here to raid, and believing your story. This is for the chief to decide. But until then, you'll want to explain what your purpose is here, and why, exactly, if you're trying to reach the Halls, you're rummaging around way down here in the south."

They spent a while explaining what led them to being derailed, how the forces of Light were after them. Obviously, they kept a lot hidden, such as their Dark cards and the fact that the inquisitors were able to sniff out their presence. They still weren't too clear about the status of wielders of Dark cards among the Furyborn, but if they were anything like the rest of Ordei, that part wasn't going to earn them any immediate adulation. Still, the part about them being enemies of the Light did earn them a grudging nod from the old man. Regarding their tasks, they obviously couldn't tell him what the message was, because they didn't know it themselves. Showing off the wooden creation earned only a grunt and a shrug.

Eventually, he spat on the ground and let his gaze roam over them all. "All right. There's clearly more to this than what you're telling. I don't care—you can tell the chief yourself. For now, we'll bring you back with us, then we'll see what happens." With that, he turned around and walked up the incline, shouting, "Naley! If you can't bring him around, you're carrying Slate."

"What?" The young voice that had spoken up against Slate now had a complaining twinge to it. "But he was acting insane."

"This isn't a punishment. You're the strongest, with Slate out. I can make up a punishment if you'd like?"

The owner of the voice didn't respond. Instead, she leapt over the edge of the depression and crossed to where Slate had fallen. She was a young Furyborn, taller than average, with her long locks tied in a multitude of braids.

Less than a minute later, they started the march. It was almost dizzying to Chase how quick the shift had come. Just a moment ago, the existence of the Furyborn nation had been mostly theoretical, and now they were being led into their midst. Granted, they were definitely far from being fully accepted—the Furyborn spread out to encompass their smaller group as they walked, and were clearly watching them as much as they were scouting their surroundings.

The old man stuck around as they walked, clearly in a bid to keep any issues from appearing before they made it to their goal. The other Furyborn roamed about in what seemed like a confusing manner, people coming and going without any apparent order or reason.

Chase and the others didn't talk much on the march. Instead, they used the chance to take in anything and everything they could about the Furyborn.

Their clothes looked like crap. Of course, covered in clay as everything was, anything would look bad. Still, the quality, the wear and tear... everything looked rather bad. Coming from the Waves, their group knew about bad clothing—and this definitely wasn't good. Hard-wearing was the nicest you could say about it. That, by itself, gave the appearance of them coming from a poor society. However, their weapons were anything *but* poor quality. On top of that, their footwear looked to be sturdy and good.

The Furyborn were very much on home turf. They kept a fast pace, didn't falter, and didn't look like they had any doubts about where they were going. Their steps were silent, and they managed the progress with an eerie efficiency, striding over the hardpacked surface of the clay and dirt like ghosts, where Chase and the others squelched through muddy patches and caused pebbles to clack across the earth.

Above them, a flying beast kept pace with them, solemnly sliding through the sky. Chase eventually matched them to the old man, recognizing the half-vacant look of somebody managing their summons. Interesting. So, there were at least two card wielders among the lot.

At first, they tried to talk to the old man. However, beyond giving them his name, Ephraim, he maintained that he shouldn't talk too much with them, before the chief had actually agreed on whether they were enemies or not. A man of his word, he clammed up, even though his demeanor was agreeable enough. Thus, they were left to follow their guides through an unfamiliar terrain.

Slate woke up at some point. It took a good while before they were able to get him to quiet down and continue with the march. Continue they did, though they agreed among themselves to keep an eye on the aggressive fighter.

The terrain they traversed was familiar enough. After all, they had stumbled through this terrain for days now. What was nowhere near as familiar were the increasing signs of habitation. At first, it was just the occasional movement in the distance, a hint of something moving far away. Then, they started to see other signs. A solitary pole with markings top to bottom in what almost looked like claw markings. A small cave filled with ash from past bonfires. A set of scuffed footprints.

Six hours in, they saw the first dwelling, a crude hut: clearly long abandoned, with the roof caved in. A while after that, they started seeing man-made paths worn into the hard clay. Finally, once the sun had set, they spotted some scrawny fruit trees, thin and low to the ground. Even so, the dozen trees were clearly an orchard, and not wild growth. They'd made it and were about to enter Furyborn lands proper.

Chapter 9

"There is a lot we cannot say about the societies of the Furyborn, even should we want to. For one simple reason: We are not them. The Furyborn place a lot of emphasis on the importance of blood, of family. Even those of us who have been accepted into their cities are not of the blood, and there will never be any doubt. Even so, we have done what we can, even if we will forever remain outsiders." That is so sad. This book delivers the knowledge I'm looking for at times, but more than anything else it makes me want to learn more! (Page 15.)

"This is where we'll need to blindfold you." Ephraim had stopped on the path before them and now addressed them solemnly, with his arms folded and brow creased.

Kith snort-laughed. "Yeah, that's not happening."

Ephraim didn't back down. "If you plan to enter our home, it is. I am ready to give you all a chance, have you enter our lands without any sort of approval. Yet, I'm not going to show you our defenses." The man spat, his weather-creased face scrounged up in a lopsided grin. "Besides, it makes no difference for you. You might be tough as nails, but even if you were to make it inside, you'd be outnumbered and outmatched. So, make up your minds. We have reinforcements surrounding us anyway. I will give you my word you'll be led in unharmed, though."

"Don't be a jerk, Kith," Chase said. "Their house, their rules. Besides, it makes sense that they're cautious. They don't know us yet."

Kith grumbled, but eventually relented. They were all blindfolded and made to whirl about until they nearly spewed. Then, the Furyborn led them by the shoulders for an indeterminate period, as they clumsily stumbled along.

Chase couldn't see anything, of course. He reconciled himself to being powerless—a harder task than he initially imagined. Having gone from being a nobody to somebody, and then being at somebody else's mercy... it rankled. He busied himself, trying to obtain as much information as he could by listening intently. Of course, knowing that Kith would surely be sneakily watching through his shadows helped a bit.

The first real sign that they'd made it to actual civilization was an absence of sound. At this point, following weeks of trekking through the wilderness, they'd become accustomed to the sounds of the wilds. A yellow-stomached lizard was prone to piercing, clicking trills. Birds cried out in challenge and recognition. Also, a certain species of clay-colored squirrels had the most annoying "nek nek nek" sound. Now, they all disappeared and were, little by little, replaced by other sounds. The sounds of digging. A wheeled contraption crunching pebbles underneath as it passed. The unmistakable lowing of a caarnath.

Eventually, voices replaced even those, as people cried out in greeting, and the inevitable astonishment of seeing what their people had dragged home.

At long last, his guiding hand let go of Chase, letting him come to a stumbling halt.

A gruff female voice rang out. "You may remove your blindfolds."

With a sigh, Chase did just that. Then he blinked and stared ahead, certain that somebody was trying to make fun of him.

He stood in front of a building. Not a large one, and it definitely didn't look like an official building, a mayor's home, or, well, anything he'd expected. Coarse bricks, rectangular shape, with clay liberally splashed on top of the bricks, but none too carefully. From within, plumes of fog escaped, carrying with them the scent of... mint?

"Well. What are you waiting for? Drop the clothes and get in!"

Chase looked around, confused. The rest of his crew looked equally baffled.

Next to him, Ephraim did just that. Without a single hint of hesitance, he proceeded to drop all his clothes and entered the building.

Liam was the first to react. With a guffaw, he took off his dirt-covered clothes and dropped them in a pile. "All right! This is my kind of party!"

Sera huffed. "Not mine! In fact, can I ask to be uninvited?"

Chase gave her a smile and then disrobed. "I... don't know exactly what's happening, but somebody once told me it was important to learn and respect the customs of other cultures."

Her eyes promised retribution, but eventually she took a deep breath and put her backpack on the ground.

One by one, they took off their clothes and entered the small building. It was, to their massive relief, a bathhouse.

Chase had heard of bathhouses in Isarn. Obviously, those were for the well-to-do, while those on the Waves usually had to make do with a bucket of water and an end of soap if you were feeling really posh. Bathhouses, meanwhile, were supposed to be temples of decadence and pandering, filled with servants catering to your every whim. Out in the wilderness, apparently, they did things rather differently.

The mud and brick hut was large, three of four sides crowded by simple wooden benches in tiers that led down to a low pool in the center. Inside the pool, a middle-aged Furyborn sat central in the pleasantly scented steam, naked as anything, arms resting on the benches behind her as she watched them entering behind lidded eyes.

The Furyborn was massive. In any perceivable way, she looked larger than life. It was hard to judge her height, but at the very least her thighs and arms matched the size of Liam's. Her skull was shaved along the sides, while the rest of her hair, so red it was closer to orange, almost reached the bottom of the pool in a long braid. Cards adorned her body—four of them, three ringed by the borders of the Fury deck, with the final one being… Light?

Chase gawked and then shook his head, as one by one, they entered the pool after Ephraim, who was already seated next to the woman. Then, he experienced the next surprise. The water from which the steam wafted was not just hot, but almost scalding. He spotted a few rocks at the center of the pool, adorned with the same claw markings he'd seen on the pole earlier. Crafted magic of some sort; it had to be. Gingerly sitting down, he let his breath slowly escape in a hiss through clenched teeth. So hot! Then, he carefully leaned back, and immediately felt the hot water and steam work at loosening up muscles and making him relax. A minute went past in uneasy silence, while the blessed heat made the awkwardness diffuse and float away.

"We Furyborn aren't much for ceremony." The gruff voice from the muscular woman made Chase almost jump in the seat. She continued. "Yet, this is one ceremony I would never do away with. Anybody who is allowed into our community—be it for a short while, or for good—will partake in a soak with me or somebody else in charge. Some call it needless exhibitionism. Some say it's simplistic. I think it is the most open, honest way of greeting others."

Chase looked at the others. When he saw that nobody knew what to say, he cleared his throat and spoke. "Well, I, for one, relish the chance at a good soak after traveling for too long." He hesitated, then added with a grin, "Also, we do appreciate you not attacking us on sight."

The big woman guffawed. "See? This is what I mean! You know, another chieftain said a while back that he thought the tradition was dated and unnecessary. Just shows how short-sighted he is."

"What do you mean?" Sera asked quietly.

The woman leaned forward and raised an arm, waving at them all. "Meeting somebody clad in their armor is just that. It has them armored, defensive in a way they know how to handle. This? It knocks people out of their comfort zone—well, outsiders, at least. Used to be it was because we didn't want any surprise attacks by people who were pretending to be weaker than they were. Now? It's an excellent way of learning more about others, even before they start talking. And you... you're an interesting lot." She beamed at them as though she'd won a gamble.

Chase couldn't help grinning. There was something infectious about the simple, good mood of the woman. "So, what can you tell about us? Apart from who is accustomed to working hard and who isn't, of course."

"Oh, almost too much." She grinned and leaned forward, letting her gaze roam lazily over each of them in turn. "I can see that the four of you are used to seeing each other naked. Your little Miss High Class there, however, isn't. She isn't used to being naked among others at all. And she has proper schooling too. Not like the rest of you." She shrugged, eyes boring into Chase's. "Almost too much to read here. You've definitely starved at some point. And that hand you've lost? It was a long time ago. Only, you don't have the scars and making of a fighter, so you were probably a criminal. Heh. I think your lives make for an interesting tale. But that's not the most important part."

Chase whistled, impressed by her insight. "It isn't?"

"No. The important part is how *powerful* you are. Four Tier threes and a Quattro? Normally, I'd attribute that to a serious attempt at spycraft. Only, nothing about that makes sense. Light *and* Elemental cards? On all of you? That tells the most interesting tale of all. One that warrants a decent retelling." She leaned back, and with a lopsided grin that came close to a sneer, spread her arms and challenged Chase. "Now. Do me."

Ignoring the phrasing and the provocative gesture—nobody from the Waves would let themselves be sidetracked by a little nudity—he took her in. "Well... clearly, what I respond with isn't as much a question of how clever or observant I am, as it is an assessment of me and my personality, and type. If I were to comment on the types and placement of all those scars, as well as guess at the meaning of those cards of yours, you'd be able to pinpoint me as a soldier or somebody who'd spent a lot of time fighting for survival. If, instead, I tried to guess at your importance in the village from your attitude and speech, and try to find hidden meanings in your words, you'll likely peg me as a political creature of sorts."

The grin on the Furyborn's face grew and grew, to where it seemed almost feral. "And if you were to compliment me on my tits?"

Chase snorted, but didn't skip a beat. "You'd probably kick my ass."

She burst into an explosive laughter.

Chase shrugged. "Honestly, like the scouts will already have told you, we didn't even mean to come here in the first place. We were forced to detour, massively, in order to avoid the forces of Light. Now, we'd very much appreciate a guide to Heart Halls, and, if possible, a couple of hints so we don't mess up too bad."

Her voice grew lower, close to a growl. "Who's to say you haven't already messed up bad?"

Chase thought about his words, then decided to go with blunt honesty. "I've seen your type before. You kill if you need to, but you don't play with your food. If you thought we were a threat to you, you'd have taken care of us already."

A glint in her eyes preceded a short nod and she intoned, in a voice that sounded a lot like ceremony, "Cleanse yourselves. Of dust, of blood, of weariness. Welcome to the village of Cemano."

Following that, the mood relaxed into something more akin to regular cordial conversation. Chase had no doubt that they were still being tested, but they'd passed whatever initial invisible test she was placing on them.

Alia, the chief—because of course she was the chief, if there'd ever been any doubt—told them a bit about the village. Then, she informed Ephraim that he was to handle living arrangements for them, for as long as they would be allowed to stay here. Following that, she asked them to repeat their tale, but the long version.

That took a bit longer. Of course, they'd agreed on what they were going to tell anybody beforehand. They stuck to a version as close to the truth as possible—a world where they'd become criminals, had earned their cards as indebted in service of the forces of Light and, following that, been forced to flee. As to their stay in the Elemental towers, they were able to stay close to the actual happenings, including the fact that they were on the run from the Lightborn, the Elementals discovered this status, and decided to guide them on their way to the Furyborn.

They did not mention Dark cards in the least, for a reason. Prejudice in Lightborn lands was hard and heavy. They didn't know how the Furyborn were taught. On top of that, the High Elementalist had opened their eyes to one disturbing fact. They were sitting on a potentially world-altering instrument. What Chase carried inside him might change the balance of Ordei as they knew it. Risking exposing all of that to somebody they didn't know, where they had no chance of predicting the reaction? That was a bad gamble.

Making the decision was easy. Sticking to their story when faced with the inquisitive and clever chief proved to be harder. She wasn't ignorant about the rest of the world and knew a good deal about both indebted and the towers. All told, they managed to answer her questions without her poking any obvious holes into their story... but, despite her amicable behavior, it became quite clear that she wasn't entirely buying it.

The muscular woman rose and reached for the ceiling, stretching to reach a woven basket suspended from a hook.

Even with the heat and the steam, Sera managed to blush an even deeper red—and even Liam blinked appreciatively.

She sat back down, revealing what she'd picked out of the basket. An apple. It was small and wrinkled, but looked juicy. "We—the Furyborn—are creatures of conviction. We are rarely political, but have a few core principles from which we *never* deviate. Four, to be exact. Independence. Integrity. Resilience. And the final one, which is key to our little chat today. Blood." She smirked at Kith. "Not like that, little brother. A little jumpy, are we?"

She laughed and continued. "Blood as in family. We care about our own. Whomever we name family, we will give anything for, protect like they are our own. If you were of the blood? I would be sharing food with all of you, proclaiming you as being kin." She took a bite of the apple and carried on, her voice even and unshakeable. "Symbolic... but they're quite juicy. You five? You have not earned that privilege. Your explanations are lacking, and I, quite simply, don't entirely trust them. Or you. The fact that you didn't cause any harm to our scouts even when threatened speaks in your favor. I doubt that you're here to actually cause harm to *my blood*, but I am not going to take the chance and help you find your way to the most hallowed of our cities just like that."

She shrugged and waved at them. "We're not going to kill you, or send you back. But we're not going to help you either."

Sera leaned forward, intent and earnest. "But we have a missive to your leader. Half-Swart the Mountain. It is imperative he receive it."

The massive Furyborn also leaned forward, nearly to the point where her face met that of Sera's. "Don't know if you weren't listening to the part with our principles, doll. *Independence.* We're not the Lightborn, here. Half-Swart is impressive, a good fighter, and a decent leader. Has a behind that's worth singing songs about. But he's just one of several elders, and he doesn't call the shots here in Cemano. No proper Furyborn would try to make that decision on behalf of our village."

She smirked at them. *"Welcome to Cemano.* Nobody is going to make you leave. Yet, nobody's going to coddle you either, or lead you by your hand to the center of our strength and give away all our secrets. If you want to earn the right to become closer to our kind and meet Half-Swart? Earn it." Her voice dropped an octave, and became laden with promises of violence. "If you intend harm on our kind? You can try your luck in my village. And I will relish the challenge."

A couple of minutes later, they had been toweled off and were dressing again outside the bathhouse.

Liam spoke up. "That is one intimidating woman."

"I have ears, you know?" The voice rang from inside.

Liam winced, then shouted back, "Don't act like you think that's an insult."

Her booming laughter followed them down the path.

Chapter 10

"Accounts of the Furyborn can be frustratingly differ-ent. Why? Because of the nature of their people. They are indi-vidualistic to a fault, and will react wildly differently to the same questions. Some may outright lie to your face if they dis-like you. To them, since you are not of the blood, they don't owe you anything." That promises to be... frustrating. Since we're never going to be part of their "blood," does that mean we should question everything they tell us? (Page 19.)

"**Y**ou're with me." The speaker stood a bit farther down the nondescript path. This girl was a mixed-race, like Cilia, with clear Liberty blood mixed with her Furyborn ancestry. The blue tinge to the otherwise earthy tones of her arms and the slight points to her ears were a dead giveaway. Apart from that, she was young, with long limbs and clearly out-lined muscles, and her hair made up in a messy bunch of braids still half-smeared in clay. She was also a Duo, both arms crossed over her chest sporting Fury cards. Her heavy pack had a mas-sive maul strapped onto it, and she radiated impatience.

Chase recognized the voice. It was the one who'd spoken up for not attacking them in the ambush. "Naley, is it? I think we owe you one."

The young woman raised one bushy eyebrow. "You might want to rethink those words, Darkskin. We can get weird about things like debts out here."

"Oh. Well, we're all ears. Even so, we thank you for step-ping up on our behalf back with... Slate, right?"

She huffed. "I didn't do it for you. It was the right thing to do. Also, Slate's a huffed-up prick who should never have had the chance to lead. If you turn out to actually help the blood, it's going to be years, if ever, before he gets the chance again. We all win."

Kith grinned and stepped forward, rubbing his hands. "All right, then. Here's to Slate getting the boot. Where are we going, what's happening, and... where in the Pits are we anyway?" He looked around. "Wasn't this supposed to be a village?"

The young woman rolled her eyes and turned around. "Follow." Her brisk pace led them farther down the well-traveled path, still one of the rare signs that they were actually near any sort of civilization.

With no other good options, they followed her.

Within a hundred feet, the terrain expanded before and below them, and they stopped, gawking.

The woman stopped, annoyed at the pause. Watching their wide-eyed expressions, her lip quirked up ever so slowly, and she let them stare.

From one step to the other, it seemed, the landscape transformed. They'd thought that the path moving uphill was natural—and maybe it was. However, they had not expected what it led to.

In front of them, a steep decline led them down into what looked more or less like a huge crater. A large depression, nearly a mile across, hid a Furyborn settlement. And what a sight! From what Cilia had read and anything else they'd managed to learn before taking off for Fury lands, they hadn't expected any real constructions—and there weren't any around, either. That was not to say that the Furyborn didn't mold their lands to fit their needs, however. First came the drop. A questionable switchback path led thirty feet nearly straight down, followed by an open potholed area where any attackers would be exposed to defensive measures from within the defenses.

As for the defenses... they had just left the Elemental towers, arguably the best defenses in the known world. Decades of construction and continuous improvement and focused attention had resulted in some massive, overpowered defenses. These... were not it.

Even so, the approach was anything but easy. Following the expanse of broken, holey soil, fit for breaking ankles and charges alike, lay a mass of brambles. Only, where brambles, in Chase's experience, were a nuisance and an annoyance, these had clearly been weaponized. Growing nearly fifteen feet tall, with thorns that were visible even from up high, the idea of trying to struggle through them was not inviting. Then followed an earth barricade in a large circle, not unlike the one they'd had back in Soil. The exception was that this one had been made more permanent, with defensive areas and guards patrolling on top. Beyond lay an unplanned chaos of singular dwellings. Chase counted a hundred huts and houses before he was interrupted.

"You coming or what?"

Following down the steep drop, Cilia couldn't contain the questions bubbling from within. "This is impressive. But... how did you make the depression? It's close to circular. Do you have somebody with Elemental cards? And what about those brambles?"

Naley waited until they were all down before turning to answer. "No Elemental cards here. You will find a few surprises, I'm sure. But in general, we manage just fine."

Liam laughed softly. "I'll say. If this is a bloody village? I'd rather try to attack Isarn than this place... and Isarn holds at least ten times as many people."

"Isarn is in the lands of Light?" she asked, curious. At the nod, she scratched her neck and shook herself almost imperceptibly. "All right. Let's get this out here straightaway. You're free to do what you want in Cemano. The scouts have all returned, and I'm sure the gossip has spread. People know who you are by now, and I'm sure you'll get some people coming by to make up their minds for themselves about you."

"But... what are we supposed to do?" Liam squinted.

"What *can* you do?" she countered. "Honestly, you do what you like. Alia said you're allowed in Cemano. That means you're free to do what you want, work with what you want. Just remember, nobody owes you anything... and don't make a mistake and try to act out, steal or something. It won't end well for you!"

Chase easily traversed the steep slope; his Agility making him feel like he was a mountain goat, able to find purchase nearly anywhere. He noted that the village below was as peaceful as he could have expected from the warmongering Furyborn. Part of the earthen embankment surrounding the village had been half torn down, a large carcass out front in the process of being dismantled by a group of people. The torn-up trail straight through the brambles showed how the beast had opted for the direct approach.

"You can stay in Surly Anne's old place. It's not much, but it should do for you. Anne won't use it where she's at." She tamped one foot at the ground to illustrate where that was.

"Appreciate it. How about you? Is there anything we can do for you?"

The tall, strong woman grinned a smile with a good deal of malevolence. "Slate always goes on about how he's a better scout than me, because he's ranged instead of a fighter. Like both aren't worth something in their own place. And putting him into *his* place? That'd do much to make a friend out of me."

Kith barked a laugh. "The big bastard tried to get us killed. That's one thing we'll do for free!"

Looking pleased with the answer, Naley nodded once. "Now, I bet you will want to relax and have something to eat."

Chase smiled. "That does sound like a wonderful plan. After all, it's been all of a day since we nearly died."

Raising an eyebrow, the scout asked, "Get nearly killed a lot?"

Kith groaned. "Yes! It's not even funny."

Naley introduced them to their new home. It was a small, low-ceilinged hut, created of a liberal mix of rough planks and clay. There were two rooms. One large, central room holding the simple kitchen, a raised sleeping area, a fireplace, and a huge, scored and pitted wooden table with benches that could comfortably seat a dozen people. The floor was made into a mostly dry surface through the mixture of, again, clay, large rocks, and rushes that desperately needed changing. The space, though large, was cluttered with items strewn about everywhere, giving it a crowded feel, even with the size suggesting otherwise. The other room was a lowered cellar for foodstuffs. Well, also for foodstuffs. The previous owner, judging from the large collection of clay jugs in the other room, haphazardly arranged on row after row, either had a serious alcohol problem or was truly an aficionado of brewing.

Questioned about the purpose, Naley rolled her eyes. "Brewing is... a bit wordy for what she did. She learned how to ferment stuff, to a point where it could get you drunk. Then she had visitors who helped her drink it and gifted her with food and company for the drink."

"Stuff?" Liam asked.

"Stuff," she answered, with a tiny shudder. "I've heard more than one person say they've seen her spit into the mixture. I think she was more interested in the end result than the actual product—getting blasted, I mean."

"What happened to this... Surly Anne?" Sera asked.

"The lost ones happened. Bunch of winged achenta dropped from the sky, when she wasn't paying attention." At the blank looks on their faces, she shook her head and added, "You'll maybe know them by... chaotic Guardians? No? Unaspected?"

"Unaspected?" Chase frowned. "But those are just normal monsters!"

"Shows how much you know. There's a lot more to the lost ones than just monsters. Take it from somebody who's fought more'n their share of unaspected. They're not just monsters, or beasts. Their threat is real, as is their intelligence. These beasts, like our own Guardians, have a drive behind them, a guiding force. Of course, we don't know what it is, or we'd have done something about it a long time ago."

She shrugged. "It's all beside the point, of course. Just know that there are large groups of lost ones, their threat is real, and sometimes they catch even the most paranoid of us unaware. Oh, and with Surly Anne gone, you'll find that some people might swing by to help you empty her stores. Do with that what you want."

"We appreciate it." Chase dropped his heavy backpack to the floor, sighing. "Mind if I ask a question?" He rolled his shoulders and faced the young woman. "Why are you helping us? Really."

The tall woman leaned against the wall, then grimaced as she noticed the large patch of mold that smeared on her armor. "Fury break that Anne." She cleared her throat. "Please disregard that. Why am I helping? Some might say it's because I'm young and impressionable. I say I'm the curious sort, who's never left the bloodied grounds. So, I'm betting if I spend an hour here and there answering your questions and bidding you welcome to Cemano, you guys are stuck answering all *my* questions in turn about the lands of Light, the towers, and the world as a whole. Sound fair?"

Chase nodded.

She grinned, this one looking liberated and free. "Good. Because I have a *lot* of questions!" She brushed off most of the mold with a scowl, then moved for the door. "You guys make yourself welcome. Do with the hut what you want—Anne didn't have any real friends or family to lay claim to the things in here. I'll go handle some stuff, then I'll be back a bit later, and you can think of what you want to know in the meantime."

Naley left, and they did just that—spent some time making the dwelling into a decent, temporary home for themselves. They'd spent enough time in the towers that the idea of having to live together in cramped conditions was a bit depressing. Even so, everybody except Serafine was used to it, and they quickly arranged the area in a manner that would allow each of them a somewhat private space. Then, following Sera's insistence, they got to cleaning. Regardless, whether their health had improved massively by reaching higher tiers, making them less susceptible to sickness, she refused to have them live in what she referred to as "the den of a mentally ill magpie."

Within the next couple of hours, they built two massive piles, one outside and one inside the building. The inside pile held items they might actually be able to use—cookware, utensils, and the like—following a thorough cleansing. The outside piles were divided into filth and non-filth, stuff that they weren't going to use but somebody else might. Following a single cautious sip by Liam, a couple of attempts by Kith, and the insistence of Sera, every single jug of drink went into the outside pile.

At that point, the neighbors started to show up to see what was going on. And their neighbors. Not like clumps of visitors—or even *like* visitors back in Isarn, who'd gawk, keep their distance, and evaluate when it'd be safest to jump in and steal your belongings. No, these were single persons or small groups, who came by unannounced and with little fanfare dropped off a few useful items, before leaving again. One scrawny grandmother left a handful of dust-filled blankets. A thickset man covered in flour carried in a handful of day-old bread. A good bunch of people snapped up a jug or two from the massive pile before taking off again. A few kids popped by as well, interrogating them on how long they were staying, what their cards did, and any random number of questions. The adults, however, were surprisingly reticent. While some did ask a few questions; most were cordial but guarded. All told, it confused Chase to no end.

When Naley came back a few hours later, the hut was drying out following the most thorough cleaning any of them had ever participated in. One strict madame of a mother, wearing a floppy hat with the dignity of a king, arrived fully armed with an armload of cleaning utensils. She insisted on staying and aiding, making sure that they completed "what that damn Anne should have done by herself years ago." Afterward, she'd just left them, amidst admonishments that they not let it get as bad ever again.

Chase immediately confronted Naley. "What *is* this place? What's wrong with people? They keep giving us stuff, and no one has asked for money! Will we have to work this off later?"

Naley, covered in a layer of dust and sweat from whatever she'd been up to in the meantime, looked utterly confused. She chuckled, then looked abashed. "This… I don't know how to explain it to you." She pulled one of her braids before putting it back behind her ear. "Did Alia tell you about our creeds?"

"Sure did. Independence, integrity, resilience, and blood," Kith said. "Last one sounded a bit ominous, but she insisted that wasn't the case. She didn't elaborate much, though. Maybe you can help?"

"I believe that will be necessary." The hunter squatted into a resting position that, though she made it look perfectly natural, made Chase's knees hurt just watching. "Blood is key." She began pulling on one of her braids again, before sneering. "Bad habit." She nodded to herself before starting to talk again, staring wistfully into the distance. "When I was six, my neighbor fell ill. Mind you, this was another village, smaller, farther inside our territory. It was less protected, but also farther from the front line." She bared her teeth at the memory.

"Old Beren was a horrible person. Surly. Scolded kids for being kids. And he smelled, like meat left out in the sun for too long, sickly sweet, even when he was healthy. My mom made us help take care of him. Gather firewood. Bring him food. Stuff like that." Her lip rose in something decidedly unlike a smile. "I *hated* it. Hated him too. I complained about it. Why were we supposed to help him? He'd never raised a finger for us. And he was sick for a *long* time before he died. Mom said he'd worked long years for the village, and that made him blood. I didn't care. Finally, I said I wasn't going to do it anymore."

With a saddened smile, she lowered her head. "They didn't force me. They just let my little brother take over my chores too. And they told anybody who would listen. Nobody ever forced me to do it... but I caved in a couple of days. It was just too much shame." She looked up at their group. "Today, I get it. We're blood. That means we work for one another, help one another, do what needs doing, because, by helping one of us, we help all of us.

"Integrity comes into play in the same way as well. We stand up for our own, help our own. Yet, we *never* aid the enemy." Now, her eyes played with fire that looked out of sorts on her young, near-innocent face. "We know what is right, and we would rather die than stray."

"But... I am a Lightborn. I also spotted one other Lightborn when we entered the village. People have been coming to give me things," Sera asked, confused.

"That's your birth. Not your personality. We know our enemy, and it's not your birthright. A few idiots tend to get the two confused, but on the whole, we know the difference. You all might be planning to backstab the lot of us... but since the chief let you in, odds are that's not happening. Meaning, making sure that you have a place to stay, have some blankets, and some food until you can get your feet under you, is the right thing to do. Simple as that. Why'd we insist somebody pay for food if they serve the blood in their own way?"

Chase marveled at the idea that somebody would give somebody else their food because *it was the right thing to do.* Sounded like insanity. "I won't say I understand what that means, really. What are the laws here?"

Naley laughed—a short, dismissive bark. "Laws. Quite clear that you come from 'civilization.' Who needs laws to tell people what's right and wrong?"

Entirely lost now, Chase looked to Sera. Her wide eyes looked as shocked as he felt. He croaked, "So, there are no laws?"

"Why would there be? People know what's right, and we follow the creed. Every other week, somebody strays from the creed, and the entire village will know. They rarely repeat it."

Meaning it was a social construct? Social pressure on anybody who didn't follow the unwritten rules entirely? He couldn't entirely make up his mind on whether this would be the best place ever or the worst. "What if they do repeat it?"

"That happens rarely. Once every other year. But the chief decides on those. Sometimes they're shunned for a few days. Sometimes they're banned from the village for a while. The stories tell of those who're proclaimed unblooded, but that never happens in real life."

Chase was starting to see the contours of how things worked. So, there were no overt laws here, and only real punishment for those who transgressed far outside the accepted norm... but plenty of social pressure to make sure people behaved. How could that possibly work, though? What about getting rich? Earning more for yourself, be it power, riches, or goods? He decided not to ask about it, though. "How about resilience?"

Naley's nostrils flared. "*Not one step back*. That's what I've learned since I was young. It's what I'll teach my kids too, once I reach motherhood." She held up her hand in an all-encompassing gesture toward their surroundings. "The reason we are still here? We Furyborn? Because we do not run. You said you were from the lands of Light, right? That means you know how they look at us." That was a statement, not a question.

There was a time to talk circles around a topic and a time to just call it. "They think you're insane. Raving madmen and -women, ready to go berserk at any point. Pits, they even look askance at any Furyborn born in the lands of Light." He nodded at Kith.

Kith sneered and shrugged. "I've gotten out of a few scrapes, simply because people looked at me like somebody who might explode at any moment."

"There you have it," Naley agreed, not unsatisfied. "Even outside our lands, people are afraid. This is because we do not back down. We do not look for the easy win. We make sure that any real struggle with our true enemies is fought to the death."

Liam shrugged. "We've been in battles to the death. It's not fun, but, yeah, sometimes there's no backing down."

The young woman tilted her head, curious, squinting, as if in doubt whether she was being mocked or not. "I do not think you understand me. What I'm saying is, we, the Furyborn, don't fight fair. We do whatever is needed to win the fight. But if the Lightborn manage to trap us, *we do not surrender*. We do not flee. We make every battle a fight to the last fighter."

Liam looked offended. "But... that's stupid. I know *I'm* not the smartest, but that right there is dumb. They could capture you, sure, but you could flee. Attack again another day. We did that."

Grinning, Naley got to her feet and walked over to face Liam. She was tall, her eyes nearly level with his. "I could. Only, I won't. Tell me, big guy. You're Lightborn."

"In flesh, perhaps. Not inside. Not with how they've treated me and mine."

She waved away his complaints. "Irrelevant. My point is, you think you could take me. One-on-one, do you believe you'd be able to kick my scrawny ass?"

Liam's eyes flickered, and he looked to the others. "I... wouldn't call it scrawny."

"Answer my question!" she demanded, suddenly icily intense.

Liam took a step back, but then gathered himself. He looked down on her physique, took in the single card on her arm and nodded. "Yes. I think I could take you."

Her cold eyes brightened, and she stepped closer to him. In a breathy voice, she asked, "But would you want to, if you knew that I'd never back down until one of us lay dead?"

He swallowed, then silently shook his head.

She did a little curtsy. "There you have it. The Furyborn and Lightborn conflict, in a nutshell. They may be bigger than us, have more powerful soldiers than us—not their regular recruits, but in their strike teams. Yet, anybody, from the most coddled noble to the lowly new recruit, knows that managing to get us against a wall will not end well. We don't back down, and we don't surrender. Meaning, they mostly try to take us on when they know they have us outmatched, outmaneuvered, and heavily outnumbered." She tapped her nose. "Leaving us a lot of time and chances to lay traps, poison their waters, riddle them with arrows, and sic our Guardians on them."

Liam blinked again, totally taken aback. He tried to speak a couple of times. Eventually, he croaked, "Are... are you single?"

Her laughter rang like sunshine over cold ale. Eyes fixed on him, she beamed, and proceeded to ignore his question. "Our final creed? Independence. Here, we're not talking about the Furyborn as a whole. Everybody knows we take care of our own. What I mean is, we don't take kindly to people trying to decide things for us. The Lightborn? They're nothing but a whole bunch of dictators, telling normal people how they're supposed to act. Nobles. Churches. City guards. All set into a system, trying to decide how you're allowed to live your life. I'd like to see them try here."

Kith spoke up, puzzled. "But... you have a chief. And we're supposed to see the main honcho, too, if you ever let us leave. You're making no sense."

"You see the chief telling me how to live my life? Which cards to pick? Where to go, how to walk, talk and dress?" she spat. "Piss on that. We make our own decisions. Chief's there to handle all the dull things, like dealing with you guys, talking to Heart Halls, counting bales of hay. Only time the chief has any real say is when somebody breaks one of the creeds."

"So, how does it work? I mean, I... might love it! But, how the Pits do you get anything done?" Kith asked.

She sneered. "Typical outsider attitude. *Oh no. If we have nobody to decide every part of our life, we'll never get anything done.* Heh. Like we need somebody in a fancy hat telling us that we need to have patrols out at all times, or have fighters standing by in case the Lightborn attack." She shrugged. "Stick around, you'll see it. Or don't. The important part is, we don't take well to anybody trying to decide our lives. We *earn* what we get. That includes going to the Halls to challenge the gauntlet and win your rights for cards, or beating the crucible to win Light cards even. We earn it."

She jumped to her feet. "That about ties it up for you as well. Because soon you'll be harping on about how to be allowed to go to Heart Halls. Instead of me trying to explain it to you and you boggling like kids having eaten their first Fire seed, let me just show you. Unless I'm in the wrong, Slate should be shouting right around now."

Chapter 11

"It's true. They are masters in hit-and-run tactics, in lay-ing traps and making the elements work for them. Yet, when they commit to battle, the Furyborn would rather die than re-treat." This boggles my mind. The level of indoctrination it would take for people to grow up and accept this? Is there reli-gion mixed up in this, or is it merely social pressure? It's insan-ity! (Page 23.)

Slate was indeed shouting.

They didn't need to go far. No part of the village was, by any measurement, far away. Admittedly, the lack of any sort of proper city planning had the path to their goal as a confusing zigzag route, with no discernable pattern behind the different kinds of buildings they passed.

According to Naley, the key to proper navigation inside the village was simply to know everything, which was of questionable help.

However, most of them were used to the chaotic mess that was the Waves. They would get used to this. Eventually. At least the center of the village was easily recognizable.

Slate stood on a raised wooden platform at the center of a decently sized cleared square of stamped earth. A handful of people had set up shop in the place as well—mostly, it looked like, people providing services for others: a smith, a leather-worker, and a single large, well-established bonfire with an el-derly man stirring the largest cookpot Chase had ever seen, sur-rounded by benches.

Slate was currently yelling for anybody who cared to hear. He named people walking by, grabbing their attention and speaking directly to anybody who paused long enough for him to continue. A couple of people stood near the edge of the plat-form, listening in.

It was a funny old world. In Isarn, Slate would've been, depending on the mood of the guards involved, beaten, fined, arrested, or any combination thereof. Here? People mostly ig-nored him.

They moved from the edge of the stamped-clay square and closer to the platform. Now, Chase started to hear what it was Slate was so up in arms about.

He pointed at a man crossing the open area. "You *know* it's right, Caddius. We've needed to spend the time and manpower on it for ages, and today just proved me right, yet again. Today, there were just five invaders, and they could march right in. If we don't get some proper traps in, prepare the terrain, maybe even set up some proper defensive positions, it's gonna cost us! Give me your token. We'll make sure they don't take us by surprise. Nobody'll die!" Slate looked... well, earnest was one thing. He also looked disheveled, still had a bit of dried blood on his neck, courtesy of Chase, and had a slightly unhinged cast to his gaze.

Caddius, which apparently was the name of the young man walking across the open area, shook his head and kept walking. "I'll tell you what I said last time, Slate. Who's gonna man those defenses you want to get set up? What about the lost ones? You'll take patrols away from them to prep elsewhere and allow them a free path to Cemano?" He passed by the platform, spat, and walked backward, still addressing Slate. "The fact that you got your ass whupped from *five damn stragglers* doesn't get you *more* trust from me, Slate, but less!"

Slate looked offended at the man. Then he made to turn around, but spotted Chase and the others. For a moment, he glared at them. With a hate-filled stare, he turned back and started to shout again. One of the people near the platform turned and walked away, shaking her head. The other one seemed to make up his mind, nodding to himself before placing something at the edge of the platform and striding away as well. Slate shouted an appreciative comment at the man, before he returned to yelling at the world at large.

Naley stopped before they got any closer. "Anybody can get up there and speak their mind. On any topic. Somebody abuses it, we make sure they stop. Slate's been yammering on about strengthening our defenses in the canyon where we ambushed you for nigh on a year now. Nobody's listening, because we have a lot of other things that come first. Besides, we all know Slate's blinded by hate."

"He has a reason to hate the Lightborn?" Sera asked softly.

Naley nodded, grim-faced. "Most of us do. But Slate more'n most. Lost his entire family to a raid. Not a rare story in these parts, but... eh. I get it."

"Okay. So, whatever order people prefer to handle the works in, Slate disagrees, and he's arguing his case." Chase listened to half a sentence. "Rather loudly and, well, spit-flecked, which I guess is why most people ignore him. What's with that... whatever the other guy gave him?"

Naley rummaged around inside the armpit of her snug, soft leather armor, before emerging with a carved piece of rock fitted to a string. "This," she said, "is my decision token. Every single person of age in Cemano has one. I can use it to apply the weight of my support to *one* decision at a time." She tilted her head up at Slate. "Big, bad and angry up there's probably collected a dozen or so at this point. He needs forty-some—can't remember the exact number right now—one for every fifty people in the village. If he gets that, whatever he's going on about will be brought before the chief, and she'll have to debate it properly with some of the lead craftsmen before they bring it up on a vote before the *full* village."

"This means anybody can suggest anything, regardless who they are? But you only get to back one topic at a time?" Sera looked intrigued.

"Exactly. If I give him my token, I can't back anything else. I can still demand my token back at any point, but... well, you see?"

Sera nodded eagerly. "It means that you are only going to back the topics you truly care about—because otherwise, you will be unable to lend your support because of something less important. Also, it means that anybody can have a good idea and have it put into motion. This is the most ingenious, open, and earnest system I have ever heard of!"

Naley blushed. "Well. Sure. Anyway, we do vote. But people don't care for the full votes, because we don't want to be interrupted all the time, so we aren't going to vote for just *anything*." Her gaze flickered to Slate, who'd started to point down at them as he yelled. She faced him and shouted back, "Shut the Pits up, you Liberty-addled moron! We lost half a scout team last week from lost ones, and you want to reinforce a direction that hasn't seen real action for more than a year?"

A number of people in and around the square burst into laughter or yelled their agreement. Slate took it less well, exploding into a belligerent outburst.

Naley turned on her heels and walked away with an offensive gesture. The others followed. The scout talked as they walked. "Besides, most everybody *except* Slate knows that the rest of our scouts are paying attention to things, constantly talking about threat levels and whatnot."

Chase took it all in. "So, basically, it means that... we'd be able to get up there and propose anything as well?"

"Yup. You could even propose you going off to Heart Halls to meet up with Half-Swart and give him a big old smooch right on his wrinkled, hairy behind." Her smile was as wicked as it was derisive. "Only, you can see how well Slate's being supported—and he's one of the blood. How many people do you think *you* can talk into supporting you?"

"Oh."

Naley left them to find their way back to their new house. When they returned, they were surprised to see that the pile of jugs and other knickknacks was almost empty, and a bunch of kids ranging from five to maybe ten were busy loading the rest of the refuse pile onto a rickety handcart.

When asked, the kids said they were going to "dump" it all, whatever that meant in local terms. The kids also had about a hundred different questions for Chase and the others, which they fired off with an impressive lack of timidness or tact.

They answered the first dozen questions, then told the kids they'd talk more later on, before retiring to prepare an early evening meal and talk over their situation.

"This is a right mess." Chase sat at the end of the long table, looking at the others, who had all installed themselves on the benches.

"Hey! I'm doing my best with the ingredients I have. Don't like it, they apparently have communal kitchens you can go eat at," Liam rumbled. He ladled a stream of thin soup into a cup and pushed it in Chase's direction.

Chase rolled his eyes, but accepted the cup, tasting the contents. "If you put the same work into your humor as your food, you'd be a world-famous jester." He made an approving sound. "The soup is better than it has a right to."

"Just like me, then." Liam preened, pursing his lips and blowing a kiss.

"If we can stay on track for a moment," Cilia blew on her own cup of soup, "Chase has a point. The system of governing they have in place is, quite frankly, entirely biased toward local issues, and at present we don't have any sort of leverage that could help us talking the locals into supporting our case."

Sera looked deep into her cup on the table, contemplative. She frowned as the surface of the soup bubbled. Then she shot back with a scream, as it expanded and… one of Kith's shadows burst out. "Kith! You! You *ass*!"

Kith nearly fell off the bench, laughing. "Sorry. Sorry. It was too good an opportunity to miss! Off you go, Raudt! You should be ashamed of yourself." The summoned shadow burst through the wall and disappeared. Kith lowered his voice and said conspiratorially, "I'm just checking to see if anybody's trying to listen in or spy on us. Doesn't look like it. They do seem kind of trusting."

Liam harrumphed. "That's a point, actually. What's to stop us from just leaving? Packing our things and going? We're not prisoners, are we?"

Cilia shook her head. "We aren't. I asked Naley. Long story short? This place, Cemano, isn't that important on the large scale. So, she thinks we'd be allowed to leave, should we choose. Only, we aren't being allowed to just waltz closer to their Heart Halls. And if security's kind of lax this far out, it only gets tighter the closer we get to their most central cities."

Liam grumbled, "Less keen to ask strangers questions in favor of attacking too, I'm guessing."

Cilia nodded sadly.

"That leaves us with two options, the way I see it," Chase mused, tapping a melody on the much-scored table. "Either we leave, try to sneak our way back to the no-man's-land between Furyborn lands and the lands of Light, move north and hope the Lightborn haven't blocked off all approaches to Heart Halls."

"Which we entirely expect that they have," Kith added. "Hence the reason we're here in this Lights-cursed village in the first place."

"Or," Chase continued, ignoring Kith, "we stay here for a while, decide to make the best of things, and do whatever's needed to convince them that we have a damn fine reason for needing to get there."

"We stay?" Kith said, with a look that made it entirely clear he believed Chase had lost his mind. "In this mess of a village, where people hate Lightborn, there's no such thing as a fellow thief, and nobody seems to want to talk to us, let alone hear what we have to say. I really need to hear the logic behind this."

Chase huffed. "You know I'd prefer a larger city too, you dolt. But it's not like we don't have reasons to stay. We wanted to learn about the Furyborn, give us the knowledge we need so we don't mess up too bad when we make it to Heart Halls? This is probably a better chance than that tome of Cilia's. Also, with what we were talking about regarding leatherworking? Cilia might actually find a place where she could learn some of the basics here. We can at least give it a month before we try to convince people to back us."

"Actually," Sera mused, "we need to get back to thinking about this properly. You are all very much used to thinking about this as a job. We have a goal in mind, and everything has to lead toward that goal, right?"

Liam shrugged, mouth full of soup. "Sounds about right."

Sera shivered. "Disgusting manners. I cannot believe that women fall for you."

"Like you're one to talk about taste," Kith sniped.

"Hey!" Chase protested.

Sera shook her head. With a tiny smile, she faced Kith. "I will grant you that one." Ignoring Chase's betrayed looks, she continued. "What we should likely agree on before we decide anything is the following: Are we in a hurry? Is there a reason for us to rush at all?"

For a moment, they were all silent. Cilia mused in a low voice, "I... guess not. I mean, the inquisitors aren't exactly likely to find us here, and we're as safe as can be. As for the agreement with the High Elementalist, it's not like we have a fixed deadline. Sure, it'd be nice if we were to be able to shoot her a message or something, but it's not like this is just a breaking and entering. This isn't something she'd expect us to handle over an afternoon..."

Chase followed the trail of thought. "Besides, even if she's been surprisingly willing to support us, this isn't her only goal. This is on *us*. We are the ones who need to find support for our plans here. I think I get what you're aiming at here, Sera. We've been rushing from one emergency to the other for all the time you've known us. We used to work simply for the day-to-day necessities - for food, shelter, and survival. Then, little by little, the odds grew, but the pressure was always there. Now? We don't actually have any pressure. We're allowed to take our time, find whatever support we can, and learn what we want to."

He rubbed his chin. "In fact, the more I consider it, the better I like it. We can take our time here, get to know people among the Furyborn, learn how they think, hone our skills and build support. That way, when we eventually move off to Heart Halls, we'll already have some Furyborn to support us. It might even be better than making it straight to that Half-Swart guy like outsiders."

Kith grimaced. "I'm not sure I agree. What the Pits are we supposed to do with ourselves here? You heard Naley. This isn't a place where we can steal stuff and expect to get away with it."

Liam rumbled, "Any place, regardless of size and location, will have need of somebody with looks, muscles, and looks."

"You said looks twice, you dolt," Cilia shot back.

"Oh yeah!" Liam winked, causing a round of groans.

In a rush, as if to avoid the conversation getting sidetracked again, Sera spoke up. "This is exactly what I was aiming at. I am certain that Liam, with his guileless charms and big arms, will be able to find something to do. I am sure that there will be the local equivalent of a healer around who I can ask to help. Cilia..."

"What Chase said." Cilia gave a brief nod. "If we're staying here for a bit, that means I'll finally have the chance to learn about leatherworking. Possibly. Based on the leather and skins they're all wearing, there's got to be somebody around who knows what they're doing. Even if my skills are abominable, free labor should be worth something."

"Hey. Don't put yourself down like that," Kith said. "Especially not when Chase is the one with nothing to offer. I mean, I'm sure I'll find something. Chase... well, they might need somebody who can chase off monsters with his ugly mug."

Chase tossed a pebble at him. "That's settled then. For now, we relax. Tomorrow, we go out and see what Cemano has to offer. That way, we'll win the love and support of the locals, try to build on what Cil's already learned about the Furyborn in that dusty tome of hers, and make sure that we'll eventually be able to make it out of here with the full support of the village."

Chapter 12

"We Elementals pride ourselves on our knowledge of card lore. We investigate, optimize, store the lore of years past and consistently try to build the best possible combinations. Our wielders are able to stand on the shoulders of giants, use our vaunted library to make the optimal choices. Yet, having known quite a few Furyborn, I question whether there is some-thing we have forgotten. The power of sheer individualism. Some of the Furyborn have carved out paths that would never even have occurred to us." I kind of hope one of the authors of this tome is somebody of importance back in the towers. The threat of stagnation when sticking to the well-worn paths should be obvious. Right? (Page 24.)

Kith

The Heart card. It always came back to that fire-scourged Heart card. Granted, growing up on the Waves didn't help. It wasn't exactly a place that put great stock in a long life expectancy. Yet, as he and the rest of his family slowly edged their way further from starvation and constant threat of death, the card had helped him learn his place. Because they all had their place, their reason for being, in their tiny circle. Liam was the body, the brawn, the one who took the beating when push came to shove. Cilia was the brains, no discussion. Anything that required proper planning, she'd handle. Chase was their heart, their compass, the one who managed to push them toward greater things than mere survival.

Kith, meanwhile, was all these things, and none. Because he didn't have what it took. He wasn't fast enough, skilled enough, or strong enough. Yet, he could be. When he used his Heart card, he could be as strong as Liam, as quick-witted as Cilia, as fast as Chase... but only for a short while. The cost was always there. Of course it was. Yet, knowing that, on the Waves, you had actual tangible power at your disposal, should you choose to call? It was a siren's song. And one that Kith could not resist.

Eight times. Eight times, he'd used the card so far. Eight years of his life, tapped away to feed a Heart card that most would deem to be monstrous. Someday, if he survived that long, he would stumble and give away the secret. He was all too aware of that. Cil always had been able to look deeper than what she showed, even if she spent half her life caught up in some book. He very well knew what that would entail. Shock, obviously. Fury, at him not telling them. Dismay at the cost he'd paid. Then, especially, the outrage when he refused to *stop* using it.

Because, he knew, that was his role in the deck of their close-knit group. He was the weighted die. The marked card. The joker, who nobody expected to truly shine. Sure, with his newfound powers as a summoner, there might eventually be the chance that he'd be able to stand up for himself and hold his weight without needing to resort to his cheat. Even so, that was still in the future. For now, Chase and Liam could still best him nine times out of ten in a straight-up duel, and both Cilia and Sera were more fundamental to their group's survival than he was. So, he would remain what he'd always been: another body to throw into the mix. And when need be? The deciding factor. At any cost.

Kith grinned to himself as he strode through the Furyborn village. Especially with Sera's new buff card. He'd almost died laughing when he saw what it did. Improving his Heart card? That it did, for sure. Only, where it might theoretically have reduced the cost, made it more palatable for him to use more often... instead, it did the opposite.

[**Cost of Life**
Heart card (amplified)
Medium duration
At what cost power? This is a question many ask themselves. You do not need to. You know the price. Whenever you need to, you have power, right at your fingertips. Upon activation of this card, your attributes are doubled for the full duration of the card, with no instant detrimental effects afterward. The only detraction? Every activation will cost you a year of your life force. Cost of Life will now also increase the rarity of all your cards by one for the full duration.
Long cooldown
"It whispers, does it not? That pulse, that promise, of strength and power, right at your disposal. You need only reach out."]

How could he not love it, even as he hated it? With this, any use of his Heart card would make it that much more likely for them to make it through whatever trouble they might find themselves in. Sera's card just made it even more likely that he would use it more often. If that meant he'd be old and decrepit before his time, so be it. It wasn't like he had a nice country home set up for his retirement anyway.

Kith stopped and asked a villager for directions. The directions, like the layout of the village itself, were a mess. Even worse than the lower city back in Isarn, which had grown out of control over time, like the boils on a drunkard's ass. The village ambled back and forth between simplicity, personal touches, and hints of war. One dwelling, easily big enough to house two families, was painted in warm colors, adorned with colored stones in murals that looked meaningful, while the hut right next to it was worn down and had a series of vertical claw marks running around the lower parts of the rickety wooden door, as though a beast, or beasts, had tried to carve their way into the place. Putting the "war" in warmth? He chuckled to himself.

When he reached his goal, he had to stop and wonder for a moment. This was the chief's home? It looked exactly like the others. A mix of poorly carved stone and timber, with plenty of the local clay ladled onto the walls for insulation. It was well maintained, sure, but there were no signs, no trappings, no obvious riches to prove that this place belonged to somebody important.

He spat. Another reason he wasn't entirely keen on them spending too much time here. Kith knew that, despite what they would claim, the others were soft. Burdened by their conscience, way too empathic for their own good. This place? It was a trap for them. A place that acted like a real family, where they put the needs of the whole over that of the single person, where anybody would be willing to sacrifice themselves for the better good? A trap. A trap of kindness and good intentions, that could get them all caught up in its strands, if they didn't distance themselves. It was his own life, writ large. He could definitely come to like the bastards... but he wasn't going to let them. His own family was enough.

"You coming in? Or are you planning to stand out there and sleep the whole day?" The loud voice boomed from within.

Kith snorted. He hadn't even noticed the wooden slits. Windows, of a sort, that could be turned to let light in, or for an easy view of the area behind him when they were near-closed. "Just wondering if you'd be naked again, or that was a one-time thing. If I should drop my pants, again. Y'know, follow custom
, stuff like that."

The slits turned to reveal the smirking face of the chief. "If you really feel like it, go right ahead. That little thing won't be a distraction. Now, come in before I grow into an old matron."

Barking a laugh, Kith did as he was ordered. The inside of the dwelling revealed a small, but well-ordered one-room building. It was warm and cozy, light and heat blossoming from a small stone fireplace set against the back wall. Besides that, there were few nods to anything but the gods of practicality. There was a single bed, a rack of weapons, a small closet and cupboard, but those were the only hints at any sort of personal life. The remaining space was taken by a large, circular wooden table, and around a dozen chairs of different make and size. Uncalled for, his mouth curled up in a small smile.

Alia's eyebrow rose as she plopped down in one of the larger chairs and waved at the other chairs. "What was that?"

Kith shrugged. "Dunno. Wasn't sure what to expect, really. It was just funny to me, to see the difference between a chief out here, and some of those who call the shots back in the lands of Light."

The other eyebrow rose to meet the first. "Oh, you've visited many nobles then? Or clergy?"

"Scoped, rather. Stole from a few." Kith shrugged. "They do tend to throw their wealth and importance in your face. Not exactly the same here, right?"

That earned a real laugh. "I hope not. Why would I need anything proclaiming how important I am? Actions are what matter. I could live in the biggest, most well-kept house, but if I didn't pull my weight, Cemano would still know."

Kith nodded. Inside, he steeled himself. Right enough, it'd be way too easy to like these people. "Can't disagree with you there." He scratched his neck. "What's the honor of your invitation then? I mean, if I'm not here to be wooed." He waggled his eyebrows.

She shook her head and leaned forward, knocking on the table before holding up her index finger. "Not buying it. Whatever simpleton act you've got going on here? Might as well save it for somebody who's spent less time with people. That Liam fellow of yours would be the one I invited otherwise. Heh. Also, if there were to be more dropping of pants."

Kith grumbled, "Save a man a little dignity, will you?" He took a deep breath before soldiering on. "But yeah. It doesn't take too much to realize that I'm the only Furyborn and the only one you asked around. Hard not to connect the two."

Alia rested her chin in her hand. Her massive arms made the large round table look like a children's playmat. Her demeanor was open and interested. "That could very well be the case." She gestured at their surroundings. "You've seen some of the people around here, by now. A handful of Lightborn and Darkborn, even a few Liberators. Double handful of mixed races. Only, you and me are the core and the vast majority. Furyborn. It's not that we have any desire to be, say, pureblood or some nonsense like what the Lightborn sometimes spout.

"Among our own, we don't truly care about race. Chance can have you born a Liberator, while your heart is entirely Furyborn. Only... those distinctions are important for those who were born or raised among the Furyborn. For outsiders, it's different. Blood does call. We do take pleasure in bidding some of our own welcome home. That was part of why I wanted to talk with you. See if you'd be interested in finding a *real* home, instead of being harassed, and considered a savage out there. Of course, it wouldn't be something that happened just overnight, but..." She spread her hands out and waited for him to respond.

"And my group?" He hid the emotion bubbling within.

She grimaced. "They're not Furyborn. Neither as a race nor in their hearts," she said, as if that answered the question.

He looked her deep in the eye. Eventually, he decided he'd found what he was looking for—some tiny, sharp, inquisitive glance amidst the guileless, open facade. "Alia, I don't know exactly what you're fishing for here. But first you go and say you think I'm clever... and then you insult me to my face?" He let a little of his outrage rise to the surface. "Even if you actually mean that to some degree, going right ahead and asking me to leave my group behind..." He chewed on his lip. "Sera would find a diplomatic way to put this, but screw you, your ancestors, *and* your bloody caarnath. Family's family."

The huge woman burst into a wide grin as the glint in her eyes turned into real warmth. "And there you go, proving my point. No real Furyborn settlement would accept another Furyborn into the family if they were this ready to leave their own family behind."

Kith growled. "I *hate* tests. Hate 'em."

Alia tapped her nose. It had definitely been broken more than once, and looked to be little more than much-mangled cartilage at this point. "Even so. By cursing me out, you pass."

He leaned back, equal parts impressed and annoyed. "Do I earn bonus points if I keep cursing you? I mean, it *is* a talent of mine." Eyes narrowing, he continued. "That can't have been the only reason for calling me here, though, can it? I mean, I'm all for luring morons into traps, but you seem like the no-nonsense type of girl, and that would feel like nonsense."

She rubbed her hands together. "Right you are again. If you can keep that up, I'll have to reconsider that whole *dropping the pants* part." Her eyes sparkled with amusement. "No. You were actually wrong, right at the start. The reason you are here isn't because you're kin. That was merely a good excuse for testing you. The real reason"—she reached across to him, tapping his biceps—"rests right there. You're a summoner."

"Right you are." Kith nodded. His mind churned, trying to gauge what implications that might have.

Some of his inner turmoil might have been visible on his face, because she smiled. "Don't worry. No more mental games today. I'll straight up tell you."

He exhaled. "Thank you. I don't mind this back-and-forth with hidden undertones, but I much prefer it when we're in a sleazy dive and I can run off if the lass takes offense to my answer."

Her laughter was rough and heartfelt. "Your friends aren't here, because this is an issue only for summoners. Or a gift, if you prefer. You'll remember the blindfold when we led you here. Quite frankly, we're taking a risk on letting in outsiders. We're trying to minimize that risk. Only, they didn't think, failed to take into account that you're a summoner, and a Pit-spawned Tier three at that, with plenty of cards."

"With you so far." Kith nodded.

"You'll find, when you get to know the rest of Cemano, that we're good people, on the whole. There'll be exceptions, of course."

"Like Slate."

"Like Slate," she agreed with a crooked smile. "Only, your people will *also* find that certain options are closed to you. Your group won't be allowed to defend our walls, join our scouts, or work outside of Cemano. That way, we are able to keep you from learning about our defenses, the numbers of our combat elements, tactics, and so on. With one simple exception."

"Ah. Me. Because I'm a summoner." It finally clicked for Kith.

"Yes. We are aware that almost every single summoner above the first Tier, let alone somebody with six cards to choose from, holds at least one summon which will let them share its senses. Usually, the range is limited. Even so, any attempt on our part to limit you to not exploring outside the village is somewhat futile."

Kith nodded in response to the unasked question in her sentence, didn't acknowledge that he actually had *nine* cards. "Makes sense."

"Instead, we're going to do two things. Well, perhaps. It depends on your capabilities. Slate went on, at great length, about your swarm of insects. Do you have any proper defensive summons?"

"Yes and no." Kith decided that this was the time for... well, if not full disclosure, at least a certain measure of honesty. "My summons are mostly geared in one of two directions. One is to halt, obscure, distract, or cause damage, like the swarm of one Elemental summon. The other direction is meant to assist me on the front lines, with summons that either boost my own capabilities or fight at my side. I'm a one-man team."

She chewed on that for a moment. "That works. Quite simply, then, trying to limit the vision of a summoner is doomed.

I rather like your little group so far, but that complicates things. I will have to assume that you are able to learn all sorts of things about our village that I would much rather keep from you. This means that the option of letting your group peacefully return to Lightborn territory is out."

Kith grimaced, but assented. It was what he would do if he were in the same situation. If somebody had secrets they'd be able to use against his family? He'd rather be a prick and force them to stay than risk their spilling the secrets. Still, succeed in their task or stay here forever? He didn't love that.

"It does also, however, mean that I'll be able to give you, specifically, a bit more leeway when it comes to possibilities. I'm not letting you join our scouts or anything like that. Yet, given that you'd be able to see outside our walls regardless, I'd be open to letting you take your turn on the walls alongside our usual defenders."

He perked up, leaning back in his chair. Kith hadn't expected that. Of course, some of what she said made sense. It wasn't like they had too many secrets from him already, and if he wanted to, his shadows would likely be able to suss out any additional information he'd want about their near surroundings and schedules. He wouldn't have to give away their Dark cards either, or the fact that their blindfolds had no effect whatsoever on his capability for leading his people back where they came from, should he need to. Of course, if she were the slightest bit of a suspicious bastard like himself, she'd already be suspecting that. In fact... "Why does it feel like you're offering me a boon here?"

"I'm not. Well, I am and I ain't."

Kith snorted. "Thank you for that clear and concise answer. I'd never be able to tell that you're a woman!"

She laughed again and stood up, slapping him on the shoulder, nearly throwing him out of his chair. "For that, I'm pairing you with Eggert on the north side."

"Thank you?"

"No. Very much not something you should thank me for." She winked and settled into a more somber tone. "I *am* throwing you a bone. Or at the least, giving you all the rope you can use to hang yourself. What I've seen of your little family so far, I like. If you're all restricted to working within the village, you'll be limited in building a reputation. With you up there on the wall, scouting and sometimes fighting for us all? That'll let you make friends a lot easier." She shrugged. "Now, it'll be up to you. Do a shit job, and you'll be stuck here for who knows how long. Impress us all, and we'll help you get to where you're going."

Kith looked her straight in the eye. The words hung unspoken between them. *"Mess with my family, and I'll end you all."* Kith didn't mind. The way he looked at things, that was an entirely reasonable stance. He spoke up. "I can't wait to get started."

Chapter 13

"For the life of me, I cannot figure out how it works. There must be some sort of ruling in place. I have traded for a decade, now, traveling back and forth between the towers and Heart Halls. Yet, while the personalities of the traders are vastly different, their approaches to trading are anything but. They care not for gems, for gold, clothing or foodstuffs. They lavish scorn on luxuries. However, for anything war-related, and any books, they will pay... indeed, overpay. It boggles the mind." No. No ruling here. If I were to guess, it's simply a matter of mentality and the difference in societies. The Furyborn may be nomadic, of a sort. Yet their settlements form a weird combination of temporary and real cities. There are no regular citizens. They are closer to war camps. War camps don't need gems. (Page 31.)

Chase was not exactly the introspective type. Over time, he'd taught himself to think a bit more about his actions, not just fling himself headlong into anything. That didn't change the fact that he felt the most free when he was mid-race, heart pumping, adrenaline rushing and shouts at his back.

This kind of felt like an introspective moment, though. A chance to take stock, to consider what had happened to get him this far. Chase knew that he didn't come from impressive beginnings. In fact, it was hard to think of anything *less* impressive than his origin. Yet, over the past months, he had felt that he was improving his lot in life, slowly making something of himself. From being a one-handed orphan living inches from starvation, to becoming the type who spoke eye to eye with spy leaders and even the High Elementalist? Something had changed, for sure.

Yet, sometimes, things just went full circle.

"Who-ee. She's a ripe one, ain't she?"

The words interrupted Chase's introspection. It came from a low-set, twisted form. A Furyborn man—no, a mixed-race, part Furyborn, part Lightborn—hobbled closer to Chase. Up close, there was nothing weird about the man. His back was bent, and it looked like his leg had set badly at some point. He moved along by the help of a short, solid stick. His hair was all gray, and his few remaining teeth hinted at a fondness for soups. Yet, with all that said and done, the old man still moved with a bounce in his step. There was fire in his eyes, beyond the color-ful sclera common to the Furyborn, and a lopsided grin twisted his mouth, though the face was rather pallid.

"Sure is. I've smelled plenty worse, though," Chase said. It was true. The stench here *was* impressive. The fumes wanted to make his eyes water, and it had clearly piled up for a while. Yet, it had nothing on the Waves during a hot spell, where the few surviving fish had to give up, bobbing to the surface to add to a truly vile soup.

The old geezer cackled heartfully. "First time I've heard that claim. But then, you're not retching yet. Might be you're telling the truth. So, what's a young, healthy Darkie like you do to be sent to old Gaven?"

"That's a really good question. Name's Chase, by the way. And I think they just didn't know what to do with me."

"So they sent ya to the arse end of... well, a lot of differ-ent beasts." He cackled again.

Chase joined the man in laughter. It did sound weird when he said it like that. Somehow, that had been the order of things, though.

They'd had a wonderful night's sleep. After being cleaned, and with the aid of a large load of simple, but soft blan-kets, their new house was surprisingly comfy. Even the fumes coming from the cellar where Surly Anne had stored her booze had mostly dissipated.

When they woke up, they found a couple of loaves left on their doorstep. Supplemented with some cooked beans from their packs, it had made for a filling breakfast, and they moved off to start their new quest—helping in Cemano and finding their separate ways to earn respect and friendship inside the village.

It started off easily enough. Cilia left them early on for the local leatherworker. Sera was pointed in the direction of the healers. Meanwhile, Kith had to go talk to the chief for some reason. That left Chase and Liam. From there, it didn't take long before a burly Furyborn with a beard big enough for Cilia to hide in dragged Liam away, blessing some god for the arrival of some-body who might keep up with him.

Only, from then on, there had been nothing but disap-pointment. Sure, the locals weren't hostile, as such. However, following one look at him, the answer to his questions was either a shake of the head, or a suggestion of another place where he might help. One place after the other, he was turned down. It felt like back in Isarn, when he'd still been fool enough to think that people would give a Darkborn kid an honest chance. Only, there wasn't the same level of hostility and judgment here. He just didn't really fit.

There was apparently no need for runners, here. All kids were put to work from a very young age. That took care of any need to send messages, carry light goods, and move quickly within the village. He was not allowed to join the scouts outside the village for some stupid security reason. On top of that, he had no craft worth talking about, and he wasn't as naturally outgoing and, well, physically imposing, as Liam. Increasingly, it felt like he was given the runaround, as people pointed him to others, who might be able to use his help. Until that final one.

Chase cleared his throat. "Well, I wanted to help, instead of sitting on my thumb. Only, I don't know my arse from my elbows, and I don't look strong. Eventually, this old lady asked if I was the squeamish sort, and when I said no, she pointed me in this direction."

"Regretting it already, are ya?"

Chase shrugged. "Nah. I don't mind honest work. It just wasn't what I expected. Are these all Guardians?"

The pen in front of them lay at the western side of Cemano, firmly pressed up against the city wall on one side. On the inside, the "fence"—if you were generous enough to use that term—consisted of wooden slats that looked like they'd been erected by somebody with the skill level of, say, Chase. Inside the fence was the reason for the confusion. And all the excrement. Dozens of beasts of various sorts, looking like species that had *no* right sitting or standing together as placidly as they did. Chase saw what looked like a fur-covered giant chicken with gargantuan claws resting serenely, nearly on top of a panther-like creature, if a panther were made out of spikes and dirt.

"Ayup. Every single one of 'em." The old man wiped sweat off his face. "Usually, there'll be a lot fewer of them at this hour of the day, only, you're not going to believe this." He waved for Chase to move closer.

Chase obliged.

"Y'know, there's this lass, Surly Anne? Heard of her?"

He blinked. "Yes?"

"Well, she upped and died. It happens, right? Only, she had a store of wonderful booze. A bit too much taste, but with the kick of a rage steed."

"Ooh." Chase started to see where this was going.

"Exactly. Not the worst o' arrangements. Then, would you believe it, some right bastard went and tossed all o' that wonderful booze to the street."

"And of course, you had to go and drink it all, so it didn't go bad." Suddenly, Chase could see it. The glassy eyes. The nearly manic grin and sweaty sheen over his face. The old man was hungover as all hells.

"Ayup!"

Chase couldn't help it. He doubled over, laughing his heart out. Eventually, he straightened. "All right, Gaven. Looks like you're a man of my heart. How can I help?"

The answer was as straightforward as it was smelly. "Shovel shit until you smell the exact same as this huge pile, boyo. Load it onto one of three rickety carts, and let me do the easy part of fastening the cart onto one of these Guardians, before somebody comes to take it away."

It was actually pretty good practice, letting him use his Clothed in Living Light as often as possible to get accustomed to using it for a second hand. Probably not what it was intended for, shoveling dung, but he'd take it.

Not that Gaven was a shirker. Not by any means. Hangover or no, he was in constant motion, going from one job to the next. Once he'd satisfied himself with the knowledge that Chase wasn't a complete slacker, and did in fact have the brains necessary to shovel dung, he focused on a series of tasks that seemed never-ending. First off was caring for the Guardians inside the pen. Second was prep work. Like he said, he fastened some of the Guardians into custom-built harnesses that allowed them to pull the massive, rickety carts.

Chase did wonder at that. Where in the Pits were they actually *taking* the dung? Sure, they hadn't exactly investigated the entire village yet, but if they had any fields that needed the fertilizer inside the huge crater, it would've been hard to miss. And those huge carts sure as Darkness weren't going up the edge of the crater, not without divine intervention. He didn't wonder too hard, though. As Gaven kept himself busy, he also kept Chase occupied, and the piles looked to have... well, piled up, for a while now.

The carts got settled into a rotation. Older kids from the village came running, somehow knowing what was needed of them. Without a single hint of fear at handling the huge beasts, they leapt onto the carts, guiding the Guardians and their burden to wherever they were going, in a northerly direction.

Then Gaven started to receive visitors. One by one, Furyborn came by—some chatting for a while, others businesslike and matter-of-fact. Regardless, most of them walked off accompanied by one or more Guardians. It was quite confusing. The animals, when led off, were relaxed, docile, and friendly. It was a weird contrast to the way Chase had first been introduced to Furyborn Guardians, that being as slavering beasts trying to drink his heart blood back when they were indebted.

After a handful of hours, they settled down for a midday meal. One of the kids, upon returning the carts, carried a package, which turned out to be some sort of animal sausage, wrapped in some large, wrinkled leaves. Watching Gaven messily digging into the meal with his few remaining teeth, Chase learned that it was supposed to be eaten in combination, leaves acting like a sort of loaf and wrapper in one. It was a bit gamy, but savory, and a lot more tender than it looked.

They sat in companionable silence on a couple of large crates next to the pens. At this point, Chase was entirely accustomed to the smell. Now, the only thing that was needed was the sound of somebody getting a beating, and possibly somebody losing their breakfast into the water, over a bad batch of home-brewed booze, and he'd feel right at home on the Waves. Chin in hand, Chase mused, "You know, Gaven, I really, really don't get those beasts!"

"That a fact? Well, I can tell you 'bout 'em, no hassle." The old man burped, leaning back on a crate. "Which ones are ya curious about?"

Chase smiled. "All of them, really... but that wasn't what I meant." He gathered his thoughts, trying to settle the point before blundering on. It was something that seemed to come a bit easier these days. Not that he was sharper, only, his mind responded snappier; it was easier to dispel some of the fuzz. "I've seen a good number of Guardians by now. Fought my fair share too. I know the basics. They're beasts, brought into being by somebody owning a deck. Only, there's quite the difference in how they act, depending on where they come from. The Lightborn Guardians are simplistic. They amble around after springing into being, growing more... solid, I'd say, until they reach a certain point. Then, they walk off to join the front lines—and that's it. The only thing left for them after that is a simple, blood-filled life, killing other Guardians or people for Ænima. They're rather mindless. I should know, having been up against some."

"Ayup. Sounds about right. I've fought a good deal myself, in my youth. Simple killers, unleashed and pointed in a direction." Gaven brushed his hands on his leather pants, though it was hard to tell whether his pants or his hands came away the cleaner for it.

"Then there's the Elemental ones. They... well, they use 'em for training. The beasts, from what I've seen, are still rather mindless, only they are able to direct them, stop them from killing, and let their wielders absorb their Ænima to grow stronger. They do use some on the front line in the same manner, but most are directly handled by trainers wearing special crafted armbands, that give them control or something like that—I'm not sure of the specifics."

"Mm-hmm." Gaven nodded merrily. From somewhere within his pocket, he'd extracted a clay bottle that looked suspiciously like those from Surly Anne's stash.

"But *your* Guardians are entirely different. They're like real animals, only, more... tamed. More placid. Also, anybody's able to direct them. Pits, that big fella with the three horns—"

"A tree stomper, that one. Fave o' mine"

"Sure. The tree stomper was led away by three kids, and the oldest couldn't have been more than *four*. There were definitely no armbands there. The kid was butt naked!"

Gaven cackled. "You got eyes. Ain't hearing no questions, though, kiddo."

Chase pursed his lips and waved his hands, including the glowing one, in the air, looking for the proper approach. "What's the deal here? Why are the Guardians so docile? I *know* you guys use yours for battle too. Only, none of these beasts look like they would fight, even if you slapped them around."

Gaven rubbed his hands together, looking thoughtful. "All right. Technically, this might just be a bit of a secret. Only, Alia ain't been by to tell me to keep my mouth shut, and you seem like a decent sort, with your head screwed on right. You'd probably be able to figure it out in a week or two anyway." He hawked and spat. "We ain't got a deck in the village. 'Course, we don't. We're too small for that, even if I think Alia'd be the right sort to wrangle one."

"She does seem like a nice, no-nonsense sort," Chase agreed and put the final bite of his meal in his mouth.

"And those knockers, am I right?"

Chase nearly choked on his food. Coughing and wheezing, he pounded his chest until he came to, glaring at Gaven.

The old man was entirely unabashed, cackling to his heart's delight. He winked and beamed. "Anyway, we get our Guardians from one of the larger cities, elsewhere. With you being all sorts o' smart, you probably know how the decks and the Guardians work?" His raised eyebrow made his entire face into a merry mess of wrinkles.

"Not entirely. I do know a bit. That you get options, can decide for yourself some details about the Guardians when you create your Wellspring."

"Ayup. You get to choose what your Guardians are supposed to be like. Not detailed-like, but enough that you can choose what you want from 'em. The Lighties want nothing more than killer beasts to toss in our direction. That's kinda telling, ain't it?" With a smirk, the old man continued. "Now, I don't know who actually made the decision, but it's been in place for as long as I've been alive, and it's a good one. Our Guardians? They're peaceful, right enough. None too bright, but that's okay. I ain't always been accused o' being the pointiest arrow in the quiver either."

Chase had to laugh at the old man's enthusiastic eyebrow-waggling.

"Only, you know how Guardians weaken?"

He searched his memory. Right enough. "I can't recall exactly who told me, but yes. The Ænima that... that gives Guardians life, that drives them, for lack of a better word, eventually runs out. At that point, they need to kill something else for their Ænima or they will eventually fade into nothingness."

"Spot on, kiddo. Only, where the tower-folks decided that meant the best approach would be to keep all that lovely Ænima for their own people to reap, we came up with a similar, but different, approach." He waved his gnarled hands enthusiastically at the village around him. "Here with us? Guardians aren't just part o' life. They're part of the family." He pointed at a gray-scaled, spindly beast that stood nine feet tall at the neck. "Jetta. Looks weak, but she's the best at boosting people onto roofs and hard-to-reach places." His hand moved onto a large, iridescent beetle, wider than it was tall, with a large, martial-looking snout. "Hedevan. Best helper you'd ever find for when you need to dig holes." The next pointed out was a group of bat-like creatures, covered in beautiful, white fur. "The toddlers. Nobody can tell 'em apart. Literally identical. Won't find nobody who's better at finding water, though."

One of them burst out in a high-pitched whine, that sounded surprisingly like the cry of a baby. Chase burst out in laughter. "*Good* name!"

"I know." He waggled his eyebrows again. "Point is, though, we decided the best way to get the most out of our Guardians was to make them truly part o' the family. They stay with us, work with us, live with us. Means they can stay for longer, too, for some reason the chiefs probably know, but I don't. Then, when they finally start to weaken, I hold a small ceremony o' sorts, bid 'em farewell and send 'em off to war proper like."

Chase nodded thoughtfully. In truth, he liked the thought of it. Sure, the Elementals had a point to their approach, especially considering they weren't exactly spoiled for living room, and would probably have trouble finding space for all those Guardians. Also, their Protectors would definitely grow stronger than the equivalent Furyborn, because of the Ænima they absorbed. Yet, compared to that, how much could a Guardian help a society during its short life? If you took it in and had it aid and toil alongside yourself, how much might that help your society as a whole? Was it even a competition? "You know... I think I prefer your approach."

"How gracious of you, good sir." The old man tipped an imaginary hat.

Chase shook his head. "Didn't mean it in a condescending way. The kids love the beasts. It's easy to see. They might just be Guardians, but the way they treat 'em looks closer to family. I like that." Musing, he continued, "There's just one thing I don't get. Back in the towers, and in the lands of Light, all Guardians were martial to a certain degree. Not entirely the same here." He nodded at a small, fat beast with a black and white fur coat, whose sole purpose seemed to be eating and looking damn cute. "Even so, there's a good bunch of beasts that look like they'd be best used for fighting and little else. What do you do with those? I saw a pack of felines stride off earlier today with a hunter, and they didn't exactly look like they were off to pull carts."

"Mmhm. Burst cats. Dangerous beasts, those. Good eyes on yer, by the by." Gaven drummed a little ditty on the clay pot, then took a thoughtful sip. The ensuing full-body shudder spoke to the taste of the concoction. "No. No, I don't think I'm allowed to tell you that. But I haven't been forbidden either." He tapped his nose. "What say we make a tiny game of it? I ain't telling... but if you figure it out, more or less, I'll give you the details."

"That sounds amazing! What should I focus on?"

"Pits kind of games do you play? Ain't a game if I give it away straightaway."

Chase laughed and patted the old man on the arm. The skin felt like a blend of bark and badly cured leather. "Worth a try."

"Y'know, I ain't never had a Darkborn servant before. I've heard they're the weak sort. Best put it to the test. No more slacking!"

Chase rolled his eyes but got up, hiding a happy smile. It felt like this gig wasn't going to stink as much as he'd feared.

<u>Chapter 14</u>

"Blood, or rather, personal connections, lie at the core of being Furyborn. Knowing who you are, what you stand for. All these years trading have paid off. My deals are nearly twice as good as those I got just starting out. Yet, compared to those actually of the blood? I get fleeced. Nobody bats an eye over it, either." This, also, makes sense. There is a definite "us vs. them" feeling everywhere here. And why wouldn't there be? With a rare few exceptions, it *is* them against the world. (Page 35.)

"**P**its! What *is* that smell?" Sera jerked back from the table. She held a hand over her nose, gagging.

"Oooh. I recognize that one." Kith perked up. He closed his eyes and snapped his fingers as he thought about it.

Liam took a deep whiff. "Ms. Catern's all-hour stew!" he said with finality from over his shoulder. He was prodding something set over the wood stove.

"That's the stuff," Kith announced. "Talk about nostalgia. Cheapest meal on the Waves, and rarely outright dangerous. Now I'm hungry."

Sera looked back and forth between the two in horror. "You lot are damaged goods."

Chase smirked. "Like you didn't already know that. Besides, the smell is me. I am the smell. We are one. I've washed, thoroughly, but it's not coming out."

"Well, you had better, or I am moving your bedroll away from mine. Out the door. Into the gutter." Sera glared daggers at him.

"Aw. You'll grow used to… fine. I'll find a solution before bedtime. Besides, there are no gutters here, so there!" He laughed and sat down at the table with an audible sigh. "I'd better anyway, because Gaven's expecting me back in the morning. You wouldn't believe how much dung twenty-two Guardians produce, but it's a *lot*."

"Twenty-two Guardians?" Cilia blinked as she raised her head from her tome. "What have you been up to?"

Chase spent a short while describing the work as well as the conclusions Gaven had helped him with. He ended his ruminations. "In time, I'll maybe find somewhere else to help. Until then, this is a decent place for me. It's honest work. Besides, now that Gaven's dangled that secret about their Guardians in front of me, I need to know."

"I found some good work too," Liam said. "Working construction. The wall around the city, as it stands, is apparently the third version since founding, and they continuously work to build on it. Meaning, they're replacing what they have right now with actual bricks. I've been shoveling clay into brick forms all day." He shrugged. "I don't know that much yet. Today was more them throwing work at me at top speed to see if they could work me into the ground." His self-satisfied smile showed how well they'd managed that. "They do seem like good people."

Kith snorted. "You say that about everybody." Pointing at Chase, he continued. "If we ever get to a place where we need to set up our own Well or whatever it's called, where we start spawning our own Guardians, knowing what we *can* do with the creatures up front sounds like a good plan." He rolled his shoulders. "Obviously, I'm not going to be able to top that kind of job. But my day was all right, I guess. I spent it learning about the defenses of Cemano and getting introduced to my own spot on the wall as a defender, keeping the village safe. You know, something worthy of a man of my stature."

Their small, warm (and somewhat smelly) room erupted into a series of dubious exclamations and questions. Eventually, they managed to get him to admit the truth.

"Still, even if I lucked into the job, it's the best that could have happened. This way, if the village is attacked, I'll have the chance to prove on behalf of all of us that we're actually ready to *help,* and that we're not afraid to put our asses on the line for them." He grimaced. "If only it weren't so blindingly *dull.* Apparently, attacks are few and far between, 'cause they have scouts out everywhere."

Cilia spoke up. "In that case, it is *crucial* that you keep focus and stay alert. You are going to work with Sera again to perfect those mental exercises that sharpen your mind and keep you awake."

"Yes, Mom." Kith rolled his eyes.

"*What?*" she snapped.

"Sorry... Mom." He whispered the word, then ducked.

With a twinkling laugh, Sera stretched her arms and rolled her shoulders. "I would love to work more with you on that, Kith. Despite what you say, I know you are putting in as much effort as anybody in this room!" Ignoring the light blush that rose on his cheeks, she shrugged. "As for me, I have been answering more questions today than the last two weeks combined. Jessel is the lead healer in Cemano, and apparently, he will not allow just anybody to assist him. It appears that I convinced him of my ability—eventually—and he will allow me to aid him starting tomorrow. I have *no* idea what the actual work will look like; yet, I believe it should aid us all. Also, for a small village, they seem to have a *lot* of badly wounded. They have two houses filled with wounded, some of them long-term."

Chase smiled. "Wounded aside, the fact that you get to have some time where you don't have to fear for your life, but can simply be a healer, probably isn't the worst either."

"That too," she admitted. "How about you, Cilia? You have been silent after you came back."

She took a moment before answering. "The rest of you remember when we were indebted. That first day. I... had never had a full day's workout. Not in the way that we had among the bait. I was beaten, I'll have to admit. To the point where I cursed Chase for insisting I get back up and keep working." She paused. "Master Benneth is more demanding than that. I have been applying tanning solutions to skins the entire day, and spending any time left practicing proper preparation of materials on spare scraps."

Kith's anger started to rise. "What a bastard. Well, you won't have to take that. We'll find somebody else for you to work with."

"What? No!" She glared at Kith, shook to her core. "That's not what's happening. Do you not know me by now?"

Liam, helpfully, jumped in. "Yeah, Kith. How are you not getting this?" Five seconds. That was how long he lasted. Then he broke down and admitted, "Okay, Cil, I'm not seeing it either. What's happening?"

"Master Benneth is, by far, the most exacting teacher I've ever had. He said that there is another leatherworker on the far side of town, who would accept me with no questions asked, should I so wish. His standards are high enough that I am unsure if I will be able to ever meet them."

"Oh. You love him," Kith finally realized.

"*Of course I do.*" Her voice was uncharacteristically frazzled. She let her hands run through her hair. Then she frowned at Kith. "No. Not in that manner, you imbecile! You don't understand. Master Benneth is something that should not exist in a village like this. He is learned. Curious. Yearns for new knowledge. And requires your best, every time. He is everything I aspire to be."

"You want to be a strict, condescending ass?" Kith shot out. Then he immediately ducked from the death glare she sent his way. "Okay, okay. Sorry. So, he's good?"

Cilia sputtered. "Good? No. He's not good. *Good* would be somebody who's practiced leatherworking their entire lives, who knows what they're doing. Master Benneth is *great*! He continually strives to improve, to learn. He asked me questions about myself, leatherworking, beasts in the lands of Light, my cards and how I've used them in my craft for *two hours* before he even considered taking me on as a helper. He's already made me realize flaws in my approach."

She frowned and kept talking, more focused and introspective. "Of course, I couldn't answer even a third of his questions. Yet, I think he was more testing my way of thinking than anything else, how I responded to deep queries. Yes." She suddenly noticed everybody else staring at her and huffed. "Yes. I like him as a teacher. And I believe the appreciation is reciprocated. He said that he would allow me to help preparing leather tomorrow. Learning how to properly skin an animal, he says, is integral to receiving the optimal result."

"Joy," Liam said, critically eyeing a large slab of meat. "But... aren't you moving backward? Is he going to take you hunting afterward?"

She ignored Liam. "I believe, if I stay with him for a while, I will learn, not only how to work with leather and other materials, but how to properly skin and treat the skin of an animal to prepare it for use. Also, with how he talked about other beasts and Guardians, he is the one the hunters go to, when they've managed to down the more exotic beasts. Picture me learning how to create armor for you from gaborn hide. What do you think I would be able to craft?"

They were silent for a while as they took that in.

Chase slowly whistled. "Yeah. We'll take that."

"Mostly, though, I believe I will learn the basics, and learn them well. Well enough to actually be able to improve by myself afterward. Of course, this is dependent on me actually keeping up with his requirements. I am unsure if I can manage that."

Wincing, Chase asked, "Don't get me wrong. I'm not trying to criticize the man, 'cause I haven't even met him, but are you sure he's all that? I mean, in this place?"

Cilia steepled her hands in front of her on the table. She closed her eyes and looked down, silent for a moment. When she looked back up, her gaze was intent and without a *hint* of prevarication. "Chase. I have spent the majority of my entire Furytorn life surrounded by fraudsters, fake-faced liars attempting to convince the rest of the world that they are something they're not. In the towers, I finally saw a few people who *had* what it took, candles in the night, illuminating the eternal shadow of unenlightenment that is everyday life in Ordei. Yet, where they were candles, this man is a *bonfire*."

Nobody said anything for a while. Sera fanned herself with a hand, while Kith looked slightly embarrassed.

Eventually, Cilia cleared her throat. "Of course, I may be wrong. If he tries anything, I will kick him."

Following a round of laughter, and Liam dividing the food around the table, they dug in.

A while later, Sera pushed her plate away, sighing. "That was wonderful. Thank you, Liam." She rested her chin in her hands, talking pensively. "I believe that should settle us nicely for the time being. Cilia will keep reading her tome and teaching us, to keep us from the worst missteps. We will be working with people from different classes and occupations, meaning that we will be able to influence quite a large part of the population in good time. As long as we apply ourselves, do not mess up and do not act out of turn, that should see us safely to our goal, with enough people ready to use their tokens to support us. Of course, the scouts seem to be very important in this city, and we will be unable to directly influence them, but both Kith, myself, and eventually Cilia should have enough interactions with them to bring them to our side as well."

Chase froze with the final piece of meat spitted on his knife. Grease dripping from the tip, he pointed incredulously at her with a low laugh. "Whoa. Where did *that* come from? That was downright insidious!"

Sera blushed. "It was not! I merely..." She searched for the words. "I am a noble. There is no escaping that. Part of what we do—a large part, granted—is influencing others. Whether that is through our actions or in other ways is immaterial. In this, I am merely trying to be aware of our actions and their eventual results. The fact that we can actually do good in the meantime is a lovely boon."

"A noble doing good?" Kith smirked. "Now I've heard it all. Color me impressed."

"Mine!" Chase waved the knife, still with meat attached, at him. "I saw her first. Find your own noble!"

"Boys." She rolled her eyes. The smile was still there, though. "Now, with that sorted, we need to handle long-term. Our end goal is unchanged. We are going to build a home, and we will need the aid of the Furyborn for that. This means that we need to keep growing stronger." She held up a hand. "*Down,* Liam."

Liam, whose arms were already half-raised toward a flex, looked caught out and embarrassed enough that they burst out in laughter.

She brushed curls behind her ears. "We will continue the paths we have chosen, and check in every once in a while, to discuss if we should be doing anything else. Cilia, do you believe you should be crafting anything in the near future?"

Cilia frowned, but eventually shook her head. "Nothing fancy. It'll be a waste of time. Like I said, Master Benneth already made me realize my approach had been erroneous. I've kept on creating stakes imbued with shadows, simply because that's how I first learned it." She wrinkled her nose. "Foolishness. The design for my fire droplets is plenty efficient for now. I will replicate that for shadow droplets and blinding droplets, and mark them clearly. That way, we will have our general kits, like we talked about, to the best effect I can create right now. Beyond that, I think I should instead be focusing on learning; and unless I'm mistaken, a month from now, I'll be able to create something for all of us that's an entirely different level than what I can today. Perhaps even something with actual permanence."

Chase nodded. "Honestly, that sounds excellent. There's no discussion that it'll be easier to use droplets at a distance than those stakes. We'll just all need some sort of belt or something so we can all carry ours safely. Now, as for me? Beyond just working, it'll be sparring and training my Strength and Toughness. There's got to be a place in the village where people spar and train."

Liam pointed at Chase, "accidentally" flexing his arm. "There is. I'll join you."

Kith rolled his eyes and eventually shook his head. "As much as it pains me, I probably won't. I need the focus on Mental Power more than anything. I've run a few loops at night of the village with Raudt and Svart, but the edge of the crater's just at the far end of my focus. I need to push that. I do know the way we got here, but I want to be able to guide us in a safe direction in case things go south and we need to hightail it out of here."

Chase nodded. "That sounds like a good plan. I'd tell you to make sure that you don't get caught with them and give away the game, but you're not a rookie."

"You still said it," Kith riposted.

"Oh, oops." Chase held up his hand innocently. Then he went serious and said conspiratorially, "I cannot stress this enough. It looks like we've landed on both feet here. Yet, we cannot give away anything. A place like this, right on the edge of everything? If they learn that we're holding back, and that we have something that—"

From one moment to the next, Kith stood up, chair clattering to the floor behind him. With a shocked look, he held up a hand, forestalling any comments. Then his arm flashed twice: once as he changed his cards, and yet again ten seconds later as his shadows slowly manifested into being. He stood frozen in place as both shadows eased through the outer walls, one on the north side and one on the east.

Eventually, he picked the chair back up and sunk back down in it with a curse. His face was pale. "Somebody was eavesdropping. I only caught them because they made a noise. They got away, though. I spotted somebody sprinting away, but then they used a card and faded away. I'm sorry. I failed."

Chase cursed, mentally going through their conversation. After a while, he shook his head. "This isn't good. I don't think it's catastrophic either. Yes, now they know we have a secret. But we didn't give away..." He leaned forward and tapped Kith's shadow card. "So, as long as we just stay silent, we should be good. I hope. Now, we just have to be extra careful. I guess we'll find out pretty soon who was listening in."

Chapter 15

"Whatever else you do, do not start a grudge with a Furyborn. You may start it, but they will end it." Oh. Yeah. That would have been a good idea. (Page 41.)

They didn't have to wonder long who was responsible. Their sleep was, blessedly, undisturbed, and for a while, they wondered whether whoever was listening in had even heard anything useful.

Yet, early morning, as Chase strode toward the day's toil with Gaven, a heavy set of footsteps joined his. He looked to the side to see Slate.

After their scuffle, the scout had looked downright furious. Even after that, the few times Chase had spotted him, he'd sported a surly look, which seemed to be his go-to mood. Today, though, his face had a manic gleam to it that was telling. The sneer that accompanied it did not bode well.

Chase decided to nip it in the bud and get a shot off early. "Ah. You're the eavesdropper. Funny. Didn't figure you for the sneaky type. Or... did you get somebody else to do your dirty work?" He laughed out loud at the infuriated look on the scout's face. "Oh, you did! Well, I don't know how much they heard. Nice of you to come straight to me, though. I'm guessing you're curious to hear more?"

"More?" Slate's growly voice was a good indicator of where his nickname came from... unless it was his real name, of course. "I am just here to tell you that I look forward to seeing you dead." The sneer only built. "Or exiled. The chief can be softhearted at times. But at the very least, I'm getting you tossed out of here."

Chase laughed and reached out with his stump to pat the shorter man's shoulder.

Slate did *not* take well to that attempt. His hand shot out and grasped Chase's forearm, crushing it painfully while his other hand eked toward the machete-like dagger at his side.

Chase didn't let the pain show. Instead, he painted a smile on his face. "Oh, Slate. I didn't know you felt that way about me. I am *so* sorry, but I'm taken. You've met her, remember? Blonde, lithe, and gorgeous?"

"Oh, I've met her." The thunder of his low voice was approaching landslide territory. "That little whore of a Lightborn *noble*? Thought you wouldn't need to let that slip, would you? How are you planning on attacking us? Which secrets do you plan to use against us?"

Fury rose within him, along with an overwhelming urge to just take the bastard down. It would be *so* easy. They were close enough that he could just step in close and then stab. One quick upward stab, into the heart from below the rib cage, or maybe the throat. Chase tamped down the anger, hard. That, at least, was one lesson he'd learned well. Those at the bottom rung of the ladder couldn't afford pride. But it was such a wonderful tool to use against others. Besides, he noticed, they were starting to attract attention. He could use that. Behind them on the muddy streets, a matronly woman with a large load of laundry had stopped to stare unabashedly at them.

Chase smirked. "Oh, little Slate. You're such a tease. Of course Sera's of the Lightborn nobility. That's no secret at all. You could've asked us and we would've straight up told you. In fact, if you go to Isarn, I think you'll find a good number of wanted posters made by her fellow nobles trying to hunt her down. So, you go ahead and spread that far and wide, mate. I doubt being wanted by Lightborn pricks will make the people of Cemano hate us."

Slate flung away Chase's arm like it was festered. "Like we will believe you. He heard you. You confessed that you have secrets—"

"*Of course* we have secrets, you over-muscled, Air-brained excuse for a spy. Who doesn't? We come straight from the towers and need to speak to the leaders of Heart Halls. You think we're going to tell you why? *You?* This is bigger than me, and definitely bigger than your tiny heartworm-sized brain can fathom."

Chase went on the offensive now, furtively enjoying Slate reeling back in confusion as the scene didn't play out as he expected. "Did your friendly little set of ears report what else we were talking about? Because I'll help you. We were talking about making friends of all of Cemano. Of showing everybody how nice we are, so nobody will object to us continuing with the goal that we already confessed we had. Dastardly enough for you? Or do I need to continue? We also talked about working hard, and not acting up or making any enemies." Chase was all up in his face now, looking down at the slightly shorter man. "How am I doing so far - friend?"

Slate was beet red, breathing hard, hands clenched into fists. "I... You... That's not what happened."

"That is absolutely what happened." Chase grinned. "Of course, you have the right to not believe me. At the same time,

I'm allowed to tell you to go sit on a stick and twirl. Now, unless you have anything else you wanted, I have some dung to fling, and you're in my way."

He didn't take being dismissed any better than he took the rest of the conversation. "You wait a Fury-damned minute, you Dark-infected pustule. I didn't say you could go."

"Good thing we're in Furyborn lands then, isn't it?" Chase said beatifically. "Independence and whatnot. *You don't get to tell me what to do, you piece of rotted garbage.*" Still smiling, he shrugged. "Now, unless you wanted to throw a punch, you'd better get on with tattling to Alia or whatever you've got filling your busy schedule."

The scout looked like there was nothing else he wanted more. Twice, his hand jerked toward his dagger—size-wise, it was more of a short sword. Eventually, the emotions on his face settled into grim acceptance. "This isn't over," he threatened.

"Oh, I realized that a while ago. You seem like somebody who needs things explained a couple of times before they stick. Don't you worry, *friend*. I'll repeat myself as often as you need, even as I realize it will be time-consuming."

Slate stalked away.

From behind him, Chase shouted, "Was it something I said? You didn't understand me? I can use shorter words, friend?" He turned and watched the matron glancing back and forth between him and Slate.

Before he could gather his thoughts, she winked at him with a saucy grin and strode off, now that the entertainment had left.

Chase shook his head. "I... probably shouldn't have done that," he murmured to himself. "Though, he was dead set against us already. Hopefully, this'll have him doing something stupid."

Slate did something stupid. He was, if nothing else, at least consistently dogged and straightforward in his approach. He marched straight to the chief, presented what he'd learned, and demanded she kick their group out of Cemano.

This, of course, was the exact wrong approach to take with Alia, who did not respond well to demands. She told him off in no uncertain terms in front of a large crowd of onlookers and proceeded to explain to him exactly why he was done leading scouting teams for the near future.

The explosive scout reacted poorly. After cussing out the chief, he became even more vocal in his opposition to their group. He changed his approach on the platform, dropping his past proposal in favor of outright warning everybody against their group and what they were planning to do. Skirting the lines of the truth, but never dipping into outright lies, he hinted at shadowy plots and them being agents for the Lightborn, sent here to spy or worse.

At first, a good deal of people listened. They were newcomers to Cemano, with two of them Lightborn. It was a natural response. The first couple of days, they received their shares of stink-eyes, and even a couple of belligerent shouts from random passersby. Nobody challenged them head-on, though. As they continued their respective work for the village, these attitudes lessened. It was one thing to cuss out a stranger, and yet another entirely to belittle somebody who'd cured your niece of her chest pains.

Naley visited them on a near-daily basis. The mixed-race scout, it turned out, was true to her word. She wasn't going to help them in their affairs—not directly, at least. That being said, she held a nigh-unquenchable curiosity for knowledge of the outside world and didn't mind in the least having to repay the curiosity of their group in turn, answering any common questions they could come up with. This was how they learned that the Furyborn, on the whole, weren't nearly as insulated as they might appear at first glance.

Naley apparently could not keep her hands still. Whatever she was doing, her hands were busy with myriad minor tasks she extracted from her leather backpack like magic—polishing a dagger, applying a dark substance to a piece of armor, or even darning socks. Right now, she was whittling a piece of wood, slowly teasing out an intricate shape from within that was beginning to look suspiciously like an idealized version of Sera.

"Hah. You really think you'd be able to keep people in the same tiny place all their life? Nah, plenty of moving going on. Some people want to live closer to the front. Those are the people right here in Cemano. Those who don't mind the danger, because they know it means they can walk the Steps faster. Others prefer a bit more safety, reach the Tier they were aiming for, become parents—any reason, really—and move further away from danger. A lot of people move." A small, lopsided smile emerged on her face. "Besides, everybody marrying their cousin is bad news. Oh, and we have the wayfarers, of course."

"The wayfarers?" Chase asked. "Never heard of those." He was scrubbing his bare arms in a bucket of tepid water. They'd traded a few hours of work for a local wonder—some locally growing shrubs that, when denuded of their bark, could be rubbed on the skin to exude trace amounts of some natural oil that would seep into the skin and overpower just about any smell. Initially, the febral sticks, as they were called, brought tears to the eyes, but after a while, the scent became rather enjoyable. Liam and Kith were off sparring with some locals, while Cilia and Sera were crafting inside their house.

"You wouldn't have. They're... well, usually, they're young people. Like me. In fact, I'm considering it myself. Talking to you doesn't help the desire to stay here, either." She shot a furtive smile at Chase before focusing on her whittling again. "There are plenty of reasons for taking off. Some want to prove themselves. Earn a reputation. Do something impressive for the blood." A shrug punctuated the sentence.

"Some of us just want to see the world. Whatever the reason, we sneak off into the world outside Furyborn territory. It's not like the Lightborn armies can be everywhere, or the lost ones. So, we just pack a bag, take a route less traveled, and go for it. Quite a few go to the Elemental towers, because there are established trade routes, and the Lightborn military usually doesn't waste their resources trying to close down the approaches entirely. Others sneak into the lands of Light. A rare few—the real risktakers—try to delve into Liberty territories. It's not like anybody trustworthy makes it back from that direction, though."

Chase took a deep breath, voice rasping a bit as the harsh minty fumes of the oil hit his nostrils. "What's the point, though? I mean, I get seeing the world, and escaping where you're at. But it sounds like that's not all there is to it."

She shook her head, tongue stuck between her teeth as she teased out a tiny chip from the figure. "Not by any means. Told you already, the blood means something to us. And here, if you're able to go out and do something impressive that will help the blood, your status in life is going to change for the better. Enough that, sometimes, people think it's worth risking their lives for."

Chase squinted, considering this. "So... they risk their lives to bring back, what? Enchanted items that your own crafters can't create?"

"That's the least of it, but sure. If you bring back a couple of weapons with permanent Light enhancements? That would earn you some renown." She waved her whittling knife at Chase's arm. "The same if you managed to earn a couple of new Light or Elemental cards for yourself. But you need to think bigger, on a wider scale. Obtaining information—*trustworthy* information—on the Lightborn, their troop movements or plans. Arranging for trade agreements. Bringing back large quantities of crafting materials that we do not have at home. That is the stuff that will aid a large number of the blood, markedly improve our situation.

"Then we have those who go above and beyond. Jetfire, who managed to kill *three* Tier four Lightborn nobles and return unharmed. The Carver, who managed to... oh. Wait, sorry, I'm likely not allowed to tell you that one. Then, there's the few who have managed to bring back decks from other aspects, letting *large* numbers of the blood improve our strengths."

The branch slipped, leaving a long, red scratch on Chase's arm. He sputtered. "Wait, what? You actually have people going off trying to find decks of other aspects?"

She nodded. "Of course we do. I mean, the odds of anybody succeeding are horrible. The Lightborn are very careful with their decks, and the Elementals are even worse—and of course, we don't want to tick off the Elementals. Also, the decks always disappear when the person who bonded the deck dies, unless you get them to hand it over willingly. Still, from time to time, some daredevils have managed. It allows us a good number of years, where those who qualify are able to earn Light cards on top of Fury cards." Naley pointed at the solitary Fury card on her arm and smiled. "Clearly, I haven't gotten there yet. But I might—either if I eventually try my hand with the crucible, or if I gamble and go out into the world."

Chase's head reeled from the new information. The Furyborn actually had Light decks? And they used them as, what, incentives? Added bonuses for those who did well? That part about the deck disappearing when the one who bonded it died was news to Chase as well. It sealed a major difference in his head—another difference between the different decks. He held secondary decks for Light and the Elements. Yet, his Deck of Darkness was an original. Meaning, it wasn't going to just fade away when he died. It would lie right there for the taking of whoever did him in.

Where did that put Chase and his family? The secondary decks could be a major boon to the Furyborn, of course, allowing Chase to grant them access to Elemental cards. It didn't sound like they already had that, and they couldn't just knife Chase for it, because it would apparently fizzle away with his life's blood. However, the Deck of Darkness? They could take it for themselves, granting the Furyborn Dark cards for perpetuity. "You're saying not everybody's allowed to get Light cards? What's it take to earn that around here?"

She paused her whittling and tutted. "Pretty sure you're not of the blood yet. Earn that, then I'll tell you. Or convince the chief she should tell you."

Chase rolled his eyes. Inside, however, turmoil roiled. He tuned out her words, as his mind considered one scenario after the other where their decks would lead to their downfall. Eventually, however, he emerged on the other side, scolding himself for exaggerating. Sure, if it came out right here and now?

There'd be no saying exactly what could happen. However, they'd already been aiming for this exact thing—revealing the Deck of Darkness to Half-Swart, along with their plans for it, and the fact that they were backed by the towers. They would just have to ensure that they didn't get outed beforehand.

<u>Chapter 16</u>

"For all their name implies, the Furyborn are really not that guided by fury. They are relentless, yes. Merciless, as well. Yet, their fury, if anything, is cold and measured. The Furyborn guide their wrath." Heh. Maybe Slate didn't hear that.
(Page 51.)

"Do you believe that your caretaker would allow you to take a small break?" The words rang out from outside the pen, melodious and warm.

Chase looked up from where he was carefully applying an ointment to the infected wound of a caarnath Guardian. He had to walk around the big beast to see that the voice did indeed belong to who he thought. "Hello, gorgeous. I'm not too sure. Gaven? What's the deal today? Are we good if I leave you for a bit?"

The old man guffawed. "Like I wasn't doing just fine before you got here, boyo. Besides, you don't let a fine piece o' woman like that wait on yer, if she's actually willing t' brave the stench. Get your Dark butt outta here."

Sera beamed a warm smile at Gaven. "I will have him back here in an hour."

"Bah. Keep 'im. He's a decent worker, that one. We've no piles waiting for him, and it's just handling the beasties when they come back." He pointed at a man who was coming his way with a couple of plain cats in tow. "Speaking of, gotta work, when the kids leave you hanging."

Chase chuckled and walked over to a conveniently waiting pair of water buckets. "Love you too, Gaven. It's been fun learning more about Guardians. Especially once we moved past dealing with their leavings." After a brisk wash and rub-down with the minty branches, Chase followed Sera away from the enclosures. "I appreciate the rescue. Where're we off to?"

She ignored him, pointing back at the caarnath Guardian he'd been treating. "What was that? I thought Guardians did not fall sick?"

He shrugged and caught up with her, reaching out for her hand. "It's - what's that word Cil uses sometimes to talk about how they're both beasts and not? Dual?"

"Duality?"

"Ah. Yes. That. The duality of their existence, or so Gaven insists. Of course, he makes a mystical wave with his hands when he says it. Anyway, according to him, Guardians aren't animals, as such, but creations of magic. However, the magic creates living, breathing beasts. Beasts that are then subject to normal rules. They don't often fall ill, because they don't have the same flawed, faulty bodies that normal beasts have, but they can be affected by stuff from the outside. Selly back there had a wound that went bad, so I was cleaning it and applying some ointment he made." He held up his hand. "Before you ask, yes it *does* make a difference if you heal them or not. A healthy Guardian fades slower than a sick or injured one. Keeping the beasties in top shape makes sure they stick around for longer."

"I was not going to ask. Guardian or not, I would never question healing somebody."

Chase looked Sera in the eye. Life in Cemano did her well. She'd always been a bit of an outlier when it came to the nobility among the Lightborn, taking pride in actually doing her job. This meant that her skin was a good deal darker than the average alabaster-statue-wannabe noble who preferred never moving outside in the sun or among people. However, following the long trip to Cemano and the ensuing last three weeks of moving among the populace of the village and staying predominantly outside, working hard to treat and heal anybody around, she'd turned into a bronze-skinned goddess, a vision of life, brimming with energy.

Chase addressed the gorgeous vision, as dryly as possible. "I'm *pretty* sure that wasn't what you said about the indebted to begin with. What were the actual words? Something about having to earn healing and Lightborn being worth more than indebted?"

"Oh, for the love of Light." She huffed. "You cannot remember what we had for dinner yesterday, but *this*, you recall?"

Chase grinned unabashedly. "Well, I've heard winning arguments is the key to a good relationship."

"Whoever told you that was a liar and a homewrecker." She grumbled for a while. Turning back to him, she asked, wide-eyed and innocent, "I believe I have something the two of us could do to pass the time. Are you in a hurry to return to work?"

"Stop that, woman!" he mock-scolded. "You know I have no defense against witchery like that." He burst into laughter and pulled her close. "I'm not going anywhere. Come what may. Though I do actually look forward to getting back to Gaven at some point later. I finally figured out what's going on with those Guardians, and I need him to tell me that I'm right."

Sera brushed a curl behind an ear and raised an eyebrow. "Do you mean the topic you were talking about some time ago?

That you failed to understand why their Guardians, even the martial ones, are so placid?"

"Exactly. Back in Isarn, the Guardians inside the city didn't really do anything—just ambled about. Here in Cemano, Gaven insists that they actually *do* use the Guardians for scouting and martial outings. Only, when they're in the fold, they're tame as pocket gazili. That one guy returning just now finally sealed it for me, or so I believe. Everybody who handles the fighting Guardians are summoners! There's got to be some card, or some *secret* that allows the Furyborn summoners to direct their Guardians into battle."

Sera blinked. "If that is true, then that is a major advantage. Lightborn Guardians can't be properly directed. Only ushered into conflict, with the vaguest of instructions."

"Yeah," Chase said, with a self-satisfied grin. "Can't wait to see if I'm right or not. *But.* That can wait. What are we up to? What's that?"

Sera smiled and held up the basket she was carrying. "Well, since you rescued me once, I figured it would be fair for me to return the favor. Today, we are, quite simply, enjoying ourselves. I found a gorgeous spot that I wanted to share with you, and the other healers helped by providing me with a few luxuries."

He didn't speak for a while, simply held her hand as they walked. "You're too good to me."

Her eyes sparkled with mirth and something warmer. "Well, I did try to betray you once. It feels like you were owed."

"Pfah. Betrayal and backstabbing are just spice. At least, according to Liam's former love interests."

They laughed and chatted as they walked, soon reaching the southwestern part of the village. It was a more subdued area, with no noisy crafters nearby. Soon, Chase discovered why, as, from one moment to the other, they arrived at a huge hole in the ground. First, he gawked at the existence of a two-hundred-foot-wide hole inside the depression of the damn village itself. Then he looked down to see what was down there, and burst out in disbelieving laughter. "What? But..."

Sera's laughter trickled as a small brook. "That was the exact reaction I was hoping for."

It was a playground. With the village already inside a huge depression, they'd clearly thought going a level deeper made sense. Inside this depression, they'd erected a landscape of rolling hills and unnaturally angled low trees that would allow kids and toddlers of any age to run free without any fear of them getting into trouble. At the edge of the hole, a handful of adults sat and chatted, while below, kids ranging from two to maybe six years old were running rampant, swinging from branches, climbing the trees, and crawling through tunnels.

"They have a caster who is able to grow and manipulate plants," Sera said, eyes lidded as she looked down on the throng of kids below. "She is the one who created the thorns outside the village too." She sat down at the edge, a good distance away from anybody else, and patted the ground next to her.

"I didn't even know that was a possibility. It sounds impressive, though. If you can steer any sort of plant life, you would be able to grow some impressive creations." Chase rolled his eyes at himself. "Like a custom-grown playground, for instance."

"True." Sera's gaze went distant. A while later, she asked, "Have you ever thought about becoming a father?"

Chase snorted. "No!"

"That was fast!" Sera exclaimed. There was a question in there.

"I can give you the long answer, too. *Pits* no!" He laughed and, seeing her guarded expression, held up his hand. "Real talk now. You know my history. I've never known my parents. Liam was the closest thing I've ever had to a dad. That doesn't exactly give me warm, fuzzy feelings when I think about fatherhood. Besides, I've barely been able to fend for myself, let alone taking care of a kid."

He held out his hand for Sera to take. Facing her head-on, he continued, his tone dead earnest. "I don't want to bring somebody into the chaos we're embroiled in. I've seen enough deadbeat parents, people who couldn't pass any tests of being a parent bar the practical one. I don't want to be like that. If ever I were to find myself in a safe situation, where I wasn't running or fighting for my life every other minute? I might change my answer then."

Sera nodded. A small smile played at the edge of her mouth. "Good answer. Should we find ourselves in that situation, we will talk."

"I look forward to that... talk." He smirked.

"We shall see if you can compete with all the other applicants by then."

"Wait, what?"

Her laughter was loud enough to make some of the parents on the far side look their way.

For a while, they talked about nothing and everything. Eventually, they turned to their progress in Cemano. "I *know*. I'm not in a position to complain. But seriously, looking at Kith being the only one to walk the Steps... I do get envious. Doesn't it itch in your fingers to get out there and test yourself?"

Sera tipped her hand back and forth. "Yes and no. I am not as enamored of combat or risk-taking as you are. I have to admit that, at times, the sensation after a fight is pleasurable. Most often, I am merely pleased I have not soiled myself." With a tight smile, she pointed at the wall where Kith would be stationed. "It does not sound like Kith enjoys his post that much either."

Chase conceded the point. "Yeah. Apparently, their scouts are too damn good at killing or diverting any Guardians before they get to the village proper. It's mostly just remnants and the occasional solitary beasts. The stories of hordes or behemoths rampaging seem to be mostly that - stories. Still, he's doing well, and a single Step for him at this point is better progress than the rest of us."

"Agreed." Sera tapped her leg. "How do you believe we are doing otherwise?"

"Hmm. Let's see. Liam's doing amazing at being Liam. Meaning, he's pretty much friends with half the village by now. Well, at least, half of the ones who like brawling, drinking, and crude jokes. And a number of the younger women too. In short, there's a good number of people who might aid us simply because Liam's a bloody wonder of a human being."

Sera snorted. "I would."

"Kith's doing good, too. He's taking this seriously. Nothing's gotten past him, he hasn't slacked due to boredom, and he hasn't even gotten into a single fight."

"Wait. That is good for him?"

Chase rolled his eyes. "Good? That's *exemplary*. Half the trouble we got into on the Waves was because he got bored and started trouble."

"And the other half?"

"Let's continue. From Cilia's never-ending praise, that Master Benneth is either sent from the gods or an actual deity. It does appear that he actually *knows* what he's talking about, in between being insanely demanding."

Sera nodded. "Cilia has shown me the improvement in her craft. Now that she has access to real tools and a teacher who demands she learn every step of the crafting process, her skills have drastically improved. There is no comparison. The quality of the leather. The stitching. Even the quality of the thread. I know nothing about leatherworking, and *I* can see the difference."

"Yeah. It's slower going than what I expected—especially with how many hours she's pouring into it. But she's right. Once we leave this place, we just need to get her a set of her own tools and a steady delivery of leather to work with, and she'll be able to produce *anything* we want, from regular clothing to hardened armor."

"I do despair of her ever learning anything about using her cards from the man. *The foundation must be solid.* That's all Master Benneth keeps repeating, apparently."

Chase grimaced. "True. But, well, when you're at the bottom of the heap, you take what you're given. Apparently, he does appreciate her work, and has started to approve some of her material work – scraped leathers, cleaned furs and the like - as being good enough for the village. That might sound like a low bar to clear, but from what people say, it's anything but. Meaning, she's starting to build up a bit of goodwill around the place as well, because, while Benneth does amazing work, he's slow, and most people have to make do with lesser work."

Sera smiled. "I believe that I am also progressing. I would not claim to be the equal to Jessel—he is a Trio, and has worked, and healed, in Cemano since its founding. He knows everything there is to know about local healing remedies and cures. That being said, I have earned the right to accompany him for any tasks, from minor infections to childbirths."

"Births?" Chase blinked. "That's new."

Wide-eyed, Sera nodded. "That was quite the experience. I have a newfound respect for midwives." She cleared her throat and continued under her breath. "Without boasting, I believe I am his equal when it comes to magical healing. He does not hold the same level of Mental Power that I do, and his choices are focused on widespread healing and boosts, rather than single-target healing like I hold."

"Hold on." Chase held up a hand. "You're telling me, that you can actually out-heal the actual Light-scoured healer of this place?" He laughed incredulously as Sera's face grew increasingly redder. "Can I pick my girls or *what*?"

"If you were listening, it is only for specific types of healing, and I could only hope to match him for practical knowledge... but yes. My healing is growing strong along with my Mental Power."

"Talented, powerful, and drop-dead gorgeous. In that case, I'll just leap straight ahead to the conclusion that you're also doing more than your part in making sure that our popularity in the village is improving. "

"Too much, in some cases." Her nostrils flared. "I had to ban old Jebediah from the premises for a while. That old lecher! He kept trying to paw at me." Her voice softened as she continued. "My main worry is that there is too much work. We get a *lot* of injuries in, and have, at this moment, two buildings filled with people who are long-term healing. Bad diseases, lost limbs, and worse. Cemano, I am afraid, is *dangerous*. But yes. People are warming to me, and I am learning a lot. Jessel and I do complement each other well."

"Do I need to worry?" Chase quirked an eyebrow. "Jessel does have that feral, too-wild-to-handle thing going for him." That was an understatement. At the best of times, the healer was hairy enough to look like a humanoid bear.

She slapped him, not too gently. "I prefer my men a tad more... groomed. Besides, I have trouble keeping just one in check."

"You really don't," he answered softly. Clearing his throat, he continued. "Anyway. For what it's worth, I'm doing well too. Old Gaven's nice, and we do get to chat with a lot of people in the village each day. It ain't like shoveling dung is going to win a lot of hearts, but I..." He trailed off. "Are you hearing that?"

"I am. Come on." Leaving the basket, they got up and ran for the commotion.

It came from the center of the village. At first, it sounded like a lot of people shouting, but when they came closer, they realized that it was a single voice, amplified to reach the entire damn village. One very familiar voice. Slate's.

Chapter 17

"The ends justify the means. A common enough saying. Yet, one that truly springs to mind when you consider the Furyborn. As long as they uphold their core principles, nothing is sacred. Poison. Child soldiers. Suicidal charges. According to the Furyborn, these are all legitimate forms of warfare." It's a quandary. What is a social construct and what is a legitimate crime? I loathe how they're exposing kids to the struggle, yet I haven't had to deal with constant attacks all my life. Who the Pits am I to judge? (Page 62.)

"Swear to the Halls, Slate. You throw away that doodad, stop yammering, and get your ass down already. My kid's trying to sleep."

Slate was on the wooden platform again. He was holding a wooden creation up—a glowing wooden block which had to be what amplified his voice—as he called people from the village to action.

As Sera and Chase came closer, they could hear that he wasn't actually monologuing—yet; he was merely shouting out to the world that he had something they all needed to hear.

He lowered the wooden object for a moment. "I will, when we've got this settled, Carmine," the burly scout answered. "But we're enough here now that we can get on with it. Won't be but a moment."

A few hecklers tried to jeer, but Slate, sneering, raised the block to his mouth again. "I know, all. You're all tired enough of me that you'd rather I never speak again. Not enough want to give me their tokens that we can actually do something about the eastern defenses either—so I won't go on about that again."

That brought up a confused murmur. According to the local gossip, that was pretty much what the man was known for. That, and an inflated opinion of his own capabilities.

"But there's one thing that's come to my attention lately that I can't with good conscience shut up about. That's why I talked to Radevan, and he agreed to lend me his amplifier this once."

A chill crawled down Chase's spine. He didn't know what this was about, but he had a really bad premonition. Not only did Slate manage to gather a huge number of villagers, with more still trickling in from the outer edges of the square, he was more collected and to the point. And Radevan, a local Tier three crafter, a woodworker, who held some esteem in the village, stood on the platform, in clear support of him. On top of that, the whole thing felt carefully crafted, like some of the mummer's farces back on the Waves, where the stronger criminals threw some weight around, trying to appear nice, when in fact everything was arranged beforehand.

Slate had been silent for the past weeks. Suspiciously silent, Chase now realized. He'd believed that the furious scout had realized that the lack of proof left him powerless. Rather, it appeared, he'd been preparing for an alternate attack.

"We all know that we have five newcomers. Worthy additions to the village, if you ask most anybody around here. They've kept their heads down, played nice and helped wherever they could. Nobody's done anything suspicious, and, to be honest, they're just here to make friends and become part of our society." Slate's voice turned venomous, as he shouted, at the top of his lungs. "Lies!" His finger aimed into the crowd, straight at where Cilia stood, next to the leathery form of old Master Benneth. "Calan. Come forward and please tell me what you heard."

A young Furyborn ambled forward from a bit farther back on the platform. He accepted the wooden block from Slate. His voice sounded out, nervous and faltering, but just as loud. "I was walking home the other day, and I was walking past Surly Anne's as I heard some voices from within. They were kind of loud and... okay, I was curious."

A few chuckles arose from the crowd. Apparently, the young man had a bit of a reputation. But nobody seemed derisive of him.

He continued. "Then I heard what they were talking about. They were talking about their *progress*." He put special emphasis on that word. "Here in the village. How they thought they were proceeding in winning us all over."

Inwardly, Chase cursed. This was bad. They were being outmaneuvered, badly. They were taking what they'd talked about and twisting it, applying it slightly out of context, making them appear cold and calculating. They didn't even lie either— just twist it; they might even have some truth detectors like those gems back in the towers. He could imagine the direction Slate would take from there, angling toward them being infiltrators, and their actions being horribly suspicious, then having them exiled or worse.

Chase shouted up at the platform. "Sure. We were talking about how we'd need to make friends if we ever wanted to gather enough tokens to be allowed to make it to Heart Halls. Like we've told *anybody* who cared to ask since we got here.

What a surprise. We were talking about succeeding in what we wanted to do since day one."

That got a few laughs and shouts of agreement. But a lot of people were holding back, observing. Judging.

Ignoring the amplifier, Slate spoke loudly. "That ain't even the point. Just the backdrop. Go on."

The kid swallowed and spoke up haltingly. "Well, that got me to thinking. If they're just, you know, using us to get what they want, or they actually are honest folk, just trying to reach their goals."

"Lil' Darkie there's worked hard as anything since 'e got here. Humor's atrocious, though." Gaven's raspy voice shot through the crowd. "I'll vouch for the bugger, one hand 'n all."

Chase could kiss the wrinkled old man. Well, if it weren't for the smell.

"That's it though, isn't it, Gaven?" The young man shrugged. "If they're actually here working for the Lightborn, trying to spy on us or worse? That's exactly what would happen. They'd keep their heads low, try to make friends. Then, when we're good and cozy..." He mimed stabbing somebody in the back. "Ain't like it's the first time the Lighties have tried something like it in our lands, is it?"

That shot through the crowd like a wave. Uncertainty. Doubt. Suspicion. Chase grimaced. At least the chief had vouched for them, and they should have enough on their side. Once Slate argued to kick them out or worse, they could—

"I think they're lying, backstabbing scum," Slate growled. He'd accepted the wooden amplifier back and was stalking around on the platform. Then he froze and held up a hand. "But I'm a suspicious type. Always have been."

What the Pits was *that?* He was changing the script now?

"Easy to argue that they're scum, trying to weasel their way into our good graces. Harder to prove, unless they care to show us the proof themselves."

"Hard to show you something that doesn't exist, isn't it?" Liam's voice arrived, loud and friendly, from the far side of the square. "Easier to just point fingers and make up conspiracies."

The crowd surrounding Liam murmured in agreement. A few jeered at Slate. Looked like the other laborers had his back.

Chase felt the mood tipping slightly. Only, then Slate went and did something entirely out of character.

He agreed with Liam. "Exactly my point." Turning for the crowd, he continued on that momentum. "That kept me up at night. How on Ordei do we prove something like that? I figured there had to be something, some middle point between just trusting their explanations and good natures, and exiling them outright due to my suspicions. Because, mind my words, I believe, with all my heart, that the chief's wrong here. Trusting their words with no damn proof?"

"We have a message from the High Elementalist herself. How is that without proof, you ignorant cretin?" Cilia shot out.

Chase winced. Calling somebody ignorant in a place of simple villagers? She'd always been the worst at working a crowd.

"A message that nobody can read or decipher!" he shot back. Shaking his head, he stood straight. "That is when it came to me. Sure, there might not be any proof we can ask of them in fairness. But we *can* demand they live up to our creed. That they uphold the same standards that *we* demand of our own. Integrity and blood? Sure. Looks like they're working for the blood, aiming to help us all. Only in the long run will we be able to prove that one way or the other. Yet, it sure looks like they're doing their part, lifting their weight. Independence?" He snorted. "Ain't seen much of that. If they're telling the truth, they're marching on behalf of the Elementals. If they ain't, they're in the thrall of somebody even worse. Resilience?" He barked a loud, derisive laugh. "Not much resilience shown in shoveling dirt now, is there?"

Disdain clear on his face, he now bellowed in full force at the enraptured audience. *"Let them prove their mettle.* We'll take them with us on the next scouting run. Show them what *real* Furyborn have to weather on a daily basis. That way, they'll be able to prove themselves as worthy to us, or die trying. Like one of the blood."

The crowd exploded in chatter and shouts. It took at least a minute before everything calmed down enough for any voices to pierce the din. When somebody eventually did, the voice belonged to Alia.

The chief was livid. "For all the Liberty-spared reaches of Ordei, *what do you think you're doing, Slate?* I welcomed these people into our midst. I heard their explanations, and I found them to be acceptable! I bid them welcome and allowed them to prove for themselves if they're good people. In here, they can't learn anything incriminating about us."

Slate didn't give an inch. He glared down at the chief. "One of them's a summoner, one's pretty enough it has to be a card, and another's a golden-haired charmer. You think we're keeping any secrets from them? I think you're an amazing, strong chief. But in this, I think you're a fool."

"You call me a fool?" Her quiet words carved through the assembled people.

He gulped, but didn't back down. "In this, Alia, yes, I do. Now, I was in the middle of something. Unless you think you should take away my option to offer a proposal to everybody here."

Her death glare promised retribution.

For a moment, Chase got his hopes up. But apparently, these people took the "independence" part seriously.

She shook her head. "You know I won't. For all you're making a fool of yourself, you have the right. But you *will* get on with it, so people can continue with their day. Also, when this is over and done with, I hope that everybody will remember my words. You are a fool, Slate. Twisted by what was done to you, unable to move on and become a whole person. It has been a long time coming, but this may be the step you take that finally takes you away from being of the blood. You should be very sure that you want to do what you aim to do."

His eyes burned with something beyond the moving colors of the Furyborn. "You know me, Alia. I do not back down." Raising his voice, he continued, addressing the crowd. "Which is why I volunteer to be in charge of the scouts who ensure that these newcomers actually uphold their end of the bargain."

An elderly Darkborn woman Chase had never talked to asked outright, "What is it exactly you're suggesting? You always say we should throw more lives at our surroundings."

"Not this time, Renna. I vote we do as we have always done. Send our regular scouts on their usual routes. But we take one of the more dangerous routes, and let it be the chance for these newcomers to prove themselves. To show if they actually have the integrity and the resilience to stand against the beasts that always threaten our lives. To prove if they're puppets dancing on faraway strings or independent people capable of acting by themselves." His grin grew wide. "And even if they fail or fall, at the least, *their* blood may protect *the* blood."

Chase wanted to curse. He wanted to howl, to rail against the injustice of it. Yet, he didn't let anything show on his face. Because he knew it was inevitable. They'd been outmaneuvered. He thought he'd been cleverer than Slate, and the crafty bastard had gone and showed them all. Because, despite the wisdom applied by the chief, the counters and objections by those they had managed to get to know in Cemano over the past weeks, Slate had managed to sway popular opinion, presenting it like an option that didn't cost anything, and carved to the bone of what being a Furyborn was—and that wasn't anything you could trump.

The first tokens were placed carefully, even reverently on the platform. That opened the flood, and, little by little, the gathered crowd turned into a wave, an unstoppable motion of people moving toward the platform to show their support that Chase and his family would need to go out and risk their lives.

Chapter 18

"That, I believe, is what leads to the major disconnect. People say 'savages,' when, really, they mean 'their values do not align with ours.' I have spent two decades in Heart Halls, and, by now, I believe that of the two peoples, we are the ones who are the least principled." Huh. At times it feels like the writers of this tome overvalue shocking comments. Yet they have a point. Of the Elementals and the Furyborn, I would likely agree that the Furyborn are the more dedicated to their core principles. As to the value of those principles and whether that suffices to call them savages... I am going to need more space for notes. (Page 70.)

"I don't get it. This is a *good* thing. Why are you all complaining?" Kith was going through the pile of shellfruits a kind neighbor had dropped off at their house, putting them aside one after the other. Finally, he came up with an acceptable selection, and sat down at the table, unsheathing one of his hand axes.

The others all lounged at the table, still reeling from the development.

Cilia, sitting next to Kith, looked down at the hand axe in Kith's hand and onward to the fruit and the hard-to-pierce shell it was named for. Her tone was colder than nighttime among the indebted, as she enunciated, without a hint of doubt, "No."

"But—"

"No. Simply, no. *No axes at the table.* At times, I wonder why we were saddled with somebody who has the mind of a five-year-old. As for your question? Because this is not what we wanted."

"But—"

"Ah-ah!" Her icy stare and raised index finger made Kith sit down with burning cheeks. "We did want to join their scouts. We are well-trained and prepared enough that, given the freedom to act on our training and own devices, we should be able to tackle nearly anything we might meet out here. Do we have said freedom?"

"Oh." Kith blinked in revelation.

"Exactly. We can't just do what we want. Anything we do on this outing will be judged by this group. Should they be impartial, that would not present a problem either. But they are not. In fact, they are more likely to present any action of ours, regardless of how small, in as unfavorable a light as possible. Even if we go out there, they'll be able to take *anything* we did on this outing and present it as proof that our values clash with the creed of the Furyborn... a creed which we do not entirely even understand. Did I sum up everything fully?"

"It's not as bad as all that." A voice emerged from the door.

They turned as one to see Naley peeking through the door. She opened it and strode in with a small smile, tossing her braids over a shoulder. "I'd say you summed it up pretty well. Only, Slate, being Slate, has made a lot of enemies. That means, even with all the tokens he got, we managed to make a few changes to his suggestions after you left because they weren't fair. He was quite clear about hating you. So, people saw the point of somebody else joining the group who actually *liked* you guys."

"You?" Liam perked up.

"Me." Naley grinned. "I'm here to tell you what you've been signed up for. And I don't mind telling you, even with me on board, you shouldn't expect to enjoy the trip."

Liam snorted. "You coming along sounds like the only thing to look forward to."

The tall scout rolled her eyes, but couldn't quite hide the blush sneaking up her neck. "You're not wrong there. Here's the deal. You're leaving in two days. Two days, that's what we have to prepare you for what you can expect to see out there, get you up to speed on how to act, how to move, and how to behave. Let's be entirely clear straightaway. *Two days is not enough.* It's not a question of whether you're going to screw up, but how much, and whether the cost is going to be in how suspicious people are going to be of you afterward, or paid in your own blood out there."

Ten minutes later, Chase closed the door behind Naley, leaned against the door, and exhaled slowly. "Well, that sucked."

Sera nodded gravely. "Two days really is not a lot of time. Does anybody else need to eat anything before Naley returns? We need our wits with us, if we need to learn about the local beasts, dangers, terrain, behavior, and..." She shook herself slightly. "Too much."

"Forget about eating. First, we need to address *the* most important thing." Chase walked over to the table and leaned over it, looking at them all one by one. "Slate is going to stab us in the back."

Kith, putting down a regular knife and triumphantly holding up a piece of shellfruit, nodded. "Yup."

"No discussion," Liam added, trying to steal the piece of fruit and failing.

"Can't say I disagree." Cilia frowned.

Sera blinked. "Are you serious? He..." She paused, took a deep breath and leaned forward, letting her curls hide her face. When she leaned back, her features were composed and serious. "I agree. Slate has already proved that he is ready to use any means at his disposal to get at us. However, he has been surprisingly measured in other ways. He could easily have lied, yet he did not. What does that mean?"

"Chalk it up to a cultural thing?" Kith shrugged, fending off another attempt from Liam at stealing his food. "He was eager enough to try to kill us and doesn't mind eavesdropping, however despicable that sort of thing is." He waggled his eyebrows, colors in his eyes roiling with mirth. "But lying is a no-no. Confusing. That's kinda the issue here, isn't it? We don't know what to expect from the bastard, making it harder for us to properly prepare. So, when Naley comes back from whatever she had to handle, we'll have to learn not only how to defend ourselves out there, but in which ways we can expect Slate to attack us."

When Naley returned about ten minutes later, it was with a promise of reinforcements. Fortunately, not everybody in Cemano believed Slate's fearmongering, and enough were on their side that they wouldn't be entirely left to fend for themselves.

First was the relief of learning that Slate and his followers hadn't been allowed to set up the details of the patrol for themselves. That wasn't how things worked in Cemano. Sure, earning all those tokens granted them a seat at the table. Whatever their proposal was, it still had to go through a process where some of the local experts would come up with demands and changes to the proposal—which was how Naley's addition to the party had been added.

It was a two-way street, though. Although Slate wasn't able to push through everything he'd want, neither could the chief, the lead scout, and some of the other experts involved in the decisions simply push aside or ignore the spirit of the proposal. A few had attempted it in the past, and the public outcry had been massive. Apparently, that went against their demand for integrity or some such.

The result, as it stood, was that they *would* indeed be demanded to go through a week-long scout patrol, pushing through some of the most dangerous areas surrounding Cemano, ones that were almost guaranteed to have them see conflict along the way. They would also be surrounded mostly by Slate's friends and favored scouts, with Naley to balance out any overt hostility. However, there also were a few concessions, due to the fact that they were not born and raised locally. They would not be demanded to handle any parts of the scouting. Nor were they expected to identify hostile creatures, ensure they had acceptable sleeping spots, drinking water, or the like. That lay on the scouts, apart from their self-inflicted task of keeping an eye on Chase and his people and making sure they behaved properly.

They wouldn't have to worry about equipment or food either. However, Cilia asked, and got permission, to start crafting complete items for herself again – not just the simple materials she'd been working on. As a requirement for taking her on, Master Benneth had demanded that she stop~~ped~~ crafting until she could live up to his exacting standards.

Apparently, survival superseded that requirement, and she was allowed to start in on the survival kits she'd been planning to create for so long.

Even if they were fortunate enough that they didn't have to worry about provisions and such, this didn't mean they could just relax and focus on any possible fights. Naley couldn't be expected to be everywhere for a full week, and if the other scouts "missed" a half-hidden threat... who was to know? And threats outside of Cemano were aplenty.

An old lady with a huge mop of steel-gray hair that looked about as unruly as a thorn bush took care of educating them about the surrounding areas. In between constantly cursing them out, berating them for being violence-happy, ignorant outsiders and preaching about youngsters of today, she informed them of the dangers of scouting and sleeping in the wilds. Dangers, which, apparently, were far from limited to the local beasts and Guardians, but extended to poisonous plants and even the damn geography at times.

As an example, one insidious venomous mole-like creature had learned that it was much easier to envenom and kill food that couldn't run away. Hence, it had taken to leaving well-disguised, deep potholes in its vicinity, perfect for breaking ankles of any creature stupid enough to run past its domain at speed.

That was but a single example. After a couple of hours with the cantankerous old woman, their heads reeled with the innumerable examples of plants and geographical phenomena that were, quite simply, out to kill them and drain their blood. The consensus of the group was to keep their hands to themselves and not touch anything they hadn't been handed by any of the scouts. Even then, they should be observant.

Also, there was the matter of the climate. Furyborn lands, when talked about by outsiders, were generally seen as wilderness, without too many details. There was a rather simple reason to that. With the expansion of the lands of Light, the Furyborn were consistently pushed back into the wilds, the less desirable reaches of Ordei. However, you would see a massive difference between the constantly wet and infested reaches of the southern marshes and the frozen north. The lands surrounding Cemano suffered from a rapidly changing climate, with but a few consistencies. The conditions ranged from wet, near-frozen, and miserable, to dry and windblown. The only constants were the winds, which could reach insane speeds and prevented most but the hardiest growths from surviving out in the open, and had a couple of implications for any scouts.

First off, the winds as well as the sudden, tempestuous rains meant that flash floods were a given. These had, over time, carved out ever-present channels throughout the landscape, leaving the soil broken and hard to traverse. Even Cemano itself had been crafted with this in mind, apparently, sporting numerous hidden channels where water could safely disperse. Outside the village, the harsh winds and landscape meant that patrols were usually traveling *within* these channels, reconciling the roundabout pathways as an acceptable cost for avoiding the winds and standing out as prey on top of the world. Traversing these channels wasn't without danger either, given that this was where many poisonous plants grew, and the harsh squalls and hard clay carried a constant risk of being caught in a flash flood. Even so, it was seen as the better alternative.

Yet another arrival came as a complete surprise to Chase. Given that Naley had only spent a couple of years as a scout, she called for another of the oldest, hardiest experts in Cemano to come educate them on the dangers of the local wildlife and which hostile Guardians they could be expected to stumble into. Said expert turned out to be Gaven. The cheery old dung slinger had lived a colorful and dangerous life in near constant struggle for survival as a scout. Although Chase had suspected him of exaggerating on many accounts, it was quickly apparent that the old man was truly knowledgeable when it came to not getting killed.

Right from the get-go, Chase was pleased to learn that he'd been right in his guesses. The Guardians of Cemano *were* in fact connected to the summoners. This was, apparently, a choice that those using their decks to establish Furyborn Wellspring in combat-rich areas nearly always made. It came at a cost, which Gaven didn't know about, but allowed any summoner to form a link to any Guardian and command them directly for as long as they were within their range. Said range depended on Mental Power and practice. This, of course, opened up an entirely new level of possible strategies for the Furyborn, which they'd fully embraced. Only the safest patrolled routes were generally traveled without the addition of carefully selected Guardians. If you moved over less traveled areas, you'd usually bring some sort of hunter with excellent vision or sense of smell. If you expected enemies, you'd bring good fighters.

Because their group was going to cross a long stretch of land in a circle ranging generally westward of Cemano that both covered a lot of area and was known as a clashing ground for regular beasts and unaspected Guardians, they'd been allowed a pack of three plain cats. That name, apparently, was a bit of a joke, considering they had nothing to do with plains, but referred to the plain, dull brown color of their skins. They were the panther-like, spikey creatures Chase spotted when he first met Gaven: consummate hunters with excellent night sight and hearing; nasty ambush predators that also had impressive pack hunting tactics.

Between Gaven and the old biddy whose name was apparently "None of your Fury-torn business, you wet-nosed runts," they were inundated with a decade's worth of knowledge about their surrounding and possible threats in a day and a half. The final half-day was taken up by Naley, who made it her business to ensure they didn't mess up trying to follow the unwritten rules of Furyborn society. That... wasn't the easiest task in the world.

Massaging her temples with steepled fingers, Sera burst out, "This is entirely unreasonable. Do you not have anything written down? No actual rules that we can memorize?" She looked pleadingly at the younger scout, who was lounging against the wall inside Surly Anne's house.

Naley snorted, twirling an arrow between her fingers. "What? Like the Lightborn? Laws and stuff, that nobles can pay to abuse or bend to their advantage?"

Kith snorted. "Naley has a point there."

Sera huffed in a, for her, very unladylike show of exasperation. "I know, I know. The laws of the lands of Light are anything but straightforward. But at least they are written down. These so-called rules constantly change depending on the person, the situation, and, it would appear, the time of day."

Naley gave her a lopsided smile. "Easiest way to learn it is living it. If you'd been here for a couple more months, half of it would be logical to you anyway."

"You are likely right. Is there not... I mean, what if people interpret these things differently? Who decides who is right?"

"Oh, every village has somebody who is well-versed in these types of things, who can decide in case of disputes."

Sera perked up. "Really? Could we not talk to her instead?"

Naley tried to hide a smirk and failed. "You already did. She left half an hour ago, after calling Kith a pest for the ages and pinching Liam on the ass."

Sera's mouth formed an O. "That was... Please lay your wisdom on us, oh all-knowing sage!"

"I figured as much." Naley gave a smug grin. "I'll try to come up with more examples, try to make things make sense for you. Though, if I had to dumb it down for you, it'd all boil down to our creed again."

"Blood, integrity, independence, and resilience," they intoned as one.

"Well done. You're about as well-trained as blue-winged boghearts." She rolled her eyes. "We don't have much time left... I'm guessing you'll want to sleep before you leave."

"If only." Cilia groaned. "I still have at least five fire droplets I need to create. Sleep is for non-crafters."

"We'll watch out for you on the march, Cil," Liam assured her.

"That's all well and touching," Naley said. "Still, that leaves us with just a few short hours. Here's the way I see things. You listen, then you can ask questions, and we can try to fend off at least some of your ignorance." She twirled the arrow in a rapid flourish, then slammed it point-first into the wooden table and stood up straight.

Sera looked at the arrow as if it had just stabbed her aunt. She was *not* used to property disfigurement like this. To her credit, she managed to not say anything.

"Blood, as I've explained, means watching out for those of your kin. Helping where it's needed, doing what needs doing, and *knowing* what needs doing. For this patrol, it's kind of a given, because it's a large point of the trip itself. You guys doing your part for the blood, and proving that you're willing to do so." She paused, before adding, "Only one extra thing to remember. Whatever happens, whatever provocations they might fling at you, *do not attack any of the blood.* That will not end well."

Everybody looked at Kith.

With a wide-eyed look of innocence, he flung up his hands. "What? I didn't... ah, Liberty save me, I won't stab anybody. Even if they deserve it."

"Good. Now, as for—"

"I mean, unless... I *did* just have a fresh set of lockpicks made, and I know where Slate lives. I could—"

"No!" The chorus interrupted Kith as one. Even Naley joined the others.

"Moving on. Independence... that one will be tough for you," she assessed.

"First time I've been told I'm not independent enough," Chase said dryly. "I literally lost a hand for not following rules."

"Different world, Darkborn," Naley responded, a wry smile coming through. "The reason why I say it will be tough for you is your situation. Independence is integral to the blood because of our history, but also because of who we are. *How* we are. How can we, as a nation, improve, if we do not challenge the established ways but stay in the same ruts? A scout will, of course, learn from their elders, but inevitably try to establish their own rules, tricks, and guidance. How could it be otherwise? You would end up with human Guardians—walking, talking beasts who only acted on their orders and were incapable of thinking for themselves."

Chase thought back to the armies of Light and figured she had something of a point. There, the chain of command was writ in stone, with nobody in doubt where they were in the hierarchy. Yet, more than once, he and his friends had managed to slip by soldiers who really should have known better—and every time, it had been due to the soldiers unconditionally and mindlessly obeying orders.

The lanky scout continued. "How's this go along with your situation, where you don't know anything, where you're expected to follow orders from those who know about the dangers of your surroundings and have to do as you're said to prove that you won't be a burden to the blood, you ask? Not very damn well. I'd say the best course is this: follow orders and do as you're told, unless something sounds too stupid to be true, or you can see a better way." She corrected herself with a frown. "And even then, it's likely Slate or his friends trying to trick you into doing something stupid. In this case, as much as I dislike saying it, you're probably better off following orders."

"Probably for the best," Liam muttered as he laid his head on the table. "All of this having to watch for hidden traps and whatnot... my head hurts just thinking of it."

"Liam." Cilia's index finger stabbed down on the table and made him jump. Her voice was cold and unemotional. "I said it once back in the towers, and now I am going to say it again. You are not going to slack. You are going to pull yourself together, and you are going to do everything in your power to make sure that we can get through this safely. While you may not see the point right now, I assure you it is there. And if any of us get hurt because *you* aren't thinking, I swear, I will force-feed you fire droplets until you see the light *as it bursts from the explosion in your stomach!*"

Silence spread across the room. Eventually, Chase cleared his throat. "A little much, perhaps, Cil?"

The diminutive woman's nostrils flared, and she breathed deeply as if she'd been running. She didn't look up from the table. "I... yes. I just so detest ignorance. Especially willful ignorance." After a long pause, she continued. "I apologize, Liam. But so help me—"

"I get it, Cil," Liam said. "I wouldn't want to put any of you in danger. I'll do my part."

"Right," Naley said. "That wasn't awkward at all. Now. Integrity. You do what is needed. What is right. You don't make the easy choices. In this case, that simply means going through with the task, and never accepting any suggestions that you shirk your duties, take the easy way out, or in *any* way avoid doing what's needed. In fact, if somebody suggests it, you're allowed to react appropriately."

"I thought you said I couldn't stab them," Kith said.

"Kith!"

"Nonono." Naley interrupted the chorus. "Kith isn't entirely wrong here. Stabbing is off the table. But if anybody honestly suggests that you shirk your duties? You can threaten them, even punch them. Nobody'd look down on you for that." She frowned and looked up, before nodding to herself, satisfied. "Honestly, I think that covers that. This leads us to resilience. That's the easiest of them all."

Her gaze, often light and filled with mirth, now carried a weight they hadn't seen before. "If anything tries to go through you? You end it. Lightborn invasion? Lost ones? Landslide? Bloody god of the bloody Church of the bloody Circle born again come here for a scrap? I don't care. *You end it!* If something comes along that you can't handle? I suggest you better take your own life. Because the alternative will be worse."

"That was kind of harsh, Naley," Liam said.

"You think so? Well, let me put it to you like this. You're allowed to be clever. If you're up against stupid Guardians or regular beasties? Lead them toward the lands of Light, for all I care. But, if you let *anything*—a group of Lightborn soldiers, a solitary lost one... Pits, the smallest of windriders—sneak by you, or fight their way past you to reach Cemano? There will be no need for you to come back to Cemano. In fact, you will be *brought* back. Then, you will suffer a very, very bad time of it until you reach your all-too-early death. And I will be helping. Because right this moment, I am putting myself forward and standing up for you, in the hope that you could actually be blood. So, you had best deliver."

<u>Chapter 19</u>

"I am nobody special. Just a simple grunt. But there's one thing I've done that sets me apart. I have battled the Furyborn and lived to tell the tale. We had the numbers, the cards, and terrain on our side. They were cornered. Yet still, we lost. Their Guardians. Their leaders. Their Darkness-infected children. They all charged us, with no regard for their lives, for... propriety." Huh. I guess that's proof that the Furyborn tactics work. If they didn't all act like that, the Lightborn soldiers on the other side would likely have acted very differently. (Page 75.)

"At first glance, you'll discover the carved plains are scary as anything. Then, once you learn a bit more, you'll find they ain't as scary as all that. What you need to know, right here and now, is that the first reaction is the right one. The danger is real. You need to keep your mind with you at all times. The moment you relax is when it'll take you by surprise. I'll be pointing out the dangers as we encounter them, and the other scouts are out there, right now, finding anything big. But that part needs to stick with you. Respect the dangers, or they will claim you."

Naley walked ahead of their tight group, talking softly without glancing back at them. Her eyes never fixed on them, constantly moving, investigating, going from side to side, up, down. Every inch of their surroundings was scrutinized, categorized, and mentally marked as threat or non-threat.

They'd left right after dawn. Apparently, with the lands near Cemano being mostly safe, and most life-forms being most active late in the day or at night, they wanted to get a good head start on their journey, making it to the outskirts of the carved plains around mid-morning.

The difference in their surroundings was noticeable. The lands had, for a good while, been comprised of mostly clay, but apart from that, it had looked relatively normal to their group. They climbed up the depression that held the village of Cemano, passed through a checkpoint, and—blindfolded again—were led for a few hours before finally being allowed to walk free. From a distance, the landscape had looked unchanging, and in effect the composition of the soil didn't change much. Yet, as they walked further west and north, the land rose and started to crack, as if somebody had dropped the entire surface of the plains from great height, and left the clay broken and riddled with rifts and crevices.

At first, the cracks had been traversable, easy enough to navigate and leap. Here and there, they had to account for a deeper rift, take care that the clay could hold their weight. As they continued onward, the wind increased its ferocity, growing more insistent and constant. Dark-gray clouds on the horizon promised rain in the near future, and the air smelled clean and heavy. There were almost no trees or growths visible, and nowhere obvious for any Guardians or local beasts to hide.

After half an hour of traversing the seemingly lifeless cracked landscape, Chase had to ask. "Why are they called the carved plains? Because of those cracks we'll enter?"

"You'll see in a moment. In fact... we're about to enter. Right over there. You can see the cairn marking the entrance right ahead."

Frowning at the non-answer, Chase scanned their dull brown-gray surroundings. Right enough, a few hundred feet ahead, a larger crack in the ground was marked by a cairn—a generous description of what he'd normally call a stacked pile of rocks.

The full group pulled up right before the cairn.

Slate and the other scouts had silently moved ahead along with the Guardians until now, fully focused on their tasks, one-word commands being the limits of their interactions. Now, they turned around, facing Chase and his people. Surprisingly, Slate wasn't the one to speak up, and neither did they all stare daggers at their group. Distaste, sure, and a good deal of measured dismissal, but no overt hate. Slate, of course, didn't hide his dislike. He stood farther back, sneering, eyes lidded as they gazed over their surroundings.

Five scouts accompanied them, besides Naley. One of these, a lithe mixed-race young man with clear Darkborn features combined with his earthy Furyborn tones and colored sclera, stepped forward. He had to speak up to drown out the howling of the ever-present wind. "All right. Time to kick this off. I think we need a brief introduction here, before we go down."

Chase shared a brief look with the others. That was a lot friendlier than what he'd expected.

The smiling man continued. "I'm Beni. Once we enter, you'll see me the least. I'm the one who takes care of those beauties." He pointed at the plain cats who'd curled up next to the cairn in a huge pile of not-very-fluffy felines. "My task is to roam, to stay constantly in movement and ensure that these gorgeous beasts sniff out anything in our path, so we can take care of it.

Usually, you'll only see me when we sleep or when there's trouble."

He pointed at a woman with long, frazzled hair in a filthy ponytail. She might have been young, but there were streaks of gray in her hair, and she looked… spent. She carried a short bow and an impressive number of pouches and purses, along with a large backpack. "That's Gabby. She's our forward scout and is the one to truly look out for. If she stops, you stop. She also gathers necessary roots and whatnot for Jessel back in the village. If she starts cutting into plants, let her work. Those plants might become the remedy that saves your asses another day."

Beni inclined his head to Slate. "Slate. You might know him. Angry bastard, but he's good. He's our damage. Anything tries to take us down, he takes *it* down first, at a distance, with that over-produced monster of a crossbow."

A tap with his finger on the shoulder of the thin, near-emaciated Furyborn next to him. "Ivar. Rogue and rear scout. He makes sure nothing's trailing us, planning to ambush us. He also takes most of the night watches. He has a card."

Finally, he bowed slightly at a young, pretty woman with two long swords on her belt, a short, no-nonsense haircut, and a long scar curling along one arm like the trail of a snake left in sand. "And this beauty is who we're actually listening to. Ellie's a caster, but she's probably one of three scouts in Cemano who have the most experience traversing the carved plains."

"She's also not letting you jump her bones, no matter *how* often you try to butter her up with compliments." Ellie sneered. The other scouts laughed as if they'd seen this exchange a hundred times over. Her voice rose to a commanding pitch, a lot like Cilia when she was fed up with jokes. "All right, you lot. Listen up. I'd rather we didn't have to do this at all, but since it has to happen, this is the deal. This isn't the first time we're taking somebody new in with us. All new scouts and trainees have to start somewhere, and we bring along those who want to learn when they feel they're ready. Usually, that's around ten years of age."

Chase blinked. Cilia had told him that they didn't mess around when it came to their young ones, but ten?

"What's new is that you know *less* than nothing," Ellie continued, unperturbed. "A kid from Cemano knows what kind of dangers they're up against. They know about the plants they need to avoid and what we're most likely to experience."

"Don't hold back. Tell us what you really think." Kith smirked.

The pretty Furyborn rounded on Kith, eyes flashing. "Really? Okay. Here's what I really think. *You are wasting my time.* If it weren't for you, I could focus on keeping my people safe, training new scouts to make sure my people grow up and live.

Now, I have to waste time showing you losers around, and on top of that, you may be Lightborn traitors?" she spat.

"In short, we're used to trainees. We'll be treating you like that. Circling you to make sure you aren't taken by surprise by something you couldn't know about yet, while Naley takes care of showing you what you need to watch for. With one difference. Trainees don't fight. If we meet anything—*anything*—you get to face it. And may the buzzards pick clean the bones of those who fail to stand up to the test." Snarling the last words, she turned on her heels and strode away. She passed the cairn, looked to either side, and then climbed down *into* the rift in the ground.

Beni ducked his head apologetically. "She's actually really nice, once you get to know her."

Cilia shrugged, nodding in understanding. "I get her."

Kith stared, open-mouthed, at Cilia. "Harsh!"

With a tiny wave, Beni said, "Well, I'm off. Try not to get yourselves killed. See you in the evening at some point." He followed the path Ellie took, and the others, including the large Guardians, slowly started to follow. One of the felines walked around the cairn, while the three others followed down into the rift.

Naley nodded at them and waved for them to follow. She patted the thin Furyborn scout on the shoulder as she passed him. "Ivar will follow. You probably won't see him much. He's Darkness-blessed *scary* like that."

The thin man gave a tight smile, but didn't say anything.

They followed Naley closely until they reached the rift next to the cairn. There, she halted for a moment. "Feels weird, having to explain things like this. But here it is. You may have noticed that the wind is rather strong here."

"What? I can't hear you over the wind!" Kith complained.

"I said..." She stopped talking and squinted in exasperation at him. "Why are you like that? Anyway. You may have noticed that Ellie isn't too damn happy. We don't want to keep her waiting. The wind. Combined with the clay and the rains, it makes for a harsh landscape for plants. If you can get Gabby down there to talk, she can talk for hours about the whys and hows of it. Bottom line is that the carved plains are carved by the rains. Over time, rains and the wind have cut deep furrows into the soil. You'd think that, with the clay and all, it'd turn into rivers or streams, but we have plenty of wildlife happily carving tunnels as well, allowing the water to seep away."

She pointed down at the rift next to the tall cairn. "I'm sure, at some point, a lot of beasts preferred to stay up here on the surface. But you can see what it's like. No cover. Few plants.

Anybody and anything moving around up here will be visible from far away—and some of these rifts are *wide,* making it tough to move around. In short, most things have moved into the rifts. Up here, you'll find flying predators and the occasional winged Guardian, trying to spot anything they can pick off from above, and little else. Down there? That's where the life is."

Chase took that in. He looked at the broken landscape ahead of him. True enough, the cracks seemed wider than they'd been farther east, the rifts more widespread and common. "I get that. And you explained this already. But why don't you just scout up here then? Wait. No, I get it. I can't even see what's happening in this rift from up here. If we walked around on top, we'd miss half of what was down there."

She gave him a tight smile. "That, and some of the local fliers are *fast*. We cull their populations where we can, but they're tough to handle. On top of that, this is just where the rifts start. Farther on, they are wider and larger than what's left on top. Being a scout out here, west of Cemano, means knowing how to navigate the carved plains and the major cracks and tunnels. If you wanted to be able to navigate on top? You'd need wings."

Within the next few hours, they started to earn a solid appreciation of the truth of that. At first, navigating the rift was claustrophobic, with the walls pressing in on either side. However, the walls soon widened, and the rifts expanded, showing them an entirely new world. Where the world aboveground was dull, brown, and gray, the soil hardened by the constant gusts of wind, down here, nature had found a niche. And it thrived. Both on the ground and within cracks in the sides of the walls, nature had taken a hold and did not let go. Vibrant colors battled with the browns and grays for dominance, leading to a kaleidoscopic, discordant scene that was hard to adjust to for the untrained eye.

Naley spent a bunch of time that first day trying to deal with this. She pointed out which plants were poisonous, which had nasty thorns and which were common hiding grounds for some of the ambush predators lurking in the deep. From her explanations, it seemed like most beasts out here were predators in one way or the other. Even so, they weren't attacked or beset by anything, and they passed the time learning and marching. Eventually, they started to relax, just a bit.

That was when they met their first enemy.

Slate marched back to them. He didn't bother to hide the distaste on his face. "All right, traitors. Time to get to work. Nest of dawn vipers up ahead and to the left." He promptly sat down and extracted a piece of dried meat from a pocket and started to gnaw on it.

Naley nodded. "Part of the job. You'll find that there are a *lot* of threats down here. Most of them, we don't deal with. Regular beasts that don't threaten anything, just try to live their lives? We leave them be, and they leave us be, as long as we don't stomp on 'em. Huge threats, swarms or behemoths, we try to steer away, let them waste their strength on Lightborn Guardians. Dawn vipers, though? They're nasty business. They're mostly active around dawn, when a lot of the regular wildlife rests. They also have a nasty venom and multiply *fast*. Left unchecked, their brood can expand to the point where it's a real problem, with a hundred or more vipers in a clutch."

Liam nodded, adjusted his shield and unclasped his truncheon from the belt. "Any advice on how to deal with them?"

"Don't get bitten. That's about it. They're deceptively fast when they strike, but otherwise not too slow or tough. The real threat can be in the numbers. They swarm."

They were lucky. The clutch they uncovered had around forty vipers, half of them young ones. The grown ones were rather impressive, reaching nearly ten feet in length.

However, having been forewarned, they were able to handle them with no issues. Kith called his Crescendo of Might summon; Liam stood as backup, limbs covered with Become the Clay to fend from any fangs, while Chase covered them with his sling and Squall Sling for ranged attacks. Sera and Cilia remained on standby, heals and fire droplets ready for the attack.

It turned out to be entirely unnecessary. The venom from the vipers might be effective, but against Kith's short-lived summon, it did absolutely nothing. The bulky summon cheerily waded among the winding, slithering clutch, smashing anything that moved, while rocks flew out to hit anything it missed. When, eventually, the nest lay still and the summon faded into nothingness, Liam strode into their midst, shield ready, and rummaged around to make sure that nothing survived.

When he walked back to the others a short while later, Chase carefully carved open the single viper hanging stuck in the clay covering Liam's arm. "You missed one!"

That was the first encounter they had that day. It wasn't the last. Once, they had to clear away and burn a carpet of fast-growing, blood-drinking ivy that had expanded to cover the rift they were traversing. At another point, they had to climb up the side of the wall of the rift to deal with a member of a particularly aggressive and massive hawk species that had decided to nest at the crossroad of several different rifts, attacking anything that came near. Once they ruined the nest, the hawk took off, and the scouts assured them it'd soon find another place to nest that wasn't an inconvenience for the scouts. The beast wasn't a problem for Cemano; they just couldn't let it harass their patrols.

The rifts constantly changed, growing and tightening, rising and falling, expanding into side tunnels and combining with others. At the widest, they were nearly a hundred feet wide, and some of them grew more than thirty feet deep. Naley told them how some of them turned into massive tunnel systems, usually due to some critter or other. But they avoided delving into those wherever possible, because the cramped confines were trouble, and the delvers hadn't proved an issue so far. In the evening, they camped out in a half-cave in one wall of the rift.

"You've done well, so far." Naley folded up her hood to use as a pillow. The others prepared for the night at the other end of the cave, out of earshot. "No unnecessary risks. No fancy stuff. Simply dealing with issues as they come." She lowered her voice, glancing at the other scouts. "I don't know exactly what's going on here. I hadn't expected Gabby and Ellie to be here. I do know Beni and Ivar hang out with Slate a lot, so I am kind of surprised they haven't come at you harder. I... maybe Slate was being honest, and he just wanted you to prove yourself."

Chase snorted. "I've seen bastards like him. Back when I kicked his ass? He didn't care one whit for creeds or rules or anything. He wanted to kill me, and damn the rest. He's just waiting for us to lower our guard, then he'll strike. At least, that's what I think. If I'm wrong, we spend this entire round trip stressed out and jumping at shadows. Still, I prefer that to relaxing and getting stabbed in the back."

"That's... probably not the worst approach," she admitted. "Now, you've seen some of what the plains have to offer. You have been fortunate and avoided both Guardians and flash floods, so far, yet you've had your first taste. With new trainees, we'd be circling back right now, talking about what they did wrong and what they did right. What do you think about the place?"

"Hold that thought." Kith held up a hand. "Guardians, sure. We get those. What in the watery depths of the Pits are flash floods?"

"Did you not pay attention back in Cemano?" Her voice was exasperated.

Kith grimaced. "'Course I did. There was just a lot to take in, and little time to do so."

She rolled her eyes. "How anybody can grow up without learning about flash floods, I can't imagine. But... pay attention now." She grimaced and looked into the distance. Then she nodded to herself and indicated the cave around them. "You'll have noticed by now that the clay here is kind of dense. It's absolutely horrid at letting water seep through. That, combined with some of the heavy rainfalls we get now and then..."

"You'd better not be saying what I think you're saying," Kith murmured. "Monsters and Guardians, I get. Now we have to be afraid of being drowned in our sleep too?"

"No. Not at all. Just be... aware." Naley gave a weak smile. "It barely ever happens. We know the areas, which pathways are low enough to be flooded, and we don't camp there. Of course, sometimes some of the tunneling beasts create blockages or carve tunnels to lead water in new directions, but yeah. Almost never. When it happens, though..." She shuddered. "You can get trapped inside a rift with no aid to get you out, heavy currents bearing down on you to smash you against walls and rocks. It's an ugly end."

Kith glared out into the growing darkness. "I hate this place."

Chapter 20

"I have been a scout for a decade now. Having observed at least thirty clashes between Lightborn and, Furyborn I can say three things with certainty. One, they have a bond with their Guardians we cannot start to comprehend. Two, their fighters are, on average, nearly as strong as our elites. Three, we are winning." Written by a Lightborn scout three years ago, apparently. Huh. On first instinct, I'd have to agree. There's no discussing they've been pushed back everywhere. Only... do they really *seem* like they're at a disadvantage? Have the Lightborn just culled the weaker ones? (Page 72.)

The next three days went off without any major hitches. They performed an approximate half-circle around the western area bordering on Cemano, going northwest first and then beginning to veer west and increasingly southward. Apparently, the route they took would never be the exact same, because they needed to stay on top of things, ensure that they caught any budding issues, beast nests, or Guardian infestations. Taking the same route every time could lead to serious issues in the long run.

Their days were varied and never dull. Sometimes, they'd walk for hours in silence. At others, they'd stop every other moment for discussion, for their ranged or caster to take out smaller beasts, scouts to sneak ahead to check out specific positions, or any number of things.

One day, they spent several hours painstakingly cutting down and dispersing a blockade of assorted branches, rocks, and worse that the scouts told them had been carried along and deposited inside one of the rifts by a flash flood. As it stood, the large pile could be circumnavigated, but with enough additional rains, it could lead to a serious issue further down the line. Also, such piles apparently attracted certain beasts who loved nothing more than central hiding places they could use for ambush spots.

Later the same day, they spent half an hour being literally bombarded by crap from an insanely aggressive family of carrion gulls—a local pest. The near-dozen birds weren't truly dangerous—they were rarely carnivorous, even though they were ridiculously territorial. However, left to their own devices, they would grow in numbers and start taking on bigger prey, like humans. The birds stayed high enough aloft their cards and arrows couldn't reach them, yet they never relented in their attack. Eventually, though, they managed to locate their nests and Liam, covered in a veritable soup of filth, tore the nests apart and smashed their eggs.

Once, a sudden squall turned their passage into something that could have been an issue. They were in a deep part of a rift when a heavy rainfall hit. Gabby fell back to inform them that their position was compromised, with the nearest runoff point for flash floods being two miles back. The Furyborn scouts joined their ranks, but nobody, not even Naley, helped with any further hints. After a short discussion, Cilia pointed to her preferred solution—a solid rock ledge about ten feet above the canyon floor. There was no way to get up there, but a brief sprint and Chase's Steps of Brilliance had that covered. Then, it was only a matter of lifting everybody up with their ropes, followed by a long, unpleasant wait in the pouring rain until the risk of being caught up in a flood had passed them by.

The Furyborn scouts were, on the whole, standoffish, but apart from Slate, they weren't actually outright hostile. Gabby, the taciturn older woman who helped Jessel gather herbs, surprisingly turned out to be the kindest among them. Once she learned how well-versed Sera was in all things plant-oriented, they started talking up a storm during their rare breaks.

Ellie initially kept her distance. The caster, who apparently was the one in charge, seemed to have a naturally distant personality. However, after the first couple of days, Liam, being Liam, started getting to her, and soon she agreed to share her wisdom from countless outings on the plains.

Ivar didn't socialize. He barely did so with the other Furyborn, and definitely not with the newcomers. It seemed to be more a matter of personality than actual distrust or dislike, though they did sense his gaze on them here and there.

Beni was a talker, and the most outgoing of the lot. However, he was also, like he'd initially stated, out and about almost the entire time. He left early, arrived late, and even then, only stayed for food and brief updates. Then he and his large felines were off again, to sniff out any threats and lurking hostiles.

Naley, of course, was constantly there. She helped them avoid issues before they formed, taught them the basics, and, where the others were more of the "sink or swim" approach, taught them enough that they'd be able to build on it and learn proper scout behavior for themselves.

Slate made up for the rest when it came to hostility. He constantly stared back toward them, lidded eyes watching, judging. Once, it even looked like Ellie took him to task over it, facing him down in a heated discussion well out of hearing range. Following that, his expression soured even further, though he did keep his attention more fixed on the path ahead of them.

Somewhere around the western-most edge of their circuit, however, Beni came racing back. All four of his cats loped along with him, two in front and one slinking along, peering back every once in a while. His hands flashed as he ran, gesturing something.

Gabby immediately joined him, racing back toward the others, who, within seconds, had their weapons ready as they met in a huddle bristling with weapons.

Half a minute later, Ellie rose from the huddle and walked at a no-nonsense stride over to them. "This is it. Hope you've learned what you needed to. Because this is the challenge you were looking for."

Kith looked as if he were about to say something smartass, but Cilia's glare kept him silent.

Ellie pointed into the distance. "Time for you to become properly introduced to the lost ones."

They climbed to the top of one of the plateaus. This far out on the plain, what was originally the surface of the plains was reduced to numerous flat-topped cliffs and plateaus overlooking the labyrinth of rifts, caverns, and passages crisscrossing the plains below. Gabby had cleared the approximate area of any overtly hostile fliers, and they carefully sidled their way to the edge of their plateau to see the reason for this.

"Cleansing Fires of the Pits, what *is* that?" Cilia exclaimed.

"That," Beni said, not moving his eyes from the vision below, "is the reason that we're out here. It's also the reason why scouts rarely make it past their fifth year on the job. Lost ones."

Cilia shook her head in denial. "The unaspected are supposed to be just that. Mindless manifestations of magic spontaneously appearing in areas that aren't suffused with magic of any of the other aspects."

"I understood *some* of that." Beni grinned. "Listen, I don't know what your books or Lightborn scholars have or haven't taught you. I only know what my eyes and my people have learned, risking our own lives out here. Those things? They're not mindless. They can think. Sometimes, they attack in numbers, with species you wouldn't see working together attacking at the same time. Sometimes, they sneak around for some unknown reasons." He grimaced and pointed downward. "Then, sometimes, you get an infestation."

Below them lay a crossroads. One of a thousand similar meeting points, where several rifts crossed, creating an open area where you could get a slightly better overview of your surroundings. Sometimes, these were tight confines, the splitting rifts and tunnels little more than claustrophobia-inducing shafts barely wide enough for a small child. At other times, they were grand areas, wide enough that you could camp out in safety, with hundreds of feet of clear vision in all directions.

This had been a massive one. However, what might have been a large, open area, was now anything but. It looked like somebody had taken a thousand oversized strands of slime and played around with them inside the crossroads, carefully stringing the glistening, green strands from one side to the other in a nasty display of creativity. Within the chaotic, messy display of disgusting strands and what looked like a toddler's snot bubbles placed everywhere, half-seen shadows slithered about, only occasionally letting themselves be seen.

"What *are* those?" Chase asked, equal parts disgusted and intrigued. "They look like a mole made love to a cockroach."

"Only if they shared the bed with a scorpion then." Beni shuddered. "Hive scabs are disgusting, surprisingly fast and venomous. You don't want to get hit by their claws."

"They are also a real threat. Once they truly start building their hive and get the outer shell up, they're an absolute *pain*. Those strands are nowhere near as thin as they look. Sometimes, they're hardened. Sometimes, they're sticky." Ellie sneered down on the half-seen beasts.

Chase frowned down at the vision, tapping his bottom lip. "So, in order to take them out, you have to go into that confusing mess of a labyrinth and take them on. Looks like they're fast climbers too?"

Beni just waggled his eyebrows.

"Well, ain't that a nice gift they went and wrapped for us," Kith drawled. "We get to push our way through a playground built of snot, with hundreds of venomous, ugly things just waiting to welcome us properly."

"You're the ones who wanted to come to our lands. Nobody invited you. We can go home right now, and you get to leave this all behind," Slate growled, an undercurrent of satisfaction all too audible.

"*Such* a helper," Cilia said coldly. "How are they with fire?"

"Don't you know *anything*?" Slate barked.

Ignoring him, Naley shuddered. "Awful. Just awful. Anything they've built just goes up like *phoosht*." Forestalling the inevitable comment, she continued, "Only, fire out here on the plains is like a lodestone. You'll have every Dark-cursed critter under the sun either popping their nose in to see if there's anything worth eating, or running away as fast as their legs can carry them because they're that afraid of fire. It's chaos."

"So if we—" Kith started.

Naley cut him off. "Chaos that can sometimes spread for *miles*, with hundreds or thousands of beasts going berserk. You don't want to try that."

Kith blinked. "Fire's out. Gotcha. I'm guessing you're not going to share your regular tactics with us either?"

Ellie patted Liam's shoulder. "I would. But it would defeat the point. We'll tell you what you need to know about the hive scabs. Then you get to prove yourself, or not. We'll be in the background, to make sure things don't spiral out of control, whatever else happens to you."

Chase had a sudden realization. "Good. That way, even if we fail, it's not going to have any backlash on Cemano."

She narrowed her eyes but nodded at him. "Just so."

"Okay. Not gonna lie. Fire would've been nice. But I can't help but think we can handle this in a way that won't get us killed. Let's ask all the questions we can come up with, then see if we can't figure out a decent plan."

Half an hour later, they were slowly making their way down the plateau again, at a decent distance from the hive. They'd learned quite a few things about the scabs. Fortunately, the beasts themselves, individually, weren't the toughest fighters. They were fast, slippery, and especially agile within the hive, but they had no natural armor, their strength was less than overwhelming, and the front claws were their only weapons. That was the good news.

The bad news was the reason that they *needed* to take them on. Being Guardians, the beasts in the hive weren't going to just settle down and relax. They were going to continually build and expand the hive, taking in any hostile beasts as food and building materials in a never-ceasing cycle of expansion until they hit human lands. In times past, on two occasions, the Furyborn had had to resort to fire to deal with especially fast-growing or large hives, regardless of the issues. It would seem that something within the beasts, some innate intelligence, automatically steered them toward constant expansion, wild bloodlust, and, eventually, Furyborn areas.

Liam strode forward, truncheon in hand. He had his shield raised, looking as comfortable on his arm as if it were a part of his body. Become the Clay was active, covering him in a heavy layer of defensive material, on top of the current layer of leather armor and chainmail. Cleansing Fire covered him with a sheen of nigh-invisible flames that would grant him a layer of constant weak heals and cleansing (without actually being at risk of causing a fire), while Convince the Unbeliever created a halo effect around the mountain of muscle, at the same time as it added to the healing effect along with a slowly increasing Agility boost.

On his right side, three steps back, stood Kith, lazily twirling his hand axes. He looked almost lackadaisical, relaxed, entirely at odds with the tone of the battle to come. For once, he had no physical summons alongside him. One, the Divine Mentor, was currently an internalized presence, guiding his every move, making him stronger, faster, more precise. It made him ooze *danger*. On top of that, his Twice the Fun card combined with his Tier three Light card, Sacrificial Saints, to give him a wholly disturbing look. At the moment, a plethora of see-through spectral figures swirled around him like a graveyard of ghostly soldiers called back into service, each of them ready to take a mortal blow for him.

Chase stood on his left. He balanced out Kith's lack of nerves, jumping up and down, grinning nervously, and clutching his short sword, waiting for that blessed moment where the blissful rush of action took over and flushed the stress away. He had Steps of Brilliance ready for added ease of movement in-battle, along with Clothed in Living Light. Today, he had the malleable light turned into a layer of armor, while the majority of the material went to turning his left hand into a gloved fist with long spikes.

Where the three formed a loose half-circle, Cilia stood dead center behind the three. The belts crisscrossing her torso were filled to bursting with crafted items ready to be used; though they had been carefully emptied of any fire droplets, lest she pick one by accident. Her face was a lesson in focus and concentration, eyes constantly moving, not accepting any chances of surprise.

Sera was rear guard. A floating warhammer swirled lazily around her, ready to defend her or slam down on any enemies coming too close. On top of that, she held her sword breakers for any personal defense. She still needed to create the best possible all-out defense for herself. Besides Warhammer of the Ancients for self-defense, she had Warmth of the Circle and Unexpected Spillage ready, prepared to heal or outright divert any damage caused.

The lack of noise from the hive in front of them was disturbing, unnatural. Where, just minutes earlier, it had been an incessant whizzing of movement, a backdrop of constant wet sounds and skittering, now it was completely, unnaturally silent.

"They know we're here," Chase said. "I know, no need to even mention it. Still, looks like what they told us holds up. When they're faced off with enemies, unless they're easy prey, they'll hold back and wait for them to enter the hive." He rolled his shoulders. "Which is when they'll come rushing in, steamrolling us all in an overwhelming tide of filth and poison."

"And snot. Don't forget the snot," Kith added, helpfully.

"I was trying to." Chase laughed. "You know the drill. Wake 'em up, then pull back and hold. Take no chances. Liam's front and center for a reason."

Cilia added, "Also, no single step forward unless the surrounding hive is smashed into bits."

"That too." Chase gritted his teeth. "This doesn't have to be fast. It doesn't have to be pretty either. We can pull back and rest if we need to. Just needs to *work*."

The situation was oppressive. From a few hundred feet away, the looming threat was undeniable. From fifty feet's distance, it was palpable. Chase started to spot the occasional gleaming eye and wrinkled skin within. They stopped at thirty feet away, right at the edge of his range, and Chase asked, "Are we ready?"

The chorus of assent came immediately—testy, but firm.

Chase mentally flexed a muscle. His Among the Raindrops card activated promptly, as smoothly as if he were bending a finger. A split second later, the foremost area of the hive, including the few first feet outside the hive itself, were covered in liquid. Slippery, oily liquid that'd make it truly hard for the hive scabs to move. Also, there was the acidic element, and the part where it stuck to the enemies. Couldn't rightfully forget about that.

The hive erupted in an ear-splitting cacophony of screeches. The world went insane.

Chase wasn't the type to suffer from nightmares. He was still young, but his short lifetime had been filled with threats and experiences that might be traumatic to some. His tolerance for danger, blood, and filth was high. Even so, the sudden vision of the labyrinthine, confusing chaos of the glistening, lurking hive erupting into one huge, overwhelming wave of claws, lidded eyes, folded skin, and ugly, dirty mouths—all howling for blood— would stay with him, sometimes making him wake up in a cold sweat.

As one, they stepped a few feet back, slimy liquid still erupting from Chase's card, covering the clay of the area ahead of them, and making it hard to traverse. Then they settled, ready to face the enemy.

That first charge contained at least thirty Guardians. It looked like one large mass of unbroken ugly flesh, falling over itself and rearranging itself, in the rush to get at them.

"Eyes!" Cilia's shout was barely heard over the howls. Yet, they knew it was coming, and shut their eyes. One carefully crafted leather ball ranged out, followed by another, a few seconds later. The entire breadth of the rift, from one second to the next, was covered in blinding darkness from Cilia's droplets. The screeching intensified even further, along with the growing sounds of Guardians falling over themselves to get at them. They all wanted to open their eyes, but didn't, knowing what was inbound.

A sound of skittering ensued, followed by a grunt from Liam. A solid thud announced that whatever had hit him had been flung back.

The canyon erupted in blinding light.

Where, before, the screeches had been furious and piercing, now, they were pain-filled and *deafening*. Chase felt pain in one ear. At the count of ten, he finally opened his eyes.

The rift in front of them was chaos. Guardians flung themselves about on the ground, blinded and howling in pain. More were inbound from within the hive itself, but there were fewer than the first wave.

"Kill, then reset!" Liam's loud shout was barely audible beyond the din.

Chase, Kith, and Liam rushed forward, stabbing out with abandon at downed and blinded beasts.

The scouts had been right. As individuals, the hive scabs were weak. Their only real weapons, though scary, were their claws. Blinded and covered in the slippery, acidic liquid from Chase's card, they were barely a threat. In an unrelenting rush of stabbing, slashing, and clubbing, the trio fell on the downed beasts like a runaway gaborn.

Liam cursed in relief as the damage from a downward claw was diverted back upon the scab's own body by Sera's Unexpected Spillage. He punted it away before it could strike again.

"Back, now!" Cilia, taking to her role as the eyes of the group, briskly commanded.

They obeyed, falling back into their original position, ready for the next wave of creatures to attack.

These scabs were less hindered than the first wave. They had clearly done better at avoiding Chase's slippery acid, and had still been at the edge of the hive when the blinding effect took hold. Yet, they were less numerous, came separately as opposed to the first massive wave of flesh and chitin, and were unable to truly work up speed on the now slippery clay of the rift. They struck, claws scrabbling and searching for soft flesh, throwing themselves at the group with abandon, trying to overwhelm them with their suicidal charge.

They broke themselves on that front line. Liam took not a single step back, meeting their charges with the shield, the clay of his armor, or economical strikes of his truncheon. Any beast attempting to move past him was met with entirely different approaches, where Chase danced among them, too fast to strike down, or Kith, less flamboyant in his movements, portrayed a level of competence and surgical precision above and beyond his regular level, while glowing like a god.

A minute and a half. That was all it took, until the last scab of the second wave curled up with Kith's hand axe buried deep in its abdomen. Beyond, the few surviving beasts of the first wave slithered back into the hive, mewling, open sores on their bodies from where the acidic effect of Among the Raindrops was starting to have an impact.

Chase took a deep breath, flicking his short sword to clear it of a globule of thick-flowing blood. "Well done!" he called out. "Anybody hit?"

Kith, Cilia, and Sera called out in the negative.

Liam grunted. "One of the little buggers got past my shield and got my ankle. Any minute now." He let out a hiss of relief. "Yup. Cleansing Fire just took care of it. Good as new."

"All right." Chase grinned at them, only slightly maniacal. "This is working. We've *got* this. We'll clean ourselves of the slime, wait for the water to disperse, then move in."

This time, they had to move even closer. The beasts drew back within their hive, having now learned that charging outside was a good way to get killed. Chase stood right outside the hive and managed to splash a couple of scabs right at the edge of his card. Only, instead of attacking, they pulled farther back, lurking.

"What the scouts said about the limited intelligence is clearly true. They're waiting for us to enter their domain, where we can't run away quickly. How about instead we ruin their day?"

Liam, taking in the intricacies of the hive in front of them, nodded. He looked up at where it strained toward the sky, reaching ten to twelve feet at the tallest points. "This is going to be quite a bit of work." He grasped his truncheon and, with another glance at the Guardians looming within, slammed it down hard on a strand reaching from the ground to the far edge of the rift. His weapon made a deafening *snap* noise, but bounced back, making him curse loudly. Two more strikes, and the strand broke, making the entire hive tremble. Liam sneered. "A *lot* of work."

Kith stepped forward, cracking his knuckles. "Better get started then."

It was a lot of work. In the end, however, that was what it devolved into. Work. Compared to some of the near-death experiences they'd had, this was a lot less stressful. At first, the hive scabs hovered out of reach, not reacting as Chase, Liam, and Kith chopped into their home beyond loud howls and screeches. As they, slowly but surely, expanded on the safe area, however, the Guardians did react and charged to attack.

This was where the *limited* part of their intelligence came forth, however. Whatever made decisions on behalf of the hive clearly was unable to plan long-term or consider numbers and tactics. If it could, it would have seen the inevitable collapse of the hive, and either pulled back entirely to start over elsewhere, or rushed ahead with every single Guardian at its disposal. Instead, it looked like it was operating with some sort of basic preservation instincts, only daring to empty out part of its troops at a time.

As such, they only had to deal with a dozen of the beasts attacking at a time—twenty the one time—and they perfected their strategy. Their group pulled back, Chase kept up applying the slippery liquid, and, once they were out on the firm ground in front of the hive, they'd brace and hold. Beyond that first charge, they didn't even need to use any of Cilia's creations.

They took their time. They knew they weren't in any rush. As long as they could finish the job before nightfall, they'd be unlikely to run into further trouble, considering the hive scabs were known to kill off all wildlife in range. Hence, they rested between each fight, kept an eye on the cooldown of their cards and reactivated wherever needed. Once, they took a longer break, as Chase had slipped in his own raindrops and one of the scabs managed to nick him on the arm. They all pulled back far enough they were in no danger of setting anything on fire, before Sera switched her card to Tongues of Pride, letting her cleanse the venom. Following that was the hour-long wait before she could switch back to her healing card again, since they didn't dare fight with the fire-damage buff of Tongues of Pride active.

At a certain point, the end result became evident. Over the next hours, they cleared half the hive, then two-thirds, and the population of the ugly Guardians kept dwindling. Eventually, with less than a fifth of the glistening strands remaining, the last beasts, huddled in what their limited minds clearly perceived as some sort of safe shelter, finally rushed out to take them down.

That attack became the largest of them all. Almost fifty of the small beasts thundered out as one, attempting to slay their attackers. As all those before them, the scabs failed.

Envenomed, pierced, slashed, covered in bile, blood, and worse, their group stood. Not a one of them had evaded that last attack without a wound. Yet, they stood. Defiant. Proud. Triumphant. Closer to the next Tier. From the heights above, the accompanying scouts looked on in silence, judging, assessing.

Chapter 21

"Anybody wishing to establish a trade route with Heart Halls should acknowledge this. You get one chance. One opportunity to make a good impression. Following that, the damage is done. The towers pride themselves on the knowledge stored in their library. Well, it has nothing on the preternatural ability of Furyborn to know about you, your tricks, and any trades made in bad faith." Some of these authors should have been vetted better. Of course, the Furyborn will talk. Merchants of Earth's Ward trade with anybody. Those in Heart Halls mostly just trade with the Elementals. How could they *not* gossip?
(Page 79.)

The following days marked a noticeable change for them. Following their approach to the demolition of the hive scabs, and the subsequent grueling dismantling of the remaining strands that still obstructed normal passage of the rift, the demeanor of the scouts finally tipped toward the positive.

They didn't flip their behavior from one moment to the next. But the next time they camped, Gabby put down her bedroll a lot closer to them, and animatedly talked about some of the plants they'd manage to find along the way. Ellie caved, and shared the evening meal with them, ostensibly to plot the course for the following days. In practice, however, she spent most of the time talking to Liam, progressively inching closer to the handsome fighter. Her initial standoffishness slowly burned away by Liam's insistent good-natured flirting.

The spilling over toward the tipping point continued over the next couple of days as they traveled their circuit, until the camps of the scouts and their family were close enough you could hardly tell them apart.

The sole difference, as expected, was in Slate. Even as they hit the most westward part of their circular path and started trekking south and east, he kept up both his distance and hostility. Yet, with the other scouts growing closer to their team, that marked him as the outsider, both physically and mentally, as he demonstratively put his bedroll as far apart from them as possible.

At this point, they didn't care much. They knew that he wasn't going to change. But with most of the scout group clearly positive toward them, and having done well so far, they knew that things were finally going their way. So, they enjoyed themselves, growing closer to the other scouts, and absorbed as much knowledge about their surroundings as they possibly could. With the walls tumbling down, and their group eager students, the scouts became willing teachers.

The fourth and fifth days of the outing taught them much about the wilderness surrounding Cemano. It also, inevitably, brought many stories about past clashes of the scouts, and eventually carried along a greater understanding of what the Furyborn faced on a daily basis out on the outskirts of what the Lightborn considered livable territory.

The local beasts were not as much a challenge for the scouts as they were a fact of life. They were bloodthirsty, sure, and could be tough, numerous, and wily. However, they were still beasts, and among their numbers, they tended to give each other enough competition that they rarely grew to become real threats. With the Furyborn present to cull the numbers of specific threats, they would not be an issue.

Lightborn, as well, weren't as much of a threat as expected. Sure, it was a constant sword hanging over their heads, and the fact remained that any moment now, a Lightborn army or squad might decide that their territory was ripe for an invasion. However, Cemano was in constant communication with other Furyborn settlements and could call for assistance if they were in overwhelming need. Most often, what the Lightborn sent were nothing but indebted, poor bastards sent to prod for responses, to check for weaknesses. If those didn't die by themselves, they'd be easy pickings for any scout group. True Lightborn scouting groups were rarer occasions and demanded a stronger response. However, historically, they'd managed to wait them out and ambush them once they were deep inside Furyborn territory.

The real threat lay in the lost ones. The unaspected Guardians that their group had finally crossed blades with in the hive scabs. Although the unaspected most often lived up to their reputation as unpredictable, spawning in an untold number of shapes, generally dangerous, and bloodthirsty, the scouts were able to tell them about the other side of them. The fact that they sometimes spawned with limited intellect, like the hive scabs. That they most often turned up in horribly impractical and unfortunate places, specifically in weaker or less patrolled areas. That they seemed to be *steered*.

Between themselves, Chase and the others spent a good while debating whether there was any real truth to this, a greater intellect guiding the unaspected, or it was a consequence of the scouts being forced into clashing with the dangerous beasts so often. They didn't settle on any conclusion, though it was hard to argue with the wisdom built up over years and years.

The clash with the Guardians had been good for them all, progress-wise. The monsters might be weak, but there were so many of them that the Ænima harvested by Liam especially, but also Chase and Kith, built up to decent progress. All three of them managed to gain a full Step, with Liam stating that he was certain he was damn close to Step eighteen. Cilia and Sera had both eventually had to step in and fight as well, but neither had gained a Step, though Cilia earned a point to Toughness. The others poured their free points into their chosen paths. Liam went for further Strength, while Kith continued to play catch-up with Cilia and Sera on Mental Power. Chase sought higher-rarity cards by adding another point to Potential and had earned a rare point to Mental Power during the confrontation.

Of course, Slate didn't ease up on them. He challenged them, time and again, on tiny things. Sometimes, it was a matter of attempting to make them do his bidding on smaller occasions. Innocuous things, where they'd have to decide whether they could be seen as shirking their duty, or they'd be seen as unthinking creatures not fit for independent thought. At other times, he gave them orders that might be misconstrued, and could lead to them making mistakes and performing their tasks badly—such as erecting their camps in a manner that would lead them open to night ambushes. That part, however, became easier the more experienced they became in the work of a scout and the way they operated.

On the evening of the fifth day, it culminated when Ellie called out to Slate to "cease his idiocy" as he tried to lure them into building up their smokeless fire to the point where it could be seen from faraway and entice monsters. Chastised, the hostile scout subsided into a sullen silence and, for once, didn't prod them further.

Apart from Slate, the sensation among the scouts was one of relief. Apparently, this point of the circuit, where their southward direction stopped and they started to move slightly north and east back toward Cemano, was where they typically started to see less adversaries. It wasn't *safe*, but definitely announced a departure from the most dangerous parts of their trek.

They stayed up a bit later than usual, chatting merrily about what they planned to do when they came back to Cemano over a good meal cooked by a combination of plentiful meat caught by Beni's felines, greens located by Ellie, and Liam's experimental cooking. The good food made for a joyful occasion, and the scouts were keen to talk.

Apparently, the life of a scout was one of working hard and playing hard. With the exception of Gabby, who had four kids and a husband back in the village, the others were single and spent their free time getting drunk, lazing about, sparring, and, quite often, getting in trouble.

Chase couldn't blame them in the least. With what they had to face out here on the plains, a chance of rest and recreation was, in his eyes, more than well-earned. He spent the evening with Sera, daydreaming about all the equipment they wanted to have Cilia craft when she'd finally finished her apprenticeship with Master Benneth. It ended up as an extensive list, most of which were likely quite impossible. Chase had to admit that the odds of finding another gaborn, skinning it, *and* making sure to get the horrible smell out of its skin might be beyond Cilia, even when she completed her training. Eventually, though, they went to rest, at ease, positive about the development and the coming days.

They awoke to mortal danger.

Chase's mind was still in that halfway place between dreams and sleep, when he heard the shouted words coming at him. Only a life on the Waves made him surface fast enough that his brain somehow made sense of things—and even so, it took a couple of seconds before the rest of his body caught up to reality.

"We're under attack! Wake up and defend yourselves!"

The words were Slate's, growled with impatience, but also with an underlying current of... fear?

Chase leapt up to see nothing at all. Within the shortest of moments, however, he heard the noises beyond the groans and curses from the other scouts. Bestial noises—growls, clicks, and cries.

They hurriedly helped one another don their armor. Meanwhile, the Furyborn scouts were huddled nearby, with two of the large plain cats pacing back and forth, growling.

Ellie strode over to them, as they finished readying the last of their weaponry. Behind her, Naley gesticulated wildly at Slate. Snippets of their discussion reached them—mostly curse words, but it sounded like Naley accused Slate of something.

Ellie's features were back to how she'd looked when they first met her. Standoffish, distant, and dismissive. Only her eyes betrayed anything beyond that. "This is bad luck for you. It's not often we see a swarm this close to Cemano."

"What does that mean? What's happening and what do we do about it?" Chase asked.

"It's a swarm." Ellie grimaced. "Sometimes, for some reason, the wildlife can get all riled up. It can be a flash flood, a larger predator, a lost one's attack - anything. Point is, there's a swarm incoming, every local creature fleeing or charging right here, and you're the ones who're going to try to stop it. We'd steer it off, but they're heading in the direction of Cemano. Good luck and... I'm sorry." Having said that, she strode off into the darkness with nothing but a compassionate glance and unsaid words behind her scowl.

The other Furyborn scouts followed her, Naley still arguing but clearly losing the argument.

For a moment, there was silence, punctuated by the growing noise of the incoming swarm, whatever that meant in practice.

Chase snarled, pointing at the retreating backs of the scouts. "We're on our own. Time's running out. We don't know what we're facing. We *do* know if we run, that's it with the Furyborn. Anybody for running?"

As one, they looked unsettled, but defiant.

Well, apart from Kith, who grinned like a loon. "They're running. That means we get to finally let loose. Properly, I mean. Nobody watching and cover of darkness means... all cards are a go."

Chase hesitated, but nodded. "Anything to survive. From the sound of it, we'll need it. What's our approach?"

Cilia growled, "Kith said it. Hold nothing back. Everything, including fire, is on the table. With the way they're already enraged, we have every beast in the neighborhood in the charge. That means you get to use everything in the kits I've given you. Just make sure you throw them far enough away that they won't impede us. That means *don't blind me, Kith!*" Ducking her head, she added, "From the sound of things, even using our kits won't be enough either. We need to find a tighter spot. Somewhere defensible."

"That's a good plan. Outrun them until we reach a space we can hold, then dig in." Liam glanced at the backpacks still on the ground. "Leave our shit behind. If we survive, we'll see what remains afterward."

As one, they turned and loped off into the darkness.

The ensuing race would end up as one of the creepiest experiences of Chase's life. It wasn't like he was afraid of the darkness. In fact, he was very well acquainted with it, more familiar with operating by night than most people. However, the experience of racing through the rift by dead of night, their only light the weak glow of the moon on the lightly clouded night, as well as the nigh-imperceptible shine from Liam's and Sera's bodies, while the roars, hisses, and sometimes curdling howls of pain and worse from behind them was not one he'd want to repeat any time soon.

Ten minutes in, they found what they wanted. It wasn't perfect. It was, however, the best they could hope for in their present situation. And not knowing anything further about the terrain of the rift beyond, they decided to make this their stand.

The bottom of the canyon they stood in was a depression, a natural dip in the landscape that had parts of the rift under water, with only a tight space on either side of the water holding a slightly submerged walkway, allowing somebody to wade through without diving fully into the water. It wouldn't work to block any beasts from diving into the water, but would hopefully guide most of them to wade through the shallows at the side of the rift, instead of swimming straight through. Then, they'd be able to meet the beasts with their feet fixed on dry land, while any attackers would be awkward, feet set on muddy soil and underwater.

They quickly divided their attention, Liam holding one side, and Kith and Chase ready on the other, with Chase ready to race back and forth in case Liam needed help. Cilia and Sera took their places centrally, at the edge of the basin, where they'd have the best line of sight and be able to fend off any beasts that decided to ignore the walkways and swim right through.

"Initial wave's bound to be the worst," Chase said breathlessly. "We don't hold back for that. Blind them, followed up with fire droplets. If we can bunch 'em up hard enough, we might stop them entirely. Break the momentum. If we don't manage that, we're in trouble."

The sounds of the impending swarm grew louder. Now, they could hear specific cries, recognize a few species they'd clashed with over the past days. The worst, however, was how *many* different species were present. There were cries, hisses, clicks, squawks, howls, and worse.

They didn't talk tactics beyond what they'd already mentioned. By now, they knew what to do, how best to use their cards to the full advantage. Flashes lit up the dark canyon, as they activated their cards, one by one. Among the Raindrops was out in full effect, already making the surface on the far end of the shallow basin slippery, slowly building up an acidic welcome. On top of that, Kith summoned his Tainted Earth, the ground ready to hold down and drain any beast unfortunate enough to slip and fall.

Liam was in it for the long haul. Become the Clay covered his extremities, while Convince the Unbeliever lit him up from within, promising increased Agility over time.

Cilia patted her well-stocked crisscrossed belts, then nodded to herself; Sera grunted, letting Blessing of the Night come into effect, increasing any buffs any of them might have active. On top of that, Warhammer of the Ancients flashed into force, the large, glowing, ornate warhammer floating in a menacing arc around the healer.

Chase rolled his shoulders, selecting his cards. For this, he decided, Winds of Change was a given. He'd want to be able to switch cards fast if circumstances changed. On top of that, he readied Sticky Fingers, prepared to improve his own attributes as rapidly as possible. He contemplated Clothed in Living Light, but held off for a moment, looking at the basin of muddied water in front of them. He grinned. *There* was a better way to bid them welcome. "Slight change," he called. "Hold back on your throwing. I'll stop them cold! *Then*, you throw everything you've got!"

The nearest bend in the rift was a bit over a hundred feet away. His words were almost drowned out by the growing cacophony. Shadows started to play on the canyon walls.

"How are you going to do that?" Kith cried out, trying to make himself heard.

"If they attack as a wave," Chase laughed, eyes aglow with a wild fire to rival any Furyborn, "it's only fair to welcome them with a wave."

It was probably the least practiced of his cards. He'd barely used it in conflict, given how it required the right setup. However, there was the one thing that people all over Ordei kept repeating—how the real divide in force started around Tier four. That this was where you stopped being a powerful individual, and started to become a Power.

[A Friendly Wave
Rare, Elemental rogue
Tier four
Active, short duration
Rogues, more than any other class, are aware of their surroundings. They learn how to use the terrain to their advantage, always on the outlook for cover, for hiding places and terrain that will aid them and work against their enemies. This card allows the wielder to take a more direct hand in adjusting the surroundings to their advantage. For a short duration after activation, the wielder is able to command any water in their surroundings, making the water splash onto pursuers, soak clothes, ruin footing and even drown an unlucky pursuer.
Medium cooldown

"Getting your hands dirty is part of being a criminal, they say. But... look at me. My hands have never been cleaner!" A crime scene is swept clean by a rogue wave.]

Swept clean by a rogue wave. That was a horrible pun. Yet, Chase found himself grinning madly as he stared at the forms growing sharper in the darkness ahead. They really thought they were going to sweep them away? Well, today, the beasts of the carved plains were going to learn that others could play at this game. And Chase preferred playing with a rigged deck.

He tapped the card. Within seconds, a strange sensation erupted within him, like a third limb attaching to him, allowing him to reach out and move something else, something... more. It would have been utterly overwhelming, if it hadn't been for his constant practice with his new limb of Light. As it stood, he sensed two bodies of water, right within reach, ready to move at his slightest nudge.

Chase didn't just nudge. He grabbed hold and he *shoved*. With all his willpower he strained, throwing the water of the basin into a whirl, making it race around the shallow basin. Once, twice - he let the momentum and speed build, waiting for the swarm to move closer.

As the beasts grew into definition, their group braced, readying themselves for impact. Nobody moved too early. At this point, they'd fought together enough times that they were a well-oiled mechanism, trusting in one another.

They were close enough.

Chase grasped the metaphorical existence of the waters in the basin. He ignored the presence of the smaller body of water summoned from his Among the Raindrops card, taking full hold of the swirling waters. In one powerful push, he *heaved*.

Whatever the reason the swarming beasts of the plains might have for swarming, they'd arisen, as a tooth-filled, hostile, slavering mass. Now, the waters of the basin arose to answer their cry. And it drowned them out.

The wave rose, halfway to the edges of the canyon, and rammed down upon the monster tide swarming their way. Monster wave met actual wave. The flesh gave way. In an impressive example of nature's dominance, the wave grasped every single beast at the forefront of the animals' rush and carried them along back down where they came from. The mass of bodies and water clashed with even more beasts, making them fall end over end—hurt, frustrated, or outright killed by the sudden show of force.

Chase had closed his eyes to fully focus on guiding the wave. He pulled hard on it, making it rush back into the basin, even as he kept it separate from the acidic waters of his other card. It created a schizophrenic experience, as the liquids wanted to mix, and only his mental strength kept them apart. Finally, the waters rushed back into the basin, filling it most of the way back up. "Now!" he cried at the top of his lungs.

Five blinding pouches flew through the air. Night turned to day, beasts crying out in pain and confusion. Their group didn't relent for a moment, unleashing fire droplets one after the other, welcoming the attackers with unquenchable flame. A rare few larger beasts had managed to keep their footing against the first wave. Within seconds, every single one was burning or burned. Steam rose from scorched flesh.

The world burst into outright insanity. What seconds before had been a cohesive, maddened mass had been slammed back with unmatched force, and now turned on itself, exploding to all sides—blinded, on fire, or pushed to mindless panic from the sudden emergence of deadly fires. On top of that, the fulminating heat met the water, bursting into steam that filled the narrow canyon walls and obscured the vision for all the animals still rushing toward them. The first pain-filled cries of beasts barreling into and falling over other downed beasts arose.

Chase almost felt bad for what he was about to do. Clasping down hard, he ignored the sentiment, grasped and pulled. The liquid from Among the Raindrops that had been amassing ever since he activated it now reacted to his A Friendly Wave card, letting itself be guided where he wanted. It moved now, a much lesser wave than the first one. Where the first wave was built for size and force, this wave was much more shallow and went for width and movement.

The acidic wave rushed down the entire breadth of the canyon. Wherever it met the incoming beasts, the liquid acted according to the characteristics granted to it by the magic of the card and *stuck* to them. Acid painfully sizzled away at the fur, skin, or carapace of whatever it encountered.

Letting the wave of acid run out its natural course, Chase dismissed the Tier four card, switching over to his Clothed in Living Light. While his left arm lit up, a shield of light growing into being, he shot his first Sticky Fingers at a random beast. They'd stopped the initial charge. The additional point to Toughness, doubled by Sera's Blessing of the Night, made him feel a bit more solid, ready for whatever was to come.

He was *not* ready for what was to come.

Over the next couple of days, they would try to compare stories, mention what they'd experienced throughout the battle. Yet, they never came to the same conclusions. The sheer randomness of beasts caught within the canyon, their separate placement, and the speed at which everything proceeded ensured that their experiences were wildly different. The only thing they agreed on was the sheer brain-scrambling *chaos* of it.

The final single card that Chase recognized before the battle erupted was Kith's Apian God, as a near-solid mass of insects descended upon the downed and hurt beasts. From then on, he was forced to fight for his life.

Chase's spot on the right side of the, now somewhat lower, basin was less exposed than Liam's left side. It was a bit narrower, and the path was riddled with rocks to ruin the footing of incoming enemies. Kith flanked him, the Tainted Earth active in front of both, managing to hold back some of the impeding beasts.

They'd managed to cause a good deal of chaos already. Even so, there was movement *everywhere*. One moment, he nearly got skewered as a gazelle-like beast with a hammer-nosed snout leapt halfway over the basin, only to fall short by a couple of feet and slide awkwardly down into the muddy waters. The next, he stabbed in frenzy as a boar-like beast *that was still on fire* rushed up, trying to catch him with its tusks.

Every single chance he had, he used his Sticky Fingers, building his attributes higher and higher. On top of that, he kept renewing his Among the Raindrops at the far end of the basin, spreading out its area to make sure that the momentum of any new beasts arriving was ruined. Beyond that, his entire concentration was focused on stabbing out at hostile beasts and *not dying*.

At first, he didn't even see any of the others except Kith. The first time he noticed anything apart from his own struggles was when a shield interspersed itself between him and a large frog-like creature covered in enough oozing acid wounds that it looked like it had almost died. The beast hit hard, then succumbed, sliding down on the see-through shield. Chase ran it through with his short sword. A split second later, a wave of painful warmth ran through him as healing forced a series of claw marks on his arm, that he hadn't even noticed receiving, closed.

An undeterminable while later, the pressure against Chase lessened a little. He managed to spot Kith at his side. He dodged and weaved, hand axes performing intricate and deadly silhouettes in the air. No beasts rushing against him came along unhindered. They all had small flocks of insects surrounding their heads—biting, stinging, distracting.

On the far side of the basin, Liam stood strong, unmatched. Where Chase and Kith were in constant movement—dodging, leaping, evading—Liam barely moved. A single step here, a leaning forward there. Yet, where the beasts tried to advance, they broke against him. He matched strength against strength, accepting their attacks, angling his shield or extremities to avoid the worst damage, in order to be able to lash out in devastating strikes. And he made them pay. The basin on his side was in constant turmoil from the beasts being smashed down into the water and struggling to get back up and face him again… dying, drowning, pushing each other under. Meanwhile, his Draining Ward and Become the Clay kept growing his powers and attributes, while his Convince the Unbeliever kept his health topped up along with its slowly increasing Agility boost.

In the center, Cilia went from a silent statue to a blur of motion as she assessed the situation and acted with impunity. Whenever a sufficiently menacing beast threatened to rampage straight through the basin, she'd meet it head-on—blinding it or wrapping it in a fire droplet. On top of that, every thirty seconds, she sent a blinding pouch farther down the rift at full strength, blinding and disorienting any new groups to arrive.

Sera was in constant action. Where the three close-combat fighters kept their eyes on the beasts ahead, she kept her eyes on *them*. She judged and acted, her Cry for Blood throwing shields, heals, and buffs where needed, as the beasts arrived and died. Every time a tired beast managed to cross the basin, she was there, sword breakers and Warhammer of the Ancients raining down to send it sliding back into the basin, its body another impediment to the incoming beasts attempting to wade or swim through.

They barely noticed when the numbers of the swarm started to dwindle. Chase's mind was fully taken with the need to keep on stealing attributes, summoning new acidic puddles, and fending off attackers that he only took heed when he stabbed down into the skull of a young plain cat, stepped to the side and saw… nothing. The canyon hadn't suddenly emptied out. However, from one moment to the next, it seemed, the impetus that kept them charging was dying down. The remaining few dozen beasts of different species on the far side of the basin huddled there, as if unsure whether to keep advancing or attempt to flee back down the rift where they came from.

"Did we make it? Are we safe?" Sera asked hoarsely. Liquid dripped from her sword breakers, as she stood at the water's edge, panting.

A thundering rumble answered her question.

Chapter 22

"One-Thousand-Blades. Domain of Fury. Shara the Fleshcaller. At least twenty known Furyborn over time have reached Tier six and crossed that invisible threshold of infamy. There is little common ground between their powers, bar one detail. The majority of their numbers hold a connection to the Furyborn lands and beasts that even we Elementals lack." That really is interesting. Elementals, with their limited space, could very much gain from a strong connection to their lands and wildlife. A difference between symbiosis and subjugation? Needs further study. (Page 82.)

"**O**h no."

Chase had once attended the performance of a mummer's group in Isarn. Sure, he'd been picking pockets at the time, but given that he was waiting for his mark to be thoroughly enthralled (and grease-covered) by his caarnath kabob before striking, his cover of being engrossed in the story turned out ninety percent true. Gifted actors, wearing wigs and elaborate masks portraying the faces of whom they were playing, their number had also included a talented musician. A veritable one-woman band, this multi-talented person had switched effortlessly between a weeping string instrument for the romantic parts, flutes for innocence, and a jaw harp for comedic effect. Yet, right at this moment, it was one specific scene that came to mind: when she'd thoroughly punished a simple wooden drum to add the impetus of a large threat incoming to their scene.

Right now, this moment, it was the same. Slow, booming sounds came from right around the bend in the rift, along with a deep reverberating purr, a stomach-clenching constant rumble.

Then it cleared the bend.

The monster looked like something that had evolved in order to dominate the rifts. A predator through and through, grown to thrice the size of what it should truly be. The wide, tall form made it large enough to almost reach the edge of the rift if it stood on its hind legs, while the massive legs led to an oversized carnivore's mouth... a nightmare of sharp, jagged teeth, made for ripping into flesh. It looked like a giant bear had mated with a frog, and was then summoned into being through the panicked mind of an over-stimulated child. The matted fur carried some other substance within, as if it had rolled in dark clay to make it a second skin. Even on all fours, the horror was twice as tall as Liam.

"A plain behemoth," Cilia breathed.

"I'm getting them confused, right? Those weren't the squadron-killers that made everything out here live in fear. The ones big enough to eat a man in a mouthful and tough enough to withstand a crossbow bolt. Tell me I'm wrong." Kith's eyes remained fixed on the huge form navigating the bend.

"The one time in your life you're actually right, has to be now. Typical." Chase kept up the banter, even as his bladder threatened to let out on him.

The beast's massive head swiveled with unnatural speed, fixing on the vast number of bodies inside the rift. A deep-set, scrunched-up, ugly face, lacking a nose, resembled that of a bat. Then it roared. It wasn't a *loud* sound. However, it was pervasive, a force that thrummed through the air, made something deep within the body vibrate, threatening to loosen bowels and morals alike.

Chase took a deep breath. "I'm sorry, Cil. No time for a proper plan. Just tell me, everybody. Run or fight?"

In the background, the beast slowly started to lope into a run. It was anything but graceful. Yet it was faster than it had any right to be.

"Nothing's changed. We fight," Kith growled.

"It's just a few feet taller than the gaborn. Fight." Liam's bravado sounded hollow.

"Fight," Cilia said simply. Then she ruined it by adding, "My legs are too short to outrun that thing."

"I will protect us," Sera added.

For a few seconds, Chase simply observed the encroaching behemoth, drinking in all its details. How its gaze was engrossed on the animal corpses strewn on the ground, even to the point of ignoring their group. Those claws at the end of its long, wide legs, at least a foot long. The way that matted fur covered every part of its huge body, except for its ugly face and pale underbelly. How every part of its undeniable stride covered the ground *too* fast, promising speed and a long reach.

He grimaced and spoke up. "Sera. We are going to need your Heart of Hearts."

"Done." The card gave off a murky light under her shirt as it activated.

Kith growled and murmured something under his breath.

"Face and stomach. Those are the two spots we might be able to damage. No time for anything fancy. Throw in everything you have and do it straightaway. I'm aiming for the face. Hopefully, that'll bring it off-balance and you can go for the stomach." He aimed a feverish grin at them. "Please don't die."

With a soft half-forgotten prayer, he switched Among the Raindrops to Race of Life, granting a small additional boost to Agility. He'd need every little bit for this. He activated his Heart card as he started to move, feeling it take effect in the pit of his stomach. That sensation of being nobody important. Of being eminently dismissible, ignorable to the point of near invisibility. He ran, keeping to the right side of the basin, leaping corpses and splashing through puddles of bloodied water.

"That. Goes. For you too! Don't you *dare* die! Light incoming." Cilia grunted as she lobbed one item after another into the air at the oncoming beast.

Chase didn't have time to answer. He was already gone, racing alongside the canyon wall. Behind him, he heard Liam's heavy footsteps following him, and softer, lighter loping steps that had to be Kith. For now, the behemoth ignored him entirely; enough that he could spare a moment to think about the insanity of what he was doing. Charging at a beast that probably weighed forty times what he did, that was infamous for killing entire *groups* of scouts? What in the Pits was he even thinking? They could still run, climb the edge of a rift, and escape. Move back to the lands of Light and...

Chase narrowed his eyes and ignored what his brain was trying to do. He'd been through that mental discussion over and over again. This was the path forward. If he had to carve that path straight through the ugly face of an obscene, primeval monstrosity, then so be it. At least he had the best possible status for it. His mental nudge quickly brought up his current attributes.

> Personal Info:
> Name: Chase
> Title: Dark/Elemental/Light rogue
> Step: 21 (Tier 4)
> Strength: 18 (+1 Tier bonus) (+38) = 57
> Agility: 21 (+13 Tier bonus) (+48) = 90
> Toughness: 18 (+1 Tier bonus) (+38) = 57
> Mental Power: 19 (+1 Tier bonus) (+40) = 60
> Potential: 30 (+1 Tier bonus) = 31

Yeah. It might be suicide, but if ever he was going to have a chance, it would be now. Every single one of his attributes was past the regular invisible limit to Sticky Fingers, doubling his natural attributes. As if that wouldn't be insane enough already, Tier bonuses and Sera's Blessing of the Night allowing him to triple, reach even loftier heights. His body felt unnaturally light, yet solid, holding a degree of power he'd never thought possible.

Each step was a burst of power, a tiny explosion. Each thought came faster, clearer, brought more details and nuances with it.

Pouches hit the canyon floor ahead of him. Chase screwed his eyes shut, mentally taking in the next steps so he didn't stumble. Beyond his eyelids, the world went dark, then light.

Too soon. He'd opened his eyes too soon. That, or his increased Mental Power made him take in more details and more light than he usually would. The entire world was a mess of blobs, colored circles, and pain. Yet, he focused, pressed on, pushing himself onward, nearly stumbling, then catching himself and racing on. If he was blinded, the damn beast had to have it even worse.

The behemoth's pained growl seemed to reverberate back and forth inside the rift. Yet, Chase could fixate on it, sort of, giving him something near-solid to aim for. He raced forward, suicidally fast on the grounds covered with fallen shapes, navigating more by intuition and half-remembered positions than actual sight.

Slowly, painfully slowly, the world stepped back into clarity. Before him, a large shadowy shape towered high, nearly drowning out the light of the moon.

As he'd thought, the behemoth *was* even worse off. It stood on three legs, one massive limb pawing at its eyes, as if trying to rub the invasive lights away. Yet, its huge ears still twitched and moved, as if listening for what was happening even as it tried to regain its bearings. It had not spotted Chase yet, though.

In one massive leap, Chase raced ahead and leapt, hitting the behemoth's knee and using it as a springboard to propel himself even higher. He soared through the air, his entire being focused on his arc, on the carrion stench of the beast's mouth coming closer. Just another second, and its unprotected face would be within strike range.

He wasn't sure whether it was because of the sensation on its knee or it had spotted him somehow, but he felt the protection of Nothing to See Here burst apart, like a fake pearl necklace tearing apart under an ill-timed grasp.

The beast's mouth shot forward, too fast for something of its size, aiming to snap him right out of the air. He barely had the time to interpose the shining protection of his Tier four card between himself and the massive jaws. It wasn't going to be enough, though. Those teeth could gulp him down in a single, massive mouthful, and they bore down on him with ridiculous speed.

Something shot past him and placed itself between him and the beast. Some energy that tore past him, robbing the momentum of those huge jaws. Inexplicably, a fountain of dirty blood sprung from the beast's stomach, spilling out below Chase to strike the ground in a nauseating, rancid waterfall.

He found himself miraculously unhurt, stuck with the magical shining shield granted by his card within the teeth of the beast, hanging from one glowing arm, the rest of the body suspended in front of the behemoth from that single point of contact. The sudden realization that Sera had somehow managed to use her Unexpected Spillage to turn the damage of the beast back on itself, and that he'd have likely been a late-night snack otherwise, struck his mind and was promptly pushed to the background in favor of the knowledge that he was, right this moment, actually exactly where he needed to be. In mortal danger, sure, but right within reach.

Acting before he had any chance to really look at the insanity of what he was doing, Chase braced both feet against the lower face of the monster. Then he pushed off with all of his strength, dismissed the Clothed in Living Light card to get himself unstuck right as he started his upward momentum, and, the moment he spotted the large, glinting presence of the behemoth's eyes, twisted his body and stabbed out with all he had.

The short sword entered the beast's left eyeball without any sort of resistance. Still turning in the air from the twist, the sword turned with him. He struck something deep within the eye. Then gravity took hold of him. That spiteful bitch.

Chase hit the ground, and it nearly rattled his skull. There were only two semi-coherent thoughts rummaging around inside his head, beside incredulity that he'd actually managed to wound the huge monster and a certainty that he was about to die.

One was the need to get *away*. The other was that this was going to be his only chance. Sight swimming, everything hurting, he dismissed Winds of Change, letting go of the versatility of being able to swap cards indefinitely, and changed it for Free of Perdition.

Above him, the monster roared with pain and rose to both hind legs. Its shape was outlined against the night sky, larger than anything he'd ever seen—larger than the gaborn, deadlier than Instructor Boneridge. Before, its roar had been deafening. Now, it was tangible, pushing against him like a wall of sound, feeling like a fist grasped hold of his insides and held *tight*.

Scrabbling away on the ground, he kept trying to activate Free of Perdition. The card took forever to switch. He heard footsteps from behind him as Liam and Kith came running. Then it clicked. Free of Perdition activated, and his life force burgeoned, growing solid as a tree trunk, stability settling him to the point where it felt like he'd be able to headbutt the beast and be the one still standing.

The card had taken. He'd managed to steal the behemoth's Toughness for himself. Only, he didn't know whether the second part had taken. Whether the Mental Power of the beast was massive enough that it would be able to keep itself from having its own Toughness replaced with Chase's own, in comparison, feeble numbers.

Liam's challenging roar nearly rivaled the hurt cry of the behemoth. He rampaged forward like a messenger of doom, like an enchanted missile launched from the towers—implacable, unstoppable. He was wrapped in waves of shining light; Waterfall of Light made him hard to follow as the card granted him additional impetus and the ability to stun or trample. On top of that, his already brawny arms were monstrously inflated; veins stood out under the short-lived effect of his Earthen Might; fire and ice whirled around his truncheon from his Unleash the Elements. That avalanche of unstoppable might and momentum all focused into the full force of his truncheon, slamming down on the back part of the behemoth's hind leg.

The behemoth, rearing in pain, was already off-balance. That implacable strike, added to the trample effect, made something *crack* in its leg. The beast toppled, like a huge tree that had been felled, seemingly taking forever to hit the ground.

They were not in the clear. It was hurt. It was off-balance, unable to strike back right this moment. Yet, the beast had already proved faster than it looked, and the massive body was sure to hold insane strength—even disregarding its famed ability to devour beasts for additional life force.

Kith did not grant it a chance. Even as the beast toppled, the pale-blue light of the moon casting the scene into a pallid, unreal setting turned dark as a thousand separate forms converged on the falling body. The buzzing sounds drowned out Liam, the behemoth, everything, as they arose to an overpowering hum. For a second, it looked as if the fur of the fallen behemoth had come alive, as a living, contorting carpet of insects crawled, slithered, and flew across the beast's wounded torso. It started to pound and scratch its own chest, claws raking insects away. Then, from one second to the next, the mass slithered *inside* the open wound in its stomach. Once in there, they erupted.

The pale light of the moon faded before the burgeoning light of the explosion bursting from the monster's unprotected stomach, as Kith activated Fiery End and every single summoned insect burst into a tiny conflagration within the fleshy insides of the behemoth.

At this, the monster turned insane. It hit the ground and lashed out uncontrollably, almost spastically, at anything and everything nearby. Its surprising speed and long reach made it near impossible for anybody to be able to come near and hurt it.

Cilia, of course, didn't mind. She rained down the remaining fire droplets she had from afar. Chase and Liam, as well, pulled back and used the single fire droplet they had to add flames and destruction to the beast's frenzied lunges. Fire and pain-filled roars filled the sky.

Only, the huge beast did not lie down and die. It slavered and howled, kicked and snarled, twisted and bit. And it did not relent. The blinding lights of the fires within it were dying, and its spasmodic struggles relaxing. With the sound of somebody trying to breathe through a glass of water, it flopped onto its side, then tried to get back up. Parts of the fur on its back and neck were still on fire, yet it barely deigned to notice it, as it struggled to get back up. Torched, blinded, with a massive hole scorched within its abdomen, it still did not relent.

There was only one thing keeping it down.

Kith, in a dance of death.

It could not be described in any other way. With a graceful dip, he leapt near the behemoth and slammed his axe down into one front paw. Then he leapt back, just far enough to be able to punish another paw instinctually trying to slap him down from another side. Seemingly able to anticipate its movements, he dodged and dipped, leaping and sliding to avoid its clumsy slashes and strikes, disrupting its balance and momentum. And every other second, his axes carved into its massive hamstrings and tendons—cutting, snapping, ruining its movement.

Hurting, reeling, half-blinded, with any attempt at regaining its equilibrium countered and punished, the gargantuan beast's control grew less and less focused.

Meanwhile, Chase got back on his feet. He and Liam circled the beast, looking for openings. Once, then twice, Chase leapt forward and slashed the beast's hide and flanks, carving bloody rends in its body. Free of Perdition had clearly taken effect. The monster's insane Toughness was made void, or at least mitigated.

The end came faster than anticipated.

Sera called out, "Take the hit, Kith! Everybody, ready to attack."

Unquestioning, Kith stood in front of the next uncontrolled lunge of the beast, blood-dripping hand axes spread out to either side, screaming in defiance as a torn and bloodied paw the size of his torso rushed sideways at him.

Unexpected Spillage stepped into effect again. What should have resulted in Kith's chest caving in and him being flung through the air ended with the paw repelled, stopping as if it had hit a brick wall, while another deep wound tore open on the behemoth's body.

At that, they all leapt to the attack.

Cilia dropped her final two fire droplets on its squirming shape.

Kith, still reeling, belatedly hit the retreating paw with a glancing blow.

Chase leapt in and burrowed the short sword to its hilt in the beast's back, nearly taking a bout of flame to the face from one of the fire droplets.

Liam, truncheon multicolored with Unleash the Elements, brought his truncheon down hard upon the ugly, massive skull. With a shocked cry, he overbalanced and nearly fell, as his weapon penetrated whatever resistance the forehead retained and sank foot-deep into the head. A gush of fire erupted from within.

The behemoth opened its eyes wide, jaws clenching shut, before opening again, claws reaching out to devour the morsel just within its reach. Its tongue lolled out and with a glassy-eyed stare it died.

Chapter 23

"Whatever else, I did not see this coming. I must admit I am not the prettiest. Yet, in the past week, after saving a scout's life, I have had nothing less than three different Furyborn proposition me." Huh. Is that how it works? Should I expect Furyborn hunks throwing themselves at me when I get back to Cemano? (Page 91.)

"I can't believe I'm still alive." Liam let his hands wander over his face and neck, as if unsure whether everything was still attached.

"You can say that again." Chase nodded, letting his head slump back against his pillow. He grimaced, rummaging around to try to arrange his recline more comfortably.

"I can't believe I'm still alive," Liam repeated, deadpan.

"I, for one, can hardly believe we managed to tear through that huge beast like that. We've gotten *strong*!" Kith exclaimed in a husky voice.

"*I* cannot believe you are abusing that poor beast like that, Chase. Allow it some grace in death," Sera admonished.

Chase finally managed to arrange the soft, floppy ear of the carved-up, fur-covered behemoth to grant him a better pillow. "Pits, no. A while ago, it was trying to gore me and damn near succeeded. It's only fair that, in death, it grants me a bit of rest and relaxation."

Relaxation had been slow in arriving. Although it felt like the stampede had brought along every single beast and Guardian in miles, the scouts had been entirely right when it came to fire on the plains. Their final, fiery conflagration had brought in surrounding beasts for hours to come, straggling in in ones and twos—once an entire pack of frog-like beasts.

Following the demise of the behemoth, the group of Furyborn scouts had trickled back. They took a long look at the gore-covered, corpse-strewn canyon floor and, after a short, terse discussion, sprang into motion. In the hours to come, the scouts helped them spot and eliminate the monsters that fell upon them or tried to drag away any of the easily available luncheons they'd arranged. The Furyborn, while lower in Tier than their group, made up for it with their teamwork and in knowing exactly how to tackle the different beasts.

Chase and his group did help here and there, but generally, following the battle, they were in little shape to continue fighting. Especially Chase, who had crashed *hard* once the boost from his Sticky Fingers ran out. He woke up lying half inside a four-inch-deep puddle of cooling blood.

Eventually, in the early hours of the morning, Ellie approached them, following another discussion with the other scouts. Her demeanor was, if anything, stiffer than earlier, and she pointedly kept her eyes from meeting Liam's. She cleared her throat twice before saying anything. "I... Look, we should be safe now. We're changing the plan from here on."

Kith rubbed his face, unaware, or uncaring, that dried blood flaked from between his hands. His eyes were distant, unfocused. "Oh? No more looking for Slate to backstab us?"

Ellie's glance traveled over the rift behind her. Her uneasy smile grew increasingly stilted. She exhaled noisily. "Listen. Slate had a point. If you guys were slackers, it wouldn't be right letting you stay in Cemano. But you took down a behemoth by yourselves, and..." She gestured at the bodies filling the canyon floor. "You're good. Seriously. He can say what he wants. We'll back you up."

"Agreed. Also, their break is done." Gabby's voice intruded over Ellie's.

"What? What break? I just—" Kith's complaint was cut off by a whoof of air.

"What needs doing?" Liam asked from next to him.

"A windfall like this isn't something that can be ignored." Gabby's no-nonsense voice left no room for debate. "One thing is that we'll likely have a safe spot in this part of the plains for *years* unless something new and scary moves in. But we can't just let all these bodies spoil. We've already sent Beni's cats rushing back to Cemano with messages requesting Guardians and carriers. This will keep the entire *village* in meat for weeks or more, as long as we keep everything from spoiling. That's beyond all the parts that Jessel is going to want me to collect and preserve for healing purposes. You believe that fight was hard? The next couple of days are going to be even harder. I am going to work you to the *bone*." A ferocious grin erupted on her face. "And then, when we're back in Cemano, I'm going to feed you until you're fit to burst. You're in my good books now. I'm sure you'll hate it!"

She didn't lie. For the next three days, the older Furyborn worked them all to the bone, scouts or not, in order to salvage as much as possible of the gifts that nature had decided to throw after them. None of them complained, though, as Gabby worked herself harder than anybody else. They bled animals, gutted and skinned them. Some, they carved up and seared over large fires they erected then and there—again, deviating from their regular rules. Others, they left for later, according to some order that only existed inside Gabby's head. From time to time, Gabby would instruct one of them on some specific task, and they could be stuck working for hours trying to carve out natural crystals set inside a malice mole's innards, or, once, harvesting and washing the toenails of a species of pigs.

Yet, something had changed. The Furyborn worked *beside* them, not around them, at all times assessing them to see how they would do. Fending off roaming pests attracted by the scent of blood, trying to gore airborne carrion birds attempting to get away with choice morsels from their kills: all was made easier, knowing that they had passed the eye of the needle and didn't have to look for hidden traps in every conversation and situation, as long as they pulled their own weight.

That weight, by itself, was nothing to scoff at. Although the local predators at this point were mostly down to smaller pests and birds, there were a *lot* of them. That, on top of the burden of the massive load of work, left them constantly active. Liam earned himself a point to Toughness, and both Sera and Cilia one to Strength. Seeing the writing on the wall, Chase switched back to Spoils of the Undeserving and gained both a point to Toughness and one to Mental Power—from having to stay constantly alert, he judged.

That was but the latest in the lovely number of gains from their battles. The hordes of beasts had predominantly been regular animals, hence, granting no Ænima to aid them in walking the Steps, but there had been a fair share of Guardians caught within the swarm. Liam, Chase, and Kith all earned a single Step, leaving Chase at twenty-two, Liam at eighteen, and Kith at nineteen. Sera didn't earn any, while Cilia's fire droplets had earned her *two* Steps, leaving her at nineteen.

Although they spent a good while grumbling about the behemoth not actually being a Guardian—especially Kith, who'd put his life on the line going toe-to-toe with it—but a regular beast that earned them nothing, there was no discussion about their overall trend. They were improving. Tier four suddenly seemed just a question of time for all of them, and even Tier five didn't sound like a fever dream. *Tier five.* That was the providence of higher-class citizens, of generals, those who earned their places in the footnotes of the history books as Somebodies. Having been nobodies for most of their lives, that seemed entirely insane.

Their attributes matched the pace. Their meteoric rise, the training from the towers, and Cilia constantly pestering them to keep up improving had done them a world of good.

Personal info:

Name: Chase
Title: Dark/Elemental/Light rogue
Step: 22 (Tier 4)
Strength: 18 (+1 Tier bonus) = 19
Agility: 21 (+13 Tier bonus) = 34
Toughness: 19 (+1 Tier bonus) = 20
Mental Power: 20 (+1 Tier bonus) = 21
Potential: 31 (+1 Tier bonus) = 32

No other changes for Chase, except for the single temporary point to Mental Power from Sticky Fingers that became permanent. In the long run, that card along with his training card were going to see him aim for the skies. Well, or see him dead. That felt kind of prophetic to him. He did feel amazing about his Potential nearly tying with his Agility for first place. Any future cards earned were bound to be of a high rarity.

Personal info:
Name: Liam
Title: Dark/Elemental/Light fighter
Step: 18 (Tier 3)
Strength: 18 (+11 Tier bonus) = 29
Agility: 14 (+1 Tier bonus) = 15
Toughness: 26 (+1 Tier bonus) = 27
Mental Power: 13 (+1 Tier bonus) = 14
Potential: 10 (+1 Tier bonus) = 11

No real changes for Liam either, except for the fact that his Strength and Toughness kept climbing.

Personal info:
Name: Kith
Title: Dark/Elemental/Light summoner
Step: 19 (Tier 3)
Strength: 17 (+1 Tier bonus) = 18
Agility: 18 (+1 Tier bonus) = 19
Toughness: 14 (+1 Tier bonus) = 15
Mental Power: 21 (+1 Tier bonus) = 22
Potential: 11 (+11 Tier bonus) = 22

Kith probably had the most balanced build of them all. Yet, that belied the fact that Mental Power had once been his lowest attribute. Now, he was reaching entirely new heights mentally and was able to guide his summons alongside himself in battle nearly without issues. Add to that his Potential hitting twenty-two, and his, well, potential, for lack of a better word, was sky-high. If they ever managed to be offered Furyborn cards, or when he hit Tier four, the new cards would be amazing. Any day now.

> Personal info:
> Name: Cilia
> Title: Dark/Elemental/Light crafter
> Step: 19 (Tier 3)
> Strength: 13 (+1 Tier bonus) = 14
> Agility: 19 (+1 Tier bonus) = 20
> Toughness: 15 (+1 Tier bonus) = 16
> Mental Power: 29 (+11 Tier bonus) = 40
> Potential: 11 (+1 Tier bonus) = 12

If Kith's development was impressive, Cilia's focus had to be downright criminal. Forty Mental Power. *Forty!* Sure, her other attributes, ignoring Agility, were falling behind. However, that was the exact plan for her. As she shared her attributes, her normally cold eyes shone with unshed tears. Where her upbringing, race, and family used to amount to nothing but barriers for her potential, now everything had come together to unleash a shining star who might shake the world when she came into her own.

> Personal Info:
> Name: Serafine
> Title: Dark/Elemental/Light healer
> Step: 17 (Tier 3)
> Strength: 15 (+1 Tier bonus) = 16
> Agility: 17 (+1 Tier bonus) = 18
> Toughness: 16 (+1 Tier bonus) = 17
> Mental Power: 32 (+11 Tier bonus) = 43
> Potential: 12 (+1 Tier bonus) = 13

Some might say that Sera's progress was falling behind that of the others. In some ways, it was. Considering the training she'd received growing up, nearly all of her attributes were falling behind the average of their group. Yet her Mental Power more than made up for it. Her every card hit harder, worked better, boosted their attributes higher. Once they managed to work up a proper defensive strategy for her, she would be a powerhouse to reckon with.

All told, at this point, they figured that there'd be less than a handful of wielders, if that, in the entire village of Cemano who'd be able to match their Steps and Tier. And with their constant training and focus on attributes, likely, only the chief might be able to match their attributes. They had grown *strong*.

Nearly strong enough to match Gabby's intensity and pace at the task of protecting their spoils and preserving dozens of beasts for slaughter. They did complain, yet even Kith's complaints died down when he watched the hardy Furyborn spend hours *inside* the behemoth's stinking carcass, dressing it down, removing offal and carving off slabs of meat to be dried or seared.

Gabby insisted that Kith use his Apian God card as often as possible, because it grasped control over nearby insects. It granted them a rare few minutes bereft of the constant stinging and buzzing menaces around them that threatened to infest and spoil their meat. Kith started to experiment with different methods of removing the insects entirely: having them fly as far away as possible, having them attack each other, drown themselves. Eventually he settled for gathering as large an insect cloud as possible, before having them self-immolate using his Fiery End in the farthest depths of a nearby half-cave, unseen from their surroundings. After a while, that managed to keep down the number of airborne pests.

At long last, their work came to an end. A loud, merry shout proclaimed the arrival of not one, but *three* groups of Furyborn. Not the regular hard-bitten scouts, these. Sure, they all had the hardy looks of people who'd spent the vast majority of their lives outside. These weren't the ropy, wiry muscles of the scouts, but massive brawn of people used to working hard at all times. Relief had come for them all.

"I am not one to complain." Sera groaned. "Yet, even my cramps have cramps. I doubt that I have ever worked as hard in my life. Even Instructor Boneridge would be hard-pressed to keep up with Gabby."

They were resting in the early evening, reclined against a canyon wall, well away from the slaughter site and the cloying scent of blood.

"I know," Kith agreed. "I'm not one to complain either—"

A chorus of laughter and heckling overpowered his lie.

"But I think Gabby could personally scare away half the applicants of the towers in the first week. No, the first *day*."

"How are we all doing, though?" Chase asked. "Not talking about weary muscles or Kith's constant whining. How do you feel about where we're at? What about the locals? Are we doing good? Is there anything we're missing or should focus on? I'd hate for us to get away with the purse and get caught because we're too busy patting our own backs."

Sera spoke up thoughtfully. "I have been paying attention. I know that I do not have your practice working crowds, spotting con men and whatever you call it. Yet, I have been trained to look out for nuances, beliefs, and hidden agendas. I see none. None of the scouts have attempted anything that I might classify as underhanded."

"Have you all been keeping away from using the *other* cards?" Cilia asked.

"Yes, Mum," Chase and Liam intoned. Even Sera joined in. It had been one of the earliest agreements after the fight, hoping that nobody'd noticed anything untoward in the battle and keeping away from temptation and the risk to get spotted and having their secret revealed. No Dark cards!

"Good." Cilia continued, brow furrowed. "Sera. You likely have not noticed, because Slate has been avoiding you and Liam worse than before. He has not changed. If anything, he has become even more hostile to us. He has attempted, on several occasions, to make me do his work, and challenged Chase's knowledge and Kith's temper."

Both Liam and Kith nodded. Sera's eyes widened at this revelation.

Cilia gave a tight smile. "I believe this is desperation. He has proved himself horribly mistaken, and seeks to find some late redemption. Just stay level and don't tip the raft. Once we're back in Cemano, he'll lose the last bit of hold over us, and we'll be free to be ourselves again. I can't see us having any trouble finding supporters and tokens after this."

Their group relaxed for a bit, lost in the luxury of not having to work or even stay alert as the newly arrived work teams handled the heavy toil.

Eventually, Kith, sitting on a rock with his back against the canyon wall, cleared his throat. "So, maybe I've been using *one* of my cards."

"*Kith!*" Cilia's tone was equal parts incensed, afraid, and insulted.

Kith looked around to either side of their group, a droplet of sweat dripping down his face. "Please don't kill me. I did it for a good reason. I think." He spat, then tapped his temple as he looked down between his legs. "It was the timing. What were the odds that, just when we were about to make it to safer parts, a swarm would bear down upon us? By sheer happenstance?"

Sera shook her head. "The scouts have already explained it. Our scent alone could have been enough to alert any of the beasts, let alone the fights we have had. A series of escalating encounters, and that is how swarms are born. Nothing suspicious."

He sneered. "Princess, if you believe that, I've got a legendary deck I'd like to sell you. Only slightly used. Ignoring perfectly good suspicions is how you get stabbed in the butt."

Liam scowled. "One time. Why do you always—"

"I believe," Cilia said with a voice that would make an Elemental caster specializing in ice proud. "He was about to tell us why he ignored what we'd all solemnly agreed."

Kith ducked his head. "Because of Slate, all right? He's a stubborn ass. I get that. But I've asked around with the others. I think he's either seen something, or he suspects. He's been lurking about a lot, glaring at us from afar."

"Why? Liberty, bereft of reason, if that's true, then *why* have you taken any chances?" Cilia asked.

Kith leaned forward, intently looking at them all. "I told you. Because it didn't make sense. What's the chance that a swarm would attack us right at that point? So, when I knew where Slate was, I had my *friends* look around nearby at night, see if I could spot something out of the ordinary." Facing the furious look on Cilia's face, he barked, "*I was right*, Cil. Took me awhile to catch it. My range has improved a lot along with my Mental Power, but it was half a mile away and not easy to spot. I found a branch, wrapped with a piece of cloth. It was half-trodden into the clay. It had been burnt, like a torch."

Chase launched into a series of curses, long and hard.

Liam frowned. "What?"

"What he means," Chase said in sepulchral tones, "is that the swarm was *led* here. Somebody—obviously Slate, that murderous prick—lit a torch, knowing the fire would attract monsters. Then he sprinted, monsters on his ass, in our direction, where he took the time to warn the scouts and leave us in a right mess."

"Earth bury him in a low grave!" Liam exclaimed. "That rat bastard hung us out to dry. Are we sure—"

Eyes fixed on the ground again, Kith murmured, "Took me awhile, but I found a second one too, farther out."

For a while, an uneasy silence spread over their group.

Chase was the one to speak up first. "First off... well done, Kith. You did what you had to do."

Cilia, still scowling, didn't say anything.

"Second... this doesn't change a lot." He held up a finger at the outbursts trying to drown him out. "It doesn't. It's not like we can call Slate out. Our word against his, over a couple of burnt branches? Not going to paint us in a good light. We can't move against him, either. He's still one of theirs, while we're on a trial. The only thing it changes is in us knowing that we need to stay alert and not mess up, for as long as we're in Cemano."

"We have to walk alongside him and act as if nothing has changed?" Sera tapped her lip and nodded. "Okay."

"Just okay? He tried to *kill* us." Liam gawked.

"Did it take?" She smirked. "Apologies, Liam. But I am used to keeping up appearances when it comes to enemies and loathsome people. Acting would not seem so untoward for you either, would it?"

"I *guess*." Liam sulked. "I'd rather punch him, though."

"We all have to sacrifice something for the greater good, it seems." Chase grinned, but then pointed at Kith. "We're *done* with the other cards, though. You hear? You did good, but Cilia's going to murder you, and you know what she's like when she wants something."

"I'll behave," he said. "Please don't do with the murdering."

"I promise nothing." Cilia raised her chin.

The trip back to the village took forever. Although their next few days became a whole lot easier, as villagers circled in to help, pick up meat and ingredients and depart, weighed down by heavy burdens, the task ahead of them was still enormous. Eventually, the slowest and biggest of the Guardians arrived from Cemano, along with a grinning Gaven. They were going to carry the majority of the remaining burdens, including the behemoth's meat and the bones, which apparently were exquisite material for both carving and crafting.

They still had to leave a lot behind. Huge, stinking piles of offal and discarded parts that nobody could find a use for. A number of the carcasses had also spoiled, either gone bad because they hadn't been dressed properly in time, or because insects got to them. Yet, Gabby insisted that they'd salvaged the majority and their fight would create a seriously comfortable buffer for Cemano in the weeks and months to come. As to the remnants, she just shrugged. Nature would take care of that.

<u>Chapter 24</u>

"Furyborn are the most racially cognizant of all aspects. Note that I do not call them racists. Yet, you will find that being born with any aspect but that of Fury, you will invariably be subject to a higher degree of scrutiny and criticism. This is the way of life out here. They know what they like and what friends look like. I know that being a Furyborn, even one coming from Earth's Ward, has made my life a lot easier here." That's... exactly what calling them racist means. Of course it is. Does he not know what the word means? That's it. I am writing the library back in Earth's Ward for addendums. Edit: He's not exactly wrong in calling them racist, either. He should just be honest about it. (Page 41.)

"With that in mind, I hope that you will all help us and support us. We've been sworn to silence from the High Elementalist, but I *can* say that the end result should be something advantageous both for the Furyborn and Elementals. And the Lightborn are going to *hate* it. Now, we've done what we can to prove that we're actually here to help, and not to... stab you all in the back or something. Honestly, if I were a traitor, I'd probably ask to help somewhere that didn't have me handling this much crap another time."

"You're rambling again, Darkie!" a voice shouted from in front of the platform. "Best get back to shoveling dung."

"Aaand thank you so much, Gaven," Chase answered dryly, before turning back to address the rest of the small crowd. "I *am* rambling. And to be honest, half of me doesn't even want to move on, dung or no. I've come to like Cemano. A lot. Except, this is important. If we need to stay here another year to convince you all that we're honest about it, so be it. But I hope you will accept my words for what they are."

Another voice shouted out in mock affront. "That was *clearly* a threat. That bastard threatened us with staying here for another year. How low can you go?"

Chase laughed. "Thank you, Ellie. Yes, with how much time you've spent with Liam lately, you'd absolutely *hate* it if we stayed, right?"

She sputtered unintelligibly in response.

Chase continued above her protests. "Honestly, though, that's all I had, everybody. I'm not going to waste your time any further. Help us, if you think we deserve it. Talk to anybody, if you're in doubt. Except Slate. Please don't talk to Slate."

Eventually, the ribbing and good-natured back-and-forth subsided, and the crowd slowly dwindled away. A good number among them, before leaving, moved to the platform to leave their token. Chase counted the first thirty-eight, and smiled at Naley, who, winking, put down her own token next to the others before leaving the square. This was just the morning crowd. Going by the regular flow of Cemano, enough people would walk by over the day, including the evening surge when people gathered to talk, debate and eat together, they would comfortably make it past the numbers they needed... easily double it, even.

Chase observed the calm center of Cemano as its people went about their business. He was going to wait awhile before addressing some of the crafters who usually set up in the square a bit later in the day. The spare time allowed him something as rare as a moment of introspection.

The past month and a half since they'd returned from the scouting route had been good to them. Surprisingly good. Chase had never expected that he was going to be sad to see the last of the village. Yet there he was. The people of Cemano? They were good people. Not even simple. Pits, most of the people of the Waves had been dumb as dirt, ruined by a life of cheap thrills, too many blows to the head, or, often as not, both. Here? They weren't learned. But they were curious, eager to learn, and they were anything but limited in their mindsets. Stubbornly, *insanely* independent, sure. *Aggressively* eager to challenge any preconceived notions in others, which they believed didn't hold up, very much so. Yet, they never dismissed any knowledge or opinion simply for deriving from a specific source or person.

In short, he'd come to like the place. He liked stubborn old Gaven and his ill-conceived notion that he'd be able to drink any challenger under the table, regardless of weight and build. He liked Naley and her burning desire to see the world. He liked the crafty chief, Alia, with her wise eyes, quick wit, and coarse humor.

Cemano had been good to them.

Following the scouting route and their success, they'd all been cleared and accepted to join the scouts for any further tours. The general mood of the populace toward them had warmed considerably. Yet, Alia had cautioned them to stay the course and stay for a while longer. Ostensibly because they weren't going to send a caravan toward Heart Halls for a while anyway. Deep down, Chase suspected her of simply wanting to make the most of their stay, milk them of everything they were worth. He didn't mind at all. Underhanded or not, she'd been true to them, and been among the first to put her token up in their support.

He wasn't going to begrudge the time spent in the village. Not a single moment. Sure, burning his work clothes would likely be the only way to get the smell of dung out of them, but he'd learned so much. About the Furyborn. About their temper, their Guardians, how they lived in so close a companionship with their Guardians and the surrounding landscape, that sometimes they'd even move an entire village to follow migrating animals or soil that needed a break from farming. About their fighters, their skills, and how they seemed to perceive everything, up to and including life itself, as a damn challenge they weren't going to back down from.

Kith had kept up his work as a defender on the walls of Cemano. Yet, with their place in the village unchallenged, the floodgates had opened and he'd slowly gotten to know the other defenders, especially the summoners. It had been a learning experience for him, though their approach to being a summoner was drastically different from the utilitarian one that the rest of Ordei seemed to adopt.

Yet, as the local Furyborn kept insisting their way was superior, he followed along and learned from them, slowly realizing that there were indeed certain advantages to their way of life. Sure, Furyborn summoners mostly mastered few actual summons, leaving them underpowered, should they find themselves in conflict without any Guardians nearby. Yet, their mastery over and cards helping them control and boost the local Guardians was undeniable, often leaving the Guardians stronger than the equivalent Tier of a summoner's creatures in the rest of the world. Apart from that, there was also another branch of local summoners, the beast master, where they'd adopt and guide a local beast, or several, granting those additional powers.

Cilia majorly disliked all Kith's speculations regarding summoners. Mostly because the locals refused to share any explanations as to *why* things were the way they were for summoners—that, or they simply didn't know. And if there was one thing Cilia loathed, it was not knowing.

Fortunately, the summoner theories were among the only details she was unable to learn *anything* about. She returned to her studies with Master Benneth with a vengeance, and learned everything there was to learn about leatherworking. She learned how to tan leather, cut, measure, and dye it, about the different needles and myriad other tools needed for proper leatherwork, about different types of stitching and thread and their advantages. When Chase finally climbed on that platform to put up his proposal to have them travel to Heart Halls, she had just finished a round of visiting different crafters in Cemano, allowing her to assist in the creations of her own set of tools. She was, in the words of Master Benneth, actually in a position where she held the knowledge and capability to learn how to properly create something.

The fact that she'd worked for several months and still hadn't been allowed to properly craft a single gods-cursed new item was enough to send Liam into hysterics. Only... not when Cilia was around, because criticizing Master Benneth was not done.

Liam himself had never seemed happier. He operated the way he preferred it, with his brain mostly turned off, simply enjoying life. He worked hard, he trained hard, drank hard, and he... spent a lot of time with Ellie. The two hit it off, drinking, sparring, and hanging out whenever she was back from one of her scouting trips.

Sera, as well, was caught up in a twofold world of learning. Part was completing what she'd started with Gabby on their trip, learning all about the local wildlife and plants and what they could provide in medicine. The other and, to her, most important part was learning about all the degrees of healing that had nothing to do with actual card magic, and everything to do with knowing about bodies, rehabilitation, nutrition, and such. It was a world she'd only seen through the lens of dry learning back in Isarn, and now she learned it in practice. She assessed that the practice had already made her a much better healer, and went at it with passion.

Beyond that, though, their little group had simply had the chance to relax, to get accustomed to a simpler lifestyle and a day-to-day situation where they didn't have to fight for survival every other moment.

Now and again, in the evening, one of them would speculate on whether staying in Cemano would be so bad. Whether a simple life like this, where they only had to worry about their little village and limited wants and desires wouldn't be nicer than the challenges they'd inevitably meet when they moved on. Except, nobody actually pushed on the topic. Because, when all was said and done, they knew what they were fighting for. Sometimes, Chase would take out the High Elementalist's message and put it on the table. They'd argue how it actually worked and what it said. But they never suggested simply dropping it. Because, even if it would be a large undertaking, it was also something else. Something more.

Staying in Cemano would mean bowing down to the pressure of the world around them, accepting that this was how the world would remain. The Lightborn would be at the center of the world, with Elementals, Darkborn, Liberators, and Furyborn pushed back into simple survival. Meanwhile, that message symbolized the chance to change all that. To strive for a dream where they wouldn't have to make do, with the need to bow. And Chase suspected that this streak of independence, of railing against authority, was one reason why he got along so well with most Furyborn.

For all their enjoyment, it wasn't like they'd just relaxed in their time in the village. They trained on a daily basis, either sparring between themselves or with the locals, or with Sera and Cilia as guides, following what they'd learned in the towers. They refrained from taking any long scouting circles. Having that one eventful trip was enough for them. Yet, some of them did take the occasional one-day trip with other scouts, to relieve them of boredom.

Sera was the one who pushed herself the most here. She knew that it was harder for her to walk the Steps than the others, hence the short trips where she'd see the chance of action with a decent degree of control was optimal for her. Eventually, she did manage to be the sole person to gain another Step, catching up to Liam at eighteen.

The results of their persistent training did not fail in showing up either. Kith earned a hard-won point to Mental Power and another to Agility.

Liam managed another point to Agility as well, on top of a point to Toughness. His training bouts with Ellie were becoming something of an attraction, as caster flung soil and plant life at fighter, pitting Agility and magic against Strength, sometimes for hours on end.

Chase yet again praised his Spoils of the Undeserving as he gained two points to Mental Power and one to Strength and Toughness.

Sera, with her major focus on healing and her outings, only managed a single point to Toughness, while Cilia, utterly caught up in her learning processes, managed two whole points to Mental Power.

Slate, of course, did not just disappear into nothingness, simply because his proposal had been defeated. He did, however, fade away from the public eye a bit and stopped making a spectacle of himself. After the initial shaming, that was. For a few days after returning, he was a laughingstock, suffering biting comments and derision wherever he went. Once the worst of it was over, he acted as if nothing had changed and started to pop up everywhere, "coincidentally" hanging out near them.

Chase didn't trust it, or him, one bit. To their advantage, the young man who'd eavesdropped on them via a card seemed to have stopped listening to Slate after his embarrassment. This meant they'd likely only have to deal with the mean-spirited scout himself. Following a few initial careful whispered discussions among his crew, they agreed to a few simple rules.

— No talking about, or using, Dark cards. At all. No exceptions, outside of sheer survival needs.

— No discussing their plan, except in very vague terms. Adding to that, don't talk about the subsequent plan of continuing into Liberty territory.

— Any specific plotting would have to be absolutely necessary, and agreed upon so they could handle it in as safe a setting as possible.

Their precautions seemed to have worked. There were no whispered rumors, no shouted accusations. Whatever Slate might be plotting, he kept it to himself.

Following their successful proposal, Liam carried a hefty bag of small tokens to Alia's home—at least twice the minimum needed for them to consider what they asked. The brawny chief accepted the bag graciously, made a few lewd, outlandish comments and returned to her work. The day after, they were all invited to sit with her, and deal with the result.

***

The main Church of the Circle, Inner Sanctuary.

"I understand." The bald figure made no outward sign of his understanding. His visage—bald, thin to the point of emaciation, with the skin pulled tight and sunken eyes—made his head look like a skull.

Archbishop Desahl tapped the side of his throne. A real throne—ostentatious, glittering... a sign of *power*. Not like the dull thing the old archbishop used to sit on. "Please repeat to me exactly what it is you understand, Inquisitor Vorbis. We would not like any misunderstandings like last time."

"I understand that you require me to elaborate on my desire to leave." Seconds ticked by, until he finally broke the silence again. "We expect the *fugitives*"—the inquisitor spat the word as though it were poison on his lips—"to have evaded our scouting groups, wandering inquisitors, and our best efforts at pursuit. We also believe they were involved in a... situation in the village of Lillybrook."

"Lillybrook? Where is that? And why believe that they were involved?"

"It lies about a hundred and twenty miles south of their expected approach toward Heart Halls. Somebody robbed large quantities of foodstuffs from the mayor, a Mister Emperlinger's house. Right around that time, a group of wielders defeated a large force of unaspected Guardians to the west of the village."

"Ah." Archbishop Desahl tapped the side of the throne again. He would really need to order some additional pillows. Luxurious or not, the throne was rather uncomfortable. Though, they would have to be well crafted to not make him look less visually imposing. He refocused. "That does fit with their regular methodology. Impractical, poorly planned, and with a penchant toward trying to impress the unwashed masses with their heroics. Now, that would put them outside the reaches of our closest patrols, and within reach of the Furyborn lands. How old is this information?"

"Two weeks. The scout who spotted the aftermath was of the misguided conviction that they deserved a chance to run for saving the village." A fire lit in his deep-set eyes. "He was kind enough to provide the village with an example of how that was not the right approach."

"Right. Right." The archbishop sighed. "That means they are now beyond our reach. We know the Furyborn have settlements nearby, and we do not have enough forces nearby to invade currently. Hence, your desire to leave?"

Vorbis bowed. The movement looked unnatural on the gaunt man, like a stick figure that was more liable to crack in two than bend. "Yes. It is as you say. They are likely to have reached their goal. Instead of trying to force our way in, I would cast a wider web, increase our presence east of Heart Halls, and catch them when they eventually try to leave."

The archbishop nodded. "Permission granted. As is your desire to bring more of your brothers to the front and use some of the local soldiers. We will *not* let them slip through our fingers. Dismissed."

Vorbis bowed again. Then he left, without a single glance to either side.

A chuckle rang out from behind him. The archbishop froze. Slowly, he looked over his shoulder.

Lord Beforant rested his arm on the back of the throne. One perfectly arched eyebrow rose high in amusement at the man who'd just left. "I *do* so love fanatics."

"My Lord Beforant. I was not aware that you were going to be here today." The noble had taken the secret entrance too, the one reserved only for the highest echelon of the Church.

"Oh, I like to surprise, *Esteemed Father*."

His voice truly was a work of art. The warmth seemed real, but the hints of disdain and menace lay right behind the layer, hinting at darker things.

"That, I would say, is what separates players from the playing pieces." He strode around the throne and sat down on the armrest, putting his foot up and resting his elbow on Archbishop Desahl's shoulder. "You don't mind, do you? I like to sit while I pontificate." The titter was incongruous with the perfect vision of a nobleman in control.

"Of course I do not mind." The archbishop lied.

"Good. Good. Fanatics. I love them. They are predictable. Packages of belief sets, perfect to be set off with a single touch of an emotional trigger. You know exactly what you're going to get. Look at that absolute beauty of a fanatic who just left." He waved lazily at the gate. "You need so little to control a specimen like that. Heretic. Blasphemy. Any hint that somebody is straying from the 'right' path, and he will go at them like a mad dog, ignoring how much he himself desecrates his own teachings in the process."

He chuckled. "A man like him will never be a player. Players are those who take a step back, truly *see* the pieces, and learn how best to apply them." The noble's elbow pressed down painfully on the archbishop's shoulder blade. "Of course, the game is more subtle than that. The same goes for players. Some may believe they are players, and fail to realize that they are, in fact, but a more efficient playing piece. Often, that realization comes with a sudden, sharp drop."

The archbishop grimaced. At times, Lord Beforant was like this. He would be amiable, then turn on the screws, to remind those he believed subservient of their place. "Good point." He bowed his head. "The former archbishop is a good reminder of what happens when you think yourself untouchable. One I have taken to heart." There. That was as clear as he was going to be. He would play the good little pet, right until he had the power to escape the clutches of the noble.

Lord Beforant leaned in over the throne, turning toward him. In a pleased purr, he said, "Oh, that is just *wonderful* to hear, Esteemed Father. In fact, that is so wonderful, that I am going to include it in one of my coming plays."

The archbishop blinked. "Plays, Lord Beforant?"

"Oh yes. Not a political play either. You may not have heard. It's been the truth for years, but I've finally made it official. I am now the largest contributor to the arts in all the lands of Light." Lord Beforant leapt off the armrest and glanced about, until his eyes converged on the bowl on the small table next to the throne. He frowned deeply, before picking up a grape and squishing it between two fingers. "Grapes? Really? The entire church in your pocket and you indulge in grapes and... cherry tomatoes?"

He tsked, shaking his head softly. "Even if you discard the waste of not abusing your power, that is just too much. It would be *so* easy for somebody to take all of this—gaudy throne, blood-red cherry tomatoes and all—and paint you as a classic villain." He merrily tapped the side of his well-shaped nose. "Players need to think of these things. But then, you'd have to make enemies of somebody with an army of bards in their pay, which would just be *ridiculous*."

"Yes. Ridiculous." Archbishop Desahl reeled. Why was Beforant so actively hostile? What did he suspect? What did he *know*? He tried to change the subject. "What else do we do, then? About the... *heretics?*"

Beforant tapped the armrest of the throne for a while in a discordant pattern. He smiled, yet the smile did not reach his eyes. "Yes. Them. Your informants and mine are both to blame for being late in telling me about their departure from Earth's Ward. I will not miss this chance again. We will double our army's presence on the western front, especially near Heart Halls, increase our covert presences in all western villages and cities, and offer double pay for informants."

"Should we also increase our smaller intrusions into the Fury lands?"

"Grand idea." Lord Beforant paused and let his hand rest on the shoulder of Desahl. "The numbers among our indebted are near to bursting. We can offer a few hundred of them clemency for anything useful. Perhaps a thousand, over time." The hand grasped tighter, growing nearly painful. "The bloody *bitch* of a High Elementalist gave them an Elemental Deck. Do you see it? Do you have *any* idea what kind of power they could give me?"

Me. Not "the Church" or even "our Wellspring." Archbishop Desahl, not for the first time, reconsidered whether his decision to ally with the popular noble was going to spectacularly backfire. He nodded and said something noncommittal. For now, it was all he had. He'd hang on tight and hope Lord Beforant didn't drag them both over a cliff in his rush for power. Besides, he *could* see a world where he spearheaded a church presiding over all Furyborn, Dark, Light, *and* Elemental aspects. Perhaps, then, they'd even be able to bring Liberty back into the fold. That would almost be worth the pain of kneeling to this dreadful noble.

Chapter 25

"Yesterday, I was asked about traveling in the Furyborn Lands. What insanity. Let us for a moment ignore the pointed fact that the Furyborn will not take kindly to any unwanted stragglers on their lands. Even so, it would still mean traveling within lands so hostile the Lightborn have withdrawn from them. The risk of death would be immense." I will have to write a chapter or two myself, it seems. Even when the writers take to sheer speculation, they're being stupid about it. "Lands so hostile the Lightborn..." Pfah. Are they forgetting that the Furyborn move about out here? Stupid, stupid, stupid. (Page 14.)

"**S**he said yes! Woo!" Kith leapt about, flinging his arms up in the air in triumph.

"We heard you the first fourteen times." Liam snorted. "Now, would it *kill* you to lend a helping hand?" He waved a hand at several covered pots next to him, even as he stirred another huge pot, from which enticing smells emerged. "Oh yeah. This is good."

"It might? Kill me, that is."

"*We* may hurt you if you don't start working already," Sera said tersely. "Besides, we are throwing a farewell party. Celebrating that you are leaving these people is in bad form."

"Be that way." Kith sniffed and grabbed a pot. On his way out the door, he turned around. "It's not like I'm happy to get away from here. It's just... have you got any idea how wonderful it will be to *never have another guard duty* on the walls again? I doubt anybody who's ever tried it will fault me for being happy I can escape from those Pits of boredom."

The others grabbed pots and pans and followed him outside. Right in the middle of the street, an area had been taken over by a hodgepodge assembly of furniture and people. There were tables, chairs, and benches that had clearly been dragged out from people's houses. A large group of people were standing and seated, moving around in amiable confusion, with others bringing foodstuffs, drink, and other additions with little rhyme or reason.

On one nearby chair right outside their house, Ellie leaned back, spearing a slice of roasted meat on her knife. "I sure won't blame him. Guard duty's the worst! The only reason I became a scout in the first place was to get away from that tedium." As Liam placed his large pot on the table close to her, she grabbed his sleeve and dragged him down for a long, deep kiss. Eyes sparkling, she spoke up again. "The only reason I'm blaming any of you is that you're going to drag away my little toy."

Liam righted himself, holding a hand to his chest, affecting affront. "Is that all I am to you, woman? A plaything, to be used only for his brawn, beautiful face, and near-limitless stamina?"

"Sure ain't for the humility," Beni drawled on the bench right next to Ellie.

"Of course you're more than that, love. Those calves. Oomph." The tall, wiry caster winked at Liam over the roar of laughter that exploded around them. Her eyes glinted with untold emotions, though.

They shared the meal in an unmitigated chaos of conversations, pranks and shouting. That was one thing they'd learned rather quickly, to Sera's dismay and complaint. There was no such thing as proper etiquette in Furyborn lands. Or rather, the etiquette was that meals were supposed to be a time of laughter, enjoyment, and no rules whatsoever. The single exception was the one untold rule which tied into the point: no heavy discussion topics mid-meal. Food was for life and laughter. The time for seriousness came afterward.

Dirty clay dishes and plates piled up on the tables. Close to a hundred people were still around. Most of the children had abandoned ship and left in a screaming, joyful horde to play elsewhere. Plumes of dense smoke rose from the few pipe owners who enjoyed the crass, but aromatic verdant leaf that grew locally. Somebody had managed to find a few clay jugs of Surly Anne's old stash, which made locals either cluster around or flee from the stench.

"All right." Chase clapped his hand on the table and spoke up. "If I can have your attention?"

"Have it? Sure. Keep it fixed? Depends how much you're yappin'." Gaven squinted as he poured a tall drink from a jug to the protests of the others at his table.

"I'll keep it short, then. Not unlike you, Gaven."

A few laughs arose.

"You all know by now we didn't mean to come by here. It was a whim of fate, as our planned route was disrupted. Instead, what started as a detour and a way to evade the Lightborn has proved to be a stroke of luck."

"That sounds about right. You probably wouldn't find other villages willing to let in somebody as suspicious-looking as your lot!" Alia shouted.

"Exactly! Thank you!" Chase bowed. "A naive chief—"

"Hey!"

"And a bunch of rubes who'd let themselves be convinced that somebody as obviously conniving as our lot are actually here to do some good."

Ellie, sitting on Liam's lap, trying to kiss him into submission, surfaced for air. "Oh yes. Conniving. That's Liam." Then she attacked him again.

"Seriously, people. Thank you so much for giving us a chance. You have *no* idea what that means to us. Where we grew up, it was every person for themselves. There was no such thing as family, except the one you'd choose for yourself—and even then, they'd be every bit as likely to stab you in the back as to offer you help." Chase waved his arm at the village surrounding them. "Finding a place, such as this, where people help each other without even being asked, where the community's the most important thing? It's been an eye-opener. Thank you ever so much for that!"

People smiled and nodded at his words. A few cheered.

"He does like to hear himself talk, doesn't he?" Alia smirked.

A few shouts of "Speech! Speech!" arose to meet her.

She grimaced. "Do I really have to?" Seeing the cheers, raised fists, and clapping from Chase and the others, she bowed her head. "Okay then. Have it your way. You know I'm horrible at these things."

"Ayup! That's what makes it *fun*!" An already inebriated Gaven raised his mug at her.

Alia shook a huge fist at him good-naturedly. Then she turned serious. "Chieftains do speak together, now and again. We meet up, share tales, offer advice. Sometimes, the advice is simple, but useful, like knowing which traveling minstrels you shouldn't bed for waking up itching all over."

"She didn't lie about being horrible at this," Kith drily remarked, before taking a bread roll to the face and almost falling off his chair.

"At *other* times," she continued, ignoring his comment while brushing crumbs off her hands, "it's telling stories about what's worked in other villages and what hasn't, which kinds of lost ones we've battled, what combinations of cards we've seen arise that made a difference. Stuff we can apply here in Cemano, if we like what we're hearing." She cracked her knuckles. "Mostly, I forget about half of it before I'm out the door. We're not like the Elementals, too timid to carve their own paths, following the exact choices of their forefathers without changing anything. But, at our last chat, there was one thing I took to heart. It was on the topic of Lightborn infiltrators."

A hush fell over the crowd. The good-natured ribbing faded away, as people leaned forward, attentive.

"They've tried many times over the years. Most often with solitary travelers, and never with groups as weird as yours. Yet, they have tried a lot of different approaches. Groups of non-Lightborn. Groups without cards or where none of them held any Light cards whatsoever. Yet, there was one detail that consistently reappeared among the attempts, and it was this. While they had different strategies, they would inevitably attempt to bargain. To come up with an acceptable trade. *If we do this, you will let us in.*" She shook her head with a smirk. "Like we would just put up a price for them to be accepted among us."

She turned on Chase and his crew now, the colors in her eyes brimming with warmth. "You started out like that. Because that was where you came from. But over time, you showed that there was more to you. That you did not shy from doing what was needed, even if there was no immediate gain from it. That you *understood* what it's like to be a Furyborn, even if you do not know the words." She paused, tapped her lip and added in a dry rasp, "That, or you're just *really* into shoveling shit."

The crowd erupted into laughter and heckling.

Once silence fell over them again, Alia extracted a hemp basket from under the table. "When I first met you, I teased you. I told you how, if you'd been of the blood, I'd be sharing food with you, offering you official welcome to my lands, except you hadn't earned that." She removed the cloth folded over the basket, revealing six small, wrinkled apples. "You are still not of the blood. That is not something that I can grant you here. Possibly, you will never earn that. However, I *will* offer you welcome to my lands. Should you ever return, you will have a place here. Though... not Surly Anne's place. You've fixed that up nicely, and I've already got people asking to move in. You get to fix a new ruin." She smirked at them.

With wide smiles, they all accepted an apple from the chief and bit into them. The skin was wrinkled, and the apples were small. Yet, they tasted like victory.

Hoarse with emotion, Chase had to try to speak a few times before he managed, "Thank you very much, Alia. Right at this moment, I feel terrible that I can't tell you exactly what we're going to do." He glanced at his crew. Kith's smirk, Sera's warm smile, and Cilia's curt nod made him continue. "I will say this. If we succeed in our plan? We'll be back at some point. And we will have something to give back to Cemano for everything you've given us. We had a home here for a while, and it was a damn good one."

As the hours passed by, the feast slowly faded into a party and people came by to say goodbye to them all, share a few final words, or simply enjoy their final hours together. Oh, and there were gifts. So many gifts. Small ones—of rations for the journey, changes of clothes, or everyday items you'd want for a prolonged journey. The true gifts arrived with little fanfare, as singular givers dragged them aside one-on-one.

Jessel surprised Sera with a wrapped parcel, entirely filled with dried herbs and plants, fit to help cure dozens of people of a wide variety of ailments.

Eggert, a surly, young summoner with horrible skin and worse hygiene, shyly gave Kith a proper sheath for his hand axes, allowing him to draw them a lot faster.

A bunch of workers gave Liam a large skin of alcohol, which they swore was better than "that swill from Surly Anne." Ellie dragged him off into the darkness to give him her present— which was the last anybody saw of the pair that night.

Master Benneth gave Cilia a tome. Or rather, a leather-wrapped folder, self-made, holding blueprints, written by hand, on different leather creations. He followed that gift with a long-winded series of admonishments on what to do and specifically not to do, that had anybody but Cilia herself rolling their eyes.

Finally, in the early hours of the morning, Gaven plopped down on the bench next to Chase. "Whoeee. Somebody hold on to the world. It's spinning something fierce!"

Chase laughed. "Better lie down on the ground, mate. That way you won't have far to fall!"

The grizzly animal handler blew a raspberry and leaned back, almost overbalancing. "Bah. That's one thing you'll need to learn. How to hold your drink."

"Also, how to keep it away from you."

Gaven guffawed. "Y'ain't wrong there." He squinted at Chase. "Y'know, I figured I was going to get you the best gift ever, but then I thought to m'self, you'd had the pleasure of my company for months. Don't get any better'n that!"

"That's a truly depressing sentence. Only, I actually do agree. Please don't ever change, Gaven. And whoever shows up to help you after me, give 'em just as much crap as you did me."

The old man burst into laughter. "Good one!"

They sat in silence for a moment, watching Kith try, and fail, to match a few of the local fighters in arm wrestling. Finally, Gaven spoke up again, this time serious, nearly sober. "I did have one gift in mind. Not for you. That scrawny twerp of yours there."

"Kith?"

"He's the one. Been watching 'im. Sharper 'n he looks, he is. So're you, of course. You'd have to be."

"Feels like you're getting sidetracked here, old-timer." Chase smirked.

"Only 'cause I choose to. Where was I?"

"You were saying how you'd miss me so much, you had a gift for Kith."

Gaven guffawed and hit Chase in the shoulder. "This is for all of you. Ain't spoiling the surprise neither. Here it is."

Chase looked at the tiny item the old man put in his palm. It was a small, intricately carved gemstone, shaped in the form of what looked to be a duck. "I thought you guys had no use for gems? This looks valuable, Gaven."

"It is and it ain't." He barked a laugh. "No clue what it's worth outside of our lands. Here, it's worth a lot, but only to the right sort. You make it to Heart Halls, 'n earn your cards. Once you've got that, you go to Germina's, tell her I sent you, and she'll set you up."

"Germina's. I mean... what does that mean?"

"Allow an old man his fun. You give this to that scrawny kid, and let him guess his heart out. If you figure it out, don't tell 'im, though. It'll be even better if it's a surprise."

Chase tapped the gem thoughtfully. "You're telling me that I should hold it over his head like it's a secret, make him rack his mind every day trying to figure out what it is, and not give an inch, for my own amusement?" He looked right into the old man's eyes. Then he enfolded him in a big hug. "It's like you're the dad I never had."

Gaven stiffened, then hugged him back. "You're damaged goods, kid. But you're not the worst."

"Right back at you." The hug went on for a while. "You know, you really should start rubbing your skin with these febral sticks. They help with the smell."

Gaven snorted. "You're not letting go, though."

"Meh. If I let go of family just because they were a bit crap, I wouldn't have any."

Chapter 26

"The Lightborn have sent scouts, of course. Yet, with their regular tenacity, the Furyborn find them and erase them from the face of the earth. Yet, now and again, somebody returns, filled with rumors about the unexpected. Constructions where you'd expect none, well-trodden roads, cart traffic, systems... signs that organization exists where most believe chaos rules. I tend to agree. The Furyborn cannot have survived on tenacity alone for this long." Oh. He did get the point. It just took him two chapters and thousands of words. (Page 26.)

They didn't leave early in the morning. Celebrations had spread, leading to some rather hefty hangovers. Not everybody was blessed with high Toughness, and locating everybody, waking them up, *and* getting them to a state where they'd be ready to leave led to more groans than Rita's Raft O' Pleasure back on the Waves.

Eventually, they managed, and just before noon, they took off for Heart Halls.

It was a much bigger procession than Chase expected. There were about forty people outside of their own group, all gathered in the central square of Cemano, surrounded by four large carts loaded to the brim with crates, barrels, and more—huge backpacks, weaponry, a handful of large Guardians Chase had spent months catering to, including the two caarnath Guardians of the village. Around them all milled family, friends, and others who'd shown up to say goodbye, matching the size of the celebration from the day before. The mood was joyful and free, excitement mixed with sadness. It was merry enough that it kind of reminded Chase of the few times they'd teamed up with other, larger groups to plan heists.

Right up until one stick-thin, older Furyborn with a shaved head, a loud voice, and an attitude that would've matched the armsmaster for ferocity, took charge. "All right. Because you lot decided that today was going to start late, I went and decided that it's going to *end* late as well. We're not getting behind schedule because you couldn't hold your drink." A chorus of groans met her statement, but nobody talked back. She veered on Chase and the others, who, on the whole, looked markedly fresher than most of the others. "Everybody here knows me. I'm Misandria. No 'Missy.' No endearments. Misandria. Go right ahead and tell me who you think should decide how things work on this trip."

Kith gulped, but his brain apparently won out, as he put forward the only acceptable answer. "You should?"

"Damn straight. Now, the chief, in her wisdom, decided that since you lot are traveling with us, we won't need any further protection. That leaves me with only two scouts who know what they're doing and few fighters. Are you going to help or be trouble for me?"

"Help, of course," Chase said. "We're clueless when it comes to scouting, but we can fight. You tell us where you want us, we'll hold our own."

She sneered but nodded. "Best prove that, or I swear by the soil of my birth, I'll march you right back to Cemano and trade you in, and paddle your behind like a toddler in the process."

Misandria, it seemed, was a harsh mistress. She was, however, quite effective, and with short notice, she'd managed to chase away all the family and well-wishers, organized the members of their caravan into an order she found acceptable, and they were on the way. The caarnath and two other Guardians were strapped to the carts, every one of them had one person assigned to guide a cart, and the final Guardian, Cherro, the largest plain cat of Cemano, plodded alongside a summoner.

Shortly, they arrived at the edges of the large depression that surrounded Cemano. There, Chase finally got an answer to his question regarding approaches to the village for anybody who wasn't on foot, as they revealed a well-hidden long tunnel that led through the soil and up to the surface. That village just kept on surprising.

The change was a bit of a shock. Right before noon, they were still at the center of things, chatting with passersby. An hour later, they were out of view of the village—and suddenly it was like they'd never left the wilderness, with only a poorly maintained path to show that anybody had ever preceded them along that route.

The mood switched too. The moment they left the outskirts of Cemano, every Furyborn went into serious mode, weapons ready, eyeing their surroundings for anything of note.

Chase and the others, however, had quickly come up with one rule for this trip that'd be the single guidance: just follow whatever Misandria says and does. For every moment out there, every part of what they knew told them that was the way. This was not a case of somebody being clueless, yet self-assured to act like she know what she was doing. She was utterly, undeniably in control. This was also clearly seen in the others on the trip, who *also* looked toward her for guidance. Where the others were tense and clearly out of their element, Misandria led their caravan, focused but relaxed, a straight-necked vision of certainty and guidance.

"I am trying to figure this out," Sera mused after they had walked like this for an hour. "I believe I have most here on the march pegged for what they are, however, there are some I cannot entirely figure out."

"Have you tried, like, asking people?" Kith smirked. "Sometimes they answer. I know, it's probably a bit far-fetched for somebody as learned as you."

"Oh, stop yourself." Sera rolled her eyes. "First off, I am not going to go horsing around in the procession and making a bad impression of myself for Misandria."

"Okay, that part I get." Kith grinned.

"Second, it is a way to pass the time. So, tell me, oh savvy child of the slums. What do *you* believe the different members of our outing are here for?"

Kith rubbed his chin. "It's like that, is it? Okay, princess. Street smarts versus overpriced tutors. We take turns, and guess. Then we see what's what. I go first?"

"Be my guest." She pointed at the first small group of people accompanying the foremost wagon. It was a low-set man with a paunch, surrounded by a taller woman and two younger women in their late teens.

"Tossing me an easy target, eh?" Kith smirked. "I'll take it. Merchants. Or, rather, merchant and his workers. You can see they work for him, because they keep following his lead, asking him for advice and stuff. Also, they keep focusing on the wagons, ensuring everything's properly fastened. How's that for street smarts, then, princess?"

"Not bad. Not bad. Of course, you could have added that they are related."

"Oh." Kith's eyes darted sideways before returning to Sera. "Sure. I knew that."

"Of course you did." She nodded forward to a looser grouping, eight people walking and conversing softly. They were disparate in looks, clothing, and equipment. "The next group is both more and less complex. More, because they seem to not have much in common. Less, because they do stick together, walk together, and seem to get along."

"That's a lot of speculation and no answers."

She waggled a finger. "I am just adding the qualifiers for my answer. They are specialists and crafters who, for some reason or other, have an errand in Heart Halls."

Kith's lip quirked up. "Doesn't exactly change my comment."

She shrugged. "Well, I do recognize most of them. So that helps."

"So do I," Cilia added in. "There's a farmer, a potter, the bowyer, and that weird woman who keeps coming around Master Benneth's to talk about cloth. Definitely crafters."

Kith made a disgusted noise. "That's just cheating. Anyway. Next group." He indicated the next batch of people, six strong. Noisier, less restricted and less nervous, they were also, on the whole, more muscular. "Liam's kind of people." He winked. "Simple folk. Helpers. They're here to give a hand, carry heavy stuff and not think too much. Probably pick up a weapon if it's needed."

Liam, who'd been withdrawn throughout the entire day after bidding Ellie farewell, looked up and snorted. "You're more right than you know. I've worked with some of them. Adem there is strong and fast enough to keep you on your toes, but... let's just say, even knowing the entire village, he would lose this game. Not a thinker."

Sera acknowledged the point, and his answer, with a gracious half-bow. Then she frowned. "The next group is the one that was troubling me." She indicated four people, three women and one man, clearly walking together. "They are clearly ready for combat. Their weapons are prepared, they are aware and focused, yet they are experienced enough that they do not look nervous. All of them are wielders too. And that one's Ivar. Only, Misandria said that we would be the protection on this trip. So what is their task? I must admit I am stumped. Misandria did say that we were low on scouts, so it cannot be that."

"Oh. That's easy. They're... no-" Kith squinted, opened his mouth, then reconsidered and murmured something under his breath. "Okay, I'm not entirely sure. But I can guess. Look to the next group."

Sera followed his gaze. The next unfocused clump formed the largest of the groups. Sixteen total, they were mostly young, ranging from about fifteen to twenty, with two exceptions in their later twenties. One and all, they were in good shape, often scarred, though the quality of their equipment ranged from well-made to none at all.

Kith harrumphed. "Those have got to be the challengers. You've heard about those, right?"

"Those who decide they want to prove their worth and become wielders?"

He tapped his nose. "Spot on, princess. Look at their arms. Not a single card among 'em. Also, they're loud, prouder than a gambling Lightborn noble down on his luck, about to cause a mess."

"They have something to prove, you mean?" She raised an eyebrow. "Ah. I see where you are going. Regardless of how ebullient they are, they do follow that group in front, look to their guidance and respect their commands. Are they superiors?"

Kith squinted at her for a moment, then nodded to himself. "You're not too slow." He turned to Chase. "Good luck. We won't have to trade her in." Turning back to Sera, reveling in her scowl, he nodded. "Hadn't noticed the respect myself. They're not superiors, though. Remember Furyborn and independence? No. This is something different. Somebody back in the village mentioned something about other decks. I think this is it. About them attempting to beat the crucible, whatever that means, and earn the right to be granted cards from one of those other decks they've managed to snag from the Lightborn over time."

Sera opened her mouth in an O. "That is an excellent observation. It would explain their mannerisms and pride. Yes. Well considered. You do realize, that with a bit of book learning, you might have what it takes to become a scholar?"

Kith snorted. "Well, with a bit of naughty underwear and a flimsy dress, you might have what it takes to—"

"Kith!" Cilia smacked him over the head.

"Just saying," Kith complained, rubbing his head. "Just because I have the parts doesn't mean anything but a threat on my life would make me do it."

"It was a compliment, you dolt," Sera said, not unkindly. "Take it as it was meant."

"So was mine?" Kith laughed. "Okay, sorry. Last group? Nah. Too easy. A hunter and two cooks."

"Too true. Ah. There goes the entertainment." Sera shook her head in disappointment.

"Oh, running out of *entertainment*, are we? I seem to remember somebody saying that they needed to keep their lead in Mental Power. And somebody else claiming they would do whatever was needed to make sure they'd be able to protect us. Does that only mean when we're in actual danger? Or does it extend to when you could be *training* instead of lounging about?"

Cilia's pointed barb brought with it a handful of groans.

She didn't even register their complaints. "Now, I managed to trade Gabby a fire droplet before we left, and she showed me an exercise I believe would be good practice for most of us. Pay attention. What you do is, you focus your concentration on a mental problem. Math, language, whatever you've got that can keep yourself entirely occupied. Then, at the *same* time, you take your hand and run it through a series of exercises, like this..."

Intermingled with complaints, jabs, and laughter, the miles soon faded under their feet, as they embarked on their journey. Within each one of them there was a tiny flame. Of excitement, nerves, and elation. At long last, they were going to Heart Halls, to the center of the Furyborn lands. They would actually be able to move on with their attempt to earn Furyborn cards and eventually win a home for themselves.

Chapter 27

"Considering that they are often called savages, there are an impressive number of social gaffes you can make pertaining to the Furyborn. Most of these are eminently ignorable. The Furyborn are aware that you do not live by their creed. However, one thing to always avoid: never, ever pull rank. At best, it will lead to mockery. Often, blood." Finally, some useful advice! I think I will pen down a list of their creed and how it should pertain to your behavior. (Page 36.)

Their elation didn't last long. Truth be told, they hadn't expected it to. They entirely expected the trip to be a continuation of their scouting circle—fighting Guardians, horrible terrain, and hostile local beasts every step of the way—only, this time it would be with the added difficulty of trying to keep forty other people safe.

The actual challenge proved to be an entirely different one.

"Him! What the Pits is *he* doing here?" Chase couldn't hold back his outburst at the surprise of the person who waited on the path ahead of them. A dirty, low-set, muscular figure with a massive crossbow on his back and a constant frown on his face.

"Slate? But..." Liam groaned. "I was so sure we'd finally seen the last of him."

Cilia scowled. "Some frustrations are harder to get rid of than you hope for."

"Heh. Like that rash you got, Liam, back when you visited—"

"Kith, dammit," Liam cursed. "Why'd you have to mention that? Now, it's itching like it's back to stay."

"I hope he's not back to stay." Chase frowned. "He's talking to Misandria, though. That's bad, isn't it?"

"We are *right* here, Chase. We know exactly the same as what you do. He is done talking to her now, however. I think I will go talk to him. We might as well be aware what we are facing." Having said that, Sera strode off toward Slate with an open expression on her face.

The rest of them watched as he spotted her, waited until she joined him, and they exchanged a few terse, but civil, comments. Sera walked back to them. Outwardly, she appeared calm, but they knew her well enough to recognize that the

Lightborn had been shaken. Slate, behind her, had it even worse, looking pale like she'd punched him in the kidney.

"It is exactly what it looks like. One of two scouts allotted to the caravan is no one else but Slate."

"Well, ain't that a lovely surprise?" Liam said.

"Like a slap in the groin." Kith nodded. "So, he joined to mess with us?"

"He was quite open about it." Sera's eyes flickered to those walking closest and lowered her voice. "He believed that we were a threat to Heart Halls. With... our secrets and plots and so forth. Obviously, he knows nothing, but he suspects the worst. He *will* attempt to make our lives difficult."

"That goddamn piece of wave scum!" Chase burst out. "Just when we thought we'd gotten away from him!" He massaged his temples, pacing back and forth. "What's the plan then? Back to more of the same from our scouting trip? It's supposed be three weeks. That's going to be a *long* three weeks."

Sera exhaled. "No. We are not repeating that. Hence why I told him that we discovered what he had done on the trip. The torches and everything."

The others looked at her, stunned into silence. "You..." Kith pointed at her.

Sera blushed and looked down. "I may have overreached. However, it was a calculated gesture. Obviously, I did not tell him about our cards or *how* we learned. Only that we found him out, and that we were ready to reveal him, should he try something similar. Besides, on our circuit, he could hide behind the other scouts. Here, he is the main scout, given that Ivar is mingling with the others trying for the crucible. Everything will point to him, if he attempts something."

Cilia grimaced. "I wish you'd talked to us first. This could be bad. He might hit us with something completely new, now."

"He might," Sera admitted. "Only, I have had to deal with a *lot* of powerful people over time, seen a lot of fragile egos. Most, when challenged directly, will back down."

Kith swallowed and looked down. "My experience is that most, when challenged directly, will back *off.* Then they'll sneak over and cut the bindings on your raft when you're sleeping. I hope you're right, though."

"Time will tell, I suppose," she assented. "At the very least, he should be busy enough to stay away from the caravan most of the time."

Surprisingly, that turned out to be entirely the case. For the first couple of days, they only saw Slate sparingly in the evening, when they camped, and even then, he kept to himself, even bedding by his lonesome, away from Ivar.

Their group had plenty of time to speculate about why that was, because for once, they weren't kept busy with work or guard duty every waking moment. At first, they didn't quite understand why that was, and how come the expected clashes failed to appear.

The daily routine of the caravan was simple. They woke up bright and early, right around dawn. At that point, the cook had already been awake for an hour's time, preparing a filling meal for everybody. Following a quick meal, they spent between half an hour and an hour on prepping for departure—loading what had been unloaded back on the wagons, planning the day's journey, informing everybody what was bound to happen, and plotting their route with Slate.

Then it was off. They might have expected some sort of arguments about the order of marching, discussions, fights... whatever was apt to happen when different personalities were bound together and forced to spend every moment in close proximities for weeks on end. What they found was different. Misandria made damn sure of that. Any sort of unruliness was punished with extra duties, instantly and severely. To her, there was no hierarchy. There was simply her, and everybody else who'd fall in, or else. Independence was all well and good. Misandria was all for that, as long as independence fell in line and did what she said.

They found time for a short, cold, midday rest every day, eaten without unpacking anything. Then it was off again, constantly on the move; the slow pace nevertheless eating up miles. Following the first day, where they'd marched within the well-traveled reaches of Cemano, they'd all had spots assigned to them. Their group were to march right near the front... only, not *in* front, so as not to disturb those who knew which dangers to look for on a trip like this.

In the evening, they'd stop at pre-arranged, sporadically maintained campsites that were set up with defence in mind, granting them a good view of the surrounding area. Usually, it was something simple, like some raised earth banks. Sometimes, there were actual limited fortifications. Whatever the situation, their evenings were a mix of socializing, relaxing, and handling all repairs, maintenance, and a million other tiny tasks that accrued over a day of marching.

The first full day of marching was tense. The next one as well, though the tenseness and need to stay focused mixed with a growing sense of boredom. Following that, boredom started to dominate the mix. Nothing happened. *Nothing!*

Going west to reach the carved plains had been a harsh experience, with the punishing wind and the ever-changing climate. Going north was very different. Not only was the route easier and better maintained, the landscape did not break into the myriad rifts and canyon paths optimal for local beasts to hide, ready to ambush them. Their surroundings were generally open, with the occasional forest of crooked, hard-lived trees and flat-topped mesas dotting the plains.

As their surroundings slowly changed, they got into a discussion as to why.

Cilia was the one who came up with the initial theory. "Of course, I could be wrong, but all signs point to this. It's a layered defense of sorts."

"Like pikemen first, followed by archers and then casters? Not sure I follow." Liam frowned.

"No. That's not it," Cilia said, not unkindly. "It's like - take Isarn, right? We constantly had the army running around, and we had the local Guardians standing in line just outside the city. Why? Because they were needed to fend off the threats that kept appearing. Now, remember that tiny hamlet we passed through on our way to Earth's Ward. What was it called?" She snapped her fingers several times. "You know, the one with the *really* forgetful innkeeper?"

Liam chuckled. "Ah, yeah. Inn's name was the Broken Wheel. All-day fish stew. Only, the nearest stream must've been three hundred miles away." He shuddered.

"*That's* what you recall? Anyway, you remember how peaceful the hamlet was? One bored constable, and not a single Guardian. And how often do you think they'd see the armies of Light there? Never, that's how often." She spread her hand toward the surrounding lands. "This is what's going on here, but better hidden. Or so I think, at least."

Kith frowned and looked about. "Not sure I get your point. We haven't seen a single village since we left."

"Wrong. They don't announce their presence. But they're out there. If you look for the signs, they are there." She pointed behind her. "Half an hour ago, we passed another trail, leading east. A well-trodden one, with caarnath footprints and cleared of plants. That doesn't happen by itself. Then we have the clear signs of cultivation."

"What? Where?"

Sera laughed, before holding a hand in front of her mouth. "Apologies, Kith. But... I believe I will have to force you to learn a bit about plant life. That, right there, is a field. You can *see* the rectangular shape and the darker soil, mostly unbroken by rocks. And over there, we have an orchard. Note how the trees are planted in a line? That does not happen naturally."

"Oh. *Oh!* Yeah, I do see that!" Kith scratched his nose. "And I guess the increased number of people in the distance was a bit of a dead giveaway too."

Sera blushed and cleared her throat. "Those, *I* did not spot. Perhaps we should exchange notes."

They continued their journey, now keeping an eye out for developments to confirm Cilia's theory. In the evenings, they often spent time with some of the other travelers, relaxing and talking about their lives, their surroundings, everything. Eventually, the image became clearer.

"Why do you think we call our lands the bloodied grounds?"

Cilia was helping maintain some leather armor on some of the Furyborn traveling to obtain their cards and had eventually decided to ask them about her theories. Teaghan, the thirty-year-old hard-bitten woman with just eight and a half fingers, answered with a question, though there was no belligerence to be heard in her tone.

Cilia shrugged. "Right until now, I'd guessed that it was for the reddish-brown nuances we see in the clay here and there."

The Furyborn scratched the buzz-cut on her head and nodded. "That's part of it, of course. But it's also because Furyborn have spilled our blood for every single foot of land we've managed to guard from the Lightborn conquerors." She spat on the ground. "Exaggerating, of course. But every home, every village we have out here? It's hard-won. And with Lightborn pressing us on one side and the lost ones trying to carve out slabs of our meat everywhere else... it's less exaggeration than any of us would like."

"So, how do you manage?" Cilia scooted forward, fingers continuing their mending automatically as her gaze fixed on the older woman. "You have impressive scouts. That, I've seen. But I've been an indebted in the forces of Light. I've seen the kind of numbers they throw around. Teams of scouts, however powerful and talented, are not able to stand against that."

"Sad to say, but you're right." She grinned, revealing a mouth that had teeth missing on one side. "Standing up directly against their numbers would be a losing game. So, we don't." Her grin grew into a smirk. "But them Lightborn, they like their - what's it called - chains of command and whatnot. Lots of paper going back and forth, important people needing to accept orders before anything can happen."

"Bureaucracy?

"Yeah. That's it. Before any proper order goes out, whole towns will know about it. And we have eyes and ears everywhere. So, when they move in numbers, we're ready for them." The big woman shrugged and cursed as her own needle escaped her grasp. "Hate these tiny things. Anyway, that's just part, of course. Other part's the way we do things with our homes and towns."

"Oh. I had been wondering about that." Cilia shared her own guesses on how they handled things, keeping their defenses and military on the outside of their lines. "Is that it?"

"Well, you're not entirely off. That's probably how they'd do it among the Lightborn. We do not let everybody just dictate how to do things."

"I've noticed," Cilia said dryly.

Teaghan grinned. "Oh yeah. You probably would have. Not many would gainsay an order from the chief, or nobility or mayors or whatever they're called where you come from, right?"

"That's debatable," Cilia agreed darkly. "We had nobility, and people acted like they were in charge. Only, the ones who really called the shots were the wielders, the thugs who'd gotten a measure of power. Regardless who you're talking about, disobeying them often came with, well, bad results."

"Not so here. We take our independence seriously." Teaghan tapped the card on her left arm, showing a woman proudly brandishing a sword in defiance. "We also take our defense seriously, though. Meaning, nobody turns their back on the blood."

"I'll be honest here. I can't quite follow what this all has to do with your villages and defenses?"

"Well, it's like this." Teaghan tossed the half-repaired bracer to the side with a scoff. Then she knelt, took out her knife, and started to draw in the soil ahead of her. First, she slashed a foot-long line in the clay. "Left side, our side. Right side, east, filthy Lightborn. Follow?"

Cilia nodded, smirking.

On the left side of the line, far removed from the line itself, Teaghan carved a large circle. "Heart Halls. Most attacked city of the bloodied grounds. It's also where our best wielders stand up against the oppressors. Being allowed to join their ranks is an honor." Teaghan raised her hand, mutilated little finger and ring finger raised with the others in a gesture of patience. "I know, I know. It doesn't explain much. Patience."

She pointed back to the soil and added a bunch of smaller circles in a sort of wedge shape moving closer and closer to the "border" between the two races. "By itself," she started, "Heart Halls wouldn't be able to hold the lines against their forces.

These are all cities and villages where those who are willing to fight settle down. They each have their forces and troops, ready to act independently, harass and damage any incoming armies. Seasoned veterans, most of them, with plenty of crafted goods and support from Heart Halls."

Cilia nodded at the explanation, frowning, but did not interrupt.

Teaghan moved on, adding additional, smaller circles all the way farther up and down along the line, circling around to form a rough outer circle. "All the border cities and villages are used to conflict as well. They don't get attacked near as often as Heart Halls, and less, the farther away we get. Yet there's always *something*, be it Guardians, armies, or beasts. Cemano is a border village, sort of, only we're far from the regular routes and larger Lightborn cities, meaning, we see more Guardians than armies. Out here, you get a lot of families who want to raise their people in safety, people who're past their prime but still want to make a difference, or those who, for some reason or other, are never going to be able to reach the pinnacles of power."

The circles formed a very rough outer border encircling the entire Furyborn lands. Haphazardly, the rugged woman added cross marks all over the place behind the outer border. "These... are our safe places. Here, you can grow old. Or you can dedicate your life to crafting, or if you, for some stupid reason, think that nonviolence is the way to go." She shrugged. "They're not bad places. Good places to rest and get better. Few people want to settle down there for good, though. I grew up in one of those." She jabbed a finger at an X somewhere far north of their current position. "Of course, once I wanted to learn how to fight and do my part, I had to move to a place that matched my Step and power."

She pointed to a tiny circle, even farther south and a bit west from Cemano. "Deluge is a rough place, but a good place to challenge yourself and learn. I earned a few Steps there, even did well enough that I could visit Heart Halls, beat the gauntlet and earn my cards." She moved her finger to tap fondly on the large circle that constituted their capitol. "Eventually, I got hurt, though. Bad day, bad weather, bad judgment, bad everything." She held up her hand again, wiggling the damaged fingers, before indicating one of the crosses just north of Cemano. "So, I spent half a year recuperating. Then I needed to get back into it, which brought me to Cemano." She shrugged. "I've gotten used to fighting again with less fingers, and earned my second Tier. I think I'm ready to challenge the crucible for my pick of the Light cards."

Cilia nodded, following the explanation and the convoluted description of the woman's travels around Furyborn lands. Suddenly, she bit off a curse and sat back on her heels.

"Jab yourself?" Teaghan asked. "I do that all the time."

"No. It's just... what you've done here. Is that normal? What I mean is, didn't your family want to move with you?"

Teaghan shook her head. "Dad's dead. Mom had a close call with a squad of Lightborn casters and lost her taste for it. She's up here." Her foot lightly tapped an X almost dead center in their territory. "I visit her, sometimes." She shrugged. "Different families make different choices. Some accept the risk to follow their kids on their journey. Others follow their own path. We're all blood, though."

Cilia rubbed her forehead, trying to take in what the older woman was explaining. "You're telling me, that you've created a world where every single person moves around as they grow and develop, in order to better aid the Furyborn."

"It's how it works. Why would we want a lot of rookies on the walls of Heart Halls? That'd only lead to death. Facing off against dawn vipers and carrion gulls will much better teach them good reflexes, caution, and wisdom. Yet, having true veterans in Cemano would also be a waste. There's rarely something that can't be headed off by experienced low- and mid-Tiers."

Cilia reeled, trying and failing to explain exactly what was so crazy about this system to her. "But... that's insane. Does that mean the only constants here are the cities?"

"Of course not. They're just dirt and stone. Why would they be constant?" She scoffed. "If we have a bad outbreak of lost ones that cannot be contained by a village, we leave, wait for other villages to add their forces to ours, and then we handle it, before we can move back, or construct a new village."

"You're telling me that you will move entire villages if need be."

"Guardians. Villages. Cities. We do what the blood needs. To do anything else would mean to not be Furyborn."

"They're insane! Fire-scourged, Darkness-infested, Water-washed, Fury-rended *insane*." Cilia spat the words vehemently, but at a low enough tone that anybody outside of their own group would not hear.

Liam snuggled deeper into his bedroll, rearranging his wadded-up shirt as a pillow below his head. "I thought that was why we liked them? They're willing to go up against the Lightborn? That's my kind of insanity."

"Not. My. Point. They've actually gone and created a sort of nomadic system where everybody moves according to the demands and needs of the nation as a whole, instead of what the individual person wants. We're not just talking about moving with the seasons, which would make sense. We're talking about entire cities just packing a cart and moving if it's better for their society. And they do it *freely*, not because nobles or people in charge demand it!"

Kith yawned. "I'm not sure I understood any of that. Or why you're so upset about it. People doing things of their own volition is good, right?"

"Yes. No!" Cilia clasped her head. "It feels like they're brainwashed. Listen. If, tomorrow, they found out that a huge army of Lightborn were on the march for Cemano? Half the damn Furyborn would get up, leave their homes and move to fight them. If the battle were unlikely to be won, they'd just pack Cemano up and abandon it. Just like that!"

"That's drastic and all." Chase cracked his neck thoughtfully. "Still, I think I'm with Kith here. So what, if they're raised to think like that? Beats having nobles conscript you."

"It's... But... The scope..."

"Isn't it you who always says that we need to improve?" Liam asked. "Sounds like they've improved and you're just jealous of their efficiency."

"*That is not what is happening,*" she hissed.

Chapter 28

"There is something that does not add up. The Furyborn lands are dangerous, yes. They are in constant opposition with the Lightborn. Even so, with their numbers, and lack of proper formations, they should simply not be able to stand up to their oppressors." True. Unless, of course their entire damn populace is indoctrinated into growing as strong as possible because that is what you do! I am not getting over this! (Page 62.)

About a week into their trip, they had their own introduction to the efficiency of the Furyborn. It started with a flying beast.

Mid-morning, they were just past the point of their trek where the body had gotten its initial exercise, muscles were growing less stiff and the worst of the haze of waking up had faded. The day was proving to be a dull, gray one, with a gloomy layer of clouds providing a drizzle—light, but looking like it was planning to keep it up for the entire day.

Suddenly, a loud shout from Misandria had them all halting and preparing weapons, as they took in an approaching beast.

It was a flier. Half the length of a gaborn, it nonetheless dwarfed even their largest caarnath in length and approached with a grace and speed that a gaborn could only dream of. It was a slender creature, however, looking more like a huge dawn viper had sprouted feathers: a long beak, four long, spindly limbs, and large, bat-like wings. It descended from the gray backdrop and hovered about a hundred feet above them, before slowly diving closer.

"Don't attack. Messenger Guardian!" Misandria's shout carried across the entire caravan.

The beast hit the ground, ran a couple of steps to slow its forward motion, and then lay down on all fours like an obedient pup.

Misandria marched forward, ignoring the sharp teeth present in the flier's beak. She nuzzled its feathers, grasped at something settled around the beast's neck, twisted, and removed a small container. She read the thing, cursed, and shouted. "Challengers. Initiates. And you lot." She pointed at

Chase. "Approach. Meanwhile, Simeon. Food for this lovely thing!" She patted the Guardian with more warmth than she'd shown anybody in the caravan so far, while their cook dashed off.

Chase and his crew sprinted up to join her. They were soon followed by the veteran prospects and the young challengers who would be testing for their cards.

Misandria didn't mess about with any introductions. "We have a hostile Guardian that's gotten past the ring of outer villages." She pointed off into the distance. "It's gotten at least five people so far. The village has been evacuated. Just a few scouts remaining to make sure it doesn't go into hiding again."

Teaghan spoke up, all business. "What are we looking at?"

"Night emerald." A few shocked exclamations rang out across the group; Misandria ignored them all. "A night emerald's the apex of ambush predators. It's big, fast, silent, and practically impossible to take down because its skin is highly resistant to nearly any sort of damage."

"What can we do then?" One of the young initiates spoke up, her eyes gleaming with equal parts excitement and stark-naked fear.

"Depends. We were alerted because Heart Halls knew we were nearby and our numbers. If half of us volunteer, we should stay back. If we all go, though - once the skin of a night emerald is broken, it's as soft as any other beast. A combined barrage should be able to down it, quickly. But if you all don't think you're up for it, we will give answer, and they will pull back and gather a slower, larger force."

Chase saw Cilia's eyebrows shoot into the air as she was once again shocked at the systems of the Furyborn. This time around, so was he. They were tracking who moved where? Sending Guardians, which both had to be connected to summoners to be able to move as intellectually as this one had, and have an *insane* range to be able to fly messages from Heart Halls. "What's likely to happen if we don't go?"

Misandria shrugged. "A couple weeks wasted. They'll likely be able to take it down from afar with few issues. The village might be a loss, though, along with all provisions and a lot of equipment. Night emeralds have good senses for food and don't much respect walls. It'll tear apart the place in search of food."

Chase shared a look with the others. Inwardly, he winced. Slate had been on his best behavior, so far. No hostile whispers, no ambushes, no ugly surprises. Yet, they were still far from where they needed to be, and he'd be sure to paint any lack of proper behavior in a bad light. If they refused, he'd use it. "Count us in."

Eventually, everybody volunteered, though a few of them, like Teaghan, with her damaged dominant hand, would not participate in any ranged attacks but rather stay back in case the beast made it past the first barrage. The rest of the caravan would stay and wait for a full day, before they'd move on by themselves.

As the fighters continued onward, they shared cards, options, and tactics. Misandria and a few others also shared what they knew of night emeralds.

A scarred, low-set caster sneered as they walked. "Forget about the size. They're huge, sure, but that just makes them easier to hit. What makes them trouble is that they're nighttime predators and near invisible at night. They have a skill that makes them blend into shadows. If we can find them during the day—"

Misandria interrupted. "Oh, we can. Slate is already out there. He knows that if he messes up, his chances of joining me again are gone."

Chase cursed inwardly, but didn't say anything. If Slate were to try something, this would be a decent chance. They'd better prepare as much as they could. "How aggressive are they?"

"Mindlessly." The caster snorted. "If you catch them during the day, that's your main issue. They'll try to kill you straightaway, and won't relent until they or you are done. And since they're pretty fast and their armor is that good, you only really get one good chance to take it down. Then it's on you and about to mess up your day."

"That's brilliant."

"Yeah, it's... wait, what?" The caster stopped, looking at Chase as though he'd lost it.

"I mean it. Intelligent beasts are the *worst*. I'll take mindless and homicidal any day." Chase rubbed his hands together. He pointed at Sera, Cilia, and then himself. "We've got cards to boost my Agility and help me evade better. Then we have a few surprises on top of that to make sure the damn thing keeps its focus on me, while the rest of you take it down. Anybody else have any useful cards?"

Chase entered the village of Tibali by himself. He could see the parallels to Cemano, no discussion. The same materials—mostly wood, clay, and stone—had been used here for the construction of the housing, with a few marked differences. Especially the defenses. They had cleared the area for a few hundred feet outside the village, had a large, simple earth embankment surrounding the place, and a scout tower set dead center in the village, and that was it. Approaches weren't obfuscated like they'd been in Cemano. The village wasn't lowered into the ground to make it even harder to spot from far away. No thrice-improved city wall.

It felt eerily quiet as he crept along. His footsteps only echoed inside his mind. One of the scouts, a rogue, had a card that boosted the stealth of his approach, and it was pretty unnerving. On top of that, he kept his Heart card active.

Tibali looked as though it had been frozen in time. Like, from one second to the next, some grim feat of magic had whisked away all people, leaving everything else untouched. A ripple of clean clothes, now thoroughly dampened by rain, flapped on a line. A couple of chairs had been dragged into the streets, next to a game involving colored stones. Doors and windows were open, as if the owner'd *just* popped out to grab something.

The constant light rain and layer of light-gray clouds covering everything left the scene with a shadowy blur, like a dream; hazy and unrealistic. Chase could easily picture falling into a dream and emerging right here, wandering around, lost, until his mind resurfaced in the waking world.

Regardless of the lack of proper defenses and the weird mood, Chase found himself impressed by the village. It carried with it a sense of... care, that had been lacking in Cemano. Buildings were created with better eye for the details and for the visuals. People had crafted personal gardens with a show of flowers, added decorative touches beyond the merely practical ones. Where Cemano had been a place to stay, this was a place to *live*, to settle down and grow old, with decades of care going into buildings and gardens. He felt an unexpected pang of anger at the thought of people looking to escape the constant strife surrounding Furyborn lands *still* having their lives uprooted, simply because of some stupid Guardian looking for food and easy targets.

A hundred feet into the village, Chase found the beast's trail. What looked like a stack of firewood, inexpertly stacked, turned out to be a clutter of bones, meticulously sucked clean of any trace of flesh. Even coming in prepared, that vision left him momentarily reeling—but then he grounded himself and focused. The bones were too large to be human. Simple local beasts, or Guardians, who'd either been set upon the night emerald to cover the retreat of the townspeople, or left behind because they couldn't flee fast enough. There was a large stain of blood on the ground underneath the stack of bones, indicating that it had been killed right there. From then on, Chase stayed on full alert, cautiously moving ahead and staying in hiding where he could, even with the stealth boost.

It turned out that was entirely unnecessary. Another street down, the trail of the beast became blindingly obvious. He reckoned even Liam would have been able to follow it. He spotted a series of houses, leading all the way to the edge of the village, that had been entirely thrashed and spilled onto the street. In the other direction, a loud crash rang. Chase allowed himself a grim smile. He didn't mind the occasional stroke of luck. Now, he just needed to spot the damn thing and catch its attention.

Chase cursed his luck as he ran. He knew very well that he volunteered for this task. He didn't resent anybody for agreeing, and it wasn't like they'd lied about what he was going into. Only... maybe they could have insisted on going a bit more into detail about the damn beast! Say, explain that its sheer existence was enough to make you doubt your eyes. Or, maybe, explain the fact that it was less animal and more... no, later!

He moved on. Cursed himself for his lack of focus and set his gaze on the street ahead of him instead of thinking about the unnatural crackling, splitting, expanding and shrinking, multi-faceted dark-skinned creation of insanity rolling along behind him. One thing made sense now: how it took a lot of people to take it down. He'd planned to start out properly, give it some real damage with his Squall Sling and a fire droplet. Maybe even manage to hit it in the mouth, create a conflagration *inside* it. Wouldn't that be a nice surprise? Show everybody that he'd been able to take out the thing by himself!

A loud sound erupted from behind Chase. Something whizzed over his ear. He ducked and nearly slipped on the wet surface of the street as the bricks of half a gods-cursed wall launched into the air and crashed down ahead of him.

His experience kept him from looking back. Basic rule. Never look back. You'll just ruin your pace and risk your footing. Besides, he didn't *need* to look back to picture the twisted, mind-boggling imagery of the abomination of nature pursuing him, hard, faceted sides churning around as the only means of propelling it forward. The damn thing hadn't even *had* a proper mouth. Instead, its many sides twisted and turned, shrunk and grew, capable of tearing apart stone walls or swallow a caarnath whole, however it should like.

Chase focused on the landscape ahead of him, eyes sweeping out to find... *there!* There they were, in the distance, every single one of the others, hiding in a large shrubbery on the far side of the earth embankment. Liam stood off to the side, shield and truncheon clenched in his grip, ready to step in if things went sideways. Chase truly hoped they wouldn't. Having to take on this *thing* in close combat would be devastating.

Among the Raindrops had been active since the start, right from the second he'd released the fire droplet—failing to hit anything inside it, but very much succeeding in grabbing its attention. Unfortunately, the usually-so-effective card had entirely failed to have *any* effect whatsoever on the night emerald so far. Its faceted sides churned through the pools of liquid with all the grace of a hundred-sided carved die rolling down a hill. It might be its bulk, that it was simply too heavy to slip and slide around, or it might be something about the surface of its sides that increased its friction. Whatever the cause, the only effect his card had so far was that the layer of liquid on the beast was slowly accumulating as it stuck to its sides, building thicker and more glistening.

Chase raced up the back of the earth embankment and leapt down the other side without pause. A single, bright platform grew into being mid-air, and he hit the ground in stride, veering off to the side. "Wait for it!" he shouted, as he passed by the waiting group, running right and pacing his approach.

The night emerald continually churned forward, unstoppable, unflappable. It was fast, for damn sure. It was also unnatural, must have weighed several tons, and still aiming straight for Chase.

"Now!" His shout rang out over the cleared area, as he slid to a halt, readying his next attack.

Instantly, a singular surge of projectiles and effects flew in a concerted wave from the others. A burst of dark energy: six arrows—two glistening with some sort of effect—two crossbow bolts, and one head-sized boulder, courtesy of Liam's already prodigious Strength, increased by his Earthen Might.

A few missed. The rest impacted the hardened sides of the night emerald in a crescendo of different sounds. The crack of the boulder punctuated the assault. Yet, the attack stopped just like it had started, not a one of them continuing beyond the first. Just like they'd agreed.

Chase shouted unintelligibly at the same time as he let go of another fire droplet. It struck right at the front, where it was starting to slow down and aim its attention at the ambushers. He yelled, "Come on, you loaded-die-looking freak. *Come eat me!*"

The night emerald obliged. In a move that looked physically impossible, it shifted some of its facets and slammed down and back. A split second later, the entire bulk of a thing that must outweigh their whole group, armor and all, flew through the air, covering half the distance to him in a single, ridiculous bound.

Chase made an involuntary sound somewhere between a scream and a shout, turned around and ran for his life. Seconds later, he was pushing his speed, forcing the distance between him and his pursuer. Then, once he was satisfied that the thing didn't have any hidden reserves or ways to catch up to him all at once, he started to run in a long half-circle to lead the Guardian back to the waiting group again.

The caster had said that night emeralds were dumb. That was not an exaggeration. If anything, he was downplaying it some. The creature of ugliness and angles doggedly kept pursuing Chase to the point where one of the barrages from the waiting ambushers wasn't even enough to garner its attention. That first attack was proof of concept. The rest was simply the necessary repetition needed for getting the job done. Between downtimes, he let Among the Raindrops cool down, reactivating it the moment it was ready again.

On the second round, a few arrows found their ways into cracks between its sides. The shafts were ground apart right away, but the points still remained on the inside.

On the third attack, something cracked inside one of its facets, splitting one of the many hardened surfaces in half. Following that, and likely owing to the fact that a layer of acidic water covered its entire surface, it slowed down slightly.

Just when they were readying themselves for the fifth attack, the beast slowed down further, nearly stopping entirely. A full-body shudder ran through its bulk. Then it screamed.

Chase nearly soiled himself at that point.

It hadn't given *any* signs of even having the capability of producing sounds. Yet, the grinding, high-pitched noise rose, increasing in strength. It started forward, haltingly; yet, as it did so, it left behind two of its plates. Then, the screaming *really* started.

Once the armor started to fall off, loosened either by the slowly building effect of the acid or the increasing damage from the attacks, the liquid was able to properly enter the body within. Then, things really started taking off. The pitch built to where it became physically uncomfortable.

Chase decided to move things along. With a mental nudge, he activated A Friendly Wave. Then he grasped all the liquid gathered on the ground behind him and on the night emerald. With every scrap of concentration he had, he *pushed*, sending all the acidic water rushing toward the openings in its body. The screaming increased, as what had to be tons of water rushed to force its way inside the holes of the armored thing and burn it out from the inside.

It never moved from the spot. Thirty seconds later, the damn thing made a final full-body shudder and simply stopped. The screaming evolved into keening, then a barely audible whine. Finally, it died, deflating like a tall pillow emptied of its stuffing.

The aftermath of the battle was a happy affair. They celebrated, clapping one another's backs and shouting happily. Chase, as well, earned a lot of praise, though the Furyborn were rather subdued when they approached him. He didn't quite get that.

Kith eventually explained it to him. He slapped the half-molten plates surrounding the carcass of the night emerald, gagging at the stench that had started to emanate from it. "Mate. Look at this thing. *Look at it.* This is the stuff nightmares are made of. Like Liam, this beastie here is ugly and dangerous enough to make grown men cry. He..." Kith looked around, then realized Liam wasn't anywhere close. "Urg. It's no fun when he's not here. Stupid, sexy Liam. Anyway. You took something plucked out from a bad horror story and *made it melt from the inside.*"

Chase looked at the ground, uncomfortable. "I didn't do it by myself. I was buffed to my eyebrows and everybody helped break the shields. You think the acid would've been able to get inside this Fury-torn thing without somebody to break the plates?"

Kith pivoted from him to the deflated carcass. "Yes. Yes, I think it would have. Eventually. It'd have taken forever, and you'd be in danger of getting complacent and messing up. Of course, if you'd been able to use *some other cards*, you'd have slowly robbed it of its attributes and been able to windmill around it with a smile on your face forever... and you'd still have been able to eventually melt the damn thing to ooze. That's not my point, though." He nudged Chase with his shoulder and turned around to the others, who were discussing something in a circle, Liam beaming happily, arms all over the place with extravagant gestures. "You remember Stolothem, back on the Waves?"

"Like I'm going to forget him. I didn't even *see* what he did to Sister Emera, and I still got nightmares."

Kith flung his arm around Chase's neck. "That's my point, brother. Somebody like Stolothem? You'd be able to take him on right now, without preparation, without a damn *weapon* even, and you'd still be able to wreck him. You've gotten powerful."

"*We* have gotten powerful."

Kith scoffed. "Not my point. Point is, you've managed to do it *without* turning into a monster. That right there? There's fear in there, for sure. But there's awe too. That rogue fella with the stealth card asked me if I would ask you for some pointers on Agility training. Didn't ask you directly, though. Not because he was afraid, but because, right now, in his eyes, you've become something else. Something bigger."

"Bullshit." Chase turned to the group and watched. Only, despite his initial disbelief, he couldn't deny what he was seeing. Everybody loved Liam, obviously, because he was Liam. Except, even there, with people talking to and laughing with the brawny fighter, the adoration and friendliness was tinged with something else—a standoffishness, a distance you'd normally never see with the big lump.

He looked at the others too. Damn. That caster was there, talking to Cilia. Except his posture said it all. Slightly hunched shoulders, eyes downcast, inoffensive smile. Sera, too, had three young initiates surrounding her, hanging on her every word. Beyond them all lurked Slate, glaring at their mirth. His eyes met Chase's, boring into him with undiluted hatred. Chase blew him a kiss. He shouldn't have. It felt amazing. At least some things never changed.

There was one other person whose demeanor didn't change in the least either.

"You did what you needed to do. Now get back to the caravan. If something happens because we were dallying, congratulating each other, I will personally ensure that your lives become a trip to the Pits!" Misandria sneered, as she stepped over to the corpse of the night emerald and kicked it, hard. "Such a waste of energy. This Fire-roasted thing was dead the moment it stepped onto our lands. And with what you've done to it, those armored plates aren't fit for crafting anymore, either. A waste on all counts."

"Oh. They can be used for crafting usually?" Chase asked.

"They can. Takes talent to work with. It's somewhere between stone and leather. Malleable but somehow porous. Yet, you've seen the forces they can withstand. Also, they take rather well to magic." Another kick made one of its plates crack in two. "Doubt we're going to salvage any of this, though." She snorted. "Also, I don't care much. People from Tibali will be able to go back home, and there weren't too many people or homes lost. That's all that matters." Her growled tones softened, just for a second. "Now git, Darkspawn. You've done what I asked of you."

Chapter 29

"There is one thing I recommend. Do not learn too much about Heart Halls before arriving there in the first place. The experience should not be cheapened." What nonsense is this? The authors are the sort of people who enjoy surprise parties and filled pastries with no description. Heathens! This tome is supposed to be educational. Educate, dammit! (Page 65.)

With the astounding quantities of acid he'd been able to push into the center of the night emerald, Chase was not extremely surprised by him being the one who got credit for the kill and absorbing its Ænima. He *was* surprised to learn that he only gained a single Step from it, landing him at twenty-three. Still, any growth was growth. He immediately deposited the point into Potential, dreaming about which rarities and which insane effects he might gain when and if he reached Tier five.

It wasn't going to be on this trip, though. The rest of the march took place in utmost peace, with no monster sightings, no signs of anything untoward, not a single attack. The most adrenaline-fueled experience was when everybody with ranged weapons were buffed and sneakily ushered into a position where they'd be able to attack and take down a brace of gristle ducks—an ugly animal, that, despite its name, had some thoroughly enjoyable meat on it. They ate well that day.

Most of their group's focus during the trip was on remaining attentive despite the lack of excitement, and on their training. Whatever else was going to happen when they hit Heart Halls, they knew that they would likely have to prove themselves in one way or the other. Furyborn seemed to set a good deal of importance to people proving themselves in front of the world and your peers, and they would be *ready* for it.

They also spent a good deal of time trying to take in what they were seeing. As the miles passed beneath their soles, the landscape continually changed for the better. Gone was the wind-swept harshness of the carved plains, now but a faded memory. What grew in its place was different. Not idyllic. Nobody would ever compare the colored clay of the bloodied grounds to any sort of paradise. Yet, the place did hold a beauty to it, and the farther into Furyborn territory they came, the more the locals seemed to tease it out. Not by means of art, extravagance, or any sort of luxuries. But in that the deeper they went, the more the dwellings, villages, and cities seemed to be created in thriving symbiosis with the land.

Where earlier on, villages had been hidden away, obscured from prying eyes or anybody who might potentially be out to get them, now singular buildings started to appear—outliers and solitary persons or family. In the crook of an old, still living tree, they'd find an entire wooden building, carved, it seemed, from the tree as it still grew. A low clay hillock turned out to be a low, long hall, crafted in clay, sun playing in the subtle nuances of the clay itself. A small tree grove had been carefully maintained and trimmed to craft an inviting cozy corner, covered from the wind and rain, where their caravan could camp for the night in comfort. Everywhere they went, nature had been... nudged along, to be more accommodating and welcoming. Villages and cities were still removed from the beaten path, off where travelers wouldn't just stumble upon them by accident. Entirely on purpose, according to their Furyborn compatriots.

It wasn't just buildings that slowly went through a transformation. The roads grew wider, better maintained as they traveled. Other people started to appear on the roads—messengers, villagers, sometimes just travelers with no obvious purpose or workers toiling away. They were met with warmth everywhere, and, at the start, every other traveler spent a brief while chatting with Misandria, exchanging knowledge on the roads and surroundings.

Then, the road grew even more trafficked. Every so often, two smaller roads would meet, and the road leading on from there would inevitably be larger, with a few additional people traveling. One day, the well-traveled and maintained hard-packed clay road switched over to being paved. The others on the caravan explained that it was like this in the entirety of the bloodied grounds. "All roads lead to the Heart." Every single village, no matter how remote, was connected to the expanding, ever-changing network of roads that crisscrossed their lands. And this time of year, the roads would be even fuller, given that the next gauntlet was soon to be due.

As if in answer to this prediction, within a span of two days, the roads went from near abandoned to packed with Furyborn traveling everywhere. Yet, the vast majority of the traffic went in one direction only. Toward Heart Halls.

Three weeks, the entire trip was supposed to take. With their focus on self-improvement and Cilia constantly toiling to keep them at it, they all managed to improve, in one way or the other.

All of them focused on the Mental Power and Agility exercises Cilia had gotten them. They were, on the whole, wonderfully efficient.

Kith managed to increase his Agility. Liam hit an increase in Agility and one to Mental Power. Sera managed Agility, along with a boost to Toughness; Cilia got a single point to Agility as well. Chase managed to earn a rare increase to his already monstrous Agility, along with Mental Power and a point to Toughness—from the hard trek, he guessed.

One evening, just before they usually turned in, Misandria cut off the talented young man entertaining them all on a carved bone flute and—with a complete lack of fanfare—announced that they'd hit Heart Halls the following day and they should pack and prepare accordingly. Having said that, she tossed a sack to the nearest person and strode off to discuss something with their cook.

Their group watched in growing confusion, as the woman with the sack made the rounds to every person in their caravan. Each individual received, and was told to take care of, a small branch or sprig, still green and living.

Chase held up his own branch, completely confused. "What's this for? And what does that even mean?" Chase asked one of the young prospects. "Prepare accordingly?"

The caster, Povel, smiled and dipped his head. "You'll see tomorrow. As for the preparation, she said that in benefit to our group, really. Challengers and prospects. We're expected to prove our worth before we're allowed entry to Heart Halls. It'd be a shame to arrive with an unhealed wound, weak from an effect or something similar and fail the test. Anybody who needs more time will have to camp out here a few nights until they feel up to it."

Chase scratched his neck. "But I thought there was some time until the tests started. Couldn't you just find an inn or something, rest and prepare there?"

Povel snorted before holding a hand over his mouth. "Sorry. I sometimes forget that you guys aren't from here." He grasped at words, clearly failed, then grabbed the young rogue who was walking past them. "Cato. Help me here. He's asking why somebody hurt or unprepared couldn't just get a room at an inn to rest and prepare."

The young man's eyes widened and slid over to fix on Chase. He blinked rapidly and opened his mouth, then frowned. "He... doesn't know about the seashells?"

"He doesn't know about the seashells," Povel said with incredulity, raising his hands as if to say *Where do I even start?*

"I can see how that can be confusing." Cato tapped his lip, then said, "How have you paid for anything in Cemano?"

Taken aback, Chase frowned. "We... haven't. We've offered our help wherever we could, but people kept giving us stuff, just like that. Nobody's ever asked for money."

"That's because we don't *use* money."

Still frowning, Chase shrugged. "Sure. Cilia guessed at that after a while. I guess that's kinda normal in villages. I don't see—"

"No." Cato interrupted. "*We*—the Furyborn—do not use money."

Chase took a step back, glared at the young rogue. "That—" He sat down, feeling as if somebody'd slugged him around the head. "What? No. What?" He cleared his throat. "Repeat that to me. The *entire*. Liberty-forsaken. Furyborn. People. Do not use money. Is that what you're trying to tell me? Because I do *not* like being made a fool of."

Povel held a hand over his heart. "On the blood, I swear. Sure, if we take down some Lightborn who have money, we send it on to Heart Halls. The merchants there use it to buy things that we all need, to be divided out into our lands. But why would anybody need money on the bloodied grounds? We take care of our own. If a hunter needs help tracking down an elusive prey, Cato will help. If somebody needs help burning away brush for an expansion, my card can do the trick. And if Cato and I need to have our clothes mended, or get something to eat... why would we hunger or walk unclothed? The blood takes care of our own."

Chase just blinked, as everything he knew about everything was undermined. "Listen. No. Besides, what would that have to do with seashells?"

Povel snorted. "There are a few tests to tell if you're ready to be initiated, or face the challenges. The seashells are one of them." He grunted. "Listen. I get it. This may be weird to you. But it makes sense. I don't have any family in Heart Halls. If I just run around the place, somebody'll need to feed me. And why should they do that if I don't have a shot at the crucible?" He shrugged. "As long as I pass the tests, there are places that will open their doors to me, keep me fed and warm until the actual gauntlet."

"And if you can't handle the crucible? You're cut off and nobody'll feed you?"

Now, Povel started to look outright offended. "No. Then I'd starve. You think my people would let me starve? Why... Listen. Why would I risk the crucible if I wasn't ready? Those tests are there for a reason. If I were to try anyway, I'd just get myself killed or injured. Then, I'd be a burden on healers and others for even longer, until I got better again. No. I do my part. I've already proved myself once, passed the gauntlet. And when I enter, soon, I'll pass the initial tests, then I'll prepare myself for the real crucible and hopefully be able to earn another set of cards for me. Five years from now, I could be a defender in Heart Halls."

Chase spent a moment trying to take it all in. He failed, massively. Then he went back to the others to complain.

"So that's why I have to conclude that all the Furyborn are Liberty-forsworn, Water-logged, Light-blindedly *insane*. Any questions?" Chase finished, panting from the rant.

Liam yawned. "Are you going to let me sleep any time soon?"

Sera, holding a hand in front of her mouth, *very* nearly hiding her amusement, added, "Did it feel good to get that out?"

"Y'know, actually, it did!" Chase ducked his head and spread his arms wide. "But seriously. Can you believe it?"

Cilia slowly nodded. "Actually, I can. Consider the situation. The Furyborn, as a whole, are extremely united. I know, I know, independence is part of their creed, but it is still independence *within* the greater ruleset they operate by."

Liam squinted. "If you're going to insist on keeping me up... I'm not sure I get it. Are you saying that even if Furyborn won't let anybody throw orders left and right, because of the whole independence thing, everybody still tries to follow the creed?"

"That's *exactly* what I'm saying!" Cilia shot a rare smile at Liam. "Back on the Waves, nobody gave a crap about what the Lightborn were spouting about bettering yourself and growing strong in order to reap the benefits you'd earn, because we knew it was a lie." Her lip curled up in a sneer. "Or, at best, a truth that only benefited those with funds or born into 'proper' families. But still, there, young Lightborn learned that you should work for those in charge because it'd benefit yourself. Here? They all learn that you should work for the sake of the greater good, because that includes yourself."

Chase cocked his head, mulling it over. "It feels like we've gotten pretty far from the part where I said there's no money here."

"We really haven't. The only reason they would have been able to implement a system where there's no money is that it isn't what's worth striving for here. *They don't care about money.* They care about growing stronger, helping others and bettering themselves, because working for the common good and contributing as much as you can *is* the point here. Oh, sure, you're bound to find a lot of people who aren't entirely altruistic, but since there's people everywhere who're ready to call out anybody who tries to mess with the system, if you try to be too selfish, the system's going to come crashing down on you."

"Huh," Kith said thoughtfully into the evening sky, bedroll pulled right up under his nose. "That means the vast majority of everybody is either going to work as hard as they can to help their neighbors and everybody else because they truly believe in it, or... what?"

"Find a smaller village out of the worst war zones and make a decent living for themselves there, I guess." Cilia shrugged. "That way, the pressure won't be too bad, and everybody around them are still going to ensure that they contribute to the system and to Furyborn on the whole."

"That's a whole lot of words just to agree with me that they're insane." Chase laughed and placed his own bedroll on the soil. "Okay, fair enough. Maybe not insane. The system works. That's pretty obvious. It's just weird. No money, except for what they might find on invaders, and Povel said they're sending that to Heart Halls for the merchants to use anyway. What does that change for us? I mean, except for the fact that we aren't going to be able to use what little money we have to buy items."

Sera nodded appreciatively and placed her own bedroll next to his. "Honestly? Very little, I would say. What we intend to propose should already work in favor of the Furyborn as a whole. Hopefully, the High Elementalist has framed her message as such. It really only cuts down on the use of underhanded methods in reaching our goals."

"But I *love* underhanded methods," Kith complained. "It's what I do best."

"I know you do, sweetie. I know you do." Sera smiled. "Now, there is no way that we are fortunate enough to be simply granted what we desire. While it would be refreshing for them to simply grant us Furyborn cards and offer support, I cannot see it happening." A series of snorts and eyerolling were the only response. "However, as long as we continue in the vein we already have, are honest and forthright and work for the betterment of everybody, we shall succeed in our endeavors."

Kith pulled his bedroll all the way over his head. From underneath, his muffled voice said, "Chase. I blame you for bringing her in. She's sucking *all* the fun out of life!"

Chapter 30

"It all boils down to one defining battle. The Siege of the Halls. Picture this. The Furyborn once ruled the entire known western divide in relative peace with the other aspects. For years upon years following the Church of the Circle ousting the Darkborn clergy, this changed, until they were forced back to this one stronghold. The entirety of the Furyborn resistance, defending from the Lightborn armies. Only, back then, they were not called Heart Halls." Really. I find that hard to believe. A single stronghold, somehow able to stand up against the entire damn Lightborn force? (Page 72.)

"**W**hat is this?"

Chase's question went unanswered. He turned around to see that his crew shared his confusion, all as one staring at the landscape in front of them with equal parts disbelief and wonderment.

A group of the challengers and prospects from their caravan passed them by. Povel chortled and halted, patting Chase on the back. "Glorious, isn't it? Of course, I knew about it when I first came here, years ago. Knowing about it and seeing it are two different things, though."

"Sure, sure." Chase nodded amiably. His voice didn't quite break. "Just one tiny question. *Where are the Lights-damned halls?*"

Povel doubled over laughing. "You know, I heard about the defenders of the Halls fighting to get put on scout duty, just so they can take in the reaction of newcomers. I never quite believed it, but now I see it!" He waved his hand at the landscape beyond. "These *are* Heart Halls. The halls at the heart of the bloodied grounds. Our roof just isn't tiled like a lot of guests expect."

That was quite the understatement. They'd gotten up with the sun and crested a large hill to greet the view in the morning sun. What spread out ahead of them was, exactly as stated, not a tiled roof. Instead, it was a roof of leaves, covering a massive forest that stretched off into the distance, as far as the eye could see. With the green and brown nuances forming a never-ending carpet of movement, distance and sizes were hard to discern, but the individual trees looked absolutely massive, at least compared to the scrawny growths that Chase knew from their journeys around Isarn. "Okay. I'll admit it. You got us, man.

Good joke. So, we have to waltz through a huge forest before we get to Heart Halls."

"Nooo," Kith slowly drawled. "Look closer, mate. There's buildings and stuff in between the trees. I think these *are* the Halls."

Chase looked closer and did indeed spot wooden buildings and clay walls here and there in between trunks. He blinked as he had to revisit his initial estimates of the sizes. Either some of these buildings were tiny, or the trees were hundreds of feet tall. Was that an earthen wall stretching in between tree trunks to create a weird, winding wall? "Nah. That can't be, Kith. Because the Furyborn are a lot of things, but they aren't dumb. They wouldn't place the heart of their power, their vaunted defensive stronghold at risk of being erased by a single Lightborn with a grudge and a torch."

Povel slapped Chase on his back, wiping tears from his eyes. "This is better than when I earned my first card. Thanks for being such a good sport about it. Come along, I'll tell you the story as my mom told me."

In front of them, Misandria and the others were already ranging ahead, following some unseen path along the downward slope and into the forest beyond. Their group crowded around Povel as they started their own descent.

The caster preened at the attention, his rough voice booming with mirth and pride as they walked closer to the trees. "You ask anybody who's most important in the history of our kind, you'll get a lot of different answers, depending on class and temper. Lot of ranged adore Awelia, the Ever Arrow. Plenty of chieftains and summoners are going to say we owe our lives to Body-As-One—that's the chief who invented the system we have with our Guardians and figured out how to train them and make it work. Me, I've always been partial to the stories about Nerissa, or Earthsea, as they called her. Without her control of nature and our soil, we'd never have been able to adjust our grounds and stand against such overwhelming numbers as those we've faced."

"Except, unless you're going to explain how a *forest* of all things is your central defense, none of those people seem to be part of the explanation." Chase frowned.

Povel laughed again. "You're not wrong. Okay. The Acorn and the Root. The way I've heard the story told is that the Acorn was an unassuming man. A crafter, with a wonderful connection to nature and a lot of dedication to his craft, but little else. He'd spent his time on the front lines and earned a good deal of cards. Only, his true talents weren't even noticed for the first long part of his life. His life partner, the Root, was the chief of their city, and the one who got all the attention—a stalwart defender, hard as nails."

His mirth died down. "We'd been losing for a long time. Year after year, we'd been pulling back, erecting strongholds only to lose them to the overwhelming Lightborn armies. Our couple here were far behind the lines of defense to begin with, only, as our forces were slaughtered all across the bloodied ground, the front of the war eventually reached their home. Entire armies marched along, ready to trample their city and continue to end our kind once and for all. That was when the Lightborn learned what real resilience looks like!"

Povel glowed with pride. "The Acorn and the Root, it turned out, had not been idle. For years on end, they had been cultivating and growing a forest. Not like you see it today. It was a young forest, saplings and small trees, with the buildings of the Halls much easier to spot, the defenses less developed. There were people everywhere, however—entire cities' worth of less combative Furyborn displaced and moved back as the fronts moved."

The caster turned around as they walked and indicated the higher ground they'd just vacated. "Picture this. Every single one of these hills, covered with Lightborn soldiers, indebted in their thousands, along with plenty of high-Tier wielders, strengthened from years of slaughtering the blood. Many of them back then even had Furyborn cards, from all the decks lost to battle, treason, or torture." He turned around and faced the large forest again. The scent of the greenery carried with it a sense of life, of energy. "Now imagine this place, only there were maybe a fourth of the trees, the largest of them reaching perhaps twenty-five feet of height. It looked a lot less sparse. The armies could just roll in and over us." He smirked. "At least, that's what they thought."

He gestured animatedly with both hands, indicating movement from everywhere on the hills all converging on the forest. "They came in their thousands. At first, they didn't even bother to properly amass their armies for an efficient strike because our defenses looked that weak. Then... they disappeared." Povel shook his head in amazement. "Every child born on the bloodied grounds have heard dozens, hundreds of stories from that first clash. Yet, what it all boils down to is that the Lightborn soldiers were caught out. When they attacked, they failed to see what they were up against. That first conflict became a slaughter, and the trees were watered with blood. Lightborn blood. They tried to overwhelm us with numbers and failed. They tried to torch us out, and failed. Nature itself rose and swallowed them."

"This is the part where you tell us the trick," Cilia said. "This Acorn of yours has to have done something massive in order to manage that."

Povel nodded. "It's not a trick. But it *was* massive. The Acorn, through a very specific combination of cards, managed to obtain some unique powers. Namely, that he was able to permanently displace powers from Furyborn and give them to the trees. With the Root as an in-between to properly explain it to people, for years, they convinced numerous wielders lying on their deathbed or ready to lay down their arms after a lifetime of strife to instead sacrifice their amassed powers to the trees. Oh, and even back then, we had strong enough casters to protect the forests from fire."

They stood, stunned. Nobody said anything or even made any sound, as they tried to wrap their minds around the enormity of that claim.

Finally, Kith said hoarsely, "Are you trying to tell me that all those trees down there are Light-scoured *wielders*?"

Povel fended off the idea with raised hands. "No. That's not how it works. However, depending on the wielder and their powers, the trees *are* imbued with certain powers derived from their Tier and cards. Oh, and before you ask—outsiders tend to ask that—nobody lays down their lives. They can still live out the rest of their lives in peace. They simply give up their cards, for the good of all. Communion can be a hard choice, and is irreversible, but it is bloodless. And it is what has granted us our living trees."

"So... what's it do? And is that why we all have a tiny little tree friend?" Chase raised his own branch.

"Spot on, my friend." Povel laughed. "That branch will identify you as a friend. The alternative is ugly." He shrugged. "I have only been here once, and I have never been in any battles... but the capabilities of the living trees are supposed to be very different. Some actually *do* move, flailing and striking with their branches, grasping with their roots. Others bestow powers on Furyborn or other trees, manipulate the soil or smaller plants, command wildlife. Some even heal. The variety is too long to tell, and only those fighting for Heart Halls hold something approaching a full list."

Drily, Kith added, "Also, asking too many detailed questions as an outsider is pro-ba-bly frowned upon."

Povel bowed his head in assent, tapping his nose.

Sera, meanwhile, stared at the forest with an awestruck gaze. "This means that the Furyborn, for years upon years, have allowed this forest to grow, and had your people retire their powers into the embrace of the land?"

"I like the sound of that. You have a way with words, lass. And yeah."

"Light above." She breathed. "No wonder the Lightborn paint you all as maniacs. If they enter your forests, and have no idea if the trees will hold hidden enemies, will heal your enemies, or reach out and tear you apart..." She expelled her breath in a long, whistling wheeze.

"Hasn't stopped them from trying, of course." Povel smirked. "Well, for the first many years. We haven't seen any takers the last dozen years or so. Nowadays, they tend to prod the rest of our lands for weaknesses, which just shows they aren't *complete* morons."

Chase considered the idea, nodding along. Of course they wouldn't try. If the forest was resistant to fire, and the Furyborn retirees would continue sacrificing their powers to the cause—which he did not doubt for a second—it was no wonder that the forest had grown as massive and intimidating as it had. "Okay. Should we just enter then? Or is there something we need to do as outsiders?"

"Step onward, brother," Povel said. "Heart Halls awaits."

At first, Heart Halls seemed to be a massive misnomer. The heart part made sense, of course, given that a lot of people had extracted that closest to their hearts to feed the powers of the trees. As they walked among the outermost, solitary younger trees, the second part was well-hidden. Within the next hours, however, the logic slowly came to light.

They soon realized that the trees were not just organically grown. Each tree, oaks and birches mostly, had a good deal of distance surrounding it, yet the crowns of the trees joined above, close enough to conjoin their branches and create the illusion of a roof above, which still, in most places, allowed subtle sunlight to peek in from between the canopy above. That, along with the silence in the relative lack of undergrowth, allowed for a somber sensation, as if they were walking hallowed halls. Hallowed halls which, at any time, might take umbrage with their presence, reach out and rend their flesh...

Recognizing living trees was an art form. As they walked, they started to debate which trees had entered communion and which hadn't. Povel, as the unbiased judge, settled their discussions. They soon realized that there *was* something to set the trees with powers apart from the rest, though it was hard to define. It was slightly, but not exactly, like the infinitesimal glow surrounding Lightborn people, which could only truly be seen in pitch darkness. Eventually, Cilia settled the matter by calling it an aura of vitality, which seemed to fit the bill. Living trees just seemed more alive, more vibrant, even if the color scheme was the exact same.

After a while, they saw constructions interspersed between the trees. Some were unobtrusive and hard to spot, like the occasional archery platform, while others, like the earthen walls they'd spotted from the distance, were disruptive, forcing them to change their route. Soon, these walls grew in presence, and they realized that this was entirely on purpose, creating a labyrinth of sorts where any potential invader would have to run back and forth in tangled routes to keep intruding, forcing them past a great many different trees.

They spotted defenders, too. Not many. Whatever else was needed to become an official defender of Heart Halls, apparently a great deal of camouflage knowledge seemed to be part of it. The first time Chase spotted a pair of unblinking eyes staring from between a leafy patch of the canopy thirty feet above, he almost wet himself. From then on, he spotted them here and there—unblinking, unflinching, silent, and, frankly, intimidating as the Pits.

A couple of hours in, their surroundings changed slightly. Not the forest. It remained a presence of widely distanced trees. Also, the paths kept winding, these older earthen embankments overgrown with grass and mosses. It would appear that they kept adding further defenses as the forest expanded, forcing any attacker to have to make their way through a seemingly endless series of defenses and detours. However, in here, the defenders were farther between. Instead of that, the city itself appeared.

There was no obvious limit or point. Yet from one moment to the next, they spotted a building nestled between two huge oaks—a nice, wooden home large enough for an extended family. Outside the building, racks held drying meat, and a stone oven gave off an aromatic scent.

That was the first of many. From then on, slowly, Heart Halls unveiled its center. The bright-green halls with the solemn mood slowly grew warmer with the noise of people running about, tending to their daily business.

"How the Pits do you find your way around in here, mate?" Chase asked Povel. "I can find my way around in a city, but this isn't a city. 'Go left at the tree and then right at the third tree' doesn't exactly feel like it'd be easy."

"You ask." Povel grinned. "A lot. I'm told it gets easier, but I'm not sure I buy it. Memorizing the specific buildings helps. Of course, once we get deeper toward the center, the buildings grow more... memorable."

"I'll take your word for it." Chase huffed. "I'll take a normal city any day over this." A slight breeze caressed his face and he ducked, glancing about nervously and seeing nothing. "Erm. No offense, tree."

The security checkpoint was more checkpoint than actual security. That part made sense, of course, given all the layers of security they'd already navigated. Really, it was more of an extended, massive table set in the center of a clearing, with a bunch of people waiting to attend to any newcomers.

Misandria's caravan was halted and the caravan guide unceremoniously launched into a discussion with one of the people behind the table. What followed was a brief, unemotional split, as their grouping was carved up into several smaller groups, allotted a local to guide them to where they were going and immediately sent off, one group after the other. With the exception of a single cart, all the carts stayed near the checkpoint, with no-nonsense locals already going through and debating over the contents.

Chase and his crew were among the last to be allocated.

Their guide, Lassenta, was a spry, older woman, wearing a dark-gray, short-sleeved leather shirt, showing off her cards. Chase couldn't help his gaze from slipping to her arms. Both showed cards, yet the cards were not vibrant and life-filled like regular cards, but a gray, dull imprint, as if charcoal sketches of actual living, active cards.

"You can ask, young'n. I don't bite. Besides, it's like that with every newcomer."

"I'm sorry." Chase introduced each of them in turn. Then he chuckled and went for it. "I'm sure it's annoying as hell, but I *am* extremely intrigued. Have you given over your cards to the forest?"

"Communed." She nodded. "Wasn't a tough choice. We all know it'll help the forest protect us and keep those damn Lightborn from killing us all—no offense, hot stuff." That last part was in the direction of Liam, along with an incredibly saucy wink. "But it's true. When I gave my cards—my essence—over? It wasn't a one-sided thing. I got something back. Not in the means of power or anything like that—I still have my attributes, even if I'm growing weaker with age—but I got a sense of... belonging, in return. Of peace, of affinity with these old, gnarled woods. Heh. Of course, that might just be because of my own gnarled old limbs." She patted the trunk of a tree as she passed it, with something like real fondness in her gaze.

Lassenta led them on through the forest. Increasingly, their path crossed that of other people, and regular homes and buildings showing signs of belonging to one craft or another increased in number. It never became industrial or officious like the trade district in Isarn. Even at its busiest, Heart Halls felt like a gathering of like-minded people who'd come together to handle a few things that needed doing—and the best place to meet just so happened to be in the middle of a forest village.

Some things beggared belief. At one place, loud clanging introduced a smithy that had been erected at the core of a living, thriving oak. The massive roots swept up like the tentacles of a monstrous octopus, and, by all rights, Cilia insisted that the heat emanating from the forge should have killed off any life within the branches and torched everything. Yet, the tree towered high above, providing the perfect airy shelter for the thickset woman toiling within.

Once, loud rustling preceded something gargantuan swaying along in the background. The spread-out trees prevented them from seeing exactly what was there. However, the half-seen vision had Chase gaping and doubting his mind. A walking, twenty-foot-tall tree was not out of the realm of possibility. Not in this place. However, the single Furyborn ensconced *within* the crown of the tree, as if she were the head of the creation? That was something out of this realm. He turned to Lassenta to ask.

In response, the old woman cackled and winked. "Leave us some secrets, kid."

As they followed their guide, she led them unerringly in the wanted direction, though it soon became clear that their goal was nowhere near. Kith asked, and Lassenta laughed in response. "You afraid of a little walk, son? You shouldn't have come to the halls, then! Everything's far here!"

They took a short break after a few hours, with Lassenta calmly waiting for them to eat a bit of hard-crusted bread. Then they continued, as did the never-ending expanse of forest.

Finally, at a vague guess, following a five-hour march since their start at dawn, the terrain did change somewhat.

With a self-satisfied smirk, Lassenta strode ahead of them, onto a short earth knoll and gestured at the sight behind her. "Welcome—to the Heart."

Chapter 31

"Want to tick off a Furyborn? Deign to disparage Heart Halls. The adoration that they lend to their central home is nothing short of mythical. Mess with it at your own risk." Yeah. That Acorn fellow managed to save their entire race. No wonder they are attached to the place. (Page 70.)

It was a city. *The* city. In front of them lay the city that had once been the foundation and salvation of the entire Furyborn race. It had to be. For one, the place showed no sign of being erected, like the rest of the place they'd seen, in a form of symbiosis with nature. There stood a wall. An actual city wall, not some amalgamation of clay and magic. Beyond lay streets—slightly chaotic and unplanned in the Furyborn way, but still, regular streets—with houses cheek by jowl with one another. For another, the trees right on the outside of the walls were enormous. Ridiculously so, and gleaming with eldritch power from within.

The city itself wasn't huge. Neither did it look anything special. In actuality, it looked more like they'd taken Cemano, minus the whole 'hiding the place within a huge depression' part, and expanded it by two or three times. Also, it felt off.

"Lassenta? Is this really it? I mean, people have built it up for a while. I have to admit, that I expected something bigger." Chase shrugged apologetically.

"You're not the first to say that, son." She smiled. "They've kept the place pretty much unchanged. To show everybody where we came from. Now, stop gawking. We'll have to go see if Half-Swart has time for a bunch of outsiders carrying heavy mysteries."

The city unfolded before them. Again, there was little to set the place apart from Cemano. There were no luxuries, no ornate adornments on the buildings. If they had to point out one thing that made the place stand out, it would be the people. Every single person crossing their path was a wielder, or a former wielder. Arms, and the occasional legs, sported cards as a testament to the presence of a large number of high-Tier people. Also, they were alert and looked to be in amazing shape and almost uniformly well-equipped. Cilia gawked at some of the creations people wore—light on ornamentation, but gleaming with innate magic.

Eventually, they made their way to where they needed to go. It was not what they'd been expecting, at all.

"This is like a mess hall. It's like... no, it *is* the exact same as that communal place in Cemano, just a lot bigger. I think they even have the same giant cook pot." Kith gawked, pointing at a large pot, where a low-set and wide, bald, mixed-race cook was stirring the pot and occasionally spooning out solid servings to people arriving.

Chase patted Kith's shoulder and followed Lassenta. He spoke to Kith over his shoulder. "Not as fancy as the High Elementalist's own quarters, is it? Still, we knew these folks aren't fans of fancy. I, for one, enjoy that they're so down-to-earth."

"I guess." Kith shrugged, as he shook himself out of his reverie and followed along. "I'm guessing that's our guy?" He pointed to a table near the far wall, where a near-dozen of heavily armed people were listening to a slab of a Furyborn, the first they'd seen in ages with actual metal armor, and an axe leaning against the wall behind him that was about the size of Sera.

Lassenta snorted, then she grabbed a clay bowl and spoon from a stacked pile and gestured for them to do the same. She led them to the cook, talking all the while. "He's busy right now. We'll eat first. That way, we won't have empty stomachs growling to interrupt the conversation. So, what do you know of Half-Swart?"

Cilia was the first to find her words. She nodded at the cook and took an appreciative sniff of the contents of the bowl. "Honestly? Very little. You Furyborn do not exactly let a lot of information about your home and people spread out past your borders. There're a few details I've read in this tome that lead me to believe he's an absolute terror on the battlefield. Apparently, he's changed the course of several battles by himself."

Kith looked behind Cilia to the armor-wearing fighter, who was now pounding the table, roaring with laughter. The massive wooden table shook from the impact. "I can entirely believe that. He looks like a terror. Doesn't look too bright, though."

With her spoon in her mouth, Cilia reached back and slapped him. "Behave. It's not like you're the epitome of learning yourself."

The cook barked with laughter as he ladled a serving to Liam, then looked at him and topped up the bowl. "New here? Wait. No need to answer. It's not that hard to tell." He leaned forward with his hands on the table, which was spattered with spills from the thick, deep-brown stew and stage-whispered,

"You're not wrong, though. He's not the brightest spark in Ordei." He grimaced at the stew on his hands, and wiped them on his already much-abused apron.

Chase chortled as he held out his own bowl, but it turned into a half-choked noise along the way. He took in the cook. *Really* took him in. The middle-aged man was part Darkborn, like himself, and part Furyborn. The dusky tones to the skin weren't easily spotted behind the warm, earthy color, and his bald head didn't betray anything. The heavy beard was dark, with a bit of gray growing into it. Also, where most Darkborn were lithe, this man was almost impossibly wide, though he stood well below even Chase in height. Only, the tilt to his ears were a dead giveaway. "No!" he exclaimed. "I honestly think you're wrong. I think this Half-Swart is a bit of a sneak, trying to catch newcomers off-guard, gauge their behavior before they're officially introduced."

The cook's laughter rang out even louder. Then he brushed up one sleeve to show off a card, ringed with the thorns of a Furyborn deck. The card was simple, in brown tones, depicting a man, screaming defiance, in front of a large mountain. The skin beneath, however, was clearly that of somebody with Darkborn blood. "Well, you got me there. I guess the 'Half-Swart' part of things is a bit of a giveaway." He gestured at his ears and winked at Chase. "I do like to see the difference in people's behavior before they approach me officially. Tells you a lot about them, really—the difference when they think they're dealing with underlings and the leaders. Especially when there's Lightborn among 'em." He raised an eyebrow. "No offense, eh?"

Sera laughed. "If you are looking for the regular snobbishness of Lightborn nobility, I am afraid we will have to disappoint. I used to be a noble, and I have long despaired of teaching this band any manners. If anything, their unruliness has worsened."

Half-Swart's eyebrow rose even higher and stayed. "And your own manners, miss..."

"*Much* deteriorated as well. I apologize. I am Serafine. Formerly de Valerian. Now, a member of this merry gang of fools." Her hand reached out to settle on Chase's biceps. "I would not have it any other way."

"Huh." He let his gaze roam appraisingly over them. With a brief nod, he said, "All right. I've been told that you have a delivery from Tatiana Skysworn. You guys sit down and eat your brown, then we'll go to my home. Lassenta, you mind taking over duty for me here?"

The old scout snorted. "Suddenly you're all business, eh, Half-Swart? You usually prefer it when you can string 'em along for a while longer." She waved his denials off. "Of course, I'll take over. As long as you get that filthy apron away from me. That's just a disease waiting to happen."

They sat down to eat in a half-tense mood, with Half-Swart joining them, asking about their journey from Cemano. He nodded good-naturedly and asked follow-up questions here and there. That he asked directly about the night emerald before they mentioned it themselves didn't pass them by—clearly he'd been prepped on them and their endeavors.

Finally, they finished and he guided them toward his house. It was a small house, clearly for a bachelor, with everything about his existence spelling out that there was but one person living there. The only details to make him stand out from any other Furyborn they'd met were a set of leather armor on a rack—much-used but well-cared for, and gleaming deeply with bright energy—and a side room with a table and benches large enough to seat around twenty people.

Half-Swart rummaged around in a cupboard beside his bed while he told them to sit down and take their packs off. The wide man sneezed and emerged with a dusty bottle and a wooden contraption that looked somewhere between a tinkerer's challenge and a child's toy. Once he wiped it down, they could see a weird creation with interlocking wooden wheels, metal wiring, elaborate runes, and a circular hole in the front. He set it down on the table in front of them and went off to pick up a handful of small tumblers, which he also placed on the table. He cracked his knuckles. Then he uncorked the bottle and poured a measure into each tumbler. A smell of flowers, honey, and summer filled the room. With a satisfied sigh, he sat down across the table from them, took a tumbler for himself, and raised it. "First things first. Welcome to Heart Halls. May you survive your stay."

Uncertain, they took a tumbler each and drank.

Kith made a sound almost like a purr deep in his throat. "That's like honey, but for my soul. What *is* it?"

"Local mead. The brewer's a Tier three crafter, and a damn fine one at that. Enjoy the side effects." Half-Swart chuckled.

Chase checked his attributes and noted that his physical attributes were all increased by three points. He whistled softly. "We appreciate the welcome. Erm. *May you survive your stay?*"

"Heh. It's an older greeting. In the first years of the Halls, any Furyborn visiting knew that they would be in danger, because of constant raids, attacks, barrages, and whatnot. It's not as fitting anymore, but I still like it."

Kith put a finger into the tumbler to extract the final drops. "Me too. It's simple and easy. I also like the mead! Beats a long-winded speech."

"Kith!" Sera scolded.

Half-Swart laughed. "A man of my heart. If you'd been welcomed by any of the other leaders here, especially Naian, you'd get all the speeches you wanted. However, since you say you come from the Elementals, you get to talk to me, and I prefer mead. Besides, speeches aren't going to change what the core of this meeting is about. You come from the High Elementalist, you say?" He steepled his hands and leaned forward to face them intently.

Sera nodded stoically. "We do. And we carry a message for you. I... am not sure how this works. However, she insisted that we let her start the introductions, before we talk about what we have in store and what it could mean for the Furyborn." She pulled out the wooden peg from her pack and held it toward him.

He grunted appreciatively. With a hand, he indicated the wooden contraption he'd extracted. "Former High Elementalist made this. Tier six. A crafter, she was, and ridiculously talented, back from when the first unofficial agreements between the Furyborn and Elementals came into being."

"I thought you didn't *have* any agreements. From what I've read, that's pretty much the backbone behind the peace treaties between the Elementals and the Lightborn?" Cilia frowned.

Half-Swart waved a massive paw of a hand dismissively. "I did say unofficial, didn't I? Listen, everybody knows that the peace deals between Lightborn and Elementals are more proof of the stalemate between them, than any actual desire for peace. *The Lightborn have attacked the Elementals for decades on end.* How are you going to call that peace?" He shrugged. "They bicker and change tiny details in their agreements, but the peace is there in name alone, until something changes. *Of course* the Elementals have been talking to us. We're the same as them, only our fight is more out in the open."

Cilia, frown slowly lifting, started to nod as he talked. "And you can't make any peace talks between them and you official, because it would damage what good the Elementals do derive from the agreement." She paused and grimaced. "Why tell us this?"

The wide man shrugged. "I recognize this. It's definitely from Tatiana, meaning I can trust the contents to be real, to a certain extent. Also, if you *were* trying to do some damage here, you'd have to find something different. It's not like the Lightborn aren't aware that we communicate. They're not dumb, you know." He grinned. "If they had something tangible to prove that the Elementals were trying to stab them in the back, maybe it'd change a bit... but then again, not that much. You think they'd let all those smugglers travel from Earth's Ward to the Halls and back otherwise? Nah. They keep up enough defenses that it doesn't cost too much, knowing that those traders aren't going to be able to affect the situation, and they try to beat us into submission. Nothing much ever changes, though." He lapsed into a momentary silence, before noisily clearing his throat.

"All right. This thingy. They are paired devices. Tatiana has one; we have the other. You can record and play voice messages on them, and nobody else is able to listen in. They're tiny wonders. The real wonder is that the messages themselves..." He tapped the wooden peg on the table. "Aren't magical. Only the devices themselves. Meaning, you can give them to anybody you trust, and as long as they know how to operate them, they can work them without magic, anywhere. Any final comments?"

Disregarding the ambiguity of that statement, they shook their heads.

Half-Swart slowly inserted the peg into the hole in the contraption. Then he let his fingers play in a deft sequence across the surface and side of it. Instantly, the cogs started to spin. A few seconds later, the voice of the High Elementalist appeared from within the device, as clearly as if she were sitting right next to them. They all sat back, listening intently.

"Greetings from Earth's Ward, dear Half-Swart. This is a message of two parts. The second half will contain the usual information. Offers for trade and purchases, information on troop movement, Lightborn changes, and some pertinent information on their latest attempt to steal our original Elemental Deck."

The wide man blinked and tapped the device again. The message stopped. "They did what now?" he growled.

Chase answered. "Well. That's at least a good part of why we're here in the first place, and not hiding out in the towers. I think she's about to explain."

Half-Swart glared at him for a moment, as if trying to figure him out. Then he tapped the device again, and her voice resumed.

"This first half, however, is going to cover exactly why I have let the largest chance of improving the power of the Elemental towers slip out of my grasp, why I insist that you should do the same, and how it is going to provide the best chance that both our races have ever had of escaping the yoke of the Lightborn."

He didn't stop the message this time. He did scowl at them all as if he were bearing witness to a forgery.

"This young Darkborn before you, the one with the slight arm incident, holds the Deck of Darkness. Not *a* Deck of Darkness. The original."

Half-Swart's eyebrows shot up. His scowl deepened at the same time, making him look almost unhinged.

"If we—either of us, really, either the Elementals or the Furyborn—were to appropriate the deck, we would add a powerful weapon to our kind. A weapon that, given enough time and practice, might be enough to affect the power balance between us and the Lightborn. However, let there be no secret between us at this moment. *I do not believe it is enough.* As we have debated before, on too rare occasions, I am afraid that the Lightborn are winning. With the towers as entrenched as we are, and the Furyborn as challenged everywhere but inside Heart Halls, even something as unexpected and powerful as another deck, spread wide to our entire populace, would only delay the inevitable. The Lightborn are too many, too powerful, and hold too much infrastructure and too many wielders and Wellsprings to defeat like this."

There was another pause now. Not because Half-Swart stopped the recording. You could hear the High Elementalist's soft breathing, as if she were hesitant to continue. Her voice was strong and decisive as it reappeared, however. "What we need is a way to blindside them. To tilt the current equilibrium, or to build up a *new* power, to the point where it would be able to ruin their chokehold on the central parts of Ordei. I will add to my reasoning in the second part of the message, but this one time, I will be blunt where they, the young wielders, can overhear as well.

"*Neither of us should have this power.* Not only because it will not suffice to do what we need, but because we, as separate powers with differing interests, cannot entirely trust each other. We, inside the towers, have both our isolationists who believe we should let the Furyborn drown by themselves, and our weakhearted collaborators who would rather keep negotiating for a peace with the Lightborn that we shall never see. You, spread across the bloodied grounds, have your share of isolationists and racists, to the point where you would have trouble convincing them to trust in the towers."

Now the wide leader did stop the recording. With his gaze flickering between the contraption and them, he let his hands glide nervously over his shaved head before grasping onto his thick beard and pulling softly. "She. Why—" He closed his eyes and stopped himself. He took a deep breath. "I will hear her out," he said out loud, whether to himself or to them.

"As anybody with access to real power, you know what a limiting factor our Wellsprings are. Limiting enough that the Lightborn might have been able to eventually topple the towers, had they succeeded in stealing one of our decks. Adding further aspected decks to Wellsprings allows them to grow stronger. Yet, even strengthened, our respective Wellsprings will not provide enough, given that both the Furyborn and Elementals are constantly pressured by the Lightborn."

Her voice grew in power now, and emotion. "What we need is another pressure point. Another Wellspring, established as far from Lightborn presences as possible, where Elementals, Darkborn, *and* Furyborn may live in peace, to grow and eventually reach a power level that will allow them to become a changing factor in this war. These young prodigies, whose talent, integrity, and fervor I will personally vouch for, have somehow, on top of the Deck of Darkness, managed to gather a Deck of Light, to which I have added an Elemental Deck. It may seem premature to divest the towers of that kind of power, but—"

"What the *Pits* is this? There's no way that you..." Half-Swart slammed a fist down on the table, only to stare as Sera bared her arms, showing Elemental and Light cards. The others followed her example, adding their own mix of Dark, Light, and Elemental.

Stunned, he shook his head slowly, before returning his attention to the voice, still talking.

"My own reaction. Seeing that the Deck of Darkness exists was a shock, and an eye-opener as well. Therefore, dear Half-Swart, my fervent hope is that you see the point of my plan. That you will be able to talk your fellow leaders into matching our offer, to grant them a Deck of Fury and allow them to march onward to Liberty lands. There, with their amassed strength, your support, and all the cards at their disposal, it is my hope that they will either be able to rouse the Liberators out of their self-imposed isolation and will lend their strength to the cause or, lacking this, that the group will be able to steal a Liberty Deck for themselves.

"Imagine it, Half-Swart. Picture a Wellspring, hidden from the Lightborn, strengthened by decks from *all the aspects*. You have heard the legends, just as I have. Can you even fathom the kind of strength that could grow from this fount? Can you picture what this could do? *Can you see our salvation?* Because I can."

Half-Swart didn't reply at once. He stopped the recording and visibly struggled to collect himself, eyes flickering from one exposed arm to the next. He cleared his throat several times before speaking. And when he did, his voice sounded vulnerable and shaken, entirely at odds with the sturdy, strong man before them. "What are your Tier bonuses from the decks?"

"We gain a plus two to our class attributes from the Deck of Darkness. Then we gained a boost to our health and reduction to any detrimental effects from the Light Deck, and an additional plus one to all attributes from the Elemental one," Chase said.

"And the Wellspring?" he pressed. "Which additional bonuses does it grant you?"

Kith snorted. "Listen, mate. I think even Liam here can see what you're doing, and he's a bit slow."

"Hey!" Liam protested. "I can totally see it. You don't believe us, man! That's actually kind of hurtful!"

"We've been running for our lives since we got this deck, months ago. It's just been one thing after the other. Our time in Cemano has been the first actual break we've had... and it's not like it would be the optimal place to establish a Wellspring now, is it?" Kith smiled, not unkindly. "We haven't got the *faintest* clue what the Wellsprings do in practice, except for the vague notifications Chase here received. But we'll answer any questions you have, as well as we're able. Then... no, wait. I think maybe you'll want another drink right now, and we'll take it from there. We have nowhere to be right now, except in this exact place. Ask your questions and maybe please don't have us killed and our corpses looted."

Sera groaned and hid her face. "Why do we ever let him speak?"

Chapter 32

"The reason behind why Elementals, on the whole, sympathize with Furyborn? Cutting to the bone, we are in the same situation. Our cage is gilded and contains more luxuries, while theirs is larger. Cages, nonetheless." That went dark. Can't say I disagree, though. Also, surprisingly insightful. I might have to attempt to isolate the additions of this specific author and focus on those. (Page 6.)

Half-Swart took his time. He also had another tumbler of mead and, nudged by Liam, shared with them. Then he asked every question he could come up with. Regarding all the messages Chase had received regarding the Deck of Darkness. The information about the Wellspring, the Tier bonuses, everything. He spent a *lot* of time and effort going over the attack on the towers.

Eventually, he asked them to step outside his home, while he listened to the second part of the message. With a worn, haunted look, he ducked inside.

They stood there, awkwardly, unsure how to take everything, while the minutes passed.

Finally, Half-Swart opened the door again and bid them back in. The jovial, good-natured leader looked as though he'd aged a decade in an hour. For a while, he simply sat at the table, lost in thought. Then, he tapped the message device and the second part of the message started to play.

"I thought we were not supposed to hear this?" Sera asked.

"Because it's not especially relevant to you. Not because you were banned from it." A muscle under his eye twitched, and he massaged the spot with his fingers.

They listened through the message in absolute silence, unsure how to deal with the situation and what was going to happen. It was, as stated, a lot of high-scale information regarding the lands of Light, troop movements, city development, political choices, and musings from the High Elementalist. Where it was possible, she also elaborated on the countermoves performed by the Elementals, practical or diplomatic moves made. The red thread among the entire discussion was the need to stop the Lightborn from grasping onto even more power. She also elaborated, in detail, on the attack on the towers, where that left the Elementals, and speculated on the costs—economical, diplomatic, and in manpower. She did not attempt to hide the damage caused to the Protector system and the repercussions this would have in years to come, both with the increased mistrust against Lightborn and the loss of so many Protectors.

Eventually, she went into more details about why she believed that Half-Swart should go along with their plan to build a safe place for everybody, painting a picture of their group and everything she'd gathered about them. Listening to the collected intellectual argue passionately for the plan, and present them as generally simple, but earnest, people, made them cringe and avoid one another's eyes.

When her voice eventually stopped, an uncomfortable silence filled the otherwise cozy house. Half-Swart seemed lost in his own thoughts, a deep frown creasing his brow. After several minutes, Chase cleared his throat.

The leader made a small jolt, then nodded to himself. Rubbing his eyes, he sighed, and then looked at them, one by one. "I," he started, in sepulchral tones, "am not one for half measures. So, when I trust, I do not hold back."

"Fury tear me a new one," Kith interrupted. Shaking his head, he addressed the wide man. "Could you maybe give us a Lights-be-damned *hint* another time? I still wasn't sure if you were going to have us killed or not." He shuddered. "Trust. I like that. No killing. Please continue."

"You thought I was…" Half-Swart chuckled, then covered his mouth. "Please accept my utmost apologies. Let me make this clear. I am *not* going to harm you in any way. As a matter of fact, I am going to support you as much as I can. However, I'll be blunt. Having my world view turned upside down was *not* how I expected my day to go!"

He held up a hand, forestalling any outbursts. "I am coming to terms with what you and Tatiana claim. The fact that there is a new player on the scene was not the issue. The issue was that I needed to walk through the alternatives before I could decide exactly where to go from here." He tapped the table in front of the speaking device. "She speaks a lot, but there are also a *lot* of things she does not talk about. For good reasons. For all that we agree on holding back the Lightborn and trying to bring back an Ordeï where all kinds can coexist, we don't see eye to eye on all topics, and do not discuss everything.

"The fact that she entrusted me – *me* - with the temptation of having you in my grasp means that she's willing to go further for that goal than I'd thought before. Yet, the temptation is undeniable. What if I were to kill you and take the deck from you? What if I were to empower Heart Halls, train for years, then surprise the Lightborn with Guardians and wielders suddenly wielding unknown powers? Or if I co-opted her idea of establishing a new Wellspring in a remote area, but within the bloodied grounds, under our full control?"

He exhaled forcefully and sank down in his chair. "I had to work my way through these scenarios, to know where I stood, to understand myself. I am no genius to grasp these things in a split second. And for all that the High Elementalist may be a genius, she does not know our kind. Even so, she is not wrong. It would be too much, and not enough. We would still be unable to push back their forces. And eventually, we would fail. On top of that, while we are not as racist or divided as she thinks, the lost ones are becoming a threat on the far reaches of our territory." He groaned and let his hands rub over his bald pate. "I was supposed to *serve food* today! No. Do not stress. I am not going to make any easy choices. Like I said, I'm going to trust you and do my best to help you. However, that requires some things from you as well."

"Name it," Chase said.

"I am going to have to gather the other leaders of Heart Halls. The entire council of elders, in fact. Normally, I am the only one who deals with the towers, but they are all going to have to listen to this and decide. This is not a situation that can be hurried. We will have to plot our approach. We will be talking to a lot of the people you have spent time with in the bloodied grounds. You might as well grow accustomed to the fact that you'll be questioned, likely several times over. Some of us may want to see proof, see your cards in effect."

Half-Swart pulled his beard softly. "I can't picture how it's all going to play out. People aren't going to be happy, that's for sure—but when is it ever like that with change?" He chuckled darkly. "I will tell you this in advance, and I will not apologize for it. You had your chance to relax in Cemano. Be glad for it. Because from here on out, if the elders are going to put their trust and support behind you? You will have to earn it."

Chase leaned forward himself, catching Half-Swart's eyes. "We've told you where we come from and what we've gone through. We've been forcibly inducted into the forces of Light. We've tangled with a crazed survivor of the original Dark path of the Church of the Circle. We've fought and killed inquisitors. Three, so far. *I jumped from the goddamn top of the Elemental tower and lived.*" Chase's smile showed off all his teeth, and he could not be bothered in the least to hide his challenge. "Bring it!"

Of course, Kith had to go and ruin it all by groaning, "Don't get us all killed. Please?"

Half-Swart's eyes didn't move off Chase's. Something lit up in them, and one side of his mouth inched up. His finger stabbed out at Chase. "I need you to stay that cocky. And I need you to be able to match that cockiness in actual skill." He narrowed his eyes. "You are going to move to the challengers' pens. If anybody asks why, when you're un-initiated outsiders, tell 'em to talk to me. There, you will be able to train to your heart's delight. Don't slack. I don't know what the next days and weeks will bring, but *you will need it.*"

"Some of us need more than just practice." Cilia raised her head in challenge. "If we are to prove our best, I will need to be able to *craft.* I will need materials and tools."

"You won't be the only crafter there. Tell them what you need. Obviously, you will not be able to get everything you want, but we make sure that there are stores of the more common materials available." Half-Swart nodded to himself. "If that is all, I have my work cut out for me. I have a bunch of stubborn bastards to convince to take the chance of their lives. Of all our lives."

Kith smoothly jumped in. "So, this isn't the time to tell that Liam there's actually an inquisitor?" His innocent gaze portrayed no deception whatsoever. Only the humor playing in his eyes did.

The tic returned on Half-Swart's cheek. With impressive poise, he put up a hand to calm the muscle. "I *have* already agreed to support your group. I have not decided whether you all need to live for it."

With her face hidden behind her hands, Cilia added, "I've had the same thoughts plenty of times. If you need plans, just tell me."

They managed to finish their talk without any of their number being designated for outright murder. Following that, they walked back to the communal kitchen and Lassenta agreed to aid them to their new destination. They quickly left the actual city behind and moved into the wilderness beyond. Originally, they'd come in from the east, and now they left for the west. The general layout didn't change, though. Defenses everywhere, as well as countless empowered trees. They spotted fewer defenders going west, but had no doubt that they were there.

They chatted with Lassenta as they walked. According to her, the constant defenses were a simple conclusion of the way that Heart Halls had originated and developed over time. Following that first, massive clash, the city had actually been surrounded, hence they added defenses in all directions. For the first couple of years, until they'd fought back the Lightborn forces and opened access for other Furyborn to join their ranks and help in the battle, they'd had to be prepared everywhere. It was only later on, when they'd established proper battle lines, that they started to concentrate their defenses eastward.

In the early afternoon, a couple of hours after leaving the city proper, they reached the edge of those early battle expansions. From then on, the forest started to expand more naturally, with fewer defenses, fewer disorienting detours and clay walls and more actual nature. For a while, the forest actually became a bit *more* oppressive, because it had been allowed to grow naturally toward the west, including more underbrush, and a canopy that closed up and drowned out most sunlight.

"Ah. But quit your complaining, kids. Your young legs should be able to handle a tiny walk, should they not? You have cards and all. Meanwhile, little old me has to get by with just the memories of my glory days, and the joy of being able to assist such wayward youngsters as yourselves in your endeavors." Lassenta held a hand over her heart.

"Little old me," Liam grumbled. "We had somebody, back on the Waves. Tilly. Most innocent-looking old biddy you could think of. Also, she mixed the meanest concoctions. She didn't even have any cards, but if you wanted a potion of any kind to make life the Pits for somebody? You'd go to her. What I'm trying to say is that she also made the same sounds that you just did... and I've watched her give somebody the runs for two weeks straight, just by jabbing them with a knitting needle smeared in some of her stuff."

"Yeah. You're overselling it, woman," Kith added. "If you want any pointers on how to look *truly* innocent, just talk to Sera here. She can't help it."

Lassenta cackled. "You lot are hilarious. I'm almost sorry that I will have to let you go. We're getting there now. You can hear all the meatheads beyond."

"Meatheads?" Cilia frowned. "I thought around here, people were fonder of those who are ready to fight for the Furyborn?"

The old Furyborn snorted. "Oh, we are. They are wonderful people, who risk their lives on behalf of us all. Also, I've spent half my life as one of their number. I'm allowed." In the driest voice one could imagine, she added, "Besides. These are the challengers. The prospective defenders. There's a *lot* of stupidity and weakness that needs to be weeded out from among their number before you find the actual defenders among the lot."

Chase laughed. "I am getting the weirdest flashbacks from the towers again. You wouldn't happen to have a long-lost Elemental half-sister by the name of, erm, Brookwatch, would you? She used to go out and shout *'Death to stupidity'* every so often, to try to get through to the slowest of the initiates."

"I don't think so... but I do love it. *'Death to stupidity!'*" She chuckled.

The path they were following slowly opened up, and the canopy lessened and eventually faded into individual treetops instead. The terrain opened up as well, introducing them to...

"The challenger pens," Lassenta said fondly. "Where you lot can eat, get your head smacked silly, get healed, and construct your own longbow, without having to walk longer than you can spit. Oh, and get laid, of course."

"Lassenta!" Sera said.

"What? Don't be a prude. I was young and gorgeous too, once. Didn't have your golden curls, of course, more's the shame. Even so, I had legs that went on for days. It'd be a shame to not use them for their intended purpose." Her cackle scared a bird out of the tree above them.

Liam stared at her. Slowly, he shook his head. "I never knew my mother. If I had, though, I'd want her to be exactly like you."

"Oh, shush."

"I mean, absolutely mental!"

She cackled again. After she was done, she had to stop and lean on a tree while she regained her breath. Finally, she stood and pointed down the slope. "The pens. I'll be introducing you to the people on watch, then I'm off. Is there anything you want to know?"

They looked at the place below. Now, there were clear sounds to go with the sight. Yet, it was a bit confusing. Because what they saw was an imposing barricade, made out of large trees planted right next to each other in a huge square area nearly a mile across. Some of the trees were smaller than others, or different kinds, creating an odd lopsided visual and allowing them to peek inside.

"So...that's definitely a training area, on the far left." Liam tiptoed to try to see more. "What are the other spots? And what's with the trees?"

Lassenta pointed, moving her hand counterclockwise as she mentioned them. "Training area, just like you said. Mess hall. Barracks for a sleeping area. Then, urg, I can't see it, but unless I remember wrong, it's the caster area, followed by the crafter area and a place for lectures."

"You do lectures too?" Cilia perked up.

"Of course we do. We may not have fancy libraries like the Elementals, or be all dressed up nice and shiny like the Lightborn, but we teach our own. Sometimes, they're led by other challengers or prospects. Sometimes, we have some of the local defenders swing by and show what they've learned." She beamed. "I don't know what the towers were like, but I'd bet it beats having your nose buried in a book all the time. Here? We like to keep things practical."

"That sounds wonderful." Kith grinned.

"It is. I couldn't picture having to spend every day reading about fighting instead of actually fighting." Lassenta ignored Cilia, who tried to interrupt and correct her. "As for the trees? Well, those are what we have that sets us apart from what all those other fancy institutions might have. I bet even the towers would love to copy this." She leaned forward and fake whispered, "You see, in the early days, we didn't really know what the results would be when we communed with the trees. There's an art form to it."

She rolled her eyes. "At least, so they say. The proof is down there, though. As long as you're inside the pens? You will learn faster, recuperate faster, *heal* faster... some of the trees even have some effects that are supposed to help with crafting, though I'll be damned if I know how they work. Fact is, when you're in the pens? You'd better work your asses off, because it'll be worth it!"

Chapter 33

"Of course, they suffer debilitating defeats too. Over the course of a conflict of decades, no power could be convinced to continue fighting if they did not have victories to point out. Disregarding the initial campaign of the Lightborn, which almost quelled the Furyborn entirely, there have been incredible victories for the Lightborn over the years. The Aetero campaign. The destruction of the marshland. The Givel reconquest. Most of these point to one specific flaw among their kind. The lack of proper training in any sort of formation fighting." Huh. That is one incredibly logical issue. With their strategies and customs based on small-group tactics, ambushes and the like, along with their fight-to-the-death approach, they have few possibilities of obtaining these skills. Maybe... no. (Page 81.)

The introduction to the challengers was incredibly easy. They simply walked in, and everything was opened to them. One of the attendants had some questions, because they hadn't received any notice that they'd be joining the pens, but once he heard that he should ask Half-Swart... that was it. Whatever the mixed-race leader explained to them was enough to quench any unnecessary questions to their plans.

With that handled, they settled in among the unruly lot that were the challengers of Heart Halls. It didn't go over quietly. Every day in the pens was chaotic, messy, and often bloody.

Upon their arrival, there were about a hundred and twenty challengers around, waiting, improving, and practicing in preparation of their challenges. Considering that the trials were only held twice a year, these seemed like low numbers—that is, until they learned that the number of challengers was less than one in ten compared to the number of wannabe challengers who were currently testing or preparing for the tests to earn their first cards elsewhere. Cilia crunched the numbers, and confirmed that, with the expected attrition and people failing the tests, the number of people who ended up earning cards or earning access to Light cards on top of their Furyborn cards would easily double the output of the Elemental towers.

During the first days, the former Waves-dwellers questioned why people had to go through tests in the first place— why they didn't just give cards to everybody. Surely, that would improve the strength of the Furyborn as a whole. However, the response, apart from the general opinion that cards *needed* to be earned or they wouldn't be appreciated, was that it wasn't just a test—it was a matter of ensuring that people were ready. Physically ready, with the attributes needed to survive in the bloodied grounds. Mentally ready, where they wouldn't freeze up the first time they had to spill blood or had their own blood spilled. Prepared with enough training to ensure they did not get themselves killed through rookie mistakes. Considering the point that nearly all the initiates were young, it was hard for them to argue with a system that took care in making sure their young were prepared properly.

They were accepted among the other challengers without any incidents. The people in the camp were incredibly diverse when it came to age, class, and attitude; their mixed group fit right in. There was no discussion that the vast majority of challengers were pure Furyborn, but only the occasional outlier made any difference between the races, and that behavior was put down hard.

Initially, there were a few murmurs against their group, given that they were outsiders and their place in the group wasn't as clear-cut as everybody else. Yet, within the first days, that faded away as they proved themselves by working as hard or harder than anybody else present.

The mood in the pens was one of focused (and often raucous) concentration and determination. Nobody here had arrived without first spending years among the scouts, fighting and navigating amongst lost ones, Lightborn Guardians, and, in some cases, skirmishes or outright battles with Lightborn soldiers. The point being, these weren't innocent youths, but hardened veterans. Their experience differed, of course. Not many were as used to actual conflict as their own group. Many were vastly more experienced in scouting, avoidance, stealth, and wilderness survival than they were in battle. Yet, they were, one and all, experienced and committed.

Also, the pens differed completely from the towers in one aspect. Here, they weren't competing against one another. They were preparing for and struggling against the vaunted test to come. Gauntlet or crucible, they were mythical tests, which nobody would divulge any details about.

The result from this deviation was that, where the towers had students fighting, trying to one-up and snipe at one another, here, the only interest lay in bettering oneself. As such, there was an inherent understanding that everybody, in general, tried to help one another.

Perhaps it was part of growing up among Furyborn, where everybody was expected to help one another, aid where you could and add value according to your capabilities. But where any attempt, both among the Lightborn and the Elementals, to establish a training camp such as the pens, would've seen egos clashing and people trying to put down competitors, here there was a general understanding and acceptance of the fact that you'd never be the best at everything, but you'd damn well better try to improve.

The sensation from walking into the pens for the first time was insane. The moment they entered the semi-claustrophobic confines, with those huge trees looking down on them from all sides, they felt it coming, in waves. Like the sensation of suddenly being inundated with several different buff cards activated at the same moment, waves of energy pushed out from the trees, making their minds feel crisper, their eyes sharper, footsteps lighter. It was physically possible to spend time in the pens and not learn, but you had every chance. The onus lay on you. The effects from what had to be dozens of Furyborn communing, giving their hard-earned powers back to the land and somehow focused into more than a dozen overlapping boosting effects, was entirely undeniable and, at first, quite distractible.

They soon settled into daily rhythms inside the pens. Lassenta had forgotten to mention one area, which ended up dominating several hours of the day for each of them. A large segment, given entirely over to a massive obstacle course: huge blocks of wood and metal for lifting, swinging and throwing, harnesses to add weight to their bodies—in short, anything you'd need to push your attributes to the limit. Just like that, they found themselves right at home. There was no Instructor Boneridge yelling at them, but the sentiment was the same.

The fighter area, as Lassenta had called it, was actually divided into several different smaller sections. Depending on what you wanted to train, you had different terrains. There was the straightforward packed-clay dueling area, a place with a sloped gravel surface, a fifty-by-fifty-foot square with mud deep enough to pull at your boots, and even a mini-forest containing dozens of smaller, much-abused, yet still living, trees you could hide behind as you fought. Some jester had even created a wheel of fortune, where you could let the vagaries of fate decide which terrain you'd be fighting on. On top of that, the place held a massive number of weapons to choose from, blunted for practice purposes and otherwise.

Among the challengers, there was never any lack of takers for dueling practice. At least half the challengers were always in the fighter area, either resting up from a bout, waiting for a matchup they wanted, or simply looking to be entertained. It was usually a matter of minutes to find somebody to test yourself against, regardless of whether you wanted the thrill of a full dozen going against one another or a one-on-one.

The caster area and ranged areas were more straightforward. However, there had also been some work done, with pulley systems and other inventions, allowing casters and ranged fighters to practice distance effects on simulated enemies both at a distance, in movement, and in simulated swarms and groups.

The healing tent was never empty. Putting more than a hundred eager youths in close quarters and telling them to improve their fighting skills was never going to end bloodlessly. Fortunately, the challengers saw their fair share of healers among the lot, and they collaborated to improve their skills and knowledge about the human body. Broken bones, stab wounds, charred nerves... nothing was beyond the eager healers preparing for their challenges. Yet, practice subjects rarely went willingly - the sight of a dozen healers eagerly peering at an open wound and debating the best way to handle it felt unnerving to even the hardiest of fighters.

The lecture area did not entirely live up to its name. Or, it did, but it was so much more. After the first couple of days, even Kith was forced to admit that he liked it. There was nothing to the area. It was simply a cordoned-off site of packed dirt under the overreaching crown of a gnarly, twisted tree. Yet, in practice, it was often as lively as the dueling areas. Lecturers came in from the defenders working every day to keep Heart Halls safe, local experts, and crafters. They would get up and talk on their chosen expertise or simply a matter of interest to them. Sometimes, it could be the best techniques to harry an incoming Lightborn army. At other times, it could be an exposition on the kinds of Guardians you could expect to meet, and the optimal ways of fighting them. Yet, it could also be something as low-practical as proper preparation, packing the right things in the right way to ensure you'd be ready for your scouting tours.

It wasn't just the defenders giving one-sided speeches, though. Any challenger could also get up and expound on something they believed they mastered well enough to talk about. Challenger, defender, or expert - lectures were never just about listening. Challengers were vocal in their approval and disapproval, questioning, demanding examples from the speakers. Where the lectures in the towers had been about experts showing what was right and proper and students accepting it, here, you wouldn't get away with a claim without proving it, or explaining exactly how come you were right. The lectures were not always useful. Yet, they were *never* dull.

The crafters' area was a source of contention in the camp. More than a few challengers argued that it really didn't belong. That their tinkering, by rights, was a contribution to the *proper* challengers, and as such, they should be separate. Of course, most challengers, knowing that the crafters would have to risk their lives alongside any other class to walk the Steps, scoffed at the notion.

Regardless of what the opinion was on their presence, their area was the noisiest, busiest, most chaotic part of the pens. Smiths, woodworkers, tinkerers, armorers, and alchemists competed with one another to make the noisiest, smelliest, and flagrantly outrageous showings. For regular crafters back in Isarn? That could be overwhelming enough, with painters, smiths, and others making a spectacle of themselves. For carded crafters, trying to push themselves to improve, while trying to one-up and impress all others nearby? It was insane.

More than once during their stay, something exploded or started a fire. At least once a day, a combination would create an unforeseen reaction, earning panicked responses and an immediate call to arms, with all crafters uniting, scouting from a safe distance to decide whether they should fetch water, healers, blankets to warm up a cold effect gone wrong... or simply get their friends so they could all laugh at an experiment gone hilariously wrong.

Cilia immediately joined the crafters' ranks. As a bit of a loner, she didn't immediately feel at home in the chaotic confines. However, the moment she picked up on the ever-present desire—no, *need*—to learn and improve among their ranks, she opened up, taking part in many discussions on the subject of combinations and optimal enforcement of Mental Power. As the sole crafter present who'd learned in the towers, outside of a single painter who didn't come by often, she found that she was actually in a situation to have a learned opinion on most topics.

At first, she spent her time between fighting practice, attribute building, and working to restore the items they'd used on the road to Heart Halls. A single day after their arrival, however, she was blindsided as she received a gift. Following that, she spent nearly all her time planning, preparing, and crafting, roping in Sera to stay nearby and use her buffs to improve attributes for the parts where she had to infuse aspects into her items. She refused to talk about the gift, however.

Kith was a man possessed. Learning that not only would their senses be improved, but that the odds of them retaining additional attributes from their training was somehow improved, he *lived* in the practice areas. He only deigned to spend time on anything not training-related when the others pulled him in for dueling practice, or if a particular lecture was extraordinarily well-suited for him. Seeing him alone in the training area even after dark, toiling by himself or teamed up with a low-set Furyborn fighter with a disturbing damage-reflecting card became the rule rather than the exception.

Liam, meanwhile, took his lessons from Lassenta. He definitely didn't slack, putting in a good deal of hours sweating alongside Kith, learning about tactics or practical issues as a fighter or testing himself against others in the dueling areas. Yet, he openly admitted that he spent more than his allotted time simply hanging out and making friends with the locals. After everything that occurred in Cemano, he believed that cultivating a new group of friends and acquaintances who would stand up for them could more than pay back the investment in the long run. Of course, he just phrased it as "wanting to make friends."

Sera spent a lot of time together with Chase. Not in any carnal sense—there was no such thing as privacy in the pens, a fact which a number of the younger Furyborn very obviously didn't care about—but working to improve the metaphorical arsenal of their group. She did spend a good deal of time initially working with the other healers, but soon concluded that her learning from her tutors and Jessel meant that she had mostly outgrown their discussions. As such, she stuck to training her body, her mind, and her combat mindset. She also made her first attempts at trying to create a fighting style for herself that was fully defensive.

Chase, for himself, took a step back and tried to consider the possibilities. The chance to improve attributes faster than usual would be less efficient for somebody like him who already had a card to gift the same effect. The lectures, as well, were interesting, but they were also far from focused. A lecture one day might be something they'd be able to use, with the next three days being filled with superfluous information, useful to Furyborn, scouts, and defenders in the making, but not to people like them. Hence, he took the unexpected gift of the dueling area, and decided to make the absolute most of it.

At first, he flung himself into one-on-one duels, optimizing his capabilities and improving his approach against different classes and types of enemies. He expanded from there, and started to fight against two, three, or even four Furyborn at once. Sure, he got his ass handed to him as often as not, but that was not the point. This was all about learning, about knowing what to do so he didn't freeze when he found himself in the same situation in actual combat. The more he built on it, the more he found that he had to learn, and soon, he and Sera sat down every single day after partaking in duels, either as a partial group, or their full group, working to discover and improve their use of their cards.

At first, it was more about experimenting on and improving their general approaches. Deciding exactly which combinations of cards they should use in specific situations.

For instance, if they were preparing an ambush? They'd have Kith's Shadow Master for scouting and Coils of Shadow for attacking. Combined with Liam's Waterfall of Light and Earthen Might, Steps of Brilliance for ambushing from above and Free of Perdition to ruin any really powerful enemies, they would be able to do a *lot* of damage in little time. Add to that Cilia's improved Heart card, and they'd be able to cut any targets off from screaming for help. Or if they were looking into a drawn-out fight, they could center everything around either Kith's Tainted Earth and Chase's Among the Raindrops if they needed to stay on the move and out of reach, or the same cards, added to Liam's Become the Clay and Draining Ward, if they were okay with getting bogged down.

The two debated back-and-forth, weighing pros and cons of different cards in different situations. Then, they got more situational, creating combinations that would serve them well in specific situations. Combinations that they might be able to switch to, in order to surprise enemies, create battle-ending, or—in some scenarios—life-saving changes.

As an example, if anybody but Sera was downed or incapacitated? Sera could use Cry for Blood or Unexpected Spillage to keep enemies from finishing them. Cilia would be able to follow up with a blinding pouch, or Kith could do the same, sacrificing his Divine Mentor. Meanwhile, Chase could waltz in, using Steps of Brilliance to carry them to safety or Liam could use the trample effect from Waterfall of Light to smash their way through anybody trying to keep them trapped.

Some of the combinations and discoveries were more theoretical or funny than actually practical. For instance, Chase figured out that his Steps of Brilliance, although limited to carrying himself, didn't actually have a weight limit. Meaning, theoretically, he'd actually be able to carry Cilia on his back and move about mid-air while she dropped crafted items on their enemies... only, the odds of it not going horribly wrong in a stressful situation weren't excellent.

Yet others were absolutely devastating. For instance, they learned that if Kith summoned his Apian God, combined with his Twice the Fun card, doubling the number of summons *and* Sera added her Tongues of Pride card, they ended up with a ridiculously oversized swarm of insects *who did fire damage*. Against thick-skinned Guardians, this might not be a game changer. However, against, say, a group of ranged or caster enemies? It would be a killer—and for casters, Liam could use Ravenous Shadows to devour their magic to add insult to injury.

Some combinations were incredibly dependent on terrain. Through experimentation and a single, well-timed increase to Mental Power for Chase, they confirmed that the power of his

A Friendly Wave card grew along with his mental attribute. Suddenly, the liquid from the water trough he'd been able to shape into a focused wave going thirty feet managed nearly two additional feet. Sure, in dry areas, the card was basically useless, unless he combined it with Among the Raindrops. In muddy and overly wet terrain, however, he learned that he could slightly manipulate the liquid in the soil and worsen or improve the terrain with some effort. And near rivers, lakes, or the like, it was *incredibly* powerful. By itself, it could knock enemies off their feet, keep them out of commission for the duration of the wave. In combination with other crowd control cards like Tainted Earth or Draining Ward? It could theoretically down and incapacitate entire groups of enemies, without them even having to risk getting stabbed.

There was also the combination from their fight with the behemoth they decided to simply dub "the Finisher," to be applied against especially powerful enemies. Chase would use Free of Perdition, stealing the target's Toughness and hopefully replacing it with his own. Following that, they'd add a two-punch combo of Liam with Earthen Might and Waterfall of Light, while Kith used Twice the Fun combined with A Fiery End to summon a large number of smaller summons, which would then sacrifice themselves in a fiery inferno.

They were still limited in their practice. Given that they were still under orders to operate in hiding until the leaders had made their decision, they couldn't use their Dark cards in the open. That didn't stop them from theory-crafting—and they had a variety of opponents, builds, and classes to practice against that they'd be hard-pressed to find again.

For a full two weeks, they flung themselves into training, trying to spot any weaknesses and build their strengths. There was no news; nobody came by to interrogate them or bring them to justice. They knew, just like the rest of the challengers, that their time here was limited, and as such did what they could to make the most of it.

Yet, when the time did come, they were not prepared.

Chapter 34

"I've met one person ever who was accepted as a Furyborn and granted cards. One. Of course, he wouldn't reveal what he had to do to become one of them. I need to know. What did he pay? Which elaborate items did he craft? From my experience, I will wager that it was something momentous, something that made a real difference to their kind." Wrong. At this point, I believe it's more a question of integrity than extravagant spending. If they found somebody, who seemed like they were willing to actually become of the blood and do what needs doing... Darkness hide me, am I going native? (Page 83.)

"Get *down*, Cilia!" Liam bellowed the words, even as he raised an arm.

She flung herself to the ground.

His clay-covered limb intercepted an arrow covered in a fluorescent effect streaming at her. The arrow impacted his arm. The color spread across its entirety, scintillating colors traveling higher. He grunted, and simply ignored it.

Liam and Sera were forming a protective circle, both of them facing off against any outside attackers. Between them, Kith and—a now, supine and cursing—Cilia were doing their best to make a difference in a different situation.

They were all up to their ankles in the mud and bogged down something fierce. Both from their front and back, attackers lurked behind trees or crept along in the mud to minimize their profiles. Ten of them, ranged attackers mostly, along with a caster, two healers and two fighters. They worked together, divided into two equal groups, and laid down pressure on Chase's group. Blunted missiles rained upon them, fighters holding back to fend off any attacks, while the caster grabbed and flung shards of dirt that affixed themselves to whoever was hit and hardened to freeze them up and lock muscles. On top of that, both of the enemies' groups had a healer and a fighter, to make it more difficult for them to close with them.

It was all progressing as they'd planned for.

Chase raced around in the air, keeping his distance as he stayed aloft from the clinging mud, traversing solely on his shimmering platforms. The ranged attackers tried to take him out of the air; missiles whizzed at him whenever he came too close. Yet as long as he stayed back, he was not in any real danger. They were all, with one exception, Tier one or two, with the attributes to match, and only one of the ranged attackers was Agility-focused. For whichever Liberty-forsworn reason, he'd decided to focus on throwing daggers, of all things. It did *not* serve the man well when he was at a longer distance.

"They're not closing in. We'll have to go on the offensive!" Kith yelled, a hint of panic in his voice.

"Of course we're not getting any closer," one of the Furyborn shouted back. "Have you *seen* Liam's arms?"

"Screw this. I'm taking us in. Liam, guard our backs!"

Kith strode forward, aiming straight for the group facing Sera head-on. His Crescendo of Might summon burst into existence; its huge, shapeless form grew, ambling forward, as it ignored the clinging mud. Half-hidden behind its shape, it would be hard for any attackers to spot the shining gleam that had started to glow from within Kith's own body—the only overt sign of his Divine Mentor summon guiding his every movement. To the attackers, there would just be a mounting frustration that the squat summoner managed to evade or deflect their every missile, hidden behind the bulk of the ugly creature as he was.

Liam did as he was told, keeping Kith's back clear, even as he worked overtime trying to defend Cilia and Sera. Already, several missiles were embedded in the clay on his shoulders, making him look like a particularly handsome pincushion.

Sera held her own and helped keep Cilia half-hidden behind the massive tower shield she carried, even as her buffs and self-buffs made her move faster and spread the love to the others.

Kith moved closer, now, and the attackers prepared to face off against him. The fighter in front of him shone with a rich, earthen brown, and started to pulsate slowly, before a subtle orange layered itself on him, as his group layered buffs and card effects. He raised a long sword, tapping his oval bronze shield invitingly before pointing it beyond the Crescendo of Might summon at Kith in a wordless challenge.

In response, the bulky summon threw itself to the side, and Kith exploded.

At least, that was what it looked like from a distance. Even knowing that it was coming, Chase got half an eyeful of the blinding effect as Kith sacrificed his Divine Mentor in a radiant burst of brilliant light. He blinked furiously, trying to make the dots disappear, even as he made his move. After hearing Kith's cue, he'd climbed high into the air, footstep after footstep taking him higher. Now, he spread out the platforms from Steps of Brilliance, every foothold far ahead and below him, as he sprinted downhill, building speed with every step. Piece by piece, card by card, he watched their battle plan unfold beneath him as he hurtled to the attack.

The Crescendo of Might summon was back on its tree trunk-like feet, ambling toward the half-blinded attackers again. Kith was already leaving it behind, racing ahead, flourishing his hand axes in anticipation.

Chase focused, activating A Friendly Wave, grinning wildly as he *felt* the welcoming sensation of the water on all sides bidding him to come play. With a mental tug, he grasped hold of all the moisture in the mud around the five Furyborn, condensing it into actual water and *pulling* it away.

Cries rang out, as the five attackers turned defenders suddenly found themselves stuck with their legs in quick-hardening soil. Then they changed pitch as Kith and his summons barreled down on them.

At that point, with the enemies all stuck or trying to break out of the soil, preparing for Kith's charge, Chase performed his final flourish as he reached the healer's shield at breakneck speed. He grasped all the water displaced from the mud, and told it to *move.* In a span of heartbeats, the large pool of mud-brown water swelled and rose into the air, before the growing, tall wave crested, right on top of the healer. There, it stopped, unnaturally holding at the peak of the crest, with the healer hidden within, mud at neck level.

The healer's shield burst apart like a gambler's self-control in front of a pair of dice. Mud slid down on top of him like a particularly dirty waterfall.

Chase planned his path forward. One platform there, letting him arrive at the now-hardened clay at top speed. A hard strike, hitting the helmeted dagger-thrower with the hilt of his dagger. Two more platforms, two more steps, as he barreled into the still-blinded caster shoulder-first, regained his balance on the hard clay, and climbed into the air again to avoid the archer with the short bow who was turning, blinking. Then he was past, and Chase let the wave drop right as he arrived. He finished his charge in a dive, readying to strike the now unshielded healer, only to realize the man was already gasping and sputtering with his hands in the air, mud near sealing him in.

The ground squelched as Chase landed, slipping and nearly overbalancing in the wet mud.

"You're out!" he told the healer, though he had to repeat the phrase before the healer's panicked face slumped in realization and defeat. He nodded, sighing as the thick layer of mud now clinging to his clothes started to slowly slide off from Chase's mental nudge.

Chase turned, grinning, to take on the rest of the defenders.

He need not have bothered.

Kith had continued his enthusiastic, massively distracting, charge. His axes, on top of the blinding effect and the clinging hardened clay around his feet, had the enemy fighter entirely outmaneuvered, kneeling in surrender while rubbing his shoulder. The Crescendo of Might summon had already moved past the beaten fighter, and was reaching the peak of its growth.

The remaining archer took one look at the towering hulk of the summon and carefully held his hands up in surrender. The caster, getting back up from being tackled by Chase, didn't have time to do the same, before Kith had him on his ass, tapping him three times in short succession on his shoulder, stomach, and pelvis.

Staring from the far end of the dueling grounds, the other five-person team flung down their weapons in surrender.

"A fair fight? You made a wave appear out of nowhere and drowned me! *How is that fair?*" The healer had a dagger out and was trying to scrape mud from his soft leather jacket. He sighed in disgust, even as laughter and chuckles arose from the other Furyborn.

"Just be happy that Kith didn't summon those fire mosquitos." The jovial fighter cracked his neck and slapped his face. "I'll tell you. Trying to concentrate on an enemy, when you've got small fiery beasts trying to climb into your nethers and sting you... that's an experience I'd wish only on my worst enemy."

"It's a combination of cards, actually," Cilia added. "Sera's buff adds the fire damage. It gets *really* interesting when Kith uses Twice the Fun to double the number of summons, though. And if we're in an area with other insects, they get pulled into the effect too."

The fighter shuddered. "It's a war crime is what it is. Hey, you want to go another round, Kith? I'd like to take you on, just one-on-one. I think I could take that huge shambling thing of yours alongside you, if everybody else weren't trying to ruin my day."

"I think that maybe it will have to wait." Sera nudged Chase. "It looks like something is going down."

"Outsiders!" A voice bellowed from the edge of the dueling area, its uncaring tone in strict opposition to the relaxed banter of the teams resting within. A gaunt Furyborn stood on the edge, a scroll case clutched in his hands. He had long, thin, and patchy light-brown hair blowing in the breeze. Even from this far away, the colors in his eyes swirled cold. "You have been summoned before the elders, immediately."

Chase looked at his crew, at the thick layer of mud covering them all. His hand froze where it was scratching at his scalp, crusted-in flakes falling off him. "Well, that's one first impression we're not coming back from."

They tried. They argued for the chance to, at the very least, take a quick sponge bath and put on some different clothes. Yet, the officious messenger shot them down, one by one. He had been given a task, and the task was going to be carried out, irrespective of their desires. Before that unstoppable force, there was no refuge, and they soon found the mud drying on their skin as they strode toward their meeting.

The messenger didn't deign to tell them anything. That had not been part of his instructions, and even Sera, politely asking him for a bit of information so they could prepare properly, was merely scoffed at and ignored. Eventually, he demanded silence from all of them.

They finally settled down into simply following, while sharing uncomfortable glances with one another. Of course, they knew what this was about. Yet, if this was the way they were being introduced to their hour of judgment, what could they expect? Running was not an option. Not at this point. They'd come this far, and they'd damn well done a good job. Nervous glances became fixed miens of defiance and stubbornness as they moved toward their destination.

To begin with, that destination was rather unclear. Over the last few weeks, they'd learned a *lot* about their surroundings, at least what they'd been able to glean through the stories of the challengers. Heart Halls might be a strangely created place. Not a village, not a proper city, but somewhere in between, albeit dominated by its defenses. However, although it was stretched over a swathe of land that seemed improbable for its citizen count, it did boast a lot of different crafters and possibilities, and Heart Halls demanded the best of the best. The place had the best fletchers, armorers, smiths, traders, woodworkers, alchemists... whatever you could name, as long as it was focused on utility or combat, the city was bound to have it. Somewhere. Except, none of the larger places seemed to coincide with where the messenger was taking them.

Then, they spotted the tree. Or, rather, the fortress. Or...

Chase felt comfortable enough about his own personality, attributes, and upbringing to know that he had a bunch of flaws. He was easily distracted, had trouble sitting still, and could be a bit too enamored of the thrill of quick action. Yet, he rarely found that he had trouble finding words. Except for now.

Chase had seen this type of thing before, but hadn't gotten a proper look. The *thing* ahead of them had been a tree, once. What it was now was harder to describe. The base shape was that of a tree, no discussion. The twenty-foot-tall tree-like creation had a clearly defined trunk and a crown with verdant, green leaves shining with health. So far, so good. Yet, that was where any similarities with an actual tree ended. To begin with, it had a driver... or a rider, maybe. Settled deep within the trunk, the face of a woman was clearly visible through a number of deeply carved openings. Her eyes emotionlessly scanned the surroundings as the tree took one ground-eating step after the other, moving at a sedate, pendular pace that nonetheless carried it far. Because, yes, it had feet. Or roots. Whatever they were, their gnarled base was wide, flared, and allowed the tree to move in a sure-footed, unstoppable way that clearly told that nothing short of an actual mountain would stop its forward motion.

That in itself was weird, wonderful, and outlandish. Yet, at this point, they'd experienced wonders and amazing creations around Ordei that a walking tree with a human controlling it would be fathomable. It was the creation added *to* the tree that took the existence from outlandish to unreal.

It was hard to tell where the tree itself stopped and the creation started. The two were clearly separate, but still intertwined. Separate, but united in purpose. Either it was something they'd managed to grow from the tree itself, or the creator had somehow managed to match it closely enough to the tree that it was practically impossible to tell the differences. It was armor; it was a building; it was the tree itself. The darkened wood was layered thickly, tapered on top of the tree itself, reinforcing its structures, and looked thick enough it would be able to weather the strike of a gaborn. Farther up the tree, the armor widened, sporting a number of platforms, replete with handholds and waist-high defenses, allowing archers to stand and shoot down upon any intruders. Yet, that wasn't all. The farther up you followed the creation, the more it tapered out, growing to be at least twice as wide as it was tall.

With a sound somewhere between the creaking of a bough and the heavy thud of the stone of a fortress wall rocking into place, the tree came to a halt, right in front of them.

Chase couldn't help but feel that the tree itself was looking at him, judging him. His gaze met the emotionless eyes of the Furyborn hidden away deep within.

Their guide didn't bother with awe. "As summoned by the elders, so we arrive," he announced loudly and officiously.

A barely discernible muttering from above preceded a clattering, as a long rope ladder unfurled, reaching just above the ground. The messenger climbed up without a single glance back. They shared a look before following him. Chase went last, with a single prayer of gratitude as he activated Clothed in Living Light. He did not care to think about how annoying climbing this would've been with just one hand.

Chapter 35

"Are the courts of the Furyborn fair? Nobody knows. We have never seen, let alone heard of, a single judgment called down on any criminals. I can only say that those who do not abide by their rules tend to disappear." How lovely. Yet another place where I'll be able to school the scholars of the towers. If we live to tell the tale, of course. So. Many. Notes. (Page 83.)

The rope ladder emerged onto a wooden platform, placed just underneath the lovely awning of the living, vibrant tree crown. That part was undeniably correct. Yet, it also failed at properly painting the image of what the newcomers saw. Calling the top of the wooden behemoth a platform seemed about as sacrilegious as calling a king's throne a chair. The warm colors of the wide wooden area played in a subtle contrast that made the eye relax and the heart smile; the surface somehow looked as soft and inviting as a feather mattress, and every single part of it looked brand sparkling new.

Yet even as his eyes trailed from edge to edge, taking in everything—the railings that could easily double as battlements, the group of five people lounging on pillows at the center in front of the central trunk—Chase couldn't spot a *single* place sporting a nail, a joint, or two different boards meeting. It looked entirely like the whole damn thing had been grown, arrow slits and all, from a tiny baby tree. Which, of course, he couldn't entirely dismiss.

The elders of Heart Halls did not rise to meet them. At first, Chase reckoned that it was simply a matter of power, of showing them who was in charge. Yet, the stares of the elders told a different story. Their glances flickered over each of them in turn, over their clothes, before eventually coming to rest in one specific spot. On the straight-backed, officious Furyborn with the patchy hair bowing deeply before them.

Half-Swart groaned deeply before rubbing the bridge of his nose. "For the love of the Halls, Evan, not again!"

It turned out that Evan, the messenger supposed to fetch them, had a bit of a history of making his own choices when it came to properly preparing any "supplicants," as he called them, to be introduced to the elders. He had most definitely not been tasked in denying them the chance to clean, change their sweaty clothes, or spend half a minute preparing mentally. The man took his scolding stoically, with no sign of admission that he was going to change his ways, before removing himself from the platform.

One of the elders addressed them with a sigh. She was a Furyborn, like the other elders, except Half-Swart, and a single Lightborn woman. She looked like what Gunnha, the proprietor of the Busy Hand back in Isarn, might look like after a decade of easy living. She was compact, but soft, looking so much like somebody's nice granny that you'd almost expect her to be wearing an apron and offering cookies. In actuality, she wore long, flowing garbs not too far off from the official robes of the Elementals of the towers. "My name is Elder Naian. I apologize on behalf of everybody. Evan is very... conscientious." She cleared her throat. "Now. Usually, I'd give you the chance to go back to the pens, bathe, and prepare properly. Only, since you're here, and this is a serious matter, we should proceed."

"Also, we *need* to get back to the eastern front." The Lightborn's hoarse, raspy voice sounded like a permanent fixture, and was entirely at odds with her looks. She was a tiny thing, gorgeous and doll-like, with perfect hair and a girlish blue dress. She didn't look one bit over twenty-five. Also, every other second, she... flickered, as if her presence was ephemeral, or an illusion.

"That too, Elder Madaline." She inclined her head. Her robes moved strangely, as if independently of her own movements. She stood and faced them, head held high and face impassive. With her deep-set laugh lines and four foot ten of height, the look was a bit off. "Your arrival to Heart Halls has not been unnoticed." She glared at Elder Madaline, who snorted and rolled her eyes. "Not only do we rarely allow an entire group like yours access to Heart Halls, but you come bringing a proposal from High Elementalist Tatiana Skysworn. A proposal that is not just unprecedented, but frankly unheard of in all Furyborn history."

The Lightborn, Elder Madaline, rolled her eyes again. "Naian. Could we get on with it?"

Huffing, Elder Naian's mouth turned downward. "This is a historic moment. I'm just trying to add a touch of gravitas."

"Gravity's what you got, woman. Not gravitas." A hint of a smile curled on her lips.

"*Madaline Gregorian de Satine.* You behave, or I am going to recite your entire genealogy as a formal introduction." She cleared her throat and fixed her blushing face on their group again. "The proposal is, as stated, unheard of. It makes a number of logical leaps and implies a propensity for risk-taking that goes beyond anything that past collaboration and mutual help between the Elementals and the Furyborn has seen. To sum up, the High Elementalist proposes." She held up a hand and started to count on her fingers.

"That we not only grant cards to you, but an entire secondary deck, that will cost the Furyborn and be yours for the remainder of your life.

"That we aid you with manpower, provisions, and equipment.

"That we let you walk away with these gifts, free and separate, with no way to control what you intend to do with this."

Her voice grew slightly strangled, as if she couldn't really believe her own words.

"As if this weren't enough, she suggests that we should then let you walk into what these days is seen as close to certain death—walking in to Liberty lands, with the intention of also gaining a Deck of Liberty." She shook her head. "In return, she refers to promises that you would be able and willing to then establish a Wellspring open to anybody, with the inherent powers needed to withstand the accumulated powers of the Lightborn." The strict words and severity of the woman burned away the former jolly mood.

They wilted under her strict, scrutinizing gaze. Put like that, it definitely sounded like an insane ask.

"High Elementalist Skysworn does not mince her words. She claims elements of racism and weakness in our ranks that should keep us from taking your deck for ourselves. Also, there is a lot left unsaid in this proposal." She continued, "She does not *quite* threaten us. Neither does she spend any time debating what the Elementals might do, if we were to do so... *but it is implied*. This level of overt hostility from an outside power, even an ally, is quite frankly unbelievable."

Sera was crestfallen. Kith looked like he was about to start spewing sarcastic comments.

"We *have* agreed that we are not going to take away your cards—"

"I still say it's the only choice," a wiry Furyborn woman, whose matted, gray-streaked red hair looked more like a lion's mane, burst out hotly. "Screw the towers. They can't help us from up there, and it's not like they'd be able to get back at us. The strength—"

"Will not be enough, Elder Yassia, *as we have already voted on*," Elder Naian announced with finality, "compared to the Lightborn forces, and the cost of the goodwill, information freely given, the trade, and frankly necessary aid from the Elementals that would disappear, were we to do so." Elder Naian's glare caused the feral Furyborn to subside, and she turned back to face them. "What you, and she, offer, is simply not enough. Vague promises, yet little in actuality. As such, we wanted only to hear from you, judge your ideas for ourselves, before sending you back. Perhaps, in time, we might be able to find a compromise that could work for all of us. Meanwhile, we will wait and hold our own, like the Furyborn have always done."

For a while, nobody said anything. Chase blinked. Then he snorted.

"Find something funny, boy?" Elder Yassia growled.

"Frankly? Yeah. Quite a lot of things, really." He pointed east, or, at least, where he thought east was. With the subtle, pendulous movements of the tree underneath him, it was hard to tell. "First, there's the idea that sending us back out there isn't a risk in itself. *They're amassing the inquisitors to hunt us.* And those sanctimonious pricks have a skill that let them spot Dark cards, if they get close. The High Elementalist's already said that she can't take us in, because that would likely lead to open war with the Lightborn. I don't know enough about this stuff to tell if she's right, but that still leaves us out, in the middle of the open, with threats all over."

He growled now, having talked himself warm. "What exactly do you think happens if the Lightborn catch us and get a hold of the deck? How long do you think it's going to take for them to expand their *own* forces with Dark cards? They already have Furyborn decks, of course, from all your battles. How long is it going to take them to decide to take the towers, to have a complete collection of decks? How will the Furyborn fare by then?"

"Now, listen here—" Elder Yassia started.

Chase ignored her, looking Elder Naian straight in the eye. "What's really funny, though? *We never wanted any of this.* Back in Isarn? We were nothing. Lower than low, living on the Waves, running in the slums, surviving any way we could. But what we're looking for, somehow, even as we've walked the Steps and climbed the Tiers, hasn't changed one tiny bit. We just want a Light-scoured *home*. If you want any fancy plans, or elaborate schemes for how we'd intend to build the Wellspring and make things ready to face the Lightborn? We can't help you. I'm sure the High Elementalist has a ton of plans already. We'd be willing to work with her—and with you, of course—and would *need* guidance. But that's the one thing that we crave, above all. A home. All we want is a home. And we'd be ready to open it to all, and fight where needed, to make sure that it'd be a good and safe one."

Silence spread after that. Chase felt a hand on his shoulder and, surprised, saw that it was Cilia's. He clasped the hand.

Eventually, with an inscrutable expression, Elder Naian turned to the single heretofore unnamed elder and asked, "Was that enough for you, Elder Nightbranch?"

Cilia's hand on Chase's shoulder clasped down, and she made a strangled sound, for some reason.

The Furyborn, oldest among the lot, and seemingly badly hit with arthritis, judging from the way his bony hands cradled on his lap, stood up. His eyes were steel-set but warm, even as his voice had the shaky timbre of an old man. "It was."

He nodded at Chase and smiled. "In short, apart from Elder Yassia, we did not actually intend to throw you back out. There would be no boon to this, and no need. We have asked around among the people you have encountered on your journeys, and had messages sent to Cemano. With a very few exceptions, they have praised your conduct.

"Also, the fact that the Elementals hold you in high enough esteem to grant you a deck is telling. Yet, we Furyborn prize other characteristics than the Elementals. If we are to lend you our support in truth, we would want you to hold true to *our* core values, not just those of the towers. Your speech would not do well among the Lightborn nobility... but to me, it does show your resolution to aid the blood, and that you would do it *your* way, not just be a hand puppet with the High Elementalist's hand lodged with her grip halfway up your insides. I will agree to see your true colors."

Elder Naian shot a recriminating look at the elderly man, which he entirely ignored.

Chase reeled, unsure whether he was catching this. "Does that mean—"

Elder Naian held up a hand, stopping his question. "We have found that we agree with the High Elementalist on the whole. Something needs to happen, unless the Furyborn and Elementals are to slowly succumb to the growing powers of the lost ones and the Lightborn." The grandmotherly woman let an inkling of warmth show in her mien. "Since Elder Nightbranch agrees, we can move to the next phase. Because everything among the Furyborn is earned. We have had outsiders before, asking for boons, for help, to become one of us. Never anything as groundbreaking as this. If we aid you in this, not only do we risk the cost of a Deck of Fury, a price that will be reclaimed with time and new wielders—no, we also risk the Lightborn, even the Liberators, obtaining the original Deck of Darkness. The end result of that would be unknown, but it could only spell disaster for us all. As such, independence and blood are all well and good. We will also need to test your integrity and your resilience."

Their group shared uncertain looks.

Sera asked, "What exactly does that mean?"

Elder Yassia shot them a smile that would not have looked out of place on a charging gaborn. *Good* teeth. "It means we're cooking up something special for you kids. Either you get to prove your mettle and I was wrong... or you prove you don't have what it takes. Then we either send you packing, or take your cards off your cold bodies."

"Out of line, Elder Yassia," Elder Nightbranch admonished. He smiled, showing a gap-toothed grin. "Not wrong, though. If you want to be part of us? Prove it!"

Elder Naian nodded. "Our challengers will meet their own tests a week from now. Your own trial will be different. It will be harder. If you intend to join forces with the Furyborn for the future, you will need to bring everything you have to the table. We will need..."

"Three days," Elder Madaline said.

The matronly Furyborn assented. "We will need three days to get your trial ready and inform the inhabitants of Heart Halls what is happening. Do whatever you need to prepare in the meantime. Because if you are not ready, it *will* be your final test."

Chapter 36

"We do get Furyborn out here, outside their lands, now and again. Yet, they tend to be the unwanted ones, the weak ones, those who disagree with how their lands are run. We take their truths with a grain of salt... yet we still lap it up, since information about the bloodied grounds is so hard to come by. I am sure the Lightborn do the same." Huh. That's probably accurate. Troublemakers and failures are more likely to leave and try to make a living selling information. Likely, the Lightborn know a lot more about their lands than the Furyborn realize. (Page 85.)

Initially, they'd simply celebrated. What, at first, had seemed an insane fever dream, now had a chance to actually come true. Even if they'd been dropped off the weald walker (which was apparently the proper name for the tree-like construct, an amalgamation between a communion and a very specific Furyborn summoner build), they shouted loud enough that they were sure the elders could hear them rejoicing.

Following that, however, their situation became clear, and their moods dampened. Now, not only would they have to prove themselves in front of the elders and... well, likely the entirety of Heart Halls, in what was likely to be some huge gladiatorial combat setup or similar... their secret was also, finally and irrevocably, out.

In a very, very short while, all of Heart Halls would know their secret. This wouldn't be like back in Isarn, or among the towers, where a small-ish, select group were introduced to the secret. No, here, it would be a general update, and *everybody* would know they had Dark cards.

They decided to split up and get as many preparations done before the news spread. Cilia went back to whatever craft she'd been working on, with the promise that she *would* reveal it soon. Liam flung himself headfirst back into training, with the desire to carve out as much from the added bonuses in the challenger pens as possible. Kith decided he'd rather spend the time getting reacquainted with his Dark summons, even if it meant the secret would be out for him earlier than for the others.

That left Sera and Chase, who were sent on a mission on behalf of their entire group. A mission to take every single coin they had and spend it in Heart Halls markets, buying any damn thing they might find use of in the tests to come. Yet, after spending an hour and a half marching to find the right place, their mood was anything but burdened by stress.

"I must admit. Going on a shopping spree was not how I imagined celebrating our success... not that I am complaining." Sera laughed, linking her arm with Chase's.

"Do I know how to treat my women or what?" Chase smirked.

"Women, plural? Is it really time for a neutering?" One eyebrow quirked up.

Chase laughed. "You're a lot less timid than I took you for, the first time I saw you."

Sera snorted and blew a curl from in front of her eyes. "You aren't exactly what I pictured either... which is probably a good thing, considering that I wanted to stab you, right then and there, among all the other indebted. Light's truth, you were so infuriating!"

He drew her in for a quick kiss. "It's a gift." Looking around, his grin turned into a frown. "Speaking of things that aren't what I pictured... this is quite far from what I expected from the vaunted Heart Halls market. I expected, at the very least, a small city where the outsiders were escorted in by defenders and wouldn't be allowed to leave under pain of death. Instead, we get a small street market, not half the size of Isarn's lower market. What's that about?"

She smiled. "Truth be told, I expect we should be thankful for this much. There will likely not be many people attempting to come here and trade, and those who do are bound to have had trouble slinking by the Lightborn forces. I fear that we will have to overpay to get anything good."

"You're probably right. Wait. Is that—"

"You. Dark-soiled filth." The voice was filled with scorn, laden with dark promises and extremely recognizable.

Chase felt a warm sensation in his entire body, as his Toughness increased by a decent number. He praised Sera in his mind. Then he plastered a warm, welcoming smile on his face. "Slate! Mate! Did you ever notice that those two rhyme? No way that's a coincidence, you know, what with your warm and friendly attitude."

The irate Furyborn scout stalked closer to the pair. His arms were taut with coiled tension and veins stood out on his neck. "How did you do it?" he demanded.

Chase surreptitiously switched to Free of Perdition and Circle of Darkness, ready to steal Slate's Agility and dump him in magical darkness at any sudden movement. His eyes roamed, alert to any unexpected maneuver, yet he kept his tone warm and bubbly. "Ooh. That's a deep question, my friend. A good one, too. The right woman *can* change your life. First, I treated Sera *right.* I didn't come on too strong, but let my natural good looks do the work. Obviously, that approach won't work for you, but—"

"How did you convince the elders to give you a chance? *You?*" It wasn't quite a shout, but the snarl was definitely loud enough that heads turned around them.

He sighed and let his false cheer drop. "Listen. Have you ever considered, that if you're the only one who wants to see us all dead... maybe it's not us who are the problem? Alia and everybody else back in Cemano accepted us. Misandria accepted us. Even your elders have accepted us and have given us the chance to prove ourselves."

"*They didn't all accept you! Elder Yassia saw through your lies! You were carrying Dark cards all along and lied about it.*" Spittle flew from his lips.

Chase noted that tiny detail. The elders *had* noted that there'd been some people talking up against them. It wasn't like it was a huge surprise. He lowered his voice to a calming tone. "Yes. We did omit the fact that we had Dark cards back in Cemano. It's just like we've said right from the start. The High Elementalist did not want us to disclose everything before we met the elders. And *yes*, Elder Yassia wanted to take our cards for the Furyborn. But the rest of the elders voted against that. Can't you respect their decision? They're your leaders, man." The moment he'd said that, Chase realized that it was the wrong thing to say.

Slate froze up, fury crystallizing into something deeper, darker. "So, I should just bow my head and ignore my heart? Like a good. Little. Lightborn?" His chest rose and fell with panting breaths, as if he'd been sprinting.

People around them started to idle closer, in that very human attraction to a commotion.

Sera, cutting through the tension, stated coldly, "Slate. We do not care for your company. We never did. Yet, we have things to do. So, either attack us or move on, because we cannot be bothered to spend any more time on you, you vacuous, good-for-nothing chest infection!"

The scout blinked. His eyes narrowed, and he ignored Sera, pointing straight at Chase. "You think you've gotten away with it. You think if you complete your trial, nobody's going to be able to touch you. I'll see you mistaken. I'm not letting you hurt the blood!" His final words nearly unintelligible from how he snarled, he turned on his heels and stalked off.

For a while, they just stood there, watching the furious scout nearly collide with another pedestrian before he strode away. Slowly, Chase's lip curled up until he couldn't restrain himself any further. "Chest infection, eh?"

Sera slapped his shoulder. "I rarely curse. And less, when I am angry. Also, I seem to have heard something about you courting me? Not coming on too strong? Letting your natural good looks do the work? That is not how I recall it."

The banter did a lot to wash away the black clouds that Slate had thrown over the day's triumph. They would still have to warn the others that the damn bastard might come up with something to try to blindside them... yet even that knowledge couldn't quite ruin the jubilant mood.

Soon, they found themselves strolling through the markets in search of equipment and items that would help them defeat whatever the elders might cook up against them. And they found that, for all that Heart Halls markets looked a lot less impressive than what they'd envisioned, looks were deceiving.

Basically, the place consisted of a large, open space at the edge of the forest, blanketed by a tall wooden fence surrounded by watchful Furyborn defenders. The watchful defenders were certain to ensure that visitors behaved and nobody stole away into the forest to discern the secrets of Heart Halls. Within the fence was a cleared area holding rows upon rows of stalls. The stalls had simple wooden walls, were ugly but durable, with slanted awnings over each stall to keep away rain, and tiny, fenced-off areas behind each stall for carts, wares, and the like. There were nearly a hundred stalls present, yet only about a third of them were occupied, the rest of them closed off.

A Furyborn vendor displaying a selection of the finest bows Chase had ever seen explained it. "It's all in flux, really. People from all across the bloodied grounds build up stores and travel to Heart Halls to trade off what they've built. Some of us just leave their goods here for others to trade with the traveling merchants. I like to trade 'em off myself, because I know what they're worth. Regardless, how many people are here depends on what's happening, the weather... a lot of other things. Now, with the Lightborn forces gallivanting about to the east, not as many traders will chance the approach... but with the challenges upcoming, we will see more arriving in the next few weeks."

They soon learned that Povel hadn't lied when he said that the Furyborn didn't use money. Any Furyborn vendors present only considered accepting any of the money they'd earned, stolen, or gained in the towers, if they had an inkling that they were overpaying to a degree where they would be able to easily earn it back from the outsider tradesmen present. In short, that was a losing proposition, even if Sera sent longing glances at a tall, hardened tower shield that was constructed of some sort of lightweight monster hide and enchanted.

For ease of navigation, Furyborn vendors were placed at one end of the area, and outsiders at the far end. Once they were done looking over the items available for trade, Chase and Sera strolled to the other end, ready to take on the part where they were more likely to come back with something they'd actually be able to buy.

"Nah. I'm not saying Kith's wrong. We definitely could do with better weapons on the whole. I'm just saying we're used to what we have right now, and three days isn't enough to properly get accustomed to a new weapon, unless they're *really* similar to our old ones."

Sera agreed amiably. "Fair point. That would, in my opinion, shift our priorities toward consumables. Food, potions, or the like. Though we are not likely to be able to afford much, that might grant us—"

"Shush." Chase held up his hand.

"What? No! You did not just—"

Eyes wide in shock, Chase held a finger to his lips and pointed surreptitiously. Frowning, she fell quiet and watched.

It was a stall like any of the others. Nothing special about it. If there was anything to set it apart, it would be the plumes of aromatic smoke rising from the fenced-off area behind the stall. That, and the voice coming from within the stall. "Now, good sir. Please take a mouthful and let it roll around in your mouth. Like so, exactly. What you, as a discerning client, will note, is the absolute lack of contaminants and distracting taste elements. This is because the ale has been aged in an absolute vacuum for eight months—a trade secret of mine that I am particularly proud of."

"No. Fire-charred. Way," Sera breathed. "It cannot be."

"It is." Chase's brow furrowed and he rolled his shoulders, and put one hand on his short sword as he barreled his way forward, past the prospective Furyborn customer who spat out his mouthful of alcohol and blubbered out in annoyance. Chase growled. "You!"

Brewer Nordon did not look like the type who'd be taken aback by... anything, really. His jovial face, flowing black locks, and warm demeanor was disarming and distracted from the fact that his powerful build indicated somebody who didn't spend all his time taste testing alcohol. As ever, his Elemental cards were on open display on his arms underneath his rolled-up sleeves, revealing water-aspected cards on top of slightly pale and clammy, blue-tinged skin. The man blinked from under his meticulously polished goggles, looking from his customer, to Chase, over to Sera, and then back to Chase. "Chase? Erm. What a... coincidence!"

"Did you *really* have to scare my customer off? His face said that he was already sold, and I had the perfect pitch ready for him," Nordon complained.

Chase and Sera half-dragged the protesting brewer back into the small fenced-off area behind his stall. It was filled with barrels stacked up next to the same extravagant setup of pipes, glass bottles, boilers, and beakers they'd had back in Soil. Chase tried to keep himself from hitting the taller man, but the temptation was growing. "Yes, we had to! *Why did you follow us here? How did you find us?*"

Nordon looked at them both, his skin pale and sweating. His eyes twitched and he took a deep breath. "Okay. So... maybe I kind of followed you here." He hurriedly added, *"But it's not what it looks like."*

Coldly, Sera asked, "Then you had better explain what it actually is. Because right now, it very much looks like you are following us around wherever we move and spying on us."

"I... well... yes." The big man harrumphed, frowned, then slapped his cheeks. He muttered under his breath. "Come now. I'm more eloquent than this." Spreading his arms, he asked, "Do you remember when I met you in Soil? You approached me, and said that you were there, both for the best booze and for information. I actually thought that you knew more than you let on right then. But then, when I met your clever friend, that Cilia in Earth's Ward, I realized that this was not the case. Those two first times? It was a coincidence that I met you. But then, with the chaos that followed, I started looking into you. And I learned a *lot*."

"What do you mean?" Chase growled.

"Please. Two people can keep a secret if you stab the other in the back and absorb his Ænima." The derision in his voice was tangible. He shook his head. "A *hundred* people in the towers suddenly gained Dark cards; you spent time in the company of the High Elementalist herself and were then snuck out the back door. On top of that, you are wanted by any inquisitor on top of a lot of Lightborn thrill seekers and bounty hunters—and you believe you can keep it a secret? Come now! Be real."

Sera and Chase shared a glance. That was not what they'd expected to hear.

The large Elemental took a beaker, dipped it in a large pot. "I am a crafter and a brewer. That is my job, and I'm *good* at my job." He took a sip from the beaker. Grimacing, he shuddered. "Usually. That was foul. Less nutmeg." He cleared his throat. "Brewing is not my passion, however. I am, by heart, an aficionado of information, and a bit of a thrill seeker. Learning that the Deck of Darkness was alive and kicking, and in the hands of a bunch of nobodies—no offense—does it really surprise you that I followed?"

"But how did you know to come here?" Sera asked.

"Please." He waved her off. "It's not like you could go anywhere else. Besides, I'd already visited a few times. I *like* the Furyborn. They're straightforward to deal with." He leaned forward. "And a bit simple, if I have to be honest. But I always bring them good stuff. My alcohols, and a hidden cache of well-crafted items from Earth's Ward. What really surprised me was that *you* weren't here when I arrived. My sources didn't come up with anything, and I honestly thought that you'd been caught. Yet here you are, just as I hoped."

Chase guardedly folded his arms. "Yes, here we are. Now, what are your intentions? You told Cilia back in the towers that you weren't in the market for blackmail. Has that changed?"

Nordon's eyes shone with an intense light. "I find a wielder, or wielders perhaps, of Dark cards. The first in centuries. And you think that I would stoop to *blackmail*?" He chortled. "Never! Just think of it. The secrets you must have. The stories you can tell. *The information you must hold is the kind that can topple rulers and move borders.*" He cleared his throat and winked. "And of course, I wouldn't mind a set of cards for myself, eh?"

Sera erupted in a tinkling laughter. "I bet you would not."

Chase didn't let off. "So, what exactly is it you want?"

"I want to milk you for information. I want to know everything that's happened to you, everything you know about Dark cards, their history and *your* history. I want cards for myself, I want a deck for myself, I want..." He took a deep breath, and exhaled with a grin. "A lot."

"And in return?" Chase asked.

"In return, you'd get anything I could possibly offer." His gaze fixed on Chase, unwavering. "Anything. No exceptions. My expertise as a crafter, my services as a brewer... I'd shine your Fury-damned boots every morning." He chuckled. "I'd offer you my services in bed, but I can see that's off the table. Yet, these aren't even the useful services I can offer. I will lay bare *any* information I have for your perusal. How do you think I made it here, even though the Lightborn are swarming like bees when you're running off with their honey? How have I learned which cards you and your friends have, according to the annals of the towers? How do I know you stole a deck in Isarn? Because of my connections. All I have and all I've guessed, I will make available to you, at no cost."

Chase and Sera looked at each other. It wasn't like Nordon looked especially trustworthy. Rather, at the moment, he looked pretty manic, eyes glinting with undisguised avarice. Also, the fact that he'd crossed something close to a war zone, risked his life, wares, and riches, at the chance of knowledge... did that make him less believable or more? He had been right in his estimates, in the end...

Eventually, Chase hazarded, "Where I'm from... we don't trust easy."

Matter-of-factly, Nordon nodded. "Trust is an easy way to an early grave. Reciprocal relationships is where it's at."

"Reci-what-now?"

"Give and take." Sera smiled.

Warily, Chase said, "This isn't the sort of thing we decide on a whim. Also, we kind of have a tiny task we need to handle first. But then... we may talk."

"That works for me. I managed an agreement to age a batch of rum for added attribute boosts. Meaning, they're not kicking me out for at least another three weeks."

Chase pursed his lips. "Hmm. What's your take on giving away bribes without gaining anything solid in return except possible goodwill?"

Nordon performed a half-bow with an added flourish. "I believe it is a wonderful love language that anybody in my position needs to master."

"In that case, we would love to hear more about anything you can offer that grants additional attributes. Also, an update about what is moving outside of the bloodied grounds."

Nordon rubbed his hands together merrily. "I think we are going to end up with a wonderful relationship. Sit down and let me tell you the myriad ways in which I may bribe you."

Chapter 37

"Before you try the tenacity of a Furyborn, recall this: They went to war with the Lightborn, not because of themselves, but because they mistreated the Darkborn. Does that sound like mettle you want to test?" That sounds like half a story. Then again, with the Furyborn we've met, I can believe it. (Page 89.)

The mess hall of the challengers' pen was... a mess. More people had started arriving for the challenges, and the cooks were working overtime. Tempers flared and people clashed, as Furyborn from all over met and disagreed.

Sera sat, gesturing elegantly with a fork, as her meal of overcooked boiled vegetables cooled on the table in front of her. "Meaning, there has been an actual change of leadership in the Church of the Circle because we repelled their attempt to steal the Elemental decks. The nobility has all but taken over control of the church in practice, with a Lord Beforant in charge. Nordon says that he has people—regular people—working both with and in the church, reporting to him. For now, however, it looks like there is a shift from them going after all heretics to them seeking the Dark cards for profit's sake. Now, for what that means for us? He cannot be entirely sure, yet." Sera paused, and frowned. "He also told us a good deal about troop movements outside the bloodied grounds, that likely would bore Liam and not mean a lot to the rest of us, just yet at least."

Kith grumbled, "You're telling me, that he gave you *all* that information for nothing... *and* he gave you a bunch of Strength- and Toughness-boosting potions—"

"Brews." Chase interrupted. "All of his stuff is alcohol."

"That only makes it better. He gave you all of that, for nothing?"

Sera waggled a finger. "Not at all. He is bribing us in order to get into our good books. Establishing an amiable future relationship. It just shows he knows how the world works."

Kith scoffed. "I don't trust him. Not one bit. We should do something about him."

"Even if we were ready to stab the man in cold blood, which I wouldn't do without a reason," Cilia scolded, "it makes a *lot* more sense to milk him for everything he's got. Now that everybody knows we have Dark cards, we might as well use them. Take him for all his knowledge and items, in return for a few cards. There's nobody who says we need to follow his advice, but at the very least, we should take the chance to learn."

"You're just saying that because he offered to teach you about crafting again." Chase laughed. "Not that I disagree. I think he's got a lot to offer that we want. Walking around blindly hasn't exactly been the best experience. Also, he kept hinting at having knowledge about the Liberators. I don't know if he knows something or he's just guessing. Whichever it is, if he can save us from walking into a death trap on Liberty lands, I say we listen."

Liam knocked on the table. "That's all well and good. It also doesn't matter at all." Ignoring their exclamations, he pushed away his empty plate. "It doesn't. Now, I know that I don't always think enough. Well, you, you and you." He pointed at Cilia, Chase and Sera in turn. "Think too much. You're stuffing your head with theories and rumors that are just going to get you *less* focused for the challenges we have ahead of us. In short, well done on getting us some boosting brews. Now, let's focus on what we need for the trial. Did you even look at anything else in the markets?"

Cilia looked like she was about to blow up. Sera blinked owlishly, while Chase grimaced.

Eventually, Cilia cursed. "Damn the decks, he's right."

"Yeah. It feels horrible. Like the world's been turned on its head." Chase shook his head. "Liam has a point. Who would ever think it would come to this?" He ducked the slap from Liam, only to take one from Cilia next to him. "Ow. Dammit! Okay. Who's first?"

"Let us go in turns," Sera offered. "Each of us says where we are at, what we have gained, and any thoughts we have." She looked around the table at the others, who nodded in turn. "In that case, my gains have been minimal. Even with the effect from the trees in place, I have only gained a single increase to Toughness from getting hit around with a shield."

She outlined her attributes:

Personal Info:
Name: Serafine
Title: Dark/Elemental/Light healer
Step: 18 (Tier 3)
Strength: 15 (+1 Tier bonus) = 16
Agility: 18 (+1 Tier bonus) = 19
Toughness: 18 (+1 Tier bonus) = 19
Mental Power: 34 (+11 Tier bonus) = 45
Potential: 12 (+1 Tier bonus) = 13

Chase wrinkled his nose. "That's downplaying it quite a bit. You're also getting a lot better at going fully defensive from all the dueling practice. Also, you've helped Cilia and helped *me* with all the different card combinations."

Sera ceded the point.

Chase took over. "That's pretty much me as well, though I've focused more on the dueling aspect. I've gotten a boost to Agility to go with Toughness, though. One thing I'll add... just a thought. I believe that whatever we're going to face isn't going to be like in the towers. What I mean is, I have no clue what we'll meet, but I don't think they're going to throw Guardians at us, mostly because that would mean throwing away their own resources."

Personal info:
Name: Chase
Title: Dark/Elemental/Light rogue
Step: 23 (Tier 4)
Strength: 19 (+1 Tier bonus) = 20
Agility: 23 (+13 Tier bonus) = 36
Toughness: 22 (+1 Tier bonus) = 23
Mental Power: 23 (+1 Tier bonus) = 24
Potential: 32 (+1 Tier bonus) = 33

Kith whistled. "Thirty-six Agility. This is getting ridiculous. I'm not threatening you, mate, but if I could carve that training card off your arm and take it for myself, I would."

Chase snorted. "Going feral, are we? Putting the fury in Furyborn?"

He rolled his eyes. "That was horrible. Now, I haven't slacked off like those two. And it's paid off. I've earned a point to Toughness, one to Strength, and *two* to Agility. I feel I'm on the cusp of another point to Mental Power too. Whatever we're going to face, I'll be ready. I believe I'll spend the remainder of the time with any of you who want to get the teamwork, erm, working properly, now that we can use our Dark cards freely."

Personal info:
Name: Kith
Title: Dark/Elemental/Light summoner
Step: 19 (Tier 3)
Strength: 18 (+1 Tier bonus) = 19
Agility: 22 (+1 Tier bonus) = 23
Toughness: 15 (+1 Tier bonus) = 16
Mental Power: 22 (+1 Tier bonus) = 23
Potential: 11 (+11 Tier bonus) = 22

"That's not looking bad at all." Liam clapped him on the back. "I have no clue how you can keep advancing all of that at the same time, but keep it up. It's clearly working. Now, I have only earned a point to Agility for myself. But I think I've done my fair share of work... and I'll keep on doing it the next couple of days, making sure we stay friendly with everybody, now that the secret's out."

Personal info:
Name: Liam
Title: Dark/Elemental/Light fighter
Step: 18 (Tier 3)
Strength: 18 (+11 Tier bonus) = 29
Agility: 17 (+1 Tier bonus) = 18
Toughness: 27 (+1 Tier bonus) = 28
Mental Power: 14 (+1 Tier bonus) = 15
Potential: 10 (+1 Tier bonus) = 11

Chase nodded. "I hadn't even thought of that. You're totally right, though. If you can keep them from stabbing us in the back from prejudice or fear or... I dunno, the desire to steal our cards, I think you've done everything we could possibly ask of you. Also, you are getting to be a damn powerhouse, big guy!"

Liam smiled. "I will. Don't you stress over it. I know the other challengers by now. They're good people. A few of 'em just need... a nudge in the right direction."

Sera smiled and let her hand intertwine with Chase's. "Sometimes, that is all it takes."

Cilia cleared her throat, for once not even deigning to ignore the soppy flirting with an eyeroll. Her gaze was different from her usual direct, challenging stare. She extracted a large burlap sack from under the table. "Like you know, I have been mostly hidden away, crafting. Hence, the only thing I have advanced is my Mental Power."

Personal info:
Name: Cilia
Title: Dark/Elemental/Light crafter
Step: 19 (Tier 3)
Strength: 13 (+1 Tier bonus) = 14
Agility: 20 (+1 Tier bonus) = 21
Toughness: 15 (+1 Tier bonus) = 16
Mental Power: 32 (+11 Tier bonus) = 43
Potential: 11 (+1 Tier bonus) = 12

"Only, she says. And it's at frigging forty-three!" Kith made a choking sound.

Ignoring him, Cilia continued. "My lack of progress is not due to laziness. Yet, I haven't exactly been forthcoming about what I've worked on, for one reason. This was my first truly ambitious project, and I was unsure if I actually had the skills to pull it off."

Liam scoffed. "Come now, Cil. You have the highest Mental Power of all of us"

"*Next* highest, thank you," Sera pointed out with a challenging tilt to her upper lip.

"*Ignoring* Sera now. Also, your dedication to improving has been more impressive than any one of us. I, for one, would never go through the mind-breaking torture that your Master Benneth calls rote learning."

"Building the foundations to an acceptable level is—"

"Key to becoming a good leatherworker," they all chorused, Liam with his mouth full again.

Cilia glared at them. "This is not a simple lack of self-esteem. I am not Chase. I know my value, and am not afraid to own it."

"That's hurtful!" Chase proclaimed. Then he scrounged up his face in confusion. "Probably?"

"This was an actual case of not knowing whether my skills, as of yet, properly untested, even with a decent Mental Power, even with my fire focus and Ritual of Fire card, *even with Sera's buffs on top* were enough for me to manage what I wanted to create."

Their table fell silent.

Kith was the one to find his words first. "Cil. That was a mouthful. What exactly have you been working on?"

Her slight smile grew, turning brilliant. "Chase. You recall the night emerald?"

Chase's eager demeanor turned into a confused stare. "Wow. I think I just got emotional whiplash from you changing topics so fast. Do I remember the insanely strong, adaptable, nearly impenetrable nightmarish horror of a multi-ton monster that almost jumped on top of me? Why yes, yes I do."

"The day after arriving to the pens, I got a visitor. Misandria. Apparently, she'd told you that the monster's skin was ruined from all the acidic liquid you'd bathed it in."

Chase narrowed his eyes. "Yeees?"

"Turns out that was a bit of an exaggeration. She didn't *know* if the skin was ruined. She had it carried with us, took it to a local leatherworker here in Heart Halls after arriving. Apparently, they were able to salvage a good deal of it, cure and treat it—and since Misandria knew I'd apprenticed with Master Benneth, she gave it to us, for going above and beyond."

Chase made a strangled noise deep in his throat. "The night emerald skin? Those armored plates that *all* the archers, regardless of Tier, could only pierce after using several cards, after we'd debuffed and struck it dozens of times? Those are what you've been working with?"

"And enhancing." She took the burlap sack and upended it; an unwieldy, large pile of darkened items clunked out onto the table. "Liam. See what you think. I stole some clothes of yours to check the size."

He ignored the comment about theft, looking at the massive pile of material on the table. "For me?"

"Come on, you big lug. You're not that daft. Who else would we want to carry a suit made out of a nearly impenetrable material? Pick it up already," Cilia scolded.

With a look approaching awe, he grasped the largest item on the table. Then he grabbed onto it with his other hand as well, to avoid overbalancing. "Heavy." He grunted. Unfolding it, he held it up for all to see. It was a body armor, created to cover the entire upper body, including the arms. Yet, the armor was clunky, with large squarish items somehow grafted onto the material underneath. Inspecting it closer, he mused, "This is regular leather?"

"Sort of. The base armor is capracine leather. It's a local, hardy rodent that's fairly common around here. A pest, really. Wasn't hard to get. The material's decent, but you can get better. The good part is that, like the plates, the material takes well to enhancing."

Liam grunted, as he held it in one hand and knocked with a knuckle on one of the plates on the leather. It made a muted ringing sound, like knocking on the side of a solid granite wall. "This is the night emerald skin, then? It... doesn't feel like stone."

Cilia smiled proudly. "I sure hope not." She grabbed the sleeve and let her hand run lovingly up the bumpy material. "Two hundred and sixty-eight plates of night emerald skin sown onto the leather with special needles. Each and every one of these plates has been imbued with fire, granting it enough malleability for me to work with it, and align with the leather underneath, even as it retains its hardness."

"Darkness steal my sight." Liam put down the armor reverently. "Imbued with fire. Is that why it has that color?" The leather underneath was a dark brown, yet the plates on top retained the near black of the night emerald. However, they looked alive, as if a tiny flame had come alive inside each plate of monster skin.

"It is. It's also why wearing the armor should grant you something... more," Cilia hinted. "Put it on already. I want to see how I've done."

A short scene of chaos followed, with the locals hooting at the show, as Liam unabashedly dropped his shirt to don the heavy armor. The chaos only increased as he dropped his pants, adding catcalls and whistles to the mix. After a short moment of admiring the craftsmanship, he added the leather gloves, with plates on *both* sides of the glove. Lastly, Cilia helped him clasp the gorget in place and secure it. Finally, the skin-tight helm clasped in place, leaving his face free for optimal vision.

The tall Lightborn rolled his shoulders, jumped up and down a few times, ran in the spot and windmilled his arms to test his range of motion. His frown grew deeper. "There's something..." he murmured. His eyes grew distant for a moment, then his eyebrows shot up in shock. "Cilia," he breathed.

Her laughter was the sound of weeks of stress relieved in a single breath, with a hint of tears. "Yes! Liberty break my chains, I did it! How much?"

Half-strangled, Liam sounded disbelieving. "Seven. It grants me seven points to Agility."

A hush filled the room. Then shouts erupted.

It took a while to calm the room down again. Following that, they had to insist that Cilia wasn't taking any orders right now. Eventually, they were forced to leave the mess hall in order to continue their conversation.

"I believe it's because I imbued each piece of night emerald skin as a piece of the whole. Intent matters. I wanted the material to be durable, malleable, and aid your movement," Cilia explained as they walked back to their cots. "Also, with the material as... greedy as it was—I know. It's a poor explanation, but those are the words that feel right. They sucked in the enhancements and wanted more. I doubt a full set of regular leather would be able to hold more than a single point or two."

"It works. It really, really works," Liam said, awestruck. He couldn't stand still, performing lunges, quick sprints, jumps mid-conversation. Slightly out of breath, he mused, cheeks rosy with exertion, "It's heavy. I wouldn't want to try putting it on with a Strength below twenty, that's for sure. It's also rather stiff, of course. With the plates everywhere, even with the enhancements, it really should limit my movement. But... seven Agility! I feel like one of those dancers with the feathers and the bells. And the protection should be amazing." He blinked. "Is this going to be porous? You said its skin was somewhat like rock."

"Don't be daft, Liam." Kith snorted. "You saw the thing move. You think it was going to crumble apart if you hit it with your old truncheon?"

"He's not entirely wrong, Kith," Cilia said. "The armor will be more vulnerable to blunt damage. The Guardian had vastly larger mass behind it to absorb any blows. The smaller plates and your, obviously, weaker body, won't have the same resistance. And any broken fragments will have to be replaced entirely, since they crumble. Also." She sighed and exhaled in disgust. "It's not permanent. I was *this* close. I could feel it. Only, I'd have to change my focus somewhat for it to be permanent. It will hold onto its enhancements for months. Three, at least. Six, at the outside. Then it will start fading away. Maybe I can re-enhance it at that point. I hope so." Her voice grew a bit frantic at this point. "I did manage to include one thing I wanted. Took extra care with the inside of the gloves. There are tiny plates both in the palm and on the inside of the fingers. You should be able to catch unenhanced blades at no risk to your fingers now. Also—"

Liam grasped onto her. The tiny woman almost disappeared as he enfolded her in a massive bear hug. "Cilia. This is the *best* damn gift I have ever received. That I'm ever *going* to receive, most likely!" He stopped, looking down at the smaller woman, who was blushing wildly, looking straight down to avoid his gaze. He didn't relent. He took his massive paw, now even larger with the thick, padded gloves, and put it under her chin, gently lifting it upward. "We don't say this enough. Cilia. You are brilliant. Not just clever. Brilliant enough that you're going to make a huge impact, wherever you go."

"It's just an arm—"

"It's *not* just an armor!" Liam roared. He let go of the startled woman and pointed back at the mess hall they'd just left. "Didn't you just see them? Clamoring for your attention, for you to help craft something for any of them." He took two deep breaths before closing his eyes and spreading out his hands in a calming gesture. "You, Cilia, are Tier three. Not Tier five. Not the daughter of some legendary hero, waited on hand and foot, taught by the best of tutors, but a stubborn, mixed-race brat grown up in the worst of circumstances. And with a few weeks of work and the right materials, you've changed the way I fight completely. *That's a good thing.* I am faster; I can take more risks, absorb more hits. Like this? I am free. Free to keep us all safe." Liam's voice was hoarse, and his eyes shone. "You, Cilia, when you grow with us, are going to change the world."

Cilia ducked down to avoid his gaze. She started to walk again, and the others followed. For a long while, she didn't answer, merely walked, head bowed. When she spoke, it was nearly too low to catch. "I'll try, Liam. I'll try."

They arrived at the barracks and started to prepare for the night.

Sitting on the edge of her cot, Sera looked troubled. "I... hesitate to mention this, but I believe there is one final thing we should discuss."

"Now what?" Liam yawned. "I'm nearly asleep. All this excitement has worn me out and I need to be well-rested to break in my new armor tomorrow! Along with all the challengers I'm going to make cry."

She ignored his claims. "It revolves around our trial. I believe there is a point we have missed." Sera looked at the floor, disturbed, but focused.

The others stopped what they were doing and gathered around Sera.

Kith asked, "What's that then, princess? Apart from what Chase said about the Guardians, that is. I can't really see how we can guess more about what we're going to meet."

"You might not have been paying attention, then." Sera smiled, taking the sting from her comment. "The elders said it themselves. They are going to be testing us according to their creed." She walked over to the opposite cot to pat Liam's massive biceps. "Resilience is all well and good. But how are they going to test our integrity and independence on an obstacle course?" Sera wrinkled her nose. "No. This will be the same situation that Naley pointed out all over again. We are going to be put into awkward situations, somehow, and expected to act according to what makes sense for the Furyborn."

"But they *don't* make sense!"

"I know." Sera huffed. "No laws? Kids get conscripted at ten years of age?"

"No money!" Kith shuddered. "Everybody *shares*."

"Enough," Chase said. "I hate to be the voice of reason here. It's not really my thing. But Sera's right. That's *exactly* the infuriating crap we'll need to prepare for. Only, we can't afford to spend all our time yammering about theories. We should get some rest, and then tomorrow, we can find ourselves a new Naley."

"A new Naley. I like that. Naley was hot," Kith said dreamily.

Cilia's fist crashed into his shoulder. She cursed. "Ow. Damnit. You're getting too boney. I should make a set of gloves for myself."

Chapter 38

"The reason my trade campaign failed? Not because of their stubborn refusal to accept Elemental or Lightborn coinage. Not because of my trading skills. No, it was their damn expectations. So mercurial. Sometimes, they would expect humility. At other times, they were forthright to the point of insult. To this day, I am unsure whether they actively bankrupted me or it was my lack of understanding." I sympathize with her, even if I deem the cause her ignorance. She should have asked more questions, researched deeper. Yet, the Furyborn *are* hard to comprehend. (Page 41.)

The three days went by way too fast. They didn't find a "New Naley," yet Liam had a good talk with some of the challengers he'd befriended earlier. To them, having outsiders who were actually interested in learning how to behave "properly" was a welcome novelty. Hence, for the full three days, a handful of different challengers took time out of their own training to help them understand the conundrum that was Furyborn mentality.

At times, it seemed self-contradictory. The desire for absolute independence and refusal that anybody, even your damn chief or elder, was the ultimate boss of your life, weighed against the degree to which they toiled for the blood, for instance, seemed absurd. Yet, it made sense to the Furyborn. And the more time the crew spent among them, the less weird their idiosyncrasies seemed.

It wasn't like they spent their time just chatting. Just as planned, they spent the vast majority of their time in actual training, except Liam, who was their one-man goodwill generator. When he wasn't humiliating other duelists in his new armor, Liam spent half the day in the mess hall or walking around the pens, chatting with the challengers.

Of course, that didn't clear them of all belligerence. Regardless of what the official attitude was toward the Dark cards, some people definitely equated Darkness with evil. On top of that was the fact that they'd been keeping a third of their cards secret from everybody. The argument that the elders had asked them to do so until they'd made their decision had some weight, but they were embroiled in some heated moments along the way.

Still, they did find a good deal of time to actually train. When morning came on the third day, and Half-Swart himself came to pick them up and bring them to their trial, Kith had managed to get the additional point in Mental Power he was chasing, and Cilia earned herself another point to Agility. They felt ready for anything the elders threw at them.

Cue their confusion, when Half-Swart didn't really throw *anything* at them. He just came to meet them, right at the entrance to the pens.

All packed up, wearing their best gear and packs filled with food and any items they could imagine using, they felt as ready as they could be. Challengers, attracted by the elder's arrival and the commotion of their crew finally setting out on their trial, crowded the opening in the huge tree barricade.

Half-Swart rolled his massive shoulders. Happy to have an audience, he grinned unabashedly as he spoke in a voice loud enough to carry. "Trial starts now. You have two days to find and return the Deck of Fury. It's a real deck. Obviously not a primary deck, but still, a functioning, ready-to-use deck, kept under guard in the village of Heath, about three and a half hours' march that way." He pointed northwest. "Nobody in the village has been told that a trial is ongoing. They've been informed that the deck is going to be theirs, to be used to establish a Wellspring in Heath soon, and that they're supposed to keep an eye on it." He chuckled. "We weren't even lying either. If they manage to protect the deck, they're keeping it. That'll be a nice growth spurt for the village."

"Wait," Kith said. "No battles, no traps, no... elaborate obstacle courses or devious puzzles? And you're telling me they don't even *know* we're coming?"

"We sure didn't tell them anything."

"That's not..." Kith huffed and tried again. "What's the bloody trial in this, then? Can we just walk in and *run away* with the deck? Or absorb it?"

"You can sure try to just sprint away. No absorbing it, though. You need to bring the deck back." Half-Swart truly looked like he was enjoying himself.

Cilia growled. All business, she barked, "Kith. Hush. Sera. Boost our Heart cards."

Sera blinked, but a second later, the card flashed on her leg.

Following a moment after that, they experienced the sounds from the outside world fading away, as Cilia's Heart card activated, leaving them cut off from the noise of the outside world.

Half-Swart put his little finger in his ear and rummaged around. "Well, that's uncomfortable," he murmured.

Cilia sighed. "No more uncomfortable than you telling everybody present what is going to happen so they can warn their friends."

"Oh." Kith slapped his forehead as he realized what was going on.

"Oh, indeed." Half-Swart smirked. "I wish you good luck on your trial. Of course, we will be watching. You will be judged on your performance. On your choices. On everything you do from here on out. You catching on to the point this fast is a good start. But the real trial is only just starting. I recommend that you get any questions out of the way quickly."

Chase grimaced and rubbed his chin. "Are there any limitations, apart from the deadline? Anything we're not allowed to do?"

"Are there any limitations in real life?" the elder responded, an eyebrow raised.

"Okay, so this is going to be judging us on what we do, how we succeed... *how* exactly are we being observed?" Kith asked.

Half-Swart guffawed. "Naughty, naughty. Already trying to cheat the system, are we?"

"You can't prove that," Kith shot back, then laughed.

"You've informed the villagers about the deck and that they're supposed to guard it. Can we expect any intervention from any other groups or persons?" Chase's brow furrowed in thought. "From outside the village, I mean?"

Half-Swart tapped his nose. "Good thinking, Darkie. Let me answer it like this. *We* haven't arranged any additional defenders." He looked behind them. "Anything else? It looks like part of the crowd is peeling away."

Chase looked behind them and cursed. A few onlookers were indeed slipping away, one deeper into the pens, while another was sidling past them en route to the outside. "That deck. Is it just a simple deck, or does it have any defenses or traps?"

"Oh, come now. Life wouldn't be the same without *some* surprises now, would it?"

"You're enjoying yourself *way* too much, Half-Swart," Liam scolded. "Are we off?"

They took a rapid discussion right there, rearranging the bubble without Half-Swart in their center. Swiftly, they came to the unfortunate conclusion that trying to keep the challengers from spreading the news would be a losing fight. Even *if* they were able to talk the challengers into supporting them over their own families and friends in Heath—a questionable proposal at best—the secret had already been spilled. There'd be messenger Guardians, communication cards, rogues and summoners with cards to let them outrun even Chase… all sorts of ways they'd be able to get the news to Heath before they made it there. Even if that weren't the case, they all knew that the velocity of rumors beat that of the flight speed of the average gaborn.

With all that in mind, they decided they might as well take their time and prepare properly. In this case, that meant using their secret weapon. They prepared and released the best card they had that could help them gather information, garner goodwill, and obtain secrets that could help them on their way. Not an actual card, this time.

Liam.

It took nearly twenty minutes, while the rest of their crew double-checked their equipment, debated whether they should start downing some of Nordon's brews and decided they'd rather wait. Kith spent most of the time with his eyes closed, already deep within the senses of his Shadow Master summons, making sure that there were no ambushes waiting for them right outside the pens.

Liam didn't look entirely pleased when he returned to them. He huffed in displeasure, then grimaced as Cilia's bubble of silence settled over them again. "Okay, the good news first… because there's not that much of it." He nudged his chin at the challengers' pens. "Some are definitely already racing off to warn friends or family in Heath that we're coming—"

"How is that *good* news?" Kith exclaimed.

"The good news is that I managed to talk enough of them into giving us a chance and not team up to kick our asses right this moment! It was a close thing, too. Earning a Wellspring for remote family sounds a good deal better than granting a half-stranger a fair chance."

"Oh." Kith looked chastised and cleared his throat. "Well done then."

"The only other piece of good news is that a few of them were nice enough to tell me about Heath—how to get there, what it looks like, and what the defenses are like—oh, and an alternate route back here, in case we're being chased. The bad news lies in what Heath *is*. Which is a nice place for local defenders who've fought for their entire lives to retire to enjoy some well-earned years of rest in peace."

Cilia groaned. "Meaning, it's bound to be filled with high-tier veterans."

Liam nodded grimly. "Except for the ones who've communed, yeah. That's exactly it. The village also doubles as a nearby fount of reserve soldiers in the rare case of the Lightborn showing up with large numbers of forces, so they're bound to be well-trained too, rather than slacking. Now, the defenses are supposed to be minimal, but that probably doesn't matter as much if they have high-Tier wielders everywhere."

They mused over this for a moment. Then Chase laughed. "This is amazing."

As one, they turned to him, and he raised his arms defensively. "No, really. It is. Think about it. Sure, the secret's out. But right this moment, we'll still be on the offensive. Even if they know we're coming, we'll have the element of surprise, of being able to see what's happening, prepare surprises and distractions, catch them out, while they'll be caught trying to defend from an unknown attacker."

"Oh." Liam slapped his forehead and beamed. "This isn't an attack. It's a job."

"Damn straight it is." Chase whooped. "We're about to go steal a deck from a village of Furyborn veterans who know we're coming. But they expect attackers, not thieves. This is going to be amazing!"

The first couple of hours of marching were anything but amazing. It was a tense trek, with their group jumping at shadows, ready to react to anything at any moment. Kith spent every moment inside the eyes of his shadows, scanning for anything and anybody, with no reaction whatsoever. Oh, it wasn't like they were alone. They were still slowly exiting the outskirts of Heart Halls, and the trees and sporadic defenses sported watchful defenders. Only, the defenders didn't seem to care in the least about their passage.

Liam had gotten a good description of the path they were supposed to take, which was fortunate. Even though the western path lay far from the current front against the Lightborn, the approach remained as twisting, turning, and inconstant as the one they'd arrived by. If they'd had to attempt the road themselves, they might as well have spent a full day simply navigating the approach.

As it stood, Liam judged that they might actually make it there in the three and a half hours that Half-Swart estimated. They made good speed, enjoying how they all, at this point, had enough Toughness that they were able to march at a rapid pace for a full day without getting winded. Even Cilia was at sixteen Toughness by now and was only slightly flushed by the exertion. As for the proclaimed watchers, they hadn't spotted any yet. Sera did say that she had a constant itching sensation of being watched, and they speculated it might be an invisibility card or the like, by somebody with a ridiculously high Mental Power.

They had maybe an hour to go, when Kith suddenly hissed, catching all their attention and pulling them up short. He pointed at Cilia, miming a bubble, and they huddled around him.

"It's up. What's going on?" Cilia said.

"We've got something... weird going on." Kith frowned, his eyes closed eyes and fingers twitching.

"Weird how? Ambush weird, trap weird, ancient wielder of Darkness gone insane about to flood all of Ordei with Dark Guardians weird?" Chase noticed their looks and shrugged. "What? I only want that sprung on me once."

"Just... weird weird, I think," Kith said. "There's somebody hiding in the bushes, a minute ahead, about twenty feet from the path. And if it's an ambush, it's the weirdest one ever. Whoever she is, she's half-dug into the ground, has pulled half a bush on top of herself, and it looks like she might be bleeding to death. And... I think she's a Lightborn."

"Get out here!" Liam's voice bellowed into the under-growth. "Now. I can see you, and I *know* you've seen me. And keep away from any weapons. There's four of us, and we're armed."

"That's one way to spring an ambush, I guess," Kith murmured.

They spread out, preparing. Kith and Chase entered their regular positions, trailing Liam. Sera stayed back a bit, ready to act with Unexpected Spillage in case the hiding Lightborn did anything surprising.

After a few seconds, the bushes started to move. The movement soon turned into a figure, which limped out toward them. It was a sorry figure that approached them, hands held up in surrender.

She was a Lightborn, no discussion. Yet, she wore no Lightborn insignia, and her clothes were nondescript, dirty and sodden. "Please. Don't attack."

Chase shared a glance with Cilia, whose scowl showed exactly what she thought of the chance encounter. "Right back at ya, lady. Now, if you don't mind, please kneel about ten feet away, and we'll have a nice, civil chat. Kith? Are we still uninter-rupted?"

"Not a soul to see."

"Good. Please proceed, ma'am."

She staggered ahead, nearly fell, and slid gracelessly to her knees.

Chase nodded. "You have any weapons? Please get rid of those. Just fling them ahead."

With an awkward motion, she unclasped the button on her hilt, extracted a large, machete-like dagger, and tossed it onto the ground. She wavered and looked like she nearly fell over.

"Thank you," Chase said, less harshly. "I think maybe we can afford for Sera to give a helping hand here. It'd be a waste if our chat was cut short by an untimely case of death. Anybody disagree?"

Nobody said anything, and a few seconds later, a light glow settled on the Lightborn and faded into her body. She gave a high-pitched gasp and nearly fell forward in a full-body shudder. When she sat up a moment later, her eyes fixated on Chase's, before darting onward to the others, watching, assessing.

Chase spoke up again. "Before any introductions, I think I'd like for you to raise your sleeves and show us your cards."

The woman grimaced, but did as she was told. Her left arm was empty, but her right held a single card, bordered in bright, merry sunlight.

"If you don't mind, this would probably be a good time for you to show us that you're actually a friend with the Furyborn, and have some Fury cards as well."

She grunted, half in amusement and half in dismay. Her voice, when it emerged, was cracked and despondent. "That's not going to happen. Name's Lissy. I'm... well, the polite word's a forward scout. Most would call me a spy."

The words hung in the air for a moment. Chase exhaled and cursed softly to himself. "So. Let me get this straight. You're a spy, sent to Heart Halls to..." He waved with his hand for her to continue.

"To map out the surroundings of the city, find less defended approaches than the ones they already know."

Chase rubbed the bridge of his nose. "Fury plow my fallow fields," he murmured to himself. "Okay then. And what in the *Pits* are you doing right now?"

The woman looked about to fall apart. She raised her arms. "I honestly haven't got a clue. I... listen, I'm an indebted. They said they'd allow me cards and let me keep them if I did this. It was either this or a short life that'd end under some Guardian's claws. You probably won't get this, but... I knew this was a chance, but it was the only chance I've ever gotten. I had to take it. There was a tree. A bloody tree! It swiped at me, and..." Finally, it looked like she *saw* them properly. Her eyebrows rose comically high, moving from one to the next, spotting the Dark cards visible on Kith's and Cilia's arms. "Who—what— in the Pits are you?"

They interrogated her for a short while. It turned out that Lissy didn't have anything to offer them. She was, by all accounts, simply somebody doing her best, yet caught in a horrible situation and knew nothing about Heath, except that it was a place she should shy away from given how many people lived there. They spent awhile discussing the situation under the hiding influence of Cilia's Heart card before coming to a conclusion. Then they dropped the silence effect, gathering around Lissy.

"All right, Lissy. It might seem at first glance it's anything *but* your lucky day," Chase started.

The Lightborn hadn't moved at all. She was still kneeling, eyes downcast, the very image of hopelessness. What she muttered under her breath sounded like affirmation of his comment.

"You see, we're in the middle of a trial of sorts for the Furyborn right now. One, where we're being observed every waking moment, or so they claim. This means that any chance you might think you had at secrecy is long gone. They already know you're here. Meaning, even if we wanted to let you go, it'd be moot."

Chase raised his voice to the skies and spoke up. "We're giving it even odds that this is some twisted scheme to test our integrity, see if we'd aid a Lightborn who looked innocent." He ignored Lissy, who looked suitably confused. "If that is the case, then *screw you!* Integrity isn't just about acting in favor of the Furyborn against all else. It's also a case of not being a horrible monster. If you came up with this, *do better!*" He took a deep breath and glanced at the others, who nodded at him to continue.

Chase spoke straight to the kneeling woman. "If this is real... if *you're* real, I'm so sorry, Lissy. They'll already have seen what's happening and will be on their way to pick you up. I doubt you deserve what's going to happen." He raised his neck to the skies again. "If there's any honor to you. Please be merciful. She didn't want this. Indebted don't get any chances. Everybody deserves at least one chance in life."

Chapter 39

"I do say. If there is one emotion that has been at the fore of my stay in Furyborn lands, it is that of wonder. All races have wonders. Lightborn make theirs exclusive to the few. We Elementals flaunt ours, showing them off in a competition to show everybody who's best and richest. The Furyborn? They hide it in plain sight. I have seen villages with defenses worthy of Earth's Ward. I have seen old gaffers sporting powers that would have the towers falling over themselves to offer them a chance at Protectorship. Everywhere, there is beauty, hidden among the bloodied clay." For once, I agree entirely. I expected uncultured wilds. I found something worth love and adoration. (Page 86.)

"I hate this place," Liam said.

"Really?" Sera asked. "I have rarely seen you angry or downcast with all your friends and acquaintances."

They were farther along their path, getting closer to Heath and slowing down, on the lookout for any scouts, any action, anything that might alert the locals.

Liam shook his head with a sad smile. "Sometimes, I lie, Sera."

"What?" She looked taken aback. "You?"

"Of course I do," the big man said. "I like people, but it's not like I naturally agree with everybody. Some people are just disagreeable. That's where I lie. A lot. And even here, among a people who seem to spend a good deal of time and energy to support their own kind, you get the usual... pettiness, bad tempers, and just horrible assholes. Even so, this, what we just did? It feels wrong. I think that's one of the few things I absolutely loathe about this place. That they're letting their war with the forces of Light spill over to the Lightborn race as a whole."

Sera nodded and patted his shoulder. "I agree with you there, Liam. Nothing justifies leaving a young girl hog-tied like that, uncertain of what is to come."

Kith snorted and butted in. "I mean, it depends. Sometimes, they ask for it..."

"Kith!" Sera scolded.

"Sorry." His grin was strained. "I know, it's a crap situation, and I don't like it either. Still, I needed to knock you out of your rut. We're there and we need to focus. Keeping the elders from executing some poor bastard needs to take a back seat for now."

"There" meant the outskirts of Heath. Following Kith's shadows who roamed around out front, they decided to move away from the path and hide in the underbrush so they could properly scout out the village. Then, they'd be able to see what they were up against and judge the best possible approach. Soon, they struggled their way into a clearing, well-hidden behind a mess of thorny bushes and brambles, and settled down to see what they had to work with.

The village of Heath was nothing special. At least, that's what it looked like at a distant glance. A small, idyllic village consisting of a few hundred houses placed with the care of a drunken dice toss. There was no rhyme or reason, no carefully planned streets and plazas like in the fancier districts of Isarn. There were few defenses, as well. The entire village was surrounded by a wooden palisade with a low ditch dug in front and what looked like thorny brambles covering the wall. There also were a couple of guards patrolling on a raised walkway on the palisade and a single guard handling the gate in the palisade. Yet that was it. No internal battlements, no soldiers or scouts on the streets, no Guardians in view. Just a regular old village, with the villagers going about their business.

The village was centered on a hill, with a squat wooden tower watching over the remainder of the village and the ground slowly rising to that point. Apart from the palisade wall, said tower looked like the only defensive structure of the entire place: solid and ugly construction with rust-colored iron plates covering the lower third of the tower. The top level was open to the elements, with a single person placed looking out. There was something gleaming right next to him.

"You've got to be kidding me," Cilia announced, deadpan. "They have it right there? At the top of the tower?"

Sera nodded. "It sure does look like it. I have to admit, though. I expected a better trap."

The others fell silent and stared at her.

"What? You are the ones who have taught me to be distrustful." She exasperatedly blew a lock of hair away from her eyes. "They know we are coming. They are aware that we will most likely try to scout them out. Yet, they place the deck in the exact location anybody would be able to spot from a distance, with but a single defender? Come now."

Liam took a deep breath. Then he sniffed and wiped at his eyes. "They grow up so fast these days."

Kith patted him on the back. "There, there. I know. Any day now, she'll start running with boys, and won't that be a horror? We'll have suitors everywhere."

"They can sure try," Chase grumbled. "Now, while I enjoy tormenting Sera as much as the next man, and probably a few extra men, maybe we should focus on what's in front of us? Yes, clearly that's a trap. What are we thinking? Illusion? Fake deck? Or real deck, but with an elaborate ambush waiting for us?"

"I think...that we need to wait for night," Cilia decided. "Yes, Liam. Waiting is a pain, especially when we're on a deadline. Yet, the way I see it, the only real chance we have of scouting the place properly and knowing what we're facing lies with Kith's shadows. If we try to have the shadows scout the place in clear daylight? We'll get caught. So, even if they're bound to be ready for us, and expect a nighttime attack, I think it's the right choice."

Liam shrugged. "I'm not complaining. I could do with a nap."

"You can scope out the village and watch out for scouts with the rest of us!" Cilia snapped.

He smirked and waggled his eyebrows at her, before settling down on top of an old half-rotten tree trunk.

The day passed with little fanfare. There was little to discover. Solitary Furyborn passed into and out of the village—some looking like scouts, others carrying baskets as if for gathering berries or mushrooms—with a single wagon driver bringing in his load of firewood being the exception. In the streets, there was little activity: people ambling about, talking, working, gathering in small groups and breaking apart. The busiest part of the day was during the evening, when a central building had somebody carry two tables into the streets to carry on a celebration of sorts.

The guards on the palisade changed shifts once in the early afternoon, and again at nightfall. Whomever was lurking in the tower, there was never more than one person visible at any time, though they did move about a lot. All told, however, everything about the village spelled calm relaxation and a place in a state of harmony with itself.

"This... is one humongous trap." Kith spat on the ground, underscoring his words. He wiped drizzle from his face. At one point in the afternoon, a light rain had started—the kind that started out unobtrusive, but ended up soaking all your clothes, equipment, and your very being. Following nightfall, it had only intensified, and now visibility was severely hampered.

"I knew it. I absolutely knew it." Liam stood up and punched the air. "These are supposed to be hardened veterans. Yet it just looks like everybody's walking around enjoying their day, with nothing happening? No training. No real guards worth talking about."

Chase snorted. "Calm your shiny ass. We all knew it was a trap. Even Sera said so."

"*Even* Sera?" Sera said.

Chase mouthed "Sorry" to her, but spoke to Liam. "It was like we said earlier. If they knew we were coming, why wouldn't they prepare a proper defense? No. They've got an ambush ready. Now, hit us with it, Kith. How bad is it?"

Kith exhaled and shook his head with a dark look. "I've had Sable and Raven roaming for—"

A collective groan erupted from the rest.

"Please, now," Sera said. "Those are just other words for darkness. Might I not help you with some names? Please? This is hurtful, both to your summons and the rest of us."

He scowled. "They *like* their names. I can tell. Anyway. I've had them roaming for a couple of hours now, peeking into every building, trying to figure out what's going on. The good news? Most of the village is actually just in a lazy, relaxed state. Most go about their business with no stress, looking like nothing is going on. I doubt they've told everybody what's happening."

"That *is* good news," Cilia mused. "Having to escape hundreds of pursuers who know the terrain and surroundings would be a pain."

"Belay that happiness." Kith rubbed his hands together for warmth. "Because the ones who do know? They're ready for us. And I don't exactly know how to approach this. Because we've got three decks waiting for us, and all of them are defended."

Once they got past the initial confusion, Kith explained the issues. There were actually three different positions holding a glowing, shining deck, and each of them had groups of alert, carded people ready to move into action at any moment. The tower itself that they'd scoped out was the one that had the heaviest guard contingency, with a full dozen of defenders ready, out of sight on the lower floors of the tower. Apart from that, a tavern also held ten hard-bitten elderly people, all fully armed and armored, seated around a central table with a glowing deck visible through the windows. Finally, one of just a handful of stone houses in the entire village, with a hardy construction and steel-banded door, had a deck visible through the bars of the window, and six guards lurking in the cellar.

On top of that, Kith could disclose another half-hidden fact. As was the case with many places they'd seen in and around Heart Halls, Heath was constructed close to nature, with trees, shrubs, and bushes being a natural part of the village itself. Yet, as Kith's summoned shadows came closer, he noticed that at least three of the larger trees shared the subtle glow of a living tree, promising hidden capabilities and an area to avoid, if at all possible.

Kith finished his elaboration, his voice growing vexed. "So, we've got three targets, and the real one could be any of them. We have no clue *how* they're creating the extras, and I can't get my shadows close enough to try to spot any fakes, meaning, we have to decide which one's more likely to be our real target." He flung up his hands in disgust. "And regardless if we even hit the right one, we'd need to somehow beat all of them without making any noise, because otherwise, we'll have all of the groups on our asses in minutes."

Sera nodded. "You are right. They are bound to have some sort of warning system set up between them. Meaning, we will need to be able to find the right place, and, on top of that, we will need to pull off our attempt flawlessly and silently. Even if we *were* able to slash our way through their forces, I doubt the elders are going to judge wholesale slaughter kindly."

"I *know* I'm right." Kith groaned. "How is this an actual trial? It's impossible is what it is! They're trying to get us to fail, without saying as much. *Why are you laughing, you bastards?*"

Chase held a hand over his mouth from where he'd shared a soundless piece of mimicry with Liam. He couldn't quite drown his good mood, though. "Listen, mate. I'll tell you what's going on, and I'll speak really slowly so you have a chance to understand it."

"Oh yeah? Can you still speak with my foot up your ass?" Kith growled.

Cilia, watching from the side, suddenly blinked and slapped her forehead.

Chase grinned and pointed at Cilia. "She just got it, too."

"*Got what?*" Kith asked, exasperated.

"Listen. You're on the docks in Isarn and somebody challenges you to a shell game."

Kith groaned deeply.

"A shell game?" Sera asked.

"Three shells. One ball. The dealer moved the ball about as fast as he can, then challenges you to spot the shell with the ball, for a wager." He beamed at Sera. "You're pretty damn sure it's under the left shell. Which shell do you pick?"

Sera looked strangely at all of them. "I am clearly missing something here. I... would likely pick the center or right one then, because the dealer is faster than my eyes?"

Cursing, Kith shook his head. "No, Sera. You don't pick *either of them*, because the ball's not in either shell. It's all a setup. I can't believe I didn't see it. Every one of these decks out in the open with defenders for any attacker to see. So regardless which one we pick, we're getting away with a fake, or trying to grab an illusion or something. Clever."

"What about the real one, then?" Liam mused. "Where is that one?"

"That's the real question," Chase said. "Is Kith right? Is the deck buried in a root cellar? Are they trying to set us up to fail here? Also, should I really be speaking suspicions like that out loud if they're watching us right this second?"

"If Half-Swart's listening in right this moment, he's probably laughing his ass off." Liam snorted. "He's not the type to be easily insulted. To be fair, I don't think they're the types to set us up for failure either. Regardless what you think about 'em, they do have honor."

Cilia tapped a finger on her leg a few times. Her brows rose, as did her finger, pointing at Liam. "That's it." She looked at their expectant looks and huffed. "No. I haven't found the damn deck. It's not like *I* have magical shadows with weird names. But Liam's right. They *do* have honor. Integrity."

"Resilience, independence, and blood," Chase said. "What's your point?"

"That their kind of integrity isn't automatically the same as it'd be with the Elementals or the Lightborn. Now. What can we speculate from that?" She ticked off on her fingers. "They want to test that we're resilient, meaning, that we've got the guts and the power to succeed. They want to test whether we respect the blood, in that we don't blow up the damn village and kill everybody in there. Whatever we do, it can't be allowed to overly weaken the blood. Possibly also in that we turn over a poor indebted to be interrogated because letting her go might be a threat to the Furyborn."

"*Still* not happy about that," Liam growled.

"Integrity is part of the same. Do what is right. Do not fold to temptation. Stand up for our own. Never help the enemy. Do not take the easy choice. And finally, independence. Each person chooses for themselves, thinks for themselves. They told us what our task was. But they didn't tell us what we were supposed to do. Meaning, we have to prove we can think for ourselves, not just act on orders." Triumphantly, Cilia raised an eyebrow. "Do either of you see what I'm getting at?"

Liam harrumphed. "Well, it's kinda like back in Cemano, isn't it? They tell us a task, but it isn't just the task that's important—it's also how we complete it."

"I won't tease you any further, but you're nearly there. Because, it isn't so much about what they said, but how they said it. Just like the very first thing Half-Swart mentioned. Remember? Kith, you asked whether they'd know we were coming, and he said—"

"*We sure didn't tell them anything,*" Kith breathed. "Cil, you clever devil. So, they're not going to lie to us, but they don't mind playing around with us, to see if we can think for ourselves. What was the other thing he said about our task?"

Sera blinked. "He said that the deck would be under guard. And also, that they were under orders to keep an eye on it."

Kith slapped his thigh. "*There* we go. That means, the deck *is* actually somewhere, where people are keeping an eye on it. If we're sure it's a shell game?"

"Yes," Cilia, Liam, and Chase said in unison.

"All right. Then, my dear shades simply need to find others who are actively awake and guarding something." He chuckled. "In the middle of the night, in a two-cart excuse for a village? That should be doable."

<u>Chapter 40</u>

"Why do we even do it, they say? Why trade with the Furyborn, when they are, in all aspects, poorer, more challenged for proper materials than we are? The answer is nature. Their connection to soil, to the nature, to Ordei herself? It is beyond compare. I saw a bow, last year, made by a Furyborn. I readily admit, I cried. It was pure. A piece of living nature, still living, brought to purpose." Men and their toys. (Page 93.)

For all his cockiness, it took him more than an hour to locate it. Not only was the village filled with cellars, sheds, stables, outhouses, and other buildings, Kith's shades were also limited by trying to evade detection—meaning, they could never just use the fastest approach everywhere, if there were lights, people, or any of the awakened trees nearby, for fear of getting spotted.

The others were wet, uncomfortable, and bored, staring out into the darkness on all sides, watching out for any scouts. Liam started to yawn and couldn't stop, his every jaw-cracking yawn growing larger than the last.

Finally, Kith breathed with closed eyes, "I got it. Light blind my eyes, I found it!"

The others huddled around him.

He opened his eyes, blinked in surprise to see them all clustered around him and chortled. "Pits are you hugging me for? It's not like I can show you with an illusion or anything." He pointed out into the night, somewhere in the cluster of occasional lights within the village. "It's... right around there. Bit south of that central tower... come to think of it, it's also more or less dead center between the three fake decks. That's not a coincidence."

Liam grunted. "So, if we mess up, they'll come rushing in from all sides?"

"Yup. Took me forever to spot it, though. You know why? The bastards parked it *right out in the open.*" He shook his head in amazement. "Remember that cart with firewood arriving earlier today? That's what tipped me off. Why wouldn't they pull it into shelter instead of letting it stand out in the pouring rain? Well, that's because there's a crate hidden right underneath. A crate, filled with straw, and one, barely perceptible glowing item."

Liam nodded, bemused. "The balls it takes to pull off something like that. Hidden in plain sight, eh? How the Pits did you find it?"

"It was the 'under guard' thing. There's a stable boy pretending to sleep next to a couple of Guardians right nearby. That was the first tip. Then I started to spot the others. One woman's watching from a second-story window. Another's lurking in a root cellar with the door cracked open. Finally, my favorite, a guy's sleeping off a bender under a tree. He went so far as to actually pour half of a bottle of something onto his shirt, and he's *really* selling the act."

Kith shrugged. "There's also one other, around the corner on a stool inside a shed. A bookish lady, looking like she's fighting hard to stay awake. She can't see the cart, though." He shrugged. "Those are all, though. Just two people and a boy, really, ignoring the one around the corner. If we hit 'em hard, we might be able to grab the deck and race off before they know what hit 'em. Still, that'll leave us with half a village on our asses, as we race for Heart Halls. Fighting in the rain, in the dark, in a forest our opponents know a lot better than us. Probably won't be fun."

Sera laughed softly. "You do have a gift for understatement, Kith. Fortunately, this is what Chase and I were working on. Considering combinations of cards to use for different circumstances." She rubbed her hands together. "One question first. The palisade. You mentioned brambles. Is it something we might climb, or is it too dangerous?"

Kith snorted and looked at the whole group. "Sera's the one with the lowest combined Strength and Agility here, and she still has sixteen and nineteen respectively. She could jump it and do a handstand on top, just for kicks. The wall guards are about as attentive as old Fathom back in Isarn too. Slipping past them is child's play."

Sera continued. "Great. That leaves us in the village. With my Heart of Hearts engaged, that will allow Cilia to use her Heart card to keep *any* noise from coming from us, as long as we stay close together. Added to Chase's Circle of Darkness, we will be clothed in darkness *and* preternaturally silent. This should take us all the way to our target. Kith? Can you find a place for us nearby, where we can lay low for a few minutes?"

"I... sure. There's a tool shed right around the southern corner that'll shelter us. Looks unlocked, as far as I can tell."

"Good. The rest of you can hide out there. Liam will wait there, while the rest of us continue slowly around the corner, and I can use *my* Heart card to investigate the four watchers from a distance and see which builds they have, and, hopefully, enough of their cards and active abilities that we can estimate what we are dealing with. Following that, we decide exactly how we get the deck—if we can sneak it out somehow, or if we need to go with Kith's approach." Sera squinted, eyes unfocused as she thought it over. She nodded to herself, then started as she saw the others looking at her, slack-jawed. "What?"

Chase burst out, "That was damn sexy! Where did that come from?"

Kith pointed at Chase. "What he said! We've had to deal with Chase's crappy plans for years. This could actually *work*. Right, Cil?"

Cilia frowned, opened her mouth, and then shut it again, nodding. "Honestly, I would prefer having a fully-fledged plan before entering the village, but knowing their classes and builds? That's likely to change things. Besides, we've only got about three hours until the sun comes up. Having to wait for tomorrow night would... not be preferrable. We would be in a rush to get back to Heart Halls in time, that way. If we manage it today, we'll still have time to get sidetracked with pursuit."

Chase rubbed his hand over his pants eagerly. "This is amazing. Cil always spends *hours* getting on my nerves with the tiniest corrections. I can't believe that you're such a natural at this! Or, maybe we're just being such a good influence on you..."

"Good influence." Sera let the words drag out. "Letting me plan a theft." The only reaction she got was Cilia's wry smile. The others simply nodded or waited expectantly. "You are all the worst." In a small, warm voice, she continued, "I am glad I met you."

Liam rushed forward and enfolded her in a massive bear hug. "So are we. Good alone. Better together! Now, let's go rob the elderly!"

Chase raced first, closely followed by the others. He didn't slow down as they reached the trench, merely activated his Steps of Brilliance and ran right across the obstruction, climbing higher to be able to leap past the palisade wall as well. As he passed the wall with nearly a foot of air to spare, he let his bedroll drop, covering the thorny brambles for the others to cross easier. He dropped down softly on the far side, slipped slightly in the wet clay, and hurried back to stand underneath the drop. Mere seconds later, Sera arrived, hoisted over the palisade by Liam. Chase was ready with a steadying hand to soften her drop and keep her from falling. Cilia and Kith followed in short succession before a grunt preceded Liam dragging himself up over.

Liam landed heavily, but with his feet spread wide, with perfect balance.

Chase hurried to activate Steps of Brilliance again, climbed back up onto the walkway on the palisade wall, and grasped onto his bedroll again to remove it. It caught on the brambles for a second, and as he pulled hard on the material, he felt something. A sensation, an emotion of sorts. It stemmed from... the brambles? He rushed to pull back, even as invisible tendrils brushed at his mind. Not a true mind, but an animalistic vibe of inquisitiveness, trying to ascertain whether he was friend, foe, or food.

He almost slipped and fell off on the far side, but managed to get his platforms up and running, landing an awkward, jolted descent.

The others stared at him, as he rolled up the bedroll again. He snarled and moved closer to ensure he was within the range of the silence effect from Cilia's Heart card. "The brambles. They're... awakened. Or a Guardian beast or some summoner card effect. I don't know."

They froze up. Seconds went past in silence. "Have we been made?" Kith whispered.

After half a minute, Chase exhaled. "I doubt it. It didn't feel like a person. Not truly intelligent. I think, maybe, we just don't want to try jumping over, if the thing's been alerted."

All business, Cilia clapped her hands. "Good. Now. *Complete* focus from here on. Kith. Shadows in front. Steer us the right way, away from any direct observers. Chase. Keep your shadows centered on us. The rest of you, stay close. Nobody leaves the distance of my Heart card."

They took off. At a rapid pace, they trotted through the silent streets of Heath, following Kith's directions.

At first, they took additional care to ensure that they moved silently, and listened for any signs of movement, before realizing that the silence effect worked both ways. Their sounds didn't spread, but outside sounds didn't enter the affected area either.

Chase worked with the effect of his card as he moved. He allocated a tiny bit of his concentration to simply following the others. Yet, most of his attention went to adjusting his Circle of Darkness as they progressed. When first he'd received the card, it had seemed like a wonderful thing for battle and ambushes, an area effect he could slam down on any enemies to keep them blind and off-kilter. It was that. Yet, it was also *so much more*.

Chase had few chances for really testing out the card, but now, he attempted to optimize it as he went, and what he experienced was an absolute thrill. The level of control of the circle was near-absolute. Not only could he adjust the depth of darkness inside the circle, he was also able to layer and adjust as he went, creating differences within the circle. That was a lot better than what he'd hoped for. A circle of complete darkness? That would be surprisingly hard to hide. Given that darkness in real life was never absolute, a circle of full darkness would stand out, especially to the trained eye. Yet, a circle of shadows which he could gradate from one depth level of darkness into another inside the circle and attune to the surroundings outside? That was a whole other level.

Their progress was swift, unhindered, and felt entirely unnatural, with how all outside noises were blocked out. Once, Kith abruptly veered from one direction to another, yet less than ten minutes later, he pushed open the unlocked door to the tool shed they'd selected for their hiding spot.

Liam settled down within, grumbling a bit that he had to stay behind, but they'd agreed that the less people they brought, the better, and his cards weren't needed just now.

The others moved on ahead, Kith in the lead again, quietly moving around the block, ensuring that they'd be able to find angles where Sera could use her powers on the people lurking, watching the deck.

This time around, their progress was clunkier, a lot slower, and with several stops and starts, as Kith assessed and found the right places for Sera to stand, still within the Circle of Shadows, where she could use her Heart card and learn what they were up against. Eventually, after circling the entire street once to get to the guy lurking near the fountain, they returned to the tool shed.

With her face carefully composed, Sera asked, "Are we still covered? No cards about to reach the limits of their duration?" Head shakes answered her question. Then, she slowly folded up and burst into silent laughter.

"What's going on? What am I missing? Did you guys have all the fun out there?" Liam asked.

"Not that I noticed," Chase added, equally confused.

Sera wiped away a tear and took a deep, shuddering breath. "Okay. Starting from most to least dangerous. That guy in the cellar. He's a fighter, carries a nasty wood axe, heavily Strength- and Toughness-based. He also has three cards running."

"Three? Damn. And those are just the active ones. I guess we can count on this being the right place then?" Kith asked.

"Yes. Judging from his attributes, I would put him at Tier four. As for the cards, they are Strength of the Blood, Soil to Sand, and Body of Iron. That's one Strength boost and an armor boost, but I don't know that middle one."

"Soil to Sand?" Chase asked. "Oh, a rogue had it back in the pens. It changes the footing in your surrounding area. Makes it better for you, worse for enemies. Completely unfair in duels."

"Thank you. The woman watching from the window above is ranged, Agility-based, and has a short bow nocked and ready. No active cards, but I'd put her at Tier three. Then there's the kid in the stable. He's actually a summoner, and the Guardians next to him look like they're his. But both the Guardians are heavy, slow, and tough. One's a caarnath; the other looks like a plow animal. And they're fully asleep."

"Sounds like they are still dangerous." Liam rubbed his chin.

"Sure. If we stick around. But the kid is only Tier one, maybe just into Tier two. And his attributes are heavily skewed toward Mental Power. Since we are not planning to fight the city, he is not that much of a threat."

"Fair enough." Liam conceded the point. "And the last guy?"

Sera swallowed another chuckle. "Apparently, he is uncarded. Also, he is unconscious."

"What?" Cilia said flatly.

A snort escaped Sera's mouth involuntarily. "That was my first reaction. On this very evening, just before a martial reckoning, Heath's miller decided to go and get dead drunk, and now he's sleeping."

Kith stared. "So, that guy is out there, sleeping it off, when the place could turn into a battleground at any moment? Heath's miller knows how to *party.*"

"Would you focus?" Cilia snapped. "That does leave us a bit better off than expected. We only have to handle the three wielders, and the Guardians, possibly. The question is, how do we manage that in a quiet way?"

They settled into silence.

Kith was the first to respond. "That's where things get difficult. I just had Slither slide over to check. And the kid and archer can see each other."

They groaned.

"Are we thinking a smash and grab, then? Or simply covering myself in shadows, followed by a grab under the cart, hoping they won't spot it? I should be fast enough to do it in a couple of seconds."

"We could time it," Kith speculated. "But that archer looks horribly focused... and there are three of them, keeping watch."

Liam growled, his deep voice reverberating in the stuffy shed. "We want to avoid combat. We don't want to be spotted. But it's not bloody likely we'll grab it without getting spotted.

Meaning, we need to grasp one of the good old Waves' tricks. It's been a while since we pulled a bloody roach, isn't it?"

Three of them perked up. Sera just looked confused.

Chase chuckled. "A bloody roach isn't what it sounds like. Or rather, it can be. It can be any sort of insect or filthy, disgusting thing. Sometimes, you don't even need a prop. You just want the outcry. Just think about it, Sera. What happens if you're at a fancy dive, and some fellow next to you starts yelling 'Aaah. It's a bloody roach!'"

They shared a laugh. Liam smiled into the distance, as if far away.

Sera bowed her head in understanding. "You get the attention of anybody present. Of course."

"Even better if there *is* a roach or three racing about. In the meantime, you'll be free to act. Not many people are able to keep their cool when disgusting insects are involved." His smile grew deeper, more diabolical. "We don't have any roaches. But we have something even better."

Kith's Coils of Shadow moved through the village of Heath, unseen under the cloak of night. The short vipers slithered alongside buildings, keeping their movements slow and unobtrusive. Their dark scales seemed to draw in the light, making them near impossible to spot, even as they left the cover of Chase's Circle of Darkness.

"They're nearly in position." Kith's eyes were closed, brow furrowed in concentration. "Are you sure we want to do this? If they catch us, we'll have people milling everywhere. We'll have to knock out half the damn village to escape."

"We're sure. It's how people work. Are *you* sure you can handle things on your end? There will be a lot of different tasks for you to handle," Cilia asked, tense.

Kith snorted and cracked his neck. "Please. It'll be easier than pushing Dead Weight Donni off his raft. They won't see anything." He took a deep breath. "That's it. We're ready. We go?"

"Go!"

Kith clenched his jaw in concentration as he spoke under his breath. "There. That should... no. How about this, then? I... What in the Pits? How does anybody, drunk or not, just keep on sleeping while a snake slithers over their *face*?"

The others shuddered.

Kith continued. "Kid gloves off, then. How about *this*, then?"

An ear-piercing scream cut through the night.

Kith grinned. "Ah. That did the trick. The nostril. Poor miller." Despite his light tone, his brow was furrowed in concentration, and his head moved slightly, as if he were looking around. "And they're off. That archer jumped *out* the damn window! Impressive. Fighter's right behind her. Come on, kid... yes!"

Tensely, they all waited. In several spots on their street, candles were lit inside rooms, and people cracked open windows, yelling for silence, or asking what was going on.

"They're *really* rushing in now. Whew. There were more people waiting for us around the place than I'd spotted. Thirty, forty, nearly fifty of them. Whew. Aaand they've reached him. Coincidentally..." His face lit up in a huge smile. "Our guests have also reached us. Would you be so kind as to crack open the door slightly?"

Liam did just that, opening the door a handful of inches. Hopefully not enough to get spotted. Just enough, that a tiny bundle of undulating movement managed to enter. It was a bed of snakes, moving together in unnatural unison. Equally unnatural was the fact that they were carrying something. A lightly glowing deck of cards.

Liam softly closed the door again, as the others stared at Kith in amazement.

Kith didn't even open his eyes. "Now comes the important part. We're out of immediate eyeshot from the cart. But how they react is going to decide if we sprint, or if we take it slow and sweet." He waited with bated breath, before suddenly punching the air twice. "Yes! They're laughing at the miller. Somebody's scolding him. Come. Activate every card you can, and we're out of here, but slowly. First move is just left and a hundred feet down the street. There's an empty stable. Move... now!"

In stops and starts, they started to move under the cover of silence and darkness from hideout to hideout, ever closer to the gate. They moved as fast as possible, stopping only to hide from moving feet, inquisitive villagers, and others cursing at being woken up. Even so, it took less than fifteen minutes before they were within a stone's throw of the palisade.

Kith held up a hand. "We'll need to hold for this. Our watchers—the ones keeping an eye on the deck—were delayed by having to explain to everybody what was going on. Now, they're moving back to their posts, though. They... Oh. Liberty steer me true. It's bloody happening."

"What?" Liam whispered. "What's bloody happening?"

Mirth bubbled from Kith, who jumped from foot to foot in tiny, excitable leaps. "They didn't bother to bloody check the crate. They're just moving back to their positions. We made it!"

Regardless of what karma might usually say about these things, they suffered no last-second mishaps. They easily cleared the walls as the two guards on the night shift shared a quiet pipe far away. Following that, they made off into the night. Like thieves.

<u>Chapter 41</u>

"For anybody meaning to trade with the Furyborn, there are many worries. Selecting the right goods. Evading Lightborn patrols. Avoiding the occasional raiders preying on merchants. Finding trustworthy guards. Making a good deal. Yet, there is one thing that you should never worry about. Because the Furyborn do not cheat, and always honor their deal. Well. According to their own sense of honor, at least." He had to. He just *had* to add that last part, didn't he? (Page 32.)

The return trip was, blessedly, uneventful. After making it into the brushes surrounding the village, they traveled under the effects of their cards until the sun came up. At that point, they eschewed any sort of caution and focused on speed. Of course, they knew that somebody would discover their bait and switch at some point, but as long as they were far enough away, they reckoned they might make it back without having to knock any pursuers on their asses.

To their absolute surprise... they actually managed. They made it back to Heart Halls and returned to the challenger pens, where an officious Evan was momentarily knocked out of his usual haughty expression, as they gave the deck over for him to deliver to the elders. Then, they waited. They slept, showered, ate, and did absolutely nothing, while they waited for the reaction.

It took nearly a full day.

After a very late breakfast, they sat in their cots, too stressed out to start doing something productive. Liam kept talking about training to get rid of the nervous energy at least every ten minutes, but never got up.

Drums split the air. Deep, sonorous booms thundered, loud enough to make everybody, even the dueling teams, pause whatever they were doing.

They got up and left the sleeping area. Everywhere, people were listening, looking around in confusion.

A few locals looked like they knew what was going on. Challengers clustered around them, to ask what was happening.

Then they started to see them. Furyborn, rushing by, running, leaping, whooping as they passed by the pens, in one direction.

"Pit's going on?" one of the challengers yelled.

One tiny Furyborn, seated on a large, avian-like quadruped, twisted in her saddle and laughed, shrill and merry. "It's a Convocation! Come on, you ignorants! We're all summoned. Maybe we're going to war again!"

Liam turned to the others. "She sounded happy about that. Why'd she sound so happy?"

"Dunno. But we'd better follow. I'd be surprised if it didn't have anything to do with us."

They followed the crowds, eastward, growing increasingly astonished at the sheer number of people around them. What started out as a trickle of people moving alone and in small groups grew to a stream, and then a flood. The trees grew rarer again, and the foliage slowly parted, inviting in the rays of the sun from above.

Then they saw it. The wooden amalgamation—part fortress, part living tree of the elders—sat at the center of the plain, nearly a mile out from the edge of the forest. On top of it, a small figure, covered in vibrant paint and surrounded by a golden haze that had to be something created by a card, stood tall, brandishing something in his hands. Half-Swart, standing above a duo of drums reaching taller than his waist, wielded a set of massive beaters. He screamed—a sound of abandon, of challenge and fury. His arms descended again, and the drums resumed, a challenging, frenzied, vibrant pitch.

Around the behemoth, a grand mass of people milled about, shouting, dancing, and yelling with abandon. Some brought instruments, adding to the kinetic scent of the vibrant energy in the air. There had to be hundreds, verging on a thousand. Still more kept appearing from within the forest in a steady stream.

In a choked voice, Liam said, "I thought we agreed there weren't actually that many people in Heart Halls."

"Well, it looks like they don't know." Chase frowned. "I have a bad feeling about this. What's going on? Why so public?"

"It doesn't matter," Cilia said, matter-of-factly. "Whatever happens, happens. We've done everything we could. Now, it's just a question of riding the wave, and hopefully we don't end up drowning."

Kith, looking past the wooden behemoth, gave a dark chuckle and pointed. "At least we're not the only ones who're peeing ourselves from not knowing. Look."

In the far distance, bright spots and indistinct dots on the horizon showed a few Lightborn patrols following along with the day's happenings. On the plain as well, a smaller, colorful group of people standing close together indicated the Elemental traders having followed. Whatever was going to happen, the world would know.

For a full hour, at least, the music continued. Constantly, more people joined the throng, until they had to be several thousand strong. Five thousand, perhaps. More? The numbers of the plain seemed to grow every moment, and the energy grew increasingly frenzied, nearly tangible.

They decided to move a bit closer to the living tree. They didn't want to miss whatever was going down.

Eventually, as jugs of alcohol started to be passed around the crowd, the mood was hitting a fevered pitch, when the drums culminated in an eardrum-shattering tumultuous finale and grew still. The crowd, as one, turned with shining eyes toward the behemoth.

"Brethren. Friends. Stalwart defenders of Heart Halls. *We have called a Convocation of the Blood!*" Elder Naian's voice rang out, strong, warm, heartfelt. Some creation or card was in effect, because her voice rang out easily over everybody present—maybe even to where the Lightborn scouts could hear it.

The crowd erupted in cheers. Exactly what they were cheering, Chase couldn't tell, but there was meaning there.

"Too long. It has been too long since the last Convocation. We have been embroiled in defending ourselves, in holding the line, in making sure our daughters get to grow up as safe as we can, at *any* cost."

People grew more subdued, nodding and grasping friends, some with wet eyes as an admission of the cost.

"Yet, we have seen little but stagnation. There has been individual growth, sure. Some villages thrive. Some defenders rise to the top, grow strong, lead the blood to victory." Elder Naian's voice was pained. "*But it is not enough.* Some would argue the point. Yet, those of us on the front lines see what is happening. How the Lightborn ignore the Halls, yet, their raids on outlying villages and cities grow evermore bold. How the lost ones take a toll in blood and lives, running over settlements that have stood for decades. Here, at the center, we have grown strong. Yet, is it of the blood to relax at the cost of others?" That last sentence she yelled, challenging.

"No!" the plains responded as one.

"It is not!" Elder Naian shouted in confirmation, a voice so filled with challenge that it had a physical presence. The idea that the voice belonged to the small woman with the grandmotherly presence seemed confusing, incongruous with the slight shape on the edge of the behemoth's platform shouting defiance. "We have gathered you here today to tell you all that is about to change. No longer will we allow ourselves to be pushed farther back, with no release in sight, while the Lightborn expand their forces, live on the choicest land, and slowly take over the entirety of Ordei. No. We finally have a way to fight back!"

Oh. Chase felt a sinking sensation at the pit of his stomach. He could tell where this was going.

"We have allied with a wielder... of a Deck of Darkness!" Her voice, triumphant and vibrant, was loud enough that it caused those nearby to shield their ears.

The crowd, eager, eyes gleaming, fell into a hush, interspersed with shouts of doubt and demands for more.

The far-off elder didn't hold back. "Convocations are usually held as a prelude to war, to attacks. We also tend to keep them secret from the enemy. Not today." She held up a fist, challenging, at the distant Lightborn. "You hear me, you Fire-scoured traitors? You listen good, and tremble. Because from today, the world changes. We will bring the powers of Darkness against you. Come to our borders and challenge us at your peril! *Run to your masters and tattle, for the bloodied grounds will lie waiting for you. And a shadow will cover our lands, waiting to swallow you all!"*

Chase just stood there, wide-eyed. Their group shared glances, uncertain, disturbed. Even Kith was unable to find a smart-ass comment for the moment. It was probably for the best. The Furyborn around them were ready to go on the warpath, right at that moment. If the elders said so, they'd probably launch right into a charge at the far-off Lightborn, who did seem to have reduced their numbers already.

"Why do we inform you of this, my brethren? Because we are doing this. Right now! Four days from now, when the first challengers complete their gauntlet? They will be offered, not only Light cards, but also Dark cards. *But that is not all!* For now, we are not going to *stop* with the challenges. For the next unforeseen period of time, we will continuously hold challenges, seeking to spread the Dark cards as widely as possible to those who are worthy. And we want you all to become part of it. We want you to accept the challenge, to spread the word, to grow in strength as we all grow. *Right now,* the call is going out to every village to send their best, and have them return, better, stronger, ready to defend the blood."

She paused. Every single person was hanging on her word, eager, afraid to miss even the tiniest detail, aware of just how momentous a situation this was.

Softly, lovingly, she asked, "Kin. Do I have your aid?"

The plain erupted into chaos. Shouts, proclamations, war songs, snippets of music, and sometimes, unintelligible frenzied screams were everywhere.

Elder Naian took this in the way it was presented. "My people. I thank you. We elders have revealed our Heart cards to you... and you have answered. May we never forget this day, when the balance finally tilted back in favor of our kind." Her voice lifted, becoming one of joy, of undiluted pleasure. "As such, we declare this day a celebration. A national feast, never to be forgotten. Drink and eat today, for tomorrow, the Furyborn prepare for war!"

From the edge of the forest, carts appeared, holding large barrels and foodstuffs, fruits, meats... any kind of luxury that you could imagine. Within the span of minutes, a full-blown feast erupted on the plains outside Heart Halls. A feast to celebrate the end of secrecy, and the escalation into full-blown war.

Their tiny group seemed the only one apart from the festivities, caught up in introspection, trying—and failing—to perceive exactly what this would mean to them.

Sera spoke up first. "Does this mean that we completed our trial?"

Kith snorted. "Of course it does. Unless... nah. They wouldn't. We're definitely safe! I think."

"Guys," Chase said. "Whatever we are, we're about to find out."

They slowly turned around, watching Evan standing behind them, hands behind his back and his face set in an emotionless expression.

"Gah. Could you not do that? How long have you been standing there?" Kith snarled.

"Long enough to hear you contemplate if the elders would take away your bounty, as would be their prerogative." He motioned for the wooden behemoth, swaying softly at the center of the now-busy plain. "Should we find out?"

Half-Swart shouted in unadulterated joy, and let the beaters in his hands descend in a merciless onslaught, subjecting the large, wooden drums to a pounding, joyful rhythm, as they climbed up the rope ladder. He finished with a full-body slam that unleashed a sound wave to be felt as much as heard and grinned, sweat staining his face. He turned to them, half sweaty, half hair, all feral. "Ah. If it ain't the guests of honor."

They emerged one after the other, settling on their feet in front of the seated elders, who had clearly already started to partake of the feast.

"So, are you stabbing us in the back or what?" Chase challenged.

Sera expelled her breath in a whuff. Even Liam blinked and raised his brows.

Kith merely snorted. "What? We all thought it. Chase just said it. Elder Yassia there definitely wouldn't be against it either.

Nothing wrong with speaking your mind here among the blood, is there? Besides, whatever you're planning, it's not like you stopped to ask us for our opinion, meaning, the jig's up already. So, what'll it be?" he asked Half-Swart.

The half-Darkborn threw his head back and laughed uproariously. "I *like* these kids," he said to the other elders. "When we get outsiders, they're always so obsequious and reverent. Not these ones."

Elder Yassia sneered at them. "I'm not impressed."

Half-Swart rolled his eyes at her and turned back, putting the large beaters aside before standing up, leaning over the large wooden drums. "You're right. We didn't stop to ask your opinion, or even your agreement. We just went ahead with our plans... because we're being mighty clever."

Elder Naian sighed. "What our beloved elder here is trying to say is that the time for secrecy is over. We are about to make history. With you at the center."

Chase frowned. "But... that will mean that the Lightborn learn? About everything. You will—"

"We will ensure that our kin grow stronger, while granting you everything you need." Elder Naian raised her head proudly. "Furyborn are not honorless."

"I believe that," Chase said. "But... the Lightborn are going to come in force, now! You would have us linger in Heart Halls, granting cards to challengers and prospects for the next full year?"

Cilia cursed. Then she shook her head vehemently. "No. That's not what this is."

Half-Swart laughed, pointing at Cilia. "Good head on that one. Do tell them."

She stood up and looked out at the, by now, thousands celebrating, dancing, eating and drinking on all sides of the towering, moving tree. "You just painted a massive target on your own backs. Whatever else happens, the Lightborn are going to know that you have Dark cards, and they're going to double their efforts at killing you all." She winced. "Do you have any idea how many people are going to die from this?"

Half-Swart stood tall, facing Cilia. He nodded slowly. "We are very well aware. We debated our approach for a good long while. Secrecy—true secrecy—as you well know, is already out of the question. The Lightborn know of your existence. It's just a question of what they think is happening. Right now, instead of trying to keep you secret? We decided to shout to the world exactly what will be happening. That way, when you're ready to take off for Liberty lands, the Lightborn will be too busy trying new ways to attack us to look at you sneaking off to create a solution that can truly blindside them."

"So... you're actually letting us go?" Chase blinked. "Sorry. I must be slow today."

"Clearly." Half-Swart smirked. "Let me explain it to you explicitly. First, we are going to officially congratulate you on completing your trial. Then, we are going to very officially and publicly let you become part of Heart Halls, here to grant cards to all of us for eternity. Following that, you will be called upon from time to time, to, very publicly, grant cards to worthy challengers who earn it. Now, you stated that the limit to gain another deck was four hundred additional wielders? That should take around... two weeks for challengers to complete?"

"Three weeks," Elder Madaline stated. "That should be doable, solely with the challengers who will accept here in Heart Halls, and the nearest towns."

"Good," Half-Swart said. "A few weeks from now, you will become a bit more reclusive, tired of all the attention. Following that, you will retire from all the attention somewhat, but still grant challengers cards from behind a privacy screen in your new house. Ostensibly, this will continue for months and months. In practice, as soon as we can, you will give us the new deck, and we will take over granting new cards, still behind the privacy screen, allowing you to take off on your mission. There are wielders who can ensure you leave in secret. We will guide you, aid you, grant you what equipment we can—and then, we are going to bloody the Lightborn's noses and keep their attention on us, while you go secure a future for *all* Ordei."

They fell silent for a while. Eventually, Liam ventured, "Cilia was right. *So* many people are going to die from this. Yet, you're still planning to go through with it?"

Half-Swart's smile slipped for a moment, became a half-ironic smirk. "Integrity can be costly—but it's worth it in the end. Or so we've found. Besides, Elder Naian did not lie. We *are* stagnating, while the Lightborn flourish. Perhaps, the Dark cards in themselves will be enough to grant us an edge against the Lightborn. And if it wasn't? We would rather go out swinging, doing the right thing. Exactly like our forefathers decided."

Kith scratched in his thick hair, obviously ill at ease with the entire situation. "Well, we'll try to make sure that it's all worth the price. When we eventually manage to claim the final deck, we are going to pay it back, and then some." He cleared his throat. "I mean, when we figure out where to start."

"We already know that Wellsprings created with an original deck is stronger. But, if the legends are right, the Wellspring of yours created with decks of all five aspects? It will be something else. A refuge for all, and a bulwark against the Lightborn."

Elder Yassia interrupted him. "Don't you worry about the wheres and whats. None of us expect you to have the wits or connections to arrange something like this. Like I have already clearly stated, more than once, I would rather cut you out of everything and handle it solely with our kin. Yet, I have been outvoted. So, we'll make sure you're outfitted. That you have a guide. And that you have backup."

She waved her hand dismissively. "We aren't going to send any of our few Tier fives with you. Regardless of my likes and dislikes, your success will rely on secrecy. But we will make sure that you have the best chance you can have. Also, while you run around, risking the power balance of Furyborn and Elementals alike, we will be in touch with High Elementalist Skysworn to ensure that we have the plans properly in place for our fortress." She snarled, "If we're going to risk the blood, we are going to do it right. We will create a wall, upon which the Lightborn will break their necks."

"That's nice," Liam said awkwardly. "So... since we're already pretty deep into the awkward, bloodthirsty part of our day—do you mind telling us what you did with Lissy? Or was it a setup? Because we didn't appreciate that at *all*."

Whatever they'd expected, that was clearly not it.

Elder Yassia simply asked, "Who?"

Elder Madaline, however, gave a tight-lipped smile. "I am glad you asked. And it is typical of Elder Half-Swart to just skip past the official parts of your trial, simply because he does not care for it. Let me handle that part."

She looked from one to the other. "You showed a good deal of heart and an understanding of the needs of the blood, in how you aimed very obviously and carefully for non-lethal approaches. Even had you tried to abscond with one of the fake decks, I would have passed you, simply for that. You have shown impressive degrees of resilience, both back in Cemano, and in how you do not back down from any challenge, but power through regardless. Your integrity is impressive. You are outsiders, very obviously so, yet you have made it a priority to think of the blood at every point."

Half-Swart snorted. "Yeah, yeah. Also, they're too independent for their own damn good."

"They are *impressively* independent, and think on their own instead of bowing to titles, finery, or riches. In everything, you have earned what you receive. As for our newfound guest? You may not know, but this is not a new strategy on the Light's side. It costs them little, and the rewards for a success outweigh the theoretical cost in letting a potential, low-Tier wielder die.

"That Lissy of yours sends her regards. She was more than willing to tell us everything she knew, which was not very much. She is even now traveling toward one of our border villages. She will have the same experience that you had in Cemano. If she wants to, she can fight to earn the right to take our trial and truly become one of us. Or she can choose another career and become a boon to the blood elsewhere. Regardless of her choice, she will be better off here among the Furyborn than back with her own kind." The Lightborn's face split in the first heartfelt smile they'd seen from her. "A small, but not unimportant, number of us started our real lives like that. Does that answer your question?"

"Erm. I… guess it does." Liam frowned. "Where do we go from here, then? When do we start?"

Half-Swart's eyes glinted with deep-set humor. His voice grew husky, and his smile was more than a little disturbing. "Now!"

Chapter 42

"Ah, but the allure of it. The Furyborn decks. The Lightborn have secured a few during their history, jealously safeguarded until the wearer died. Yet, outside of that, almost nobody has ever earned cards. If only they would see reason." For once, I entirely agree. Furyborn and Elementals should exchange cards more. Peace balance or not, it would be to the advantage of both. (Page 27.)

"Pits do you mean, now?" Chase asked, too taken aback to even try.

"Gilly? Bring the new deck down," Half-Swart said.

Suddenly, the large behemoth shuddered, moving more than just the gentle swaying and creaking that had been the backdrop of their conversation until now. A large branch moved down from above, prehensile movements stretching the limb further than they'd expect to be possible from a normal tree. Tied to the branch was a simple burlap bag, glowing ever so slightly from within.

Elder Naian moved past them, facing the revelry below, which was showing signs of burgeoning from the realms of partying into debauched revelries. Her voice rang out. "Kin! I have one final announcement to make. One thing for you all to know, before our new dawn starts. Behind me stands a group of five, outsiders all, only one of them Furyborn by race. Even so, they have proved themselves to be Furyborn by heart. They have risked their lives, putting themselves in jeopardy for the blood, when they could have retreated safely. They have proved stalwart, accepting challenges that would make fully-fledged defenders of Heart Halls blanch. They have proved a capability of thinking for themselves instead of blindly following orders. And finally, they have proved that they think of the many before the few."

She paused, letting the scattered groups of celebraters dotting the ground settle into murmurs and questions. Then she asked softly, her voice traveling to all corners, subtle smile audible to anybody. "Why do we bring them up? Outsiders earning our full acceptance is monumental. But at this hour? Right when we go to war? What do they have that makes their involvement worth mentioning? My blood and bone, my dearest children. I will tell you right now." She flung her hands up. "They brought us the deck!" Her voice grew into a triumphant shout, inching higher to an insistent crescendo. "They hold the Deck of Darkness. They will be the catalysts, the deliverers, staying right here in Heart Halls to grant each of you who earns the privilege your very own Dark cards."

Shouts and cheers rose, drowning out even her amplified voice for several minutes. Eventually, they subsided, and she continued, intensively, eyes blazing as she walked the edge of the platform, looking out at the gathered on all sides. "What think you? Once, we were part of the Coalition, a happy union with the other aspects, all considered equal. Yet, as every child is told, we split, when the Lightborn, hiding under the veil of the Church, struck at the Darkborn and the wielders of Dark cards. We recognized their attempt to grasp all power for themselves. And now, we have the chance to finally strike back, with the very Dark cards that caused the Lightborn to create the schism in the first place. *Does it not feel right?*" Her words were intense, nearly sexual.

The answer was a roar, drowning out any attempt at speech, and, indeed, independent thought.

Eventually, Elder Naian turned back to their group with a smile, and droplets of sweat running down her amiable features. She grasped the deck from the branch and walked back to the edge of the platform.

A hush spread, as people recognized the glowing shape.

She flung her arms wide open, her words still going out to the entire crowd. "So, I ask you, my dearest of friends. In order to welcome those who would sacrifice all chance at ever leaving Furyborn lands again—should we pay them back in kind? *Should we make them part of the blood?*"

The soundwave this time was physical, roars pushing down upon them from all sides.

Elder Naian turned around to them, and beckoned Chase forward.

Slowly, he walked toward her. Among the Elementals, even the Lightborn, he would've knelt, showing (or faking) his respect to those in charge. Yet here, that didn't feel right. Head held high, he strode to face her head-on, doing his very best to appear levelheaded, in control, strong enough to be worth the honor.

With a fond smile, Elder Naian whispered, "Make us proud, kid." Her voice rose, and she intoned, "Being of the blood has never been about race. Nor is it some sort of vendetta against the Lightborn. It is simply a matter of choosing sides. Of deciding to stand up for the side of what is right, whatever the cost. These young men and women have proved beyond any doubt, that they are willing to pay the price. So, I say to you, take this. Our deepest, most sincere sign of acceptance. Accept, and become part of the blood."

"Join the blood." The chorus was unanimous, deafening.

Chase took a step forward, and accepted the glowing deck. He spent a second admiring the sheer beauty of it. The details—the thorns, running along the edges of the deck, the living colors... even the scent was one of healthy soil after the rain, of sheer, untethered, vibrant *life*.

He accepted the notification with a sigh of relief.

[You have located a Deck of Fury. As the holder of a Deck of Darkness, you have the option to accept cards from it or bond with the deck, absorbing it. Which do you choose?]

Absorb. Clearly.

[You have bonded with a Deck of Fury. From now on, through you, anybody may share in the gifts of Fury. In addition, any Wellspring you create will be strengthened, carrying attributes and granting bonuses born of Dark, Light, the Elements, and Fury.]

Finally. They'd worked so hard to get here. To earn this boon. Now, they received it. Chase let the sensation of Fury run through his body. It felt like life, like unbridled energy, like sheer, savage *strength*.

[You have continued working to restore the balance. Absorbing additional decks from other aspects and adding them to the wielders of the Deck of Darkness further tips the scale in the right direction. As a reward, the first ten card wielders of Darkness are granted an additional bonus to their Title based on their class.

You have received +2 to Agility per Tier from the rogue class.

From the secondary Deck absorbed, Light, you have received a boost to your health. Detrimental effects to your attributes and mentality last only half as long, and you are much less likely to fall ill.

From the third Deck added, Elemental, you have received a bonus of +1 to all attributes.

From the fourth Deck added, Fury, you have received the power of the soil. Whenever you are in the vicinity of soil blessed with the strength of a Wellspring with which you are aspected, you will gain an additional temporary +5 boost to all attributes.]

Liberty fend! Chase shuddered. That sensation of empowerment wasn't simply founded in the moment, or in the newfound magic entering his system. It was *real*, an actual improvement to his situation, and that of the rest of his crew. An instant boost that increased every single one of their attributes with half of a normal, uncarded person's attributes. He mentally checked his attributes, and gawked. *It bloody worked on Potential too!* Meaning, as long as he was in a place connected to a Wellspring of anything but Liberty, any new cards for him and the others were likely to be of a higher rarity.

Elder Naian gave him a kind smile. "Do you have anything you would like to tell the blood?"

He inclined his head and thought furiously. "Simply this. Tell them that we are going to repay this honor in kind. We will make sure that the blood grows stronger."

She assented and relayed his words. The answering roar was one of approval. Then she laughed, merrily, with a fire that belied her age. "Tomorrow brings war. War, and the opportunity to finally pay back our enemies what they have unleashed upon us for years and years. For today? Joy and celebration. Live, my kin—live, love, and show the world the joy of being of the blood!"

The elderly Furyborn turned back to them. Then she took off a bronze earring, shaped like a caterpillar, and shuddered. "Liberty fend. That always feels so wrong. Now, our people are going to be caught up in celebration for the near future. Once they wake up with heavy, *heavy* hangovers, you are likely to be inundated with attention. So, right now, I recommend that you accept your new cards... and then I say, we all join the celebrations. We *are* creating history right now, for good or ill. If that isn't deserving of a night of debauchery, I don't know what is."

Kith was the first to shake himself out of his reverie. He blundered over to the edge of the platform, nearly stumbled, before catching himself on the edge of the wooden battlements. "I... I'm not made for this," he said hoarsely. "I'm the lookout, for Darkness's sake. The distraction. Not the bloody center of attention." He closed his eyes and visibly pulled himself together. With a deep breath, his lips slowly spread in a semblance of his normal devil-may-care grin. "But I'm not one to say no to new cards. Hit me, Chase."

Not one to let such an easy opening slide, Chase slapped Kith on the cheek. *Then* he triggered the Deck of Fury.

Kith's look of outrage swiftly merged into one of pure astonishment as he took in what was being offered. Shortly, he closed his eyes, minute expressions on his face switching from disappointment over joy, dismissal into other emotions one split second to the next. Eventually, he settled into a look of dogged decision and nodded, once.

A full-body shudder ran through him, from head to toe. "Gah. I swear, this only gets weirder every time. Or maybe it's just that we get so many cards at once. Also... what's with this Tier boost? That's insane!"

"Don't tell 'em." Chase grinned. "Let them experience it for themselves."

Kith grinned. "That's mean. I like it." He shook himself like a dog before adopting a less self-assured posture. "Cilia. Before I tell you what I got, just know that I *really* gave my choices a lot of thought."

Cilia rubbed her temples. "Why do you do this to me? If you already know that I'm going to... you know what? Just get it over with!"

"Okay. My Tier one pick? That one was easy."

[Let Them Go
Epic, Fury summoner
Tier one
Active, medium duration
Any summoner worth their salt knows when to dig deep to protect a summon, and when to let it go. With this card, the summoner can actively sacrifice a summon or group of summoned creatures. The energy tied up in the creatures will be spread out as a passive temporary boost to all attributes except Potential to every other person or summoned creature in the group. Any bound Guardian sacrificed will grant triple the boost.
"Let them go, and we will rise like the break of dawn." The High Elementalist surrenders control for personal gain.]

Kith grinned unabashedly. "This is going to be amazing. Say that I've got the Crescendo of Might out, but it's falling apart? Now, I can sacrifice it to give *all* of us a boost, and then I can switch to another summon. Along with A Fiery End, I can make sure that my summons will always help, in life as in death, whether it's by causing damage to our enemies or boosting us."

"Epic rarity. Damn. Probably means the boost will be impressive too. Any bound Guardian... what does that mean?" Chase asked.

"Well, my Tier two card should explain that one," Kith said.

[Ties That Bind
Rare, Fury summoner
Tier two
Passive, permanent
Most summons are temporary, restricted to when the card is active. Yet, with the right choices for a Wellspring, any summoner earning new cards may choose a card like this. With permission from the owner of the Wellspring, you will be able to bond with any resident Guardian. This Guardian will then be permanently

attached to you like a regular summon, until the Ænima powering it runs out. The effect of this card will remain active, regardless whether you switch to another Tier two card.

In addition to the Guardian's own attributes, it will be awarded a permanent increase to its Agility, with one point for each three points of your own Agility.

"What do you mean, I cannot summon this again once I let it die? Go away, you ridiculous little man." The summoner of Naz has an ugly eye-opener.]

He turned to the elders. "I know, nobody okayed anything like this. But I figured this might be the perfect chance. If you could connect me with a flying Guardian, we'd actually have a way to communicate over long distances."

Cilia sputtered, "You just *expected* them to give you a Guardian, because you asked?"

"We will," Half-Swart interrupted. "At Tier two, you will not be able to bond with a flying Guardian, but we will find a suitable choice. It's in our own interest to have a way to communicate."

"See, Cil? It's in their own interest!" He grinned weakly, and moved to the side to put Liam between him and Cilia. "Besides, even if it weren't possible, think about it. We'd be able to use this, when we establish our own Wellspring. It will let me command and communicate with a Guardian *permanently*, and I won't have to spend a card slot for it. There's no way I wouldn't pick that."

Cilia scowled at him, but didn't say anything.

He chose to take that as agreement. "My last card... well, I'll let the words speak for themselves."

[From Out of the Pits
Rare, Fury summoner
Tier three
Active, instant
At the core of the Furyborn lies the concept of blood. Of being ready to sacrifice for your kin, should the path take you straight to the Pits themselves. Yet, if you are fast and crafty enough, you can extract enough to let you and your kin live another day.
Activating this card allows the summoner to sacrifice a third of their own health. Doing so will grant the same health to each and every person in their group, including their summons. There is no natural limiter to the usage of this card. The summoner may die from using this card.
Medium cooldown
"I would do anything for love. I would also do this." Rolat Polpettone dies for his beloved.]

"You're *damn* right, I don't approve of this card," Cilia snarled. "This is a surefire way to get yourself killed."

"I knew you'd say that. But just listen. If I use this, and Sera heals me afterward? That will heal *everybody* in our group, at the cost of just one card. If we're all hard-pressed? That's a lifesaver. Could you imagine if we'd had this in our battle against that behemoth on the plains? I could've stayed behind with Sera, and we could keep everybody topped up in tandem, safely."

"I..." Cilia sighed and bowed her head. "I won't deny that you have a point. Please use it with responsibility. Wait. Forget that. *Please don't kill yourself!*"

"I would never—"

"Yeaaah, my turn. We all know how this is going to play out." Liam smirked. "Twenty minutes from now, we'll finally get you to admit that perhaps, sometimes, in the wrong situations, you can be the tiniest bit irresponsible. Do as Cil says. Don't be daft. We need you around."

"That was surprisingly nice of him," Sera whispered to Chase.

Chase, fighting down a grin, waggled his eyebrows. "Wait for it."

"I mean, your blunders make for the *best* stories. I've made half the challengers back in the pen cry with laughter, just from the cinna berry story."

Somebody cleared their throat. Liam and Kith both turned around.

Elder Naian stood with her arms folded and an eyebrow raised. She didn't say anything.

Liam shot her a fake grin. "Well. Time waits for no man. Should we get on with it?"

"Indeed." The elder's voice could have caused seas to dry out.

Chase activated the deck.

Liam's gaze, as it turned inward and he closed his eyes, was more expressionless than Kith's, more stalwart. His only acknowledgment of any sensations was, after a full minute of consideration, a slow exhale, before he opened his eyes again.

"That boost was a lovely surprise." He smiled to Cilia and Sera. "You have something to look forward to. As for my cards... At this point, I believe that I am covered, more or less, when it comes to defensive cards. I can stand up to almost everything but the biggest, baddest things out there. Where I feel myself outmatched, especially, is on mobility, and especially on offense."

"You have been at it for less than a year, Liam. You cannot be expected to match up directly with somebody who has trained for their entire life," Sera offered.

Liam gave her a sad smile. "I'd agree. Only, life seems to throw us into those situations anyway. My choices reflect that."

[Optimal Offense
Uncommon, Fury fighter
Tier one
Active, medium duration
The best offense is a good defense. Or was it the other way around? Regardless which school of thought you adhere to, you now get to double down on your choices. Upon activation of this card, you get to increase the strength of your offense by a full thirty percent, at the cost of a twenty percent reduction in defense, or vice versa. Whichever choice you make lasts for the full duration of the card, and cannot be willfully canceled.
Short cooldown
"I am getting bored. Are you all getting bored? You have been trying to get through my armor for a while. Should we finish this?"]

Chase frowned. "I like the defensive aspect. The offensive, not so much. It leaves you open to a lot of instant damage… but then again, if we need to go all-out, it might be worth it."

"My thought exactly," Liam said. "I don't have to like it. But I can definitely see where it could be useful. Charging the entrenched positions in the towers? I could've used the defense. And back in Isarn, with the gaborn? I could barely hurt it." He shrugged. "In combination with the next card, however, I believe that it can truly shine."

[Escalating Defenses
Rare, Fury fighter
Tier two
Active, short duration
It can be *so* hard to truly let loose. To unleash the constant need for personal protection and focus on attacking. This card is for those who desire to leave the boring, self-restraining back-and-forth of regular combat behind and opt for something more… exhilarating. For every successful attack on an enemy, regardless of damage inflicted, you summon a single magical shield for you to control mentally, up to a maximum of three shields.
"Hey, wait. That's not fair." Arghan the Butcher faces five archers.]

Sera beamed at him. "*Well* chosen. I am unsure how many other combinations of yours it would work for, but combining those two cards would grant you some much needed defense, even as you massively boost your offense."

"Thank you so much." Liam looked half-surprised at the praise.

"Of course, for the shields to work properly, you will need additional Mental Power training."

"And there we have it," Liam grumbled. He waved off Sera. "I know, I know. I'll put in the time. Promise." His frown slowly built up into a lopsided smile. "Also, I saved the best for last. My Tier three card is wonderful."

[All Out
Rare, Fury fighter
Tier three
Passive
Sometimes, simplicity is key. That principle is the foundation of this card as well. As long as the card is equipped, any offensive cards equipped by the wielder have their offensive effects increased by forty-five percent.
I am too weak, you say? Allow me to slip into something more suitable." Grandstanding turns violent.]

Kith choked. "What? No downsides? That's just cheating!"

Cilia cut in. "The efficiency depends on a lot. Now, it does look like an excellent fit, since your other Tier three cards have been somewhat situational. Yet, you would have to drop another Tier three card, and Unleash the Elements is an amazing offensive choice."

"Agreed. However, a blanket increase is impressive. Combined with Optimal Offense, you would wind up with an increase to your damage of between, let us see, seventy-five or nearly ninety percent, depending on whether the effect is additive or multiplicative." Sera looked thoughtful. "Also, the effect of Waterfall of Light would be interesting. Improving the trample and stun effects. Oh. And I wager that it would increase your temporary strength gain from Earthen Might as well. Your Strength is twenty-nine right now, is it not? Doubled, and with a forty-five percent increase, followed by a thirty percent increase, the end result could be either seventy-nine or..." Her brow furrowed.

"I... what? Please stop multiplying," Liam said. "I just wanted to grow stronger, not do numbers!"

Sera chuckled. "You are not getting off so easy. This will need extensive testing and a lot of calculation. Well chosen, though. Is it my turn now?" At their assent, she focused inward and grew still.

They waited. And waited. Several minutes passed by.

"Oooh that tickles." Sera laughed, before growing more somber. "Cilia. They were being ridiculous not telling us. The Title increase is a temporary plus five to our attributes while we are near a Wellspring with which we are aspected."

Cilia harrumphed. "That means near almost *any* Wellspring at this point. Does that include Potential?"

Sera nodded. "It does. You will be offered better cards and should be mentally prepared to plan for that. Silly boys." Lips drawing into a tight line, she turned to the others. "Now, Cilia has spoken about aspected affinities before." She sighed. "Stop rolling your eyes, Kith. You could do with improving your vocabulary too. I am talking about how the different aspects have a predilection for certain effects. Like Light cards tend toward healing, blinding, stunning, and protective effects, while Dark enjoys weakening, shadows, and the like."

"I knew that," Kith grumbled, not meeting her eyes.

"I believe that the Fury cards align with the Furyborn sensibilities in this. Meaning, it is no surprise that we see cards heavy on the choice of sacrifice, an adoration of strength and staying power, and connection to the land. This, in turn, allowed me to guide my strategy, to add another aspect to what I already have." She gave a slight smile. "I am at a decent level of competence and versatility, when it comes to healing, shielding, and boosting us all. As such, what I desired was utility and long-term prospects."

"Long-term?" Even Cilia looked confused.

"I will get back to that. My first card was simplicity itself."

[Natural Decomposition
Rare, Fury healer
Tier one
Active, variable duration
Over time, nature will break down anything. This card allows the wielder to target any enemy, who will see any active defensive effects up to Tier three break down. The time needed depends on the Tier of the effect and the Mental Power of the healer and the target. With matched Mental Power, Tier one is instant, Tier two takes fifteen seconds, while Tier three takes thirty seconds. *"Missed? My dear nemesis, I do not miss. Nature simply takes its time. Now, be kind enough to hurry and succumb."*]

"Yes!" Liam pumped his fist. "That's amazing!"

Sera blushed. "Granted, it is limited to Tier three and not instant."

"Pfah. If there's anything we've proved, it's that we're stubborn. What's thirty seconds? At least now, we *have* something against enemy effects beside my Ravenous Shadows. Also, your own Mental Power is ridiculous."

"Agreed. It is situational, but should be a lifesaver in the right situation." She shot them a small smile. "Besides, it's Rare. At Epic or even Legendary, it might allow me to target higher Tiers. My new Tier two card is nearly the opposite. Useable in almost any situation, yet not as life-changing."

[Nature's Shield
Uncommon, Fury healer
Tier two
Instant, medium duration
Part of a healer's job is taking care of damage. Yet, an even better approach is ensuring that the damage never happens in the first place. Some healers weaken enemies or shield their allies to ensure the damaging blows can never land. Yet, ensuring that the enemy never arrives in the first place is surely preferable to either approach. Upon activation of this card, the wielder calls upon nature to raise, shape, and place a few lengths of thorny underbrush. The height and toughness of the raised plants depend on the Mental Power of the healer.
"Oh, you're stuck? How sad. Maybe you shouldn't have tried to kill my friends!"]

Chase whistled. "That honestly sounds like it's veering into caster or summoner territory. But... yeah, I can think of a few situations where that could come in handy."

Kith grimaced. "I don't know, man. Plants. They're not going to stop something like the night emerald, are they?"

From behind them, Half-Swart guffawed. "Kid. Nothing short of a Tier four card is going to stop a night emerald in their tracks. But, a Nature's Shield with decent Mental Power—and by that, I mean above twenty—can become a pain for smaller or unarmored Guardians, not to mention anything about us soft-skinned humans. We're talking full hedges and six-inch thorns here."

Sera made a tiny squeaking sound in her throat. She mouthed the word "twenty" with wide eyes.

Chase grinned appreciatively. He couldn't wait to see what it would look like with her Mental Power at forty-five!

Clearing her throat, she continued. "Well. That will be fun to play with. Until then, this is my Tier three card."

[Home Defender
Rare, Fury healer
Tier three
Passive, permanent
Some people do not care about home. Others will take what they have and defend it to the last. This lets you designate an area with a one-mile radius for yourself, where you will always have the upper hand against any intruders. Inside that area, your attributes, except Potential, and the attributes of those allied with you, will be increased by +3.
The effect of the card will remain active, regardless whether you switch to another Tier three card. Once activated, you cannot establish a new home area for a full month.
"I was unaware the Wind-torn Healer lived here... Lads. I'm sorry. Put those weapons away. We're going home." A sergeant saves his men.]

"That's just ridiculous," Liam breathed.

"Ridiculous how?" Sera looked apprehensive, as if unsure how they were going to take it.

"Ridiculously *good*, obviously. Those are free points! You can use it, and *anybody* nearby is going to get a boost."

"You *kids* are ridiculous." The voice made them all turn around toward the sight of the haughty, doll-like Lightborn elder striding for them.

Half-Swart began, warningly, "Madaline..."

"No. They need somebody to tell them this, and if you're not going to, I will." Somehow, the tiny woman managed to loom over them, even being a head shorter than Kith. "You. Kids. Are. Ridiculous. I've been watching this for long enough to realize that you have no concept of exactly what you are."

"That seems harsh," Liam said.

She snorted. "If anything, I'm underplaying it. You lot may have a decent idea of balancing cards and whatnot. You have *no* idea just how rare you are. Home Defender isn't a special card in the least. Lots of people have it offered. Less than one of every hundred healers accept it."

They fell silent. Gawking at one another, none of them could see what the elder was getting at.

Kith tried. "But... why?"

She rolled her eyes, then took the last few steps, reached up and tapped Kith on the nose. "One in a hundred Furyborn manage to reach Tier three. Sometimes more, sometimes less. Of those who reach Tier three, less than half complete their trials to earn a Tier three Light card. *And you talk about spending a Tier three card choice for a passive boost as if it were a given!"* Her voice grew into a shrill screech, showing her outrage.

"People get so few cards, they *need* to make their choices count. Anybody who actually were to choose Home Defender at the cost of an active card they could use for their own survival? I'd push with all my influence to ensure they became a chief, even if they got it at Common rarity. Preferably in a frontier village. That single card could save numerous lives and make lives immeasurably easier for an entire village. *It would mean a difference of four Steps to every villager. That is just at Common with a plus one bonus!*" She exhaled, gritting her teeth. "Somehow—somehow, you've managed to beat the odds and survive for long enough to earn cards from four separate decks. But never think that this is normal."

Half-Swart's voice rose, mellow and happy. "What the honored Elder Madaline is *trying* to say is that that's an excellent choice—especially for when you eventually establish your Wellspring. Also, if you ever hit Tier four, you should consider increasing the rarity of that card. Though we've never seen anybody with an Epic rarity version of the card, the bonus does increase with the rarity."

That left their heads swimming. Chase considered the fact, and suddenly realized just how ridiculous the card could be. Sera could single-handedly improve the attributes of hundreds of allies with what amounted to twelve Steps. He croaked, "I... guess that settles that. Are you going next, Cil? Or you want me to pick?"

Blinking as she came out of a stunned reverie, Cilia agreed. "You go next. I have an idea of the types of cards I could be offered, and I'm going to think it over a bit more. In fact..." Her chest flashed, as she applied her Heart card, shutting herself in and removing the distractions.

Chase blinked. "Okay. That settled that, I guess." He took a deep breath and sat down, crossing his legs. "Here goes."

A minute in, a grin spread on his face, and only grew, until it looked as if his head were about to pop off. Slowly, like a felled tree, he tilted backward, until his back hit the platform. The grin never left his face.

He slowly opened his eyes, looking up into the sky. "Ouch. That was incredible." Still lying on his back, he stretched. "This was worth it all. Fury cards truly are something else, aren't they? Especially when you have a high enough Potential."

Chase's head was eclipsed by the arrival of Liam, standing over him with folded arms. "We've played nice. No wasting our time, now—or *the entire damn council of elders!*"

Cilia, clearly reacting to Liam's threatening posture, disengaged her heart card again, eyebrows raised.

"Oh. Okay. So, I liked what Sera said about utility. I have a number of cards that will make me faster, move better, allow me to grow stronger over the course of a conflict, and, as you know, manipulate our surroundings... but I am fairly underwhelming when it comes to direct damage, especially for tougher enemies. That was my first card."

[Unending Decay
Epic, Fury rogue
Tier one
Instant, medium duration
A tree rarely topples from a single stroke with an axe. Animals are rarely taken down with one bite or swipe of a claw. With this card equipped, every single strike of your weapon following the first on the same enemy will result in fifteen percent additional damage, to a maximum of an additional one hundred and fifty percent damage. Striking other enemies will reset the count.
Medium cooldown
"I done told ya, didn't I? Mess with me, and regret it later." The hangman wins his duel, twenty minutes in.]

Kith snorted. "That's ridiculous. Just... absolutely ridiculous. You'd even be able to pierce through that behemoth's skin by yourself."

"The requirement is dangerous. Striking something, or someone, consecutively, brings you into a lot of danger," Sera mused, frowning deeply. "Yet, in the right situation, it can make the difference."

Chase nodded. "Yeah. That was what I thought. Not for every battle, but in the right circumstances, it could make a decisive difference. My Tier two card is... well. Quite different."

[Fight Another Day
Rare, Fury rogue
Tier two
Instant, medium duration
Some wielders make history. Their approaches, tempers, and cards vary wildly. They all have one thing in common, however. They lived to grow strong. Reaching that point sometimes means a tactical retreat.
Upon activation of this card you, and anybody grouped with you, receive a marked increase to running speed as long as you are running away from enemies.
Long cooldown
"Stand and fight? I mean, I could. But... I'm not going to." The Lion of Tekarn has yet to earn his moniker.]

"Chase! This is the single best card you have ever picked!" Cilia's eyes glowed with intensity.

"O-kay? I mean, it's practical, but—"

"Screw practical. It's a possible escape route for *all* of us. We've needed that so much. That was so amazing, I don't even care about that ridiculous slashing card you picked first!"

Chase grinned weakly. "Well. I hope you keep that attitude with my third card."

[Home Turf Advantage
Epic, Fury rogue
Tier three
Passive, permanent
Any successful rogue is a distrustful rogue. They need to be alert, awake, perceptive, and cautious, ready to catch any danger to themselves and their kin. Yet, nobody can live their life in constant alertness without losing their edge.
This card, when wielded, allows the rogue, and anybody in their group, added benefits while resting. They will recuperate easier, their wounds close faster, and they will need less sleep to stay sharp. Also, any food and drink consumed will be more nourishing.
"It's like I said. Food just doesn't taste the same when you're away from home."]

Chase grimaced. "I know. How is that going to help us survive combat? Well, it isn't. It's... honestly, I don't know entirely why I picked it. Probably because of what Sera said, about thinking ahead, planning for the future. At this point, well, I can actually see a future for us, when we earn an actual home. And I don't want to just get by. I want an actual good life. I want to feel good, to enjoy myself, to feel *safe...*" Chase shrugged sheepishly.

Cilia narrowed her eyes, nodded brusquely. "I understand. Don't let it happen again. We still need to get there."

Her voice might be hard and direct, yet the tone spoke volumes. If Cilia thought you'd done a really bad job, she'd damn well tell you.

From behind them, Elder Madaline cleared her throat. "The title of the card is misleading. That card is one we love to see on any roaming scouts. It actually works anywhere. Meaning, even if you're out scouting, you will need less rest and less provisions. You will be able to switch to the card when you stop for the day, enjoy its full advantages, then switch back in the morning."

Chase tried, and failed, to keep from smiling as he cleared his throat. "Oh. Thank you. Here I was counting on showing my Tier four card off to make amends."

[One with the Soil
Epic, Fury rogue
Tier four
Instant, long duration
The stories all tell us about the massive fireballs, the summoned swarms of locusts and ground-breaking attack cards. Yet, they neglect to remember one thing: that is not how most fights are won or lost. The slip of a foot. A patch of gravel or slippery mud. These are the small things that spell the end for a huge number of fighters. With this card, you and your group will retain perfect balance, regardless of footing and weather.
"Dear Lord Baluz. It takes more than a punch to the chin, a muddy slope, a dozen summoned simians, and an Agility debuff to throw me off my feet. Admittedly, not that much more. Call it a tie?"]

Chase smirked. "In itself, it might be a bit underwhelming, at least for a Tier four card. But with my Winds of Change card for Tier three, I'll be able to switch back and forth between this one and A Friendly Wave."

Cilia tapped her lip. "First you create a muddy, slippery surface difficult to navigate—"

"That happens to stick to enemies and is acidic for them because of Among the Raindrops," Chase added, merrily.

"Following which you switch back to ensure that our footing is impeccable and we can move at will, while our enemies are left floundering. Rinse and repeat as necessary." She nodded curtly. "You were right. This is acceptable."

Elder Madaline's voice was strained. "Acceptable. She calls it acceptable. It can wipe out..." The doll-like Lightborn noticed their gazes aligning on her and waved a hand dismissively. "Move along. I'm not even here."

Chase chanced a glance at the elders. Four of them were still seated in their half-circle, with Elder Madaline right next to them. Half-Swart looked on with an amused glance, as if this were the best entertainment to ever grace Heart Halls. Elder Naian looked as if she were trying hard not to scold them for acting like...well, like the young people they were. She still sported a kindly smile that reached her eyes. Elder Madaline had the glazed look of somebody who'd seen too much and really just needed a cup of warm tea with rum, only she might leave out the tea entirely. Elder Nightbranch toed the line between being impressed and entertained, with a dash of annoyance at their antics. Elder Yassia looked like somebody who'd inadvertently stepped in a pile of caarnath leavings.

Chase had worked intensely with caarnaths in Cemano. He was intimately familiar with the look.

Cilia clasped her hands together. Her shoulders looked tight and bunched up, but her gaze was resolute. "My turn."

She closed her eyes, still standing. A minute passed by. Three. She stumbled forward and caught herself right before falling. With a strained noise close to a wail, she turned and tossed herself at Elder Madaline, who caught and held her with surprising strength for her size. Without any explanation, not a single word, Cilia burst into tears.

They were all shocked to their core, stunned, unaware where to turn or what to do. Cilia. The core of their group. The dependable, savvy, ever brilliant mind of their group, who was always slightly distanced in her displays of emotion, both physically and verbally, hung in Elder Madaline's embrace, sobbing like she'd been whipped bloody.

The Lightborn elder looked over Cilia's shoulder. She mouthed words at them that Chase couldn't decipher. The meaning was clear, though: equal parts "Help me!" and "What is going on?"

"Hey. Cil. Are you okay? Did you get some bad choices? Talk to us." Liam's voice was calm and careful, like somebody trying to approach a scared animal.

Cilia's sobbing subsided slowly. Still clinging on the elder's shoulders, her shuddering breaths deepened and the forlorn sounds slowly faded. With an effort, she brushed tears and worse off the elder's shoulder, then took one measured step back. She inclined her head deeply before the elder, then turned to the others and did the same. "From the core of my heart, I thank you all."

She didn't bother to wipe the tears from her face as she turned back to the others. Contemplatively, she mused, "Crying was liberating. I might resort to that another time. Something to remember. Now. You may have questions about my outburst."

Kith's expression, exquisitely frozen somewhere between sarcastic, stunned, and entertained, preceded a half-restrained laugh. "Questions. Yes. We have those." Quite clearly, it cost him to not elaborate any further.

"I have been feeling stuck. I apologize that I have not spoken to you about this. Yet, the sensation was there, constantly. A fear that, when we continue on this path, I would start lagging behind you all." She didn't look down, didn't avert her gaze, but the insecurity was there, for all to see.

Liam frowned. "But...the fire droplets? And my armor? My beautiful armor! You've made sure that I'm way more likely to survive!"

Chase snorted. "Besides, you're the one who fixes our plans to make sure we don't die."

"And learn dull stuff so we don't have to." Kith smirked.

"Do not, for a single Light-deprived moment, believe that comment is going away unnoticed, Kith," Cilia said, her eyes packed with menace. "Also, I know that what I do brings value to our tiny family. I'm not bereft of logic. Only, I'm not blind either."

Her head held high; her eyes sparkled as she spoke. "Our near future's not going to be peaceful. Walking into Liberty territory. The inevitable conflict with the lands of Light. Regardless of the outcome, even if we win, there will be an aftermath. Clashes. Attempts on our lives. Yet, I am no stronger than, say, a Tier two fighter in combat since I have no active combat cards. Possibly a Tier three if I see them coming and have my kit ready. Yet, my attributes are not geared for it. The evidence was there. Were we to continue like this, I would either have to cease going into combat with you or end up dead."

Chase gaped, mouth opening and closing like a fish caught out of water. His voice wavered, as he ventured, "Well. That's... you found another way, then?"

"I did," she said calmly. "Hence my reaction." She smiled beatifically. "The Title increase raising my Potential was the icing on top of the cake. Yet, my cards should be self-explanatory."

[**Manipulate Fury**
Common, Fury crafter
Tier one
Passive, permanent
This card lets you connect to the world around you, allowing you to manipulate the Fury aspect within you, in the soil and the air and, eventually, add them to your crafts. Manipulating your aspect will drain your stamina.
Take a dash of home. Add a splash of family, of heat and hearth. Season with that rage you hold so dear. This concoction is an ember, just waiting to burn. Fury brewer Darintas addresses the crowd.]

"Nothing special here, of course. A tad less... distanced than other aspect manipulation cards, but that was to be expected."

[**From Farm to Table**
Uncommon, Fury crafter
Tier two
Passive, permanent
The vast majority of crafters prioritize. They outsource, purchase goods, ingredients, and materials, purchase semi-finished products. It allows them to trade on the craftsmanship of others and craft a lot faster.
Yet, there is a joy in handling every part of the process, a certainty in knowing, intimately, every tiny item that you include. With this card, throughout the entire gathering and crafting process, you are able to imbue minute quantities of magic into the materials. Hence, the enhanced effects of the final product will be improved, based on how large a part of the process you have handled yourself, up to a maximum increase of sixty percent.
"Get yer filthy hands off me kill. That'll be a coat worthy of a king, it will!"]

After a moment, Liam apologetically raised his hands. "Sorry, Cil. I don't see it. At Tier two, you already had that Ritual of Fire thing where you could make things better."

"It raises my Mental Power while crafting, yes, Liam. To a maximum additional fifty percent, further boosted by Sera's buffs, which at this point lands me about ninety-five Mental Power in total."

"*Ninety-!*" The outburst came from Half-Swart, who, blinking, waved them off. "Sorry. That... sorry. Continue."

Cilia beamed. "It's all about the wording, like Sera told us. This card increases the effects, based on how large a part of the process I create myself. Nowhere does it state that I need to have the card equipped for the entire process."

"Oh, you *filthy* cheat," Chase said. "You are so good! So, you're saying that you can carve, clean, and handle the skins of your own kills, prepare them for crafting, switch to Ritual of Fire for the actual crafting, and still get most of the residual boost?"

"I've scrutinized the text more than a dozen times. It should work. Meaning, anything I craft from scratch should contain a perhaps forty to fifty percent stronger magical effect than what I can already craft at a calculated ninety-five Mental Power. *And this isn't the good card.*"

The silence on the platform was absolute. From below, the sounds of revelry were reaching a ridiculous pitch: thunderous drumbeats, howls, cries, and chants mixing with songs and shouts of defiance and, often enough, pleasure.

A low laughter made Cilia turn around.

Elder Madaline was shaking her head and looked her dead in the eye. Clearly and slowly, she enunciated, "Ri-di-cu-lous. I told you. Now, get on with it, child. If you are right in this, it will be something for my kids to hear. Then, I intend to get *so* drunk!"

Cilia - unflappable Cilia, who always had an answer - blushed. She turned back to the others.

[A Familiar Tool
Rare, Fury crafter
Tier three
Active, medium duration
No one knows the hammer like the smith himself. This old adage rings with truth. If you created an item, worked with it intimately, you *will* know it beyond somebody who simply bought it from a market stall. You will be aware of the imperfections beyond simple look, the strength hidden in the grain of the fabric, the stress they can and cannot handle.
This card takes that strength of knowledge and cements it into being. Any item created by the crafter themselves will have fifty percent added to their magical effect in combat, be it offensive or defensive, as long as the crafter is the one to wield it.
"They said that poison could not defeat the tainted count. And I laughed. For did I not create this poison myself? Now, stab me and be done with it, you cretin, for you are already dead."]

Sera laughed. Her eyes bulged, as she clamped her hands over her mouth, laughing hysterically. "Cilia! This is insanity! You are aware of that, right?"

Cilia nodded, eyes shining with joy. "With this, I won't be afraid to join you in battle, because my droplets and other utility items will be strong enough to stand up to *anything*. Any armor I craft for myself will be better at saving my life. As I grow in power, so will they. These are not easy cards to use. They require a lot of planning, demand that I handle large parts of the process that could be expedited a lot simpler or faster and will reduce my potential output. That being said, I believe that Master Benneth would approve." She showed her teeth in a savage grin. "And I can't *wait* to see what I can craft with this."

Elder Naian took that as her cue. She stepped forward and held up a hand to them. "We have had reservations. Of course we have. Taking a chance such as this, risking our entire domain on a gamble… it is not a decision easily made. Yet, having seen your decisions, your thoughts, and your sheer joyful exuberance at watching your closest grow stronger—it is a relief and a promise."

Her smile lit up her entire being as she enfolded all of them in an open-armed gesture. "Yet, we can't have youngsters like you spending *all* your time with such heavy thoughts. You've made it. You've gotten stronger. And now, we need for you all to leave. You need to go out there, relax, get roaring drunk and make some horrible mistakes."

They didn't wait for her to repeat herself.

Chapter 43

"Listen. Who would you rather have in your corner? A Lightborn, well-taught and civilized? An Elemental, educated in the towers by the best? Or a Furyborn, off their leash and snarling for blood?" That is horribly racist. But still, I agree. The ferocity and tenacity of a lot of Furyborn grant them a large advantage over others, even if it may only be in our heads. (Page 21.)

Elder Naian would be proud of them. They made a *lot* of youthful mistakes that night. Stupid drinking games. Some flavorful meat that did taste a little off. Some mushrooms that were supposed to bring enlightenment. In Liam's case, twins. Yet, when the smoke cleared, headaches faded, and stomachs settled, they could look back to that day through a wishful haze of joy and slight disbelief.

They made it! They'd managed to convince the Furyborn, earn new powers, and would soon be able to take off for Liberty lands in the search of the final deck to add to their Wellspring, and erect a home for them all. *An actual home.* As if that weren't enough, they would not have to make it by themselves. Behind them, they'd have the full power of the Furyborn, as well as whatever covert aid and information the Elementals would be able to bring to the table.

Even now, scouts and merchants turned informants were racing for Earth's Ward, carrying duplicates of Half-Swart's messages for the High Elementalist, professions of agreement, explanations, and queries. It also carried a long message that Chase and his friends had recorded themselves, stating, beyond a doubt, that they were doing this of their own free will, including a code word Tatiana had given them so long ago.

Yes. They might have to go off into the unknown, brave a border that was known to swallow anybody who crossed it and never again spit them out, and somehow steal or earn a deck that nobody else had ever managed to purloin—and still make it back out. Only, the difference between acting on their own and with the full weight and knowledge of the Furyborn behind them, was a weight off their shoulders.

For now, they were simply told to relax, to take some time for themselves and enjoy the downtime, while the elders prepared, gathered information, and had crafters prepare anything they could come up with to help. They were offered a house for all of them, along with improved accommodations.

That lasted for a full day. Then they got antsy and started training again.

Of course, there was also the newfound experience of being celebrities. It was a good thing that the council of elders had planned for them to become "tired" of the attention and fade from public view. (And, covertly, away from the bloodied grounds entirely.) Because it was damn well going to happen regardless.

Not only were they asked to tell their stories, again and again, the sudden adulation they were subjected to was an entirely new experience for them, and not one they enjoyed. It was easier for them to deal with the rarer examples of people who disbelieved their achievements, who disliked them for not being Furyborn, who wanted to put them in their place. The first couple of duels they won did quite a lot to reduce the number of those.

Rumors, of course, grew wild, and the pens were anything but exempt from those. Certain details quickly became fact, however. Such as Heart Halls soon becoming the target for a *massive* influx of new challengers. All around the challengers' pen, Furyborn toiled day and night to expand the premises and make room for newcomers who wanted to prove their worth and challenge the right to earn Dark cards. Tried and true systems were suddenly put to the test as they scrambled to fit in more, and still ensure they weren't just handing out the cards.

In their private conversations, they did wonder out loud why it was that the damn Furyborn didn't do just that—open up distribution to anybody, and ensure that any person who wanted got cards. It would guarantee that their people as a whole got a massive power boost. Of course, it would also go against the entire mentality of their people, but... power!

While most of them trained, and Liam reveled in the massive boost of attention and, frankly, love they were getting from all sides, Cilia faded from view entirely. Through the elders, she made arrangements with a local leatherworker to soon accompany them on very specific hunts that would allow her to build a stockpile of different types of high-quality leathers, skins, sinew, and furs. While the leatherworkers and the elders tried to work out the optimal schedule and targets, she planned. She sequestered herself in a corner of the crafting section, embroiled in the isolating effect of her Heart card, plotting and planning creations, only emerging to eat and discuss her plans with Sera. She didn't start crafting beyond building their regular stock of droplets. Not yet. But her vague promises and evasions promised massive results when she eventually would.

***

Their downtime came to an end the third day after the announcement. Chase strode into the confines of the crafting section of the challengers' pen and paused. He'd been there several times over, of course. He'd never get used to just how *noisy* it was, though. He had imagined that a lot of crafts were dependent on the ability to concentrate, in order to craft the optimal result. Well, that sure wasn't happening here. They had the ring of hammers from smithies right next to the stench of alchemists, while clothiers did their best to ignore a pack of brewers arguing over the best way to enhance ale.

Chase ignored the looks he got, and the cautious smiles. At this point, he was used to it. If he didn't get moving, he'd soon find himself beset by curious people asking to see the cards, to hear about his experiences and, more or less subtly, attempt to convince him to give them cards. There was always one. Ignoring the fact that he might learn to know how best to enhance ale from one of the resident crafters, he moved past the entrance, walking deeper into the building.

It was a huge creation, easily bigger than any warehouses he'd visited back in Isarn, during work hours or not. The theory behind its construction was exactly the same as back there: tall walls, high-set windows that let light into the huge area, and the occasional load-bearing pillar holding up the roof. The only difference being that here, everything was created in clay, somehow strengthened enough to not fall down on their heads. Even the "windows" were clay, somehow made translucent.

Cilia was exactly where he'd last seen her: in the far corner of the building, seated on a stool, surrounded by tables and parchment on all sides. A subtle glow enfolded her on all sides, the silencing effect ensuring that she could concentrate in peace. Her only nod to the existence of all the other crafters was the fact that she faced the rest of the warehouse, and not any of the walls. Of course, that might also be attributed to just how many times Kith had managed to scare her, leaping from nowhere into the range of her Heart card under the pretext of calling her to dinner or other even worse reasons.

Chase didn't do any of that. He didn't find the same satisfaction in childish pranks like that. No, you'd want to lull the target into the belief that they were safe. *Then* you hit them out of nowhere. So, as he got closer to her, he stayed right in the direction she was facing, waving slightly to catch Cilia's eye and avoid shocking her.

Entering the bubble of silence was the same, unsettling sense as it had always been. A slight popping of the ears, and a weird sensation of having moved farther than just a step, as the noise and smells of their surroundings faded.

Cilia didn't look up from her work, barely moved to acknowledge his arrival. A charcoal sketch on parchment, detailing something that looked like... wings, possibly? "I've eaten today," she said dismissively.

Chase laughed. "I know, Cil. That's not it. You need to come."

Now she looked up, frowning in disapproval. "*Need* demands an explanation, or I'm not moving. I'm actually getting closer to finishing the plans for my own armor. If I can't finish those plans, I can't ask the leatherworker to hunt for the right materials. If I can't get the right materials, I'll be forced to create something subpar. If I end up creating something subpar... Master Benneth would be disappointed."

The way she said that, it sounded like a fate worse than death. "Can't have that," he quickly agreed. "Only, I was sent to get you. Kith's off to fetch Liam from his cohorts of fans."

"What *is* going on?"

"Dunno. But Evan's here, says he has orders from the elders."

"Oh."

In short order, they were off again; wandering through the Halls and heading eastward in pursuit of the elders. Evan, in his regular taciturn ways, did not see fit to include them in what information he had.

The woods were definitely becoming more crowded. More carts moved in and out, bringing in the provisions needed to feed an increasing number of inhabitants. More travel-weary, dirty travelers arrived, wide eyes taking in everything. The only thing that hadn't changed so far, or so it seemed, was the number of defenders.

Kith, annoyed at the loss of an undisclosed number of hours he could've used to improve his training, pressed Evan as they walked. "Listen, bub. Did you hear where we're supposed to help the council and all damn Furyborn in the world? We're not your Darkness-smothered average outsiders who come here, trying to trade bits and bobs with you at hiked-up prices. We're trying to help. Now, could you at least help us a little in return so we know what's going on and how long we'll be gone?"

Evan's face froze in an expression that entirely failed to hide the disdain he felt. "Sir. I understand your frustration." He looked down as he walked before nodding to himself. With an earnest grimace, he started to roll up his left sleeve. "You have been informed of our creeds, have you not?"

Kith snorted. "More than anything else, I'd say, yeah. Resilience, integrity, independence, and blood."

"Good. That makes it easier for me to tell you. You might not know. However, certain cards actually correspond to certain creeds. You see this card? It attests to one of the most important messages of the creeds." He indicated the card on his arm. It was a lovely depiction of a partly see-through procession moving through a clearing, with vaguely threatening creatures everywhere, surrounding them but not seeing them.

Before, Kith had mostly been annoyed. Now, he was entirely intrigued, taking in the card and nodding eagerly. "I see it. What does it mean?"

Evan bowed slightly. "The exact definition can be hard to explain to an outsider, so I will try to make the meaning as clear as I can." He cleared his throat. Then his finger shot out and stopped right before Kith's nose. "It means *I'm not your Light-cursed servant, boy, and I don't care who you are, so quit your yammering and keep walking.*" He turned on his heels and continued to walk.

For a moment, they were all too shocked to react. Then Liam burst into helpless peals of laughter. The others joined in… all except for Kith, who strode after Evan, demanding he stop, and, when he didn't, subsided into cursing under his breath.

Their walk turned into a long hike. Long enough that they started to talk about food. At this point, they'd been on enough longer excursions, and knew that distances in the Halls could be extensive. Sera had actually thought far enough ahead to pack a bag of fruits and nuts and shared as they went. They all went armed. Of course they did. Regardless whether these were the Halls, they were *also* the bloodied grounds, and everybody they met had their own weapons handy in case of stumbling upon a feral Guardian or beast, or some sort of emergency.

They kept moving east and, after the first couple of hours, started to veer north. Eventually, the trees started to thin, along with the number of defenders, and they recognized that they were approaching the edge of Heart Halls leading up to Lightborn territory.

Finally, they spotted somebody. The clearly recognizable form of Elder Yassia stood, gazing out at the distant lands of Light with her back to them. Evan gave a curt nod to her back, turned on his heels, and walked away.

Kith watched him leave. "Fury cleave my skull, that man's infuriating. Please tell me I can kick his ass," he fumed.

Liam chuckled. "I don't know, man. He's growing on me. *I'm not your servant, boy.*"

"Somebody really takes the independence part of their creeds seriously." Chase smirked. "Good thing he's Furyborn, eh? I wouldn't give him good odds of surviving working for any of the nobles back in Isarn."

Sera snorted, then held a hand over her mouth. "Could you picture it? Or in the towers? Telling the High Elementalist to make her own damn tea if she is so thirsty?"

"Could we get on with it?" Cilia asked. "I know it doesn't really feel like it, but we're on a schedule. I *really* want to get back and continue working on my armor."

"I guess." Chase grimaced and started to walk. "Wonder what the angry old biddy wants with us. She didn't exactly seem like she was a fan."

"She isn't!" the Elder shouted from nearly fifty feet away. "But she does know a few things. So maybe you should start moving already."

Chase winced and raised his hand apologetically at the others. "Oops. Guess we'd better get to it."

"Ya think?" Kith grinned. "You could also spend awhile calling her names first..."

"Kith," Cilia said. "Enough."

"All right." He gave in with a sigh.

They reached the elder, who still stared off into the distance. Her wild mane of red and gray hair flowed in the light breeze, making her frozen, slight shape look like something out of a painting. Slowly, she turned to face them. Without talking, she took them in, her grim expression not giving anything away. *Really* looked at them, as if she were trying to fathom their inner workings, simply by looking. "Do you know how many times the Lightborn have attempted to enter our lands?"

"And a *mighty* fine day to you too, Elder Yassia," Chase said. "Listen. I know it's probably super fun to interrupt the day for a handful of others and make them hike through half a forest, but unless you have a point—"

"I *do* have a point, you tiny pest, so shut up!" she exploded. Closing her eyes, she visibly gathered her composure and then repeated herself. "Do you know?"

"How many times?" Sera mused. "My tutor spoke of four major campaigns against the Furyborn."

The elder scoffed. "Eighty-two times. This last year alone."

Stunned, they shared looks.

"Some are simple infiltrators, like the one you chanced upon. The most regular approach is a single group of fast-moving attackers rushing in, trying to take out a single tree with axes, acid, or fire, before moving back to safety." She snorted in disdain. "We are many in the Halls, yet we can't be everywhere. Sometimes, they get away with it. Yet, at least once a year, we get a larger force attacking. Sometimes as few as twenty. Sometimes in the hundreds. Those are the real challenges."

She started to walk, without looking back to see whether they followed. Her arm shot out to indicate a tree, right at the edge of the forest line. It glowed slightly with that innate vibrancy that announced a living tree. "Look at that. They have attempted felling that tree twice now. More than a dozen people have lost their lives in the attempt to make such a tiny inroad into our lands. Of course, the forces of Light have no lack of recruits or indebted to throw at us."

The tree did look it. Half its side looked green and verdant, shining softly with the color of an awakened tree. The other side was dominated by a series of deep cuts into the thick trunk of the wood, and dead splotches on the wood and discolorations in the surrounding soil marked some sort of attempt, acidic or otherwise, to ruin the tree using some card or other.

"Elder Yassia? We get it," Chase said in a somber voice. "The Lightborn have it out for you. Pits, it's not like we haven't had our clashes with them. We've told you as much. Dead inquisitors. Wanted posters. Remember?"

"No. You clearly do not see the point."

They'd left the edge of the trees behind now. The rolling hills beyond looked green and alive with tall grasses, though they had blemishes, weird discolorations, and entire areas that were simply dead. "To you, these lands are simply the means to an end. You came here, you were able to convince the elders to give you what you wanted, and now, soon, you are off again, leaving behind the blood to fend for themselves."

She fell into a pregnant silence as she continued to march straight ahead.

Chase couldn't help but think that something was horribly off about the elder. Back with the other elders, she'd been belligerent—openly hostile, to be frank—but she hadn't looked as *lost* as she did right now. As if she were in mourning. Perhaps this was her attempt to convince them to turn back. Regardless of his hopes and suspicions, Chase kept his hand close to his weapon, and noticed the others doing the same.

Elder Yassia ignored them all. "I tried to convince them. I truly did. I learned about some very differing opinions on your behavior. Most believed that you were genuine, that you wanted exactly what you said and were willing to pay the price for it. That you took to our values like you had been born here. Meanwhile, others figured that you were faking it. That you merely learned how we thought and said exactly what you knew we would *want* to hear. What is easiest to believe?" she mused. "That a disparate group, ostensibly from different walks of life, with *four* different races operating in harmony somehow all understand and agree with our culture... or that you are all dirty, filthy liars?"

Chase froze. He stopped, hand coming to a rest on the hilt of his short sword. "Okay, that's enough. We've gone far enough, and we're not going to just stand here and be insulted for your amusement. Either you tell us what the Pits we're doing out here, and make it good, or we're turning around and leaving, right this moment."

The elder turned around and looked at them. Her eyes were not as hostile as her words might assume. Rather, they were tired, sad. "Okay. What I truly wanted to show you today is simple. It is one fact I've learned over the years, that truly has been tested over the past weeks. Namely, that there is *nothing* I would not sacrifice for my kin. My life. My dignity. My position."

"What are you trying to say?" Liam growled. His shield was in place on his arm, hand on his truncheon.

"I think she's saying that it's about time I showed my face," a very familiar voice rasped close to their position. A drawling, hostile snarl of a voice, filled with ominous portent. Slate rose from a nearby patch of grass.

In a single second, they all had their weapons ready, pointing at the emerged scout. His only reaction was a deep sneer.

"Slate," Chase snarled. "I should've known that you'd team up with this wicked old *bitch*. What are you planning?"

Slate bared his teeth in a carnivorous display of hostility. "Exactly the same as I've tried right from the start. Make sure that you don't turn the bloodied grounds into a charred hellscape."

Chase assessed the two. Slate was exactly the same as he'd always been. A Tier two ranged fighter—capable, but not overwhelming, with a focus on Strength and Toughness. He hadn't even bothered to arm himself with the heavy crossbow he preferred. Meaning, he had other plans.

His gaze swung to Elder Yassia. The woman looked frail and unimpressive, thin, like a weather-bitten old tree that refused to die. Yet you surely didn't become an elder if you didn't have some sort of competence. Her sensible, well-worn leather outfit covered any cards she had. At least there were no cards displayed at her throat, meaning, she was Tier five at most. Tier five, they could handle. Probably. Yet, she didn't look like she was preparing for battle either. Meaning... there was another threat out there.

"All right. Lay it on us. Where are they hiding? Who or what have you got lurking out there?"

Yassia's gaze shot to Slate's.

He shook his head softly. "Right. For all that you're in this only to backstab us all, I won't deny that you're quick on the uptake."

Elder Yassia raised a hand, and he stopped talking. "We do not have that much time. Let me give you one simple choice. You claim to understand our values, right? Well, right now. This moment. You get to prove it." Her eyes bored into Chase's. "Show me your integrity. Would you lay down your life for your group? *This is not a rhetorical question.*"

Chase froze. Cold sweat erupted all over his body.

Kith's voice interrupted at the same time as his hand landed heavily on Chase's shoulder. "Nice try, Old Wrinkly. Like we're going to give up any of our own for any damn reason." He twirled a hand axe in his left hand before pointing it at Yassia. "You want him? You'll go through me. And... I'm thinking a swarm of bees. Yeah. Exploding bees sounds about right."

"You think this a joke?" Elder Yassia spat. "I am giving you a chance. Waste it or don't. You can all walk away, right now. Stride off, away from the bloodied grounds, and you can still live. Only this young Darkborn needs to die."

Liam stepped up on Chase right side. "Sorry. Sorry to hear that your wits are going with old age. We're leaving now. If you want to try to stop us? Go right ahead."

Slate's wicked smile deepened, as his feverish eyes followed the exchange. When he eventually spoke up, it sounded like a purr. "I am glad that was your choice." He put his fingers in his mouth and whistled—a shrill, piercing sound that tore through the air.

On all sides, the air itself shimmered, like a heat haze traveling over the lands. Then it faded, leaving Lightborn soldiers to appear in its wake.

Chapter 44

"I used to think them barbarians. I scorned their prac- tices, their brutality. Then, I saw what became of survivors, of any Furyborn too weak to kill themselves rather than fall in the hands of the Lightborn. Now, I know the real barbarians." I'm honestly surprised they dared introduce this to the tome. The Lightborn would not be happy to read this. (Page 96.)

Ten. Twelve. Fourteen. Seventeen Lightborn soldiers, most heavily armed and armored, with the looks of veterans. Chase's fingers twitched. *Fight? Run for it? Wait and see if an opening appeared?*

"Ah. You came through, Elder Yassia." The voice was warm and charismatic. It fit like a glove with the owner, a tall and wide, muscular man with a rugged, handsome face and a wild blond beard. "To be entirely honest, I expected this to be an attempt at stabbing us in the back."

Yassia spat, "I don't change. If I try to stab you, it will be in the face, Armsmaster Rillek."

The tall Lightborn bowed sarcastically. "Appreciate the gesture." He made a sweeping gesture. "These are the kids who have caused so much trouble for us all, then?"

She nodded.

"I have to admit," the soldier mused, "I was slightly con- fused at your offer in the first place. I knew that some of our soldiers had ways of communicating with you barbarians. But you reaching out to tell us that you were willing to hand over who we were waiting for, as long as we took care of him? That, I didn't expect. Care to enlighten me?"

Yassia scoffed. "It's simple. Simple enough that even a killer like you should understand. These kids have managed to convince the other elders that we should protect them."

Rillek's warm laughter rang out. "Oh, that *is* grand. So, you call upon the loathed Lightborn to make your problem go away, and it can all go back to normal." He was silent for a mo- ment, before asking, in a conspicuously light tone, "You don't even want the deck, then?"

Yassia scoffed. "That damn deck. It's caused us all no end of trouble. *No*, I don't want the deck. I want it to disappear. I want you to take it far away, and do with it what you want. That way, when you start fighting over all the power it promises, you'll leave us the Pits alone."

"How very altruistic of you." He smiled. "There can be no doubt that the nobles back in Stradeburg will have a field day over this."

"They will not. The capitol will be up in arms. That deck is anathema. It is sin, crystallized into being. The Church will see the deck destroyed." The words came from a gaunt, bald figure right behind Rillek. He was the only one to not carry armor, but a long, brilliantly white robe instead. And a card shone from beneath the brilliant white of his stomach. Tier five!

"Of course, Inquisitor Vorbis," the soldier said. "Let's leave that for the higher-ups to handle. Meanwhile, we just make sure that everything goes according to protocol." With a flamboyant wave worthy of a noble, he turned on Elder Yassia again. "On that note. I *will* be entirely honest. I am slightly disappointed with you, honored elder."

"How do you mean?" The old woman tensed, everything in her body showing her readiness to act.

"Well, there I was, ready to believe in the goodness of your heart, in a newfound willingness in the Furyborn to avoid conflict, to settle peacefully, when a few of my scouts noticed something strange. A large group of defenders, heavily armed, hidden away, almost like they were ready to go on the attack."

"Armsmaster Rillek—"

"I mean, really now, Elder Yassia? What was the plan? Allow us to grasp hold of this young cripple, start moving him away, and then you would get to sweep in and save your lands, defeat some Lightborn in the process, and ensure that the Darkborn, sadly, got himself killed?"

Elder Yassia didn't answer. She just glared darkly at him.

He chuckled. "Oh, that is rich. That was it exactly. Now, listen here, hag—"

"No, *you* listen," she barked. "You think you can fend off all my men? There are enough to ensure that you all end up enriching the soils of the bloodied grounds. Back away, take the rest of his group, and leave the Darkborn behind. No one will have to die."

"Oh, it's much too late for that." His tone grew as smug as a feline settling in with an entire stolen fish. "See, I may have lied a little. Because I was going to backstab you too. I was just going to do it better. Now, I could still let you go and take my prize home. Only, I'm not going to. The prize I will earn for bringing home a Deck of Darkness may overwhelm my rewards for ending an elder of Heart Halls... but every little bit helps."

He raised a finger, and a brilliant light started to shine from it. A tiny sphere of brilliance came into being and swiftly rose into the air, settling mid-air dozens of feet up. His tone became sepulchral. "That was my signal." His eyes never left hers. A few hundred feet away, loud *whoomphs* erupted, several in quick succession. Instantly, flames rose into the air, tall enough to be seen from far away. Half-drowned in the sound of the explosion were heart-rending screams. "And those were your vaunted scouts." The tip of his tongue ran across his lips.

For a split second, Yassia didn't even react. Then she screamed, and the world exploded. Earth flew everywhere, obscuring the sun.

The armsmaster's voice rang through the sounds of explosions, loud, and in command. "Whatever else happens, keep them here!"

Chase pulled back, weapons ready, looking into a world that had suddenly become dark from dirt flying everywhere as his friends closed up around him. "What do we do?" he shouted.

"We run!" Kith yelled.

They turned on their heels, started to move.

Chase activated his Fight Another Day card.

Dirt rained down onto the ground all around them, as the eruption settled, allowing them to see.

To see Elder Yassia attacking Armsmaster Rillek—wide, sweeping movements of her arms making the soil follow her every bidding.

To see Slate go down under the onslaught of several soldiers.

To see the inquisitor stalking in their direction, death in his eyes.

To see the remaining soldiers closing in on their position, from all directions. First in their dozens. Then, as they appeared from within the high grasses in the distance, more than a hundred. All wielders, all armed, all entirely focused on their group. There was nowhere to run.

Elder Yassia's end was protracted. It was hard-won. But it was never, ever in question. Had it only been her against the armsmaster, she might have won. In the bloody, gore-filled minutes they fought, she unleashed an onslaught of nature's fury they had never witnessed before. The entirety of the grasslands was at the beck and call of the thin, elderly woman, it seemed, and she wielded it like armor, weapons, distractions, and as an aid to her movement, all portraying a mastery built up over years and decades of strife.

Chase had thought her Tier three or four at most. Now, he adapted his estimations, stunned by the swiftness of her movements and ease of control. She had to be Tier five. An entire *wave* of soil rose to bury the armsmaster at a simple gesture, even as she struck at the ground, carving out a furrow that shaped itself into a rough spear.

Only, she wasn't fighting the armsmaster one-on-one. The wave of soil struck a brilliant shield and broke apart, erupting into its myriad components. A blast hit the ground at her feet, ruining her footing, even as a shining butterfly landed on the spear and burst, breaking it apart.

Arrows, summons, shield effects, and Light magic: all the armsmaster's soldiers unleashed violence on Yassia, and healed and shielded him, while ruining every chance Yassia had to fight on even grounds with him.

While they clashed, the circle around Chase and his friends drew tighter, battle-ready soldiers preparing themselves for any action. Several times over, Chase nearly urged them to run for it. Except, there were simply too many enemies... and the unsettling inquisitor, Vorbis, lurked right behind them, hands glowing in a menacing hum, breathing hard, as his deep-set eyes dared them to move, to do *anything*.

It took less than two minutes for the Lightborn to defeat Yassia. By then, they had her panting, bleeding from myriad cuts on arms, legs, and stomach. Her hair, already messy, had been half shorn from her head, and her scalp bled profusely, blood running freely down over her face, blinding one eye.

Armsmaster Rillek settled back, chest rising and falling steadily. There was a gleam of joy in his eyes as he held up a hand and shouted, "Nobody kill her." Turning to her, he ordered, "Surrender already, you old hag. Your life isn't going to be enviable, but at least it will be life."

She gasped, forcing air into her lungs. "Life under the Lightborn?" Closing her eyes, she breathed deep... once, twice. Then her eyes opened again, and her eyes shone bright, every single facet of dark, bloody hatred. "That would not be life." She fell to her knees, both hands tearing into the ground; the soil, twisting, formed itself into twin daggers of earth. Both hands shot out... at her own throat.

One caster reacted in time. A dagger burst apart into dirt. They failed to stop the other. The dagger tore into her throat, point first, opening a wide, jagged wound, from which blood poured forth in a torrent.

Slowly, Elder Yassia sank down on her knees, still facing the armsmaster. A golden glow surrounded her, as a healer tried to save her life. Yet, the dagger was still inside the wound, Yassia's fist feverishly tight on the rough hilt. The wound refused to close. Seconds later, she breathed her last.

The following minutes were tense. Armsmaster Rillek didn't waste much time over Yassia, merely cursing over her death. Then he moved into action, snapping orders left and right, forcing everybody into action, demanding updates on the ambush on the Furyborn.

They were roughly disarmed, following a short period of standoff between them, the inquisitor, and the encroaching soldiers. With a lot of shouted threats and not a little prodding, they were then corralled in an eastward direction at spearpoint.

Chase's mind reeled at the sudden reversal of their fortunes. Just a few hours earlier, they'd been set and safe, nearly ready to move onto the next chapter of their lives. Now, they were, what? Sacrifices? Heading for the block? Or, more likely, bound to be interrogated and tortured first, before they could be done in as the party favor in some nice political to-do in Lightborn lands.

Should they have fought? Would that have changed anything? They were stronger than the Lightborn soldiers, no discussion. Yet, that inquisitor was *right* there, and a Tier five to boot. On top of that, the numbers of the Lightborn were enough to drown them. No. Surrendering was the right choice. They were weeks of hard marching away from any larger Lightborn settlement. As long as they weren't outright slaughtered, they'd have the opportunity to spot their chance to escape. On top of that, they knew that Elder Yassia's death wouldn't have gone unnoticed. Even if there would be some delay, they were sure to send forces after them—if anything, to keep the Lightborn from appropriating the deck.

They weren't outright slaughtered. Instead, they were hurried through the ranks of Lightborn soldiers, every single one of them looking at them with expressions ranging from hate over outright disgust to undisguised greed. Apparently, the armsmaster wasn't the only one with high hopes for what their capture would do to his career.

There were no camps this close to the bloodied grounds. Less than half an hour into their flight, they were ungently corralled past a gentle hill and down a slope into what was clearly a small staging ground. Here, they had gathered a few pack animals, carts, even a healer's tent with healers standing by for anything. Everything, including the healer's tent, looked like it was ready to pack up at minutes' notice.

Which was exactly what happened. Less than ten minutes transpired, before the carts were packed and attached to the caarnaths, who accepted their burdens with placid grunts. Wounded soldiers—because apparently, whatever ambush they'd sprung on Elder Yassia's scouts hadn't gone off blood-lessly—on one cart, provisions on another. The third cart of four? That one was for them.

Chase almost felt honored. This cart was something out of the ordinary—not just the regular slapdash of cheap wood and nails, hammered together to make for a squeaky, but efficient way of transporting your goods. This had been carefully crafted and painstakingly put together. Not for looks, nor for comfort. For security. It was a flatbed cart, drawn by yet another caar-nath. The bottom of the cart looked to be made from one entire piece of wood, and it shone with a bright glow that attested to it being imbued with some sort of magic. Apart from the bottom, there were no frills or additions to the cart, except the one dom-inating piece. One long, lightly glowing chain, snaking its way from one end to the other, locked into place on either end with two heavy rings that looked like they weighed twenty pounds apiece.

The inquisitor, along with nearly a dozen soldiers, looked on with badly disguised bloodlust, while a dirty, soot-smeared laborer clamped heavy iron cuffs on all their wrists and ankles. Once those were all in place, the soldiers nudged them onto the cart, where they painstakingly trailed the chain through each shackle attached to every cuff. When they thought they were done, a couple of soldiers walked up, carrying an unconscious Slate, who was cuffed and chained as the second in line, with Sera as the last. Finally, they pulled the chain taut, ensuring that their limbs were all pulled uncomfortably tight to the floor of the cart.

With a satisfied grunt, the laborer said something to the inquisitor and walked off. The inquisitor remained standing, gleaming eyes fixed directly on them as if he planned to stay there forever. He procured a heavy, multi-headed whip from somewhere, and his eyes shone with eagerness to use it.

A few minutes later, a shout rang out, and the cart jolted into motion. Around them, the entire force split into motion, ex-cept for about a third staying put. Chase, turning his head every which way, put the numbers of the remaining surrounding sol-diers at maybe a hundred total.

Once, Kith started to whisper. However, the moment he did, the inquisitor barked out for silence, slamming the flail down on the cart bed. One of the corded whip heads lashed across Kith's leg, leaving a long, thin line of blood. They got the message after that.

The journey swiftly became one of uncomfortable tedium. Their trappings weren't torturous. Yet they were anything but comfortable. The cuffs were tightened hard enough that they ached, and being unable to move their hands or feet more than ten inches from the ground made it so they were wholly unable to find a really comfortable position. Slate remained unconscious.

The arrival of the armsmaster cut their musings short.

"Inquisitor Vorbis. I need you to join the sleeping cart to rest," he said without preamble.

"My place is with these heretics," Vorbis answered. His burning eyes didn't even waver.

"Of course it is," the armsmaster acknowledged. "Yet, we need to focus on the distance here. You will be needed above all during the long hours of the night. Where anybody else may flag in their vigilance, I know you'll remain alert—and it's a long two weeks back to civilized lands. Get your rest now, while we're safe."

The inquisitor looked the muscular leader straight in the eye, with no hint as to whether he was going to follow his order. Then he turned on his heels and walked to find a resting place on one of the following carts.

Armsmaster Rillek followed him with his eyes as he departed. As the gaunt inquisitor lay down, he sighed deeply, with a satisfied smile. He shook his head slightly to himself. "God, I love fanatics."

Chapter 45

"I congratulate you for your tenacity in reaching the end of this tome. We are aware that much of the contents may appear spurious. Yet, with so little information readily available, we have included everything we deemed viable. Please remember, dear reader. The single most important thing about the Furyborn? They are better as allies than as enemies." Did… he just admit they didn't even know which parts of the tome are true? (Page 104.)

Chase cleared his throat. "You want to run that by us again?"

Armsmaster Rillek laughed. His eyes gleamed with heartfelt amusement. "Oh, come now. You heard me. And you're from Isarn, right? Frontier city. Clergy are even less reasonable there than in the inner cities."

"Yet you said you *loved* fanatics," Liam tried, frowning deeply.

"Of *course* I do. They're so bloody useful, aren't they? Well-taught, powerful, and so damn easy to steer. Like grimbolds, but able to grasp intelligent commands. Well, mostly."

"Are you supposed to tell us that?" Chase indicated the cart behind him with a tilt of his head. "Fever gaze back there looks like he'd take offense to being called a grimbold."

Rillek laughed even louder at that. "Oh, please. Like he would trust your words. You're Darkborn and are *the* heretics who have killed his brethren and caused the latest turmoil in the church. If you were on fire, he would likely be toasting sausages over you." The tall, charismatic man sighed happily. "Besides, I've really looked forward to this talk. Because you lot and me? We're about to become the best of friends, for the remainder of our trip." Another guffaw at their shocked looks. "Oh, yes we are. Now, I realize there will be an adjustment period. Of course there will. Yet, you'll come around. Because, you see, I'll be the only thing standing between you," he nodded at Chase, "and those poor followers of yours getting butchered. So, I *do* hope we can become friends."

"What?" Chase snapped.

"Oh, come now. You've managed to play tricks on the entire Lightborn society for months. Don't act like you're a village clown. You know how it works. These poor losers? They're collateral. Bonus prices. Spoils of war." He eyed Sera appreciatively as he said that. "While there'll be a bonus in there if I bring them back, their corpses will do just as fine. I would be a poor leader not to use leverage like that, would I not?"

"You hurt one hair on their—" Kith snarled, only to freeze in his tracks.

With a warm smile, the armsmaster very slowly extracted a knife. It was nothing special. An everyday knife like you'd use for anything on the road. He held the knife softly by two fingers and slowly dragged it across his own arm. It didn't cut. Then he took proper hold of the knife and slowly placed it edge down on Cilia's lower leg, gently dragging it across her skin as he pushed down slightly. A thin, red line followed the trail of the knife. His eyes didn't leave Kith's, though the tip of his tongue protruded slightly from between his lips.

"Leverage. Leverage makes all the difference. And you don't have it. So, do me a favor and shush, my furious little boy." He wiped his knife on her leggings and put it back in its sheath. He scratched his neck. "Where was I? Oh. Right." He looked at Chase, something dark gleaming behind his eyes. "Your friends are dead, unless somebody intervenes. That, you will have to adjust to. They have nothing that cannot be found elsewhere. Your crafter friend there? Sure, she has Dark cards, as do the rest of you. Only, there is but *one* of you who holds the deck. Or should I say decks?" He grinned.

"How do you even know that?" Chase asked.

"Please. There are a hundred Elementals who gained Dark cards from you. Do you really believe that could stay a secret? We Lightborn have our contacts. Also, we know that you stole a Deck of Light from High Priest de Merion in Isarn, and were granted an Elemental Deck in the towers. From the blank look on your faces, I think I will need to spell this out, so there is no doubt as to my meaning."

He leaned forward, his warm smile looking plastered on as he hovered over the cart. "If I kill you all right now and simply take the Deck of Darkness and hand it in? I'm going to earn a promotion. Likely an estate, a bag full of gold for me to spend when I'm done with my service." He waved the notion away. "Only, that would be *such* a waste. Decks, outside of the original decks, fade away with the death of the holder, unless they are handed over voluntarily. That means that this wonderful Elemental Deck you hold would just fade away into nothingness. Do you have *any* idea what the upper crust would pay to receive both a Dark *and* an Elemental Deck, all wrapped with a bow? I don't either. But I must admit I'm rather salivating at the thought. So, what I need to do is to turn you over to my superiors with you ready to cooperate."

He sighed theatrically. "Now, I have been informed that some of you are in fact from the lower walks of life. That makes my position a tad more difficult, because you won't just believe any old lies I could come up with, citing honor or promises or such nonsense. You are aware that handing over the decks entirely would just lead to your subsequent death, likely in a huge public spectacle meant to show you off as a monster. With you aware of this, any torture or threats on my side would be made even more difficult—and I do so hate difficulties. With that in mind, I am going with the other option. Circling us back to..." He gestured in the air, performing a circle that went back to its starting point. "Leverage. Meaning, you have an option here. Chase, was it not? Dreadful name. Yet so very appropriate."

"What option?" Chase growled.

"Be a nice little puppet." Rillek grinned, leaning over to pat him on the head. "My superiors would love to have the Dark, Light, and Elemental decks all wrapped up in one convenient package. In fact, creating a Wellspring from three full decks would make them positively ecstatic. You can offer them this. Of course, you would be a prisoner for the rest of your natural life. Also, you wouldn't be acting on your own ever again. In fact, you'd have the nobility's hands so far up your ass you could really appreciate their expensive manicures. But you'd live. And so would your friends, kept alive for the simple reason of maintaining leverage against you."

Chase reeled. The idea of being trapped, again, with no way to escape, took the wind out of his sails. "So... I'd create a Wellspring for the Church?" he asked, trying to buy time.

"Yes. Or for the nobles. I'm not really sure who's in charge these days. Doesn't matter much either, as long as I'm getting rewarded. You would create a Wellspring. Make the exact choices for the Wellspring they'd want to. Summon whatever Guardians they'd require. Dance, sing, and humble yourself at their request. And I'm sure they'll have plenty of requests."

He shrugged. "But you'd be safe. Set for life. Fed. Protected. And so would your friends." He grinned down at Slate, who was still out. "Not so for this treacherous little Furyborn. He's bound for a short, ugly time with the local questioners, who will milk him for all he's got."

"Listen here, you psychopathic—"

"Kith!" Chase snapped. "Please, Armsmaster Rillek. We'll need some time to think it over."

"Of course you do." The man nodded pleasantly. "Take whatever time you want. I'll be right here, as will my trusted men. Listening to anything you have to say. Don't take it personally. I would just be so very disappointed if you decided to abuse my hospitality by conspiring to do something stupid."

That being said, he did fall back to walk right behind the cart, whistling under his breath. Even *that* was melodic and pretty.

For nearly a minute, they succumbed to a melancholic silence. Eventually, Kith burst out, "I *knew* we should've killed Slate, back in Cemano. At least we can make up for that now."

"Kith—" Sera started.

"Don't *Kith* me. See where it's taken us. We made it, even though he fought us every step of the way, made everything harder than it had to be. And now, he's ensured that we're all as good as dead. Or, even if we survive, we'll be trapped for the rest of our lives, and bring about the fall of the Furyborn. *My kin!*"

A low chuckle from next to the cart interrupted his words. Rillek coughed. "Oh, never mind me. This is better than a full team of mummers. Just act like I'm not here."

They subsided into a sullen silence after that, each of them trapped in their own recursive spiral of dark thoughts, self-recrimination, and half-formed plans of escape. After half an hour, Slate awoke from his unconsciousness, groaning and holding his bloodied head. Once he figured out what was going on, his expression vacillated between horror at his situation, what had been done to the elder and outright hatred for their party. He didn't talk, though.

A few hours went by. They were each given a large squirt of water from a waterskin, but were told that they weren't being fed until that evening. With the armsmaster there, they couldn't find it in them to discuss their situation.

At long last, the silence lifted. It was Cilia who broke it. She lay down, curled upon herself in the fetal position, with her hands over her face, obscuring her mouth. Her words were loud and intense, even as the sounds of the world around them faded into nothingness. "Slate. You cannot talk. You cannot give *any* sign that you hear this. But I have a question for you. Give a small nod if you understand."

The scout had frozen, unmoving. For a while, it seemed as if he wasn't going to react. Eventually, his head lowered in an intimation of a nod.

Cilia remained lying perfectly still on the wooden bed of the cart. You'd have to be really close to see her lips moving. "My Heart card allows me to create a circle of silence. No sound comes in *or* out. Meaning, we can only use it sparingly, or they'll notice it. My question is simple, though. What would you rather—help us all escape and have the possibility to stab us in the back later? Or see the Lightborn gain all the decks and let them torture you for your secrets?"

His voice, when it arrived, was pain-filled, close to a growl. But the answer was straightforward. "I'll help."

The following couple of hours were a stressful mess, as their group, now including the recalcitrant Slate, invented a system that would let them talk without getting spotted by their guards. Even though they could, theoretically, talk as much as they wanted, anybody finding out that they were plotting in secret would lead to further security measures. Besides, even though sound didn't escape from Cilia's circle, it also didn't enter, and it would be too easy to get blindsided by something, if they weren't attentive. So, they figured out a system where Liam and Chase would watch either side of the cart and reach out with a foot to touch Cilia's leg if it wasn't safe to talk. It led to some near misses, and some jumbled, broken talks, but they did manage to agree on the basics.

Judging from the gossip of nearby soldiers, these weren't one established army, but a bunch of disparate groups, brought together at short notice on Inquisitor Vorbis and Armsmaster Rillek's orders. They were also well and truly trapped. According to Cilia, a few blacksmiths back in Isarn sold enhanced iron, touting it as thrice as strong as the regular kind. The chain that had them all awkwardly trapped looked suspiciously like that very iron.

Liam believed that, using his Earthen Might, All Out, and Optimal Offense cards at the same time, along with every buff they had, he might possibly be able to pull apart the cuffs themselves, which were unenhanced. He didn't sound too hopeful, though. After agreeing that there were no easy solutions to be found here, they agreed to wait for the evening, until they camped down, to try to have a more in-depth chat in secret. Chase was harboring an idea for maybe using acid on the cart itself.

Except they never did stop. The carts kept on plodding onward, and the Lightborn guards took turns ambling off to join a cart and take some hours of bouncing sleep, even as they distanced themselves from the bloodied grounds. The armsmaster came by a few times to check on them and talk to the guards. Eventually, a couple of guards loudly complaining led to them realizing that the first handful of days would be a never-ending march to take them deeper into the lands of Light and away from any pursuit. The third of the soldiers who had stayed behind would be working to disguise their tracks, lay false tracks, and defend against any Furyborn who tried to follow. The Lightborn soldiers laughed in relief at not being part of what they clearly perceived as a sacrificial group.

Evening came and went. Twilight arrived, the near darkness making it hard for any watchers to see exactly what was going on.

"Now is the time. We can hide our talks right now, as long as we are alert. But the inquisitor is bound to arrive for his night shift soon, so we need to hurry," Cilia said.

"Why do you even include me?" Slate's voice rasped. "Don't act like you want to save me or some crap like that."

Cilia scoffed. "Why would we? You've tried to get us killed, what, three times now?"

"Four." He didn't back down, didn't apologize.

"Right. If I had the choice, I, would leave you to die right here... Only, my Heart card doesn't work like that. I can decide how big the circle of silence is, but not the shape. Since Sera needs to know what's happening, that means you're included too. Now, Slate. This is the moment you choose. You could either blow our cover and let everything the armsmaster explained to us come to pass. The Lightborn would take us in and keep us as slaves, and you'd be resigned to torture and a quick death. Or, you throw in all you have, help us get away and back to the bloodied grounds. Decide."

His snarl was as feral as they came. "On the blood, I swear. If I can, I will help you escape. But I will not let you get away with working against the blood. I will follow you and keep an eye on you. If any of you try to betray the Furyborn, I will see you dead."

Kith blinked. "Did we... just earn a pet?"

Ignoring him, Cilia glanced at the guards walking next to them and said, "Silence." Lowering the barrier, they listened for a few seconds to secure that nobody was trying to address them and nobody was approaching. With a curt nod that was almost imperceptible in the growing darkness, she said, "Status. We have three guards surrounding the cart at all times, Tier two and above. The inquisitor will arrive soon, and the armsmaster is also bound to spend a lot of time around us. In short, we can expect to be heavily guarded at all times. In addition to this, we have more than a hundred Lightborn surrounding us, estimating at least eighty of these are wielders and combat classes. What else?"

"I've kept an eye on them. These aren't indebted or rookies. They look like veterans. Even the Tier ones will be tough bastards," Kith growled.

"Plenty of ranged and caster classes too," Liam added. "If we run, we will be moving targets. Though... I suppose we just need to get past the opening salvo, and then we'd be good?"

"Forget it." Slate's rasping voice was sullen. "We've got a lot of combat classes there, but at least half will be the veteran hunters who like to hang out around our lands. They know the terrain better than you do, have cards to help them hide or move quickly, and are fully equipped. We've got several hours' running back to safety and no gear. No way we'd make it."

"Wait with the planning," Cilia admonished. "For now, we need facts."

"Our weapons are on the hindmost cart," Chase said. "I can see the handle on Liam's truncheon from here."

"Facts," Sera mused aloud. "The inquisitor really seemed peeved at the idea of leaving us alive. That might be an opening between the armsmaster and the inquisitor."

"That's true." Chase perked up. "If he learns that we'll be pampered and kept back in the capitol... that may be worth looking into."

"Fact," Liam grumbled, silently straining, ignoring their hypotheticals. "I've changed my mind. There's no give in these chains. With all cards and buffs active, I might be able to tear the shackles on our cuffs open, but the chain itself, and the massive rings it's fastened to, are too tough. Meaning, we're not going anywhere. Least they didn't get my armor off before we got shackled."

"You want facts." Kith smirked and scratched behind his ear. He held up a hand, and something tiny glinted in the near-dark. "Fact is, I'm amazing. I'll handle the locks, as long as Sera makes sure that her Heart of Hearts card is active."

They shared looks. Heart of Hearts boosted all their Heart cards. Would they actually, finally learn what Kith's Heart card did?

He barreled on, not waiting for any questions. "Once the locks are done, we can pull the chain through all the cuffs. We'll still need a solid distraction."

"I can manage the distraction," Sera said, her voice decisive. "Yet, even if we get free of the cart, evade, or beat down the nearby guards, we still need to make it back to that last cart and get our weapons. Attempting to run weaponless feels like suicide."

"Brute force paired with distractions? *Please.* Liam and I have done that since we were ten. I've got the distractions, Liam has the force." Kith grinned.

"If you get me back to my crafted items on my belts, I can force space for us, get us away from the surrounding soldiers," Cilia said. "Even if it costs me every single item I've crafted, I can do it."

"Which, again, leaves us in the same position as last. Running from veteran hunters, in a land we don't know." Liam grimaced.

"I've got that speed boost for running away?" Chase hazarded.

Slate cut them off. "I will make sure we get away."

They looked at him dubiously.

Kith frowned. "Okay. And how exactly do you plan to do that?"

The scout snarled, "You claim you can magic these chains off and get to our weapons? Then I can keep any hunters off us."

They argued and discussed their plans, debating timing, approaches, the advantages and disadvantages of different cards for a while until they started to rehash discussions they'd already been over. They watched the guards constantly, and Cilia made sure to drop the effect of her Heart card at intervals to ensure that they weren't being spoken to. Eventually, the inquisitor arrived, and they settled in to get some sleep, knowing damn well they'd need the energy in the morning.

Chapter 46

*"Postscript: We have tried, numerous times, to have Fu-
ryborn add to the tome, to confirm or deny what's hidden
within. As one, they have declined, bar a few who have been
deemed untrustworthy."* What a surprise. Would you like to
give away the secrets of the blood for a paltry fee? No? That's
so weird... (Page 105.)

"Ah. Armsmaster Rillek. A word, if you would?"
Sera's loud words broke the early morning silence.
"We would like to talk about accommodations."

The armsmaster looked a bit taken aback at the loudness
of her question, and couldn't quite hide the side glance he sent
the inquisitor. "I don't mind talking with you lot. First, I think
we should allow Inquisitor Vorbis the chance to get some breakfast after his nightly vigils."

Vorbis didn't give an inch. His stony gaze fixed on Rillek's
and stayed there. "Accommodations?" The distaste in the sepulchral tones sounded as though he'd bitten into a pastry and
found a dead mouse inside.

Ignoring the look on Rillek's face, Sera barreled on. She
leaned forward as far as she could on the edge of the cart, facing
him where he was arriving from the left. "Yes. Of course. Accommodations. I mean, if Rillek says we'll be housed and kept in
Stradeburg as a reward for our cooperation, we will want to
know if it is worth it."

If his expression had been stony before, now it settled
into a look of distaste worthy of being preserved as a statue.
"Explain!"

The armsmaster's half-hidden glance promised retribution. However, he turned to Vorbis with a light smile. "Listen.
Clearly, this lot doesn't know what they're talking about. You
and I both know that we're taking them back to the city for the
church to decide what will happen."

The discussion between the two swiftly deteriorated.
Once Vorbis realized that Rillek wouldn't expressly promise that
the party of filthy blasphemers was going to die, he pressed the
armsmaster hard, threatening to execute them right then and
there.

On the cart, they all rushed forward, sliding their cuffs
along the chain so they could follow the discussion from as close

up as possible. Outwardly, at least, that was the case. In practice, they all bunched up to hide Kith's movement with their bodies.

Not that the guards paid any attention. Any soldier worth their salt knew that shit trickled downward, and knowing your leader's disposition and adjusting accordingly would make the difference between your day being business as usual or being assigned to permanent latrine duty. As such, their attention was riveted to the ongoing discussion between the two most powerful people among their number and didn't deviate.

Chase kept watch. For this crucial moment, that was all he could do. He watched the situation, glancing from guard to guard, ready to kick Kith in case any of them started taking an interest in what was going on atop the cart. From out of the corner of his eye, he spotted something weird on Kith himself.

One second, Kith was frowning, then he glanced about himself. The next, his chest flashed, and suddenly, he seemed to... relax. His movements sped up, and he settled into action. Seconds later, he leaned back and tapped Liam twice on the leg. His work was done.

That led them to the trickiest part of the entire plan. They had to move, and they had to be entirely sure that their targets were distracted.

Currently, the guards, the armsmaster, and the inquisitor were all engrossed in the discussion. Yet, they were also consummate professionals, veterans at their craft. If they mistimed this attack, they weren't about to get any do-overs.

Liam pulled back slightly, put both his hands on the chain and braced his feet. Then he kicked Kith with one leg, and Cilia with the other.

Instantly, the noise of the argument between the two Lightborn disappeared into nothingness, as Cilia's Heart card stepped into effect. Liam waited, eyes fixed on the horizon, tenseness written in every line of his taut back.

Dots appeared in the distance, in the open air. Around them, silent figures turned and stared. Somebody pointed, saying something they couldn't hear. Rillek and Vorbis turned toward the disturbance.

"Now!" Chase yelled.

As one, they placed their arms and legs on the bed of the cart, trying to line them up as much as possible.

Liam grunted, card flashing on his left arm as he activated Earthen Might, doubling his strength for a moment. The chain pulled taut, trying to drag limbs with it. But they braced as much as they could, and the long, heavy chains slithered through one shackle after the other, clinking and clacking loud enough to wake the dead. But Cilia's Heart card did not allow a single sound to escape, and the final link of the chains clinked onto the floor of the cart, allowing Liam to free himself last.

"Now!" Chase repeated, and flung himself from the cart, followed by all the others.

The dots on the horizon grew closer, solidifying into a cloud of dark insects, visible to all—buzzing, descending upon a cart a hundred feet ahead of their own to sting the Lightborn leading the cart. They were loud, impossible to ignore, and eminently distracting.

They were enough. Mostly.

At the last moment, Inquisitor Vorbis noticed something. Perhaps it was a noise from when they left the noise canceling effect of Cilia's Heart card, vaulting to the attack. Perhaps it was a card or some ingrown instinct. Whatever the reason, he chose that exact moment to look over his shoulder. A bright light erupted on his arm, a shield growing into being.

With a cry, Sera activated Natural Decomposition, and the burgeoning shield faded away into nothingness.

This very moment, they had everything activated that could possibly give them an edge.

Sera had Spark of Divinity to boost their Strength attributes, Heart of Hearts to improve their Heart cards, and she'd used her own Heart card to assess both Rillek and Vorbis, assuring that they didn't have any active protective cards beforehand.

Chase had Unending Decay activated, adding incremental damage to subsequent attacks, Race of Life for that bit of extra Agility, Winds of Change so he could adapt in a split second, and Clothed in Living Light shining from his left arm, granting him an eight-inch-long punch dagger growing from his stump.

Kith sent his Apian God summons running amok elsewhere, providing insectile distractions farther ahead among the soldiers, even as he himself arrived, fists rising and falling.

Cilia and Slate had nothing. Nothing activated to aid them. Even so, they did not hold back.

Liam... Liam came in last. Yet, he combined Earthen Might with Optimal Offense and All Out to eschew defense entirely and cause as much damage as possible.

They swarmed over Vorbis and Rillek, like cockroaches on offal. Fists fell—elbows, knees, even the shackles on their cuffs rose and fell as they hit the two unsuspecting Lightborn.

They were unarmed, sure. Yet, they had surprise on their side. What was more, everybody except Slate had spent months living through the most grueling training schemes, fighting for survival, with no quarters given. When they rose fifteen seconds later, the steaming, bloody bodies of Rillek and Vorbis were barely recognizable as humans.

For one frozen moment, the surrounding guards were stunned, looking from one attacker to the other. What had, half a minute ago, been pacified prisoners, were now blood-smeared savages: Liam holding Rillek's dagger, Slate grasping the whip that had apparently been the inquisitor's only weapon and showing blood-smeared lips from where he'd torn into the inquisitor's neck with his damn teeth.

"Alarm! The prisoners are escaping!" One guard yelling broke the standoff. Only, Cilia's ferocious snarl made no doubt of just how much his shouting was going to help him.

Chase took a split second to take in the situation. The three nearby guards were all rushing at them, bearing weapons. From around them, as well as both ahead and farther back in their procession, people were slowly realizing what was going on, readying themselves to join the fray. He growled, "We're going *dark*!"

The world changed around him, even as his punch dagger faded away into nothingness. It was like a slate of fog covering his surroundings, fifteen feet on every side. Except, that was only for him. For anybody else who didn't happen to have any cards or effects to counteract the Tier four card, it would be an absolutely impenetrable layer of darkness that kept them from seeing anything from even an inch away. The three guards surrounding the cart stalled and stumbled as they were left blinded.

Chase didn't waste his time. He barreled ahead straight at the cart holding their equipment. He didn't check to see whether the others were with him. He knew they'd be following, keeping right at the edge of the shadow circle, to be able to see what they were doing and still remain mostly hidden. They'd debated creeping onward *inside* the darkness, but ended up vying for speed instead. The odds of some caster or healer being able to burst apart the shadows or landing some area effect on them halfway there was simply too high.

Now, the ranks of the Lightborn were truly waking up. All around them, soldiers shouted orders and questions, sometimes just yelled at the sight of Apian God summons diving, biting, stinging, all around their ranks. Not that the summons were that effective. Kith kept to the plan, making sure that they spread out as much as possible, causing chaos rather than damage. Already, healers were summoning blanket effects to drown out the tiny pests, with other classes easily taking down individual insects; some casters used cards to take out entire groups.

Chase kept on racing straight ahead. Speed was of the essence now, rather than silence. Ahead of him, on all sides, insects buzzed, diving down to attack anything and anybody between them and their items. First one, then another Lightborn soldier disappeared into Chase's Circle of Darkness. Their looks were almost comically surprised, eyes wide open in shock as, to them, the early morning transformed into rank darkness. He welcomed each of them with swift strikes, disabling them without taking them out, but didn't dare to slow down for a second.

He made it to the cart and leapt up, eyes frantically searching. Behind him, the pulling caarnath lowed in shock, and the cart driver cursed. Two soldiers, prepping their weapons for his arrival, dropped back defensively, one stumbling away in fear, when they were left blind. Chase didn't bother to engage. *Where was it? There!* One nearly full burlap bag sported the hilt of Liam's truncheon. Chase grasped onto the bag, grunting at the weight, leapt down and moved away from the cart.

A bright blast erupted into being right above him. He felt something like a sensation of loss, of cleansing, as the shadows evaporated from one moment to the next. Damn. Somebody'd managed to realize what was going on. Probably the healer pointing at him from fifty feet away and shouting something hostile. He resummoned the punch dagger with Clothed in Living Light again.

Chase upended the bag onto the ground next to the cart. He unceremoniously picked up his own short sword and moved on to take care of the single remaining guard, who was blinking confusedly and focusing on his arrival.

The Lightborn guard was good. He was clearly well-trained, carried armor that was well-cared for, and the spearhead swiveling in Chase's direction didn't waver. However, Chase had one thing going for him that the man just couldn't match. Attributes. At this point, his boosted Agility was high enough that the soldier, hardened and effective though he might be, looked as if he were wading through molasses. Chase knocked aside the spear tip with his short sword, stepped in, and struck the man right in the throat with the punch dagger. For a split second, his eyes locked with those of the cart driver, who, wide-eyed, held up his hands in surrender. Chase gritted his teeth and turned away, rushing to meet the others.

They were crowding over the bag, rummaging around inside to get to their weapons and equipment.

A short, sharp pain hit Chase. Something clattered onto the ground beside him. He looked over his shoulder, saw the cart driver with his arm outstretched. The man yelped, and rushed to sprint away. Chase ignored the pain—the throwing dagger had hit awkwardly, and the wound could be a lot worse. Sera would take care of it.

What *was* bad was the situation. Around them, the Lightborn soldiers were waking up to the state of affairs, alerted and ready to act. At least with Rillek and Vorbis dead, there were no leaders who'd stepped up so far—but it was only a matter of time. Behind the mass of Lightborn lay freedom and salvation—but there were between thirty and forty soldiers getting into formation, boosting and hurriedly preparing themselves who they'd have to go through first.

Cilia cried out in triumph, as she draped a belt across her shoulders, before grabbing the other belt and fastening it around her waist. An ugly light lit in her eyes, as she commanded, "Next step. Follow me. I promised I'd get you through. Now watch this!" She grasped a shadow droplet in either hand, turned, and took a deep breath. Then she shouted, improbably loud for her slight stature, *"Move aside or die!"*

A slight woman, unarmored, holding no weapon, charged three dozen veteran soldiers on an early morning. What went through their minds at that moment? Was it confusion? Amusement? The slightest hint of self-doubt?

They would never get a chance to learn. What they did know was that, behind them, the following Lightborn were ramping up to charge, finally realizing in full that their prisoners were attempting to get away. On top of that, after the surprise and distractions, their ranged attackers and casters were finally starting to rain down attacks on them.

The rest of their team didn't wait to see what would happen with Cilia. Liam loped ahead, banging his truncheon against the edge of his shield in a dull, threatening rhythm. Sera switched her Spark of Divinity boost to Agility, running with her own shield ready to fend off any ranged attacks. An ugly shape emerged from a glowing portal, showing that Kith had moved on to the next step of the plan as well. The insects of his Apian God card had served their purpose. Now, it was time to forge ahead in strength, and Kith glowed with inner strength and purpose from his Divine Mentor card, even as the Crescendo of Might summon forged ahead on... shambling, misshapen limbs growing all the while. Slate, touting his oversized crossbow, raced along, silently scowling, eyes fixed on the ranks of soldiers waiting ahead.

Chase dropped his Race of Life card, swapping the boost to Agility for Among the Raindrops and building up puddles of sticky, acidic water behind them to fend off the forces amassing behind them. Then he dropped Unending Decay and activated his first Sticky Fingers, grinning at the familiar sensation of stolen attributes boosting his well-being.

The Lightborn struck first. Arrows and ranged spells rained down among them. A splash of liquid light blanketed Liam's shield, sizzling over the shield's surface as well as his arm. An arrow impacted with Sera's left thigh, momentarily left open as she shielded herself from another attack. Warmth of the

Circle pushed the arrow out and closed most of the wound. The Crescendo of Might summon took a near-dozen arrows and a long, sizzling stream of too-bright fire, leaving it near falling apart before it even made it halfway to the defenders. Chase knocked aside two arrows meant to pierce his body without losing his speed.

Then Cilia yelled in rage, as she used her full power to toss the twin droplets of shadow ahead of them, one slanted left and one right. From one second to the next, the entire formation of Lightborn soldiers, solidly arrayed to receive their charge, disappeared into a living circle of darkness.

For five seconds, the battlefield took on an almost supernatural sensation, where they felt alone in the world as they raced on unchallenged.

Knowing what came next, Chase dropped back a few steps to run next to Slate. "Close your eyes!" he yelled over the screams and shouts from the soldiers.

"Why?" Slate growled.

"Just do it, damn you!"

The following droplets of light erupted just a hundred feet before they hit the ranks of the Lightborn. The shadows were torn apart as the brilliant, blinding light reached the heavens and turned localized night into day. At Tier one, Cilia's blinding effect barely managed to blind a thirty-foot circle. This, Chase was sure, could be seen back in Heart Halls.

The confused yells from before turned into true, pain-filled screams as the Lightborn almost as one were blinded from the incoming effects. Seconds later, the first fire droplets landed, and the screams grew louder.

Twenty seconds earlier, the Lightborn soldiers looked like the pride of the forces of Light: arrayed in full formation; defensive, prepared to fend off anything the world might throw at them; Light, arrows, and effects rushing from them in organized salvos. Their formation was lacking, without their leaders standing safely at the back to unleash devastating high-Tier cards and efficiently direct their attacks, because they weren't as used to acting independently. But they *were* a well-oiled, well-trained machine.

Half a minute later had them looking like the victims of a devastating ambush. A robed healer sprinted blindly through the center of their formation, entirely on fire, until she collided with another soldier and dragged him down to the ground with her. Their screams were bestial, like something out of the Pits.

The fire droplets raining over their ranks, like tears from a jilted god, ruined cohesion and practiced calm. Being dropped into shadow was one thing. Having that replaced with actual blindness was a step worse. But going from being prepared and in control to blind and having your pants set on fire? No training could prepare you for that.

Liam tore through their ranks first. His cards were still entirely set on offense, and it showed. Sprinting straight for the gap between two smaller clumps of soldiers, his truncheon whipped out left and right. Two soldiers collapsed, one with a leg bent entirely the wrong way, and the other with a helmet dented so badly, there was no hope for the head underneath.

Chase followed on his heels on his right side, Kith on his left. Chase stabbed at everything in reach with his short sword and punch dagger, caring more about speed than efficiency. A slice at a tendon would be just as good, if not better, at keeping an enemy far behind them than a stab to the torso. On top of that, every fifteen seconds, his Sticky Fingers went off, robbing their enemies of their strengths and buoying his own.

Kith, meanwhile, was an engine of death. With Divine Mentor internalized, his movements were crisp and precise, his hand axes a menace to anybody nearby. The axes performed tight, deadly arcs, tearing into any enemies in reach with efficient abandon. Where Chase disabled, he killed, methodically and horrifyingly.

Cilia, Slate, and Sera followed right behind the trio. Cilia cackled, lost in the moment, as droplets tore in every direction from her, showering their enemies with shadow, fire, and blindness. It would not last. The containers in her belts were swiftly running empty. Yet for this moment, she delivered death and chaos.

Slate had ceased his period of inaction. Here, at the center of the chaos and regular battle, it seemed he'd finally returned to a setting he was somewhat familiar with. He sprinted behind the protective fighters, stopped, aimed, and released whenever he spotted an opening or an inviting target. He eschewed trying to take down any fighters, going instead for the softer targets—archers, casters, or healers. His was not a fluent movement; it was a jerky stop-start motion, but efficient and practiced.

Sera, meanwhile, had gone in the opposite direction of everybody else. Where they were entirely focused on offense, on pushing their way through the ranks standing between them and freedom, she'd switched her cards over entirely to defensive healer cards. Her Tier one card was stuck on Natural Decomposition for the time being, because she had to switch it to deal with the inquisitor. Meanwhile, she swapped her Tier two card to Cry for Blood. The massive damage they dealt in their onslaught was enough to provide her with plenty of triggers to place shields, Toughness boosts, and heals on their party when needed.

Because it *was* needed.

The Lightborn forces might be torn into disarray, hurting, and entirely on the defensive. They were still veterans of a hundred border skirmishes and chaotic battles with Guardians and Furyborn both. While Chase and his people advanced, they had no time or chance to recuperate, so Sera was the only thing standing between them and death by a dozen smaller wounds.

Meanwhile, the Lightborn were reeling. Fighters knelt possessively over downed healers, who were busy engaging cards to cure and dispel, and to boost attributes to get them back into the fight. Here and there, casters and ranged attackers had avoided the brunt of Cilia's onslaught and were taking potshots at them, or engaging larger card effects. Yet, there was little cohesion in their actions.

A crystalline fist-sized figure floated slowly in their direction, unleashing a kaleidoscope of colors. It exploded when it came closer. Tiny, ragged crystal fragments rained off the magical shield covering Kith. Liam wasn't spared either, but a dark light suffused him seconds later, curing the worst of the cuts. Then another card struck them, dead center, long tendrils of light reaching out and touching every one of them. Where it touched, they slowed, feeling their speed sapped from them.

And then, they were through. From one moment to the next, suddenly the only things ahead of them were softly rolling hills with luscious green grass waving in the breeze. A sight so at odds with their messy struggle, it caused Liam to falter for a second. They continued running for a hundred feet.

Liam halted and waved the others ahead. "Go! I'm rear guard." His shoulders grew three inches and became more rugged and earth-like as he activated Become the Clay. Simultaneously, his weapons and armor became awash with a subtle glow as Cleansing Fire suffused him with healing and cleansing magic.

Kith cackled and wheezed. He yelled, voice infused with an unhinged maniacal tweak. "That all you got, you shiny bastards? Well, I've got more for you!" He raised his hands like a caster guiding his deathly payload. Right behind them, the Tainted Earth rose into existence, bubbling like a swamp mixed with a brewer's nightmare. Farther beyond, his Coils of Shadow came alive—small, nearly invisible vipers slithering into the groups of Lightborn beyond. He panted and backpedaled. "That's all. Beyond Divine Mentor, I'm tapped out. Let's go, already!"

Chase let his glowing punch dagger fade away. Then he activated A Friendly Wave, took all the liquid he'd summoned behind them from Among the Raindrops and churned it into a frenzy, building small waves of caustic water, making the waves travel back and forth behind them warningly. "That's *acid*, you bastards!" he yelled. "Follow, and your flesh will melt right off! That's the power of Darkness right there." He turned to the others with a grin. "That should keep them off our backs while I activate Fight Another Day and we start running!"

Chapter 47

"What will be the end, then? Will the Furyborn succumb to the Lightborn in time? Will they ally fully with the Elementals or even the Liberators? Nobody knows. The only thing I know for certain is that they will never surrender." This leaves a bittersweet taste, but I agree. Whatever else, the Furyborn will not go quietly. I hope beyond hope that we can help them avoid the grisly fate threatened by the Lightborn. (Page 104.)

Chase's display of power did not warn them off. That would have been too easy. Rather, the group of Lightborn who had been racing on their heels—the ones who had formerly been leading the caravan of Lightborn—caught up to the ones they'd broken through, and joined ranks with them. Following that, they went on the prowl.

Over the following half hour, as they fled, things went from tough to dire. With the incoming wave of Lightborn reinforcements, Kith's vipers were swiftly dispatched. The Lightborn had ample numbers of ranged, healers, and casters. At first, they tore into the Tainted Earth, light and explosions ripping apart the poor, slow summon. Then they started to harass their flight from a distance.

The group might have gotten away with Chase's Fight Another Day card active, had it not been for the single Light effect that struck them midways through their breakthrough, sapping their speed. As it was, even with the running boost engaged, they were unable to widen the gap between their group and the pursuit. On top of that, Lightborn summoners used their summons as throwaway resources, summoning them whenever they were off cooldown and sending them straight at Liam, less in an attempt to kill, and more to tire them out and bog them down.

Cilia started to use her droplets sparingly. However, the wild abandon of breaking through the Lightborn ranks had depleted her resources, and the following chase made things even worse. One by one, her pockets emptied out, leaving her usefulness strained.

Sera, for all her defensive capabilities, had nothing useful to throw against their enemies at range. Blessing of Night, which might have helped, boosting their attributes enough to let them get away and reducing the effectiveness of Light effects markedly, was unavailable. That initial switch to Natural Decomposition had *not* been planned, and now she was still in the middle of its cooldown and unable to switch back. She redoubled her attention to protect and heal whatever *did* make it through their defenses, shoring them up for the long haul.

Kith was a machine, a one-man slaughterhouse, helping Liam tear apart any summoned creatures sent at them with power and precision. Yet, his cards were on cooldown as well, and with the number of enemies arrayed against them, they would have been hard set to match them regardless. Even his surprising tenacity and efficiency was lagging.

Chase was... not enough. He tried everything he could. He switched to Squall Sling, using rocks to fling at the pursuers. Carded defenders easily picked his missiles off at a distance. He established a Circle of Darkness in the midst of the pursuit. They spread out, approaching them in smaller groups, yet remained at a distance. Among the Raindrops, as wonderful as it was at damaging and harassing enemies who were trying to close with them, was worth little against enemies who simply *refused* to get close.

Liam was stoic, a force of nature, refusing to buckle even in the slightest against the overwhelming numbers stacked up against them, tearing into summoned creatures with abandon, bearing the occasional hit with grudging acceptance and struggling on like nothing happened until Sera could heal him.

"I'm out. That was my last fire droplet," Cilia hissed. Panting, she turned back to run again, looking over her shoulder with every other step.

"I just got tagged with another Agility drain and some poison," Liam shouted with a pained grimace. He tore his truncheon down across the layer of clay on his shoulders, knocking off the four arrows jutting out, one by one. "Cleansing Fire is struggling to keep up. Can you dispel it, Sera? I'm slowing down too much." He was still running backward as he said it, shield at the ready, eyes roaming over the pursuit.

"No. I just removed one from Cilia." Sera's face was pale and drawn, but steady. "It will be about a minute before I can use it, then about ten seconds for it to work. I believe those Agility drains are Tier two!"

Chase growled. His short sword went up automatically, plucking an arrow out of the air with ease. "We're getting bogged down. It doesn't matter if our cooldowns come back, when theirs do as well... and there are still too many of them!"

It was true. They'd finished off a great deal of soldiers, or wounded them badly enough that they couldn't follow. Yet, there were still more than fifty soldiers following, using their cards at every given chance. With that many, quantity became a quality all of its own, especially when they were used to ranged combat while their prey wasn't.

He took a deep breath. "I know what we need to do. But I need your help for it. My attributes are high enough by now, that it might be possible. One final push. Give me everything you have available—boosts, backup, distractions... whatever you have. Then I'll activate Steps of Brilliance and tear into their midst. They might ignore Among the Raindrops at this distance, but once I'm among them, it'll be a different situation, especially if I can build enough to get a wave going. One minute, enough to break their cohesion, to make them pay and give us a serious head start, then I'll be back and we can get away with Fight Another Day."

Their refusals and protests erupted into the air, even as Sera ducked behind her shield, fending off a double shot aimed at her side.

Chase ignored them. "It's happening. Unless any of you have a better idea. We're not taking them head-on, that's beyond discussion. Hit them hard, make them reel, then run!"

"But Chase—" Sera's voice was small, forlorn.

A dark chuckle interrupted them all. "Such bickering. You really are kids, aren't you?"

"You have anything to bring to the table, Slate? Beyond running out of bolts, that is?" Kith snapped.

Slate barked a low laugh. "I do, *kin.*" There was no doubt the word was meant as mockery. "There's a chance I was wrong."

Those words were so unexpected that Liam completely missed his next block. The bolt of light carved a runnel into his right arm, that started weeping blood. He didn't even look at it. "What was that?"

"Your lives are on the line, yet all you worry about is protecting each other, and you care little for your own well-being." The words arrived dully, but his deep-set eyes were focused, nearly feverish. "I still think I was right... but I could have been wrong about you. So. As much as I hate it, I will need to try to save you."

"You've been able to do that all along, and—"

Sera slapped a hand over Kith's mouth, drowning out his outburst. "You can save us all?"

The mirthless chuckle contained enough dire promises to drown them all in blood. "I said that, didn't I? I saw who put that slowing effect on us. I can take him out." He unclasped the quiver at his belt, upended it, and caught the single crossbow bolt still inside. Then he carelessly tossed the quiver on the ground.

"One shot. You can really do that?" Liam asked doubtfully.

Slate grunted. "It won't be easy. I'll need to get close first. They'll probably get me good a few times. But I swear on the blood, I will take them down. You just ensure that you actually do what you promised! Make a home! Maybe name a baby after me." He snorted.

"We are not going to let you—" Sera started.

"Stow it, Lightie. You'll need to distract them first, draw their attention in several directions. Even then, it's not a sure thing. But unless you all help with that, there's no chance at all." He turned around and stood still, looking at the Lightborn soldiers following in their wake. The rough-looking Furyborn hunched his shoulders, looking like the weight of the world pushed down on him. Then he sighed and seemed to relax, cracking his neck audibly. "I still don't like any of you. Especially Chase." Then he started to run. Straight at the Lightborn soldiers.

Chase cursed. Moments later, he raced after him.

There was no time to plan, no time to arrange cards, to create a potent combination. In that moment, Chase felt only the burning need to ensure that the suicidal bastard didn't try to throw his life away unneeded. He felt, more than saw, the others chasing behind him, following, increasing the pressure on the Lightborn forces, providing them with further targets to pick from. Within the first seconds, Chase left them all behind. Ten seconds later, he overtook Slate as well.

Coming closer to the Lightborn lines, Chase had a brief window to actually think. Their groups weren't as tight and fancy as they'd been earlier. They'd learned from their losses. Now, they were spread out in smaller groups with fighters as dedicated defenders, followed by anything else farther behind where they could safely use their cards against the fleeing band. He veered right and activated his Circle of Shadows. That should damn well catch their attention, while hopefully keeping them from being too accurate in hitting him.

Too right. Within seconds, casters and ranged attackers both caught notice of him, and he was ducking and swerving through a rain of missiles and card effects. It was only testament to his massively increased attributes that he was able to avoid most of their attacks. Soon, he got close enough that their attacks got too dangerous for him to consistently avoid, and he swerved again, veering back left, activating Among the Raindrops.

He was still too far away. However, as he sprinted, the liquid started to build halfway between him and the Lightborn—

large, shiny puddles emerging out of nowhere. The soldiers saw it too, but stayed put. Good.

Slate was getting closer as well. Chase saw him, crossing his path as he raced back the other way. The Furyborn was already bleeding from a scalp wound, and his chest looked like something had exploded on him. He was grinning, though. Twisted bastard.

Chase was running out of time. Soon, Slate would be a pincushion or blown right up. His shadows burst and evaporated in an explosion of light. That damn Lightborn healer again! He halted his sprint before he'd reached more than a third of the way toward the left-most edge of the well-separated Lightborn groups. It would have to do.

Nearly slipping on the slick surface of the grass with his abrupt turn, he ran back the other way again, toward Slate and, behind him, the rightmost edge of the Lightborn troops. With a deep breath, he switched to A Friendly Wave.

Shouts erupted as Lightborn noticed him, now without his hiding shadows. He saluted them with his middle finger and sped up.

He took in the situation at a glance. One battle line of around a dozen smaller groups of Lightborn troops. Two persons, right within range and attention. A bit farther back, four more, racing closer, drawing a bit of attention. All told, a recipe for disaster. Only, now, between Chase and the Lightborn, there was also a nice, sodden patch of wetness left over from his Among the Raindrops.

Chase mentally reached out. With the stolen attributes from their drawn-out conflict, he was nearly double his usual, at a total forty-three Mental Power, and the difference was *massive*. The water beckoned his call and, all along the front that he was traversing, rose into massive waves, aiming straight for the waiting soldiers.

Chase didn't fancy himself a wicked man. However, the pain-filled sound of screams from the amassed Lightborn, after their drawn-out pursuit, felt like catharsis to him. He raced all across the battle line, directing the waves onto the enemies, forcing it to rummage around and cause as much damage there as humanly possible. It wouldn't be enough. He knew that. Their fighters were tough, their ranged attackers agile enough to avoid the attack. At any point, a caster—

The connection snapped.

He cursed. Yeah. That did it. Somebody had managed a dispel of some sort. Chase's eyes tore back toward Slate.

Slate was nearly upon the battle line. Less than a hundred feet separated them. He shouldn't be standing up. An arrow jutted from his left collarbone. An effect had carved and seared a runnel *all across the side of his damn head*. Yet he stood tall, raising his crossbow, grinning, without a care in the world.

The crystalline missile floated toward him, almost lazily.

Slate's smile only grew. Then he nodded, and released.

A second later, the crystal burst, perforating Slate's body in a hundred places.

Chase started to run back, shouting for them to flee. He risked one glance behind him. One glance, where he saw... an archer. A single archer, kneeling behind a shield, with a confused look on his face, as a healer touched his shoulder, glowing palm trying to heal him.

Failing.

The crossbow bolt dropped to the ground from the archer's wound. Yet, where it had been, bark spread outward, traveling across the archer's body, slowly encasing him in a living layer of bark, turning his skin into a horrifying semblance of a tree. The look of confusion on his face turned to horror and froze.

Between them, Slate's body lay, unmoving, broken.

Chase's step quickened. With a final exhalation that was almost a sob, he waved the others on and engaged Fight Another Day. "He did it. Flee! Flee, damn you!"

<u>Chapter 48</u>

Final notes on the ill-named *Guide to Furyborn Lands*: It is by no means a decent guide. The advice in it is questionable at best, outright wrong at worst. The information is unverified, the sources as varied and seemingly random as their opinions. Yet, there is one thing that keeps me from treating the tome as kindling or... the cruder use that Kith suggested we put it to. For lack of a better description? Its heart is in the right place, as are its conclusions. Treat the Furyborn with respect. Embrace them, and their beliefs. Honor them without subservience. Do that, and you will find a place among them.

"I can't believe we aren't at the center of a massive drunken feast right now." Kith mused. He lay down on a pile of pillows in the small earthen dwelling they'd been assigned, staring at the ceiling with a cup in his hand that idly trickled wine onto the floor. "It would seem like something they'd do." His voice, although amused, was stone weary, like he was on the verge of falling asleep.

"They just lost one of their elders," Cilia scolded.

"Exactly what I'm saying," Kith countered. "Win a battle? Party. Lose a battle? Party. Lose an elder? Party *and* perhaps an orgy."

Cilia snickered. She sat on top of her own pile of pillows, though her cup held water.

Sera closed the door behind her. The bonfire at the center of the comfortable dwelling stopped flickering, smoke rising toward the small hole at the center of the roof. "I asked them not to."

Chase, with a supernatural summoning of energy, raised a hand to beckon her over to join him on his small mountain of pillows. Spent, his hand flopped down again. "How come?"

She settled down beside him with a sigh. "Several reasons. First, I didn't want the news to spread just yet. An elder dying, no matter how you frame it, is a blow to their community. Second, we have earned this. We deserve a measure of peace, while we celebrate our accomplishments."

"But... orgies?" Liam protested weakly.

"I can't believe, after all this time, Kith can *still* be a bad influence on you," Cilia groused.

"I'm impressed too." Kith laughed. "But I do agree. I'm really not up for a lot of noise right now. Besides, maybe we don't want the world to know, just yet, how strong we've gotten."

Chase smiled warmly. "That sounds suspiciously like somebody who's hit Tier four."

"Maybeee," the Furyborn teased coquettishly, without getting up. Then he laughed tiredly. "You damn well best believe it. Tier four, dammit! Anybody else?"

Chase shook his head. "Step twenty-four. I'm *this* close to Tier five!" He laughed. "But I did manage to gain *two* permanent points to Mental Power from Sticky Fingers in the fight, so... not complaining."

"Me neither. I am close, however. Step nineteen. I got the inquisitor, but after that, I was purely on defense," Sera said.

"I wouldn't be here if you hadn't. We'll get you there with our next fight, whatever it is," Liam promised warmly. "Step twenty for me!"

Cilia nodded as well. "I will be crafting for *weeks* to replenish my stores... but it was worth it. Step twenty-one for me!"

Sera clapped softly. "Well done, all! Now, share!"

Cilia breathed deeply. "I'm going first. After this fight, I know exactly which card I'm upgrading."

"The combat one?" Liam guessed.

"A Familiar Tool. Just so. Other cards might improve my crafts, but nowhere will I gain such an increase to their efficacy in battle as there." She paused, exhaled and smiled. "And there we go. It is now Epic, and adds a full *seventy-five* percent efficiency increase when I use my items in battle. On top of that, my Title bonus has increased my Mental Power by another two, *and* I dropped every additional point into Mental Power as well."

Sera cursed.

Personal info:
Name: Cilia
Title: Dark/Elemental/Light/Furyborn crafter
Step: 21 (Tier 4)
Strength: 13 (+1 Tier bonus) (+5) = 19
Agility: 21 (+1 Tier bonus) (+5) = 27
Toughness: 15 (+1 Tier bonus) (+5) = 21
Mental Power: 34 (+13 Tier bonus) (+5) = 52
Potential: 11 (+1 Tier bonus) (+5) = 17

Cilia's eyes gleamed. "What was your Mental Power again, Sera?"

Sera didn't answer straightaway. Eventually, her voice arrived, strained. "Forty-six. Fifty-one with the boost. I..." She narrowed her eyes and lifted a trembling finger at Cilia. "This means war."

Cilia laughed. Then she closed her eyes and concentrated again. With a deep, shuddering whistle, she re-emerged awhile later. "You didn't say Tier four was *that* rough, Chase."

"Well, you're falling behind in Toughness, Cil! Toughen up!" he answered.

"Forget that." She scoffed. "Now, I've been learning from Kith and Chase."

Kith blinked, rummaged around in his ear, and focused on her. "Come again? I think I misheard."

"Shut up. My point being, with combat classes, there will often be a reason to branch out and get different card types of the same type, but for different situations. Say, attack cards for close combat, ranged attack, casters, boosting... you name it. Yet, with as many decks as we have, we reach a point where we generally have most approaches covered."

She shrugged. "It's different for crafters, since we are usually in charge of the situation when we craft. We won't have to adjust to so many different situations, and as long as we have cards to improve whichever focus we want to aim at when crafting, we're golden. Hence, any cards that are *always* active, even if you switch to other cards, may be preferrable to branching out, or, failing that, any cards that aid beyond crafting itself."

"Oh. Yeah. That's good thinking. Can't believe I came up with that." He yawned.

Cilia smirked and flicked Kith on the ear. "I simply can't believe that boost we've received. Five additional points to Potential while we're here? It makes for a world of difference, especially for those of us who haven't invested insane numbers into Potential in the first place."

Chase sniffed the air. "Do you guys smell that? I think that's the smell of... envy."

She ignored him. "My first card was unexpected, but an easy choice nonetheless."

[Touch Grass
Uncommon, Fury crafter
Tier four
Active, medium duration
In many instances, the crafting itself isn't what matters, but the circumstances surrounding the crafting. An item crafted in wind and rain with a rotting tree stump for a table will inevitably be worse quality than one made in a warm house. This card allows you to sense, shape, and direct the soil and plants around you with a speed and efficacy depending on your Mental Power.
Long cooldown

"No crafting bench, dear? Ah, but nature provides. It always does."]

"Of course, it is by no means limited to crafting. I can picture shaping a trench around a village. Hiding our presence with raised soil. Basically, all the wonderful examples we've seen from the Furyborn and Earth-aspected Elementals both. Also, adding Sera's thorn bushes to the mix should make for interesting possibilities."

"Tunneling into a dirt cellar." Chase nodded.

"Obscuring our footprints in the mud after a break-in," Liam added.

"Yeah, yeah. Jump straight to the crimes, you two," Cilia said, not unkindly. "My Elemental card is... well, not as immediately impressive. But I believe the eventual output will be even more rewarding."

[**Siphon the Source**
Rare, Elemental crafter
Tier four
Passive, permanent
The best crafters are those fully in touch with their aspects. Of course, a wind-aspected crafter performs better work when he is fully in tune with the wind itself. This card enables that connection, letting the crafter siphon connection, power, and inspiration from nearby pervasive presences of the aspect they are manipulating in their crafts. The stronger the presence, the greater the effect. The effect of the card will remain active, regardless whether you switch to another Tier four card.
"Sense it, boy. The rock around you. It steadies the hand, calms the mind. It sings, a tune to guide your mind." Elementalist-crafter Hibertus, explaining his craft.]

"No, Kith." Cilia stopped the outburst that was definitely on its way. "That doesn't mean I need to set myself on fire to improve my fire crafting. It means... think of the towers. There is no doubt that some of their higher-tiered crafters will have chosen this card or some equivalent. Of course, there is more to it—the desire to show off their power to the world, for instance—but it explains why they would go and twist their entire towers to reflect their elements. Picture... just picture the power of my fire droplets, if I were to craft them surrounded by a sea of liquid fire."

Chase cleared his throat. "I'm going to go right ahead and ignore that gleam in your eyes, because it made my balls shrivel, Cil. But yeah. I get it. It's not something we're likely to use straightaway… but if we create our own place? Setting up a small lake for watercrafts, a cave for earth, something like that? Entirely doable. And if these enhancements are *on top* of all your other cards, like Ritual of Fire…" Chase trailed off, making it a question.

"It is. It's a permanent boost, not reliant on anything else."

"Question," Sera asked. "The card says aspect, not Element. Is… that going to work with the other aspects as well? Crafting Dark-aspected items better in darkness?"

Cilia made a strangled noise. "I… hadn't even considered that. How unlike me. Maybe? It's something to look into. If it will work on all aspects…" She shook her head, as if clearing it of distractions. "Now. Since we're on the topic of enhancement cards, my final card."

[**Trail the Mirror's Edge**
Rare, Light/Dark crafter
Tier four
Active, long duration
Most cards focus on the effect, on improving the end result. This ignores the fact that most crafters focus not only on improving the end result, but also on finishing in a timely manner. With Trail the Mirror's Edge active, any Light or Dark enhancements will be completed forty percent faster. This is a dual card, working on more than one aspect.
Very long cooldown
"Any path traversed on the mirror, dark or bright side, can trail off endlessly. Trail the mirror's edge, though, and you will get there faster." The philosopher makes up vague crap to get his point across.]

Liam cleared his throat. "Did you… did you just pick a card, just so you'd have to spend less time on crafting your droplets?"

Cilia laughed. "I did! Isn't it amazing?" Remorselessly, she shrugged. "Time isn't eternal. Less time I use on those things, the more I can spend on crafting items like your armor. Also, crafting is draining. The faster I can finish, the better I can make it."

"Okay, I approve," Liam said quickly. He patted the singed, but whole, armor on the ground close to him.

"As for me I honestly don't know what I want at this point." Kith shrugged. "You've got a point, Cil. A lot of my cards revolve around being able to adapt to different situations. Now, I definitely need something ranged, judging from what we just got out of - but what else?"

"Something aimed at either Liberty or Light, perhaps?" Chase suggested. "They're the ones we're bound to clash with in the near future. If we can get more like Sera's Blessing of the Night, we wouldn't even *need* ranged options, because their cards would be useless."

Sera winced and looked away.

Chase put his hand over hers. She believed she'd failed them, when she'd failed to keep Blessing of the Night active. He knew it would take him awhile to convince her that she'd saved them, not failed them.

Kith didn't notice. "Ooh. That's a good point. I'll dig into it." He closed his eyes. "My Title improved my Potential again. Lovely. I put the remaining points into Agility, to keep up the balance with Mental Power, and Toughness, because it was falling behind."

Personal info:
Name: Kith
Title: Dark/Elemental/Light/Furyborn summoner
Step: 21 (Tier 4)
Strength: 18 (+1 Tier bonus) (+5) = 24
Agility: 23 (+1 Tier bonus) (+5) = 29
Toughness: 16 (+1 Tier bonus) (+5) = 22
Mental Power: 23 (+1 Tier bonus) (+5) = 29
Potential: 11 (+13 Tier bonus) (+5) = 29

"As for my upgrade, that one was simplicity itself. Twice the Fun now works on *three* cards."

[... **Twice the Fun**
Epic, Elemental summoner
Tier two
Passive, permanent
Sometimes, you crave something new and interesting. Sometimes, the best choice is simply more of what you already have. This card, when chosen, will double the number of summoned creatures for up to three other cards.
"You think my summoned squirrels underwhelming? Wait 'till I show you... more squirrels!"]

"So, twice the insects from Apian God, twice the creepy vipers from Coils of Shadow, and twice whatever you're about to get on Tier four... *at the same damn time?*" Chase coughed. "I can't wait to see that one at Legendary."

"You and me both, brother! I've got high hopes," Kith intoned. "Aaand I'm going under."

Watching Kith as he picked his cards was always an experience for Chase. His face underwent so many changes and emotions, he could almost feel that he was there with him on the journey. That was why the intense blushing and guilty expression did not pass him by.

Kith opened his eyes with gritted teeth. "Yeah, that's rough."

"What did you just do?" Chase asked.

"This is what's wrong in our group. I haven't even told you anything, and you assume—"

"I have eyes, Kith. You're about as good at hiding your emotions as Liam, when you pick your cards. *What did you pick?*"

Kith sighed. Then he told them.

[Ties Airbound
Rare, Fury summoner
Tier four
Passive, permanent
Most summons are temporary, restricted to when the card is active. Yet, with the right choices for a Wellspring, any summoner may choose a card like this. With permission from the owner of the Wellspring, you will be able to bond with any resident winged Guardian. This Guardian will then be permanently attached to you like a temporary summon, until the Ænima powering it runs out. The effect of the card will remain active, regardless whether you switch to another Tier four card.
In addition to the Guardian's own attributes, it will be awarded a permanent increase to its Agility and Toughness, with one point for each three points of your own Agility and Toughness.
"I know. You are kin. Do you like watching me soar?"]

Chase gaped. Then he chuckled. "I'd be embarrassed at that choice as well. Even so, I'd have made the same exact choice."

"I don't get it. This looks amazing!" Liam frowned. "A flying, permanent Guardian with both enhanced Agility *and* Toughness. What's not to like?"

Chase snorted. "The fact that we don't know if the elders are going to give up another Guardian just like that... and we don't know if it's possible to bind two at the same time, which would render his Tier two pick useless. Did I get everything?"

Kith shrugged helplessly. "I know. Rip into me later, okay? I thought perhaps it was worth the risk." He aimed a shaky smile at Cilia. "At least I know you'll approve of the next two cards."

[Crystalline Guard
Rare, Light summoner
Tier four
Passive, long duration
Most summons are both offensive and defensive to a certain extent. Not this one. The Crystalline Guard is fully passive, brought into being purely to act as a shield between the summoner and their foes. Its crystalline skin deflects most ranged and magical attacks, while the crystal shards of its body, when attacked, explode into deadly splinters, capable of piercing skin.
Long cooldown
"Listen. I... can't see you on the other side of this crystal thing. Ms. Summoner? Are you still there? I surrender. Please. I've been here for hours, and I'm wounded and tired."]

Cilia smiled with savage glee. "You bet I approve. That would have done a world of difference against the Lightborn—depending on how durable it is, of course. But a shield, that can deflect *and* will hurt any melee attackers? Also, you can summon two of them with your Twice the Fun card. Yes, please!"

[Antithesis of Light
Uncommon, Dark summoner
Tier four
Passive, long duration
Most summons are aspected, but still geared toward facing any sort of enemy. Not this summon. The Antithesis of Light is just that. A summoned entity that not only flings bolts of shadows when summoned, it also reduces the efficacy of nearby Light-aspected cards and effects by forty percent.
Long cooldown
"Come closer, morsel. I smell your terror. And I hunger."]

"It was only Uncommon. And the effect isn't as good as Cilia's. Probably because it's a summon and not a healer debuff. But I still thought it was worth taking." Kith smiled.

"You thought right." Sera nodded. "Now, we will just have to test to see if our effects stack—and if they do, if it results in a ninety percent reduction or a..." Her brows furrowed. "Seventy percent reduction."

"Yay. Testing," Kith said dryly. Then he grinned like a Waves kid who'd just gotten away with a purse. "These other choices? All for the greater good. Well, except for the flier. This final one, though? It's *all* for me."

[Pillars of Air

Rare, Elemental summoner
Tier four
Active, medium duration
Usually, summoned entities are their own individuals, with a certain degree of autonomy. The Pillars of Air are not. For as long as the twin pillars are called into being, they meld with the legs of the wielder, forming a creation that responds entirely to the whims of the wielder's movements and thoughts. This allows them to use the power of the air in their movement, leaping long distances and run like the wind. A lapse in concentration can lead to the Pillars disappearing, however.
"Wheeeeeeeeeeeeeeeeeee." The self-titled Aerial Plague leaps to his death.]

"That looks... dangerous. Efficient. Irresponsible." Cilia shook her head in dismay.

Chase grinned, raising his thumb. "Also, fun! It's very you, Kith. I mean, it sounds like something that's bound to leave you falling from great heights, but if you manage to maybe *not* die, the additional movement and surprise sounds insanely useful."

Cilia opened her mouth as if to say something, then subsided. "We will talk. At length. Liam? What do you have to offer?"

The big man had been relatively subdued following their return. "Not much. I was useless in our last fight."

Chase scoffed. "That's stupid. We'd have never gotten the chains off and broken through their ranks if it weren't for you. And you held them off longer than anybody else could have done."

"Yet, I am supposed to protect you, and I failed. In fact, it wasn't that I failed. It was that I couldn't *do* anything with them at a distance. That needs to be remedied."

His gaze went distant. Moments later, he nodded. "I upgraded Become the Clay again."

[Become the Clay
Epic, Elemental fighter
Tier one
Active, medium duration
For a while after activation, the outermost layer of your skin is converted into a thick layer of magically thickened wet clay. The clay will make it much harder for any attacks to pierce and may cause weapons to get stuck. Also, the effect of the clay becomes malleable, tied to the will of the Wielder. The layer is heavy and may make it harder for you to move if you do not have the Strength to handle the weight.
Medium cooldown

"Give that back, you stupid, filthy weapon thief." A master duelist is defeated.]

"The duration has increased… and that malleable thing." Liam frowned and got to his feet. He concentrated, and the normal, thick layer of wet clay appeared on his entire body, making him look like one of the Elemental tower golems. With a subtle sound, his entire right arm seemed to shimmer, and the clay turned hard and reflective. "Will ya look at that?" Liam muttered. He quickly grabbed a nearby fork and stabbed into his arm. With an ear-piercing shriek, it hit. He held the fork up, showing the malformed tines. "Will ya *look* at that?" he repeated. Raising an eyebrow, he met Sera's eyes. "Testing?"

"Testing," she affirmed.

Liam coughed. "So, that was fun. Probably going to be useful. On top of that, my Title improved my Strength by two, and I put one into Toughness and one in Agility to keep up."

Personal Info:
Name: Liam
Title: Dark/Elemental/Light/Furyborn fighter
Step: 20 (Tier 4)
Strength: 18 (+13 Tier bonus) (+5) = 36
Agility: 18 (+1 Tier bonus) (+5) = 24
Toughness: 28 (+1 Tier bonus) (+5) = 34
Mental Power: 14 (+1 Tier bonus) (+5) = 20
Potential: 10 (+1 Tier bonus) (+5) = 16

"Good call. And good luck, man. I know you'll get what you need," Chase said.

Liam nodded, steel-set determination on his face as his gaze went distant again. A minute later, he focused again, a brief hiss the only evidence of any discomfort. He nodded. "That will help."

[Tribune of Retribution, Blindness
Uncommon, Dark fighter
Tier four
Passive, medium duration
This card activates a punitive system, aiming to dispense karmic justice upon anybody attacking the fighter and his group. Any damage or damaging effect by an opposing force, regardless of whether the damage is nullified or not, results in an equivalent temporary reduction to their eyesight that lingers for the full duration of the card's effects. The more damage, the worse the blinding effect.

Long cooldown
"Crawl, maggots. You brought this on yourselves. Now, my friends and I will disperse justice." The Adjudicator of Dark at the Battle of Tempor.]

Chase whistled. "That is *insane*." He laughed. "A card that's based on all of us getting hit? For anybody else, that would be suicide. For us, with Sera on our side and all your summons? That's a ticket to winning. Depending on how bad the effect is, of course."

Liam smiled. "That was how I saw it, too. With all the attacks we fended off or shielded against, we would have seen half their forces blinded ten minutes into the fight." He nodded and focused. "My next choice is situational. Even so..."

[**Helping Step**
Rare, Light fighter
Tier four
Active, very short duration
Being of the Light means being there for those in need. This card, when activated, lets you move to anybody in your group currently engaged in a fight in the blink of an eye. It will, at most, let you travel forty-five feet.
"Surrender, Darkspawn. There is no point on this battlefield I do not command."]

"Sera. Will you help me train my Mental Power and ... what do you call that situation-thing again? You know, where I get better at keeping an eye on everything and everybody."

"Situational awareness. And yes. I will help you improve both. This can be a lifesaver, but I imagine it will require extensive training." She smiled warmly. "That was exactly what we need."

"I agree." He smiled. "As to my last card."

"Wait, last?" Kith said.

With a bit of his usual bluster, Liam waggled his eyebrows.

[**Tempest of the Land**
Uncommon, Fury/Elemental fighter
Tier four
Active, short duration
Natural disasters are not all bad. They roam and ravage, yet the energy unleashed in their passing can leave the soil revitalized, soon ready to easier grow to even further heights. In the same manner, sometimes, it is necessary for a fighter to unleash all their energy in one tempestuous assault. For the duration of the

card, this will imbue all their attacks with a full gamut of Elemental aspects, and grant their body the strength and fury of the soil. However, once the card runs out, it will leave the fighter weakened for a short while, unable to use any cards. This is a dual card, working on more than one aspect.
"We surrender." The Tempest of the Land is not unleashed. This time.]

Liam noticed their looks and blushed. "I know. It's dangerous. Leaving me weakened at the end of the use? Bad idea. But it can be necessary. If we'd had something like that, we wouldn't have to depend on Chase alone to wreak havoc on larger groups. The two of us, together? We might have been able to..." The unsaid ending—"to save Slate's life"—hung in the air for all of them to hear.

Sera walked over and knelt next to him. She gently grabbed his hands and stroked them. "I know. This - exactly this - is why I asked the elders to keep the situation calm for a while. There is something I need to tell you." She let her gaze slide over the others and smiled fondly. "I have been an outsider, looking in." She held up a hand, forestalling Chase's protests. "Not for a while now. I am one of you, for better or worse. Yet, I have not lived the lives you have. But I am *amazed*."

Her eyes shone with unshed tears, and her voice was rough. "Slate was an ass. Sculpted by his life, and the horrid experiences he was exposed to, definitely. He lost a daughter and a wife. I learned that earlier. Even so, he was a horrible person. Judgmental, prone to anger, quick to let go of the virtues he claimed that he was defending when it suited him. Only at the end did he find himself again. And yet, you all mourn him like he was one of yours."

"I don't." Kith scoffed. "He was a piece of filth."

Sera smiled warmly. "Liar. See, this is why I believe."

"Believe what?" Kith looked like he was waiting for a sucker punch.

"Believe in you. Believe in *us*. We have not properly come to terms with what we are wading into. We are going to face off against an aspect that nobody truly knows, walk into uncharted lands, from whence people rarely return. Yet, I truly think that we are going to make it there, make it back out, and establish a home that will endure for the ages, bring in a new era of peace, that will change Ordei as a whole."

"Listen. Sera. That's... you know we're just trying to find a place to call home, right? Not all that other stuff!" Chase avoided her eyes.

She laughed. This was no gentle titter, but a deep, amused belly laugh that shook her body and left her with tears in her eyes. "The fact that you are able to say that with a straight face explains why I needed to tell you this. You have managed to win over two separate powers to your side. You are a thorn in the eye on the strongest power in the world. Yet, you still think of yourself as lowborn and common. *That* more than anything is why I believe we will rock the world. Because I have come to believe that a foundation that is based on the common good will be able to embrace everybody."

They shared looks, part touched, part embarrassed at the warm, excessive praise.

Kith broke the silence with a snort. "Not me. I'm just in it for the bragging rights."

Cilia laughed. "No epics for me either. I just want a nice peaceful shop and crafting place."

Liam raised his hands innocently. "What? I'm in it for the girls. You knew that already."

Chase rolled his eyes. "Please. It's not like we've been planning this crap. Besides, even if we're about to go and try to steal a deck from a race that's been in seclusion for decades, it's not like I've got any weird, altruistic plans." His smile grew avaricious. "I just want to see if I can get away with it."

Sera spread her hands in surrender. "And there we have it. An epitaph for the ages. *I just want to see if I can get away with it.* May the heavens tremble in response."

The end of Theft of Decks 3, the penultimate book in the Theft of Decks series.

Card overview at the end of book three

Chase:

[Nothing to See Here
Heart card (amplified)
Active, medium duration
The attention span of the average person is a fickle thing. What will keep you interested one moment will seem dull and unimportant the next. Sometimes, to get from one to the other, all it takes is a nudge. For a limited time, become less interesting to anybody around you. Those with much higher Mental Power than yours may be less affected or unaffected.
Medium cooldown
"Now, to all those watching, I would love to extol upon you the forty-eight virtues of clean living. The first..."]

[Sticky Fingers
Legendary, Dark rogue
Tier one
Active, instant
Stealing is such a *clumsy* endeavor. Too easy. Anybody can steal a purse. This card allows you to go a step further, carefully manipulate strands of Darkness to grasp onto the key attributes of a mark, temporarily making them your own from a short distance.
There is a minuscule chance of the increase becoming permanent.
Short cooldown
"You lost what, ma'am? Your Agility? Oh. Perhaps I can help you find it near my virility and hairline?"]

[Steps of Brilliance
Rare, Light rogue
Tier one
Active, instant
This card grants you the option of creating three palm-sized platforms wherever you may choose. These platforms are visible

and tangible only to yourself, unless faced up against an adversary with much higher Mental Power than yours. The platforms only last for a short duration, but you may constantly create up to three platforms.
"I saw him, once. His was not the power of flight. No, it was a lot more unnatural. He moved like he did not belong in this world." A bystander, about the Acrobat of Virn.]

[**Squall Sling**
Rare, Elemental rogue
Tier one
Active, instant
This card allows you to create a localized brief burst of concentrated air from your hand. This will allow you to add increased impetus to thrown items, deflect incoming strikes, or even change your direction mid-air.
Very short cooldown
"Out-throw Kargar the Giant? Kargar laugh! Kargar... HOW YOU DO THAT?"]

[**Nights of Criffhaven**
Uncommon, Dark rogue
Tier two
Active, medium duration
Some rogues go for the throat right away. Others like to drag out the fun, bleed their enemies and make them truly realize their defeat before they have even lost. This card, once tapped, grants you a slow build-up for as long as you remain engaged in hostilities. Every minute you remain engaged in hostilities grants you an additional temporary point to Agility, to a maximum of +15. After fifteen minutes, you have five minutes at the maximum boost, following which the buff is deactivated.
Long cooldown
"Stop trying to hit me and hit me!"]

[**Unending Decay**
Epic, Fury rogue
Tier one
Instant, medium duration
A tree rarely topples from a single stroke with an axe. Animals are rarely taken down with one bite or swipe of a claw. With this card equipped, every single strike of your weapon following the first on the same enemy will result in fifteen percent additional damage, to a maximum of an additional one hundred and fifty percent damage. Striking other enemies will reset the count.
Medium cooldown
"I done told ya, didn't I? Mess with me, and regret it later." The hangman wins his duel, twenty minutes in.]

[Race of Life
Uncommon, Light rogue
Tier two
Active, medium duration
This card, once tapped, grants you a small boost to Agility. It can be used several times a day, making it perfect for those who often need to work in bursts.
Medium cooldown
"Some people say that life is a marathon, not a sprint. Some people are wrong. Life, the way I see it, is a marathon of sprints. And we should plan accordingly."]

[Among the Raindrops
Epic, Elemental rogue
Tier Two
Active, medium duration
Upon activation, this card will start summoning puddles for the duration of the effect in a thirty-foot radius around the wearer. The puddles of water have a triple effect, all working only against enemies. First, they have an oily, slippery effect and will make it hard to keep your equilibrium. Second, they have an acidic effect, causing ongoing damage against any exposed skin or equipment. Third, the puddles have a viscous quality, clinging to anything and anybody unlucky enough to enter.
Long cooldown
"Your fancy power is to make me stand in a puddle of water? Hah. Wait. Why are you laughing?"]

[Fight Another Day
Rare, Fury rogue
Tier two
Instant, medium duration
Some wielders make history. Their approaches, tempers and cards vary wildly. They all have one thing in common, however. They lived to grow strong. Reaching that point sometimes means a tactical retreat.
Upon activation of this card you, and anybody grouped with you, all receive a marked increase to running speed as long as you are running away from enemies.
Long cooldown
"Stand and fight? I mean, I could. But... I'm not going to." The Lion of Tekarn has yet to earn his moniker.]

[Free of Perdition
Rare, Dark rogue

Tier three
Active, medium duration
Tapping this card allows you to forcibly swap one of your chosen attributes temporarily with that of another living creature in short range. For a brief while, become as strong as an indomitable rager, as swift as a sky hare. If the target does not resist the effect, they will also see their attribute score temporarily replaced with yours. The effect remains until the cooldown runs out.
Medium cooldown
"How did you do that? Those skinny arms? It cannot be. 'The Beast' Sinclair has been brought low!"]

[Spoils of the Undeserving
Rare, Light rogue
Tier three
Passive, permanent
In this life, all good comes to those who earn it. Some people, though, are able to adjust the tendrils of fate, carve off more for themselves than what they actually deserve. With this card, the wielder will improve their attributes through training at a triple pace compared to others.
"You can tell me, man. What potions are you on? I want some."]

[Winds of Change
Rare, Elemental rogue
Tier three
Passive, permanent
Versatility is a way of life. You understand that. Most don't. However, being able to surprise others with a vast array of abilities at hand may win you the day. This card is passive, remaining in effect whenever equipped. For as long as you have it equipped, you may switch freely between all other cards. There will be no limitation except a thirty-second cooldown after switching a card from each separate Tier.
"You hear that, you gods-forsaken bastard? It's the wind. It's blowing with the winds of change."]

[Home Turf Advantage
Epic, Fury rogue
Tier three
Permanent, passive
Any successful rogue is a distrustful rogue. They need to be alert, awake, perceptive and cautious, ready to catch any danger to themselves and their kin. Yet, nobody can live their life in constant alertness without losing their edge.
This card, when wielded, allows the rogue, and anybody in their group, added benefits while resting. They will recuperate easier,

their wounds close faster and they will need less sleep to stay sharp. Also, any food and drink consumed will be more nourishing.
"It's like I said. Food just doesn't taste the same when you're away from home."]

[Circle of Darkness
Uncommon, Dark rogue
Tier four
Active, short duration
Darkness is the friend of any rogue. That is a well-known fact. This card allows a rogue to bring the Darkness with them, even in broad daylight. Upon activation, a thirty-foot circle of absolute darkness surrounds the wielder, staying with them, even if they move. Meanwhile, the darkness will be fully see-through for the rogue. Even enemies with higher Mental Power than the wielder will have trouble gazing through this short-lived circle of shadows, allowing them to get in a cheap shot, get the goods, or get away.
Short cooldown
"An eclipse? No, my stupid, stupid friend. This is theft."]

[Clothed in Living Light
Rare, Light rogue
Tier four
Active, long duration
The one constant for rogues, ironically, is a need for versatility. They need to adjust to their surroundings, often on the fly and under unhealthy or threatening conditions. This card allows the wielder that versatility. Upon activation, the card bestows the wielder with a quantity of living material that he can move, fix, and adjust with a mental nudge. A weapon? A shield? A set of skis? Any of these can be created and adjusted with this card. Any damage to the material reduces the pool of material available to the wielder. The material can be every bit as sharp as the wielder's Mental Power allows.
Long cooldown
"It's my time to shine." The Thief of Valkeer makes his move.]

[A Friendly Wave
Rare, Elemental rogue
Tier four
Active, short duration
Rogues, more than any other class, are aware of their surroundings. They learn how to use the terrain to their advantage, always on the outlook for cover, for hiding places and terrain that

will aid them and work against their enemies. This card allows the wielder to take a more direct hand in adjusting the surroundings to their advantage. For a short duration after activation, the wielder is able to command any water in their surroundings, making the water splash onto pursuers, soak clothes, ruin footing and even drown an unlucky pursuer.
Medium cooldown
"Getting your hands dirty is part of being a criminal, they say. But... look at me. My hands have never been cleaner!" A crime scene is swept clean by a rogue wave.]

[One with the Soil
Epic, Fury rogue
Tier four
Instant, long duration
The stories all tell us about the massive fireballs, the summoned swarms of locusts and ground-breaking attack cards. Yet, they neglect to remember one thing: that is not how most fights are won or lost. The slip of a foot. A patch of gravel or slippery mud. These are the small things that spell the end for a huge number of fighters. With this card, you and your group will retain perfect balance, regardless of footing and weather.
"Dear Lord Baluz. It takes more than a punch to the chin, a muddy slope, a dozen summoned simians and an Agility debuff to throw me off my feet. Admittedly, not that much more. Call it a tie?"]

Kith:

[**Cost of Life**
Heart card (amplified)
Medium duration
At what cost power? This is a question many ask themselves. You do not need to. You know the price. Whenever you need to, you have power, right at your fingertips. Upon activation of this card, your attributes are doubled for the full duration of the card, with no instant detrimental effects afterward. The only detraction? Every activation will cost you a year of your life force. Cost of Life will now also increase the rarity of all your cards by one for the full duration.
Long cooldown
"It whispers, does it not? That pulse, that promise, of strength and power, right at your disposal. You need only reach out."]

[Shadow Master
Rare, Dark summoner
Tier one

Active summon, long duration
This card allows you to manipulate your own shadow, split them into two shadows and order them around at a distance like they were your own summons. The augmented shadows are magically strengthened and enemy eyes cannot pierce them. The summoner may at any time choose to see through the shadow's eyes and speak through the shadow's mouth as if it were his own body. They can only be destroyed by magic or Elemental damage. If destroyed, there is a 12-hour cooldown for the next summon.
"It flew, I tell you. His shadow burst from his body, walked right up to me and mocked me. Threatened me. I seen it!" Careem. Denizen of the slums of Veriten.]

[**Divine Mentor**
Rare, Light summoner
Tier one
Active, medium duration
This summon brings forth a divine entity from the heavens. Internalized, the being will aid the summoner, increasing all their attributes and improving their movement speed. It can also be expended, guiding the entity to a chosen position before making it burst in a blinding light.
Long cooldown
"Behold, oh mortal. I am you. Only better, bereft of this fragile shell of yours. Follow my guidance, if you can."]

[**Apian God**
Rare, Elemental summoner
Tier one
Active, medium duration
The queens are commonly recognized as the highest ranking in a beehive. However, with the use of this card, you summon something else: an apian god, controlling hundreds of tiny air-aspected summons. They are not as large as regular bees, but still cause tiny amounts of stinging air damage.
In addition to this, depending on the Mental Power of the summoner, nearby regular flying insects may recognize the natural hierarchy of the apian god and join in the attack.
"I. Summon you. Into. Beeing!" The Court summoner finally snaps.]

[**Let Them Go**
Epic, Fury summoner
Tier one
Active, medium duration

Any summoner worth their salt knows when to dig deep to protect a summon, and when to let it go. With this card, the summoner can actively sacrifice a summon or group of summoned creatures. The energy tied up in the creatures will be spread out as a passive temporary boost to all attributes except Potential to every other person or summoned creature in the group. Any bound Guardian sacrificed will grant triple the boost.
"Let them go, and we will rise like the break of dawn." The High Elementalist surrenders control for personal gain.]

[**Tainted Earth**
Rare, Dark summoner
Tier two
Active summon, medium duration
This card allows you to awaken the soil anywhere you choose. It cannot be used directly on rock or crafted surfaces. When you tap the card, the earth grows to life in a shallow puddle of tainted earth. The earth is extremely adhesive and hard to remove. It can move, but only slowly. When touching skin, the soil drains enemies of Toughness at a slow rate. If destroyed, there is a 4-hour cooldown for the next summon.
"What's that? Get it off. Get it off!"]

[**Crescendo of Might**
Rare, Light summoner
Tier two
Active, short duration
Most summons are brought into the world with the desire to keep them present and active for as long as possible, given that they are the tools with which the summoner interacts with Ordei. This summon is the exact opposite. It comes with a time limit and the express desire to create as much damage as possible while it can.
Medium cooldown
"I am reading its mind right now. 'Rend, tear, kill!' Are you sure this is a being of Light?"]

[**... Twice the Fun**
Epic, Elemental summoner
Tier two
Passive, permanent
Sometimes, you crave something new and interesting. Sometimes, the best choice is simply more of what you already have. This card, when chosen, will double the number of summoned creatures for up to three other cards.
"You think my summoned squirrels underwhelming? Wait 'till I show you... more squirrels!"]

[Ties that Bind
Rare, Fury summoner
Tier two
Passive, permanent
Most summons are temporary, restricted to when the card is active. Yet, with the right choices for a Wellspring, any summoner earning new cards may choose a card like this. With permission from the owner of the Wellspring, you will be able to bond with any resident Guardian. This Guardian will then be permanently attached to you like a regular summon, until the Ænima powering it runs out. The effect of this card will remain active, regardless whether you switch to another Tier two card.
In addition to the Guardian's own attributes, it will be awarded a permanent increase to its Agility, with one point for each three points of your own Agility.
"What do you mean, I cannot summon this again once I let it die? Go away, you ridiculous little man." The summoner of Naz has an ugly eye-opener.]

[Coils of Shadow
Rare, Dark summoner
Tier three
Active, long duration
This card, once tapped, summons a number of small, venomous dredge spitters, calculated as one viper per two Mental Power of the summoner. These vipers are hard to spot in the dark, but vulnerable to Light powers and effects.
"Who's a lovely danger noodle? You are, my beautiful hazard spaghetti." The Valniers head chef races toward disaster.]

[Sacrificial Saints
Uncommon, Light summoner
Tier three
Passive, long duration
Nearly all summoning cards are active cards, requiring a certain degree of manipulation on behalf of the summoner. The bright saints summoned by this card do not. These are erstwhile heroes, souls so suffused with the power of self-sacrifice, that they feel the need to continue their deeds in the afterlife. Activating the card summons a random number of saints, between three and five. Each saint will attempt to block one attack against the summoner, be it magical or physical. Bear in mind that some attacks may be too powerful to be wholly blocked.
"You would not get this from any other. I will never give you up, nor let you down. We are no strangers. You know the rules, and so do I."]

[Fiery End
Uncommon, Elemental summoner
Tier three
Instant
Sometimes, in order to obtain your goal, you will have to make sacrifices. Summoned creatures are a means to an end. This card can ensure that the end in question will not be yours. Upon activation, any summoned creatures of yours explode in a violent conflagration, doing fire damage to anybody caught in their vicinity, proportional to their size and mass.
Long cooldown
"Outmaneuvered? Outmatched? One could see it that way. Only, why do you believe I have spread my summons this far out?" The last day of the city Acs Epilium.]

[From Out of the Pits
Rare, Fury summoner
Tier three
Active, instant
At the core of the Furyborn lies the concept of blood. Of being ready to sacrifice for your kin, should the path take you straight to the Pits themselves. Yet, if you are fast and crafty enough, you can extract enough to let you and your kin live another day.
Activating this card allows the summoner to sacrifice a third of their own health. Doing so will grant the same health to each and every person in their group, including their summons. There is no natural limiter to the usage of this card. The summoner may die from using this card.
Medium cooldown
"I would do anything for love. I would also do this." Rolat Polpettone dies for his beloved.]

[Antithesis of Light
Uncommon, Dark summoner
Tier four
Passive, long duration
Most summons are aspected, but still geared toward facing any sort of enemy. Not this summon. The Antithesis of Light is just that. A summoned entity that not only flings bolts of shadows when summoned, it also reduces the efficacy of nearby Light-aspected cards and effects by forty percent.
Long cooldown
"Come closer, morsel. I smell your terror. And I hunger."]

[Crystalline Guard
Rare, Light summoner
Tier four

Passive, long duration
Most summons are both offensive and defensive to a certain extent. Not this one. The Crystalline Guard is fully passive, brought into being purely to act as a shield between the summoner and their foes. Its crystalline skin deflects most ranged attacks and magical attacks, while the crystal shards of its body, when attacked, explode into deadly splinters, capable of piercing skin.
Long cooldown
"Listen. I... can't see you on the other side of this crystal thing. Ms. Summoner? Are you still there? I surrender. Please. I've been here for hours, and I'm wounded and tired."]

[Pillars of Air
Rare, Elemental summoner
Tier four
Active, medium duration
Usually, summoned entities are their own individuals, with a certain degree of autonomy. The Pillars of Air are not. For as long as the twin pillars are called into being, they meld with the legs of the wielder, forming a creation that responds entirely to the whims of the wielder's movements and thoughts. This allows them to use the power of the air in their movement, leaping long distances and run like the wind. A lapse in concentration can lead to the Pillars disappearing, however.
"Wheeeeeeeeeeeeeeeeeee." The self-titled Aerial Plague leaps to his death.]

[Ties Airbound
Rare, Fury summoner
Tier four
Passive, permanent
Most summons are temporary, restricted to when the card is active. Yet, with the right choices for a Wellspring, any summoner earning new cards may choose a card like this. With permission from the owner of the Wellspring, you will be able to bond with any resident winged Guardian. This Guardian will then be permanently attached to you like a temporary summon, until the Ænima powering it runs out. The effect of the card will remain active, regardless whether you switch to another Tier four card. In addition to the Guardian's own attributes, it will be awarded a permanent increase to its Agility and Toughness, with one point for each three points of your own Agility and Toughness.
"I know. You are kin. Do you like watching me soar?"]

Liam:

[Heart and Hearth
Heart card (amplified)
Long duration
From the heart comes that which we love. It provides life, love, and heat. For a while, you are able to control the heat around you, at short range. You may banish the cold for your loved ones, make your friends comfortable, and make annoyances overheat and leave.
Long cooldown
"Come close, love. Do you feel this? This, from my heart to yours."]

[One Heart, Opened
Uncommon, Dark fighter
Tier one
Active, instant
This card grants you a short-term Life Share ability. At your choice and direction, you may drain your own health and divide it among others, healing their wounds. Be warned that there is no upper limit here. If overused, you will drain your own heart's blood.
"I… did say I would give you my heart, did I not? Last C—" Final words of Shadow Knight Georgius Micael.]

[Waterfall of Light
Uncommon, Light fighter
Tier one
Active, instant
There are those fighters who advocate for technique, know-how, and weapon control to save the day. They tend to ignore one detail: with enough power, everything else falls at the wayside. Tapping this card causes your next attack to gain Trample. The attack will be very difficult to deflect or block, and has a medium chance to stun the enemy or knock them prone.
Short cooldown
"Rise, good sir. I was merely delivering a point. Get up… please."
The chevalier earns his exile.]

[Become the Clay
Epic, Elemental fighter
Tier one
Active, medium duration
For a while after activation, the outermost layer of your skin is converted into a thick layer of magically thickened wet clay. The clay will make it much harder for any attacks to pierce and may cause weapons to get stuck. Also, the effect of the clay becomes malleable, tied to the will of the Wielder. The layer is heavy and

may make it harder for you to move if you do not have the Strength to handle the weight.
Medium cooldown
"Give that back, you stupid, filthy weapon thief." A master duelist is defeated.]

[Optimal Offense
Uncommon, Fury Fighter
Tier one
Active, medium duration
The best offense is a good defense. Or was it the other way around? Regardless which school of thought you adhere to, you now get to double down on your choices. Upon activation of this card, you get to increase the strength of your offense by a full thirty percent, at the cost of a twenty percent reduction in defense, or vice versa. Whichever choice you make lasts for the full duration of the card, and cannot be willfully canceled.
Short cooldown
"I am getting bored. Are you all getting bored? You have been trying to get through my armor for a while. Should we finish this?"]

[Draining Ward
Common, Dark fighter
Tier two
Passive, permanent
Many fighters believe that the pathway to victory means not getting hurt. Amateurs. Veterans know that the only thing that counts is being the last one standing on the bloody field of victory. This card works on your currently worn armor and adapts it in two ways. First, it grants the armor a minor increase to its protection. Second, anybody who scores a hit against the wearer on the armor sees their Agility drained by a point.
"Hold on. A second. I've stabbed you. Three times. Why are you. Getting faster?" The death of Squire Ulrien.]

[Cleansing Fire
Uncommon, Light fighter
Tier two
Active, instant
When activated, this card sends a wave of purifying power through the body of the wielder. It cleanses the body of most diseases and hostile effects, while also granting the wielder a weak healing effect.
Medium cooldown
"Who's ready for the next round? I can keep this up forever."]

[Earthen Might
Common, Elemental fighter
Tier two
Active, very short duration
Sometimes, the best way to end a conflict is through instant, overwhelming force. How you decide to apply said force is up to you. For a brief window of time, the fighter's Strength is doubled.
Short cooldown
"Yeah, I guess I'm a bit scrawny. I 'unno. I think I can take you in arm wrestling. Care for a tiny bet?"]

[Escalating Defenses
Rare, Fury fighter
Tier two
Active, short duration
It can be so hard to truly let loose. To unleash the constant need for personal protection and focus on attacking. This card is for those who desire to leave the boring, self-restraining back-and-forth of regular combat behind and opt for something more... exhilarating. For every successful attack on an enemy, regardless of damage inflicted, you summon a single magical shield for you to control mentally, up to a maximum of three shields.
"Hey, wait. That's not fair." Arghan the Butcher faces five archers.]

[Ravenous Shadows
Uncommon, Dark fighter
Tier three
Active, very short duration
Some cards only need a single thought as you activate them, then you can forget about them. This card does not. Upon activation, it smothers the wearer in a layer of magical shadows that absorb a level of impacting magical attacks for a brief while. Once this duration has passed, any consumed energies are converted into a Strength boost with short duration for the fighter.
Medium cooldown
"You don't fight fair. But that's okay, see if I care. Hit me with your best shot!"]

[Convince the Unbeliever
Uncommon, Light fighter
Tier three
Passive

This card consists of a passive and an active element. The passive element is a weak, but constant self-heal. The active element engages at the start of any conflict, granting a +1 to the wearer's Agility for every minute, maxed at +5.
"I say to you again. My beliefs grant me the strength needed to persevere. Is that all you would send against me?"]

[Unleash the Elements
Common, Elemental fighter
Tier three
Active, long duration
Activating this card adds an Elemental aspect to your attacks. For every attack made, another Elemental aspect is added. When all four Elements are engaged, their power grows with each successive attack.
"My power is no match for yours, esteemed Protector Erfwen? Give it time."]

[All Out
Rare, Fury fighter
Tier three
Passive
Sometimes, simplicity is key. That principle is the foundation of this card as well. As long as the card is equipped, any offensive cards equipped by the wielder have their offensive effects increased by forty-five percent.
"I am too weak, you say? Allow me to slip into something more suitable." Grandstanding turns violent.]

[Tribune of Retribution, Blindness
Uncommon, Dark fighter
Tier four
Passive, medium duration
This card activates a punitive system, aiming to dispense karmic justice upon anybody attacking the fighter and his group. Any damage or damaging effect by an opposing force, regardless of whether the damage is nullified or not, results in an equivalent temporary reduction to their eyesight that lingers for the full duration of the card's effects. The more damage, the worse the blinding effect.
Long cooldown
"Crawl, maggots. You brought this on yourselves. Now, my friends and I will disperse justice." The Adjudicator of Dark at the Battle of Tempor.]

[Helping Step

Rare, Light fighter
Tier four
Active, very short duration
Being of the Light means being there for those in need. This card, when activated, lets you move to anybody in your group currently engaged in a fight in the blink of an eye. It will, at most, let you travel forty-five feet.
"Surrender, Darkspawn. There is no point on this battlefield I do not command."]

[**Tempest of the Land**
Uncommon, Fury/Elemental fighter
Tier four
Active, short duration
Natural disasters are not all bad. They roam and ravage, yet the energy unleashed in their passing can leave the soil revitalized, soon ready to easier grow to even further heights. In the same manner, sometimes, it is necessary for a fighter to unleash all their energy in one tempestuous assault. For the duration of the card, this will imbue all their attacks with a full gamut of Elemental aspects, and grant their body the strength and fury of the soil. However, once the card runs out, it will leave the fighter weakened for a short while, unable to use any cards. This is a dual card, working on more than one aspect.
"We surrender." The Tempest of the Land is not unleashed. This time.]

Cilia:

[**Death of Distractions**
Heart card (amplified)
Active, permanent
The Hand of Liberty keeps everything in check. Even distractions. Those pesky, tiny outside influences and sensual bombardments that constantly derail our thoughts, leading us to reduced productivity, minimal output, and any number of mental irrelevancies. This card can be activated at will, without cooldown. It will activate a small area of perfect control within fifty feet of the card holder, preventing anything auditory or olfactory from entering.
"Yeaaargh." The death of the scribe. He never heard the goblin sneaking up on him.]

[**Manipulate Darkness**
Uncommon, Dark crafter
Tier one
Permanent, passive

This card opens the gates, allowing you to manipulate the Dark aspect within you and, eventually, add them to your crafts in myriad ways. Manipulating your aspect will drain your stamina. *"From my soul to yours. A little shadow, a little mischief, to blanket the world and erase the tedium."* Poet-crafter Erudian Nightstone.]

[**Manipulate Light**
Common, Light crafter
Tier one
Permanent, passive
This card opens the gates, allowing you to manipulate the Light aspect within you and, eventually, add them to your crafts in myriad ways. Manipulating your aspect will drain your stamina. *"Some people hack and slash to spread Light into this world. Not us. We, my dear, create."* World-famous Light artist Everam Witteras.]

[**Manipulate Fire**
Common, Elemental crafter
Tier one
Permanent, passive
This card lights your inner furnace, allowing you to manipulate the fire aspect within you and, eventually, add them to your crafts in myriad ways. Manipulating your aspect will drain your stamina.
"Feel that? That rage, that wonderful heat. 'Tis yours, with but a thought. Feel it warm your soul."]

[**Manipulate Fury**
Common, Fury crafter
Tier one
Permanent, passive
This card lets you connect to the world around you, allowing you to manipulate the Fury aspect within you, in the soil and the air and, eventually, add them to your crafts. Manipulating your aspect will drain your stamina.
"Take a dash of home. Add a splash of family, of heat and hearth. Season with that rage you hold so dear. This concoction is an ember, just waiting to burn." Fury brewer Darintas addresses the crowd.]

A Hint of Permanence
Uncommon, Dark crafter
Tier two
Passive, permanent

The quality of your creations is decided by the deftness of your fingers and the accumulated wealth of your expertise in your chosen trade.

The grade and power of the aspect you pour into your creation is defined by your Mental Power, your concentration and mental fortitude, and your expertise at applying it to your crafting process throughout the protracted creation period.

However, one thing holds true. The longer a crafted item lasts, the better it is. People remember the eternal, the items holding permanent effects. With this card, your Mental Power sees a medium increase when attempting to craft long-lasting items or items with permanent imbues.

"Might is right. Knowledge is power. Yet, permanence outlasts them all."]

[**Apex of Growth**
Uncommon, Light crafter
Tier two
Permanent, passive
There are few ultimate truths as a crafter. One of the rare exceptions is this: Aspects do not blend well. This card ameliorates some of the natural imbalances existing between the different aspects, making it easier to craft items merging powers from different aspects. Any difficulties from crafting items with conflicting abilities or powers still remain.

"Take the cold control of Liberty. Add a splash of unbridled Fury. Mix in the pure decadence of Darkness. Oh, my friends. This sinful concoction will be unforgettable."]

[**Ritual of Fire**
Rare, Elemental crafter
Tier two
Passive, activated
Crafting by itself can be draining, both on willpower and stamina. Now, however, you can decide whether you want to sacrifice your energy for improved results. Once activated, this card will continually siphon small traces of stamina from the crafter to remain working. While in effect, for the purposes of crafting, the crafter's Mental Power is increased by seventy-five percent.

"Donande-tak, donande'tek, eru menthala-ze... damn. Candle blew out. Lousy secondhand candle makers. Kill 'em all when I rule the world."]

[**From Farm to Table**
Uncommon, Fury crafter
Tier two
Permanent, passive

The vast majority of crafters prioritize. They outsource, purchase goods, ingredients and materials, purchase semi-finished products. It allows them to trade on the craftsmanship of others and craft a lot faster.

Yet, there is a joy in handling every part of the process, a certainty in knowing, intimately, every tiny item that you include. With this card, throughout the entire gathering and crafting process, you are able to imbue minute quantities of magic into the materials. Hence, the enhanced effects of the final product will be improved, based on how large a part of the process you have handled yourself, up to a maximum increase of sixty percent.

"Get yer filthy hands off me kill. That'll be a coat worthy of a king, it will!"]

[A Dearth of Materials
Uncommon, Dark crafter
Tier three
Passive, activated
Darkness is much associated with a lack, something missing. Hence, why should it surprise people so that it is a fantastic tool for filling out those missing links? This card allows the crafter to use their magic to fill in instead of regular materials. Depending on the materials at hand, the result may even become better for it.

"Ah. We are out of thread for the needle. Magic will suture that well and tight." A proper battle doctor improvises.]

[A Testament to Light
Uncommon, Light crafter
Tier three
Passive, activated
There are cards which help with given aspects of the crafting process. Some help shut out distractions. Others help with the stamina cost. This card, instead, holds a tiny collection of recollections, from Light masters of old. These assembled tidbits of brilliance aid with any single creation that involves the use of Light magic. The boost is lower overall, yet the card will aid with every part of the process, and may even aid with intuitive leaps in the creation processes.

"They say that having voices in your head is madness. Only, when those voices keep being right and result in better creations? People shut up."]

[Chosen Focus: Fire
Common, Elemental crafter
Passive, activated

At third Tier, everybody gets this choice, for all of their decks. It can also be chosen at later Tiers, and you can only have a single focus. When activated, this will increase your control and output of Fire at any stage of the crafting process. It will allow your creations to hold more of the element, will grant you a better understanding of the bindings and will drain you less during the crafting process.
"Hearken my words, knave! There is a purity to Fire, a clarity you do not see in other elements. It burns, but it also cleanses!"
"Sire, art thou aware thou hath entered Wendie's domain?"]

[A Familiar Tool
Epic, Fury crafter
Tier three
Active, medium duration
No one knows the hammer like the smith himself. This old adage rings with truth. If you created an item, worked with it intimately, you will know it beyond somebody who simply bought it from a market stall. You will be aware of the imperfections beyond simple look, the strength hidden in the grain of the fabric, the stress they can and cannot handle.
This card takes that strength of knowledge and cements it into being. Any item created by the crafter themselves will have seventy-five percent added to their magical effect in combat, be it offensive or defensive, as long as the crafter is the one to wield it.
"They said that poison could not defeat the tainted count. And I laughed. For did I not create this poison myself? Now, stab me and be done with it, you cretin, for you are already dead."]

[Trail the Mirror's Edge
Rare, Light/Dark crafter
Tier four
Active, long duration
Most cards focus on the effect, on improving the end result. This ignores the fact that most crafters focus not only on improving the end result, but also on finishing in a timely manner. With Trail the Mirror's Edge active, any Light or Dark enhancements will be completed forty percent faster. This is a dual card, working on more than one aspect.
Very long cooldown
"Any path traversed on the mirror, dark or bright side, can trail off endlessly. Trail the mirror's edge, though, and you will get there faster." The philosopher makes up vague crap to get his point across.]

[Siphon the Source
Rare, Elemental crafter

Tier four
Passive, permanent
The best crafters are those fully in touch with their aspects. Of course, a wind-aspected crafter performs better work when he is fully in tune with the wind itself. This card enables that connection, letting the crafter siphon connection, power, and inspiration from nearby pervasive presences of the aspect they are manipulating in their crafts. The stronger the presence, the greater the effect. The effect of the card will remain active, regardless whether you switch to another Tier four card.
"Sense it, boy. The rock around you. It steadies the hand, calms the mind. It sings, a tune to guide your mind." Elementalist-crafter Hibertus, explaining his craft.]

[Touch Grass
Uncommon, Fury crafter
Tier four
Active, medium duration
In many instances, the crafting itself isn't what matters, but the circumstances surrounding the crafting. An item crafted in wind and rain with a rotting tree stump for a table will inevitably be worse quality than one made in a warm house. This card allows you to sense, shape, and direct the soil and plants around you with a speed and efficacy depending on your Mental Power.
Long cooldown
"No crafting bench, dear? Ah, but nature provides. It always does."]

Sera:

[Look Deeper
Heart card (amplified)
Instant, short duration
With a mental activation, the card wielder can pit their Mental Power against anybody, disclosing information about them up to a maximum distance of twenty feet. The higher the difference in Mental Power, the more information is disclosed about a person's Step, class, current active effects and cards, even their attributes.
Medium cooldown
"Sire. I regret to inform you that this cad has used his Mental Nudge card to influence your decisions." A merchant loses his head.]

[Blessing of the Night

Epic, Dark healer
Tier one
Passive, long duration
Once tapped, any attribute increases on you and group members in range are further boosted. Any active Light card effects of nearby hostiles are reduced to a third, sometimes outright quelled.
Long cooldown
"You dare come into this, my domain, and challenge my superiority?" The king of Fury is brought low.]

[**Warmth of the Circle**
Rare, Light healer
Tier one
Active, instant
This healing card is not the most powerful of all heals, granting a medium effect heal. However, it has an exceedingly fast effect and leaves the recipient with a small boost to Toughness that has a medium duration.
Medium cooldown
"This sensation. There is a joy here, a lingering trace of something divine. I thank you, Priestess, for this gift."]

[**Tongues of Pride**
Uncommon, Elemental healer
Tier one
Active, long duration
Once tapped, this card grants two effects. A weak fiery layer comes into being, adding itself to your weapon, as well as any allies' weapons in range. You will have weak fire damage added to your attacks. Finally, it carries a minor cleanse ability, continually working against any lower-Tier poison or debuffs used on allies.
"You ask me to bring the heat? Really? That is ironic." A Plague Knight falters.]

[**Natural Decomposition**
Rare, Fury healer
Tier one
Active, variable duration
Over time, nature will break down anything. This card allows the wielder to target any enemy, who will see any active defensive effects up to Tier three break down. The time needed depends on the Tier of the effect and the Mental Power of the healer and the target. With matched Mental Power, Tier one is instant, Tier two takes fifteen seconds, while Tier three takes thirty seconds.
"Missed? My dear nemesis, I do not miss. Nature simply takes its time. Now, be kind enough to hurry and succumb."]

[Cry for Blood
Uncommon, Dark healer
Tier two
Active, short duration (effect instant)
Tap to place marker on a chosen enemy. If that enemy dies while under the influence of Cry for Blood, you drain his life force to be redirected to a place of your choosing as one of the following:
—One-person heal, instant.
—One-person physical shield, medium duration.
—One-person increase to Toughness, medium duration.
The effectiveness of any heals, shields, or increases is determined by the enemy's Toughness.
"Do not cry, love. You may die. But I will use your essence well."]

[Spark of Divinity
Uncommon, Light healer
Tier two
Passive, long duration
Sometimes, it is less about the power of the boost than the adaptability, being able to apply what you want and where. Tapping this card allows you to select an attribute. You can then select to either apply it to a single person for a medium increase to said attribute or your entire group for a small increase. Also, for the full duration of the boost, you may change your selection.
"Ah hah hah, Lord Agravon. You have grown stronger since last we met. Allow me a second to adjust. It would not do for me to fall behind."]

[Unexpected Spillage
Uncommon, Elemental healer
Tier two
Active, instant
A battlefield is like an ocean. The waves go low and high. Sometimes, they act exactly as expected. Sometimes, you find unexpected lulls and towering waves coming from out of nowhere. Upon activation of this card, the healer may transfer one hundred percent of the force of an incoming attack, magical or physical, made on the wielder or anybody grouped with the wielder, to another being within range of the card.
Short cooldown
"Stop hitting yourself. Oh, who am I kidding? By all means, keep it up!"]

[Nature's Shield
Uncommon, Fury healer

Tier two
Instant, medium duration
Part of a healer's job is taking care of damage. Yet, an even better approach is ensuring that the damage never happens in the first place. Some healers weaken enemies or shield their allies to ensure the damaging blows can never land. Yet, ensuring that the enemy never arrives in the first place is surely preferable to either approach. Upon activation of this card, the wielder calls upon nature to raise, shape and place a few lengths of thorny underbrush. The height and toughness of the raised plants depend on the Mental Power of the healer.
"Oh, you're stuck? How sad. Maybe you shouldn't have tried to kill my friends!"]

[Heart of Hearts
Rare, Dark healer
Tier three
Passive, permanent
When equipped, this card takes that which your companions hold in their hearts and makes it stronger. Effects are drastically increased, as are durations, while cooldowns may be reduced. Beware, however, that the card may also increase existing drawbacks to the use of Heart cards.
"You've always had the power, my dears; you just had to learn it for yourself. Also, I've nudged the power along a bit." Famous high priest of the Circle to his congregation.]

[Warhammer of the Ancients
Uncommon, Light healer
Tier three
Passive, long duration
Activating this card summons the Warhammer of the Ancients. A massive, magically enhanced, though not unbreakable, Warhammer that will circle the healer for the duration of the card, fending off attacks and striking against any enemies who come too close.
Long cooldown
"What do you mean, the whooppening? That is not a word. Now draw your weapon, you imbecile." Lord Actrus of Standale, seconds before the whooppening.]

[The Flame Within
Uncommon, Elemental healer
Tier three
Active, medium duration
This card will light a boosting fire within the healer. The benevolent flames of the fire will increase all attributes of the healer,

growing in strength and effect for a full ten minutes before burning out.
Medium cooldown
"At the apex, there is a sensation of becoming... what I was supposed to be. Approaching the divine. As if I could reach out and touch it. Yet, you cannot touch this." Mareus Corex Hammer.]

[Home Defender
Rare, Fury healer
Tier three
Passive, permanent
Some people do not care about home. Others will take what they have and defend it to the last. This lets you designate an area with a one-mile radius for yourself, where you will always have the upper hand against any intruders. Inside that area, your attributes, except Potential, and the attributes of those allied with you, will be increased by +3.
The effect of the card will remain active, regardless whether you switch to another Tier three card. Once activated, you cannot establish a new home area for a full month.
"I was unaware the Wind-torn Healer lived here... Lads. I'm sorry. Put those weapons away. We're going home." A sergeant saves his men.]

The end of Theft of Decks book 3, in the Theft of Decks series.

<u>Reviews</u>

Anybody who's ever spent any time with me knows that I'm a simple creature. I prefer my beers liquid, my whiskey in a glass and my metal as extreme as humanly possible.

Yet, according to several police officers, I need to *pay* for my alcohol. The injustice!

You've already done your part to help me there, by buying my book or reading it on KU. I salute you. Now, if you're actually an angelic enough person that you're willing to help me more, (And of course you are, if you're reading the back matter, you absolute saint.) there is one thing.

Review mah book! Or somebody elses. Preferrably somebody amazing, like Rachel Ní Chuirc. Or Brian J. Nordon. Even Jez Cajiao's. Be sure to use long words – they confuse the hell out of him!

But seriously. That's the best piece of free aid you can give to writers like us. Review our books, tell the world exactly why you love them. We don't care about eloquence. But we do love you too!

Thank you so much.

-Lars

<u>Patreon!</u>

Okay then, now for those of you that don't know about Patreon, it's essentially a way to support your favorite Cheetos-smelling, sweatpants-wearing lunatics, otherwise known as writers. You can sign up for a day or a month or a year, and you get various benefits for it, ranging from my heartfelt thanks, to advance access to the books and art and more.

At the time of me writing this, the Patreon readers have access to a good deal of the final book of World of Chains which is available nowhere else.

<u>https://www.patreon.com/Moulder666</u>

Theft of Decks 4

By Lars Machmüller

One last heist. One legendary deck. One divine adversary.

Chase and his crew of unrepentant miscreants have defied impossible odds. They've broken more laws than any of them—especially Liam—can count, earning bounties from the nobility, the Lightborn church, and half the known world.

But it's been worth it. Finally, there's a chance at doing what they started all of this for; to create a permanent sanctuary.

With just one final deck in their grasp, they can establish an impregnable bulwark capable of repelling anyone—even the despised Lightborn.

Their target? Liberty. A mysterious race that vanished from public view decades ago, concealed behind impenetrable walls of fog. An enigmatic people generating more rumors than anyone else on Ordei. The one consistent thing they hear? Their leader is a literal god.

The mission might seem impossible: infiltrate unbreachable defenses, deceive an entire population, and steal a precious deck from under a literal god's watchful gaze. Except, they have the best of motivation; They really, really would like to not get lynched by all those inquisitors sniffing at their heels.

It's time for Chase and the crew to brave the borders, and risk it all, to steal a little 'Liberty' for themselves.

Coming Soon!

<u>Arise Alpha</u>

By Jez Cajiao

When you steal a hundred grand from some very bad people, the best way to survive is to stay small and quiet...

Possibly its not to save a pair of drowning girls, not go 'viral' on social media and certainly not to let the local police take your passport, trapping you on a small 'party' island in the middle of the Mediterranean Sea.

But Steve isn't the average guy, he's ex-military, ex-enforcer and ex-human. He's a one-man nanite fueled nightmare for those that cross the line, and he's decided that it's time to clean up his act. He's going to make up for the things he's done, and save 'the little guys'.

It's a nice fantasy, but even he has to admit, it's really just a justification, because he's a very bad man, with horrifying abilities, and he's only just learning what he's capable of. He needs a reason to not go to the dark, and if that's hunting down the creatures of the night and beating them to death with their own femurs?

Well, he's just the man for the job.

Stolen money. Greek Islands. Werewolves and Enforcers...
What could possibly go wrong?

<u>https://mybook.to/AriseAlpha</u>

<u>Quest Academy</u>

By Brian J. Nordon

A world infested by demons.
An Academy designed to train Heroes to save humanity
from annihilation.
A new student's power could make all the difference.

Humans have been pushed to the brink of extinction by an ever-evolving demonic threat. Portals are opening faster than ever, Towers bursting into the skies and Dungeons being mined below the last safe havens of society. The demons are winning.

Quest Academy stands defiantly against them, as a place to train the next generation of Heroes. The Guild Association is holding the line, but are in dire need of new blood and the powerful abilities they could bring to the battlefront. To be the saviors that humanity needs, they need to surpass the limits of those that came before them.

In a war with everything on the line, every power matters. With an adaptive enemy, comes the need for a constant shift in tactics. A new age of strategy is emerging, with even the unlikeliest of Heroes making an impact.

Salvatore Argento has never seen a demon.
He has never aspired to become a Hero.
Yet his power might be the one to tip the odds in humanity's favor.

<u>Buy on Amazon</u>

<u>Wandering Warrior</u>

By Michael Head

A divine quest to deliver justice.
One year to accomplish his mission.
After nineteen planets, there's something different about this one.

James Holden has reached the maximum level there is for a human. That's perfect, since he's the only one of his kind. A wandering warrior, without control of his destination, tossed between universes by gods who've failed to tell him why. James is the lone Judge on a new world in need of someone to balance the scales. He isn't afraid to do so with extreme prejudice. As the Chief Justice, he has to right the wrongs the innocent can't fix themselves.

As James quickly discovers, the roots of corruption run deep. Guilds choose to protect themselves rather than the people. Monsters roam the wilderness unchecked. Judgment is usually a decision between right and wrong, but nothing is ever that simple. This time, being the strongest human won't be enough to punish the guilty. James might have to recruit some new blood, even if he prefers to work alone.

On his twentieth world, he is going to win, no matter the cost. James will have to find a way to break past the limits of the system if he's going to have a chance at making a difference.

<u>Buy on Amazon</u>

<u>Knights of Eternity</u>

By Rachel Ní Chuirc

When Zara awoke in chains she thought she'd gone mad.

She was Zara the Fury - mistress of flame and fear. Her name was whispered across the land, from ramshackle taverns to the royal court. Even the heroic Gilded Knights thought twice before crossing her path.
She was feared—*respected*.
Now she was curled up on a dirt floor on her fiancé's orders. Valerius, leader of the Gilded, mocks her cries for help. And the kingdom is on the brink of war over the missing Lady Eternity...
But that wasn't why Zara thought she had gone mad.
The reason why is that the last thing she remembered was blood, an arcade screen, and the gun that changed everything.

But no chains can hold the Fury, and when she gets out? The world is going to *burn*.

<u>Buy on Amazon</u>

Scarlet Citadel

By Jack Fields

Gormon Hughes is 19, thin as a broom, and has—not for the first time in his life—been swept into the path of trouble. Poor, recently heartbroken, and indebted to the sort of people who file their teeth into needle points and devour wriggling bloated spiders for fun, Hughes sets his sights on salvation.

That salvation is the Scarlet Citadel, a wealthy organization of pageant fighters, monster hunters, and secret keepers. With the aid of strange oracles, rare good fortune, and a unique power that bubbles like champagne in the core of Hughes' being, he must join the Citadel and advance himself.

But the ladder of progression is harsh and dark. The rungs are slippery.

And falling means disaster...

Buy on Amazon

Facebook and Social Media

If you want to reach out, chat or just tell me my book was horrible, you can always find me on either my author page here:

https://www.facebook.com/groups/357145749698735/

_OR_

Legion recently set up a new Facebook group to spread the word about cool LitRPG books. It's dedicated to two very simple rules;

1: Let's spread the word about new and old brilliant LitRPG books.
2: Don't be a Dick!

They sound like really simple rules, but you'd be amazed...

Come join us!

https://www.facebook.com/groups/LITRPGLegion

I'm also on Discord here: **https://discord.gg/gyRkEgesH5**

In short, hit me up. I'd love to chat!

<u>Legion</u>

This is my first series with the Legion Publishers! It's run by Christine Cajiao and Geneva Agnos, who are also kind enough to let Jez Cajiao prance around in his underwear, where he can hurt nobody else.

It has, so far, been an absolutely enjoyable experience. You are welcome to reach out and ask if things have changed since I wrote this, of course. My safe word is **Jez is the nicest person in the world.**

They're taking on new authors, as we speak. So, don't be afraid to reach out.

Apart from being good people, I like that they have everything out in the open. Their contracts aren't hidden behind layers of legalese, you can find them here:

<u>https://www.legionpublishers.com/legioncontract</u>

If you want to reach out and ask any questions, get an idea of the support they offer, and possibly become part of the family? Just tap the link and fill in the form:

<u>https://www.legionpublishers.com/contact-and-submissions</u>

<u>Recommendations</u>

I'm often asked for personal recommendations, so if this book has whetted your appetite for more LitRPG, please have a look at the following, these are brilliant series by brilliant authors!

The Ten Realms by Michael Chatfield

Wandering Inn by Pirateaba

The Daily Grind by Argus

Quest Academy by Brian J. Nordon

Wandering Warrior by Michael Head

Calamity by Rachel Ni Chuirc

Codename: Freedom by Apollos Thorne

God of the Feast by Kevin Sinclair

Rise of Mankind by Jez Cajiao

<u>LITRPG!</u>

To learn more about LitRPG, talk to other authors including myself, and to just have an awesome time, please join the LitRPG Group

<u>www.facebook.com/groups/LitRPGGroup</u>

Facebook

There's also a few really active Facebook groups I'd recommend you join, as you'll get to hear about great new books, new releases and interact with all your (new) favorite authors! (I may also be there, skulking at the back and enjoying the memes...)

https://www.facebook.com/groups/LitRPGlegion/

https://www.facebook.com/groups/GamelitSociety

https://www.facebook.com/groups/LitRPG.books

https://www.facebook.com/groups/LitRPGforum/

LARS
MACHMÜLLER